LOCKWOOD
2003

DRACONOMICON™

ANDY COLLINS, SKIP WILLIAMS, JAMES WYATT

DEVELOPER
ANDY COLLINS

DESIGN ASSISTANCE
ED STARK, GWENDOLYN F.M. KESTREL

EDITORS
MICHELE CARTER, DALE DONOVAN, GWENDOLYN F.M. KESTREL, CHARLES RYAN

MANAGING EDITOR
KIM MOHAN

D&D DESIGN MANAGER
ED STARK

DIRECTOR OF RPG R&D
BILL SLAVICSEK

VICE PRESIDENT OF PUBLISHING
MARY KIRCHOFF

PROJECT MANAGER
MARTIN DURHAM

PRODUCTION MANAGER
CHAS DELONG

ART DIRECTOR
DAWN MURIN

COVER ART
TODD LOCKWOOD

INTERIOR ARTISTS
WAYNE ENGLAND, EMILY FIEGENSCHUH, LARS GRANT-WEST, REBECCA GUAY-MITCHELL, DAVID HUDNUT, JEREMY JARVIS, GINGER KUBIC, JOHN & LAURA LAKEY, TODD LOCKWOOD, DAVID MARTIN, DENNIS CRABAPPLE-MCCLAIN, MATT MITCHELL, MARK NELSON, STEVE PRESCOTT, VINOD RAMS, RICHARD SARDINHA, RON SPENCER, STEPHEN TAPPIN, JOEL THOMAS, BEN THOMPSON, SAM WOOD

GRAPHIC DESIGNERS
DAWN MURIN, MARI KOLKOWSKI

CARTOGRAPHER
TODD GAMBLE

GRAPHIC PRODUCTION SPECIALISTS
ERIN DORRIES, ANGELIKA LOKOTZ

ORIGINAL INTERIOR DESIGN
SEAN GLENN

This d20™ System game utilizes mechanics developed for the new DUNGEONS & DRAGONS® game by Jonathan Tweet, Monte Cook, Skip Williams, Richard Baker, and Peter Adkison.

Playtesters: Greg Collins, Jesse Decker, Viet Nguyen, Marc Russell, Dennis Worrell

Valuable advice provided by Todd Lockwood and Sam Wood [Dragon Anatomy and Motion], Monica Shellman and Michael S. Webster [Dragon Names]

Resources for this product [and the authors of those works] include *Atlas of Animal Anatomy* [W. Ellenburg and H. Deittrich], *Book of Eldritch Might* [Monte Cook/Malhavoc Press], *Book of Vile Darkness* [Monte Cook], *Bulfinch's Mythology* [Thomas Bulfinch], *Transformations of Myth Through Time* [Joseph Campbell], "Class Acts: Dragonkith," *Dragon Magazine* #284 [Monte Cook], *Council of Wyrms* [Bill Slavicsek], *Defenders of the Faith* [Rich Redman and James Wyatt], *AD&D® 2nd Edition Draconomicon* [Nigel Findley, Christopher Kubasik, Carl Sargent, John Terra, and William Tracy], "Dragontongue: A Draconic Language Primer," *Dragon Magazine* #284 [Owen K. C. Stephens], FORGOTTEN REALMS® *Campaign Setting* [Ed Greenwood, Sean K Reynolds, Skip Williams, and Rob Heinsoo], *The Golden Bough* [James George Frazer], *AD&D 1st Edition Monster Manual* [Gary Gygax], *Monsters of Faerun* [James Wyatt and Rob Heinsoo], *AD&D 2nd Edition Monstrous Manual*, *Oriental Adventures* [James Wyatt], *Savage Species* [Jennifer Clarke Wilkes, David Eckelberry, and Rich Redman], *Tome and Blood* [Bruce Cordell and Skip Williams].

U.S., CANADA, ASIA, PACIFIC, & LATIN AMERICA
Wizards of the Coast, Inc.
P.O. Box 707
Renton WA 98057-0707
Questions? 1-800-324-6496

EUROPEAN HEADQUARTERS
Wizards of the Coast, Belgium
T Hofveld 6d
1702 Groot-Bijgaarden
Belgium
+32-70-23-32-77

620-17668-001-EN
9 8 7 6 5 4 3 2 1
FIRST PRINTING: NOVEMBER 2003

Contents

Introduction 4

Chapter 1: All About Dragons 5
- The Dragon's Body 5
- Dragon Physiology 9
- Dragon Life Cycle 10
- Dragon Senses 17
- Flight 18
- Other Modes of Movement 19
- Combat Abilities 21
- Dragon Weaknesses 25
- Outlook and Psychology 25
- Dragon Society 26
- Language 28
- Religion 30
- Dragons by Kind 36
  - Dragon Sizes 36
  - Black Dragons 37
  - Blue Dragons 38
  - Brass Dragons 40
  - Bronze Dragons 42
  - Copper Dragons 44
  - Gold Dragons 46
  - Green Dragons 48
  - Red Dragons 50
  - Silver Dragons 53
  - White Dragons 55

Chapter 2: A DM's Guide to Dragons 57
- Dragons in the Campaign 57
- Running a Dragon Encounter 59
  - The Mechanics of Melee 59
  - Fighting on the Wing 59
  - Using a Breath Weapon 62
  - To Breathe or Not to Breathe? 63
  - Using Special Attack Forms 64
  - Dragons as Spellcasters 65
- Dragon Feats 66
- Feat Descriptions 67
- Dragon Spells 75
- Spell Descriptions 76
- Dragon Magic Items 82
  - Lair Wards 84
- Dragon Prestige Classes 86
  - Bloodscaled Fury 86
  - Disciple of Ashardalon 87
  - Dispassionate Watcher of Chronepsis 89
  - Dragon Ascendant 90
  - Elemental Master 92
  - Hidecarved Dragon 94
  - Sacred Warder of Bahamut 96
  - Unholy Ravager of Tiamat 97
- Advanced Dragons 99
  - Sample Advanced Dragon 100

Chapter 3: The Player's Perspective 101
- Fighting a Dragon 101
  - Forewarned Is Forearmed 101
  - Limit the Battlefield 101
  - The Element of Surprise 102
  - Spread Out, Concentrate Attacks 102
  - Don't Stay Too Long 103
- Feats 103
- New Spells 106
- Cleric Domains 107
- Spell Descriptions 109
- Dragonhide Armor 115
- Dragoncraft Items 116
- Magic Items 118
  - Armor 118
  - Weapons 118
  - Rings 119
  - Rods 119
  - Staffs 119
  - Wondrous Items 119
  - Minor Artifact 121
- Prestige Classes 122
  - Dracolyte 122
  - Dragonkith 123
  - Dragonrider 124
  - Dragonslayer 125
  - Dragonsong Lyrist 127
  - Dragonstalker 128
  - Hoardstealer 130
  - Initiate of the Draconic Mysteries 131
  - Platinum Knight 133
  - Talon of Tiamat 134
- Dragons in the Party 136
  - Dragons' Advantages and Disadvantages 136
  - Dragons as Mounts 136
  - Dragons as Cohorts 138
  - Dragons as Special Mounts 139
  - Dragons as Familiars 141
- Dragons as Player Characters 141

Chapter 4: New Monsters 145
- Abyssal Drake 145
- Monsters by Type (and Subtype) 146
- Dracolich 146
- Draconic Creature 149
- Dragonkin 150
- Dragonnel 150
- Elemental Drake 152
  - Air Drake 152
  - Earth Drake 153
  - Fire Drake 154
  - Ice Drake 154
  - Magma Drake 155
  - Ooze Drake 156
  - Smoke Drake 157
  - Water Drake 157
- Faerie Dragon 158
- Fang Dragon 159
- Felldrake, Spiked 160
- Ghostly Dragon 161
- Golem 163
  - Dragonbone Golem 164
  - Drakestone Golem 164
  - Ironwyrm Golem 165
- Half-Dragon 166
- Hoard Scarab 167
- Landwyrm 168
  - Desert Landwyrm 169
  - Forest Landwyrm 170
  - Hill Landwyrm 170
  - Jungle Landwyrm 171
  - Mountain Landwyrm 172
  - Plains Landwyrm 172
  - Swamp Landwyrm 173
  - Tundra Landwyrm 174
  - Underdark Landwyrm 175
- Planar Dragons 176
  - Battle Dragon 176
  - Chaos Dragon 177
  - Ethereal Dragon 179
  - Howling Dragon 180
  - Oceanus Dragon 181
  - Pyroclastic Dragon 182
  - Radiant Dragon 185
  - Rust Dragon 186
  - Styx Dragon 187
  - Tarterian Dragon 189
- Shadow Dragon 191
- Skeletal Dragon 192
- Squamous Spewer 193
- Storm Drake 194
- Vampiric Dragon 195
- Zombie Dragon 197

Chapter 5: Sample Dragons 199
- Customizing the Dragons 199
- Sample Black Dragons 201
- Sample Blue Dragons 207
- Sample Brass Dragons 216
- Sample Bronze Dragons 223
- Sample Copper Dragons 233
- Sample Gold Dragons 239
- Sample Green Dragons 247
- Sample Red Dragons 254
- Sample Silver Dragons 263
- Sample White Dragons 270

Appendix 1: The Dragon's Hoard 277

Appendix 2: Index of Dragons 286

Introduction

The dragon reared, roaring, clawing at air
And belching fire, and began to lunge down
Upon Dydd, but the druid slashed into
Ashardalon's heart, her scimitar cut
And the lifeblood began to spill. Then Dydd
Was slain, her heart wrested from her breast by
The dragon's grasping jaws, swallowed, consumed
To sustain Ashardalon's ebbing life
For a time. . . .
—The Lay of Dydd

More than any other creature, dragons are a symbol of all that is the DUNGEONS & DRAGONS® game. From the savage white to the majestic gold, dragons represent the greatest perils adventurers face at any point in their careers, as well as the greatest rewards they may hope to claim. From the tiny wyrmling at the bottom of an adventurer's very first dungeon to the colossal great wyrm he meets at the height of his career, dragons are the ultimate climactic encounter: a brutal and memorable fight that will pay off in riches from the dragon's hoard.

Dragons are creatures of myth, often described as the first sentient race to appear on a world, with life spans that stretch over hundreds of years. They symbolize the world itself and embody its history, and the oldest dragons are repositories of vast knowledge and ancient secrets. This aspect of dragons makes them much more than just a challenging combat encounter: They are sages and oracles, fonts of wisdom and prophets of things to come. Their very appearance can be an omen of good or ill fortune.

Perhaps most important, dragons are a reminder that the action of the D&D game takes place in a world of fantasy, wonder, and magic, a world far from mundane in every way. Any attempt to describe them as little more than glorified lizards with wings and breath weapons is a disservice, not only to dragons, but to the fantasy universe of D&D and the wealth of legends, myths, and heroic stories that place dragons in such an iconic position that they had to be a part of the very name of the game. Dragons are, by their very nature, epic forces in the world. Their actions, their schemes, even their dreams are felt throughout the world. From a wyrmling raiding herds of sheep to the mighty Ashardalon feasting on preincarnate souls, dragons do things that matter, whether on a small local scale or in the cosmic big picture. They are the embodiment of fantasy itself.

That, in a nutshell, is the reason for this book. Dragons are such a central part of the game that a rules reference of this nature is an essential addition to any campaign, enhancing the excitement of draconic encounters for players and Dungeon Masters alike. A DM will find information here on the powers and tactics of dragons, as well as a wealth of new feats, spells, magic items, and prestige classes designed to make dragon encounters more interesting, challenging, and unusual. In case the dragons already described in the *Monster Manual* and other books are not enough, this book also presents a variety of new dragon-related monsters of all types to include in the game. Players, meanwhile, can unearth dragonslaying tactics and take advantage of new feats and spells, magic items, and prestige classes to make their characters the ultimate dragon slayers, dragon riders, or even dragon servants.

Draconomicon is not just about the rules, tactics, and ecology of dragons, however. The illustrations in this book are intended to inspire a fresh sense of wonder and awe at the creatures that make up such an important part of the D&D game. Dragons are rapacious, arrogant, and deadly—but they are also majestic, awesome, and magnificent. A renewed sense of the grandeur of dragons might not have as concrete or noticeable an impact on your game as all the new rules you will find in this book, but its influence will surely be felt around your gaming table.

Let this book inspire you. Whether you use it to build new draconic adversaries and exciting dragon lairs stocked with legendary treasure, or to build a character who rides a silver dragon into battle against the servants of Tiamat, you are sure to find not just the rules you want, but the wonder you need to make your game more fun. Dragons are creatures of legend, and with this book you can be a part of that legend. Retell it, relive it, reshape it in your character's or your campaign's image. *Draconomicon* will show you how.

THE DIFFERENT KINDS OF DRAGONS

In the D&D game, the term "dragon" encompasses a number of different creatures, some of which bear little resemblance to the great flying creatures with breath weapons that we commonly think of as dragons.

For the most part, this book concerns itself with the ten varieties of true dragon described in the *Monster Manual*—the five chromatic dragons (black, blue, green, red, white) and the five metallic dragons (brass, bronze, copper, gold, silver). True dragons are those creatures that become more powerful as they grow older.

A number of other true dragons are described in Chapter 4 of this book. In addition, Appendix 2: Index of Dragons provides a complete list of all true dragons that have been presented in official sources.

Other creatures of the dragon type that do not advance through age categories are referred to as lesser dragons (which should not be taken to mean that they are necessarily less formidable than true dragons).

The three kinds of lesser dragon described in the *Monster Manual* are the dragon turtle, the pseudodragon, and the wyvern. Chapter 4 of this book contains a number of descriptions of other lesser dragons, and Appendix 2 lists every lesser dragon that has been described in a DUNGEONS & DRAGONS rulebook or accessory.

Illus. by L. Grant-West

A wealth of material, from bard's tales and ponderous tomes alike, has been recorded about dragons. Unfortunately for adventurers planning to confront a dragon, most of that information is wrong. The opening chapter of this book presents the truth about dragons—their types, habits, physiology, and worldview.

THE DRAGON'S BODY

"How can one imagine anything more magnificent than . . . a dragon, the paragon of creation?"

—Bheilorveilthion, red wyrm

"Nothing but a bunch of vain, glorified flying reptiles, if you ask me!"

—Hatredymaes, androsphinx

At first glance, a true dragon resembles a reptile. It has a muscular body, a long, thick neck, a horned or frilled head with a toothy mouth, and a sinuous tail. The creature walks on four powerful legs with clawed feet, and it flies using its vast, batlike wings. Heavy scales cover a dragon from the tip of its tail to end of its snout. As you'll see from the details to come, however, that first glance doesn't begin to tell the whole story about the nature of dragons.

EXTERNAL ANATOMY

Despite its scales and wings, a dragon's body has features that seem more feline than reptilian. Refer to the illustrations on the next few pages as you read on.

Like a cat's eye, a dragon's eye has a comparatively large iris with a vertical pupil. This arrangement allows the pupil to open extremely wide and admit much more light than a human eye can.

The sclera, or "white," of a dragon's eye is often yellow, gold, green, orange, red, or silver, with an iris of a darker, contrasting color.

To a casual observer, a dragon's pupils always look like vertical slits. If one were to look very closely into a dragon's eye, however, one could see a second iris and pupil within the first. The dragon can shift and rotate this inner aperture up to 90 degrees, so that the inner pupil can overlay the outer one or lie at a right angle to it. This ocular structure gives a dragon extremely accurate depth perception and focusing ability no matter how much or how little light is available.

A dragon's eye is protected by a leathery outer eyelid and three smooth inner eyelids, or nictitating membranes. The innermost membrane is crystal clear and serves to protect the eye from damage while the dragon flies, fights, swims, or burrows with its eyes open. The other two eyelids mainly serve to keep the inner membrane and the surface of the eye clean. They are thicker than the innermost membrane and less clear. A dragon can use these inner lids to protect its eyes from sudden flashes of bright light. A dragon's eyes glow in the dark, but the dragon can hide the glow by closing one or more of its inner eyelids; doing this does not affect its vision.

A dragon's ears often prove indistinguishable from the frills that frame its head, especially when the dragon is at rest. The ears of an an active dragon, however, constantly twitch and swivel as the dragon tracks sounds.

Not all dragons have external ears; burrowing and aquatic dragons usually have simple ear holes protected by an overhanging fringe.

A dragon's mouth features powerful jaws, a forked tongue, and sharp teeth. The exact number and size of a dragon's teeth depend on the dragon's age, habitat, and diet; however, a dragon's array of teeth usually includes four well-developed fangs (two upper, two lower) that curve slightly inward and have cutting edges on both the inner and outer surfaces. A dragon uses its fangs to impale and kill prey, and they serve as the dragon's primary weapons.

Immediately in front of the fangs in each jaw lie the dragon's incisors, which are oval in cross-section and have serrated edges at the top. When a dragon bites down on large prey, these teeth cut out a semicircle of flesh.

Behind the fangs in each jaw, a dragon has a row of peglike molars that help it grip prey. A dragon is not well equipped for chewing, and it typically tears prey into chunks small enough to gulp down. A dragon can create a sawing motion with its incisors by wiggling its lower jaw and shaking its head from side to side, allowing the incisors to quickly shear through flesh and bone.

Many dragons learn to seize prey and literally shake it to death. Other dragons have mastered the technique of grabbing prey and swallowing it whole.

Some dragon hunters boast that they can hold a dragon's mouth closed, preventing the creature from biting. It is true that a dragon applies more force when closing its jaws than it does when opening them; however, holding a dragon's mouth closed still requires prodigious strength. Even if an foe were to succeed in clamping its jaws shut, the dragon is likely to throw off the opponent with one flick of its head, claw its attacker to ribbons, or both.

The spines, frills, and other projections that adorn a dragon's head make the creature look fearsome, and that is their main function.

A dragon's horn is a keratinous projection growing directly from the dragon's skull. A dragon with horns that point backward can use the horns for grooming, and they also help protect the dragon's upper neck in combat. Horns projecting from the sides of a dragon's head help protect the head.

A dragon's spines are keratinous, but softer and more flexible than its horns. The spines are imbedded in the dragon's skin and anchored to the skeleton by ligaments. Most spines are located along the dragon's back and tail. Unlike horns, spines are mobile, with a range of motion that varies with the kind of dragon and the spines' location on the dragon's body. The spines along a dragon's back, for example, can only be raised or lowered, whereas the spines supporting a dragon's ears can be moved many different ways.

The frills on a dragon's back and tail help keep the dragon stable when flying or swimming.

To a scholar who knows something about the natural world, a dragon's powerful legs are decidedly nonreptilian, despite their scaly coverings. A dragon's legs are positioned more or less directly under its body, in the manner of mammals. (Most reptiles' legs tend to splay out to the sides, offering much less support and mobility than a dragon or mammal enjoys.)

A dragon's four feet resemble those of a great bird. Each foot has three or four clawed toes facing forward (the number varies, even among dragons of the same kind), plus an additional toe, also with a claw, set farther back on the foot and facing slightly inward toward the dragon's body, like a human's thumb.

Although a dragon's front feet are not truly prehensile, a dragon can grasp objects with its front feet, provided they are not too small. This grip is not precise enough for tool use, writing, or wielding a weapon, but a dragon can hold and carry objects. A dragon also is capable of wielding magical devices, such as wands, and can complete somatic

Illus. by T. Lockwood

components required for the spells it can cast (see Spellcasting, below). Some dragons are adroit enough to seize prey in their front claws and carry it aloft.

A dragon can use the "thumbs" on its rear feet to grasp as well, but the grip is less precise than that of the front feet.

A dragon's skin resembles crocodile hide—tough, leathery. and thick. Unlike a crocodile, however, a dragon has hundreds of hard, durable scales covering its body. A dragon's scales are keratinous, like its spines. Unlike the spines, however, a dragon's scales are not attached to its skeleton, and the dragon cannot make them move. The scales are much harder and less flexible than the spines, with a resistance to blows that exceeds that of steel.

A dragon's largest scales are attached to its hide along one edge and overlap their neighbors like shingles on a roof or the articulated plates in a suit of armor. These scales cover the dragon's neck, underbelly, toes, and tail. As the dragon moves its body, the scales tend to shift as the skin and muscle under them moves, and the scales' free ends sometimes rise up slightly. This phenomenon has led some observers to mistakenly conclude that a dragon can raise and lower its scales in the same manner as a bird fluffing its feathers.

The majority of a dragon's scales are smaller and attached to the skin near their centers. These scales interlock with neighboring scales, giving the surface of the body a pebbly texture. The scales are large enough to form a continuous layer of natural armor over the body even when it stretches or bulges to its greatest extent. When the body relaxes or contracts, the skin under the scales tends to fold and wrinkle, though the interlocking scales give the body a fairly smooth look.

A dragon's scales grow throughout its lifetime, albeit very slowly. Unlike most other scaled creatures, a dragon neither sheds its skin nor sheds individual scales. Instead, its individual scales grow larger, and it also grows new scales as its body gets bigger. Over the years, a scale may weather and crack near the edges, but its slow growth usually proves sufficient to replace any portion that breaks off. Dragons occasionally lose scales, especially if they become badly damaged. Old scales often litter the floors of long-occupied dragon lairs.

When a dragon loses a scale, it usually grows a new one in its place. The new scale tends to be smaller than its neighbors and usually thinner and weaker as well. This phenomenon is what gives rise to bards' tales about chinks in a dragon's armor. These tales are true as far as they go, but one new scale on a dragon's massive body seldom leaves the dragon particularly vulnerable to attack.

A dragon's long, muscular tail serves mainly as a rudder in flight. A dragon also uses its tail for propulsion when swimming, and as a weapon.

A dragon's wings consist of a membrane of scaleless hide stretched over a framework of strong but lightweight bones. Immensely powerful muscles in the dragon's chest provide power for flight.

Most dragons have wings that resemble bat wings, with a relatively short supporting alar limb, ending in a vestigial claw that juts forward. Most of the wing area comes from a membrane stretched over elongated "fingers" of bone (the alar phalanges; see Skeleton, below), which stretch far beyond the alar limb.

Some kinds of dragons have wings that run the lengths of their bodies, something like the "wings" of manta rays. This sort of wing also has an alar limb with phalanges supporting the forward third of the wing, but the remainder of the wing is supported by modified frill spines that have only a limited range of motion and muscular control.

Inside the Dragon's Eye

Most scholars remain unaware of how complex and unusual a dragon's eye really is. In addition to its four layers of eyelids and its double pupil, a dragon's eye also has a double lens. The outer lens (1) is much the same as any other creature's in form and function. The inner lens (2), however, is a mass of transparent muscle fibers that can polarize incoming light. The inner lens also serves to magnify what the dragon sees, and helps account for the dragon's superior long-distance vision.

A dragon's retinas (3) are packed with receptors for both color and black-and-white vision. Behind the retina lies the tapetum lucidum (4), a reflective layer that helps the dragon see in dim light. A dragon literally sees light twice, once when it strikes the retina and again when it is reflected back. It is the tapetum lucidum that makes a dragon's eyes seem to glow in the dark.

INTERNAL ANATOMY

As you'll see from the following section, a dragon's resemblance to a reptile is literally only skin deep. Refer to the accompanying illustrations as you read on.

Skeleton

Although complete dragon skeletons are hard to come by, most scholars agree that a little more than 500 bones comprise a dragon's skeleton, compared to slightly more than

200 bones in a human skeleton. The bones in a dragon's wings and spine account for most of the difference.

Dragon bones are immensely strong, yet exceptionally light. In cross-section they look hollow, with thick walls made up of concentric circles of small chambers staggered like brickwork. Layers of sturdy connective tissue and blood vessels run between the layers.

The accompanying diagram shows a dragon skeleton in detail. Significant parts of the skeleton are briefly discussed below.

The keel, or sternum (1), serves as an anchor for the dragon's flight muscles. The scapula draconis (2) supports the wing. The metacarpis draconis (3) and alar phalanges (4) in each wing support most of the wing's flight surface. In some dragons, the ulna draconic (5) has an extension called the alar olecranon (6) that lends extra support to the wing.

The thirteenth cervical vertebra (7) marks the base of a dragon's neck. Every true dragon, no matter how large or small, has exactly 13 cervical vertebrae, 12 thoracic vertebrae, 7 lumbar vertebrae, and 36 caudal vertebrae.

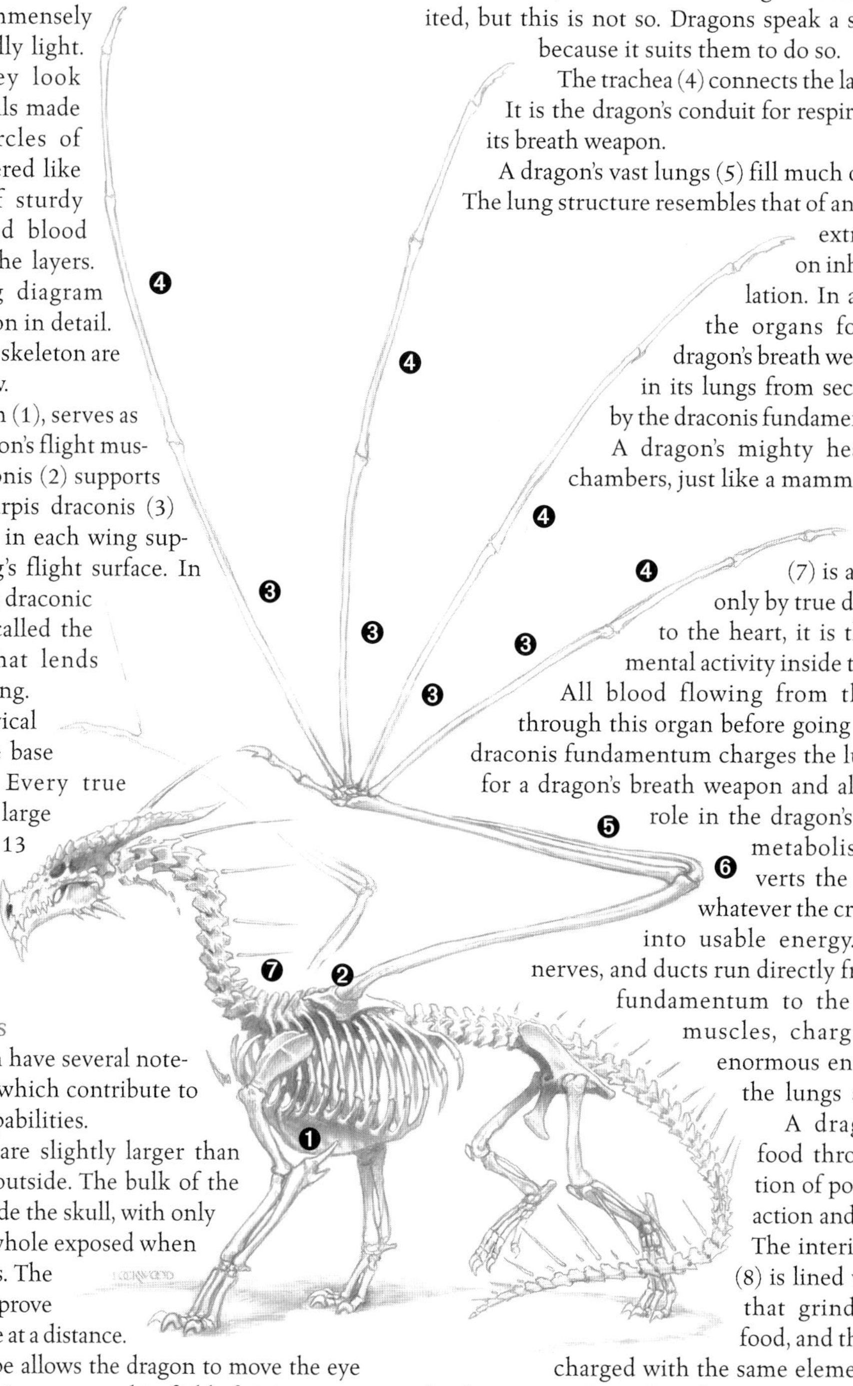

Illus. by T. Lockwood

Major Internal Organs

The insides of a dragon have several noteworthy features, all of which contribute to the dragon's unique capabilities.

A dragon's eyes (1) are slightly larger than they appear from the outside. The bulk of the eye remains buried inside the skull, with only a small portion of the whole exposed when a dragon opens its eyes. The eye's extra size helps improve the dragon's ability to see at a distance. The eye's spherical shape allows the dragon to move the eye through a wide arc, helping to expand its field of vision.

A dragon's brain (2) is exceptionally large, even for such a big creature, and it continues to grow as the dragon grows. It has highly developed sensory centers with specialized lobes that connect directly to the eyes, ears, and nasal passages. The brain also has large areas dedicated to memory and reasoning.

The larynx (3) contains numerous well-developed vocal folds that give a dragon tremendous control over the tone and pitch of its voice. A dragon's voice can be as shrill as a crow's or as deep as a giant's. Some scholars, noting that the Draconic language (see page 28) contains many harsh sounds and sibilants, conclude that a dragon's vocal capacity is limited, but this is not so. Dragons speak a strident language because it suits them to do so.

The trachea (4) connects the larynx to the lungs. It is the dragon's conduit for respiration and also for its breath weapon.

A dragon's vast lungs (5) fill much of its chest cavity. The lung structure resembles that of an avian, which can extract oxygen both on inhalation and exhalation. In addition to being the organs for respiration, a dragon's breath weapon is generated in its lungs from secretions produced by the draconis fundamentum (see below).

A dragon's mighty heart (6) has four chambers, just like a mammal's heart.

The draconis fundamentum (7) is a gland possessed only by true dragons. Attached to the heart, it is the center of elemental activity inside the dragon's body. All blood flowing from the heart passes through this organ before going to the body. The draconis fundamentum charges the lungs with power for a dragon's breath weapon and also plays a major role in the dragon's highly efficient metabolism, which converts the vast majority of whatever the creature consumes into usable energy. Blood vessels, nerves, and ducts run directly from the draconis fundamentum to the dragon's flight muscles, charging them with enormous energy, and also to the lungs and the gizzard.

A dragon digests its food through a combination of powerful muscular action and elemental force. The interior of the gizzard (8) is lined with bony plates that grind up chunks of food, and the entire organ is charged with the same elemental energy that the dragon uses for its breath weapon.

Musculature

Intact dragon carcasses are even more rare than intact dragon skeletons, making any catalog of a dragon's muscles unreliable at best. Given the number of bones in a dragon skeleton, however, a dragon's muscles must number in the thousands.

Overall, a dragon's musculature resembles that of a great cat, but with much larger muscles in the chest, neck, and tail. The illustration on page 10 identifies the major muscle groups in a dragon's body.

Illus. by M. Nelson

Of most interest to scholars are the muscles involved in flight. These muscles can exert tremendous force and consume equally tremendous amounts of energy (which the draconis fundamentum supplies). The flight muscles are located in the chest and in the wings themselves. The alar pectoral (1) is the main flight muscle and is used on the wing's downstroke. The alar lattisimus dorsai (2) draws the wing up and back. The alar deltoid (3) and alar cleidomastoid (4) draw the wings up and forward.

The muscles of the wings serve mainly to control the wing's shape, which in turn helps the dragon maneuver in the air. The alar tricep (5) and alar bicep (6) fold and unfold the wings. The alar carpi ulnaris (7) and alar carpi radialus (8) allow the wings to warp and twist.

DRAGON PHYSIOLOGY

"Dragons are scaly, they lay eggs, and they are utterly lacking in any mammalian characteristics. The notion that they are warm-blooded is silly."

—Aloysius Egon Greegier, armchair dragon scholar

"Just like a humanoid to quote three facts, get one of them wrong, and then draw an unrelated conclusion from the lot."

—Kacdaninymila, young adult gold dragon, upon reading Greegier's statement

Scholars disagree on some key aspects of dragon life, but dragons themselves have few doubts.

METABOLISM

Laypeople, and some scholars, are fond of the terms "cold-blooded" and "warm-blooded" to describe ectothermic and endothermic creatures, respectively.

An ectothermic creature lacks the ability to produce its own heat and must depend on its environment for warmth. Most ectothermic creatures seldom actually have cold blood, because they are able to find environmental heat to warm their bodies.

An endothermic creature doesn't necessarily have warm blood. What it has is a body temperature that remains more or less steady no matter how hot or cold its surroundings become.

All true dragons are endothermic. Given their elemental nature, they could hardly be otherwise. A dragon's body temperature depends on its kind and sometimes on its age. Dragons that use fire have the highest body temperatures, and dragons that use cold have the lowest. Acid- and electricity-using dragons have body temperatures that fall between the two extremes, with acid-users tending to have cooler bodies than electricity-users. Fire-using dragons literally become hotter with age. Likewise, cold-using dragons become colder as they age. Acid- and electricity-using dragons have about the same body temperature throughout their lives, with younger and smaller dragons having slightly higher temperatures than older and larger ones.

Unlike most endothermic creatures, dragons have no obvious way to shed excess body heat. They do not sweat, nor do they pant. Instead, the draconis fundamentum extracts heat from the bloodstream and stores the energy. In a sense, then, a dragon can be considered ectothermic (because it can use environmental heat). However, when a dragon is deprived of an external heat source, its metabolism and activity level do not change. Unlike a truly ectothermic creature, a dragon can generate its own body heat and is not slowed or forced into hibernation by exposure to cold.

DIET

Dragons are carnivores and top predators, though in practice they are omnivorous and eat almost anything if necessary. A dragon can literally eat rock or dirt and survive. Some dragons, particularly the metallic ones, subsist primarily on inorganic fare. Such dining habits, however, are cultural in origin.

Unfortunately for a dragon's neighbors, the difference between how much a dragon must eat and how much it is able to eat is vast. Most dragons can easily consume half their own weight in meat every day, and many gladly do so if sufficient prey is available. Even after habitual gorging, a dragon seldom gets fat. Instead, it converts its food into elemental energy and stores it for later use. Much of this stored energy is expended on breath weapons and on the numerous growth spurts (see below) that a dragon experiences throughout its life.

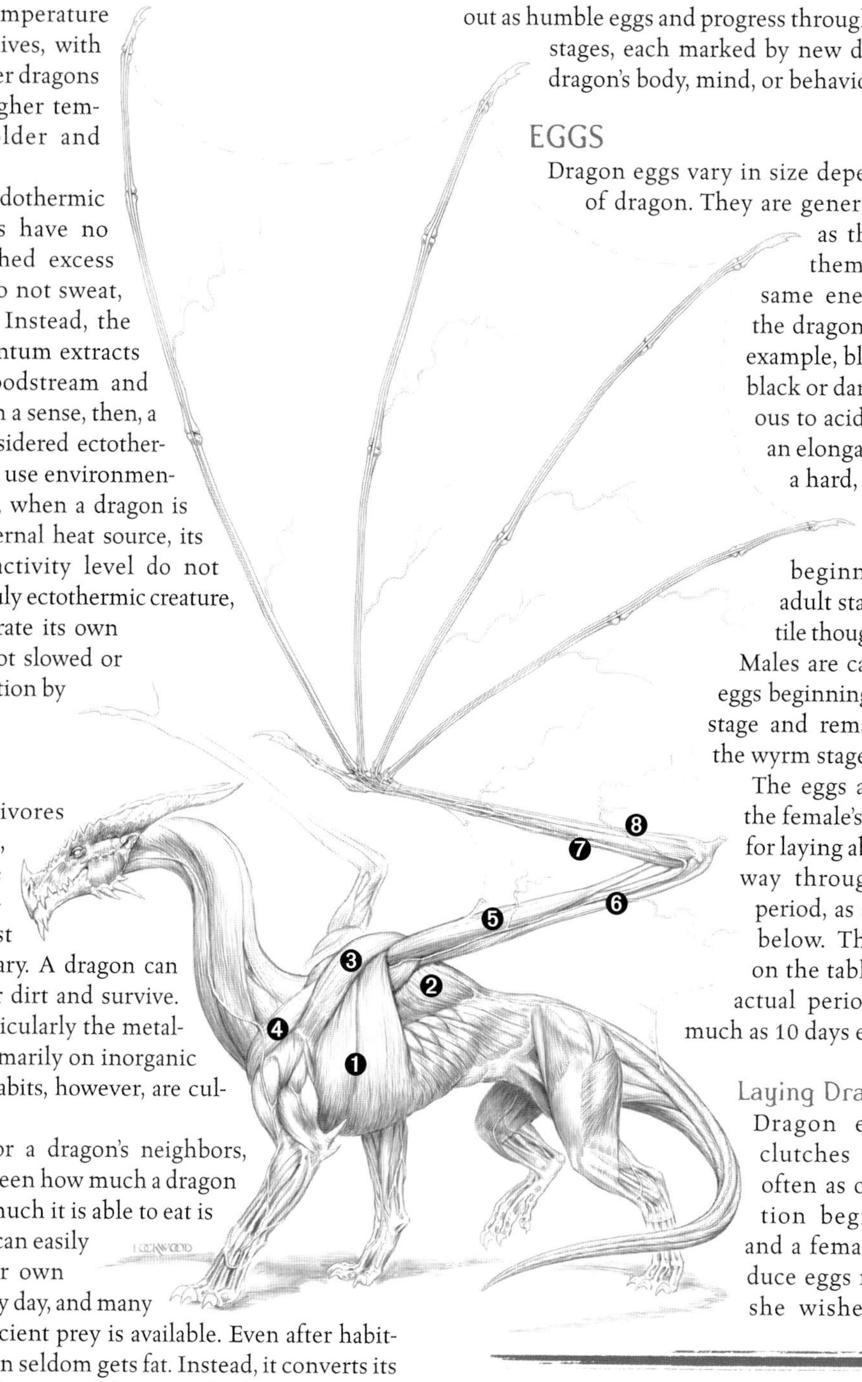

Illus. by T. Lockwood

DRAGON LIFE CYCLE

"From the tiny egg the great wyrm grows."

—Kobold proverb

Barring some misfortune, a dragon can expect to live in good health for 1,200 years, possibly even a great deal longer, depending on its general fitness. All dragons, however, start out as humble eggs and progress through twelve distinct life stages, each marked by new developments in the dragon's body, mind, or behavior.

EGGS

Dragon eggs vary in size depending on the kind of dragon. They are generally the same color as the dragon that laid them and the have the same energy immunities as the dragon that laid them (for example, black dragon eggs are black or dark gray and impervious to acid). A dragon egg has an elongated ovoid shape and a hard, stony shell.

A female dragon can produce eggs beginning at her young adult stage and remains fertile though the very old stage. Males are capable of fertilizing eggs beginning at the young adult stage and remain fertile through the wyrm stage.

The eggs are fertilized inside the female's body and are ready for laying about a quarter of the way through the incubation period, as shown on the table below. The numbers given on the table are approximate; actual periods can vary by as much as 10 days either way.

Laying Dragon Eggs

Dragon eggs are laid in clutches of two to five as often as once a year. Ovulation begins with mating, and a female dragon can produce eggs much less often, if she wishes, simply by not

RULES: DRAGON EGGS

Although it contains a living embryo, treat a dragon egg as an inanimate object with the following statistics.

Dragon Egg Game Statistics

Egg Size	Length*	Weight	Hardness/ Hit Points	Break DC
Tiny	1 ft.	1 lb.	8/10	12
Small	2 ft.	8 lb.	10/15	13
Medium	4 ft.	60 lb.	10/20	15

*A dragon egg has a maximum diameter equal to about 1/2 its length.

Table 1–1: Dragon Egg Characteristics

Color	Ready to Lay	Total Incubation	Size
Black	120 days	480 days	Tiny
Blue	150 days	600 days	Small
Brass	120 days	480 days	Tiny
Bronze	150 days	600 days	Small
Copper	135 days	540 days	Tiny
Gold	180 days	720 days	Medium
Green	120 days	480 days	Small
Red	165 days	660 days	Medium
Silver	165 days	660 days	Small
White	105 days	420 days	Tiny

mating. Mating and egg laying can happen in almost any season of the year.

Most dragon eggs are laid in a nest within the female's lair, where the parent or parents can guard and tend them. A typical nest consists of a pit or mound, with the eggs completely buried in loose material such as sand or leaves. A dragon egg's ovoid shape gives it great resistance to pressure, and the female can walk, fight, or sleep atop the nest without fear of breaking her eggs.

Dragons sometimes leave their eggs untended. In such cases, the female takes great care to keep the nest hidden. She or her mate (or both of them) may visit the area containing the nest periodically, but they take care not to approach the nest too closely unless some danger threatens the eggs.

Hatching Dragon Eggs

When a dragon egg finishes incubating, the wyrmling inside must break out of the egg. If the parents are nearby, they often assist by gently tapping on the eggshell. Otherwise, the wyrmling must break out on its own, a process that usually takes no more than a minute or two once the

Rules: Incubating Dragon Eggs

Once laid, a dragon egg requires suitable incubation conditions if it is to hatch. The basic requirements depend on the kind of dragon, as described below. The embryonic wyrmling inside a dragon egg can survive under inadequate incubation conditions, but not for long. For every hour during which incubation conditions are not met, the wyrmling must make a Constitution check (DC 15 +1 per previous check; an embryonic wyrmling has the same Constitution score as a hatched wyrmling) to survive.

An embryonic wyrmling inside a dragon egg becomes sentient as it enters the final quarter of the incubation period.

Dragon egg incubation conditions are as follows:

Black: The egg must be immersed in acid strong enough to deal at least 1d4 points of damage per round, or sunk in a swamp, bog, or marsh.

Blue: For half of each day, the egg must be kept in a temperature of 90°F to 120°F, followed by a half day at 40°F to 60°F.

Brass: The egg must be kept in an open flame or in a temperature of at least 140°F.

Bronze: The egg must be immersed in a sea or ocean or someplace where tidewaters flow over it at least twice a day.

Copper: The egg must be immersed in acid strong enough to deal at least 1d4 points of damage per round of exposure, or packed in cool sand or clay (40°F to 60°F).

Gold: The egg must be kept in an open flame or in a temperature of at least 140°F.

Green: The egg must be immersed in acid strong enough to deal at least 1d4 points of damage per round, or buried in leaves moistened with rainwater.

Red: The egg must be kept in an open flame or in a temperature of at least 140°F.

Silver: The egg must be buried in snow, encased in ice, or kept in a temperature below 0°F.

White: The egg must be buried in snow, encased in ice, or kept in a temperature below 0°F.

Rules: Hatching Dragon Eggs

To hatch, a wyrmling needs to break out of its shell. From its position inside the egg, the wyrmling cannot bite the eggshell, and the wyrmling's claws are too weak to overcome the shell's hardness. To escape the egg, the wyrmling must break the shell by making a DC 20 Strength check. Fortunately for the wyrmling, it can simply take 20 on the check, breaking the shell in about 2 minutes.

To determine the day on which the eggs in a clutch hatch, roll 1d10. On an odd number, the eggs hatch 1d10 days earlier than the norm (see Table 1–1). On an even number, the eggs hatch 1d10 days later than the norm.

If the egg has been tended by at least one of the wyrmling's parents, it needs to make no further checks to survive.

If incubation conditions have been less than ideal, however, the wyrmling must make a Constitution check to survive. The table below provides a list of circumstances and the DC of the Constitution check to survive despite the bad conditions.

In the case of a disturbed nest or an egg removed from a nest, the creature tending the egg may make a Heal check, with a +1 bonus if the creature has 5 or more ranks of Knowledge (arcana). The wyrmling can use either its own Constitution check result or the Heal check result, whichever is higher.

Opening an egg before the final quarter of the incubation period causes the wyrmling inside to die. If the egg is opened during the final quarter of the incubation period, the wyrmling can make a check to survive, but if successful it takes nonlethal damage equal to its current hit points. This damage cannot be healed until the wyrmling's normal incubation period passes, and the wyrmling remains staggered for the entire period. During this period, a prematurely hatched wyrmling must be tended in the same manner as an unhatched egg in order to survive.

Circumstance	Constitution Check DC
Undisturbed nest	—
Nest disturbed, but restored by parent	10
Nest disturbed, but restored by dragon other than parent	15
Nest disturbed, but restored by nondragon	20
Removed from nest, tended by dragon	20
Removed from nest, tended by nondragon	25
Egg opened prematurely	+5

wyrmling begins trying to escape the egg. All the eggs in a clutch hatch at about the same time.

Properly tended and incubated dragon eggs have practically a 100% hatching rate. Eggs that have been disturbed, and particularly eggs that have been removed from a nest and incubated artificially, may be much less likely to produce live wyrmlings.

WYRMLING (AGE 0–5 YEARS)

A wyrmling emerges from its egg fully formed and ready to face life. From the tip of its nose to the end of its tail, it is about twice as long as the egg that held it (the actual size of the wyrmling depends on the variety of dragon; see Chapter 5).

A newly hatched dragon emerges from its egg cramped and sodden. After about an hour, it is ready to fly, fight, and reason. It inherits a considerable body of practical knowledge from its parents, though such inherent knowledge often lies buried in the wyrmling's memory, unnoticed and unused until it is needed.

Compared to older dragons, a wyrmling seems a little awkward. Its head and feet seem slightly oversized, and its wings and tail are proportionately smaller than they are in adults.

If a parent is present at the wyrmling's hatching, the youngster has a protector and will probably enjoy a secure existence for the first decades of its life. If not, the wyrmling faces a struggle for survival.

Whether raised by another dragon or left to fend for itself, the wyrmling's first order of business is learning to be a dragon, which includes securing food, finding a lair, and understanding its own abilities (usually in that order).

A newly hatched wyrmling almost immediately searches for food. The first meal for a wyrmling left to fend for itself is often the shell from its egg. This practice not only assures the youngster a good dose of vital minerals, but also provides an alternative to attacking and consuming its nestmates. Wyrmlings reared by parents are often offered some tidbit that the variety favors. For example, copper dragons provide their offspring with monstrous centipedes or scorpions. In many cases this meal is in the form of living prey, and the wyrmling gets its first hunting lesson along with its first meal.

With its hunger satisfied, the wyrmling's next task is securing a lair. The dragon looks for some hidden and defensible cave, nook, or cranny where it can rest, hide, and begin storing treasure. Even a wyrmling under the care of a parent finds a section of the parent's lair to call its own.

Once it feels secure in its lair and reasonably sure of its food supply, the wyrmling settles down to hone its inherent abilities. It usually does so by testing itself in any way it can. It tussles with its nestmates, seeks out dangerous creatures to fight, and spends long hours in meditation. If a parent is present, the wyrmling receives instruction on draconic matters and the chance to accompany the parent during its daily activities. Wyrmlings on their own sometimes seek out older dragons of the same kind as mentors. Among good dragons, such relationships tend to be casual and often last for decades (a fairly short period by dragon standards). The youngster visits the older dragon periodically (monthly, perhaps weekly) for advice and information. Evil dragons, too, often counsel wyrmlings that are not their offspring—evil dragons lack any sense of altruism, but usually understand the role of youth in perpetuating the species.

No matter what kinds of dragons are involved, such mentor-apprentice relationships require the younger dragon to show the utmost respect and deference to the older dragon, and to bring the mentor gifts of food, information, and treasure. Should the older dragon ever come to view the apprentice as a rival, the relationship ends immediately; when evil dragons are involved, the ending is often fatal for the younger dragon.

VERY YOUNG (AGE 6–15 YEARS)

By age 6, a dragon has grown enough to double its length, though its head and feet still seem too big for the rest of its body. It becomes physically stronger and more robust. The dragon's larger size often makes finding a new lair necessary. Many dragons relocate at this stage anyway, especially if they do not have parental support. (After the dragon has hunted in an area for five years, the location of the original lair might have become known to outsiders, or the area around the lair could become depleted of prey.)

In most ways, a very young dragon remains much like a wyrmling, albeit more confident in itself.

RULES: WYRMLING ABILITIES

A newly hatched wyrmling cannot fly, takes a –2 penalty on Dexterity, and has a –2 penalty on attack rolls. These penalties disappear after an hour.

The wyrmling otherwise has all the abilities noted for wyrmlings of its kind in the *Monster Manual,* including skills and feats. Its selection of skills and feats is similar to that of its parents.

YOUNG (AGE 16–25 YEARS)

By age 16, most dragons begin a new growth spurt that eventually carries them to their adult size—though they still retain a wyrmling's overlarge head and feet. Their intellects become sharper as they gain life experience and master their innate abilities.

At this stage, a dragon begins to feel the urge to collect treasure and to establish a territory (though it might well have done both sooner). In some cases, however, a young dragon continues to share its lair and its territory with nestmates or parents. Dragons that leave the nest when they become young often range far from their home lairs, seeking locales where they can set up housekeeping on their own.

JUVENILE (AGE 26–50 YEARS)

By age 26, a dragon is well on its way to adulthood. It has nowhere near the physical power of an adult, but it has an adult's body proportions. Some species exhibit the first of their magical powers at this stage.

YOUNG ADULT (AGE 51–100 YEARS)

As it passes the half-century mark, a dragon enters adulthood (although its body keeps growing for many more years). It is ready to mate, and most dragons lose no time in doing so.

By this age, a dragon's scales have developed into armor formidable enough to turn aside all but magic weaponry or the teeth and claws of other dragons. A young adult dragon also masters its first spells and shows evidence of a formidable intellect.

A young adult dragon severs its ties with nestmates, mentors, and parents (if it has not done so already) and establishes it own lair and territory.

ADULT (AGE 101–200 YEARS)

During the second century of its life, a dragon's physical growth begins to slow—but its body is just entering its prime. With the dragon's initial growth spurt over, the dragon's body becomes even more powerful and healthy. An adult dragon continues to hone its mental faculties and masters more skills and magic.

At this stage in life, a dragon is most likely to take a long-term mate and share its lair with a mate and offspring.

MATURE ADULT (AGE 201–400 YEARS)

When a dragon passes the two-century mark, its physical and mental prowess continue to improve, though it usually

RULES: REARING A DRAGON

Being an adoptive parent to a dragon is no easy task. Even good-aligned dragons have a sense of superiority and an innate yearning for freedom. Most dragons instinctively defer to older dragons of the same kind, but they tend to regard other creatures with some disdain.

Older and wiser dragons eventually learn to respect nondragons for their abilities and accomplishments, but a newly hatched wyrmling tends to regard a nondragon foster parent as a captor—or at best as a well-meaning fool. Still, it is possible for a nondragon character to forge a bond with a newly hatched wyrmling. Accomplishing this requires the use of Diplomacy or Intimidate as well as (eventually) the Handle Animal skill.

A character seeking to rear a newly hatched wyrmling must begin with a Diplomacy or Intimidate check to persuade the dragon to accept the character's guidance; 5 or more ranks of Knowledge (arcana) gives the character a +2 bonus on the check. The character's Diplomacy or Intimidate check is opposed by a Sense Motive check by the dragon. The dragon has a +15 racial bonus on its check. Certain other conditions, such as those mentioned on the table below, can further modify the wyrmling's Sense Motive check.

Condition	Modifier
Character tended the dragon's egg while it was incubating	–2
Character was present at the dragon's hatching	–5
Each component of dragon's alignment in common with the character's[1]	–5

1 Alignment components are chaos, evil, good, law, and neutral.

This opposed check is rolled secretly by the DM, so that the player of the character does not immediately know the result of the check. If the wyrmling wins the opposed check, it regards the character as a captor and attempts to gain its freedom any way it can. (Most dragons, even newly hatched wyrmlings, are smart enough to forego an immediate attack on a more powerful being, and will wait for the right opportunity to escape.) No attempt by this character to rear this dragon can succeed. This opposed check cannot be retried.

If the character wins this opposed check, he or she can attempt to rear the dragon. The process takes 5 years, but once the rearing period begins, the character need only devote one day a week to the dragon's training. Throughout the rearing period, however, the dragon must be fed and housed at a cost of 10 gp per day.

When the rearing period has run its course, the character attempts a Handle Animal check (DC 20 + the dragon's Hit Dice at the very young stage). Only one check is made, rolled secretly by the DM. A failed check cannot be retried. If the character's Handle Animal check fails, the dragon is not successfully reared and seeks to leave, as noted above. If the check succeeds, the character can begin to train the dragon to perform tasks (the most common of which is serving as a mount; see Dragons as Mounts, page 136, and the Handle Animal skill, page 74 of the *Player's Handbook*).

For many characters, the ultimate purpose of rearing a dragon is to make it available to the character as a cohort. To rear a dragon for this reason, the character must have taken the Leadership feat (see page 106 of the *Dungeon Master's Guide*) by the time the rearing period expires, and must have a sufficiently high Leadership score to attract the dragon as a cohort at that time (using the dragon's Hit Dice at the very young stage as its cohort level). Also, the dragon's alignment must not be opposed to the character's alignment on either the law-vs.-chaos or good-vs.-evil axis (for example, a lawful good character cannot attempt to rear a chaotic evil wyrmling). For more information, see Dragons as Cohorts, page 138.

undergoes little obvious physical change. By this stage of life, a dragon is truly a force to be reckoned with—and it knows it.

Mature adults display a degree of self-confidence that younger dragons lack. Mature adults seldom seek out danger just to prove themselves (except, perhaps, against other dragons). Instead, they act with purpose and confidence, often launching schemes that take years to complete.

Because of a mature adult's power, wealth, and age, it seldom remains unnoticed in the larger world. Its name becomes known, at least among other dragons, and it often becomes the target of rival dragons or adventurers. One of a mature adult's first orders of business is to review and improve the defenses in its lair. Often, the dragon relocates as a matter of prudence. The dragon never chooses its new lair hastily, and usually includes in its plans some scheme to secure more treasure. Bards' tales of dragons destroying kingdoms and seizing their treasuries often have their roots in true accounts of what happens when a mature adult dragon is on the move.

OLD (AGE 401–600 YEARS)

By the time most dragons reach this age, their physical growth stops, though they become even more hardy, and their minds and magical powers continue to expand with the passing centuries.

Old dragons usually begin to show some outward signs of aging: Their scales begin to chip and crack at the edges and also to darken and lose their luster (though some metallic dragons actually take on a burnished appearance), and the irises in their eyes begin to fade, so that their eyes begin to resemble featureless orbs.

Most old dragons continue to hone the patient cunning they began to develop as mature adults. Though quick to defend what they regard as their own, they seldom rush into anything, preferring instead to plumb the possibilities in any situation before acting.

VERY OLD (AGE 601–800 YEARS)

After passing the six-century mark, a dragon becomes even more resistant to physical punishment. It begins mastering potent spells and magical abilities. This is the last stage of life in which female dragons remain fertile, and most females attempt to raise at least two clutches of eggs before their reproductive period runs out.

ANCIENT (AGE 801–1,000 YEARS)

By this stage, female dragons have reached the end of their reproductive years. Many females compensate by mentoring younger dragons of the species, as do many males. Ancient dragons have little to fear from much younger dragons that have not yet reached adulthood, and they have much wisdom and experience to pass on.

Most dragons at this age have minds to match the best and brightest humans, and they can tap into vast stores of knowledge, both practical and esoteric.

WYRM (AGE 1,001–1,200 YEARS)

Surviving for more than a thousand years is a grand accomplishment, even for dragons, and this stage is a great milestone in dragon life. Even among rival dragons, a wyrm commands at least grudging respect. Male dragons at this stage are reaching the end of their reproductive years, but their exalted status among dragons practically guarantees them mates. Younger females often establish territories adjacent to a male wyrm for mating, for protection, and to make it easy for the offspring to gain the wyrm as a mentor.

GREAT WYRM (AGE 1,201+ YEARS)

When a dragon passes the twelve-century mark, its mental and physical development is finally at an end, and the dragon is at the peak of its physical, mental, and magical powers.

THE TWILIGHT AND DEATH

Exactly how long a dragon can live after reaching the great wyrm stage is a matter of some debate (some scholars contend that a dragon lives forever). Unfortunately, dragons themselves are little help in this matter. They keep no birth records and are apt to exaggerate their ages.

The half-elf sages Guillaume and Cirjon de Cheirdon made a study of dragon ages by carefully noting when certain famous (and infamous) dragons reached their wyrm celebrations and then tracking their ages from there. Some later scholars suspect that Guillaume and Cirjon were silver dragons using half-elf guise, and that the speculations they published were in fact field notes. In any case, the pair eventually vanished, and their final resting places are not known. Perhaps they died in a dragon attack, or perhaps they are with us still, in other guises.

RULES: ONSET OF THE TWILIGHT AND DEATH

A dragon's maximum age is a function of its Charisma score. For a chromatic dragon, multiply the dragon's Charisma score by 50 and add the result to 1,200. This is the age when the twilight period begins for that kind of dragon. For a metallic dragon, multiply the dragon's Charisma score by 100 and add the result to 1,200. This difference reflects the fact that metallic dragons are longer-lived than chromatic dragons. Maximum ages for the dragons found in the *Monster Manual* are given on the table below.

Color	Years to Twilight	Color	Years to Twilight
Black	2,200	Brass	3,200
Blue	2,300	Bronze	3,800
Green	2,300	Copper	3,400
Red	2,500	Gold	4,400
White	2,100	Silver	4,200

When a dragon's twilight period begins, the dragon must make a DC 20 Constitution check. The dragon dies if the check fails. If the check succeeds, the dragon survives, but its Constitution score drops by 1. Each year thereafter, the dragon must succeed on another Constitution check in order to stay alive.

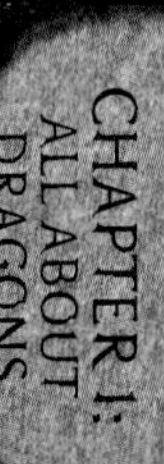

Guillaume and Cirjon established that the shortest-lived true dragon, the white, can live as long as 2,100 years. The true dragon species that lives the longest is the gold; Guillaume and Cirjon put the gold's maximum age at 4,400 years.

In addition, the sages discovered that dragons can extend their life spans to some extent by entering a state called "the twilight." That term, coined by Guillaume and Cirjon, refers to the closing phase of a dragon's life. The cessation of growth at the great wyrm stage heralds the onset of death (as it does for most creatures that grow throughout their lives). A dragon can survive for centuries after reaching the great wyrm stage, but a dragon is mortal and cannot stave off death forever. The twilight occurs when the weight of a dragon's years finally comes crashing down, forcing the dragon's physiology into a downward spiral. A dragon's twilight period can last for a number of years, but often the dragon succumbs when the twilight first sets in.

AVOIDING THE TWILIGHT

Many dragons prefer to avoid a slow descent into death and leave the mortal coil with their dignity intact. Many great wyrms seem to just disappear at the ends of their lives. No one knows exactly where they go, but scholars have identified at least three possibilities: departure, guardianship, and dracolichdom.

Departure

A dragon can simply will its spirit to depart. Upon doing so, the dragon dies, and its spirit is released into the hereafter. A dragon prepares for its departure by consuming its entire

RULES: AVOIDING TWILIGHT

Any dragon that has reached the old age category or higher can depart, become a guardian, or become a dracolich. (Details of dracolichdom can be found on page 146.)

To depart or become a guardian, a dragon must consume at least 135,000 gp worth of treasure—or at least 90% of its hoard, if the dragon possesses treasure worth more than 150,000 gp. All the treasure must be consumed in the same day, and at least 120,000 gp of this treasure must have been part of the dragon's hoard for at least 200 years.

After consuming the required amount of treasure, the dragon must find a dragon graveyard or suitable site to guard. Once it is at the graveyard or site, the dragon completes the process instantly simply by willing it to happen.

When a dragon departs, its body dies. When a dragon becomes a guardian, its body melds into the landscape. Once it has consumed the treasure, a dragon can delay departing or becoming a guardian for no more than 1 day per point of Charisma it has. If the dragon exceeds this time limit, the opportunity is lost, and the dragon cannot make another attempt to depart until it again consumes the required amount of treasure.

hoard. Most dragons also travel to a dragon graveyard and die there.

Dragon graveyards are ancient places whose origins are lost even to dragon memory. As a rule, they are accessible only to flying creatures, being situated on mountaintops, in hidden valleys (surrounded by jungle, deserts, or mountains), on islands located in windless or storm-tossed seas, or in the depths of great rifts on the earth.

Within the graveyard, dangers abound. Storms of elemental energy often wash over dragon graveyards, and elemental vortexes often appear in random spots. Some of these may belch forth groups of hostile elemental creatures or suck the unwary right off the Material Plane and onto an elemental plane. Dragon carcasses or skeletons may spontaneously animate and walk about, attacking any living creatures they meet.

Dragon graveyards also are haunted by ghostly dragons.

Despite the dangers, dragon graveyards often draw visitors. According to legend, and some reputed discoveries, not all of a departed dragon's consumed hoard is always destroyed, and many treasure hunters (showing dragonlike greed) eagerly seek out dragon graveyards for the treasures they are said to contain. Other visitors seek to obtain dragon remains for magical or alchemical purposes.

Guardianship

At the end of its normal life, a dragon can elect to become a guardian, literally transforming into part of the landscape. After the dragon consumes its hoard, it changes itself into a geographic feature: hills, mountains, lakes, swamps, and groves seem to be the most common choices.

Such areas become favorite places for dragons to lay their eggs. It is said that no nest of dragon eggs laid in such a locale will ever be disturbed. Wyrmling dragons living in the site are said to commune with the guardian spirit, receiving the knowledge they need to become strong adults.

As with dragon graveyards, legends say that some of the late dragon's treasure may still remain hidden at the site, making these features prime targets for treasure hunters. Extracting the treasure (if it exists at all) is apt to be difficult. Younger dragons living at the site usually resent intrusions, as do absentee parents who have laid eggs there (as we have seen, dragons that leave their eggs untended often still keep watch over their nests). These sites also attract

RULES: DRAGON GRAVEYARDS

A dragon graveyard presents a macabre landscape of blasted earth littered with ossified dragon bones and fresher dragon remains.

Every dragon graveyard has at least one ghostly guardian, charged with protecting the place. The graveyard's guardian is exactly like a ghostly dragon (see page 161) of a great wyrm dragon, usually a gold dragon or other dragon of lawful alignment. The guardian exists only to guard the graveyard, not to recover a lost hoard. The guardian cannot be put to rest by offering it treasure. If it is defeated in combat, the guardian reforms in 1 day.

Other ghostly dragons might be present also. These additional spirits are normal ghostly dragons.

Supernatural hazards abound in a dragon graveyard. Periodic storms of elemental energy rage through area. These storms are similar to *fire storm* spells cast by 20th-level characters (Reflex DC 23 half), except that they can be composed of acid, cold, electricity, or fire, and they cover the whole graveyard. They typically strike every 1d4 hours, but the frequency can vary widely.

Dragon graveyards also contain areas in which the fabric of the cosmos is weakened. These unstable areas can be anywhere from 5 feet to 50 feet across. Every 1d4 hours, such an area is equally likely to expel a horde of elementals (treat as an *elemental swarm* spell cast by a 20th-level character) or draw everything within the unstable area into a vortex leading to an elemental plane. This vortex lasts for 1d4 minutes. Creatures that touch or enter the unstable area during the period of the disturbance are whisked to an elemental plane.

A weak spot always has a lingering aura of conjuration magic (aura strength is overwhelming when it is active).

A dragon graveyard also has an ever-changing population of dragon skeletons and dragon zombies (see pages 192 and 197) that have become animated by the supernatural forces in the graveyard. These creatures attack any living creature they meet, except for dragons that have come to the graveyard to die.

The legends about treasure in dragon graveyards are true. A dragon graveyard typically contains triple standard treasure for the guardian's Challenge Rating. Though ghostly dragons normally do not have any treasure, a dragon graveyard accumulates bits and pieces of treasure that departing dragons have left behind and equipment from would-be looters who weren't up to the challenge.

RULES: GUARDED SITES

When a dragon becomes a guardian, it creates a geographical feature with an area of about 1 square mile per 5 points of Constitution the dragon had.

The feature created always resembles a dragon in some subtle manner. The contours of a hill might suggest a sleeping dragon, for example, or a lake might have the shape of a dragon's head or footprint.

Dragon eggs laid in a guarded area become hidden by *nondetection* and *mirage arcana* effects, provided the female laying them is of the same kind as the guardian. Both effects lasts until the eggs hatch, and neither effect has a magical aura, but otherwise they function as the spells cast by a 20th-level caster.

Any dragon of the same kind as the guardian and of juvenile age or younger can visit the area once a month and receive the benefits of a *commune* spell. Older dragons of the same kind as the guardian get the same benefit, but only once a year.

The heart of a guarded site may indeed contain a small amount of treasure left over from the guardian's transformation (hidden near the heart of the site). Such a treasure contains coins and goods only and is of a level equal to one quarter of the guardian's Challenge Rating at the time of its transformation. Removal of the treasure does not harm the guarded site, but most dragons take a dim view of such activity.

their share of ghostly dragons, adding a new element of danger for trespassers.

DRACOLICHDOM

Some evil dragons enlist the aid of others to cheat death. The dragon and its servants create an inanimate object, called a phylactery, that will hold the dragon's life force.

Next, a special brew is prepared for the dragon to consume. The potion is a lethal poison that slays the dragon for which it was prepared without fail.

Upon the death of the dragon, its spirit transfers itself to the phylactery. From the phylactery, the spirit can occupy any dead body that lies close by, including its own former body. If the body it currently inhabits is destroyed, the spirit returns to the phylactery, and from there it can occupy a new body.

See the Dracolich entry, page 146, for details on the results of this process.

DRAGON SENSES

"Dragons don't see very well in the dark. They don't hear so well, either."

—The late Aylmer Dapynto, erstwhile sage and dragon hunter

"You want to live a long and profitable life? Then don't try to sneak past a dragon!"

—Lidda, advising a young rogue

Like any predatory creature, a dragon has acute senses. These remarkable senses become even better as a dragon grows and ages, mostly because a dragon's mind becomes ever more perceptive as the centuries pass. A dragon's eyes, ears, and nose may not become any more sharper with age, but the dragon's prodigious intellect can sift increasing amounts of information from its environment.

VISION

Dragons have vision superbly adapted to hunting. They enjoy excellent depth perception, which allows them to judge distances with great accuracy, and they have outstanding peripheral vision as well. Dragons can perceive motion and detail at least twice as well as a human in daylight, and their eyes adapt quickly to harsh light and glare. A dragon can stare at the sun on a clear summer day and suffer no loss of vision. Eagles and other birds of prey can perform similar visual feats. Such creatures often have poor night vision—and it may be this fact that leads some scholars to conclude that dragons don't see well in the dark.

In fact, dragons see exceedingly well in dim light. In moonlight, dragons see as well as they can in sunlight. In even dimmer light, a dragon sees four times as far as a human can under similar conditions. Dragons can even see with no light at all.

When any illumination is present, a dragon sees in color. Its ability to discern hues is at least as good as a human's. In the absence of light, a dragon's vision is black-and-white.

RULES: DRAGON SIGHT

As noted in the *Monster Manual,* dragons see extremely well in all lighting conditions.

In normal light, a dragon sees twice as well has a human. In game terms, this means that a dragon can detect the presence of a potential encounter at twice the distance given in the *Dungeon Master's Guide* (see Stealth and Detection in a Forest, page 87, and other similar sections). Also, when a dragon makes a Spot check, it takes only half the penalty for distance: a –1 penalty per 20 feet of distance rather than the standard –1 per 10 feet of distance.

In dim light, a dragon sees four times as well as a human. The dragon's low-light vision is exactly like that of other creatures with the low-light ability, except that the dragon sees four times as far when using artificial illumination. For example, from a dragon's point of view a *light* spell produces bright illumination in a 40-foot radius around the affected object and dim light for an additional 40 feet.

In complete darkness, a dragon relies on darkvision and blindsense. Both are exactly like the standard abilities, except for the dragon's exceptional range: 120 feet for darkvision and 60 feet for blindsense.

In addition to their superior visual apparatus, dragons commonly have ranks in the Spot skill.

RULES: DRAGON SCENT

Despite their excellent sense of smell, dragons do not have the scent special ability and do not gain the game benefits of that ability, except to the extent that this sense contributes to their blindsense.

RULES: DRAGON HEARING

A dragon's ability to perceive ultrasonic or subsonic frequencies is no better than a human's. Dragons commonly have ranks in the Listen skill, and given their enormous number of skill points many hear much better than typical humans.

RULES: HOVER AND WINGOVER

Hovering is a move action, which means a dragon also can use its breath weapon, cast a spell, use a spell-like ability, or make a melee attack while hovering (but not with a wing or its tail).

If a dragon does not attack during a round when it hovers, it can instead move at half speed it any direction it likes, including straight up, straight down, or backward, no matter what its maneuverability rating is.

When a dragon stops hovering, it can turn in place and resume ordinary flight in any direction in which it could normally fly. For example, if a dragon were flying north when it stopped to hover, it could turn around and fly south afterward. It still could not fly straight up or down or fly in any other manner that its maneuverability rating does not allow.

A dragon can perform a wingover as a free action while flying. Performing a wingover consumes 10 feet of flying movement. A dragon cannot hover or gain altitude in the same round that it performs a wingover.

SCENT

A dragon's sense of smell is nearly as well developed as its vision. This refined sense of smell is only partly dependent on the dragon's sensitive nose; it also uses its forked tongue to sample the air, just as a snake does. A dragon's ability to sense the presence of other creatures by scent makes it difficult to catch a dragon unawares, and hiding from a dragon is nearly impossible once a dragon is close enough to pick up the quarry's scent.

HEARING

A dragon's ears are about as sensitive as human ears, and the range of tones a dragon can hear is similar to what a human can hear. Even the youngest of dragons, however, has sharper hearing than a typical human, thanks to its ability to recognize important sounds for what they are and to filter out background noise and focus on significant sounds.

BLINDSENSE

One outstanding example of a dragon's sensory prowess is its blindsense—the ability to "see" things that are invisible or completely obscured. By using its nose and ears, and also by noticing subtle clues such as air currents and vibrations, a dragon can sense everything in its immediate vicinity, even with its eyes closed, when shrouded in magical *darkness*, or when swathed in impenetrable fog. Of course, some phenomena are entirely visual in nature (such as color), and a dragon that cannot see cannot perceive these phenomena.

TASTE

A dragon's sense of taste is highly discriminating. Dragons can note the slightest variations in the taste of water or food, and most dragons develop some peculiar culinary preferences as a result. Copper dragons, for example, relish venomous vermin. Perhaps the most infamous draconic taste is the red dragon's preference for the flesh of young women.

Curiously, dragons don't seem to respond well to sweet flavors. Whether this is because they don't like sweets or because they have difficulty distinguishing sweet flavors is unclear. Most dragons refuse to discuss the matter.

TOUCH

Thanks to its thick, scaly hide and clawed feet, a dragon has very little tactile sense. Smaller, younger dragons who have yet to develop impressive natural armor have better senses of touch than older dragons, making touch the only one of a dragon's senses that gets less acute as a dragon grows and ages. A dragon interested in a object's texture might touch or stroke the object with its tongue. Even so, a dragon's tongue proves better at tasting than touching.

A dragon's muted sense of touch might explain its preference for nests made from piles of coins, gems, or other treasure. A bed of so many small, hard, sometimes pointy objects might prove highly uncomfortable to a human, but to a dragon such an arrangement offers a comfortable tickle, like a nubby wool blanket.

FLIGHT

"A dragon in flight? Do you call that flying?"

—Kal' ostikillam, djinni

"Dragons are stately and powerful flyers, able to stay on the wing for days."

—Yunni Cupuricus, sage

Some sages speculate that a dragon's ability to fly is partially magical; however, dragons have been known to take wing and maneuver inside antimagic areas where their spells and breath weapons do not work. A dragon owes its ability to fly, and its flight characteristics, to its peculiar anatomy and metabolism. A dragon weighs much less than a strictly terrestrial creature of the same size does, and its muscles—particularly the ones that enable it to fly—are exceptionally strong, giving the dragon's wings enough power to lift the dragon into the air.

A dragon's biggest problem in flight is just getting aloft. Given the chance, a dragon prefers to launch itself from a height, where it can

gain speed by diving initially. Failing that, a dragon takes flight by leaping into the air, giving itself a boost by snapping its tail downward and pushing off with its hind legs.

Once airborne, a dragon stays aloft with deceptively slow and stately wing beats. The wings develop tremendous lift and thrust on each stroke, allowing the dragon to coast for brief periods. To further conserve energy in flight, a dragon makes use of any updrafts it can find. Under the right conditions, a dragon can soar for hours with little effort. A dragon attempting to fly a long distance usually begins by finding an updraft and spiraling upward to a comfortable altitude, then soaring from one updraft to another. Dragons can quickly cover great distances in this manner.

A dragon in straight and level flight holds its body fairly straight, with its neck and tail extended, its front legs tucked under its chest, and its rear legs thrown back. The dragon's powerful neck and tail, along with the frills on its back, help keep it on course. Although a dragon's wings do not resemble a bird's wings, a dragon uses its wings as a bird of prey does, with smooth, steady downstrokes and quick upstrokes.

Wyrmlings are much less majestic flyers than older dragons; they have smaller wings and are forced to beat them furiously to stay aloft. They resemble fluttering bats when in flight.

Despite their vast wingspans, dragons can fly through relatively narrow openings simply by folding their wings and coasting through.

Most dragons have difficulty executing quick maneuvers in the air. They prefer to make wide, slow turns, using their tails as rudders. If a more violent maneuver is necessary, a dragon uses its head and tail to turn itself, and it can also alter the shape and stroke of its wings. Even so, a dragon has a wide turning circle, and only the smallest and most maneuverable dragon can turn within its own length.

Many dragons have perfected some acrobatic tricks to help them maneuver in tight spaces. The first of these is hovering. Normally, a dragon must maintain some forward momentum to stay in the air, but some dragons can beat their wings with enough speed and efficiency to halt their forward motion and hover in place. While hovering, a dragon can fly straight up, straight down, sideways, or even backward. Hovering takes considerable effort, however, and a dragon can do little else while it hovers. The downdraft created by a hovering dragon is considerable, and can create huge clouds of dust and debris. Some dragons can even use this downdraft as a weapon.

Other dragons can take advantage of their supple bodies to perform a wingover—a sort of aerial somersault that lets them change direction quickly. The dragon thrusts the front of its body upward and twists its body into a spin. This maneuver allows the dragon to turn in place through an arc of up to 180 degrees while maintaining its present altitude.

OTHER MODES OF MOVEMENT

"Not every dragon falls upon you like a thunderbolt from the heavens."

—Stewart Debruk, dragon hunter

A dragon doesn't have to take to the air to demonstrate amazing speed.

RUNNING OR WALKING

A dragon on the ground moves like a cat, and can be just as graceful (though the bigger dragons tend to lumber along). When it's not in a hurry, a

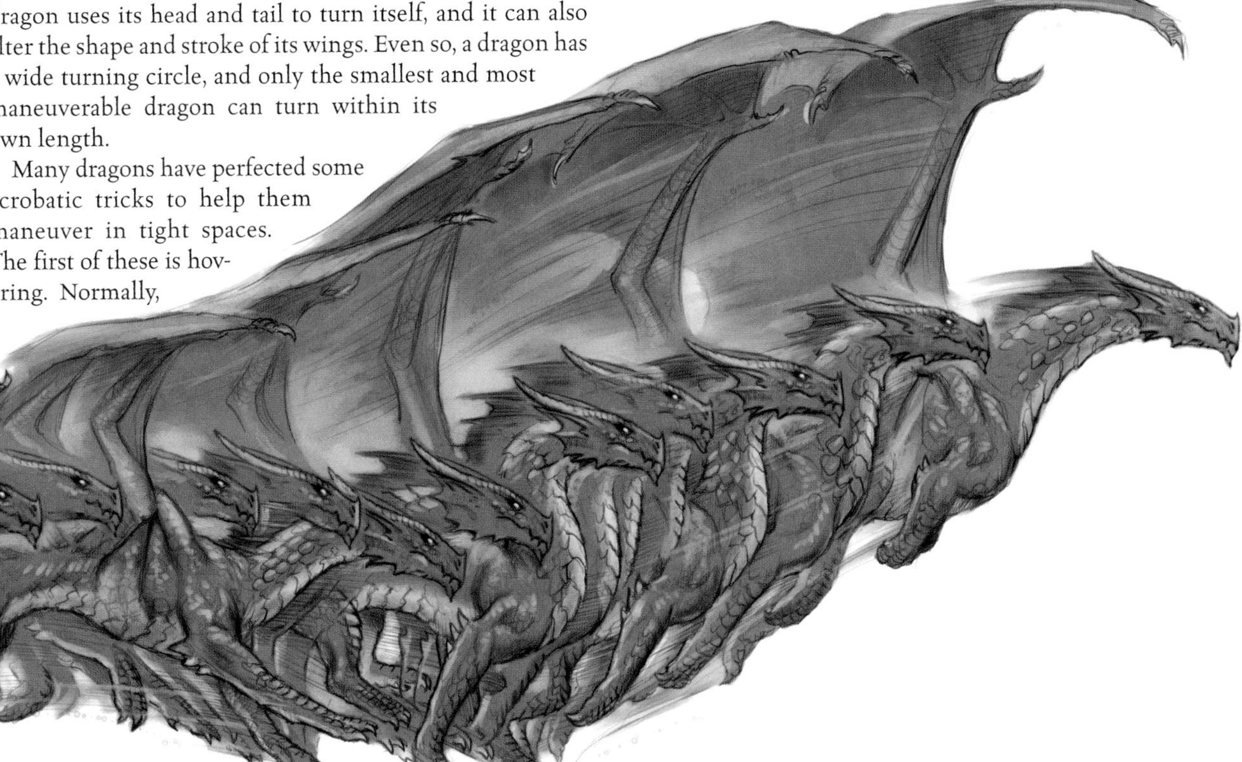

Illus. by J. Jarvis

dragon walks by moving two legs at a time. The dragon lifts one forefoot and the hind foot on the opposite side. Like a cat, with each step a dragon places its hind foot in the place where the corresponding forefoot was.

As it strides along, a dragon keeps its wings loosely furled at its side. If it is feeling lazy, it lets its tail drag behind. Usually, however, a dragon holds its tail off the ground, and the tail slowly moves from side to side in time with the dragon's gait. The motion helps the dragon keep its balance. The tail sometimes brushes the ground, but only briefly and usually well to the left or right of the dragon's body.

A running dragon can easily outpace the finest horse. It uses a galloping motion, moving both front legs together, followed by both back legs. The wings stay furled, but the dragon spreads them occasionally to maintain balance. The tail is held high.

RULES: SWIMMING DRAGONS

If a dragon has a swim speed, it can swim on the surface or below it without difficulty. It moves through water at the listed speed without making Swim checks. It has a +8 racial bonus on any Swim check to perform some special action or avoid a hazard. It can always can choose to take 10 on a Swim check, even if distracted or endangered. It can use the run action while swimming, provided it swims in a straight line.

A dragon that does not have a swim speed still can swim, but it must make Swim checks to move, and is subject to all the rules governing swimming, including taking nonlethal damage from fatigue when it swims for extended periods (see the Swim skill description, page 84 of the *Player's Handbook*).

A dragon swimming underwater must hold its breath unless it has the *water breathing* ability. A dragon with the *water breathing* ability can do anything in the water that it can do out of the water, including using its breath weapon.

A dragon holding its breath underwater must obey all the normal rules for doing so. Most dragons can hold their breathes without difficulty for quite long periods, thanks to their impressive Constitution scores. A dragon holding its breath can use its breath weapon underwater. If the breath weapon uses fire, the dragon must succeed on a DC 20 Spellcraft check to make it function properly. If the check fails, the fiery breath merely creates a few harmless bubbles of steam. No matter what kind of breath the dragon used, it stops holding its breath when it uses its breath weapon and begins to drown.

RULES: BURROWING DRAGONS

Burrowing dragons can move only through fairly soft material such as sand, loamy soil, snow, or ice. The material also must be fairly dry. A burrowing dragon cannot dig through mud, for example.

SWIMMING

All true dragons can swim, though only a few kinds can be considered truly aquatic. Aquatic dragons have long, flat tails and webbing between their toes or in their shoulder joints.

A swimming dragon usually moves like a big reptile. It folds its wings tightly against its body and throws its legs back, creating a streamlined shape. It moves its body left to right in a sinuous motion, and its tail lashes from side to side, providing propulsion. The truly aquatic dragons sometimes employ their wings as big fins in the manner of a ray or an aquatic bird.

The frill along a dragon's back helps it stay on course when swimming underwater, and also keeps the dragon from rolling over.

A swimming dragon steers with its head, tail, and feet.

A dragon swimming at the surface often holds its head and neck out of the water, which allows it to scan the surface while most of its body remains submerged. A dragon also occasionally swims with just the upper half of its head out of the water. This restricts the dragon's field of vision somewhat, but makes it practically undetectable.

Most dragons are obliged to hold their breath when submerged. However, the truly aquatic types can breathe underwater as easily as they take in water and extract oxygen from it. The dragon inhales water through its nose, and the water floods the lungs and is exhaled through the nose. The dragon handles the process as easily at it breathes air.

BURROWING

Any dragon can gouge out holes in the ground with its claws, but some dragons can also worm their way through sand or loose earth, moving as quickly as a human can move at a brisk walk.

Burrowing dragons tend to have shorter, thicker necks than other dragons, stubbier legs, and wedge-shaped heads. When burrowing, the dragon pushes with its head and uses its front feet to claw away material. The back legs kick the loosened material back past the dragon's body. The tunnel the dragon makes when burrowing usually collapses behind it.

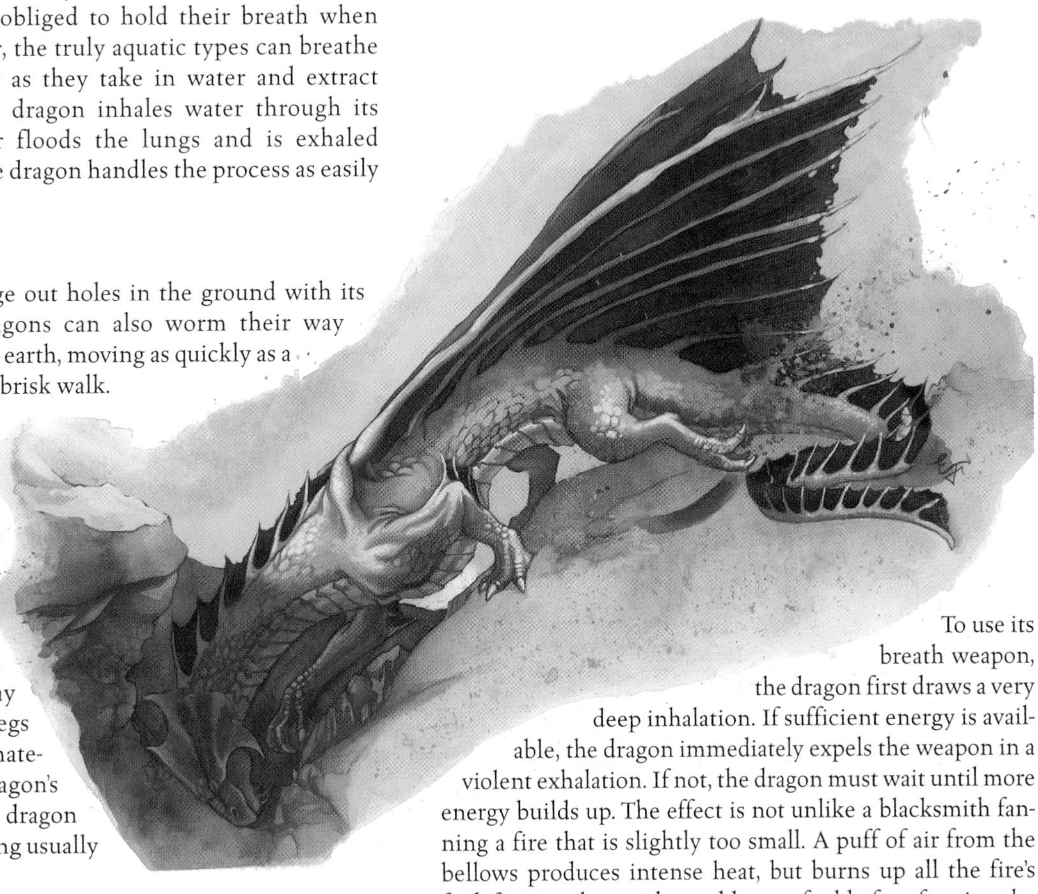

COMBAT ABILITIES

"Battle is a dragon's natural element; it is made for combat. It has teeth like spears, claws like scimitars, wings like hammers, and a tail like a battering ram. Lesser beings cower in its presence, and its breath fells armies."

— Munwithurix, red dragon

The vanity of dragons is legendary. Indeed, they have much to boast about, including a fearsome array of natural weaponry and a host of more subtle abilities that make them all but invincible in combat.

BREATH WEAPONS

The most infamous weapon in a dragon's formidable arsenal is its devastating breath. The chromatic dragons can produce blasts of elemental energy; the type of energy varies with the kind of dragon. The metallic dragons can produce elemental breath weapons, too, but they also produce a second type of breath that is nonlethal but potent in its own way.

No matter what form its breath weapon takes, a dragon generates it from deep inside its lungs, using energy generated from an organ near its heart called the draconis fundamentum (page 8). Fortunately for dragon hunters, a dragon cannot produce breath weapon effects continuously. Each breath depletes the dragon's inner reserves of energy, and it usually requires at least a few seconds to produce another breath.

To use its breath weapon, the dragon first draws a very deep inhalation. If sufficient energy is available, the dragon immediately expels the weapon in a violent exhalation. If not, the dragon must wait until more energy builds up. The effect is not unlike a blacksmith fanning a fire that is slightly too small. A puff of air from the bellows produces intense heat, but burns up all the fire's fuel, forcing the smith to add more fuel before fanning the flame again. A dragon seems to remain aware of the state of its inner energy and never tries to use its breath weapon too soon. Dragons, however, do not seem to have much control over how quickly their inner energy replenishes itself.

A dragon can discharge its breath weapon with little or no forewarning. Some dragons are adept at convincing timorous foes that a breath could come at any moment.

FRIGHTFUL PRESENCE

The mere appearance of a dragon can send pack animals fleeing in terror and shake the resolve of the most stalwart soldier. Usually, a dragon must be of at least young adult age to have this power.

Though some commentators speak of dragons inspiring supernatural fear, a dragon's frightful presence has no magical component. Dragons are simply very good at striking fear in the hearts of foes, and they can do so whenever they take any action that is the least bit aggressive.

IMMUNITIES AND DEFENSES

Though most forms of attack have at least a slim chance of working against a dragon, some attacks prove useless.

Every true dragon is immune to at least one type of elemental energy (acid, cold, electricity, or fire), usually the same type of energy as the dragon uses for its breath weapon. This immunity stems from the dragon's elemental nature. The same power that allows it to belch forth a blast of energy also keeps that energy from harming the dragon.

True dragons have superb internal temperature regulation and seldom suffer from the effects of excessive heat or cold.

In addition, all draconic creatures are not subject to effects that put them to sleep or induce paralysis; such creatures possess an unstoppable vitality.

True dragons also develop a supernatural resistance to physical blows, which can prevent nonmagical weapons from harming them at all. Bards' tales about marauding dragons enduring hails of arrows from defending archers without suffering so much as a scratch are all too true.

Thanks to their innately magical nature, true dragons also develop the power to shrug off the effects of spells. Older dragons ignore spell assaults from all but the most powerful magical practitioners.

MAGICAL ABILITIES

All dragons develop innate magical abilities as they age. Among these is the ability to cast arcane spells.

A dragon's innate magical abilities tend to reflect the character and attitudes of its species. For example, black

RULES: BREATH WEAPONS

A dragon's breath weapon is a supernatural ability. It does not work in antimagic areas. Using a breath weapon is a standard action. As noted in the *Monster Manual,* when a dragon uses a breath weapon, it must wait 1d4 rounds before it can breathe again. In this case, a round lasts until the dragon's next turn begins (see The Combat Round, page 138 of the *Player's Handbook*). For example, if a dragon breathes in the first round of combat, and the die roll for when the breath weapon can next be used is a 1, the dragon can breathe again in round 2. If the die roll is a 4, the dragon could not breathe again until round 5.

If a dragon has more than one type of breath weapon, it still can breathe only once every 1d4 rounds. The Recover Breath feat (see page 73) can shorten the time a dragon has to wait between uses of its breath weapon.

The size, shape, and effect of a breath weapon depends on the kind of dragon and its size and age, as given in the *Monster Manual.*

RULES: FRIGHTFUL PRESENCE

A dragon's frightful presence is an extraordinary ability. It works even in antimagic areas.

Frightful presence is a mind-affecting fear ability that takes effect whenever a dragon attacks, charges, or merely flies overhead. A dragon can inspire fear by flying overhead at an altitude low enough to place foes with the radius of the effect, which is 30 feet × the dragon's age category (usually at least 150 feet, since most dragons gain this ability at the young adult stage). A dragon's frightful presence also takes effect whenever the dragon charges or attacks in any way (with natural weapons, spells, or a breath weapon).

Using frightful presence is part of whatever action triggers it. A dragon does not have to take a separate action to use the power; however, a dragon can suppress its frightful presence ability as a free action.

A creature must be able to see the dragon for its frightful presence ability to take effect. If the dragon is invisible or has total concealment, the ability does not work. Once the ability takes effect, however, the consequences persist for the full duration, even if the dragon later passes from sight. Creatures within the ability's radius are not affected if they have more Hit Dice than the dragon, or if they are dragons themselves.

A potentially affected creature that succeeds on a Will save (DC 10 + 1/2 dragon's HD + dragon's Cha modifier) remains immune to that dragon's frightful presence for 24 hours. (This temporary immunity occurs only on a successful save. If a creature doesn't have to make a save because it cannot see the dragon, it is not immune and must make a save when it does see the dragon.) On a failure, creatures with 4 or fewer HD become panicked for 4d6 rounds, and those with 5 or more HD become shaken for 4d6 rounds.

As an extraordinary ability, frightful presence remains effective even when the dragon assumes a different form. Bronze, gold, and silver dragons, which have the ability to assume an alternate form, usually suppress their frightful presence ability when using assumed forms, to avoid compromising their disguises. If they wish to avoid fighting, however, they can use their frightful presence ability if they are challenged when in their assumed forms.

RULES: DRAGON IMMUNITIES

Every kind of true dragon has immunity to at least one type of energy, as noted in the *Monster Manual.*

A true dragon ignores the detrimental effects of extreme heat (110°F to 140°F) and of extreme cold (0°F to –40°F). A true dragon in these conditions does not have to make a Fortitude save every 10 minutes to avoid taking nonlethal damage.

All creatures of the dragon type are immune to magic sleep and paralysis effects, also as noted in the *Monster Manual.*

True dragons develop damage reduction as they age, as noted in the *Monster Manual.* Damage reduction is a supernatural ability and is ineffective in an antimagic field.

True dragons also develop spell resistance as they age, as noted in the *Monster Manual.*

dragons prefer damp and dismal swamps, and they also have the ability to create magical darkness. Copper dragons live in rocky hills and have the ability to shape stone. Often a dragon's innate abilities have little direct impact on combat, but the dragon can use them to defend its lair or to prepare for battle.

A dragon's spells tend to reflect its own personality. Each dragon develops a unique personal repertoire of spells (though many dragons choose similar spells for their sheer utility). No scholar has determined how dragons accomplish this, and it seems that dragons themselves don't know how they do it. Dragons simply have an inborn talent for arcane magic. They develop rudimentary spellcasting powers as they approach adulthood. Humanoid sorcerers, who often claim their magical powers stem from a dragon ancestor, usually do not develop any magical aptitude until after puberty. Some scholars take this as a sign that no connection at all exists between sorcerers and dragons. Other scholars dismiss the disparity as an inevitable result of the vast differences between draconic and humanoid life cycles.

In any case, dragons exhibit a talent that sorcerers lack: They can cast most of their spells without the physical props other spellcasters find necessary.

NATURAL ARMOR AND WEAPONRY

A dragon's panoply of overlapping scales backed by layers of hide and muscle and supported by a strong, resilient skeleton offers considerable protection from attack. Even a Tiny dragon is typically as well armored as a human wearing chainmail. A big dragon's scaly hide provides four or five times more protection than the best suit of plate armor can offer.

A dragon's primary weapon in physical combat is its bite. A dragon can bite at creatures a fair distance way, thanks to its long neck.

A dragon's claws are not as fearsome as its bite, and a dragon on the move often does not use its claws, but anyone fighting a dragon should be wary of them nevertheless.

A dragon of roughly human size or larger can strike effectively with the alar limbs at the forward edges of its wings. Though the alar limbs have vestigial claws, the wing is a bludgeoning weapon. A dragon usually keeps the "fingers" supporting the wing closed to avoid damaging the wing, much like a human clenches his fist when delivering a punch. A dragon's wings may span hundreds of feet when they are fully extended, but it uses only a fairly small portion of the wing as a weapon.

A dragon of larger than human size can use its tail

RULES: MAGICAL ABILITIES

As noted in the *Monster Manual,* creatures with innate spellcasting abilities, such as dragons, do not require material components to cast their spells. If a spell has a focus, however, a dragon or other innate spellcaster must have the focus on its person. Dragons can use the Embed Spell Focus feat to satisfy this requirement.

Except for not needing consumable material components, dragons cast their spells in the same way other arcane spellcasters do. They are subject to arcane spell failure if they wear armor. (Their own natural armor does not impose an arcane spell failure chance.) They must provide any verbal and somatic components the spell has, and they must pay any XP cost the spell entails. A dragon typically has a cushion of 100 to 600 XP times its spellcaster level. It can use these XP in spellcasting without risking the loss of a level.

Also as noted in the *Monster Manual*, a dragon's caster level for its spell-like abilities is equal to its age category or its sorcerer caster level, whichever is higher.

Although dragons cast spells as sorcerers, they are not members of the sorcerer class and receive none of that class's benefits (except for spellcasting). A dragon gains bonus spells each day for a high Charisma score. A dragon that becomes a member of the sorcerer class adds any actual sorcerer levels it has to its effective sorcerer level to determine its spellcasting ability, but uses its actual sorcerer level and character level to determine its other class abilities. For example, an old silver dragon casts spells as an 11th-level sorcerer. If the dragon becomes a 1st-level sorcerer, it casts spells as a 12th-level sorcerer, but its familiar (if it has one) has the abilities of a familiar with a 1st-level master.

As noted in the *Monster Manual,* most of a dragon's spell-like abilities function as the spells of the same name cast at a level equal to the dragon's sorcerer level or its age category, whichever is higher.

A dragon with the alternate form racial ability is proficient with all simple weapons. Other kinds of dragons have no weapon proficiencies unless they actually have levels in a character class or they use feats to become proficient.

RULES: DRAGONS AND MAGIC ITEMS

Being both very smart and very wealthy, dragons often employ magic items.

A younger dragon without any spellcasting ability—even if it has one or more spell-like abilities—cannot use spell completion items or spell trigger items.

An older dragon casts spells as a sorcerer and is an arcane spellcaster; it cannot cast a divine spell from a scroll unless it has levels in a divine spellcasting class.

Because a dragon can cast spells as a sorcerer, it can use any spell trigger item that produc es the effect of a sorcerer/wizard spell. If the dragon also can cast cleric spells as arcane spells, it can use any spell trigger item that produc es the effect of a spell from the cleric spell list or a spell from a domain to which the dragon has access.

A dragon usually lacks weapon proficiencies and fully prehensile appendages, so it cannot employ weapons. If a dragon assumes a form with prehensile appendages, it can wield weapons while in that form, but it remains nonproficient unless it has lvels in a class or a feat that makes it proficient (as noted earlier, a dragon with the alternate form racial ability is proficient with all simple weapons).

Any dragon is capable of using potions. In most circumstances, a dragon doesn't even bother opening a potion container; it simply swallows it or chews it up. Because a dragon can eat just about anything, this doesn't cause any problems for the dragon, nor does it change the effect of the potion in any way.

Because magic items that must be worn will fit users of any size, a dragon can use any magic item a humanoid character can.

A dragon can use a headband, hat, or helmet normally. In some cases, an item of this kind can be specially made for a dragon in the form of a crown, diadem, or skullcap. For example, a dragon's *helm of telepathy* may be in the form of a *skullcap of telepathy.*

Goggles and lenses made for dragons usually come in the form of cusps that fit over the dragon's eyes, or lenses the dragon places directly on its eyes, much like modern contact lenses. A humanoid character can use any special dragon item of this kind without difficulty.

A dragon can wear a cloak, cape, or mantle on its back, usually between the wings. Items of this sort can come in the form of a frill stud or spine cap instead. A humanoid character can use a frill stud or spine cap by affixing it to a cloak, cape, or mantle.

A dragon wears amulets, brooches, medallions, necklaces, and periapts around its neck, just as a humanoid does.

A dragon is not proficient with any kind of armor and usually does not bother wearing armor. In any case, armor crafted for a humanoid does not fit a dragon's body. Armor created for a dragon resembles barding and will not fit a humanoid, but will fit a quadruped of the same size as the dragon.

A dragon can wear a robe over its shoulders and upper chest. In some cases, a item of this kind can be specially made for a dragon in the form of a collar or epaulette. A humanoid can wear such an item without difficulty.

A dragon can wear a vest, vestment, or shirt draped around its wings and lower chest. In some cases, a item of this kind can be specially made for a dragon in the form of a pectoral stud or a belly stud. A humanoid can wear a magical dragon pectoral stud as though it were a vest. It can wear a belly stud in its navel.

A dragon can fit bracers or bracelets over its lower forelimbs.

A dragon can wear gloves or gauntlets on its forefeet. Specially made dragon gauntlets usually have no fingers, just holes for the dragon's claws. A humanoid can wear magical dragon gauntlets without difficulty.

A dragon can wear rings on its front claws.

A dragon can wear a belt around its midsection. Sometimes, items of this kind take the form of bands the dragon wears on its hips. A humanoid can wear such items without difficulty.

A dragon can wear boots on its hind feet. Specially made dragon boots usually resemble a dragon's gauntlets, but are shaped for the hind foot. These magic items also fit humanoid feet.

None of these items interferes with a dragon's movement, including flight.

to deliver powerful blows. To do so, the dragon curls the tip of its tail upward and uses the upturned portion as a bludgeoning weapon. The biggest dragons have enough power in their tails to sweep them from side to side, knocking over smaller foes.

Very big dragons also can use their entire bodies as weapons, crashing into smaller opponents and pinning them to the ground, whereupon the dragon literally grinds them into the dirt.

DRAGON WEAKNESSES

"Weakness? Come test thy mettle against me, hairless ape, and we shall know who is weak!"

— Lothaenorixius, blue dragon

As formidable at they are, dragons have a few vulnerabilities their foes can exploit.

Dragons often prove susceptible to attacks involving an opposing element. For example, red dragons are immune to fire but vulnerable to cold.

A dragon's elemental nature also makes it susceptible to the divine influence wielded by certain clerics, who can drive them off, compel them to render service, or even kill them outright. Dragons, however, become very powerful entities as they age, and the influence of such clerics only proves reliable against younger dragons.

OUTLOOK AND PSYCHOLOGY

"A good answer today is better than the perfect answer tomorrow."

—Human aphorism

"What's your hurry?"

—Common dragon response to the aforementioned aphorism

The most important element shaping a dragon's outlook and state of mind is time. Dragons have no desire to live for the moment; they have a vast supply of moments stretching out before them. They do not worry about wasted time. If dragons have anything in excess, it is time, and they do not concern themselves with haste.

Even the dullards among dragonkind seek to fill their time by exercising their minds. Solving puzzles is a favorite activity, though the form these puzzles take depends on the kind of dragon involved. Some, such as the bronze and the copper, seek out challenging puzzles of a benign nature. Others, such as the red and the blue, contemplate a much darker brand of conundrums. They plot ways to satisfy their greed, to defeat opponents, and to gain power over other creatures. Many scholars believe that dragons owe their natural aptitude for magic to the mental games they constantly play just to keep themselves occupied.

Many dragons also seek knowledge for its own sake. Older dragons often become repositories of ancient wisdom and lore.

Humanoid adventurers usually seek fame and fortune through three stages of their lives (adolescence, adulthood, and middle age). Even the longest-lived elf attempts to cram the bulk of his accomplishments into these phases of life. Dragons, on the other hand, through desire and necessity, seek fame and fortune from the moment they emerge from the egg to the day they finally succumb to time's eroding waves. Because it spreads its life activities out across its very long life span, a dragon takes much longer breaks between quests and adventures than a group of humanoid adventurers would take.

If a dragon were to join a group of adventurers, it might remain interested long enough to complete one or two quests. Then something else might catch its interest, and it would leave for years to engage in another activity. Upon returning, it would discover its former companions to be nearing retirement or already too old to go questing. The dragon, however, would still be young and vital, and growing stronger with each passing year. Although it would feel sadness at the loss of its companions, it would move on to new challenges.

All true dragons have great patience. They seldom hurry or rush, because they believe anything worth doing is worth doing right. For a dragon, doing something right usually involves spending a long time (from the viewpoint of shorter-lived beings) contemplating the next step.

A dragon's longevity is perhaps the major source of its vanity and arrogance. A single dragon can watch a parade of beings come and go during its long life. How can a dragon consider such creatures as anything more than inferiors when it watches so many of them enter life, grow old, and die? And all the while, the dragon grows stronger and more powerful, proving its superiority (if only in its own mind). Dragons hold at bay the powerful entity of time, whereas lesser creatures succumb and fade with nary a struggle. With such power at its command, is it any wonder that a dragon believes itself to be the very pinnacle of creation?

RULES: DRAGON WEAKNESSES

A dragon is vulnerable to the type of energy that opposes its elemental subtype, as noted in the *Monster Manual*. A dragon takes half again as much (+50%) damage as normal from attacks involving its opposing energy type, regardless of whether a saving throw is allowed, or if the save is a success or failure. The feats Overcome Weakness and Suppress Weakness (see pages 72 and 74) reduce this vulnerability.

Clerics with access to the air, earth, fire, or water domains can turn, destroy, rebuke, or command dragons of the appropriate elemental subtype. Since the effectiveness of these abilities is based on the defending creature's Hit Dice, older and larger dragons seldom fall prey to them, but they can be effective against smaller and younger dragons.

A dragon can spring into action quickly if it finds its own life in peril, or if it must protect its mate, its offspring, or its hoard. Otherwise, few problems seem urgent.

A dragon's wrath can stretch on for many human generations, matching the creature's patience. The humanoid who wrongs a dragon may escape its wrath by dying a natural death before the dragon gets around to exacting revenge. The humanoid's descendants, however, should be wary if they know about the situation, because the dragon might strike at them years or centuries after the original perpetrator has died.

DRAGON SOCIETY

"Dragons never gather without purpose."

—Kacdaninymila, gold dragon

Dragons keep to themselves, breaking their solitude only to mate, rear offspring, or obtain help in meeting some threat. Dragons of different species seldom form alliances, though they have been known to cooperate under extreme circumstances, such as when a powerful mutual threat arises.

Some scholars believe dragons suffer from xenophobia. This view is not far from the truth—any dragon simply enjoys its own company. When it becomes prudent or necessary to have a companion, a dragon seeks one out, but it prefers a companion as much like itself as possible.

Metallic dragons of different species are more apt to cooperate with each other than chromatic dragons are, though only gold and silver dragons are known to forge lasting friendships. The loquacious brass dragons enjoy the company of other metallic dragons, but most dragons (even other brass dragons) prefer to take brass dragons in small doses. Metallic dragons never cooperate with chromatic dragons.

When evil dragons of different varieties encounter one another, they usually fight to protect their territories. Good dragons are more tolerant, though also very territorial, and usually try to work out differences in a peaceful manner.

TERRITORY

A dragon usually claims all the territory within a day's flying time of its lair. The dragon will share this area with no other dragons except its mate and offspring (if it has any), and even then, younger dragons most often part after mating and leave their eggs untended.

Though chromatic dragons are not eager to share territory, they tolerate some overlap between their territories and those of neighboring dragons of the same species or alignment. These boundary areas become places where dragons can meet to parlay and exchange information. In many cases, a dragon shares overlapping territory with a mate or a potential mate.

Among dragons too young to mate, the need for security and defense usually overrides the desire for solitude. Clutches of dragons born together usually stick together until each individual is strong enough to survive on its own and establish its own lair.

CONFLICT AND INTERACTION BETWEEN DRAGONS

When dragons fight, the conflict is seldom over territory. It is much easier for a dragon to simply take wing and find an unclaimed area than to risk injury and death in a battle with another dragon. Dragons most often fight for the opportunity to loot each other's lairs. A dragon's desire to amass large amounts of treasure is legendary, even among the dragons themselves, and every dragon knows that a victory over a rival is often the best way to gain wealth. Dragons also fight over mates (such contests are not limited to males) and usually try to kill or drive away neighboring dragons of different alignments. Enmity is particularly strong among chromatic and metallic dragons that typically inhabit similar territories. Blue dragons and brass dragons, for example, both prefer to live in deserts and often come into conflict.

When two or more dragons meet and wish to avoid a conflict, they usually take to the air and circle slowly, each examining the other carefully. If the dragons are of different sizes or ages, these preliminaries end fairly quickly. Status among dragons comes with age. Older dragons know they have little to fear from younger dragons, provided the senior dragon is not already injured. Younger dragons are likewise aware that their older brethren can slay them easily, and they know that negotiating gives them the best chance of surviving the encounter.

If the dragons in an encounter are the same age or size, they tend to be much more cautious, since a sudden attack by either dragon could doom the other. The dragons might circle each other for hours.

Once the preliminaries are over, the dragons converse. If they remain suspicious of each other, they stay aloft, with the older dragon or dragons slightly higher. While aloft, the dragons are obliged to bellow at each other, since they can't easily close to conversational distance. Thanks to a dragon's keen ears and tremendous vocal capacity, this hindrance to communication doesn't present much of a problem. If the dragons become comfortable with one another, they often fly off to some high, inaccessible place where they can speak in private.

MATING

A dragon's attitude and approach to mating depend on its species and its age. Dragons follow a number of reproductive strategies to suit their needs and temperaments. These strategies help assure the continuation of a dragon's bloodline, no matter what happens to the parent or the lair.

Young adults, particularly evil or less intelligent ones, tend to lay annual clutches of eggs all around the countryside, leaving their offspring to fend for themselves. Older females sometimes lay eggs once a decade or even less often, but they usually produce at least one clutch during each age category in which they remain fertile. Often an older female lays several clutches of eggs over successive years, keeping one clutch to tend herself, giving one clutch to her mate (who carries the eggs to a separate lair), and leaving the rest untended. Sometimes a female dragon places eggs (or newly hatched wyrmlings) with nondraconic foster parents.

Adult and mature adult dragons are most likely to mate for the long term and to share the task of rearing young.

Older dragons are the most likely to mate and then raise their young on their own, and even males do so (with the female laying her eggs in the male's lair or the male carrying the eggs to his lair). Older dragons also sometimes arrange nondragon surrogate parents for their offspring. One or both parents visit the surrogates periodically to determine how well they are handling the task.

Dragon mating is not all about reproduction, however, and dragons often mate out of love. This is particularly true among metallic dragons, but love certainly exists among chromatic dragons as well. Dragons of lawful alignment often mate for life (though if one of the two dies, the other usually finds a new mate). Dragons mated for life do not always remain together. They frequently maintain separate lairs and agree to meet at intervals. Lawful dragons are not always monogamous, and they have been known to build complex intricate living and breeding arrangements with multiple partners. Such relationships usually are built around an older dragon and younger mates, and can be either polygamous or polyandrous.

Chaotic dragons tend to change mates frequently, though as they get older they often develop a preference for a single mate.

Dragons are notoriously virile, able to crossbreed with virtually any creature. Among metallic dragons, crossbreeding often occurs when the dragon assumes another shape and falls in love, however briefly, with a nondragon. Chromatic dragons may simply feel adventuresome and create crossbreeds as a result. In either case, the dragon involved usually is a young adult. A dragon almost always either abandons its half-dragon offspring or leaves it in the care of its nondragon parent. Chromatic dragons typically remain unconcerned about the half-dragon's fate. Metallic dragons believe (usually correctly) that the half-dragon will fare better among nondragons than it ever will among dragons.

Crossbreeds between dragon species are not unknown, but very rare. A hybrid dragon of this sort is usually left to fend for itself, but on occasion both parents (if they are on good terms with each other) might watch over it until it reaches adulthood.

WHY DO DRAGONS HOARD TREASURE?

"Dragons lust for treasure because, at heart, they are nothing but large, reptilian jackdaws."

—Alrod Duart, sage

"A dragon collects treasure mainly for its beauty—you don't think there can be too much beauty, do you? Besides, some treasure is very good eating."

—Kacdaninymila, gold dragon

When one thinks of a dragon piling up treasure and using it as a bed, it's easy to accuse the creature of greed. After all, what good is all that wealth doing anyone?

Some sages equate a dragon's desire to amass treasure with the behavior of jackdaws, pack rats, and other creatures that instinctively hoard bright, shiny objects. This observation is not without merit, because no dragon seems entirely able to explain why it wants to hoard treasure. Unlike a jackdaw or a pack rat, however, a dragon craves items of monetary value, not just shiny objects. Dragons are well aware of the value of their possessions. When faced with a selection of treasure, even the most virtuous dragon would like to take it all. If it has to choose, the dragon tends to favor the most valuable items. Dragons show a preference for items with intrinsic monetary value over items that are valuable because of their magic.

The sheer, primal joy a dragon derives from its hoard is nearly indescribable. In unguarded moments, a dragon will roll in a pile of treasure like a pig wallowing in the mud on a hot day, and the dragon seems to derive a similar degree of physical pleasure from the action.

A dragon also derives immense intellectual satisfaction from its hoard. It keeps an accurate mental inventory of the items in it, and a running total of the hoard's total monetary value.

The draconic preoccupation with treasure doubtless has an instinctive element that may never be fully explained, but treasure hoarding among dragons has some practical benefits.

First, having a valuable treasure at hand gives the dragon some control over the circumstances of its own death (see Avoiding the Twilight, page 15). Dragons that lose their

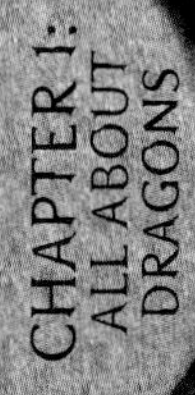

hoards often suffer so much emotional trauma that their spirits become restless even after death (see Ghostly Dragon, page 161).

Second, and more important, dragons derive status among their own kind from the richness of their hoards. Though the primary measure of status among dragons is age, the value of a dragon's hoard is what determines the relative status of dragons of the same age (when comparing hoard values, dragons consider magic items to be worth one-half their market value). A particularly large hoard can place a younger dragon on equal terms with an older dragon; a small one can demote it to an even lower status than its age alone would indicate.

DRAGONS AND THE APPRAISE SKILL

Though most dragons do not have the Appraise skill, dragons can appraise items readily, thanks to their high Intelligence scores. A dragon gains a +2 competence bonus on any Appraise check (or Intelligence check made to appraise an item) that involves studying physical aspects of the appraised item (such as fine details or weight).

Dragons with higher status have better access to mates. They have more influence among other dragons, and are more likely to be asked to render assistance or advice. This in turn increases their status even more.

Dragons tend to boast about the value of their hoards among their own kind, which is understandable, since a dragon cannot derive any status from its hoard unless other dragons know about it. Such boasting is not without peril, however, particularly among chromatic dragons, since evil dragons are not above stealing treasure from each other.

Among older dragons, treasure hoarding has an additional practical dimension. As a dragon ages, its magical aptitude gets greater, and the dragon becomes better able to employ the magic items in its hoard to its advantage.

LANGUAGE

The language of dragons is one of the oldest forms of communication. According to the dragons themselves, it is second in longevity only to the languages of the outsiders, and all mortal tongues are descended from it. Its script was likely created long after its spoken form was standardized, since dragons have less need to write than other races. Some scholars believe the written form of Draconic might have been influenced by dwarven runes, but the wise don't express this opinion within hearing of a dragon.

Many reptilian races (including kobolds, lizardfolk, and troglodytes) speak crude versions of Draconic, and present this as proof of their kinship with dragons. It is equally likely that these races were once taught or enslaved by dragons, and it is even possible that they took Draconic for their own simply to make a claim to common ancestors.

BASIC DRACONIC VOCABULARY

What follows is a selection of words from the Draconic vocabulary, along with translations and the part of speech of the word (adj=adjective, adv=adverb, conj=conjunction, n=noun, prep=preposition, pron=pronoun, v=verb).

Common	Draconic	Part of Speech
above	svern	prep
after	ghent	prep
air	thrae	n
and	vur	conj
animal	baeshra	n
armor	litrix	n
arrow	svent	n
ash	vignar	n
axe	garurt	n
bag	waeth	n
battle	vargach	n
beautiful	vorel	adj
bronze	aujir	n
before	ghoros	prep
behind	zara	prep
below	vhir	prep
beside	unsinti	prep
big	turalisj	adj
black	vutha	adj
bleed	valeij	v
blood	iejir	n
blue	ulhar	adj
bow	vaex	n
burn	valignat	v
bravery	sveargith	n
breed	maurg	v
bribe	durah	v
but	shar	conj
cave	waere	n
celestial	athear	n
century	ierikc	n
cleric	sunathaer	n
claw	gix	n
copper	rach	n
cow	rhyvos	n
coward	faessi	adj
crippled	thurgix	adj
dance	vaeri	n, v
danger	korth	n
darkvision	sverak	n
day	kear	n
dead	loex	adj
deity	urathear	n
demon	kothar	n
die	loreat	v
disembowel	gixustrat	v
dragon	darastrix	n
dwarf	tundar	n
earth	edar	n
elf	vaecaesin	n
enchanted	levex	adj
enemy	irlym	adj, n
evil	malsvir	adj
eye	sauriv	n
far	karif	adj, adv
fate	haurach	n
few	lauth	n
fire	ixen	n
flee	osvith	v
fly	austrat	v
food	achthend	n
for	ihk	prep
forest	caesin	n
fortress	hurthi	n
friend	thurirl	adj, n
gem	kethend	n
give	majak	v
gnome	terunt	n
go	gethrisj	v
gold	aurix	n
good	bensvelk	adj
green	achuak	adj
halfling	rauhiss	n
hammer	jhank	n
hate	dartak	n, v
heal	irisv	v
home	okarthel	n
human	munthrek	n
if	sjek	conj
in	persvek	prep
iron	usk	adj
kill	svent	v
leader	maekrix	n
magic	arcaniss	n
man	sthyr	n
many	throden	n
meat	rhyaex	n
mountain	verthicha	n
name	ominak	n
near	leirith	adj, adv
night	thurkear	n
no	thric	adv
nor	thur	conj
ogre	ghontix	n
on	shafaer	prep
one	ir	n
or	usv	conj
orc	ghik	n
peace	martivir	n
pillage	thadarsh	v
platinum	ux	n
rain	oposs	n
red	charir	adj
rest	ssifisv	v
scroll	sjir	n
secret	irthos	adj, n
see	ocuir	v
shadow	sjach	n
silver	orn	n
skin (hide)	molik	n
slaughter	kurik	v
small	kosj	adj
smart	othokent	adj
so	zyak	adv, conj
soar	hysvear	v
song	miirik	n
sorcerer	vorastrix	n
speak	renthisj	v
spear	ner	n
star	isk	n
steel	vyth	adj
stone	ternesj	n
stop	pok	v
storm	kepesk	n
strong	versvesh	adj
stupid	pothoc	adj
sword	caex	n
take	clax	v
talk	ukris	v
thief	virlym	n
through	erekess	prep
to	ekess	prep
tomorrow	earenk	n
travel	ossalur	v
treasure	rasvim	n
tooth	oth	n
ugly	nurh	adj
undead	kaegro	n, adj
under	onureth	prep
valley	arux	n
victory	vivex	n
want	tuor	v
war	aryte	n
water	hesjing	n
we	yth	pron
wealth	noach	n
weapon	laraek	n
white	aussir	adj
with	mrith	prep
wizard	levethix	n
woman	aesthyr	n
wood	grovisv	n
year	eorikc	n
yellow	yrev	adj
yes	axun	adv
yet	sjerit	adv
you	wux	pron

The Draconic script is also used when a written form is needed for the elemental languages Auran and Ignan. However, this use of the written form does not make it any easier for someone who knows Draconic to learn the languages of air and fire creatures.

Slight variations exist in the language used by the various kinds of chromatic dragons. These differences are similar to regional accents, with some slight differences in pronunciation from one version to the next. The accents do not hamper communication, but they are sufficiently obvious for a native speaker to know whether someone learned to speak Draconic from (for instance) a red dragon or a green dragon. The various metallic dragons have similar accents, but without any differences in pronunciation. The Draconic language has not changed significantly for hundreds, if not thousands, of years.

The spoken form of the language sounds harsh to most other creatures and includes numerous hard consonants and sibilants. It includes sounds that humans generally describe as hissing (sj, ss, and sv), as well as a noise that sounds a great deal like a beast clearing its throat (ach).

Words that modify other words are placed before and after the word they modify. The most important modifier is always placed before the word, and it might be placed directly after the word as well if additional emphasis is desired. A speaker of Draconic who wanted to say a big, black, evil dragon was approaching and doubly emphasize its evil nature would say, "Malsvir darastrix turalisj vutha gethrisj leirith" or even "Malsvir darastrix turalisj vutha malsvir gethrisj leirith."

Most Draconic words are spoken with emphasis on the first syllable. Important ideas are often expressed in spoken Draconic by emphasizing the beginning and the end of the word. In the written form, important words are marked with a special symbol of five lines radiating outward, similar to an asterisk (*). This form of emphasis is most often used by dragons when referring to themselves. The dragon Karajix, for example, might pronounce his name *Ka*-raj-*ix* and write it as *Karajix*. This form of emphasis is also sometimes used when commanding, threatening, warning, or making a point.

Draconic has no specific word for "my" or "mine," instead using several prefixes depending on the exact meaning. The name of a physical object claimed as a possession by a dragon speaker would begin with "veth" or "vethi"; the name of an individual with a relationship to the dragon (such as a friend or relative) is expressed by the prefix "er" or "ethe"; and all other forms of possessiveness are represented by putting "ar" or "ari" before a word. Thus, for a dragon to say "my sword" or "the sword is mine" he need only say "vethicaex" ("vethi" plus "caex," the word for sword), and "arirlym" translates as "my enemy" ("ar" plus "irlym," the word for enemy). When indicating possession by another, the name of the possessor is combined with the object possessed into a single word that starts with "ar" or "ari."

PIDGIN DRACONIC

Here are some sample sentences and their translations into Draconic.

Mialee, talk to the ugly elf.
Mialee, ukris vaecaesin nurh.

The elf says the magic sword we want is in the lich's tomb.
Vaecaesin ner levex caex levex yth tuor persvek arikaegrowaere.

He'll take us to the mountain of the tomb if we pay him.
Vaecaesin tuor aurix clax yth ekess ariloexokarthel verthicha.

The cave is evil and dangerous. We should go.
*Sauriv waere korth. Yth *gethrisj*.*

Shut up you stupid coward! Get in there!
*Thric ner, *pothoc* wux faessi! *Gethrisj* persvek!*

Tordek, hit the orc with your axe.
Tordek, vargach ghik mrith aritordekgarunt.

A red dragon! Scram!
*Charir *darastrix*! *Osvith*!*

Krusk is dead. He died with much bravery.
*Krusk loex. Loreat mrith *sveargith*.*

Yeah, bad luck for him.
Axun malsvir arikruskhaurach.

Check out all this gold! Tomorrow we'll be kings!
*Ocuir throden *aurix*! Earenk yth *maekrix*!*

I am not a thief!
**Thric* virlym!*

The secrets of the dragon's treasure are on this scroll.
Ardarastrixrasvim irthos shafaer sjir.

Dragon's blood flows in a sorcerer.
Aridarastrixiejir gethrisj persvek vorastrix.

Please don't disembowel the dwarf.
Martivir thric gixustratt tundar.

RELIGION

The dragon deities are all children of Io, the Ninefold Dragon who encompasses all the opposites and extremes of dragonkind.

Creatures other than dragons can worship one of the deities described here. Just as a human weaponsmith might venerate Moradin, or an elf archer pay homage to Ehlonna, so too could a dwarf, half-orc, or kobold worship a god or goddess otherwise associated with dragons. In fact, such worship is particularly common among the various reptilian (and Draconic-speaking) races, such as kobolds, lizardfolk, and troglodytes.

READING THE DEITY ENTRIES

The first section of text in each deity description contains basic information about the deity.

Table 1–2: The Draconic Pantheon

Deity	Alignment	Domains
Aasterinian, Goddess of Invention	CN	Chaos, Dragon*, Luck, Travel, Trickery (Charm, Illusion, Trade)
Astilabor, Goddess of Wealth	N	Dragon*, Protection, Wealth* (Cavern, Metal)
Bahamut, God of Good Dragonkind	LG	Air, Dragon*, Good, Luck, Protection (Nobility, Storm)
Chronepsis, God of Fate	N	Death, Dragon*, Knowledge (Fate, Planning, Time)
Falazure, God of Decay	NE	Death, Dragon*, Evil (Darkness, Undeath)
Garyx, God of Destruction	CE	Chaos, Destruction, Dragon*, Evil, Fire (Renewal)
Hlal, Goddess of Humor	CG	Chaos, Dragon*, Good, Trickery (Rune)
Io, Lord of the Gods	N	Dragon*, Knowledge, Magic, Strength, Travel, Wealth* (Spell)
Lendys, God of Justice	LN	Destruction, Dragon*, Law, Protection (Retribution)
Tamara, Goddess of Life	NG	Dragon*, Good, Healing, Strength, Sun (Family)
Tiamat, God of Evil Dragonkind	LE	Destruction, Dragon*, Evil, Greed*, Law, Trickery (Hatred, Scalykind, Tyranny)

Name: The first line gives the name by which the deity is generally known. Other names or titles attributed to the deity (if any) are given immediately below the name.

Following the name is the deity's level of power. In descending order, the levels of power are greater deity, intermediate deity, lesser deity, and demigod. These rankings do not affect the abilities of clerics, the power of the spells they cast, or most anything in the mortal world. They represent the relative levels of power among deities only.

Home Plane: The portion of the cosmos where the deity usually resides. Feel free to change these home planes as appropriate to your campaign.

Symbol: A short description of the holy or unholy symbol carried by the deity's clerics. This symbol is often used on altars or other items dedicated to the deity.

Alignment: The deity's alignment. Deities follow the same alignments as mortals do; see pages 104–106 of the *Player's Handbook*.

Portfolio: The aspects of mortal existence with which the deity is most often associated. Portfolio elements are listed roughly in their order of importance to the deity.

Worshipers: Those who worship or venerate the deity, listed roughly in order of their number and importance to the deity.

Cleric Alignments: What alignments the deity's clerics can have. As noted in the *Player's Handbook*, a cleric typically has the same alignment as his deity. Some clerics are one step away from their respective deity's alignment. For example, most clerics of Heironeous (who is lawful good) are lawful good themselves, but some are lawful neutral or neutral good. A cleric may not be neutral unless his deity is neutral.

Two alignments are within one step of each other if they appear adjacent to each other horizontally or vertically on the following chart. Alignments that are adjacent to each other on a diagonal are not within one step.

Lawful good	Neutral good	Chaotic good
Lawful neutral	Neutral	Chaotic neutral
Lawful evil	Neutral evil	Chaotic evil

Some deities do not accept clerics of all alignments that are within one step of their own. For example, Bahamut, a lawful good deity, has lawful good and neutral good clerics but does not allow lawful neutral clerics.

Domains: Clerics of the deity can choose from among the domains listed here. Domains marked with an asterisk—Dragon, Greed, and Wealth—are new domains described in this book (see page 107).

Domains that appear in parentheses are described in the *Forgotten Realms Campaign Setting*. If your campaign is set in that world, you can add these domains to the deity's list (possibly replacing other domains if desired).

Favored Weapon: The kind of weapon the deity favors. The deity's clerics generally prefer to use this weapon, and certain spells that clerics cast, such as *spiritual weapon*, may have effects that resemble this weapon.

The favored weapon line usually contains two entries. The first is for weapon-wielding clerics, while the parenthetical is for dragon clerics who don't wield weapons.

Descriptive Text

Immediately following the line-item deity entries is information about what the deity looks like and other general facts.

Dogma: The basic tenets of the deity's creed or teachings.

Clergy and Temples: This text gives details of how the deity's clerics act and the types of temples or shrines that are dedicated to the deity. It also describes any particular alliances or enmities between that faith and others.

Game Statistics

This book doesn't have the scope to contain specific game statistics and divine powers for the deities described below. Game statistics for Bahamut and Tiamat are presented in *Deities and Demigods*. You can use that book to create game statistics for the other dragon deities here if you desire such information.

AASTERINIAN

Messenger of Io
Demigod
Symbol: Grinning dragon's head
Home Plane: Outlands
Alignment: Chaotic neutral
Portfolio: Learning, invention, pleasure
Worshipers: Chaotic dragons, free thinkers
Cleric Alignments: CG, CN, CE
Domains: Chaos, Dragon*, Luck, Travel, Trickery (Charm, Illusion, Trade)
Favored Weapon: Scimitar (claw)

Aasterinian is a cheeky deity who enjoys learning through play, invention, and pleasure. She is Io's messenger, a Huge brass dragon who enjoys disturbing the status quo.

Dogma

Aasterinian is flighty and quick-witted. She encourages her followers to think for themselves, rather than relying on the word of others. The worst crime, in Aasterinian's eyes, is not trusting in yourself and your own devices.

Clergy and Temples

Aasterinian's clerics are typically wanderers who travel in disguise or secrecy. Temples to the goddess are rare in the extreme, though simple shrines dot the landscape—quiet, hidden places where worshipers can rest peacefully on their travels.

Her followers enjoy friendly relations with those of Garl Glittergold, Fharlanghn, Olidammara, and similar deities.

ASTILABOR

The Acquisitor, Hoardmistress

Lesser Deity

Symbol: A twelve-faceted gem

Home Plane: Outlands

Alignment: Neutral

Portfolio: Acquisitiveness, status, wealth

Worshipers: Dragons, those who seek wealth

Cleric Alignments: NG, LN, N, CN, NE

Domains: Dragon*, Protection, Wealth* (Cavern, Metal)

Favored Weapon: Scimitar (claw)

Astilabor represents the natural draconic desire to acquire treasure and power. She dislikes the naked greed displayed by Tiamat and her followers.

Dogma

Astilabor values wealth and power, but without any stigma of greed. She instills in dragonkind the innate need for collecting and protecting the hoard. She claims that she cannot abide thievery of any kind from her worshipers, but often turns a blind eye if such acts are performed in the name of building one's hoard.

Clergy and Temples

Astilabor accepts only clerics with a neutral aspect to their alignments, the better to remain pure to the goal of acquiring and protecting the hoard. Her clerics prefer not to get involved in conflicts between dragons, but often reward those whose hoards become large and valuable.

Astilabor is revered by dragons of all types and alignments, but actively worshiped by few. Most at least scratch out her symbol as a protective ward over their hoards.

Astilabor's worshipers are friendly toward those of Moradin and Garl Glittergold (since those gods respect the value of a gem or coin as much as anyone), but they distrust followers of Olidammara, whom they believe to be thieves at heart.

BAHAMUT

The Platinum Dragon, King of the Good Dragons, Lord of the North Wind

Lesser Deity

Symbol: Star above a milky nebula

Home Plane: Celestia

Alignment: Lawful good

Portfolio: Good dragons, wind, wisdom

Worshipers: Good dragons, anyone seeking protection from evil dragons

Cleric Alignments: LG, NG

Domains: Air, Dragon*, Good, Luck, Protection (Nobility, Storm)

Favored Weapon: Heavy pick (bite)

Bahamut is revered in many locales. Though all good dragons pay homage to Bahamut, gold, silver, and brass dragons hold him in particularly high regard. Other dragons, even evil ones (except perhaps his archrival Tiamat), respect Bahamut for his wisdom and power.

In his natural form, Bahamut is a long, sinuous dragon covered in silver-white scales that sparkle and gleam even in the dimmest light. Bahamut's catlike eyes are deep blue, as azure as a midsummer sky, some say. Others insist that Bahamut's eyes are a frosty indigo, like the heart of a glacier. Perhaps the two merely reflect the Platinum Dragon's shifting moods.

Dogma

Bahamut is stern and very disapproving of evil. He brooks no excuses for evil acts. In spite of this, he is among the most compassionate beings in the multiverse. He has limitless empathy for the downtrodden, the dispossessed, and the helpless. He urges his followers to promote the cause of good, but prefers to let beings fight their own battles when they can. To Bahamut, it is better to offer information, healing, or a (temporary) safe refuge rather than to take others' burdens upon oneself.

Bahamut is served by seven great gold wyrms that often accompany him.

Clergy and Temples

Bahamut accepts only good clerics. Clerics of Bahamut, be they dragons, half-dragons, or other beings attracted to Bahamut's philosophy, strive to take constant but subtle action on behalf of good, intervening wherever they are needed but trying to do as little harm as possible in the process.

Many gold, silver, and brass dragons maintain simple shrines to Bahamut in their lairs, usually nothing more elaborate than Bahamut's symbol scribed on a wall.

Bahamut's chief foe is Tiamat, and this enmity is reflected in their worshipers. His allies include Heironeous, Moradin, Yondalla, and other lawful good deities.

CHRONEPSIS

The Silent, The Watcher

Lesser Deity

Symbol: An unblinking draconic eye

Home Plane: Outlands

Alignment: Neutral

Portfolio: Fate, death, judgment

Worshipers: Dragons, those who would observe

Cleric Alignments: N

Domains: Death, Dragon*, Knowledge (Fate, Planning, Time)

Favored Weapon: Scythe (claw)

Chronepsis is neutral—silent, unconcerned, and dispassionate. He is the draconic deity of fate, death, and judgment. His form is colorless and without luster, marking him as an outsider to the struggles of the chromatic and metallic dragons.

Dogma

Chronepsis is a passionless observer of the world. He passes judgment on all dragons when they die, deciding where their souls go in the afterlife. Unlike Lendys (see below), Chronepsis is uninterested in justice: he merely observes what is and is not. He is also singularly uninvolved in the activities of the living, and strives to remain so. It is said that only a cataclysm of world-shaking proportions could rouse Chronepsis from his disinterest.

Clergy and Temples

Chronepsis has very few active worshipers and even fewer clerics, since most dragons don't possess the balanced outlook to avoid interfering in the events they observe.

The followers of Chronepsis count other faiths neither as allies nor enemies. Of the other deities, only Boccob the Uncaring shares a similar outlook, but neither deity cares enough to forge an alliance.

FALAZURE

The Night Dragon

Lesser Deity

Symbol: Draconic skull

Home Plane: Hades

Alignment: Neutral evil

Portfolio: Decay, undeath, exhaustion

Worshipers: Evil dragons, necromancers, undead

Cleric Alignments: LE, NE, CE

Domains: Death, Dragon*, Evil (Darkness, Undeath)

Favored Weapon: Scimitar (claw)

The terrifying Night Dragon, Falazure, is neutral evil. He is the lord of energy draining, undeath, decay, and exhaustion. Some claim he has a decaying skeletal form, but others believe that he looks like a decrepit black dragon whose flesh is pulled tight over his bones.

Dogma

Falazure teaches that even a dragon's long life span need not be the limit to a dragon's existence. Beyond the world of the living is another realm, one of undeath eternal. It is generally accepted that Falazure created (or had a hand in the creation of) the first undead dragons, such as dracoliches, vampiric dragons, and ghostly dragons (see Chapter 4).

Clergy and Temples

Among the draconic gods, perhaps only Bahamut and Tiamat have more nondragon worshipers than Falazure. Many necromancers of all races revere the Night Dragon, as well as intelligent undead such as liches and, especially, dracoliches. Temples to Falazure are always deep beneath the earth, cloaked in darkness and far from the sun and fresh air of the surface world.

The followers of Falazure count all members of good-aligned faiths as their enemies. They may occasionally ally with the forces of Nerull, but such instances are rare.

GARYX

Firelord, All-Destroyer, Cleanser of Worlds

Lesser Deity

Symbol: Reptilian eye superimposed over a flame

Home Plane: Pandemonium

Alignment: Chaotic evil
Portfolio: Fire, destruction, renewal
Worshipers: Dragons, sorcerers, warlords, some druids
Cleric Alignments: CN, NE, CE
Domains: Chaos, Destruction, Dragon*, Evil, Fire (Renewal)
Favored Weapon: Sickle (claw)

Garyx the All-Destroyer symbolizes the sheer power and destructive force of dragonkind. Some argue that Garyx is actually insane, as a result of his long occupation of the Windswept Depths of Pandemonium. He appears much like a great wyrm red dragon.

Dogma

Garyx teaches by example, periodically traveling to the Material Plane to wreak unholy swaths of destruction across the landscape. Those who revere him follow this example, using their power to bring ruin and devastation.

Clergy and Temples

Garyx pays little or no attention to his clerics and worshipers, but they care not. They believe that he grants them the power to perform acts of destruction, and that is enough. Perhaps curiously, some druids also revere the renewal aspect of Garyx, knowing that some devastation is always necessary for rejuvenation to occur. Some within the Cult of Ashardalon (see page 87) believe that the great wyrm is actually an avatar of the god Garyx.

Few temples to Garyx are known to exist, though his worshipers often carve his symbol near their handiwork.

Garyx shares traits in common with Kord and Erythnul, but has no interest in alliances.

HLAL

The Jester, The Keeper of Tales
Lesser Deity
Symbol: An open book
Home Plane: Arborea
Alignment: Chaotic good
Portfolio: Humor, storytelling, inspiration
Worshipers: Dragons, bards, performers
Cleric Alignments: NG, CG, CN
Domains: Chaos, Dragon*, Good, Trickery (Rune)
Favored Weapon: Short sword (claw)

Hlal is a sleek, copper-colored dragon with a ready grin and a happy glint in her eye. Of the dragon gods, she is the most friendly to nondragons (even Aasterinian enjoys a reputation of playful danger).

Dogma

Hlal enjoys sharing stories and songs with those who appreciate such things, regardless of the listener's race or background. She has little use for tyrants—even well-meaning ones—and even less patience for cruelty or bullying. She teaches that one must be free of restraint, whether real or psychological, in order to freely express one's opinions.

Clergy and Temples

Hlal's clerics are often multiclass cleric/bards, using music, poetry, and tall tales to spread the faith. Places of worship to Hlal are usually simple shrines, which can be packed up and moved to the next town or dragon lair at a moment's notice.

The followers of Hlal share much in common with those of Olidammara, and many characters pay homage to both deities simultaneously. Both Hextor and Vecna are among her chief enemies, because of their portfolios.

IO

The Concordant Dragon, The Great Eternal Wheel, Swallower of Shades, The Ninefold Dragon, Creator of Dragonkind
Intermediate Deity
Symbol: A multicolored metallic disk
Home Plane: Outlands
Alignment: Neutral
Portfolio: Dragonkind
Worshipers: Dragons
Cleric Alignments: LG, NG, CG, LN, N, CN, LE, NE, CE
Domains: Dragon*, Knowledge, Magic, Strength, Travel, Wealth* (Spell)
Favored Weapon: Scimitar (claw)

Io the Ninefold Dragon is neutral, for he encompasses all alignments within his aspects. He can (and does) appear as any dragon type, from the smallest pseudodragon to the largest great wyrm.

Dogma

Io cares only for his "children," the dragons, and their continued existence in the world. In some cases, this means taking the side of the dragons against other races. In other situations, Io may actually help nondragons fight against a dragon who would otherwise jeopardize the ongoing survivability of the species as a whole.

He prefers to remain uninvolved in conflicts between dragons, though if such a conflict threatens to escalate he may step in (either personally or by dispatching Aasterinian or some other servitor).

Clergy and Temples

Io has even fewer clerics or shrines than most of the other draconic deities, since his outlook is so broad and all-encompassing. Still, even the most devoted cleric of Bahamut, Tiamat, or any other dragon deity pays at least a modicum of homage to the Ninefold Dragon. He also occasionally finds clerics or adepts among the reptilian races, such as kobolds and troglodytes.

Io counts no other faiths as his enemies, knowing the value of neutrality in outlook. Even those of greatly varying alignment can find common cause under the banner of the Ninefold Dragon.

LENDYS

Scale of Justice, The Balancer, Weigher of Lives
Lesser Deity
Symbol: Sword balanced on a needle's point
Home Plane: Mechanus
Alignment: Lawful neutral
Portfolio: Balance, justice
Worshipers: Dragons
Cleric Alignments: LG, LN, LE
Domains: Destruction, Dragon*, Law, Protection (Retribution)
Favored Weapon: Longsword (claw)

Unlike Chronepsis, who judges the life of a dragon only after its death, Lendys metes out justice during a dragon's life. His scales are a tarnished silver, some say because he cares more about judging others than tending to himself.

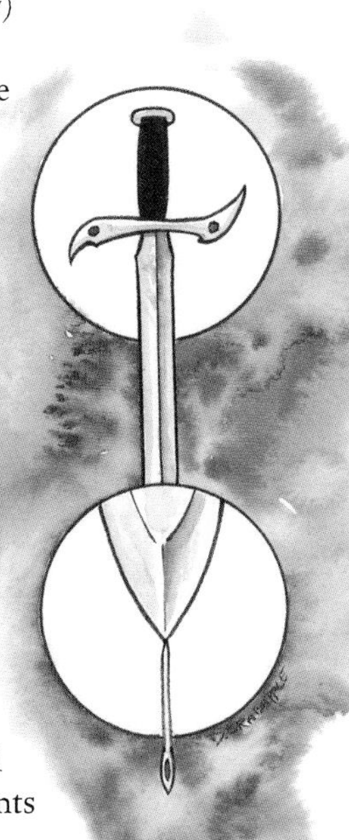

Dogma

Lendys is the arbiter of dragonkind, serving as judge, jury, and executioner alike. When a dragon has committed an injustice against dragonkind, Lendys (or one of his trio of great wyrm silver dragons) is dispatched to deal out appropriate justice. Punishments are severe, and appeals unheard of.

Clergy and Temples

The clerics and paladins of Lendys are justice-bringers as well, often serving as arbiters for local communities. In some cases, towns even rely on the local draconic worshiper of Lendys to parse out justice.

Clerics of Lendys get along well with worshipers of St. Cuthbert, and poorly with those who follow a chaotic deity such as Kord, Olidammara, or Erythnul.

TAMARA

Her Beneficence, Her Mercy
Lesser Deity
Symbol: Seven-pointed star on field of black
Home Plane: Elysium
Alignment: Neutral good
Portfolio: Life, light, mercy
Worshipers: Good dragons, healers, those desiring mercy
Cleric Alignments: LG, NG, CG
Domains: Dragon*, Good, Healing, Strength, Sun (Family)
Favored Weapon: Scimitar (claw)

Tamara is the kindest and most benevolent of the draconic deities. Some mistake this quality for weakness, though such beings don't make the same error twice. She appears as a luminously beautiful silver dragon, her eyes shining with the brightness of the sun itself.

Dogma

Tamara believes in mercy, both in life and in death. Not only does she heal the sick and tend the injured, she delivers a merciful end to those dragons nearing the end of their natural lives. She fiercely detests those who artificially prolong the life of a dragon, particularly when it is against that dragon's will.

Clergy and Temples

Tamara's clerics are healers, but also deliverers of death to those who try to escape it. They prefer to destroy any undead they encounter, particularly draconic undead (such as dracoliches).

Though a peaceful and merciful faith, the worshipers of Tamara do not hesitate to stand against evil or tyranny. Tamara counts Pelor among her staunchest allies and Falazure, Hextor, Nerull, and Erythnul among her enemies.

TIAMAT

The Chromatic Dragon, Creator of Evil Dragonkind
Lesser Deity
Symbol: Five-headed dragon
Home Plane: Baator
Alignment: Lawful evil
Portfolio: Evil dragons, conquest, greed
Worshipers: Evil dragons, conquerors
Cleric Alignments: NE, LE
Domains: Destruction, Dragon*, Evil, Greed*, Law, Trickery (Hatred, Scalykind, Tyranny)
Favored Weapon: Heavy pick (bite)

All evil dragons pay homage to Tiamat; green and blue dragons acknowledge her sovereignty the most readily. Good dragons have a healthy respect for Tiamat, though they usually avoid mentioning her or even thinking about her.

In her natural form, Tiamat is a thick-bodied dragon with five heads and a wyvern's tail. Each head is a different color: white, black, green, blue, and red. Her massive body is striped in those colors.

Tiamat has many consorts, including great wyrm dragons of the white, black, green, blue, and red varieties.

Dogma

Tiamat concerns herself with spreading evil, defeating good, and propagating evil dragons. She enjoys razing the occasional village, city, or country, but only as a diversion from more subtle, world-spanning plots. She is the villain who lurks in the shadows. Her presence is felt but seldom seen.

Tiamat constantly seeks to extend the power and dominion of evil dragons over the land, particularly when her subjects find themselves embroiled in territorial disputes with good dragons. Tiamat unfailingly demands reverence, homage, and tribute from her subjects.

Clergy and Temples

Tiamat accepts only evil clerics. Tiamat's clerics, like Tiamat herself, seek to place the world under the domination of evil dragons.

Though most evil dragons honor Tiamat, few keep shrines dedicated to her in their lairs because they don't want Tiamat's greedy eyes gazing at their treasure hoards. Instead, they dedicate vast, gloomy caverns to their deity and keep them stocked with treasure and sacrifices.

Tiamat claims not to need allies, though most believe she has bargains with many archdevils and lawful evil deities such as Hextor. Her enemies are numerous, including Heironeous, Moradin, and, of course, Bahamut.

DRAGONS BY KIND

True dragons fall into two broad categories: chromatic and metallic.

The chromatic dragons are black, blue, green, red, and white, all evil and extremely fierce. When dealing with a chromatic dragon, one must always prepare for the worst.

The metallic dragons are brass, bronze, copper, gold, and silver. They are good, usually noble, and highly respected by the wise. A metallic dragon may seem dangerous, but it will usually behave virtuously if given the chance. A fight with a metallic dragon is a fight that could have been avoided.

DRAGON SIZES

Though the dragons of popular imagination are immense, dragons come in all sizes. The smallest wyrmlings are no bigger than housecats. The largest great wyrms can dwarf a castle wall.

Although most dragons have similar body shapes, their vital statistics can vary considerably between kinds, even when they are of similar sizes. The tables included in the following sections of dragon types show a dragon's typical dimensions at each size. The terms used in the tables are defined as follows:

Overall Length: The dragon's length measured from the tip of the nose to the tip of the tail, horns or frills excluded. A living dragon usually seems shorter, particularly in a fight, because it seldom stretches itself full out. A dragon can easily curl up and shorten its overall length by as much as two-thirds, but its width increases accordingly.

Body Length: The dragon's overall length, less its neck and tail. Measured from the front of the shoulders to the base of the tail. This dimension helps define the dragon's fighting space.

Neck Length: Measured from the front of the shoulders to the tip of the nose. Burrowing dragons have stubbier necks than other dragons. This dimension may be slightly longer than the dragon's bite reach.

Tail Length: Measured from the base of the tail to the tip of the tail. Aquatic dragons have longer tails than other dragons. This dimension may be slightly longer than the radius of the dragon's tail sweep attack.

Body Width: Measured across the front shoulders, which are the widest part of the dragon. A dragon cannot fit through a space narrower than this without making a Dexterity check or an Escape Artist check (see the Escape Artist skill description, page 73 of the *Player's Handbook*). When a dragon is standing in a normal, relaxed posture, its shoulders are generally 10% to 25% wider than the indicated figure.

Standing Height: A dragon's standing height is measured from its front shoulders to the ground. To determine how high a rearing dragon can reach, add its space to its reach.

Maximum Wingspan: Measured across the tips of the fully spread wings.

Minimum Wingspan: This is the minimum space in which a dragon can flap its wings sufficiently to maintain flight. A dragon with its wings fully folded against its body has no wingspan at all.

Weight: The dragon's weight in pounds. For the larger dragons, this number is an estimate based on the dragon's measurements.

All these numbers are average values and vary by as much as 25%, up or down, for any individual dragon.

Black Dragons by Size

Size	Overall Length	Body Length	Neck Length	Tail Length	Body Width	Standing Height	Maximum Wingspan	Minimum Wingspan	Weight
Tiny	4 ft.	1 ft.	1 ft.	2 ft.	1 ft.	1 ft.	8 ft.	4 ft.	5 lb.
Small	8 ft.	2-1/2 ft.	2 ft.	3-1/2 ft.	2 ft.	2 ft.	16 ft.	8 ft.	40 lb.
Medium	16 ft.	5 ft.	5 ft.	6 ft.	3 ft.	4 ft.	24 ft.	12 ft.	320 lb.
Large	31 ft.	9 ft.	9 ft.	13 ft.	5 ft.	7 ft.	36 ft.	18 ft.	2,500 lb.
Huge	55 ft.	16 ft.	15 ft.	24 ft.	8 ft.	12 ft.	60 ft.	30 ft.	20,000 lb.
Gargantuan	85 ft.	24 ft.	23 ft.	38 ft.	10 ft.	16 ft.	80 ft.	40 ft.	160,000 lb.

BLACK DRAGONS

Black dragons are among the most evil-tempered true dragons. They prefer dismal swamps or bogs, the more stagnant and fetid the better, but can be encountered anywhere water and dense vegetation are found together—including jungles, rain forests, and moors. They have no natural enemies, though they attack and kill almost anything unfortunate enough to stumble upon them. Black dragons living in forest areas often encounter green dragons, but the two species usually manage to maintain an uneasy truce, so long as the black dragons stick to the watery areas.

Black dragons make their lairs in large, damp caves or multichambered submerged caverns. They always dwell near water, and their lairs usually have a submerged entrance and a land entrance. Older black dragons hide both entrances to their lairs with *plant growth*.

Black dragons dwelling in dungeons prefer dark, watery locations.

Black Dragon Identifiers

A black dragon has deep-socketed eyes and broad nasal openings that make its face look like a skull. It has segmented horns that curve forward and down, somewhat like a ram's horns, but not as curly. These horns are bone-colored near their bases, but darken to dead black at the tips. As the dragon ages, the flesh around the horns and cheekbones deteriorates, as though eaten by acid, leaving only thin layers of hide covering the skull. This phenomenon is not harmful to the dragon, but enhances its skeletal appearance.

Most of a black dragon's teeth protrude when the mouth is closed, and big spikes stud the lower jaw. A pair of small horns jut from the chin, and a row of hornlets crown the head. The tongue is flat, with a forked tip, and the dragon often drools acidic slime.

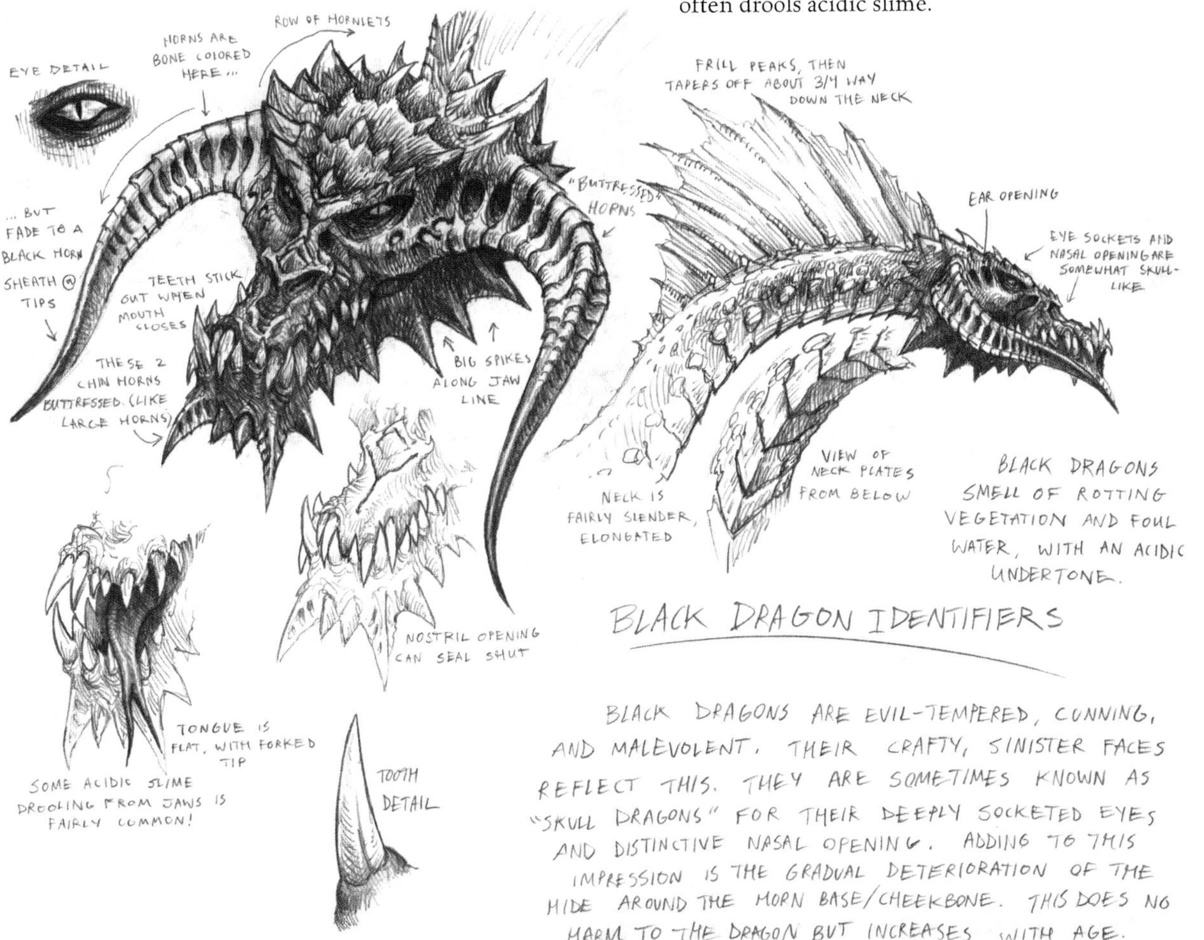

Illus. by S. Wood

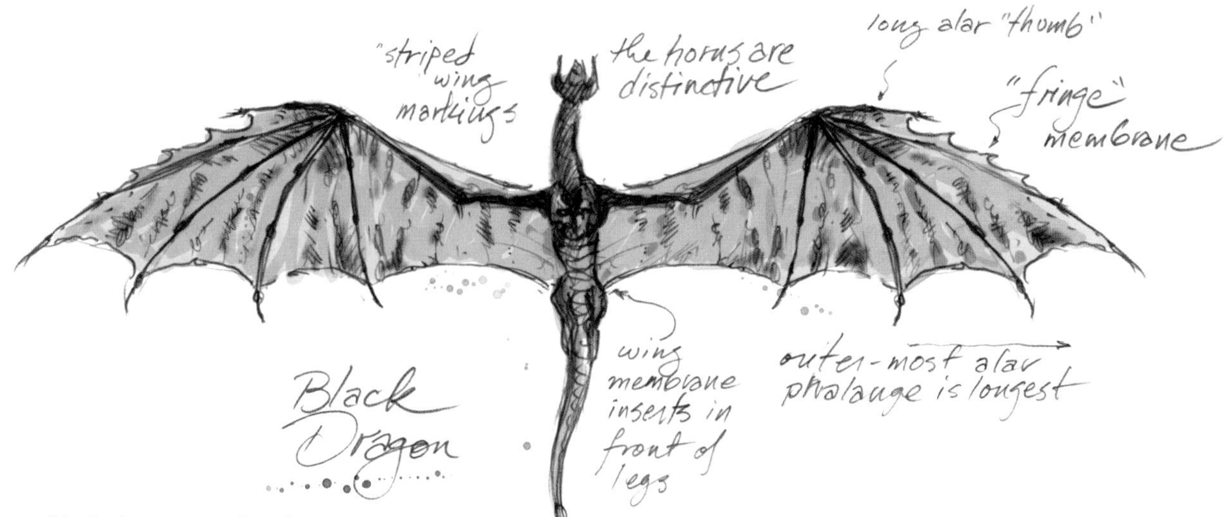

A black dragon smells of rotting vegetation and foul water, with an acidic undertone.

A black dragon flying overhead is marked by a distinctive profile. Its horns, with their characteristic forward curve, are clearly visible. The wing membranes are marked with blobby stripes, and the leading edges of the wings are fringed or scalloped near the tips. A black dragon also has exceptionally long alar thumbs. The trailing edges of the wing membranes join the body ahead of the back legs.

On hatching, a black dragon's scales are thin, small, and glossy. As the dragon ages, they become larger, thicker, and duller, helping it camouflage itself in swamps and marshes.

Habits

Black dragons dine primarily on fish, mollusks, and other aquatic creatures. They also hunt for red meat but like to "pickle" it by letting it lie in ponds within or near their lairs for days before being eaten. The rotting flesh helps make the area even more foul—just the way the dragon likes it.

Black dragons are especially fond of coins. Older and craftier dragons sometimes capture and question humanoids about stockpiles of gold, silver, and platinum coins before killing them. Others move out into nearby rivers or lakes, where they menace boat traffic and demand that passing vessels pay tribute.

In keeping with their reputation for ferocity, black dragons usually fight for their mates. The females do most of the fighting, flying far and wide to locate a desirable male and then impressing him with a victory over a rival. Eggs are usually laid near the male's lair, and the male is left to guard the young. Black dragon parents are protective, but give their offspring little support beyond the occasional bit of advice. Eventually, the parent advises its offspring to leave the area before the older dragon decides to eat the youngster.

Although capable of breathing underwater, black dragons do little actual swimming; instead, they wallow in the shallows, enjoying the feel of the mud or simply lying in wait for prey. Black dragons prefer to ambush their targets, using their surroundings as cover. When fighting in heavily forested swamps and marshes, they try to stay in the water or on the ground; trees and leafy canopies limit their aerial maneuverability. When outmatched, a black dragon attempts to fly out of sight, so as not to leave tracks, and takes refuge in the deepest water it can find.

BLUE DRAGONS

Blue dragons are vain and territorial. They favor hot, arid areas. They prefer sandy deserts, but can be found on dry steppes and in hot badlands. A blue dragon guards its territory against all potential competitors, including other monsters such as sphinxes, dragonnes, and especially brass dragons. Blue dragons detest brass dragons for their frivolous ways, chaotic alignment, and propensity to flee from battle.

Blue dragons prefer vast underground caverns for lairs—the grander the cavern, the better. They often choose lairs at the bases of cliffs where windblown sand has accumulated. The dragon burrows through the sand to reach the caves below. Most blue dragons don't bother to keep the entrances to their lairs free of sand; they simply burrow to get in or out. Many deliberately bury the entrances to their lairs before settling down to sleep or when leaving to patrol their territory.

Dungeon-dwelling blue dragons prefer fairly warm and dry areas with sand or dirt floors.

Blue Dragon Identifiers

A blue dragon is conspicuous by its dramatic frilled ears and a single, massive horn atop its short, blunt head. The horn juts forward from a base that takes up most of the top of the head, and it usually has two points. The primary point is slightly curved and reaches well forward, with a smaller, secondary point behind. Rows of hornlets line the dragon's brow ridges, and run back from the nostrils (which lie close to the eyesockets) along the entire length of the head.

A blue dragon has a short snout with an underslung lower jaw. It has a cluster of bladelike scales under its chin, and hornlets on its cheeks. Most of the dragon's teeth protrude when its mouth is closed.

A blue dragon's scales vary in color from an iridescent azure to a deep indigo, polished to a glossy finish by blowing desert sands. The size of its scales increases little as the dragon ages, although they do become thicker and harder. Its hide tends to hum and crackle faintly with built-up static

Illus. by T. Lockwood

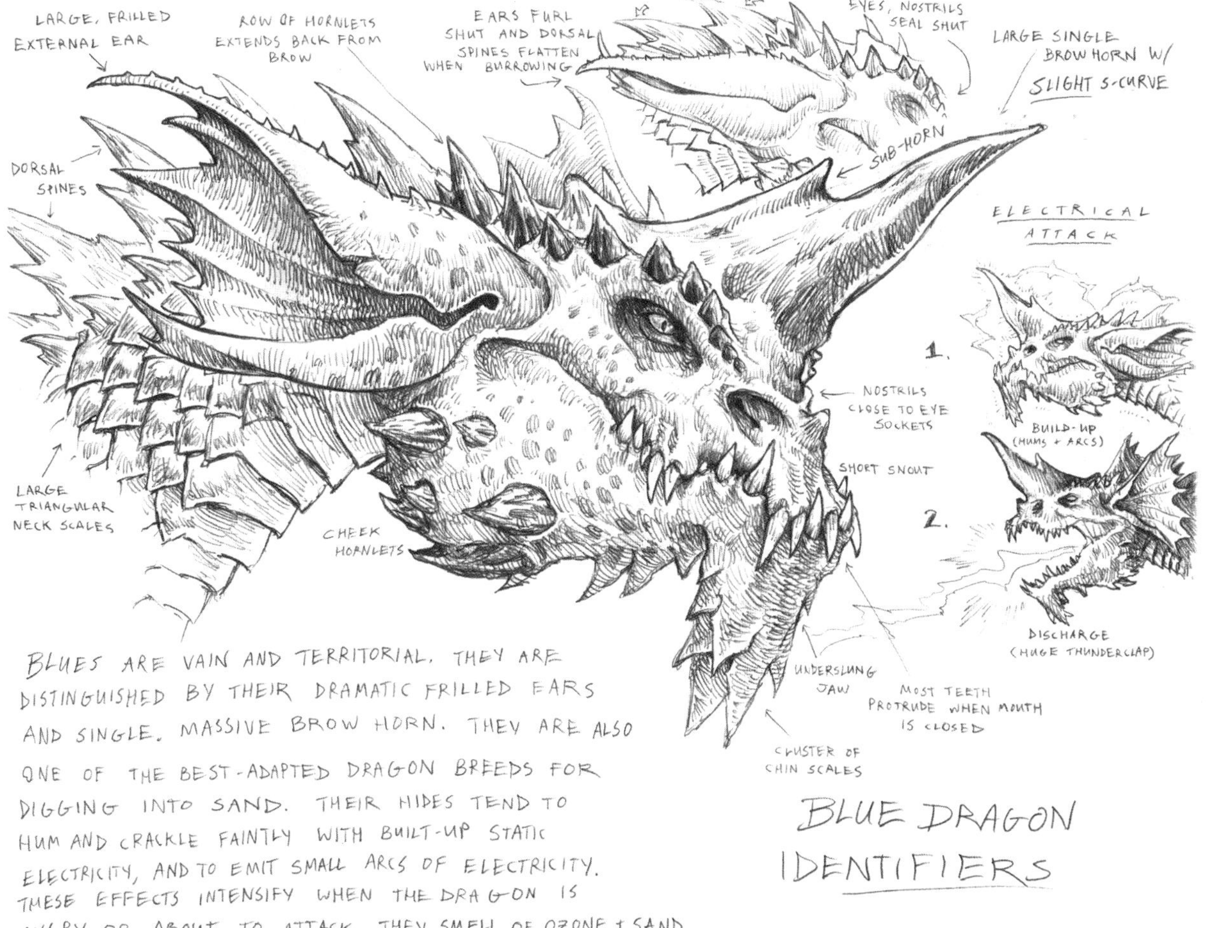

Illus. by S. Wood

electricity. These effects intensify when the dragon is angry or about to attack, giving off an odor of ozone and sand.

A blue dragon flying overhead is easily distinguished from a brass dragon by its batlike wings, which have short alar thumbs and a mottled or dappled pattern. The alar phalanges (the fingerlike bones that support the wing; see Internal Anatomy, page 7) have knobby joints, and the phalanges are all the same length, giving the wings a rounded look. The trailing edge of the wing membrane joins the body well ahead of the rear legs.

The dragon has a short, thick neck. The head is mostly featureless when viewed from below, but the ears are visible. The dragon's tail is thick and flat.

Habits

A blue dragon's vibrant color makes it easy to spot in barren desert surroundings, especially when the dragon is on the ground. When it wishes to be less conspicuous, a blue dragon burrows into the sand so that only the top of its head is exposed. This trick leaves the dragon's massive horn sticking above the surface, but from a distance the horn tends to look like a jagged rock.

Blue dragons love to soar in the hot desert air, usually flying in the daytime when temperatures are highest. Some nearly match the color of the desert sky and can be difficult to see from below.

Although they collect anything that looks valuable, blue dragons are most fond of gems—especially blue sapphires. They consider blue to be a noble hue and the most beautiful color.

Blue dragons are dedicated carnivores. They sometimes eat snakes, lizards, and even desert plants to sate their great hunger, but they especially prefer herd animals such as camels. When they get the chance, they gorge themselves on these creatures, which they cook with their lightning breath. This dining habit makes blue dragons a real threat to caravans

Blue Dragons by Size

Size	Overall Length	Body Length	Neck Length	Tail Length	Body Width	Standing Height	Maximum Wingspan	Minimum Wingspan	Weight
Small	8 ft.	3-1/2 ft.	1-1/2 ft.	3 ft.	2 ft.	2 ft.	16 ft.	8 ft.	40 lb.
Medium	16 ft.	7 ft.	4 ft.	5 ft.	3 ft.	4 ft.	24 ft.	12 ft.	320 lb.
Large	31 ft.	13 ft.	7 ft.	11 ft.	5 ft.	7 ft.	36 ft.	18 ft.	2,500 lb.
Huge	55 ft.	20 ft.	14 ft.	21 ft.	8 ft.	12 ft.	60 ft.	30 ft.	20,000 lb.
Gargantuan	85 ft.	28 ft.	22 ft.	35 ft.	10 ft.	16 ft.	80 ft.	40 ft.	160,000 lb.

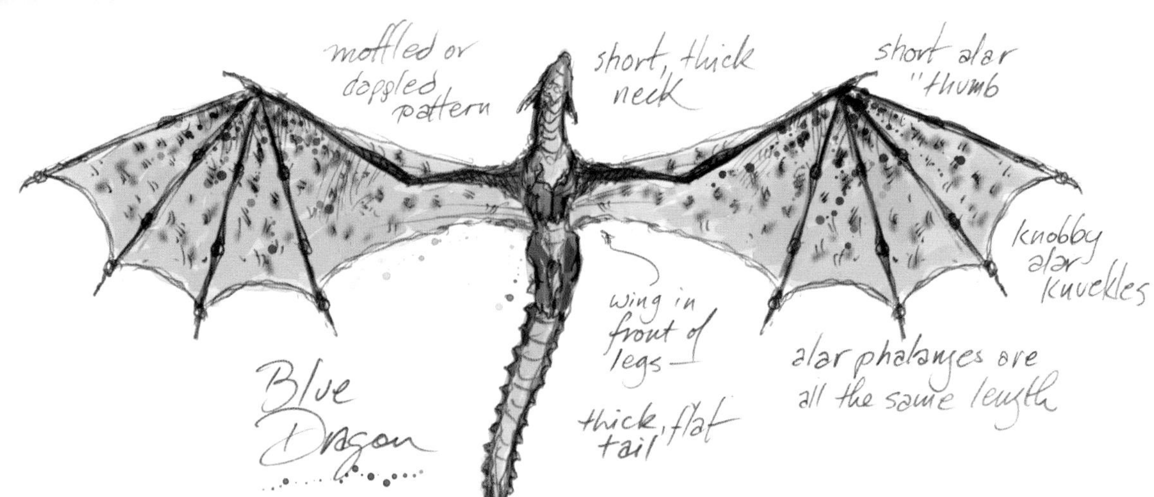

crossing the desert. The dragons think of caravans as handy collections of food and treasure, all available on the same trip.

Blue dragons have a highly developed sense of order (with themselves at the top, at least locally). The oldest blue dragon in an area acts as an overlord to all lesser blue dragons living nearby. This suzerain receives homage from its subjects and settles any disputes, particularly those involving mates or territorial boundaries. Although any blue dragon in an area can challenge the suzerain for the right to rule, this seldom happens. A blue dragon that is unhappy with its suzerain usually moves to a new area—either one with a suzerain more to its liking, or one with no suzerain at all.

Blue dragons observe elaborate courtship and mating rituals involving exchanges of food and treasure, the consent of the suzerain, and announcements to other blue dragons. Older dragons of either sex might have multiple mates, but infidelity is rare. Blue dragons are usually attentive and effective parents, and do not often leave eggs unattended.

Typically, blue dragons attack from above or burrow beneath the sands until opponents come within 100 feet. Older dragons use their special abilities, such as *hallucinatory terrain*, in concert with these tactics to mask the land and improve their chances to surprise the target. When stalking intelligent prey, they often use ventriloquism and mimicry to confuse and divide groups before closing in for the kill. A blue dragon runs from a fight only if it is severely damaged, since all blue dragons view retreat as cowardly.

Illus. by T. Lockwood

BRASS DRAGONS

The most gregarious of all the true dragons, brass dragons are famous (some would say infamous) for their love of conversation. They crave sunlight and dry heat, so they frequent hot, arid regions, particularly sandy deserts. Their choice of terrain often puts them at odds with blue dragons, which are both more powerful and more aggressive. Brass dragons usually cope with attacking blues by using their superior speed to escape, either through the air or by burrowing to safety.

Brass dragons like to make their lairs in high, rocky caves, preferably facing east so the rising run can warm the rocks. Most brass dragons also have several bolt-holes dug into the bases of cliffs where the desert winds have piled up sand. The dragons burrow tunnels parallel to the cliff face in the hard-packed sand. They can move quickly along these tunnels, exiting into subterranean caverns, or out other burrows farther down the line.

Dungeon-dwelling brass dragons often make their lairs near heavily traveled areas where they can satisfy their desire for conversation.

Brass Dragon Identifiers

A brass dragon's head has a massive, fluted plate sweeping back from its eye sockets, forehead, and cheeks. The one-piece plate is dished like a plowshare. When burrowing in the sand, the dragon often uses its head like a plow. A brass dragon also sports bladed chin horns that grow sharper with age. It has supple, expressive lips and a long forked tongue. As the dragon grows older, its pupils fade until the eyes resemble molten metal orbs.

A brass dragon has a tangy odor redolent of hot metal or desert sand.

Brass dragons have short, raylike wings that run from their shoulders all the way back past the tips of their tails. The wings get most of their support from long spines running perpendicular to the backbone. The neck is stubby and thick, with a comparatively long body. When the body is viewed from below, the chin horns are visible.

At birth, a brass dragon's scales are a dull, mottled brown. As the dragon gets older, the scales become more brassy until they reach a warm, burnished appearance. The wings and frills are mottled green where they join the body, and have reddish tints at the outer edges. These markings darken with age.

Habits

Brass dragons can and will eat almost anything if the need arises, but they normally consume very little. They seem to understand that the desert is a fragile environment, and they live lightly upon the land. They are able to get nourishment from the morning dew, a rare commodity in the desert, and they go forth at dawn to gently lift minute beads of dew off plants with their long tongues.

Though it values all precious things, a brass dragon prefers organic treasures over cold stone or metal. Its hoard often includes items made from rare woods, textiles, and

Brass Dragons by Size

Size	Overall Length	Body Length	Neck Length	Tail Length	Body Width	Standing Height	Maximum Wingspan	Minimum Wingspan	Weight
Tiny	4 ft.	1-1/2 ft.	1 ft.	1-1/2 ft.	1 ft.	1 ft.	6 ft.	4 ft.	5 lb.
Small	8 ft.	3-1/2 ft.	1-1/2 ft.	3 ft.	2 ft.	2 ft.	12 ft.	8 ft.	40 lb.
Medium	16 ft.	7 ft.	4 ft.	5 ft.	3 ft.	4 ft.	18 ft.	12 ft.	320 lb.
Large	31 ft.	13 ft.	7 ft.	11 ft.	5 ft.	7 ft.	27 ft.	18 ft.	2,500 lb.
Huge	55 ft.	21 ft.	13 ft.	21 ft.	8 ft.	12 ft.	45 ft.	30 ft.	20,000 lb.
Gargantuan	85 ft.	29 ft.	21 ft.	35 ft.	10 ft.	16 ft.	60 ft.	40 ft.	160,000 lb.

other examples of fine handicrafts rendered in exquisite materials. The warm, dry air of its lair helps keep these delicate treasures from deteriorating with age. A brass dragon takes great care to keep its fiery breath weapon well away from its delicate treasure, and often keeps its hoard in a separate chamber within its lair.

Brass dragons love intense, dry heat and spend most of their time basking in the desert sun. Their territories always contain several spots where they can sunbathe and trap unwary travelers in conversation. A brass dragon will talk for hours with any creature capable of putting two syllables together.

Many scholars believe that brass dragons are the most humble of the true dragons. While any brass dragon certainly will agree that humility is among its many virtues, a brass dragon's loquacity is really a form of draconic hubris. Brass dragons consider themselves such gifted conversationalists that they simply cannot bear to allow any sentient being to miss the benefit of their company.

For all their love of conversation, what brass dragons seem to prefer the least is the company of other brass dragons. Each one remains in loose contact with its neighbors, and brass dragons will band together whenever a common enemy threatens, but otherwise they keep to themselves.

Many brass dragons create vast networks of confidantes and informants, including djinn, jann, sphinxes, and various humanoids. The dragons use these networks to keep apprised of local events and to stay in remote communication with distant brass dragons.

Brass dragons would rather talk than fight. If an intelligent creature tries to leave without engaging in conversation, the dragon might force compliance in a fit of pique, using *suggestion* or a dose of *sleep* gas. Though basically friendly, brass dragons are quick to act if they feel threatened, and often use their nonlethal *sleep* breath to knock out aggressors. A creature put to sleep may wake to find itself pinned or buried to the neck in the sand. The dragon then

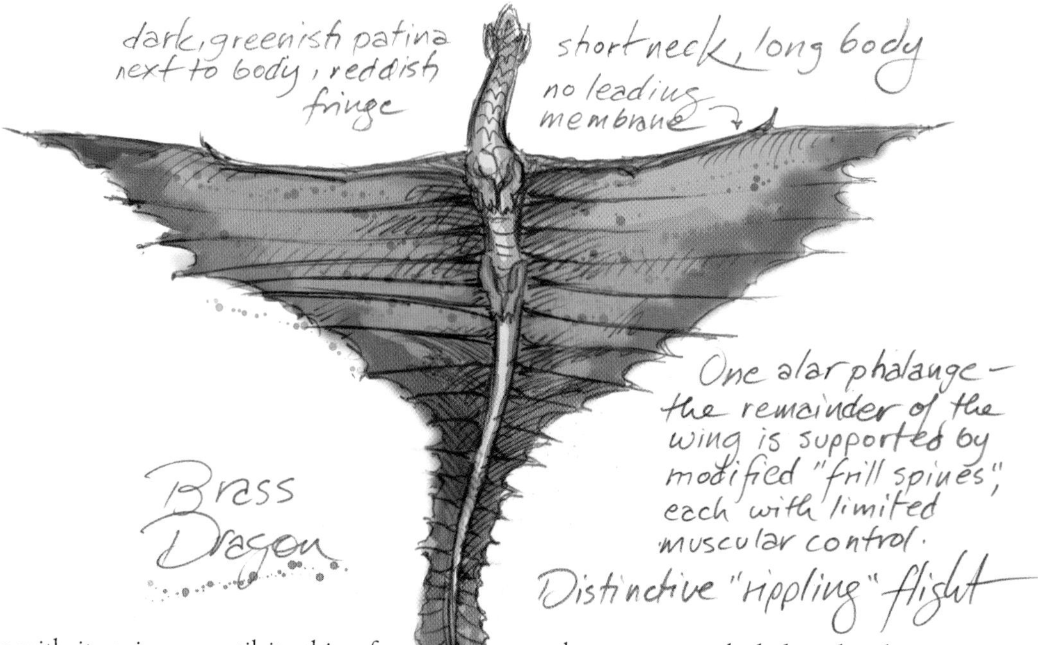

Illus. by T. Lockwood

converses with its prisoner until its thirst for small talk is slaked.

When faced with real danger, younger brass dragons fly out of sight, then hide by burrowing into the sand. Older dragons spurn this ploy but tend to avoid pitched fights unless they have some tactical advantage.

BRONZE DRAGONS

Bronze dragons have a strong sense of justice and do not tolerate cruelty or anarchy in any form. Many a pirate or robber has faced swift retribution from a bronze dragon using an innocuous disguise. Bronze dragons also have an inquisitive side and find the activities of other creatures, particularly humanoids, endlessly fascinating. They enjoy polymorphing into small, friendly animals to study such activities.

Bronze dragons like to be near deep fresh water or salt water, and are found in temperate and tropical coastal areas and islands. They often visit the depths to cool off or hunt for pearls and sunken treasure.

Bronze dragons wage a constant struggle against evil sea creatures, particularly ones that menace the coasts, such as sahuagin, merrow, and scrags. They sometime find themselves with black or green dragons for neighbors. While the bronzes are content to live and let live, the evil dragons are seldom willing to return the favor.

Bronze dragons prefer make their lairs in caves that are accessible only from the water, but their lairs are always dry—they do not lay eggs, sleep, or store treasure underwater. Often, a bronze dragon's lair has a lower area that floods at high tide and an upper area that remains dry around the clock.

Dungeon-dwelling bronze dragons often live near underground streams or lakes.

Bronze Dragon Identifiers

A bronze dragon in its true form can be recognized by the ribbed and fluted crests sweeping back from its cheeks and eyes. The ribs in the crests end in curving horns. These horns are smooth, dark, and oval in cross-section, and curve slightly inward toward the dragon's spine. The largest horns grow from the top of the head. In older dragons, the smaller horns often develop secondary points. The dragon also has small horns on its lower jaw and chin.

A bronze dragon has a beaklike snout and a pointed tongue. It has a small head frill and a tall neck frill.

A bronze dragon has webbed feet and webbing behind the forelimbs. Its scales are smooth and flat.

A bronze wyrmling's scales are yellow tinged with green, showing only a hint of bronze. As the dragon approaches adulthood, its color deepens slowly to a darker, rich bronze tone. Very old dragons develop a blue-black tint to the edges of their scales. Their pupils fade as they age, until in the oldest the eyes resemble glowing green orbs. A smell of sea spray lingers about them.

When viewed from below, a bronze dragon's wings show green mottling on the back edges. The trailing edge of the wing membrane joins the body behind the rear legs, at the point where the tail meets the pelvis.

Most of the alar phalanges are very short and form a wide frill just beyond the alar thumb. The innermost phalange is the longest, and it provides most of the support for the wings, along with a modified alar olecranon at the "elbow" of the alar limb (see page 8). This arrangement allows the dragon to use its wings as big fins underwater. A bronze dragon can flap its wings when submerged and literally fly through the water.

Habits

A bronze dragon spends much of its time in an assumed form, usually that of a small animal or an older humanoid. This charade serves the dragon's inquisitive nature by allowing it a chance to observe the world without drawing attention to itself or disrupting the flow of events. Bronze dragons value moral order and altruism.

Bronze dragons frequently congregate with others of their kind, making them among the most gregarious of the true dragons. When in their natural form, they sometimes swim or play together in the waves. They gather even more frequently when using assumed forms, particularly when observing some event of interest to them. They find warfare fascinating, and many have served in armies fighting for good causes. Afterward, they may spend decades debating the course of the war, its causes, and its consequences.

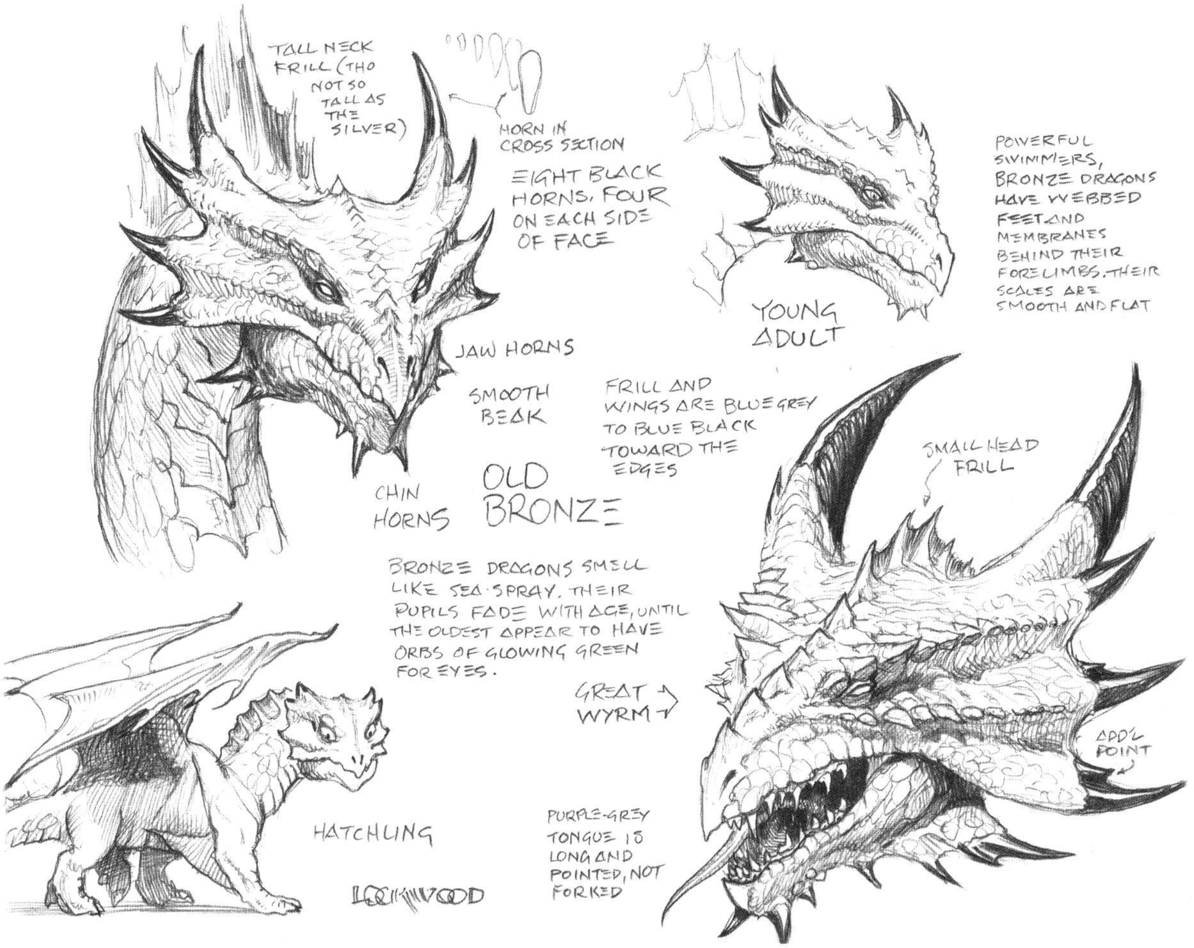

Though they have no lack of draconic pride, bronze dragons enjoy the company of humans and other humanoids. They consider these "lesser" creatures to be just as deserving of survival and happiness as themselves. When in the company of humanoids, a bronze dragon usually assumes humanoid form, both as a practical matter (it can be very hard to fit a bronze adult into a seaside cottage), and to keep the humanoids at ease. Bronze dragons delight in testing a stranger's sense of decency by posing as penniless beachcombers, shipwrecked sailors, or guileless primitives. Unscrupulous creatures who attempt to cheat, bully, rob, or kill a masquerading dragon soon find more trouble than they had bargained for when the dragon reveals itself. Creatures who conduct themselves well may never know they have actually encountered a bronze dragon. Nevertheless, good conduct earns the dragon's respect, and it is usually remembered, perhaps to be rewarded someday.

Most bronze dragons maintain a constant watch for pirates, natural disasters, and ships in distress. Many a shipwrecked mariner has been rescued by the timely intervention of a bronze dragon. Because bronze dragons usually perform such rescues while disguised as something else, the beings they save often remain unaware of exactly who their benefactor was.

Courtship and mating among bronze dragons is always a deliberate and respectful affair. Bronze dragons mate for life, and one often refuses to take a new mate after the death of the original mate. They always tend their eggs and offspring carefully and defend them to the death if necessary.

Bronze dragons eat aquatic plants and some varieties of seafood. They especially prize shark meat, and often spend days at sea hunting sharks. They also dine on the occasional

Bronze Dragons by Size

Size	Overall Length	Body Length	Neck Length	Tail Length	Body Width	Standing Height	Maximum Wingspan	Minimum Wingspan	Weight
Small	8 ft.	2 ft.	2 ft.	4 ft.	2 ft.	2 ft.	16 ft.	8 ft.	40 lb.
Medium	16 ft.	5 ft.	5 ft.	6 ft.	3 ft.	4 ft.	24 ft.	12 ft.	320 lb.
Large	31 ft.	9 ft.	9 ft.	13 ft.	5 ft.	7 ft.	36 ft.	18 ft.	2,500 lb.
Huge	55 ft.	16 ft.	15 ft.	24 ft.	8 ft.	12 ft.	60 ft.	30 ft.	20,000 lb.
Gargantuan	85 ft.	23 ft.	23 ft.	39 ft.	10 ft.	16 ft.	80 ft.	40 ft.	160,000 lb.

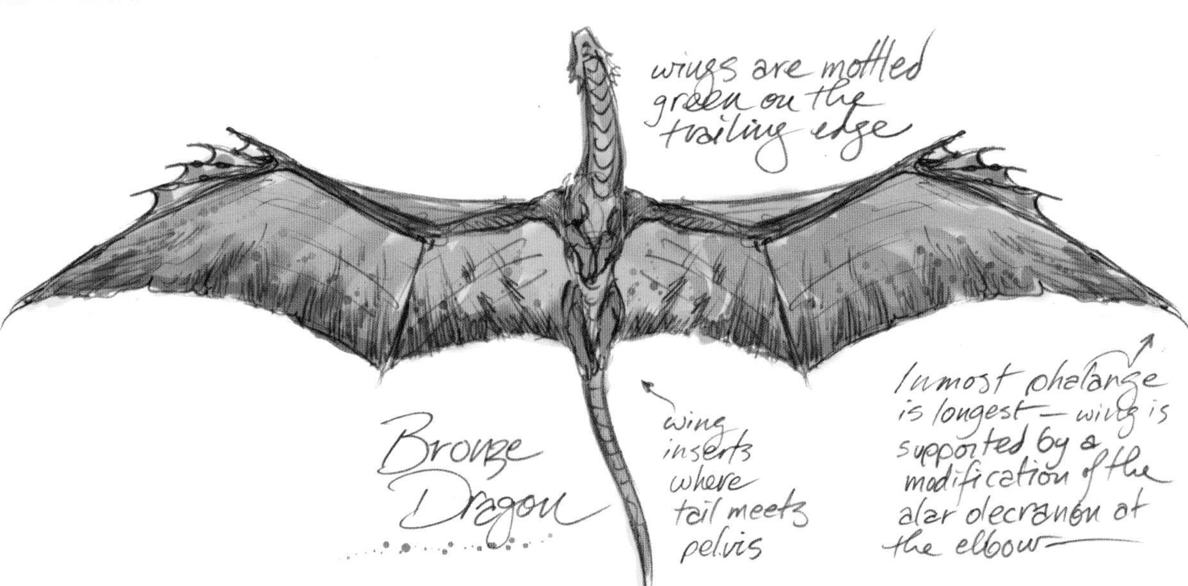

Illus. by T. Lockwood

pearl. They often keep pearls in their lairs, both as treasures and snacks. They admire other treasures from the sea as well, such as bits of rare coral and amber. Though they don't care to admit it, their favorite metal is gold, which does not tarnish in their humid lairs.

Bronze dragons usually attack only in self-defense or to defend those unable to defend themselves. They dislike killing anything they don't plan to eat, and they try especially hard to avoid killing animals that are merely defending themselves. They usually try to distract attacking animals with food, using their repulsion breath to fend them off if distractions fail. Against intelligent foes, bronze dragons usually try to negotiate, but remain wary of duplicity.

Often, a bronze dragon figures out a way to be victorious in a conflict without dealing damage, such as stranding a foe on an island or dismasting a ship at sea.

COPPER DRAGONS

Copper dragons have a well-deserved reputation as incorrigible pranksters, joke-tellers, and riddlers. They appreciate all forms of humor. Most are good-natured but also have a covetous, miserly streak.

Copper dragons like dry, rocky uplands and mountains. Their territories sometimes adjoin or overlap brass dragons' territories. The two species tend to get along well, but meetings between the two usually devolve into marathon conversations in which the copper dragons bombard the brass dragons with humor while the brass dragons blithely continue to banter. Such sessions usually end with one dragon or the other taking its leave none too gently.

Copper dragons also find themselves with silver, red, or blue dragons for neighbors. The silvers avoid too much contact with the coppers. Blue or red dragons inevitably try to slay the coppers or at least drive them away. Many a copper dragon considers the presence of a blue or red dragon as challenge, and does all it can to annoy and embarrass the evil dragon without getting itself killed.

Copper dragons make their lairs in narrow caves. They use their ability to move and shape stone to enhance their lairs, often concealing the entrances using *move earth* and *stone shape*. Within the lair, they construct twisting mazes, often with open tops that allow the dragon to fly or jump over intruders. Unlike most dragons, however, copper dragons are often happy to have cramped lairs that don't allow them space for flight; they depend instead on their ability to climb stone surfaces for mobility inside the lair.

Copper Dragon Identifiers

Copper dragons are powerful jumpers and climbers, with massive thighs and shoulders.

A copper dragon's head has a short face and no beak. Broad, smooth browplates jut over the eyes, and long, flat coppery horns extend back from the browplates in a series of segments. The dragon also has backswept cheek ridges and frills on the backs of the lower jaws that sweep forward slightly. Layers of triangular blades point down from the chin, and as the dragon gets older more layers with larger blades develop. The dragon has a long tongue that comes to a single point.

At birth, a copper dragon's scales have a ruddy brown color with a metallic tint. As the dragon gets older, the scales

Copper Dragons by Size

Size	Overall Length	Body Length	Neck Length	Tail Length	Body Width	Standing Height	Maximum Wingspan	Minimum Wingspan	Weight
Tiny	4 ft.	1-1/2 ft.	1 ft.	1-1/2 ft.	1 ft.	1 ft.	8 ft.	4 ft.	5 lb.
Small	8 ft.	3 ft.	2 ft.	3 ft.	2 ft.	2 ft.	16 ft.	8 ft.	40 lb.
Medium	16 ft.	6 ft.	5 ft.	5 ft.	3 ft.	4 ft.	24 ft.	12 ft.	320 lb.
Large	31 ft.	11 ft.	9 ft.	11 ft.	5 ft.	7 ft.	36 ft.	18 ft.	2,500 lb.
Huge	55 ft.	18 ft.	16 ft.	21 ft.	8 ft.	12 ft.	60 ft.	30 ft.	20,000 lb.
Gargantuan	85 ft.	25 ft.	25 ft.	35 ft.	10 ft.	16 ft.	80 ft.	40 ft.	160,000 lb.

become finer and more coppery, assuming a soft, warm gloss by the young adult stage. A very old dragon's scales pick up a green tint. A copper dragon's pupils fade with age, and the eyes of a great wyrm resemble glowing turquoise orbs.

Copper dragons have a stony odor.

Copper dragons have mantalike wings that show green and red mottling along the trailing edges. The upper alar limb is exceedingly short, giving the leading edges of the wings a U-shaped profile when viewed from below. The wings run down the dragon's entire body, almost to the tip of the tail.

The main portion of the wing is supported by three phalanges and a modified alar olecranon. Spines sweeping backward at an angle from the backbone support the remainder of the wing.

A copper dragon's distinctive wing profile makes it easy to distinguish from the brass dragon, which can occupy similar habitats.

Habits

A copper dragon's sense of humor compels it to seek out companionship—it takes at least two beings to share a joke. Consequently, a copper dragon is basically a social creature. Except when mating, however, copper dragons tend to avoid each other, mostly because they cannot resist getting into competition to prove which has the sharpest wit. When two or more copper dragons get together, the meeting usually escalates into verbal sparring. The dragons initially trade witticisms and banter, but the conversation eventually devolves into pointed barbs growing ever more vicious, until one of the dragons pulls away, vowing revenge. Such encounters rarely lead to violence or lasting enmity, but often create a rivalry. Rival copper dragons have carried on wars of practical jokes and colorful insults that have lasted for centuries.

Copper dragon courtship is an odd mix of tenderness and outrageous humor. Although males and females exchange small gifts of food and treasure, the real currency between copper dragons is wit. Copper dragons are attracted to mates who can make them laugh. Such liaisons are never permanent, but the couple stays together long enough to raise their offspring to adulthood. After that, each dragon's free-wheeling spirit takes over and the couple splits, with each individual going its own way.

Copper dragons are known to eat almost anything, including metal ores. However, they prize monstrous scorpions and other large poisonous creatures. (They say the venom sharpens their wit; their digestive systems can handle the venom safely, although injected venoms affect them normally.) They are determined hunters. They consider good sport at least as important as the food they get, and doggedly pursue any prey that initially eludes them.

When building hoards, copper dragons prefer treasures from the earth. Metals and precious stones are favorites, but they also value statuary and fine ceramics.

A copper dragon would rather tell a riddle or a pull a prank than fight. Any copper dragon appreciates wit wherever it can be found, and will usually not harm a creature that can relate a joke, humorous story, or riddle the dragon has not

Illus. by T. Lockwood

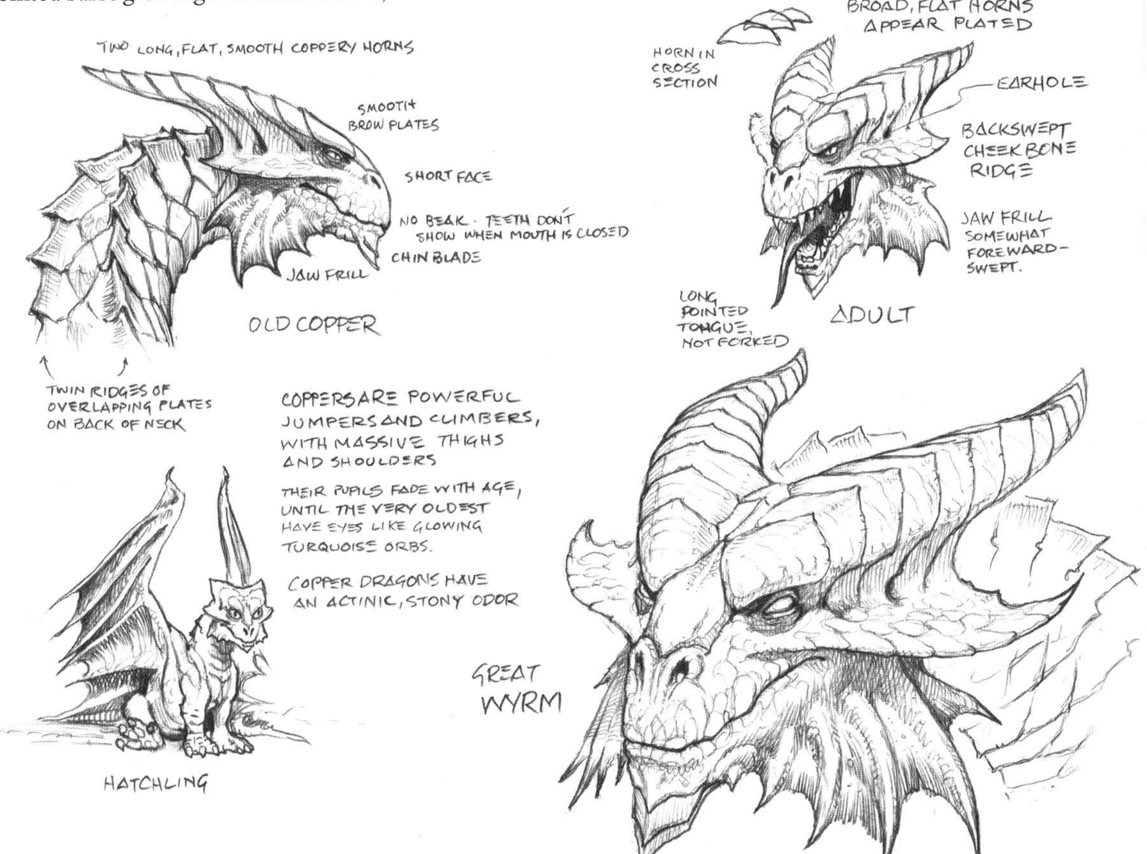

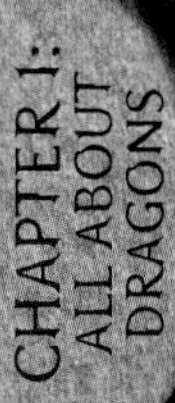

Illus. by T. Lockwood

heard before. The dragon quickly gets annoyed with anyone who doesn't laugh at its jokes or accept its tricks with good humor. Copper dragons love being the center of attention and do not appreciate being upstaged.

When cornered, a copper dragon fights tenaciously, using every trick it knows to defeat the foe. Copper dragons show similar aggression when defending lairs, mates, or offspring. In most other circumstances, a copper dragon prefers to outwit and embarrass a foe. To a copper dragon, a perfect victory comes from taunting and annoying an opponent into just giving up. In any situation, copper dragons favor thinking and planning over brute force. They often deal with superior foes, such as red dragons, by drawing them into narrow, twisting canyons or tortuous caves where they can use their climbing ability to outmaneuver the foe.

GOLD DRAGONS

Gold dragons are dedicated foes of evil and foul play. They often embark on self-appointed quests to promote good. Woe to the evildoer who earns a gold dragon's wrath. The dragon will not rest until the malefactor has been defeated and either slain or brought to justice. Gold dragons do not settle for anything less than complete victory over evil.

A gold dragon usually assumes human or animal guise, even within its own lair.

Gold dragons can live anywhere, but they prefer secluded lairs. Favorite locales include the bottoms of lakes, high plateaus, islands, and deep gorges. A gold dragon's lair is

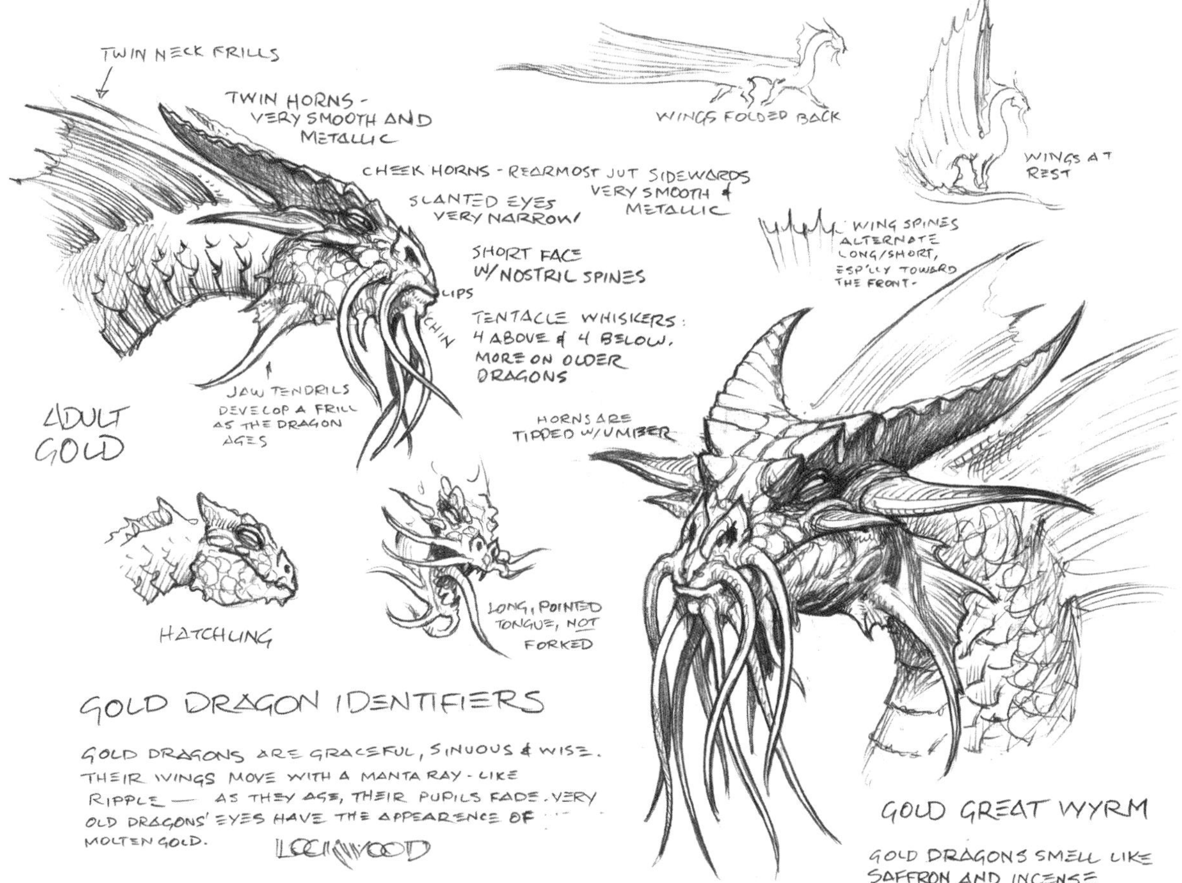

always made of stone, with numerous chambers, all beautifully decorated. The lair usually has loyal guards: animals appropriate to the terrain, storm giants, or good-aligned cloud giants.

Dungeon-dwelling gold dragons choose locations that provide them with suitable chambers.

Gold Dragon Identifiers

A gold dragon in its true form is easily recognized by its large, twin horns that are smooth and metallic, twin neck frills, and the whiskers around its mouth that look like the barbels of a catfish. Gold wyrmlings lack whiskers, but they quickly develop them as they mature. Younger dragons have eight whiskers, four on the upper jaw and four below. Older dragons have more.

A gold dragon has a short face with spines above the nostrils. The eyes are slanted and very narrow. Along with the whiskers, the eyes give the dragon a sagacious look. As the dragon ages, its pupils fade until the eyes resemble pools of molten gold. The dragon has a long, pointed tongue, backswept tendrils on the lower jaws that develop into frills with age, and cheek horns that jut out sideways.

On hatching, a gold dragon's scales are dark yellow with golden metallic flecks. The flecks get larger as the dragon matures until, at the adult stage, the scales grow completely golden. A gold dragon smells of saffron and incense.

A gold dragon has an extremely long tail and broad, mantalike wings that run all the way to the tip of the tail. When at rest, the dragon closes its wings over its back like a massive, golden moth. It folds its wings back when walking or running.

A gold dragon flies with a distinctive rippling motion, almost as if it were swimming through the air. Many scholars argue that gold dragons are the most elegant flyers of all the true dragons (and the gold dragons agree). When viewed from below, a flying gold dragon can be distinguished by its long tail and rippling wings. Its whiskers and horns also show.

Habits

A gold dragon spends most of its time in an assumed form, usually that of a nondescript human or a harmless animal common to the area in which the dragon resides. For animal forms, gold dragons often choose domestic animals, such as dogs, cats, or horses, or swift moving but fairly nonthreatening forms such as eagles. As with the bronze dragon, the assumed form allows the gold dragon to travel and observe the world without attracting undue attention to itself. When traveling in particularly dangerous areas, a gold dragon uses an especially nonthreatening form. This approach helps set at ease fellow travelers the dragon might meet, and also allows the dragon to use itself as bait for any evil creatures lurking about. Many killers and robbers who haunt the world's lonely places have met swift ends when their seemingly helpless victims turned out to be gold dragons in disguise.

Gold dragons always seek news of the wider world and local gossip about recent events. Any gold dragon is a good

Gold Dragons by Size

Size	Overall Length	Body Length	Neck Length	Tail Length	Body Width	Standing Height	Maximum Wingspan	Minimum Wingspan	Weight
Medium	16 ft.	5 ft.	5 ft.	6 ft.	3 ft.	4 ft.	27 ft.	12 ft.	320 lb.
Large	31 ft.	10 ft.	9 ft.	12 ft.	5 ft.	7 ft.	40 ft.	18 ft.	2,500 lb.
Huge	55 ft.	16 ft.	15 ft.	24 ft.	8 ft.	12 ft.	68 ft.	30 ft.	20,000 lb.
Gargantuan	85 ft.	23 ft.	23 ft.	39 ft.	10 ft.	16 ft.	90 ft.	40 ft.	160,000 lb.
Colossal	120 ft.	33 ft.	33 ft.	54 ft.	15 ft.	22 ft.	135 ft.	60 ft.	1,280,000 lb.

listener, and even the most long-winded talker does not try its patience (though even a gold dragon will draw the line if a brass dragon bends its ear for too long). The dragon usually avoids philosophical or ethical arguments with lesser beings, though it often cannot resist trumping an argument that advocates chaos with an aphorism or fable promoting law. When it encounters a being that advocates evil, a gold dragon tends to be silent, but marks the speaker for future attention.

Gold dragons have a worldwide hierarchy with a single leader at the top. This leader is elected by the whole species from the ranks of great gold wyrms and serves for life or until he or she decides to resign. Many serve until the onset of their twilight (see page 14); others serve until they believe a successor can do a better job. The leader is always addressed by the honorific "Your Resplendence."

When a vacancy occurs, every gold dragon in the world participates in the selection of the replacement, who is almost always selected by acclamation. Occasionally, two candidates of equal merit are available when the previous ruler dies or retires. In such cases, the two work out some method of sharing of office. During the past, there have been co-rulers, alternating rulers, and rulers who simply have retired early to make way for another.

The ruler's duties usually prove light because the position's authority rarely needs to exercised. Most gold dragons know how they are expected to behave, and they act accordingly. The ruler mostly serves to advise individual gold dragons on the nature and goals of their quests against evil. The ruler often can point out hidden consequences for a quest, such as the effects on the politics of lesser creatures or the impact on the local environment or the balance of power. The ruler also serves as the gold dragons' chief representative in dealing with other species (in the rare event when some matter of interest to all gold dragons arises), and as chief enforcer and judge (in the exceptionally rare case of gold dragon misconduct).

Gold dragon courtship is both deliberate and dignified. Often two prospective mates spend years debating philosophy and ethics, and go on several quests together, so as to get the full measure of one another. Once a pair agree to mate, they seek the ruler's approval as a matter of protocol. Permission to mate is rarely withheld.

Despite their lawful nature, gold dragons allow themselves remarkable freedom. Some mate for life, other only for a short time. Some are monogamous, and others have multiple mates at the same time. Gold dragons always tend and instruct their young carefully, though it is common for parents to send their offspring into the care of foster parents (always lawful good, but not always dragons) when they perceive the need. Young gold dragons may be fostered to protect them when danger threatens, to free up the parents for a quest, or simply to broaden their horizons.

Gold dragons prefer treasures that show an artisan's touch. They are particularly fond of paintings, calligraphy, sculpture, and fine porcelain. They enjoy pearls and small gems, which also are their favorite foods. Approaching a gold dragon with gifts of pearls and gems is a good way to gain favor, provided the gifts are not offered as bribes.

Gold dragons usually parley before fighting. When conversing with intelligent creatures, they use *discern lies* to help them determine if combat really will be necessary. They prefer to delay combat until they can cast preparatory spells.

GREEN DRAGONS

Green dragons are belligerent creatures and masters of intrigue, politics, and backbiting. They prefer forests; the older the forest and bigger the trees, the better. Green dragons are as territorial and aggressive as any other kind of evil dragon, but their aggression often takes the form of elaborate schemes to gain power or wealth with as little effort as possible.

Green dragons seek out caves in sheer cliffs or hillsides for their lairs. They prefer locations where the lair's entrance is hidden from prying eyes, such as behind a waterfall or near a lake, pond, or stream that provides a submerged entrance. Older green dragons often conceal their lairs with plants they have magically grown. Green dragons sometimes clash with black dragons over choice lairs. The greens frequently pretend to back down, only to wait a few decades before returning to raid the black dragon's lair and loot its hoard.

Dungeon-dwelling green dragons prefer locales with some kind of vegetable life, such as grottos filled with giant mushrooms.

Green Dragons by Size

Size	Overall Length	Body Length	Neck Length	Tail Length	Body Width	Standing Height	Maximum Wingspan	Minimum Wingspan	Weight
Small	8 ft.	2-1/2 ft.	2-1/2 ft.	3 ft.	2 ft.	2-1/2 ft.	16 ft.	8 ft.	40 lb.
Medium	16 ft.	5-1/2 ft.	6 ft.	4-1/2 ft.	3 ft.	5 ft.	24 ft.	12 ft.	320 lb.
Large	31 ft.	10 ft.	11 ft.	10 ft.	5 ft.	9 ft.	36 ft.	18 ft.	2,500 lb.
Huge	55 ft.	17 ft.	18 ft.	20 ft.	8 ft.	15 ft.	60 ft.	30 ft.	20,000 lb.
Gargantuan	85 ft.	24 ft.	28 ft.	33 ft.	10 ft.	20 ft.	80 ft.	40 ft.	160,000 lb.

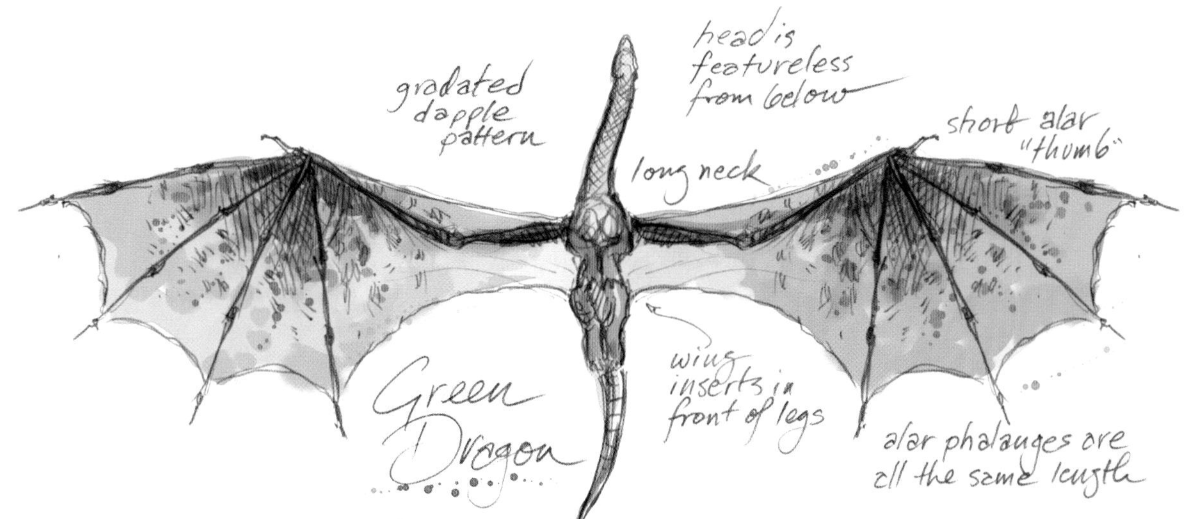

Illus. by T. Lockwood

Green Dragon Identifiers

A green dragon's notable features include a heavily curved jawline and a crest that begins near the eyes and continues down most of the dragon's spine. The crest reaches its full height just behind the skull.

A green dragon has no external ears, just ear openings and leathery plates that run down the sides of the neck, each plate edged with hornlets. The dragon also has hornlets over its brows and at the chin. The nostrils are set high on the snout, and the teeth protrude when the mouth is closed. The dragon has a long, slender, forked tongue.

The stinging odor of chlorine wafts from a green dragon.

A wyrmling green dragon's scales are thin, very small, and a deep shade of green that appears nearly black. As the dragon ages, the scales grow larger and lighter, turning shades of forest, emerald, and olive green, which helps it blend in with its wooded surroundings.

A green dragon's legs and neck are proportionately longer in relation to the rest of its body than any other chromatic or metallic dragon. When it stands on all fours, its body stays fairly high off the ground, enabling it to pass over brush or forest debris lying on the ground. The neck is often longer than the rest of the dragon's body (excluding the tail), and older dragons can peer over the tops of mature trees without rearing up.

A green dragon's long neck gives it a distinctive, swanlike profile when aloft. The head looks featureless when viewed from below.

The wings have a dappled pattern, darker near the leading edges and lighter toward the trailing edges. The alar thumb is short, and the alar phalanges are all the same length, giving the wingtips a rounded look. The trailing edge of the wing membrane joins the body well ahead of the rear legs.

Habits

A green dragon patrols its territory regularly, both on the wing and on the ground, so as to get a good look over and under the forest canopy. These patrols serve twin purposes. First, the dragon stays on the lookout for prey. Although they have been known to eat practically anything when hungry enough, including shrubs and small trees, green dragons especially prize elves and sprites.

Second, green dragons like to note anything new happening in their domains. They have a lust for power that rivals their desire to collect treasure. There is little a green dragon will not attempt to further its ambitions. Its favorite means of gaining influence over others is intimidation, but it tries more subtle manipulations when dealing with other dragons or similarly powerful creatures. Green dragons are consummate liars and masters of double talk and verbal evasion. Just talking to a green dragon can lead a being to ruin.

When dealing with most other creatures, green dragons are honey-tongued, smooth, and sophisticated. Among their own kind, they are loud, crass, and generally rude, especially when dealing with dragons of the same age and status. Younger dragons are forced to use some restraint when interacting with their elders, but the veneer of civility they adopt is paper-thin, and the dragons know it. A clear pecking order, based on age and status but with no formal hierarchy, develops among green dragons within a given area. Green dragons know each other too well to depend on any formal social structure.

Courtship among green dragons is a coarse and indelicate affair. Once a pair decide to mate, however, their lawful nature comes to the fore, and a strong bond develops between them. Parents take extreme care to invest their offspring with all the skills necessary for effective manipulation and double-dealing. A mated pair seldom leaves its first set of offspring untended, but may produce additional clutches to fend for themselves while the first clutch grows up. Once the first clutch reaches adulthood, the parents chase off the youngsters and go their separate ways. If the pair is about the same age, they divide their shared territory between them. (Such agreements usually last at least a few decades before the former mates seek ways to encroach on each other's turf.) Otherwise, the younger parent leaves at the same time the youngsters do.

Green dragons are not picky about the treasure they collect. Anything valuable will do. Among items of similar value, however, a green dragon favors the item that reminds it of a particularly noteworthy triumph.

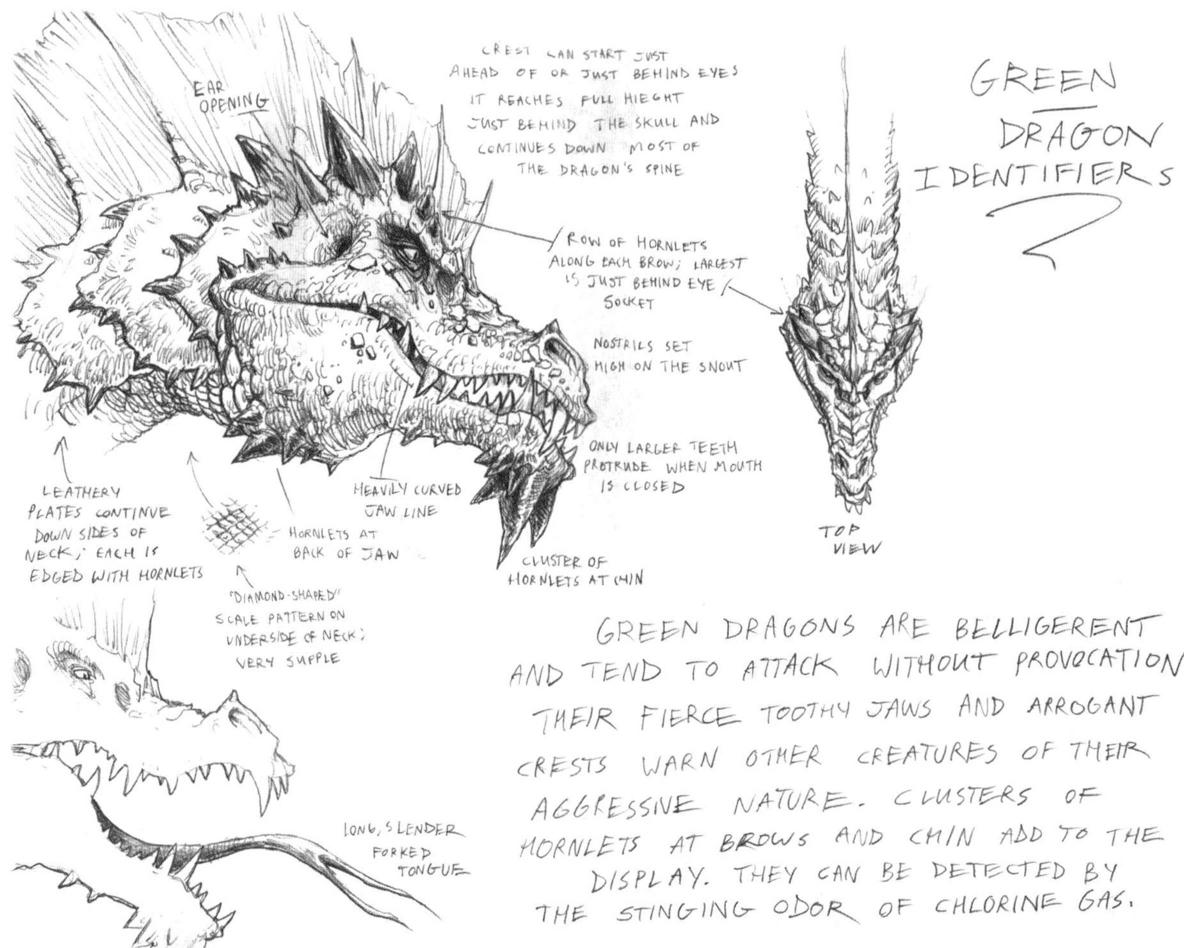

Illus. by S. Wood

Green dragons often attack with little or no provocation, especially when dealing with creatures passing through their territory. (Such creatures don't offer much opportunity for a scam or other long-term manipulation, so the dragon simply attacks.) Victory in such an encounter often nets the dragon some treasure and helps demonstrate the dragon's power to its neighbors and subjects. The dragon typically stalks its victims, studying them from afar and planning its assault. It may shadow its victims for days before attacking. If the target appears weak, the dragon makes its presence known quickly—it enjoys evoking terror. A green dragon seldom slays all its opponents, preferring instead to try to establish control over one of the survivors by using intimidation or magical enchantments. It then questions its prisoner to learn what is going on in the countryside, and if there is treasure nearby. Green dragons occasionally release such prisoners if they can arrange for a ransom payment. Otherwise, the prisoner must prove its value to the dragon daily or die.

RED DRAGONS

The most covetous of all true dragons, red dragons tirelessly seek to increase their treasure hoards. They are exceptionally vain, even for dragons, which is reflected in their proud bearing and disdainful expression.

Red dragons love mountainous terrain, but also inhabit hilly regions, badlands, and other locales where they can perch high and survey their domain. Their preference for mountain homes often brings them into conflict with silver dragons, which red dragons passionately hate. Silver dragons usually get the better of red dragons in battle, which merely serves to stoke the flames of resentment among red dragons. Red dragons also vie for territory with copper dragons from time to time, and the weaker copper dragons are often hard-pressed to survive any direct confrontation.

A red dragon seeks out a large cave that extends deep into the earth for its lair. Caves with some kind of volcanic or geothermal activity are the most highly prized. No matter what its lair is like, however, the dragon always has a high perch nearby from which to haughtily survey its territory.

Dungeon-dwelling red dragons seek out superheated or fiery areas for their lairs. Since dungeons usually lack elevated areas that offer panoramic views of the neighborhood, red dragons living in such places often settle for open spaces or areas with long corridors that offer broad views.

Red Dragon Identifiers

Two massive horns sweep back atop a red dragon's head. These horns can be straight or twisted, and can be any hue from bone white to night black. Rows of small horns run along the top of a red dragon's head, and the dragon has small horns on its cheeks and lower jaw as well.

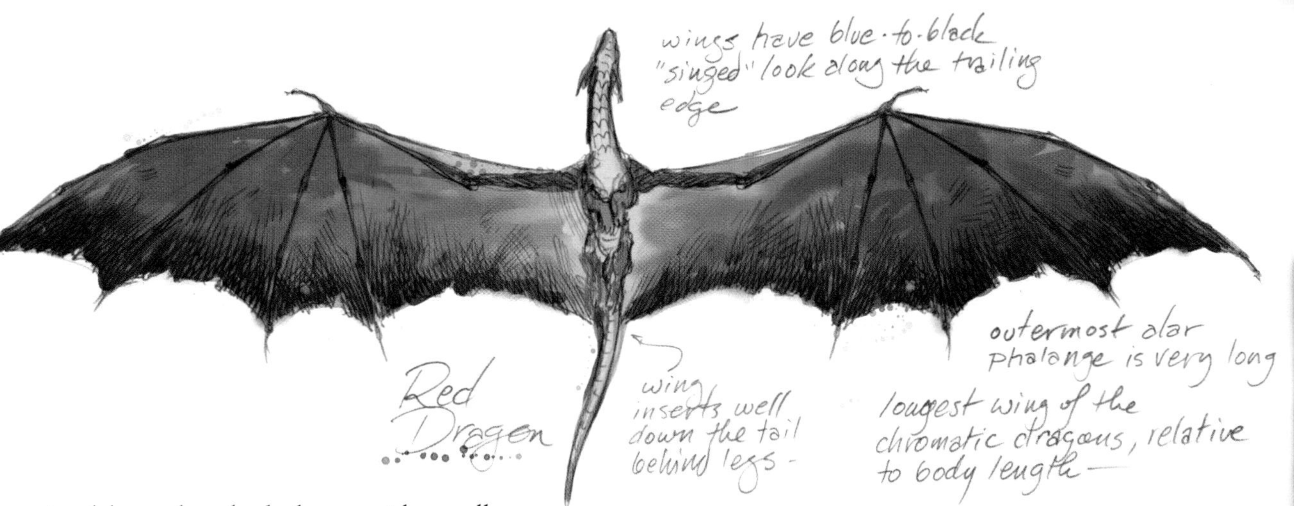

Illus. by T. Lockwood

A red dragon has a beaked snout with a small nose and chin horns. Its tongue is forked, and little flames often dance in its nostrils and eye sockets when it is angry.

The dragon has fringed ears that tend to merge with the cheek horns as the dragon ages. A red dragon's teeth protrude when its mouth is closed, and it has a single backswept frill that begins behind the head and runs all the way to the tip of the tail.

The small scales of wyrmlings are a bright glossy scarlet. Toward the end of the young stage, the scales turn a deeper red, and the glossy texture is replaced by a smooth, dull finish. As the dragon grows older, the scales become large, thick, and as strong as metal. The pupils of a red dragon fade as it ages; the oldest red dragons have eyes that resemble molten lava orbs.

The odor of sulfur and pumice surrounds a red dragon.

A red dragon has the longest wings of all chromatic dragons, both in actual measurement and in relation to body length. This is mostly due to the outermost alar phalange, which is very long and gives the wing a tapering look. The longest part of the wing is right at the trailing edge. The trailing edge of the wing membrane attaches to the dragon's body behind the rear lags and well down the tail. The wings have a bluish or blue-black tint along the trailing edge (the dragon's frills show a similar pattern); the color resembles metal burned blue in a fire.

The great horns on a red dragon's head are clearly visible from below.

Habits

Red dragons are so rapacious, ferocious, vengeful, and avaricious that scholars regard them as the archetypical evil dragons. Red dragons share this opinion of themselves. They believe that, above all other species, they are closest to the ideals of draconic nature and behavior, and that the rest of dragonkind has slipped from this purity.

Younger red dragons often find life difficult. Their vivid red scales make them dangerously conspicuous in most landscapes, and so they lurk underground by day and venture forth only at night. Older red dragons, however, are both less vividly colored and more aware of their presumed status as the epitome of dragonkind.

Red dragons are the most obsessive treasure collectors among the true dragons. They covet absolutely anything of monetary value and often can judge a bauble's worth to within a copper piece with just a glance.

Every red dragon knows the exact value of items in its hoard, along with exactly how and when the dragon obtained the item and each item's exact location in the hoard. Bards tell tales of sneak thieves who ignite a dragon's wrath just by stealing a single trinket.

Such tales are firmly grounded in fact, at least where red dragons are concerned. In some cases, in fact, the tales fall short of the mark. An adult red dragon can notice a single coin missing from its hoard, and its rage over the pettiest theft is legendary. The dragon tracks down and slays the thief if possible. If not, the dragon is sure to go on a rampage, killing anything it meets and laying waste to any town or village where the thief might have taken refuge.

All red dragons are solitary by nature and fiercely territorial; they keep constant watch for trespassers of any kind and for encroachment by other dragons. Entering a red dragon's territory uninvited is asking to be attacked. For all their ferocious independence, however, red dragons always seek to know about events in the wider world. They often

Red Dragons by Size

Size	Overall Length	Body Length	Neck Length	Tail Length	Body Width	Standing Height	Maximum Wingspan	Minimum Wingspan	Weight
Small	8 ft.	3 ft.	2 ft.	3 ft.	2 ft.	2 ft.	20 ft.	8 ft.	40 lb.
Medium	16 ft.	6 ft.	5 ft.	5 ft.	3 ft.	4 ft.	30 ft.	12 ft.	320 lb.
Large	31 ft.	11 ft.	9 ft.	11 ft.	5 ft.	7 ft.	45 ft.	18 ft.	2,500 lb.
Huge	55 ft.	18 ft.	16 ft.	21 ft.	8 ft.	12 ft.	75 ft.	30 ft.	20,000 lb.
Gargantuan	85 ft.	25 ft.	25 ft.	35 ft.	10 ft.	16 ft.	100 ft.	40 ft.	160,000 lb.
Colossal	120 ft.	35 ft.	35 ft.	50 ft.	15 ft.	22 ft.	150 ft.	60 ft.	1,280,000 lb.

make use of lesser creatures as informants, messengers, and spies. The dragons invariably adopt patronizing attitudes toward these servants, and do not hesitate to slay and eat them when they bring bad news.

A red dragon is particularly interested in news about other red dragons, mostly because its own status relative to its peers remains a top concern. A red dragon's pride is easily wounded, because any defeat or insult left unanswered causes a loss of status. This is one reason why red dragons are prone to destructive rages. A red dragon usually can recover some lost status by wreaking havoc.

Every red dragon firmly believes that no being deserves to keep anything it is not strong enough to defend. Red dragons apply this rule to their own kind. Occasionally, red dragons perceive weakness among one of their own, and the subject is not allowed to live. The victim is attacked, and its lair is stripped.

Courtship among red dragons can be a perilous affair, because most would-be suitors are treated as dangerous rivals. Successful red dragon courtship usually involves a younger dragon with fairly high status among its peers carefully approaching an older one. Females do most of the courting, but males are also known to do so. After mating, the younger dragon is usually left to guard the eggs. Most red wyrmlings are left to fend for themselves. Occasionally, two parents of about equal age mate and tend their young together.

Red dragons rarely fight for mates. Most are wise enough to know that any battle will be fatal, and prudently quit the field when a superior rival makes a claim.

Red dragons are meat-eaters by preference, and their favorite food is a human or elf youth. Their taste for the flesh of young women is well documented. The dragons steadfastly claim that such meat simply tastes better. Sometimes they force villagers into regularly sacrificing maidens to them.

Red dragons are confident fighters for whom retreat or compromise is not an option. They spend years formulating plans of attack; upon spotting potential foes, they simply choose a strategy and immediately put it into practice. Being swift but not particularly agile flyers, they often choose to fight on the ground when they can. There, red dragons often display considerable mobility and tactical savvy. They are excellent jumpers, and often leap from place or take short flights to gain the most favorable position possible when using spells or breath weapons. Any red dragon is well aware that its fiery breath can destroy treasure, and it uses its breath weapon judiciously so as to avoid incinerating the spoils of victory.

For all its legendary ferocity, a red dragon also knows when not to attack. If it recognizes a superior foe, it (reluctantly) withdraws to fight another day if it can do so without losing face. Likewise, when dealing with a clearly weaker foe, a red dragon might attempt to bully or fool the creature into rendering it some service or supplying information. In either case, the dragon gets what it wants, or the creature dies. The dragon will accept no other outcomes.

Red dragons do not slay every foe they meet in battle. Always conscious of status, they often allow a few survivors to escape and spread word of the dragon's victory.

Silver Dragons by Size

Size	Overall Length	Body Length	Neck Length	Tail Length	Body Width	Standing Height	Maximum Wingspan	Minimum Wingspan	Weight
Small	8 ft.	3 ft.	2 ft.	3 ft.	2 ft.	2 ft.	20 ft.	8 ft.	40 lb.
Medium	16 ft.	6 ft.	5 ft.	5 ft.	3 ft.	4 ft.	30 ft.	12 ft.	320 lb.
Large	31 ft.	11 ft.	9 ft.	11 ft.	5 ft.	7 ft.	45 ft.	18 ft.	2,500 lb.
Huge	55 ft.	18 ft.	16 ft.	21 ft.	8 ft.	12 ft.	75 ft.	30 ft.	20,000 lb.
Gargantuan	85 ft.	25 ft.	25 ft.	35 ft.	10 ft.	16 ft.	100 ft.	40 ft.	160,000 lb.
Colossal	120 ft.	35 ft.	35 ft.	50 ft.	15 ft.	22 ft.	150 ft.	60 ft.	1,280,000 lb.

SILVER DRAGONS

Silver dragons enjoy the company of humanoids and often take the form of kindly old men or fair damsels. They cheerfully assist good creatures in genuine need, but usually avoid interfering with other creatures until their assistance is requested or until inaction would allow something evil to come to pass. They hate injustice and cruelty, though they concern themselves less with punishing or rooting out evildoers than with protecting the innocent and healing their hurts.

Though they can be found nearly anywhere, silver dragons love high mountains and vast, open skies with billowing clouds. They enjoy flying and sometimes soar for hours just for the pleasure of it.

Silver and red dragons often come into conflict. This is only partly because they lair in similar territories. Silver dragons despise red dragons for their love of carnage and penchant for destruction. Duels between the two varieties are furious and deadly, but silver dragons generally get the upper hand, usually by working together against their foes, and often by accepting assistance from nondragons.

Silver dragons prefer aerial lairs on secluded mountain peaks or amid the clouds themselves. A cloud lair always has an enchanted area with a solid floor for laying eggs and storing treasure.

Silver dragons often dwell in towns or in dungeons. When doing so, they typically take a humanoid form and blend in with the rest of the population. They always situate themselves near one or more open areas where they have space to assume their true forms when necessary.

Silver Dragon Identifiers

A silver dragon in its true form can be recognized by the smooth, shiny plate that forms its face. The dragon also has a frill that rises high over its head and continues down the neck and back to the tip of the tail. A silver dragon has the tallest frill of any metallic or chromatic dragon. Long spines with dark tips support the frill. The dragon also has ear frills with similar spines. It has two smooth, shiny horns, also with dark tips.

A silver dragon has a beaklike nose and a strong chin with a dangling frill that some observers say looks like a goatee. It has a pointed tongue.

A silver wyrmling's scales are blue-gray with silver highlights. As the dragon approaches adulthood, its color slowly brightens until the individual scales are scarcely visible. From a distance, these dragons look as if they have been sculpted from pure metal. As a silver dragon grows older, its pupils fade until in the oldest the eyes resemble orbs of mercury. A silver dragon carries the scent of rain about it.

When viewed from below, a flying silver dragon shows a remarkably similar profile to a red dragon. It has long wings that are broadest along the trailing edge. The wing membrane attaches to the dragon's body behind the rear legs and well down the tail, and the head has clearly visible horns. The wings also show darker markings along the trailing edges, just as a red dragon's do. Fortunately, a silver dragon has one minor feature that sets it apart from a red dragon: The outer alar phalange forms a second "thumb" at the leading edge of the each wing. Viewers unable to discern the dragon's color would do well to look for this vital detail.

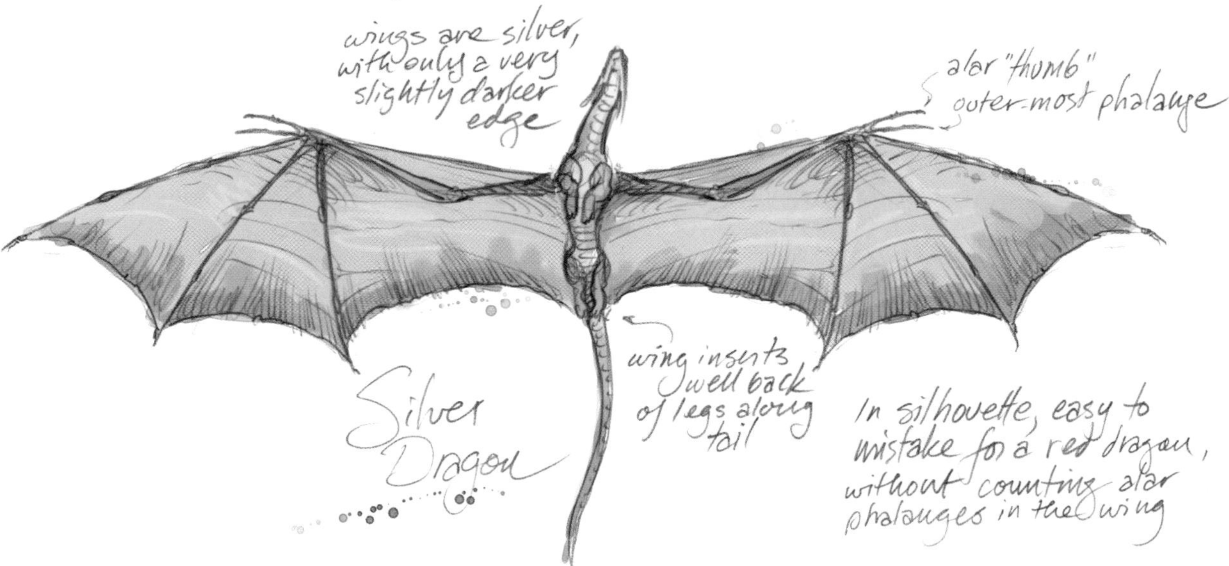

Illus. by T. Lockwood

Habits

A silver dragon often assumes a humanoid from, usually appearing as a kindly old human or a comely young elf, and spends most of its time in that form. Silver dragons do so to more readily associate with humanoids.

Some scholars maintain that silver dragons prefer the company of humans or elves to that of other silver dragons. As with most things draconic, the truth is more complex than that. Silver dragons believe themselves to be superior to most other beings, just as other kinds of dragons do. Unlike other dragons, however, silvers believe that being a dragon imposes some limitations. Many of these are practical in nature, such as their massive size and the huge living space requirements that go along with it.

What concerns silver dragons the most, however, is the draconic sense of time. They're happy to live more than 2,000 years, but they constantly fight their tendency to reflect on things and let opportunities pass them by. They understand that short-lived races such as humans must seize every opportunity that comes their way, which gives them a drive toward accomplishment that most dragons lack. Silver dragons seek to couple their own long perspective on the world with humanity's dynamism. It's a lesson silver dragons believe other dragons would do well to learn.

Though lawful and good, silver dragons have no great love for hierarchies and formal authority. They believe that living a moral life involves doing good deeds and taking no actions that bring undeserved harm to other beings. Actions that cause no harm are not their business. Silver dragons are hardly pacifists, however, and they are quick to battle other beings who would do evil or harm the innocent. They usually do not take it upon themselves to root out evil, as gold and bronze dragons tend to do. Silver dragons find that, in time, evil tends to make itself felt almost everywhere, and they seek to stamp it out whenever it appears in their vicinity. Should they discover widespread evil looming over the land, however, they are both willing and able to locate its source and tackle it there.

Silver dragons form loosely knit family units or clans with a matriarch or patriarch (called the "senior") presiding. The senior gives advice, settles disputes, and coordinates any actions the clan might take as a group. A clan of silver dragons can be spread over an entire continent, with the individual dragons in it establishing their own lairs and otherwise going about their business. Individual silver dragons might go for decades without associating directly with other clan members, but the clan takes care of its own and is always available to provide support or advice.

A silver dragon living among nondragons often develops strong attachments to its nondragon companions. When such a companion earns the dragon's trust, the dragon

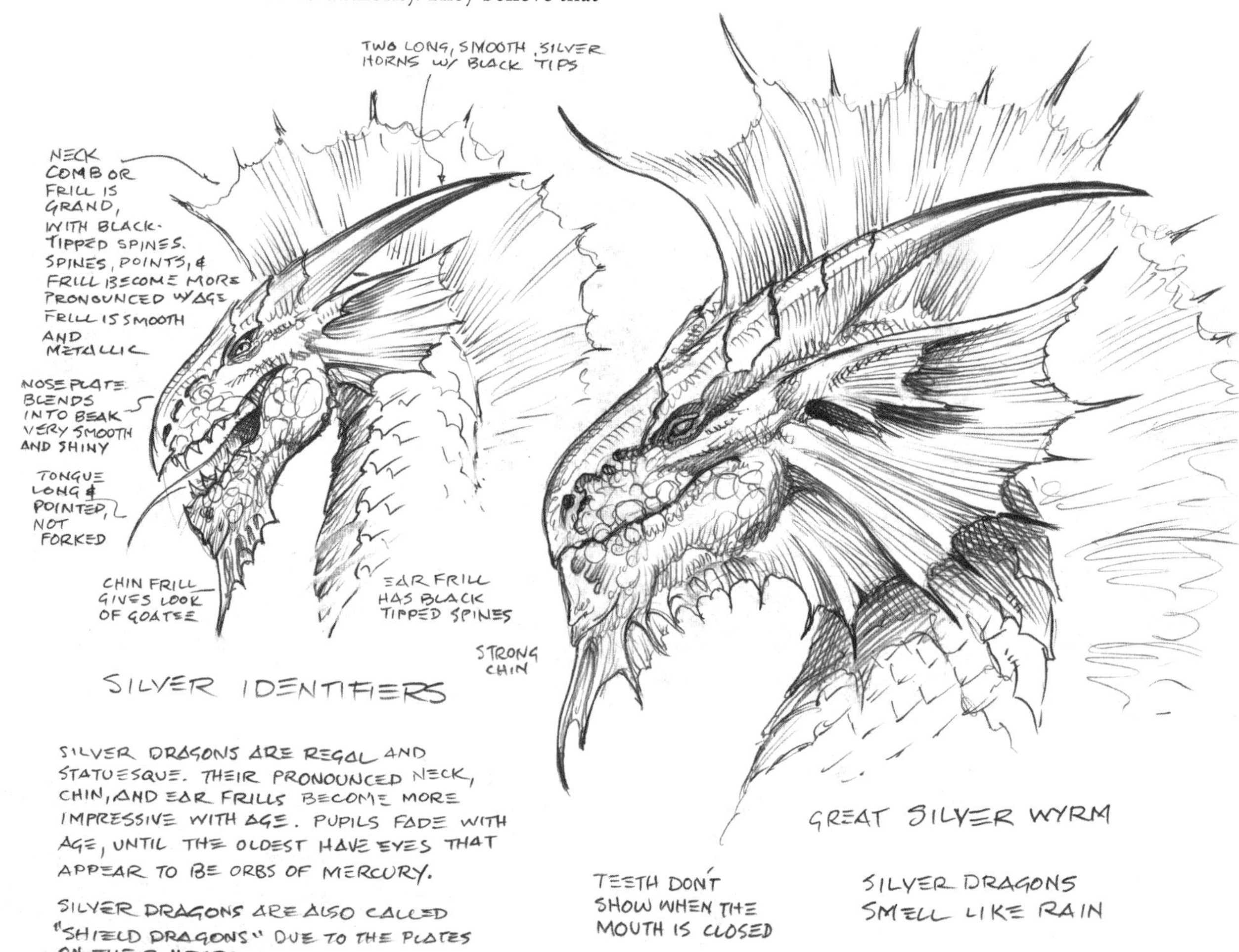

Illus. by T. Lockwood

maintains the relationship for as long as the companion lives, and may pick up the relationship with the companion's descendants. A silver dragon always eventually reveals its true nature to a trusted companion. This honesty relieves any pangs of conscience the dragon may have about deceiving its companions. It also prevents any awkwardness that may develop if the dragon has to ask some special favor of a companion, such as taking care of the dragon's abode while it embarks on some venture that might take decades to complete.

Courtship and mating among silver dragons is always a civilized and decorous affair. They always seek mates outside their own clan—mating within the clan is a serious taboo. Either sex can initiate courtship. When two silver dragons agree to be mates, they seek the approval of the seniors from both clans. The approval is largely ceremonial, and is rarely withheld (never without good reason). Many silver dragons mate for life, but not all do so. Once a courtship is completed, one of the pair leaves its clan and joins the mate's clan. Usually, the younger dragon or the dragon of lower status is the one to change clans, but this is not always so.

Silver dragons are dedicated omnivores and always seek a variety of foods. Many prefer human fare and exist on it exclusively for years without suffering any ill effects. Though many silver dragons have favorite dishes, they seldom pass up the chance to try something new.

Silver dragons prefer portable treasure that they can keep with them while living among humanoids. They especially prize items that show exceptional workmanship, everything from carefully cut gems to intricate carvings to textiles and jewelry.

Silver dragons are nonviolent and avoid combat except when faced with evil or aggressive foes. Often they remain in their assumed forms and attempt to quickly end battles using their spells and magical abilities. When fighting in their true forms, they prefer to remain airborne, and they use any clouds in the area to conceal themselves and to take advantage of their cloudwalking ability. No matter who or how they are fighting, silver dragons usually seek to eliminate the leader or the most aggressive foe first, in hopes of persuading the survivors to surrender or retreat.

WHITE DRAGONS

The smallest, least intelligent, and most animalistic of the true dragons, white dragons prefer frigid climes—usually arctic areas, but sometimes very high mountains, especially in winter. Mountain-dwelling white dragons sometimes have conflicts with red dragons living nearby, but the whites are wise enough to avoid the more powerful red dragons. Red dragons tend to consider white dragons unworthy opponents and usually are content to let a white dragon neighbor skulk out of sight (and out of mind).

White dragons' lairs are usually icy caves and deep subterranean chambers that open away from the warming rays of the sun. Dungeon-dwelling white dragons prefer cool areas and often lurk near water, where they can hide and hunt.

White Dragon Identifiers

A white dragon's face expresses a hunter's intense and single-minded ferocity. A white dragon's head has a sleek profile, with a small, sharp beak at the nose and a pointed chin. A crest supported by a single backward-curving spine tops the head. The dragon also has scaled cheeks, spiny dewlaps, and a few protruding teeth when its mouth is closed.

When viewed from below, a white dragon shows a short neck and a featureless head. Its wings appear blunted at the tips. The trailing edge of the wing shows a pink or blue tinge, and the back edge of the wing membrane joins the body near the back leg, at about mid-thigh.

The scales of a wyrmling white dragon glisten pure white. As the dragon ages, the sheen disappears, and by very old age, scales of pale blue and light gray are mixed in with the white.

Habits

A white dragon will consume only food that has been frozen. Usually a white dragon devours a creature killed by its breath weapon while the carcass is still stiff and frigid. It

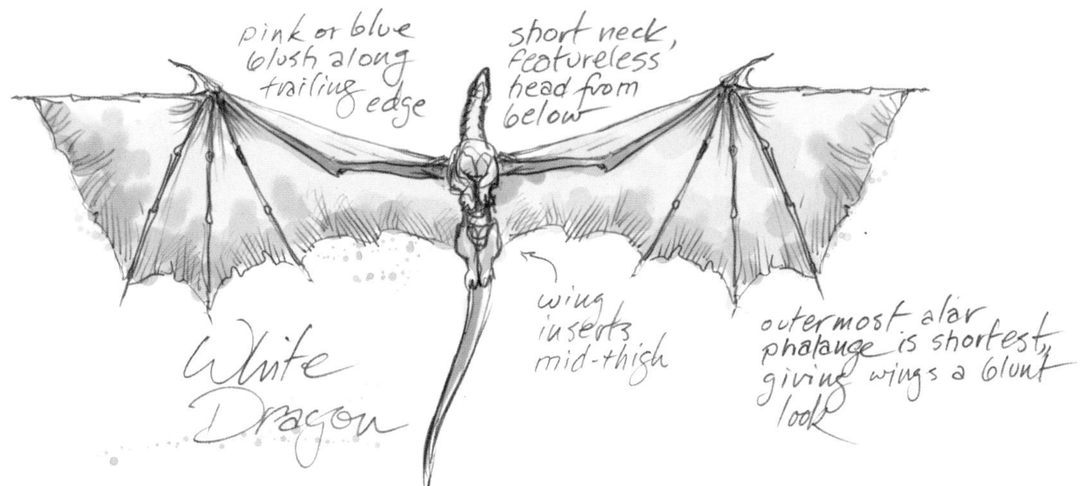

Illus. by T. Lockwood

AMONG THE SMALLEST AND LEAST INTELLIGENT OF DRAGONKIND, MOST WHITE DRAGONS ARE SIMPLY ANIMALISTIC PREDATORS. THEIR FACES EXPRESS A HUNTER'S SINGLE-MINDEDNESS AND FEROCITY RATHER THAN THE SHREWDNESS AND INSIGHT OF THE MORE POWERFUL EVIL DRAGONS. THEIR BEAKED, CRESTED HEADS ARE DISTINCTIVE. (A CRISP, FAINTLY CHEMICAL ODOR)

Illus. by S. Wood

buries other kills in snowbanks within or near its lair until they are suitably frozen. Finding such a larder is a good indication that a white dragon lives nearby.

White dragons love the cold sheen and sparkle of ice, and they favor treasure with similar qualities, particularly diamonds.

White dragons spurn the society of others of their kind, except for members of the opposite sex. They are prone to carnal pleasures and often mate just for the fun of it. They seldom tend their eggs, but they often lay their eggs near their lairs, and one or both parents allow the youngsters to move in for a time. The offspring are expected to care for themselves, but they gain some measure of protection and education from having their parents nearby.

It would be a mistake to consider a white dragon a stupid creature. Older white dragons are at least as intelligent as humans, and even younger ones are much smarter than predatory animals. Though not known for their foresight, white dragons prove cunning when hunting or defending their lairs and territories. White dragons know all the best ambush spots for miles around their lairs, and they are clever enough to pick out targets and concentrate attacks until one foe falls, then move on to the next foe. White dragons prefer sudden assaults, swooping down from aloft or bursting from beneath water, snow, or ice. They loose their breath weapons, then try to knock out a single opponent with a follow-up attack.

Although they are not pillars of intellect, white dragons have good memories, especially for events they have witnessed or experienced directly. They remember any slight or defeat and have been known to conduct malicious vendettas against beings or groups that have offended them.

White Dragons by Size

Size	Overall Length	Body Length	Neck Length	Tail Length	Body Width	Standing Height	Maximum Wingspan	Minimum Wingspan	Weight
Tiny	4 ft.	1-1/2 ft.	1 ft.	1-1/2 ft.	1 ft.	1 ft.	7 ft.	4 ft.	5 lb.
Small	8 ft.	3-1/2 ft.	1-1/2 ft.	3 ft.	2 ft.	2 ft.	14 ft.	8 ft.	40 lb.
Medium	16 ft.	7 ft.	4 ft.	5 ft.	3 ft.	4 ft.	21 ft.	12 ft.	320 lb.
Large	31 ft.	13 ft.	7 ft.	11 ft.	5 ft.	7 ft.	32 ft.	18 ft.	2,500 lb.
Huge	55 ft.	20 ft.	14 ft.	21 ft.	8 ft.	12 ft.	55 ft.	30 ft.	20,000 lb.
Gargantuan	85 ft.	23 ft.	22 ft.	35 ft.	10 ft.	16 ft.	72 ft.	40 ft.	160,000 lb.

Illus. by J. Jarvis

This chapter offers guidelines to the Dungeon Master for running the actual mechanics of an encounter with a dragon, incorporating dragons into the campaign, and developing dragons as characters with new feats, spells, magic items, and prestige classes designed specifically for dragons.

DRAGONS IN THE CAMPAIGN

It's no coincidence that the name of the game is *DUNGEONS & DRAGONS*: Dragons are iconic figures in the fantasy genre. Dragons appear at every Challenge Rating from 1 through 28 (or higher, with templates), meaning that it's quite likely characters will face them regularly throughout their careers. For some campaigns, it's enough to have dragons crop up as tough encounters in dungeons and wilderness treks. For other campaigns, spending some time to determine what role dragons will play in the campaign can be rewarding for the DM and players alike.

DRAGONS AS MONSTERS

There's nothing wrong with dragons being no more special or important than any other monster in the *Monster Manual*, at least as far as your campaign structure is concerned. Using this book will help you ensure that an encounter with a dragon is always memorable, but it need not be anything more than that—a tough fight your players will talk about for months, but not the turning point of the campaign.

If dragons are "just monsters" in the campaign, they often appear as climactic encounters in dungeons, frequently as wandering encounters in the wilderness, and only rarely as the major motivators behind adventures or campaign themes. Dragons often appear as secondary villains, the cohorts, allies, or even minions of greater, often humanoid, masterminds. As brilliant as they can be, dragons rarely appear as masterminds themselves.

Here are some possible adventure hooks to get characters involved with one or more dragons as monsters:

- A dragon is terrorizing farmland and devouring livestock, and must be stopped.
- A dragon demands tribute from a nearby village.
- A dragon has made its lair in a wilderness area formerly inhabited by other monsters, which are now moving in on civilized territory to escape the dragon.
- A good dragon disguised as a human needs help to find a magic item stolen from its hoard.
- An evil dragon is holding a paladin for ransom.

• A blackguard with a dragon cohort is tyrannizing a city.

• An epic villain has acquired one of the *Orbs of Dragonkind* and is marshaling an army of dragons to lay waste to a nation.

Some of these hooks are almost clichés of the fantasy genre, but even clichés can be satisfying experiences for players, especially newer ones, who enjoy the triumphant feeling of having vanquished a dragon.

DRAGONS AS PLOTTERS AND SCHEMERS

A campaign that features dragons as more than "just monsters" highlights their great intelligence and the unhurried perspective that comes from having a life span of fifteen centuries or more, portraying dragons as plotters and schemers. In such a campaign, dragons often work behind the scenes, generating adventure seeds less through their direct actions and more through the actions of their minions, agents, and allies, and the plans they set in motion. Dragons in such a campaign command the respect they deserve—not just from the player characters, but from NPCs as well, from commoners to aristocrats. They use that respect to build networks, lure minions, recruit agents, collect tribute, and evolve powers beyond their usual physical and magical abilities.

In their role as plotters and schemers, dragons often appear as masterminds whose plans set adventures or short campaign arcs in motion. Dragons are usually primary villains, with nondragon monsters and NPCs in the roles of secondary villains and minions.

Sample adventure hooks involving dragons as plotters and schemers might include the following:

• A thieves' guild in a major city is run by a *polymorphed* dragon.

• An evil dragon replaces a good cleric with one of its doppelganger minions.

• A dragon's bugbear minions start demanding a toll from anyone crossing a well-traveled bridge.

• A dragon's agents sow discord between two human nations, hoping to provoke war.

• A dragon allows certain items to be stolen from its hoard, knowing them to be cursed.

• An evil dragon tries to frame a good dragon for its own evil deeds, then entices adventurers to slay the supposed villain.

• A powerful green dragon sends its gang of half-dragon children to find the *Green Orb of Dragonkind* before someone else does.

DRAGONS AS MOVERS AND SHAKERS

In some campaigns, dragons are even more central forces—not only masterminds whose plans set adventures in motion, but the rulers of kingdoms, the patrons of adventurers, and the moving forces behind entire eras of history. Dragons in these campaigns are the objects of awe, terror, and reverence, the movers and shakers of the campaign world. Their intelligence, long life span, and sheer power make them the major powers of the campaign world. In some campaigns, they may even replace outsiders such as demons, devils, and celestials as the standard bearers of their alignments and the champions of the deities.

In their role as movers and shakers, dragons rarely appear as random or trivial encounters. A dragon encounter is always laden with significance.

Sample adventure hooks involving dragons as movers and shakers might include the following:

• A great wyrm who rules an evil kingdom mobilizes its forces for war against a neighboring kingdom ruled by a good dragon.

• A dragon cleric of Bahamut hires (or commands) adventurers to retrieve a draconic relic stolen by the followers of Tiamat.

• Worshipers of Tiamat begin a series of rituals designed to bring their goddess to the world.

• A disguised evil dragon acts as patron to the characters, sending them on adventures with no apparent connection to each other, all with a hidden purpose: to collect the pieces of a shattered artifact.

• A good dragon leads a rebellion against an evil dragon that rules a kingdom as a tyrant.

VARIANT RULE: SIZE BY DRAGON TYPE

To add variety to dragon encounters, consider adjusting the reach of some dragons' natural attacks as described below.

Blue: A blue dragon's relatively short neck decreases its bite reach at certain sizes, to 10 feet for a Huge dragon and 15 feet for a Gargantuan dragon.

Brass: A brass dragon's relatively short neck decreases its bite reach at certain sizes, to 10 feet for a Huge dragon and 15 feet for a Gargantuan dragon.

Deep: A deep dragon's extremely long neck increases its bite reach to 10 feet for a Medium dragon, 15 feet for a Large dragon, 20 feet for a Huge dragon, and 25 feet for a Gargantuan dragon.

Fang: A fang dragon's extremely long tail increases its tail slap reach and tail sweep radius by 50%, to 15 feet for a Large dragon, 30 feet for a Huge dragon, and 45 feet for a Gargantuan dragon.

Gold: A gold dragon's extremely long tail increases its tail slap reach and tail sweep radius by 50%, to 15 feet for a Large dragon, 30 feet for a Huge dragon, 45 feet for a Gargantuan dragon, and 60 feet for a Colossal dragon.

Green: A green dragon has a long neck and front claws. A Medium green dragon has a reach of 10 feet with its bite attack. A Large green dragon has a reach of 15 feet with its bite attack and 10 feet with its claw attacks. A Huge green dragon has a reach of 20 feet with its bite attack and 15 feet with its claw attacks. A Gargantuan green dragon has a reach of 25 feet with its bite attack and 20 feet with its claw attacks.

White: A white dragon's extremely long tail increases its tail slap reach and tail sweep radius by 50%, to 15 feet for a Large dragon, 30 feet for a Huge dragon, and 45 feet for a Gargantuan dragon.

Table 2–1: Expanded Dragon Space and Reach

Size	Space	Reach: Bite	Claw	Wing	Tail Slap	Tail Sweep Radius
Tiny	2-1/2 ft.	5 ft.	0 ft.	—	—	—
Small	5 ft.	5 ft.	5 ft.	—	—	—
Medium	5 ft.	5 ft.[1]	5 ft.	5 ft.	—	—
Large	10 ft.	10 ft.[1]	5 ft.[1]	10 ft.	10 ft.[1]	—
Huge	15 ft.	15 ft.[1]	10 ft.[1]	15 ft.	20 ft.[1]	—
Gargantuan	20 ft.	20 ft.[1]	15 ft.	20 ft.	30 ft.[1]	30 ft.[1]
Colossal	30 ft.	30 ft.[1]	20 ft.	30 ft.	40 ft.[1]	40 ft.[1]
Colossal+[2]	30 ft.+	40 ft.[1]	30 ft.	40 ft.	60 ft.[1]	60 ft.[1]

1 As an optional rule, certain dragon varieties, because of their body proportions, can exceed or fall short of these numbers. See the Size by Dragon Type sidebar.
2 The largest and oldest great wyrms gain extra reach and additional qualities; see Advanced Dragons at the end of this chapter.

• A good deity sends a gold dragon bearing a message to the ruler of a temple or kingdom.

RUNNING A DRAGON ENCOUNTER

Dragons are a nightmare in combat—sometimes as much for the DM as for the players and their characters. They possess such an extensive array of attack options, special abilities, and even movement capabilities that they can be bewildering to play. This section deals with issues of movement (including aerial combat) and hard mathematical answers to questions such as "Should the dragon incinerate Lidda and Jozan, or tear Tordek limb from limb?"

THE MECHANICS OF MELEE

As a dragon gets larger, not only does it gain additional Hit Dice, better natural armor, and increased ability scores, it gains new physical attack forms. As a result, a dragon's tactics are necessarily dependent, at least to some extent, on its size.

Table 2–1: Expanded Dragon Space and Reach summarizes the information presented in Chapter 1 for each kind of dragon.

Tiny dragons have a problem. To start with, they have only three natural attacks, with average damage (assuming three hits) of 6.5 points—most Tiny dragons don't even have a Strength bonus going for them. Getting in three hits is difficult for them, however. Though they can bite adjacent foes, their claws have no reach. Making a full attack, then, means entering an opponent's square, provoking an attack of opportunity in the process. Most Tiny wyrmlings prefer to stay out of the reach of opponents and use their breath weapons as often as possible.

Like Tiny dragons, Small dragons have only three natural attacks. However, their average damage is better—9.5 points of damage, including a +1 Strength modifier on the bite attack—and, more important, their bite and claw attacks can reach adjacent opponents. They need never enter an opponent's square to make a full attack. Even so, most Small dragons are better off using their breath weapons, employing their good speed to remain out of harm's way while strafing their foes with breath attacks.

Medium dragons gain the ability to make attacks with their wings, increasing their average damage (again, assuming five hits) to about 22.5 to 23.5, depending on the dragon's Strength bonus.

A Large dragon has reached its maximum number of natural attacks, six, with the addition of a tail slap. With six successful attacks, a Large dragon can dish out an average of 45.5 to 54.5 points of damage, or as many as 65.5 on average for red and gold dragons because of their higher Strength scores. Large dragons also gain 10 feet of reach (with all their attacks except their claws), which greatly reduces the threat of attacks of opportunity from smaller opponents. Large dragons are no longer afraid of wading right into the thick of melee, though they try to keep as many opponents as possible at neck's length (the reach of their bite attack), even if it means sacrificing claw attacks. Even Large dragons almost always lead off with their breath weapons, however, and if significantly hurt in melee they take to the air and resume their ranged breath attacks.

A Huge dragon still has six natural attacks, but now all of them have reach—including 20 feet of reach for its tail slap attack (or more, for some dragon varieties). Few opponents can close with a Huge dragon without provoking an attack of opportunity. With its impressive reach, a Huge dragon can easily attack foes spread out all over a battlefield, which are hard to catch within the area of a single breath weapon attack. Its average full attack damage (assuming six hits) is in the range of 75 to 86 points of damage (higher for a gold dragon). Dragons of this size keep their breath weapons in reserve for those special occasions when their opponents are clustered together and can all be caught in the breath weapon's area.

A Gargantuan dragon's. average damage on a full attack that scores six hits ranges from 109 to 118 points, or up to 120 or 126 points (for strong red and gold dragons).

A Colossal dragon's average full attack damage is in the neighborhood of 150 points. Dragons of Gargantuan or Colossal size fear nothing that is not divine, and are intelligent enough to make the best use of their melee attacks and all their other abilities.

FIGHTING ON THE WING

Most dragons enjoy fighting in the air, even though they are not necessarily at an advantage when doing so—particularly when fighting more maneuverable characters under the effect of *fly* spells. But the rush of air beneath the wings, the whistle

Space and Reach

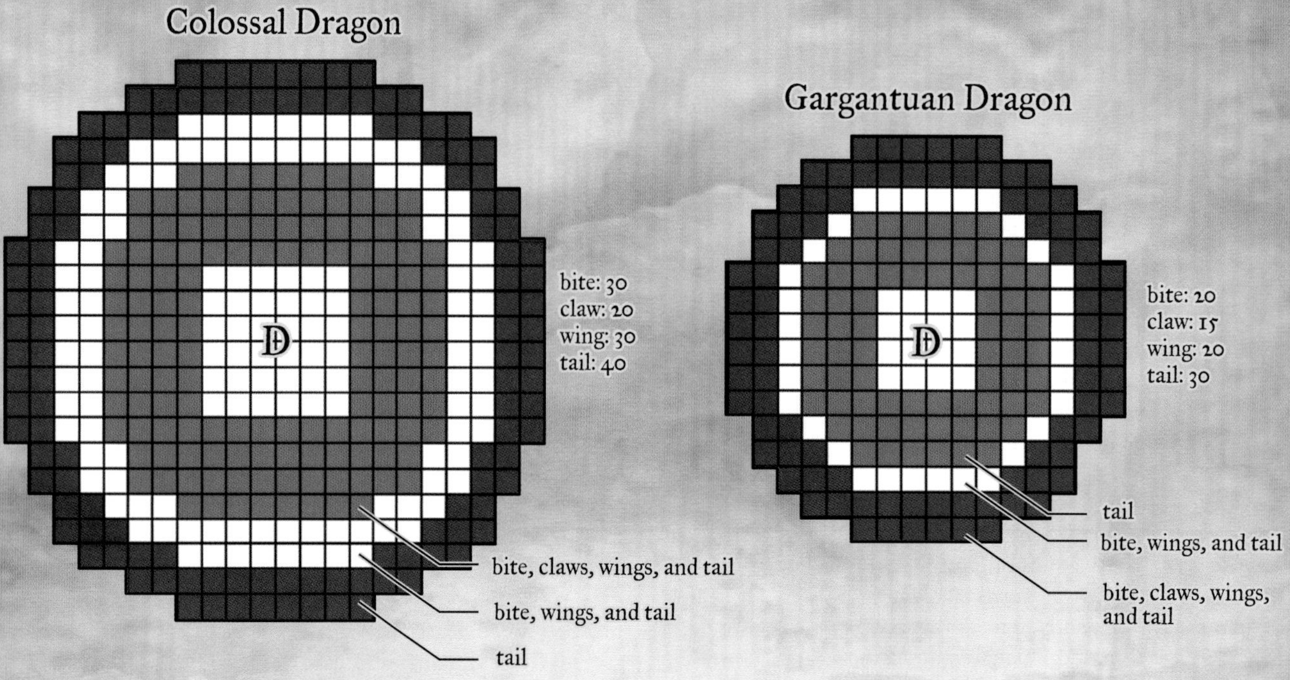

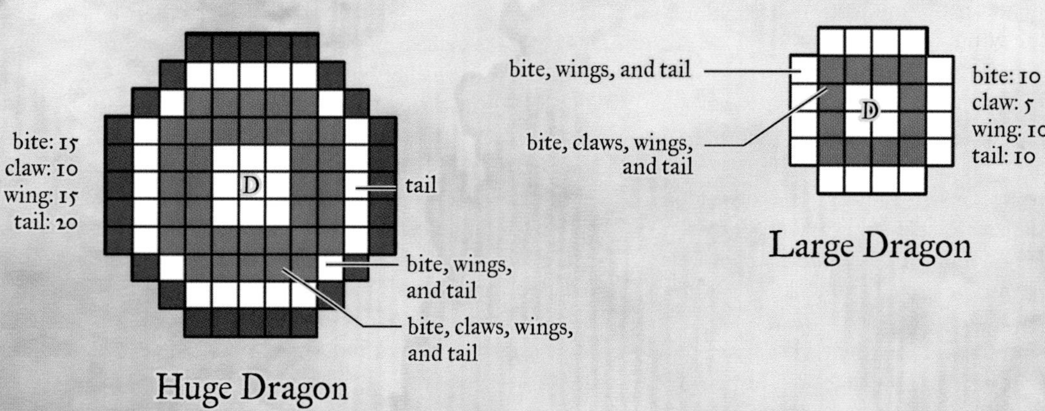

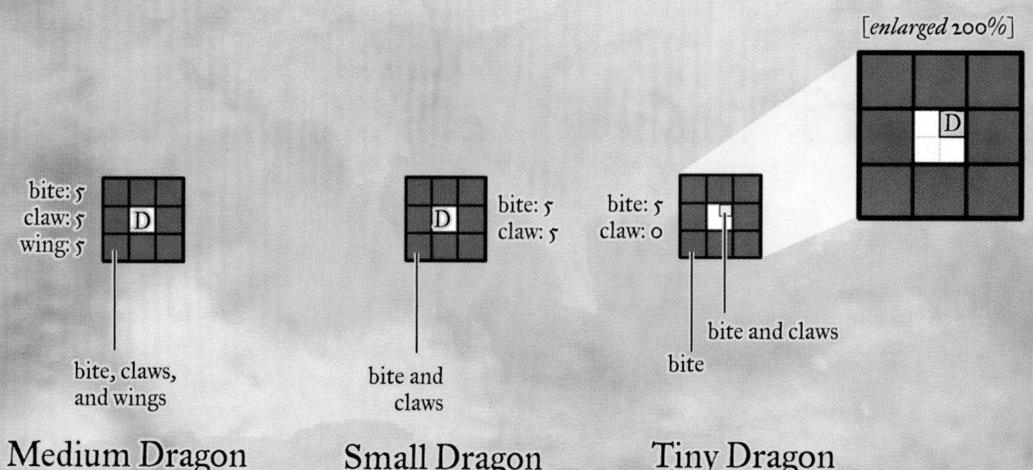

one square= 5 feet

of wind in the ears, and the sensations of diving, swooping, and soaring combine very favorably with the taste of blood and the smell of gore, at least in the estimation of most evil dragons.

The greatest limitation of a dragon fighting on the wing is its maneuverability. Only Tiny and Small dragons have even average maneuverability, which forces them to move at least half their flying speed (50–75 feet) forward every round and prevents them from turning more than 90 degrees in a single move. Of all dragons, Tiny and Small dragons are most likely to attempt aerial combat in relatively close quarters—as long as they have at least 10 feet in which to maneuver, they can fly back and forth or even in a circle to fight opponents on the ground.

A portion of the Flight diagram below shows a Small dragon making a 180-degree turn. It moves forward 5 feet and turns 45 degrees for free, then "spends" 5 feet of its speed to turn an additional 45 degrees in the same space. Then it moves forward another 5 feet, turning another 90 degrees in the same way. It has actually covered only 10 feet of distance, while using 20 feet of its movement.

Medium, Large, and Huge dragons have poor maneuverability. Like smaller dragons, they must move at least half their flying speed (75–100 feet) forward every round. They cannot turn more than 45 degrees in a single space or climb at more than a 45-degree angle, and they have to fly at least 20 feet to make a 180-degree turn. A dragon of this size won't attempt to fight on the wing unless it can move through a rectangular area at least 20 feet wide (for a Medium dragon) or 30 feet wide (for a Huge dragon) to maneuver, and at least as long as the dragon's fly speed. An area of this size allows a dragon to make strafing runs against creatures on the ground.

A portion of the Flight diagram below shows a Medium dragon making a 180-degree turn. Poor maneuverability doesn't allow the dragon to turn more than 45 degrees in a single space, so it makes a wider turn. It moves forward 5 feet while turning 45 degrees, moves 5 feet on the diagonal while turning another 45 degrees, continues another 5 feet and turns another 45 degrees, then moves along another diagonal, which counts as 10 feet (for the second diagonal), and completes the turn. It uses 25 feet of its speed to make the turn.

The Strafing Run (Poor Maneuverability) diagram on the next page shows a Medium dragon's path back and forth along a 20-foot wide chasm, using Flyby Attack to harry opponents on the ground while it flies. Assuming the dragon has a speed of 150 feet, it has two options: It can fly slowly while maintaining its minimum forward speed of 75 feet, making one run past its opponents each round and ending between runs on the location marked 75. Alternatively, it can fly at full speed, make two runs past its opponents (though it can only attack once), and end where it began, in position to do the same pattern in the next round.

Gargantuan and Colossal dragons have clumsy maneuverability, though their flying speed is tremendous. They also must move at least half their flying speed (100–125 feet) forward every round. Their turning radius is even larger: They must fly at least 40 feet to make a 180-degree turn. Dragons this enormous won't engage in aerial combat unless

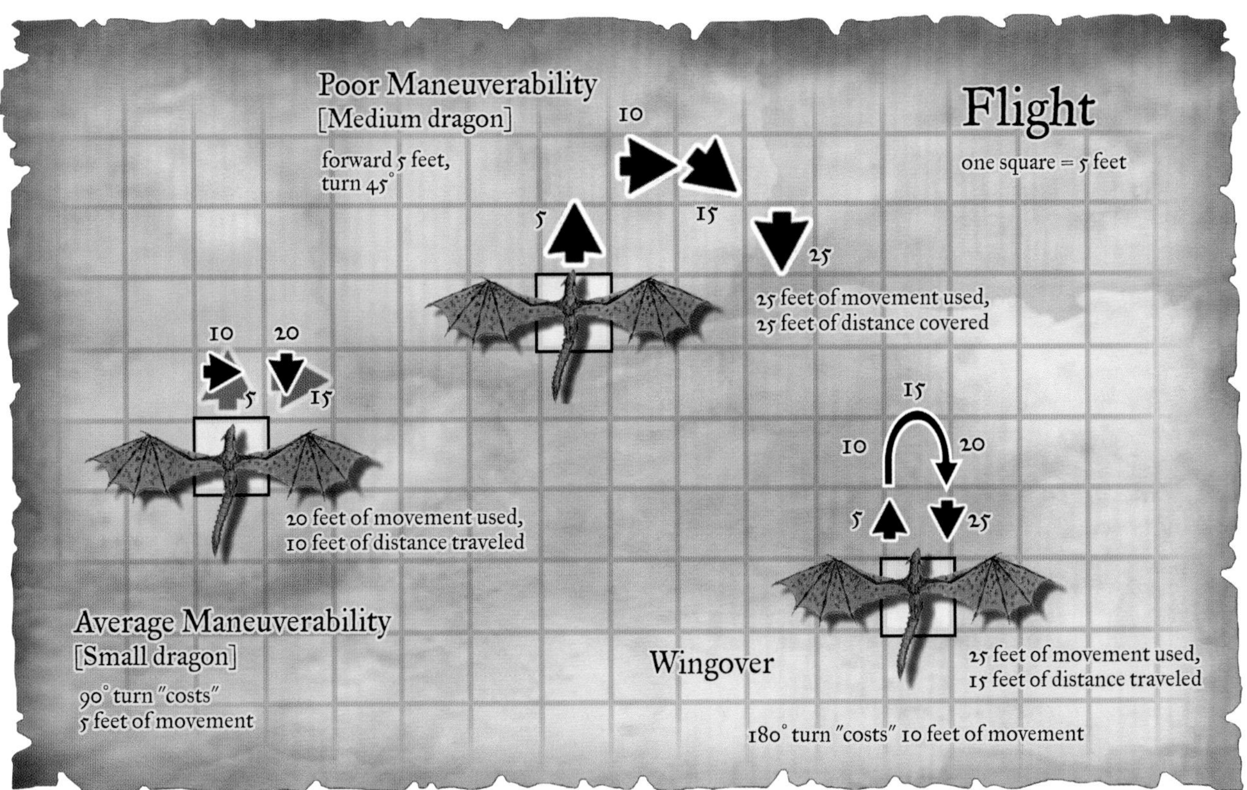

Strafing Run
[poor maneuverability]

5, 10, 15, 20, 25, 30, 35, 40, 45, 50, 55, 60, 65, 75, 80, 85, 90, 95, 100, 105, 110, 115, 120, 125, 130, 135, 140, 150

one square = 5 feet

the available space is twice as wide as they are (60 feet for a Gargantuan dragon, 120 feet for a Colossal one).

The Clumsy Maneuverability diagram below shows a Gargantuan dragon making a 180-degree turn. It must move 10 feet before it can turn 45 degrees. It starts out forward for 10 feet and turns 45 degrees. It then crosses two diagonals (15 feet) before turning another 45 degrees. It goes straight another 10 feet and turns another 45 degrees, then crosses two more diagonals (15 feet) to finish the turn. It uses 50 feet of its speed to make the turn, whipping its enormous body around behind it as it flies. (In this diagram, the movement is all counted using one square of the dragon's large space—the one right next to its head, near the center of its front face. The results are the same whichever square you use.)

The Wingover feat is a tremendous improvement to any dragon's maneuverability, allowing it to make a 180-degree turn in a single space at the cost of 10 feet of speed. In this single aspect, the dragon's maneuverability is the equivalent of perfect when it uses this feat. A portion of the Flight diagram on the previous page illustrates a Medium dragon using the Wingover feat in the course of moving 15 feet of its normal movement, at the cost of 25 feet of speed.

Flyby Attack is an all-but-essential feat for dragons, for it makes the "strafing run" possible. Using this feat, a dragon can start flying, use its breath weapon against creatures on the ground even in the air near its flight path, and continue flying, keeping out of reach. It can remain out of reach until its breath weapon is ready to use again, then return for another run. Without Flyby Attack, the dragon must make its attack either before or after it moves, which gives its opponents too much opportunity to catch up.

A dragon's rapid fly speed (two to four times as fast as a wizard with a *fly* spell cast on herself, and up to six times as fast as a heavily armored fighter with *fly*) makes it easy to remain out of reach of most opponents. A dragon that starts its turn 100 feet south of its opponents can fly right over their heads, use its breath weapon on them, and then (assuming it has Flyby Attack) continue on to a point 100 feet north of them. Lightly armored opponents (with a fly speed of 60 feet) could get within 40 feet and cast a spell, or could charge and attack the dragon once. More heavily armored characters can't even get that close. The strafing run certainly isn't a foolproof tactic for dragons, but it is a very good one.

USING A BREATH WEAPON

A dragon's breath weapon has its point of origin at any position along the outside of the dragon's space. From there, it can extend in any direction, including back into the dragon's space. All dragons are immune to the effects of their own breath weapons, so there is nothing preventing a dragon from targeting creatures in its own space with its breath weapon—after crushing them, for example.

The Cone-Shaped Breath Weapons diagram on the next page illustrates the size and shape of cone-shaped breath weapons on a grid with 5-foot squares.

After using its breath weapon, a dragon must wait at least a few seconds before it can use it again. Under normal circumstances the delay is 1d4 rounds, but the Recover Breath feat shortens that time, while the application of metabreath feats extends it. A dragon always knows how long it must wait before using its breath weapon again, and plans its tactics accordingly. If a dragon is engaged in strafing runs over a landbound group of opponents, it knows that it can fly away for half the time until it can breathe again. Then it can turn around and still reach its foes again just as its breath

weapon is ready for another use. Similarly, it can throw itself into melee for a few rounds; then, in the round before it can use its breath weapon again, it can make a single attack and change position to make best use of its breath weapon the next round.

As a rule, dragons are observant enough to notice if their opponents are not suffering the full effects of their breath weapons. After a single blast of its breath weapon, a red dragon has a good idea of who among its foes is warded with *protection from energy (fire)* and who has improved evasion. If its breath weapon is clearly ineffective against most of its opponents, any dragon is smart enough to change its tactics or even withdraw.

TO BREATHE OR NOT TO BREATHE?

A breath weapon is a dragon's most fearsome attack, but it is not always the most effective. Depending on the foes and the circumstances, using a breath weapon may or may not be the best option.

The essential difference between a breath weapon and any combination of melee attacks is that total melee damage is a fixed amount, while total breath weapon damage depends on the number of creatures caught in the breath's area. A Colossal dragon might dish out an average of 150 points of damage with a full attack action, but it has the choice of either dealing all that damage to one target or dividing it among up to six targets. A Colossal silver great wyrm can deal an average of 108 points of damage with its icy breath, but it deals the same damage to a dozen targets caught in its 70-foot cone as to a single target. If it catches ten targets, it has the potential to deal 1,080 points of damage (reduced by the possibility of successful saving throws and evasion)—and still have time to move, either to line up its targets before breathing again or to fly out of reach.

At the simplest level, this difference means it's almost always better for a dragon to use a breath weapon than to make melee attacks when facing more opponents than the dragon has natural weapons. Surrounded by two dozen militia soldiers, a Large red dragon can likely incinerate them all with a single blast of fire, while it would take 4 rounds to kill them all with melee attacks (assuming every attack was a successful kill). Of course, the fact that the breath weapon is more efficient doesn't always mean that it's preferable—an evil dragon completely unconcerned by the militia soldiers' nonmagical spears might enjoy spending the 4 rounds playing with her food.

Faced with a choice of standard actions, using the breath weapon is almost always a better option than making a single melee attack. Even if it's impossible to target more than one foe, the breath weapon will deal more damage, on average, than the bite. The only situation where this is even a close call is if the single target in question is a rogue, monk, or other character with evasion. In such a case, breathing is only marginally better than biting—and it's a small enough margin that the dragon might be better off saving its breath. If the single target has improved evasion, breathing actually becomes a worse choice than biting.

If a dragon can aim its breath weapon to catch more than one foe, there's no question about which kind of attack to

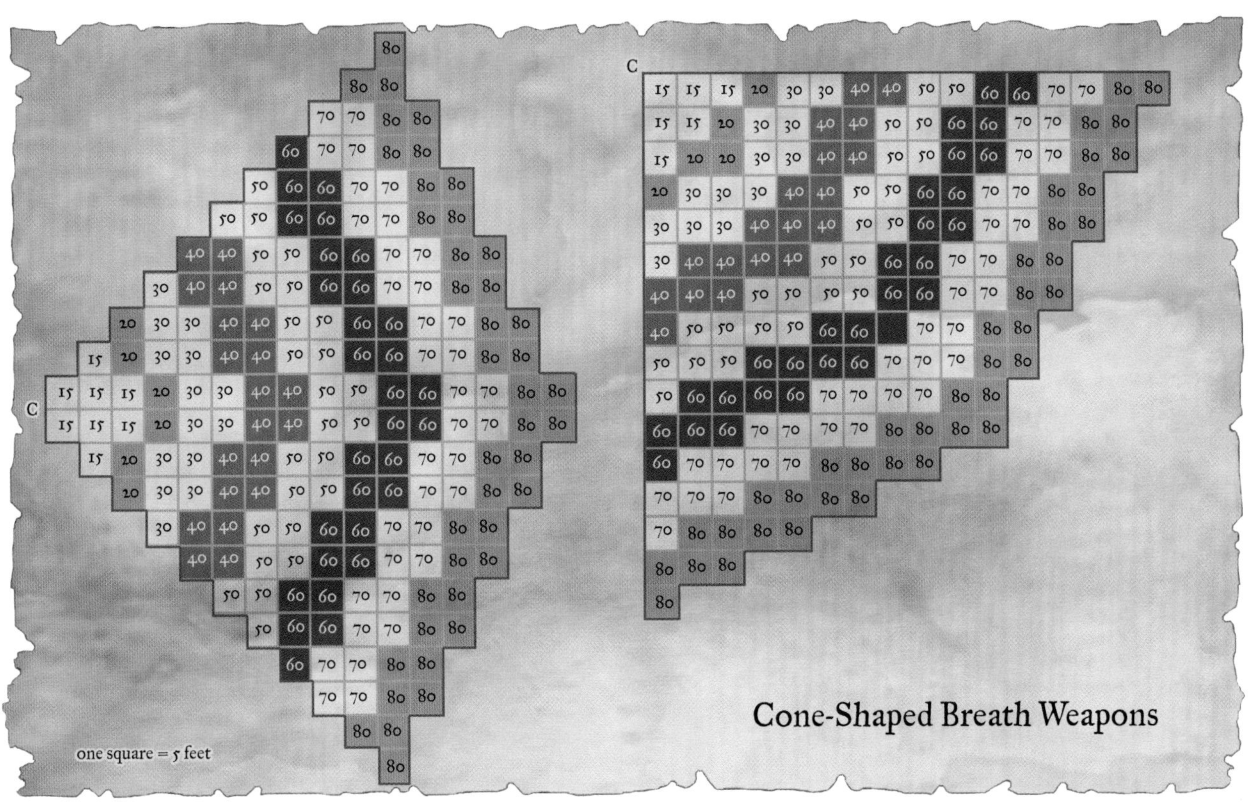

Cone-Shaped Breath Weapons

make—the breath weapon always deals superior damage against multiple foes when compared to the bite.

Faced with a choice between using a breath weapon and making a full attack on one or more foes, the choice is somewhat less clear. For a Medium or smaller dragon, the breath weapon is still a better option. For a larger dragon, the choice depends largely on how many foes it can catch with its breath weapon. If it could only breathe on one foe, it will deal more damage by making a full attack. If it can catch two or more foes in its breath weapon, breathing is a better choice.

Using a breath weapon is almost always a better option than using an area-damaging spell. The saving throw DC against a great wyrm's breath weapon is 10 to 15 higher than the save DC of its highest-level spells, and the damage potential is better as well. A bronze great wyrm that casts *delayed blast fireball* deals 19d6 points of damage with a saving throw DC of 25. The dragon is better served using its breath weapon (damage 24d6, save DC 37). A 20th-level rogue has a decent chance of failing her saving throw against the dragon's breath, but will most likely succeed against the *delayed blast fireball*.

All this logic begins to break down, however, when a dragon is facing enemies prepared to fight, particularly if the foes are expecting a dragon of a certain variety. Once a spellcaster casts *protection from energy* on the whole party, warding them against the dragon's breath weapon, the breath option becomes much weaker. However, even this depends on circumstances. If the dragon uses Flyby Attack to strafe its enemies with its breath weapon while staying mostly out of reach, two or three blasts with a breath weapon are likely to wipe out most *protection from energy* spells.

Spells can be a valuable alternative to the breath weapon in cases where opponents are protected by magic. Adventurers facing a white great wyrm are likely to be warded against cold, but they're less likely to be expecting the *chain lightning* spell the dragon has in its repertoire. Most often, though, the lower saving throw DC greatly reduces the effectiveness of a dragon's spells compared to what its breath weapon can do. A dragon is best off using spells to alter the conditions of the fight in its favor, as discussed in Dragons as Spellcasters, below.

USING SPECIAL ATTACK FORMS

Compared to the effectiveness of a breath weapon for a Huge or larger dragon, the big dragons' special melee attack forms—crush and tail sweep—are almost insignificant, though still perilous for those that get in the way. Both tactics are commonly used by confident, even cocky dragons that feel quite sure of victory, and less often by more cautious dragons. The use of the tail sweep, in particular, is often likened to the way a cat treats a mouse it isn't quite ready to eat yet. Both the crush and the tail sweep are, in effect, area melee attacks.

Crush: A crush attack can be quite fearsome, particularly because of the lingering effects of being pinned. Follow these steps to resolve a dragon's crush attack.

1) If the dragon is on the ground when it begins the attack, it makes a Jump check. The dragon must achieve enough vertical distance with the jump to clear the heads of the creatures it wants to crush.

This Colossal gold dragon's tail sweep scatters a band of hobgoblins like matchsticks.

Illus. by S. Tappin

Table 2–2: Jump DCs to Crush Opponents shows the Jump DCs required for a dragon (with a land speed of either 40 or 60 feet) to reach the required height with either a standing high jump or a running high jump.

If the dragon is flying, no Jump check is required; it simply lands on the opponents it wants to crush.

2) Determine how many creatures are in the target area. The crush attack affects any creatures located completely within the dragon's space when it lands: a 15-foot-by-15-foot square for a Huge dragon, a 20-foot-by-20-foot square for a Gargantuan dragon, or a 30-foot-by-30-foot square for a Colossal dragon.

3) After the dragon lands, each creature in the target area must roll a Reflex save against a DC equal to that of the dragon's breath weapon.

Table 2–2: Jump DCs to Crush Opponents

Target Size	Minimum Jump Height	Dragon Speed 40 ft. Standing DC	Dragon Speed 40 ft. Running DC	Dragon Speed 60 ft. Standing DC	Dragon Speed 60 ft. Running DC
Small	4 feet	18	14	10	10
Medium[1]	8 feet	34	26	26	18
Large[2]	16 feet	90	50	58	34

1 A dragon must be Gargantuan to crush Medium opponents.
2 A dragon must be Colossal to crush Large opponents.

Creatures that succeed on their saving throws take half the dragon's crush damage. They remain in their spaces—because the dragon is at least three sizes larger than they are, they can occupy the same space as the dragon. Creatures that fail their saving throws take full damage and are pinned. Roll the crush damage once and apply the result (or half of it) to each affected character.

Pinned characters cannot move. They take a –4 penalty to their Armor Class against all opponents other than the dragon, but they are not helpless.

4) On its turn, a pinned creature may try to escape. A character that makes a successful opposed grapple check (as a melee attack) or Escape Artist check (as a standard action) is no longer pinned but is still grappling with the dragon. If a character makes two successful opposed checks against the dragon, the character has escaped the grapple entirely.

5) On the dragon's next turn, it can choose to maintain the pin or to release pinned characters. If it tries to maintain the pin, it makes a single grapple check opposed by grapple checks made by all pinned opponents. Creatures who beat the dragon's grapple check take no damage, while other creatures take the dragon's full crush damage. If the dragon decides not to maintain the pin, it can act normally, without regard to the creatures that share its space (since they are necessarily at least three sizes smaller than it is).

Tail Sweep: When making a tail sweep attack, a dragon chooses half of the area it threatens with its tail slap attack—a semicircle with a radius of 30 feet if it is Gargantuan or 40 feet if it is Colossal (more for certain dragon types, notably gold and white, with their longer tails). Creatures within that area are affected if they are four or more sizes smaller than the dragon—Small or smaller for a Gargantuan dragon, Medium or smaller for a Colossal dragon. Affected creatures take the dragon's tail sweep damage (including 1-1/2 times its Strength bonus), or half that amount if they make a successful Reflex save against a DC equal to that of the dragon's breath weapon. Roll the tail sweep damage once and apply the result (or half of it) to each affected character.

Two feats, described in the next section of this chapter, can enhance a dragon's tail sweep. Whirlwind Tail Sweep allows the dragon to affect a circular area rather than a semicircle, while Tail Sweep Knockdown knocks prone any characters who fail their saving throws.

DRAGONS AS SPELLCASTERS

It is both a recognition of the limitations of dragons' innate spellcasting ability and a testament to their incredible combat prowess that, as a rule, a dragon's physical attacks and breath weapon are more effective than its spells. In general, a dragon casts spells as effectively as a sorcerer some five to eight levels lower than its Challenge Rating, so that most dragons are not the spellcasting equals of the characters they typically fight. This fact means, among other things, that a dragon's offensive spells are rarely effective in a combat against equals, as useful as they may be in terrorizing villagers. The saving throw DCs for a dragon's spells are easy for a character to make if his or her level is about the same as the dragon's CR. A dragon's best use of spells is to alter the conditions of the fight in its favor, rather than directly targeting characters who will succeed on their saving throws most of the time.

Dispel magic is a good way to remove the carefully prepared protections and wards that most adventurers cloak themselves in before venturing to fight a dragon. Unfortunately for the dragons, the disparity between their caster level and their opponents' levels makes *dispel magic* a longshot gamble. The *dispelling breath* spell (see page 78) is a slightly better option than *dispel magic*: It lets the dragon use its breath weapon and make a targeted dispel attempt against every creature that fails its saving throw against the breath. The dragon's caster level check is still going to be hard to make, but the dragon will get more chances to roll high and dispel some of the opponents' protection. Every successful dispel check is one more factor adjusted in the dragon's favor.

Altering the battlefield is another way of adjusting conditions in the dragon's favor. With its array of special abilities and immunities, a dragon's best strategy is to create conditions that hinder its opponents without hindering itself—at least not as much.

A dragon's blindsense is perhaps its single best quality for this purpose. Blindsense gives a dragon a distinct advantage over characters who rely on sight (whether regular vision or darkvision), and a smart dragon maximizes this advantage by using spells that impair its opponents' vision, such as *deeper darkness*. Dragons certainly enjoy seeing their foes' expressions of dismay, and want to be visible to inspire the proper amount of terror in their opponents, but in a tough fight, swathing the battlefield in magical darkness is functionally equivalent to *greater invisibility*.

Even a minor spell such as *obscuring mist* or *fog cloud* hinders a dragon's foes while imposing no obstacle to its blindsense, and thus offers the dragon a distinct advantage. Other fog spells, such as *stinking cloud*, *cloudkill*, and *incendiary cloud*, add injury to insult by dealing damage (or inflicting nausea) in addition to restricting vision.

Along the same lines, *solid fog* limits opponents' mobility while granting a dragon concealment. Black dragons, with their immunity to acid, naturally favor *acid fog* for the same purpose.

A dragon's energy immunity can also work to its benefit in conjunction with spellcasting. A red, brass, or gold dragon can easily attack through a *wall of fire*, taking no impairment or damage, while forcing opponents to weather the flames to reach it. This tactic can wear down *protection from energy* spells that ward the dragon's foes.

Perhaps the most dramatic means of altering the conditions of the battlefield is the *antimagic field* spell. Most dragons can function just fine in an *antimagic field*, though sacrificing their breath weapon is a difficult choice. A dragon's full attack against a character with no magical protection is simply devastating, and the complete protection from hostile magic offered by the field is worth the loss of the dragon's own spells, spell-like abilities, and even supernatural abilities (including its breath weapon and damage reduction). Dragons particularly favor this tactic when faced with opponents who are well prepared to exploit their energy vulnerability.

Of course, the most direct way for a dragon to give itself an advantage in combat through spellcasting is to cast spells on itself that enhance its abilities. *Bull's strength* and *bear's endurance* are obvious choices for any dragon. Many dragons also favor *cat's grace*, improving their average Dexterity score so they gain +2 to Armor Class and +2 on Reflex saves. *Eagle's splendor* can give a slight boost to a dragon's spell and spell-like ability saving throw DCs, and also makes its frightful presence that much harder to resist.

Dragons love *haste*, and not just for the extra (often sixth!) attack it gives them when making a full attack. A +1 bonus on attack rolls is often just that much more cushion for using Power Attack, since dragons rarely have much difficulty hitting their foes. A +1 bonus to Armor Class is always welcome, and increasing a dragon's speed by 30 feet makes it outpace every opponent that much more.

Dragons who have access to the cleric spell list (including blue and red dragons, as well as all metallic dragons) always learn *cure* spells, and learn *heal* when they can. Few events can wipe the self-confident smirks off player characters' faces like seeing a dragon who was sorely wounded suddenly recover more than 100 hit points!

Strange as it seems, dragons sometimes learn *fly* and cast it on themselves before entering battle. Relying on magic to fly reduces a dragon's speed significantly, but increases its maneuverability drastically. Particularly when faced with humanoid foes that are airborne through the same means, a dragon is often willing to trade speed for the ability to hover and turn on a dime. Other dragons prefer spells and feats that improve their maneuverability, however.

DRAGON FEATS

In addition to general feats (such as those described in Chapter 5 of the *Player's Handbook*), this book introduces a new kind of feat, the metabreath feat, and contains information on epic feats (from the *Epic Level Handbook*) and monstrous feats (from *Savage Species*).

EPIC FEATS

These feats are available to characters of 21st level or higher. Dragons of at least old age also can choose these feats even if they have no class levels. A selection of epic feats appropriate for dragons is presented here. See the *Epic Level Handbook* for more epic feats.

METABREATH FEATS

Dragons (and other creatures) have developed ways to control their breath weapons to produce varying degrees of effects, from the subtle to the conspicuous. To take a metabreath feat, a creature must have a breath weapon whose time between breaths is expressed in rounds. Therefore, a hell hound (which can breathe once every 2d4 rounds) can take metabreath feats, whereas a behir (breath weapon usable 1/minute) cannot.

Effects of Metabreath Feats: In all ways, a metabreath weapon operates in its usual fashion unless the feat specifically changes some aspect of the breath weapon.

Using a metabreath feat puts stress on a dragon's mind and body, increasing the time it must wait until the dragon can use its breath weapon again. Normally, a dragon must wait 1d4 rounds between breaths. Using a metabreath weapon increases that wait by 1 round or more. For example, if a dragon uses an enlarged breath weapon, it must wait 1d4+1 rounds before breathing again.

Multiple Metabreath Feats on a Breath Weapon: A dragon can use multiple metabreath feats on a single breath. All increases to the time the dragon must wait before breathing again are cumulative. For example, if a dragon uses an enlarged and maximized breath weapon, it must wait 1d4+4 rounds before breathing again.

A dragon can use the same metabreath feat multiple times on the same breath. In some cases, this has no additional effects. In other cases, the feat's effects are stackable. Apply the feat's effect to the base values for the breath weapon once for each time the feat is applied and add up the extra time the dragon must wait before breathing again. For example, a Small dragon with a line-shaped breath weapon could use Enlarge Breath twice on the same breath. Since the base length of the line is 40 feet, the doubly enlarged line would become 80 feet long (20 extra feet per application of the feat), and the dragon would have to wait 1d4+2 rounds before breathing again.

If a metabreath feat stacks with itself, this fact will be noted in the Special section of the feat description.

MONSTROUS FEATS

The feats in this category all require a "monstrous" form or ability as a prerequisite. Monstrous forms and abilities are unavailable to normal humanoid or animal creatures, and can include extra or nonstandard appendages and supernatural or spell-like abilities. With the DM's permission, a player may be able to choose monstrous feats if his or her character has acquired unusual abilities through transformation or by advancing in a prestige class. See *Savage Species* for more examples of monstrous feats.

FEAT DESCRIPTIONS

Below are descriptions of the feats listed in Table 2–3: Feats.

ADROIT FLYBY ATTACK [GENERAL]

You can make flyby attacks and get out of reach quickly.

Prerequisites: Fly speed 90, Flyby Attack, Hover or Wingover.

Benefit: When flying and making an attack action, you can move both before and after the attack, provided that the total distance moved is not greater than your fly speed. Your flying movement does not provoke attacks of opportunity from the creatures you attack during the round when you use this feat.

AWAKEN FRIGHTFUL PRESENCE [MONSTROUS]

You gain frightful presence.

Prerequisites: Cha 11, dragon type.

Benefit: You gain the frightful presence special ability with a radius in feet equal to 5 × 1/2 your racial Hit Dice.

The ability takes effect automatically whenever you attack, charge, or fly overhead. Creatures within the radius are subject to the effect if they can see you and have fewer Hit Dice than your racial Hit Dice.

A potentially affected creature that succeeds on a Will save (DC 10 + 1/2 your racial HD + your Cha modifier) remains immune to your frightful presence for 24 hours. On a failure, creatures with 4 or fewer Hit Dice become panicked for 4d6 rounds and those with 5 or more Hit Dice become shaken for 4d6 rounds. Dragons ignore the frightful presence of other dragons.

Special: If you have both this feat and you have (or later gain) the frightful presence ability, your frightful presence radius either increases by 50% or increases to 5 feet × 1/2 your racial Hit Dice, whichever figure is higher. The save DC against your frightful presence also increases by 2.

This silver dragon's Clinging Breath freezes targets where they stand.

AWAKEN SPELL RESISTANCE [MONSTROUS]

You gain spell resistance.

Prerequisites: Con 13, dragon type.

Benefit: You gain innate spell resistance equal to your racial Hit Dice.

Special: If your racial Hit Dice increase after you gain this feat, your spell resistance increases as well. If you have this feat and you also have (or later gain) spell resistance as a racial ability, your spell resistance is equal to your new Hit Dice total or your racial spell resistance +2, whichever is higher.

You can take this feat multiple times. Each time you take the feat, your innate spell resistance increases by 2. For example, an old silver dragon that has taken this feat twice has spell resistance 30.

CLINGING BREATH [METABREATH]

Your breath weapon clings to creatures and continues to affect them in the round after you breathe.

Prerequisites: Con 13, breath weapon.

Benefit: Your breath weapon has its normal effect, but also clings to anything caught in its area. A clinging breath weapon lasts for 1 round. In the round after you breathe, the clinging breath weapon deals half of the damage it dealt in the previous round. Creatures that avoid damage from the breath weapon (such as creatures with the evasion special quality or incorporeal creatures) do not take the extra damage. For example, an old silver dragon uses its cold breath and deals 72 points of cold damage (or 36 points against a target that makes its save). In the following round, foes that failed their saves against the breath weapon initially take an additional

Table 2–3: Dragon Feats

General Feats	Prerequisites	Benefit
Adroit Flyby Attack	Fly speed 90, Flyby Attack, Hover or Wingover	Move before and after attacking
Improved Maneuverability	Fly speed 150, Hover or Wingover	Maneuverability improves one step
Large and in Charge	Natural reach 10 feet, size Large or larger	Push back foe attempting to close
Power Climb	Str 15, fly speed (average maneuverability)	Gain altitude without losing speed
Power Dive	Str 15, fly speed (average maneuverability)	Knock down target for extra damage
Epic Feats	**Prerequisites**	**Benefit**
Dire Charge	Improved Initiative	Make full attack after charging
Epic Fortitude	—	+4 bonus on Fortitude saves
Epic Reflexes	—	+4 bonus on Reflex saves
Epic Will	—	+4 bonus on Will saves
Fast Healing	Con 25	Fast healing ability improves by 3
Improved Spell Capacity	Ability to cast spells of the normal maximum spell level in at least one spellcasting class	Gain extra spell slot
Overwhelming Critical	Str 23, Cleave, Great Cleave, Improved Critical, Power Attack, Weapon Focus	Deal extra damage on successful critical hit
Devastating Critical	Str 25, Cleave, Great Cleave, Improved Critical, Power Attack, Weapon Focus, Overwhelming Critical	Critical hit forces foe to save or die
Spellcasting Harrier	Combat Reflexes	Casting defensively becomes more difficult for casters you threaten
Metabreath Feats	**Prerequisites**	**Benefit**
Clinging Breath	Con 13, breath weapon	Breath deals extra damage 1 round later
Lingering Breath	Con 15, breath weapon, Clinging Breath	Breath remains as cloud for 1 round
Enlarge Breath	Con 13, breath weapon	Length of breath weapon increases by 50%
Heighten Breath	Con 13, breath weapon	Increase save DC against breath weapon
Maximize Breath	Con 17, breath weapon	Maximize breath weapon's variable, numeric effects
Quicken Breath	Con 19, breath weapon	Use breath weapon as free action
Recover Breath	Con 17, breath weapon	Use breath weapon more often
Shape Breath	Con 13, breath weapon, size Small or larger	Expel breath weapon as line or cone
Split Breath	Con 13, breath weapon, Shape Breath, size Small or larger	Divide breath weapon into two attacks
Spreading Breath	Con 15, breath weapon, Shape Breath, size Small or larger	Expel breath weapon as spread effect
Extend Spreading Breath	Con 15, breath weapon, Shape Breath, Spreading Breath, size Small or larger	Expel breath weapon as spread effect that can be used at range
Tempest Breath	Str 13, breath weapon, Power Attack, size Large or larger	Breath weapon also produces wind effects

36 points of cold damage, and foes that succeeded on their saves take 18 points of cold damage.

A foe can take a full-round action to attempt to remove the clinging breath weapon before taking any additional damage. It takes a successful Reflex saving throw (same DC as your normal breath weapon) to remove the effect. Rolling around on the ground grants a +2 bonus on the saving throw, but leaves the foe prone. A clinging breath weapon cannot be removed or smothered by jumping into water. A clinging breath weapon can be magically dispelled (DC equal to your breath weapon save DC).

This feat only works on a breath weapon that has instantaneous duration and that deals some kind of damage, such as energy damage (acid, cold, electricity, fire, or sonic), ability damage, or negative levels.

When you use this feat, add +1 to the number of rounds you must wait before using your breath weapon again.

Special: You can apply this feat more than once to the same breath weapon. Each time you do, the clinging breath weapon lasts an additional round.

DEVASTATING CRITICAL [EPIC]

Choose one type of melee weapon, such as a claw or bite. With that weapon, you are capable of killing any creature with a single strike.

Prerequisites: Str 25, Cleave, Great Cleave, Improved Critical (chosen weapon), Overwhelming Critical (chosen weapon), Power Attack, Weapon Focus (chosen weapon).

Benefit: Whenever you score a critical hit with the weapon you have chosen, the target must make a Fortitude save (DC 10 + 1/2 your HD + your character level + your Str modifier) or die instantly. (Creatures immune to critical hits can't be affected by this feat.)

Special: You can gain this feat multiple times. Its effects do not stack. Each time you take the feat, it applies to a new weapon.

DIRE CHARGE [EPIC]

You can make a full attack as part of a charge.

Prerequisite: Improved Initiative.

Monstrous Feats	Prerequisites	Benefit
Awaken Frightful Presence	Cha 11, dragon type	Gain frightful presence ability
Awaken Spell Resistance	Con 13, dragon type	Gain spell resistance ability
Draconic Knowledge	Int 19, true dragon, any three Knowledge skills	Bardic Knowledge like ability
Embed Spell Focus	Con 13, dragon type, ability to cast spells	Focus component becomes a part of you
Endure Blows	Con 13, dragon type, Toughness	Gain damage reduction 2/—
Improved Speed	Str 13, dragon type	Fly speed +20 ft., other speeds +10 ft.
Multiattack[1]	Three or more natural weapons	Penalty on secondary attacks lessens to –2
Improved Multiattack	Three or more natural weapons, Multiattack	No penalty on secondary attacks
Rapidstrike	Dex 9, one or more pairs of natural weapons, aberration, dragon, elemental, magical beast, or plant type, base attack bonus +10	Make one extra natural weapon attack at a –5 penalty
Improved Rapidstrike	Dex 9, one or more pairs of natural weapons, aberration, dragon, elemental, magical beast, or plant type, base attack bonus +15, Rapidstrike	Make multiple extra natural weapon attacks at a cumulative –5 penalty
Shock Wave	Str 13, dragon type, size Large, Power Attack size Huge or larger	Knock down foes by hitting ground with tail
Snatch[1]	Size Huge	Grab and hold smaller opponents
Improved Snatch	Snatch	Use snatch against bigger targets
Multisnatch	Str 17, Snatch	Penalty to maintain hold lessens to –10
Rend	Two claw attacks, Str 13, Snatch, Power Attack	Deal extra damage on claw attacks
Snatch and Swallow	Con 19, dragon type, Snatch, Improved Snatch	Swallow opponent held in mouth
Tail Constrict	Dragon, Snatch, Improved Snatch	Grab opponents with tail, deal extra tail slap damage
Suppress Weakness	Energy vulnerability, Iron Will	Lessen vulnerability to energy type
Overcome Weakness	Energy vulnerability, Iron Will, Suppress Weakness	Remove vulnerability to energy type
Tail Sweep Knockdown	Tail sweep attack	Tail sweep knocks opponents prone
Whirlwind Tail Sweep	Tail sweep attack	Tail sweep affects full circle, not semicircle
Wingstorm	Str 13, dragon type, fly speed 20, Hover, Power Attack, size Large or larger	Use wings to create wind effects against foes.

1 Multiattack and Snatch are mentioned here only because they are prerequisites for other dragon feats. The full descriptions of these feats can be found in the *Monster Manual.*

Benefit: If you charge a foe during the first round of combat (or the surprise round, if you are allowed to act in it), you can make a full attack against the opponent you charge.

Normal: Without this feat, you may only make a single attack as part of a charge.

DRACONIC KNOWLEDGE [MONSTROUS]

You are attuned to nature and the elements and can draw on deep wells of knowledge.

Prerequisites: Int 19, true dragon, any three Knowledge skills.

Benefit: This feat works much like the bard's bardic knowledge class feature, except that it relies on the scale and impact of past events rather than on how many people already share the information. You may make a special Draconic Knowledge check (d20 + your age category + your Int modifier) to see whether you know some relevant information about an item, event, or locale. This check will not reveal the powers of a magic item but may give a hint about its general function. You may not take 10 or take 20 on this check; this sort of information is essentially random. If you have a Knowledge skill that is related to or applicable to the information you seek, you receive a +1 bonus on the draconic knowledge check for every 5 ranks you have in that Knowledge skill.

The DM determines the Difficulty Class of the check by referring to the table below.

DC	Type of Knowledge	Examples
10	Something with worldwide or planetwide significance	Information about the creation of the world, worldwide cataclysms, powerful places of mystery, or gods.
15	Something with regional significance, but long-lasting or with a long-term impact	Information about empires, wars, regional disasters, or legendary individuals or groups
20	Something with regional significance, but relatively short-lived effects	Information about countries, battles, national disasters, or powerful individuals or groups
25	Something with local significance, but long-lasting or with a long-term impact	Information about a minor dynasty, a minor place of mystery, single magic item, or hero
30	Something with local significance and relatively short-lived effects	Information about a local hero, a minor battle, or a single building

DC Modifiers:	
–1	Per 10,000 gp of item's value, if an object
–5	Individual is a dragon, dragonslayer, or dragon friend
–5	Dragon has a lair in the area affected

EMBED SPELL FOCUS [MONSTROUS]

You can embed focus components required for your spells into your body.

Prerequisites: Con 13, dragon type, ability to cast spells.

Benefit: You can embed the focus component for a spell you know how to cast into your skin or hide and use the embedded focus anytime you cast the spell. You can embed a number of focuses equal to your Constitution score.

Special: The total value of expensive spell focuses a dragon has embedded in its hide should be considered part of the dragon's treasure.

ENDURE BLOWS [MONSTROUS]

You are adept at lessening the effects of blows.

Prerequisites: Con 19, dragon type, Toughness.

Benefit: You gain damage reduction 2/—. This stacks with any damage reduction you have from other sources. Damage reduction cannot reduce damage below 0.

ENLARGE BREATH [METABREATH]

Your breath weapon is larger than normal.

Prerequisites: Con 13, breath weapon.

Benefit: The length of your breath weapon increases by 50% (round down to the nearest multiple of 5). For example, an old silver dragon breathing an enlarged cone of cold produces a 75-foot cone instead of a 50-foot cone. Cone-shaped breath weapons get wider when they get longer, but line-shaped breath weapons do not.

When you use this feat, add +1 to the number of rounds you must wait before using your breath weapon again.

EPIC FORTITUDE [EPIC]

You have tremendously high fortitude.

Benefit: You gain a +4 bonus on all Fortitude saving throws.

EPIC REFLEXES [EPIC]

You have tremendously fast reflexes.

Benefit: You gain a +4 bonus on all Reflex saving throws.

EPIC WILL [EPIC]

You have tremendously strong willpower.

Benefit: You gain a +4 bonus on all Will saving throws.

EXTEND SPREADING BREATH [METABREATH]

You can convert your breath weapon into a spread effect that can be used at range.

Prerequisites: Con 15, breath weapon, Shape Breath, Spreading Breath, size Small or larger.

Benefit: You can modify your breath weapon so that it fills a spread centered anywhere within a short distance of your head. The range and size of the spread depends on your size, as shown below.

Dragon Size	Spread Radius	Spread Range
Small	10 ft.	40 ft.
Medium	15 ft.	60 ft.
Large	20 ft.	80 ft.
Huge	25 ft.	100 ft.
Gargantuan	30 ft.	120 ft.
Colossal	35 ft.	140 ft.

When you use this feat, add +2 to the number of rounds you must wait before using your breath weapon again.

FAST HEALING [EPIC]

You heal your wounds very quickly.

Prerequisite: Con 25.

Benefit: You gain fast healing 3, or your existing fast healing improves by 3. The benefit of this feat does not stack with fast healing granted by magic items or nonpermanent magical effects.

Special: This feat may be taken multiple times. Its effects stack.

HEIGHTEN BREATH [METABREATH]

Your breath weapon is even more deadly than normal.

Prerequisites: Con 13, breath weapon.

Benefit: You can increase the save DC of your breath weapon by any number up to a maximum equal to your Constitution bonus.

For each point by which you increase the save DC, add +1 to the number of rounds you must wait before using your breath weapon again.

IMPROVED MANEUVERABILITY [GENERAL]

Your maneuverability in flight improves.

Prerequisites: Fly speed 150 feet, Hover or Wingover.

Benefit: Your maneuverability improves by one category, from clumsy to poor, poor to average, or average to good (see Tactical Aerial Movement, page 20 of the *Dungeon Master's Guide*).

Special: You can take this feat multiple times. Each time you take the feat, your maneuverability improves by one category (but never becomes better than good).

IMPROVED MULTIATTACK [MONSTROUS]

You are particularly adept at using all your natural weapons at once.

Prerequisites: Three or more natural weapons, Multiattack.

Benefit: Your secondary attacks with natural weapons have no penalty on the attack roll. You still add only 1/2 your Strength bonus, if any, to damage dealt.

Normal: Without this feat, your secondary natural attacks are made at a –5 penalty (or a –2 penalty if you have the Multiattack feat).

IMPROVED RAPIDSTRIKE [MONSTROUS]

You can make multiple attacks with a natural weapon.

Prerequisites: Dex 9, one or more pairs of natural weapons, aberration, dragon, elemental, magical beast, or plant type, base attack bonus +15, Rapidstrike.

Benefit: If you have a pair of natural weapons, such as two claws, two wings, or two slams, you can make two or more extra attacks with one of those weapons, the first at a –5 penalty and the second and subsequent attacks at an additional –5, but never more than four extra attacks. Creatures with multiple limbs qualify for this feat as well, so a creature with three arms and three claw attacks qualifies for this feat.

Normal: Without this feat, you attack once with each natural weapon.

Special: You can take this feat once for each pair of natural weapons you have. For example, a Large true dragon has one bite, two claws, two wings, and one tail attacks. The dragon can take this feat twice, once for its claws and once for its wings.

IMPROVED SNATCH [GENERAL]

You can make snatch attacks against bigger opponents than other creatures can.

Prerequisite: Snatch.

Benefit: As the Snatch feat (see page 304 of the *Monster Manual*), except that you can grab a creature two size categories smaller than you with your bite or claw attack.

IMPROVED SPEED [MONSTROUS]

You are faster than others of your kind.

Prerequisites: Str 13, dragon type.

Benefit: Your fly speed (if you have one) improves by 20 feet. All other speeds you have improve by 10 feet.

IMPROVED SPELL CAPACITY [EPIC]

You can prepare spells that exceed the normal limits of spellcasting.

Prerequisite: Ability to cast spells of the normal maximum spell level in at least one spellcasting class.

Benefit: When you select this feat, you gain one spell slot per day of any level up to one level higher than the highest level spell you can already cast in a particular class. For example, if you select this feat as a 21st-level wizard, you would gain one wizard spell slot of any spell level up to 10th.

You must still have the requisite ability score (10 + spell level) to cast any spell stored in this slot. If you have a high enough ability modifier to gain one or more bonus spells for this spell level, you also gain the bonus spells for this spell level.

You must use the spell slot as a member of the class in which you can already cast spells of the normal maximum spell level. For instance, a 5th-level ranger/22nd-level sorcerer couldn't add a ranger spell slot, because he can't cast spells of the normal maximum spell level for rangers. He must add the spell slot to his sorcerer spells.

Special: You can gain this feat multiple times.

LARGE AND IN CHARGE [GENERAL]

You can prevent opponents from closing inside your reach.

Prerequisites: Natural reach of 10 feet or more, size Large or larger.

Benefit: When you make a successful attack of opportunity against an opponent that is moving inside your threatened area, you can force the opponent back to the 5-foot space it was in before it provoked the attack of opportunity. After you hit with your attack of opportunity, make an opposed Strength check against your opponent. You gain a +4 bonus for each size category larger than your opponent you are, and an additional +1 bonus for every 5 points of damage you dealt with your attack of opportunity. If you win the opposed check, your opponent is pushed back 5 feet into the space it just left. An opponent you push cannot move any farther in this round.

LINGERING BREATH [METABREATH]

Your breath weapon forms a lingering cloud.

Prerequisites: Con 15, breath weapon, Clinging Breath.

Benefit: Your breath weapon has its normal effects, but also remains as a lingering cloud of the same shape and size as the original breath weapon. This cloud lasts 1 round.

Foes caught in the breath weapon's area when you breathe take no additional damage from the lingering breath weapon, provided they leave the cloud by the shortest available route on their next turn. Otherwise, anyone who touches or enters the cloud while it lasts takes one-half of the breath weapon's normal effects; any saving throw the breath weapon normally allows still applies. Damaging breath weapons deal one-half their normal damage, and breath weapons with effects that have durations last for half the normal time. If a creature is affected by the same nondamaging breath weapon twice, the effects do not stack.

For example, an old silver dragon uses this feat on its cold breath weapon. Creatures caught in the 50-foot cone take 16d8 points of cold damage, and a DC 31 Reflex save reduces the damage by half. The 50-foot cone lingers for 1 round. While the cone lasts, anyone touching or entering it takes 8d8 points of cold damage, and a DC 31 Reflex save reduces the cold damage to 4d8 points. Creatures in the cone when the dragon breathed take no additional damage if they leave by the shortest available route on their next turn.

If the same dragon uses this feat on its paralyzing breath weapon, a creature caught in the 50-foot cone must make a DC 31 Fortitude save or be paralyzed for 1d6+8 rounds. The 50-foot cone lingers for 1 round. While the cone lasts, anyone touching or entering it must make a DC 31 Fortitude save or be paralyzed for 1d3+4 rounds. Creatures in the cone when the dragon breathed take no additional damage if they leave by the shortest available route on their next turn. Creatures paralyzed by the initial breath cannot leave the cloud, but suffer no additional effects because the paralyzing effects do not stack.

When you use this feat, add +2 to the number of rounds you must wait before using your breath weapon again.

Special: You can apply this feat more than once to the same breath weapon. Each time you do, the lingering breath lasts an additional round.

You can apply this feat to a breath weapon that also has received the Clinging Breath feat, but the resulting breath clings only to foes caught in the initial breath.

MAXIMIZE BREATH [METABREATH]

You can take a full-round action to use your breath weapon to maximum effect.

Prerequisites: Con 17, breath weapon.

Benefit: If you use your breath weapon as a full-round action, all variable, numeric effects of the attack are maximized. A maximized breath weapon deals maximum damage, lasts for the maximum time, or the like. For example, an old silver dragon using a maximized cold breath weapon (damage 16d8) deals 128 points of damage. An old silver dragon using a maximized paralysis gas breath weapon (duration 1d6+8 rounds) paralyzes creatures for 14 rounds if they fail their saving throws.

The DCs for saving throws against your breath weapon are not affected.

When you use this feat, add +3 to the number of rounds you must wait before using your breath weapon again.

This feat stacks with the effects of breath weapons enhanced with other metabreath feats, but does not maximize them. For example, a maximized breath weapon further enhanced by the Tempest Breath feat produces the type of wind effect noted in that feat description, but the velocity of the wind is not also maximized.

Special: You cannot use this feat and the Quicken Breath feat on the same breath weapon at the same time.

MULTISNATCH [GENERAL]

You can grapple enemies more firmly with only one of your natural attacks.

Prerequisites: Str 17, Snatch.

Benefit: When grappling an opponent with only the part of your body that made the attack, you take only a –10 penalty on grapple checks to maintain the hold.

Normal: Without this feat, you take a –20 penalty on grapple checks to maintain a hold with only one part of your body.

OVERCOME WEAKNESS [MONSTROUS]

You can overcome an innate vulnerability through sheer willpower.

Prerequisites: Vulnerability to energy, Iron Will, Suppress Weakness.

Benefit: You can completely suppress your vulnerability to a type of energy. When subjected to an attack based on that type of energy, you take no extra damage.

Normal: A creature vulnerable to a type of energy takes half again as much (+50%) damage as normal from that energy type, regardless of whether a saving throw is allowed, or if the save is a success or failure.

This green dragon's Power Dive knocks Lidda off her feet.

Illus. by B. Thompson

OVERWHELMING CRITICAL [EPIC]

Choose one type of melee weapon, such as claw or bite. With that weapon, you deal more damage on a critical hit.

Prerequisites: Str 23, Cleave, Great Cleave, Improved Critical (chosen weapon), Power Attack, Weapon Focus (chosen weapon).

Benefit: When using the weapon you have selected, you deal +1d6 points of extra damage on a successful critical hit. If the weapon's critical multiplier is ×3, add +2d6 points of extra damage instead, and if the multiplier is ×4, add +3d6 points of extra damage instead. (Creatures immune to critical hits can't be affected by this feat.)

Special: You can gain this feat multiple times. Its effects do not stack. Each time you take the feat, it applies to a new weapon.

POWER CLIMB [GENERAL]

If you fly in a straight line, you can gain altitude in flight more easily than others.

Prerequisites: Str 15, fly speed (average maneuverability).

Benefit: When flying, you can gain altitude and still move your full speed provided you fly in a straight line.

Normal: Without this feat, you must move at half speed to gain altitude (see Tactical Aerial Movement, page 20 of the *Dungeon Master's Guide*).

POWER DIVE [GENERAL]

You can fall upon an opponent from the sky.

Prerequisites: Str 15, fly speed (average maneuverability).

Benefit: When flying, you can dive and land on an opponent to deal extra damage. This is a standard action that can only affect creatures that are smaller than you. You make an overrun attack, but the opponent cannot choose to avoid you. If you knock down the target, you may make an additional slam attack, dealing the indicated damage plus 1-1/2 times your Strength bonus (round down). This attack is at the usual +4 bonus against prone opponents.

Size	Power Dive Damage
Fine	1d2
Diminutive	1d3
Tiny	1d4
Medium	1d6
Large	1d8
Huge	2d6
Gargantuan	2d8
Colossal	4d6

Normal: Without this feat, you can attack with just one natural weapon and do not have a chance to knock down the opponent.

Special: If you fail in the overrun attempt and are tripped in turn, you are instead knocked down and deal the indicated slam damage to yourself.

QUICKEN BREATH [METABREATH]

You can loose your breath weapon with but a thought.

Prerequisites: Con 19, breath weapon.

Benefit: Using your breath weapon is a free action.

When you use this feat, add +4 to the number of rounds you must wait before using your breath weapon again.

Special: You cannot use this feat and the Maximize Breath feat on the same weapon at the same time.

RAPIDSTRIKE [MONSTROUS]

You can attack more than once with a natural weapon.

Prerequisites: Dex 9, one or more pairs of natural weapons, aberration, dragon, elemental, magical beast, or plant type, base attack bonus +10.

Benefit: If you have a pair of natural weapons, such as two claws, two wings, or two slams, you can make one extra attack with one of those weapons at a –5 penalty. A creature with multiple limbs qualifies for this feat as well, such as a creature with three arms and three claw attacks.

Normal: Without this feat, you attack once with each natural weapon.

Special: You can take this feat once for each pair of natural weapons you have. For example, a Large dragon has one bite, two claws, two wings, and one tail attacks. The dragon can take this feat twice, once for its claws and once for its wings.

RECOVER BREATH [METABREATH]

You wait less time before being able to use your breath weapon again.

Prerequisites: Con 17, breath weapon.

Benefit: You reduce the interval between uses of your breath weapon. You wait 1 round less than usual before breathing again, but always at least 1 round. The feat stacks with the effects of metabreath feats, reducing the total time you must wait to use your breath weapon again by 1 round.

Special: If you have multiple heads with breath weapons, all breath weapons use the reduced interval.

REND [MONSTROUS]

You can rend opponents you hit with your claws.

Prerequisites: Two claw attacks, Str 13, Power Attack, Snatch, size Huge or larger.

Benefit: If you strike the same opponent with two claw attacks, you automatically deal extra damage equal to that of two claw attacks plus 1-1/2 times your Strength bonus. You cannot grab an opponent at the same time you rend that opponent.

SHAPE BREATH [METABREATH]

You can make the area of your breath weapon a cone or a line, as you see fit.

Prerequisites: Con 13, breath weapon, size Small or larger.

Benefit: If you have a line-shaped breath weapon, you can opt to shape it into a cone. Likewise, if you have a cone-shaped breath weapon, you can shape it into a line.

When you use this feat, add +1 to the number of rounds you must wait before using your breath weapon again.

Normal: Without this feat, the shape of your breath weapon is fixed.

SHOCK WAVE [MONSTROUS]

You can strike the ground with your tail so hard it knocks other creatures down.

Prerequisites: Str 13, dragon, size Large or larger, Power Attack.

Benefit: You may, as a full-round action, strike a solid surface with your tail and create a shock wave that radiates out from your space and continues for a number of feet equal to 5 × your racial Hit Dice. Make a bull rush attack by rolling once regardless of how many creatures are in the radius. Every creature in the radius makes a Strength check and compares it to your roll. Those who fail their opposed checks are knocked down.

Special: Structures and unattended objects at least partially within the shock wave take damage equal to 1d6 + your Strength bonus.

SNATCH AND SWALLOW [MONSTROUS]

You can swallow creatures you have grabbed with your bite attack.

Prerequisites: Con 19, dragon, Snatch, Improved Snatch, size Huge or larger.

Benefit: If you begin your turn with an opponent held in your mouth, you can attempt a new grapple check (as though attempting to pin the opponent). If you succeed, your opponent takes bite damage and is swallowed.

A swallowed creature is considered grappled, while you are not. A swallowed creature can try to cut its way free with any light piercing or slashing weapon (the amount of damage required to get free is noted on the table below), or it can just try to escape the grapple. If the swallowed creature chooses the latter course, success puts it back in your mouth. Any damage a swallowed creature deals is deducted from your hit points. If a creature cuts itself free, muscular action closes the hole, so that if you swallow someone again, that creature must cut itself free again. Swallowed creatures take damage in each round they remain swallowed, as shown below.

Dragon Size	Swallowed Creature Size[1]	Physical Damage[2]	Energy Damage[3]
Huge	Medium	1d8	2d8
Gargantuan	Large	2d6	4d6
Colossal	Huge	2d8	4d8

1 Maximum size of a swallowed creature. Your stomach can hold two such creatures; smaller foes count as one-quarter of a creature.
2 A swallowed foe takes bludgeoning damage in each round it spends in your stomach.
3 A swallowed foe takes energy damage in each round it spends in your stomach. The type of energy is the same as that of your breath weapon.

SPELLCASTING HARRIER [EPIC]

Spellcasters you threaten find it difficult to cast defensively.

Prerequisite: Combat Reflexes.

Benefit: Any spellcaster you threaten in melee provokes an attack of opportunity if he or she tries to cast defensively. You get a +4 bonus on this attack roll.

SPREADING BREATH [METABREATH]

You can convert your breath weapon into a spread effect.

Prerequisites: Con 15, breath weapon, Shape Breath, size Small or larger.

Benefit: You can modify your breath weapon so that it fills a spread centered on your head instead of taking its normal shape. The radius of the spread depends on your size, as shown below.

Creature Size	Spread Radius
Small	10 ft.
Medium	15 ft.
Large	20 ft.
Huge	25 ft.
Gargantuan	30 ft.
Colossal	35 ft.

When you use this feat, add +2 to the number of rounds you must wait before using your breath weapon again.

SPLIT BREATH [METABREATH]

You can split your breath weapon into a pair of weaker effects.

Prerequisites: Con 13, breath weapon, Shape Breath, size Small or larger.

Benefit: Your breath weapon retains its size and shape, but splits into two areas that you aim separately. Each portion deals half the damage the breath weapon normally deals or lasts half as long as the effect normally lasts.

For example, an old silver dragon that uses this feat on its cold breath weapon produces two 50-foot cones of cold that deal 8d8 points of cold damage each. If the same dragon used this feat on its paralyzing gas breath weapon, it would produce two cones of gas, each of which could paralyze a creature for 1d3+4 rounds.

You can aim the split breath effects so that their areas overlap. Creatures caught in the area of overlap are struck by both weapons and are affected twice, subject to all the normal rules for stacking magical effects.

When you use this feat, add +1 to the number of rounds you must wait before using your breath weapon again.

SUPPRESS WEAKNESS [MONSTROUS]

Your vulnerability to an energy type is reduced.

Prerequisites: Vulnerability to energy, Iron Will.

Benefit: You can partially suppress your vulnerability to a type of element or energy. When subjected to an attack based on that type of energy, you take one-quarter again as much (+25%) damage, regardless of whether a saving throw is allowed, or if the save is a success or failure.

Normal: A creature vulnerable to an element or energy type takes half again as much (+50%) damage as normal from that energy type.

TAIL CONSTRICT [MONSTROUS]

You can make constriction attacks with your tail.

Prerequisites: Dragon, Snatch, Improved Snatch.

Benefit: You can grab and constrict creatures you hit with your tail slap attack. This works just like a snatch attack, except that it can be used against any creature smaller than you.

If you successfully grab an opponent with your tail, you deal bludgeoning damage equal to your tail slap damage plus 1-1/2 times your Strength modifier. Each round you hold your opponent, you deal constriction damage.

You cannot make tail slap or tail sweep attacks while constricting an opponent with your tail.

TAIL SWEEP KNOCKDOWN [MONSTROUS]

Your tail sweep attack knocks opponents prone.

Prerequisite: Tail sweep attack.

Benefit: Creatures who fail their saving throws against your tail sweep attack are knocked prone in addition to taking full damage.

TEMPEST BREATH [METABREATH]

You can make your breath weapon strike with the force of a windstorm.

Prerequisites: Str 13, breath weapon, Power Attack, size Large or larger.

Benefit: When you use your breath weapon, in addition to its normal effects, creatures in the area are affected as through struck by wind effects. The force of the wind depends on your size, as indicated below. For the effects of high winds, see Table 3–24 on page 95 of the *Dungeon Master's Guide*.

Dragon Size	Wind Force
Large	Severe
Huge	Windstorm
Gargantuan	Hurricane
Colossal	Tornado

Because your breath weapon has an instantaneous duration, creatures ignore the checked effect unless they are airborne (in which case they are blown back 1d6×5 feet).

When you use this feat, add +1 to the number of rounds you must wait before using your breath weapon again.

WHIRLWIND TAIL SWEEP [MONSTROUS]

You can sweep your tail in a circular arc.

Prerequisite: Tail sweep attack.

Benefit: Your tail sweep attack affects a circle with a radius equal to your tail slap's reach.

Normal: Your tail sweep attack affects a semicircle.

WINGSTORM [MONSTROUS]

You can flatten targets with blasts of air from your wings.

Prerequisites: Str 13, dragon, fly speed 20, Hover, Power Attack, size Large or larger.

Benefit: As a full-round action, you can hover in place and use your wings to create a blast of air in a cylinder with a radius and height of 10 feet times your age category.

The wind blows from the center of your body toward the outside edge at the bottom of the cylinder.

The force of the wind depends on your size, as indicated below. For the effects of high winds, see Table 3–24 on page 95 of the *Dungeon Master's Guide.*

Dragon Size	Wind Force
Large	Severe
Huge	Windstorm
Gargantuan	Hurricane
Colossal	Tornado

Because the blast of air only lasts for your turn, creatures ignore the checked effect unless they are airborne (in which case they are blown back 1d6×5 feet).

Special: You can elect to keep the wind in effect for longer than your current turn. If you do, the wind lasts until your next turn (and you can opt to continue the effect during your next turn). Anyone in or entering the cylinder is affected. Because you are producing a continuous blast of air, the checked effect works normally while the wind lasts (checked creatures cannot move forward against the force of the wind, or they are blown back 1d6×5 feet if airborne).

DRAGON SPELLS

Over the millennia, dragons have developed a number of spells that take their special abilities and qualities into account. Despite the origin of these spells, any spellcaster can learn and use them if he or she is capable of casting spells of the indicated class and level.

METABREATH SPELLS

Similar to the metabreath feats described in the previous section, a large number of spells in this section alter a dragon's breath weapon. While metabreath feats allow mundane manipulation of a breath weapon's shape or power, metabreath spells represent significant magical enhancement of the breath weapon. A metabreath spell has a special breath (B) component listed in the spell description. Using the breath weapon is a part of casting the spell, just like making a touch attack is a part of casting a touch spell. Unlike touch spells, a dragon cannot hold the charge on a metabreath spell; it must breathe as part of the spellcasting. Casting a metabreath spell counts as a normal use of a breath weapon, and the dragon must wait the normal length of time before using it again.

A spellcaster must have a breath weapon to cast a spell with a breath component. Some metabreath spells apply only to breath weapons with a damaging, energy-based effect—so a dragon turtle's scalding breath (which deals damage with no energy descriptor) or a gorgon's petrifying breath, for example, could not be animated with *animate breath.* Either could be enhanced with fire damage using *breath weapon admixture* or replaced with electricity damage using *breath weapon substitution.* A character under the effect of an *elixir of fire breath* can use metabreath spells normally.

SORCERER/WIZARD SPELLS

1st-Level Sorcerer/Wizard Spells

Trans **Breath Flare.** Your breath weapon dazzles targets.

2nd-Level Sorcerer/Wizard Spells

Abjur **Scintillating Scales.** You gain an AC deflection bonus equal to your Constitution modifier.

Ench **Mesmerizing Glare.** Your gaze dazes creatures.

Trans **Razorfangs.** Your bite or claw attack threatens a critical hit on a 19 or 20.

Wings of Air. Target's flight maneuverability improves by one step.

3rd-Level Sorcerer/Wizard Spells

Trans **Blinding Breath.** Your breath weapon blinds targets.

4th-Level Sorcerer/Wizard Spells

Abj **Dispelling Breath.** Your breath weapon acts as a targeted dispel magic to all creatures in its area.

Evoc **Wingbind.** A net of force entangles the target, preventing it from charging, running, or flying.

Necro **Rebuking Breath.** Your breath weapon rebukes undead.

Trans **Breath Weapon Substitution.** Your breath weapon deals a different kind of damage than normal.

Sharptooth. One of your natural weapons deals damage as if you were one size larger.

Stunning Breath. Your breath weapon also stuns creatures for 1 round.

5th-Level Sorcerer/Wizard Spells

Trans **Burning Blood.** Your blood deals energy damage to nearby creatures when you are struck.

Draconic Polymorph. You change into a dragon's form.

Ethereal Breath. Your breath weapon manifests on the Ethereal Plane.

Superior Magic Fang. Your natural weapons gain +1 enhancement bonus per four levels.*

Greater Wings of Air. Target's flight maneuverability improves by two steps.

*Also a 5th-level druid spell.

6th-Level Sorcerer/Wizard Spells

Necro **Aura of Terror.** You gain an aura of fear, or your frightful presence becomes more effective.

Imperious Glare. You cause targets to cower in fear.

7th-Level Sorcerer/Wizard Spells

Ench **Hiss of Sleep.** You induce comatose slumber in targets.

Trans **Animate Breath.** Your breath weapon becomes a construct.

Greater Stunning Breath. Your breath weapon also stuns creatures for 2d4 rounds.

8th-Level Sorcerer/Wizard Spells

Ench **Maddening Whispers.** You induce confusion and madness in targets.

Necro **Enervating Breath.** Your breath weapon also bestows 2d4 negative levels.

Trans **Breath Weapon Admixture.** Your breath weapon also deals a second type of damage.

9th-Level Sorcerer/Wizard Spells

Trans **Deafening Breath.** Your breath weapon also deals sonic damage and deafens.

SPELL DESCRIPTIONS

The spells herein are presented in alphabetical order.

Animate Breath

Transmutation
Level: Sor/Wiz 7
Components: S, B
Casting Time: 1 standard action
Range: Personal
Target: You
Duration: 1 round/level

You imbue the energy of your breath weapon with coherence, mobility, and a semblance of life. The animated breath then attacks whomever or whatever you designate. The spell works only on breath weapons that deal energy (acid, cold, electricity, fire, or sonic) damage. The animated breath has the following characteristics.

Type: Construct.

Subtype: The same as yours, or the energy type of your breath weapon if you do not have a subtype.

Size: One size smaller than you.

Hit Dice: Equal to the number of dice of damage your breath weapon deals. The Hit Dice are 10-sided. Constructs also receive bonus hit points based on size:

Diminutive, Tiny: —
Small: 10
Medium: 20
Large: 30
Huge: 40
Gargantuan: 60
Colossal: 80

Speed: Varies by breath type:

Acid: 20 ft., swim 90 ft.
Cold: 30 ft.
Electricity: Fly 100 ft. (perfect)
Fire: 50 ft.
Sonic: Fly 100 ft. (perfect)

AC: The animated breath's natural armor bonus varies by size:

Diminutive or Tiny: +2
Small or Medium: +3
Large: +4
Huge: +8
Gargantuan: +10

If your breath weapon uses force energy, this bonus is an armor bonus composed of force (like that granted by *mage armor*) rather than a natural armor bonus.

Attacks: The animated breath makes slam attacks according to its Hit Dice.

Damage: Each successful hit deals bludgeoning damage (varies by size of the animated breath; see below) plus energy damage equal to one die of the same size as your breath weapon damage.

Diminutive: 1d2
Tiny: 1d3
Small: 1d4
Medium: 1d6
Large: 1d8
Huge: 2d6
Gargantuan: 2d8

For example, a Colossal red dragon's animated breath is Gargantuan in size, so it deals 2d8 points of bludgeoning damage on a successful hit—plus 1d10 points of fire damage, because d10 is the size of die used to determine a red dragon's breath weapon damage.

Special Qualities: Creatures that hit the animated breath with natural weapons or unarmed attacks take energy damage as though hit by the breath's attack.

Construct Traits: The animated breath is immune to mind-affecting effects, and to poison, magic sleep effects, paralysis, stunning, disease, death effects, necromantic effects, and any effect that requires a Fortitude save unless it also works on objects. The breath is not subject to critical hits, nonlethal damage, ability damage, ability drain, energy drain, or death from massive damage.

Saves: The animated breath has no good saves. All of its save bonuses are 1/3 of its Hit Dice plus the appropriate ability modifier.

Abilities: The animated breath has no Constitution or Intelligence score. Its Wisdom and Charisma scores are both 1. Its Strength and Dexterity vary by size:

Diminutive: Str 6, Dex 16
Tiny: Str 8, Dex 14
Small: Str 10, Dex 12
Medium: Str 12, Dex 10
Large: Str 16, Dex 10
Huge: Str 20, Dex 8
Gargantuan: Str 24, Dex 6

Alignment: Always neutral.

An old brass dragon's animated breath has the following statistics:

Large construct (fire); HD 8d10+30; hp 74; Init +0; Spd 50 ft.; AC 13, touch 9, flat-footed 13; Atk +9/+4 (1d8+1d6 fire, slam); SQ burn, construct traits; AL N; SV Fort +2, Ref +2, Will –3; Str 16, Dex 10, Con —, Int —, Wis 1, Cha 1.

An old red dragon's animated breath has the following statistics:

Huge construct (fire); HD 16d10+40; hp 128; Init –1; Spd 50 ft.; AC 15, touch 9, flat-footed 15; Atk +15/+10/+5 (2d6+1d10 fire, slam); SQ burn, construct traits; AL N; SV Fort +5, Ref +4, Will +0; Str 20, Dex 8, Con —, Int —, Wis 1, Cha 1.

Casting the spell requires a standard action, which includes using your breath weapon. When you use your breath weapon, it immediately takes animate form and attacks. It does not form as a cone or a line, and does not deal damage when it is used to cast this spell.

Aura of Terror

Necromancy [Fear, Mind-Affecting]
Level: Sor/Wiz 6
Components: V
Casting Time: 1 standard action
Range: Personal
Target: You
Duration: 1 minute/level

You become surrounded by an aura of fear. Whenever you charge or attack, you inspire fear in all creatures within 30 feet that have fewer Hit Dice than your caster level. Each potentially affected opponent must succeed on a Will save or become shaken—a condition that lasts until the opponent is out of range. A successful save leaves that opponent immune to your frightful presence for 24 hours.

If you cast this spell when you already have the frightful presence ability or a fear aura, the existing ability becomes more effective in the following ways:

• The radius of the area affected by the ability increases by 10 feet.

• The Will saving throw to resist the fear effect has a DC equal to your normal frightful presence DC or this spell's save DC, whichever is higher.

• Creatures that would normally be shaken by your fear aura are frightened instead, and creatures that would normally be frightened are panicked.

Blinding Breath

Transmutation [Light]
Level: Sor/Wiz 3

As *breath flare,* except that targets that fail their saving throws against your breath weapon are permanently blinded, rather than dazzled.

Breath Flare

Transmutation [Light]
Level: Sor/Wiz 1
Components: S, B
Casting Time: 1 standard action
Range: Personal

A brass dragon uses animate breath to produce a fiery construct.

Target: Your breath weapon
Duration: Instantaneous

If your breath weapon uses fire or electricity, it is suffused with bright light. In addition to taking the normal fire or electricity damage, creatures that fail their saving throws against the breath weapon are dazzled for 1 minute per caster level. Sightless creatures are not affected by *breath flare.* The modification applies only to the breath produced as part of casting.

Breath Weapon Admixture

Transmutation (see text)
Level: Sor/Wiz 8
Components: S, B
Casting Time: 1 standard action
Range: Personal
Target: Your breath weapon
Duration: Instantaneous

Choose one type of energy other than that normally associated with your breath weapon: acid, cold, electricity, or fire. You can modify your breath weapon to add an equal amount of the energy you choose. For example, a wyrm red dragon whose breath weapon normally deals 22d10 points of fire damage could use this spell to produce a cone dealing 22d10 points of fire damage plus 22d10 points of acid damage. Even opposed types of energy, such as fire and cold, can be combined using this spell. The modification applies only to the breath produced as part of the casting.

When you use this spell to produce acid, cold, electricity, or fire energy, it is a spell of that type. For example, *breath weapon admixture* is an acid spell when you cast it to add acid damage to your breath weapon.

Breath Weapon Substitution

Transmutation (see text)
Level: Sor/Wiz 4
Components: S, B
Casting Time: 1 standard action
Range: Personal
Target: Your breath weapon
Duration: Instantaneous

Choose one type of energy other than that normally associated with your breath weapon: acid, cold, electricity, or fire. You can modify your breath weapon to use the selected energy type instead of its normal energy type. For example, a mature adult red dragon whose breath weapon normally deals 14d10 points of fire damage could use this spell to produce a cone dealing 14d10 points of acid damage instead. The modification applies only to the breath produced as part of the casting.

When you use this spell to produce acid, cold, electricity, or fire energy, it is a spell of that type. For example, *breath weapon substitution* is an acid spell when you cast it to change your breath weapon to deal acid damage.

Burning Blood

Transmutation [see text]
Level: Sor/Wiz 5
Components: V, S
Casting Time: 1 standard action
Range: Personal
Target: You
Duration: 1 hour/level

Your blood becomes suffused with the same energy type that powers your breath weapon. (You must have a breath weapon that deals acid, cold, electricity, or fire damage to cast this spell.) Whenever you take damage from a natural or manufactured weapon, a spurt of blood erupts in a 5-foot-radius burst from the wound, dealing energy damage to creatures in its area. The energy-charged blood deals a number of points of damage equal to your caster level.

When you use this spell to produce acid, cold, electricity, or fire energy, it is a spell of that type. For example, *burning blood* is an acid spell when you cast it to suffuse your blood with acid.

Deafening Breath

Transmutation [Sonic]
Level: Sor/Wiz 9

As *breath weapon admixture,* but you add sonic energy to your breath weapon. In addition to dealing extra damage, you permanently deafen creatures that fail their saving throws against your breath.

This spell has no effect within an area of magical silence, such as that created by the *silence* spell.

Dispelling Breath

Abjuration
Level: Sor/Wiz 4
Components: S, B
Casting Time: 1 standard action
Range: Personal
Target: Your breath weapon
Duration: Instantaneous

Your breath weapon acts as a targeted *dispel magic,* possibly dispelling magical effects affecting creatures caught in its area. The modification applies only to the breath produced as part of the casting.

For each creature or object that fails its saving throw against your breath weapon and that is the target of one or more spells, you make a dispel check against each ongoing spell currently in effect on the object or creature. A dispel check is 1d20 + 1 per caster level (maximum +15) against a DC of 11 + the spell's caster level. A creature's magic items are not affected, and creatures and objects that rolled successful saving throws against your breath weapon are likewise not affected.

If a creature that is the effect of an ongoing spell (such as a monster summoned by *monster summoning*), is in the area and fails its saving throw against your breath weapon, you can also make a dispel check to end the spell that conjured the creature (returning it whence it came).

For each ongoing area or effect spell centered within the area of your breath weapon, you make a dispel check to dispel the spell.

You may choose to automatically succeed on dispel checks against any spell that you have cast.

Draconic Polymorph

Transmutation
Level: Sor/Wiz 5
Components: V
Casting Time: 1 standard action
Range: Personal
Target: You
Duration: 1 minute/level (D)

As *polymorph*, except as follows: The assumed form can have no more Hit Dice than you have, to a maximum of 20 Hit Dice. Your Strength and Constitution in the new form are above the average for the race or species into which you transform; your Strength is the average for the creature +8, and your Constitution is the average for the creature +2.

Enervating Breath

Necromancy
Level: Sor/Wiz 8
Components: S, B
Casting Time: 1 standard action
Range: Personal
Target: Your breath weapon
Duration: Instantaneous

You can modify your breath weapon so that it is laced with negative energy. In addition to the normal energy damage your breath weapon deals, creatures that fail their saving throws against the breath weapon gain 2d4 negative levels. The modification applies only to the breath produced as part of the casting.

If the subject gains at least as many negative levels as it has Hit Dice, it dies. Each negative level gives a creature the following penalties: –1 penalty on attack rolls, saving throws, skill checks, ability checks, and effective level (for determining the power, duration, DC, and other details of spells or special abilities). Additionally, a spellcaster loses one spell or spell slot from her highest available level. Negative levels stack.

Assuming the subjects survive, they regain lost levels after a number of hours equal to your caster level. Ordinarily, negative levels have a chance of permanently draining the subject's level, but the negative levels from *enervating breath* don't last long enough to do so.

If an undead creature is caught within the breath weapon, it gains 2d4×5 temporary hit points before taking damage from the breath weapon. If not immediately lost, these temporary hit points last for 1 hour.

Ethereal Breath

Transmutation
Level: Sor/Wiz 5
Components: S, B
Casting Time: 1 standard action
Range: Personal
Target: Your breath weapon
Duration: Instantaneous

You can modify your breath weapon to manifest on the Ethereal Plane instead of on the Material Plane. (You must be on the Material Plane, or on another plane with a coexistent Ethereal Plane, for this spell to function.) Your breath weapon affects ethereal creatures as if they were material, and does not affect material creatures in its area. The modification applies only to the breath produced as part of the casting.

Hiss of Sleep

Enchantment (Compulsion) [Mind-Affecting]
Level: Sor/Wiz 7
Components: V
Casting Time: 1 round
Range: Close (25 ft. + 5 ft./2 levels)
Targets: One creature/level
Duration: 1 round/level
Saving Throw: Will negates
Spell Resistance: No

Hissing and whispering softly, you lull the targets into a comatose slumber. Sleeping creatures are helpless. Slapping or wounding awakens affected creatures, but normal noise does not. Awakening a creature is a standard action (an application of the aid another action).

Hiss of sleep has no effect on creatures that can see you, creatures that have already rolled saving throws against your frightful presence, or unconscious creatures.

Imperious Glare

Necromancy [Fear, Mind-Affecting]
Level: Sor/Wiz 6
Components: S
Casting Time: 1 standard action
Range: Close (25 ft. + 5 ft./2 levels)
Targets: One living creature/level, no two of which may be more than 30 ft. apart
Duration: 1 round/level
Saving Throw: Will negates (see text)
Spell Resistance: Yes

Directing your gaze toward the target creatures, you instill terror and awe in their hearts. The targets must make successful Will saves or cower.

The saving throw DC to resist this effect is either the normal save DC for the spell or the save DC for your natural frightful presence ability, whichever is higher. You cannot cast this spell if you do not have a frightful presence ability, either natural or magically bestowed.

Maddening Whispers

Enchantment (Compulsion) [Mind-Affecting]
Level: Sor/Wiz 8
Components: V
Casting Time: 1 round
Range: Close (25 ft. + 5 ft./2 levels)
Targets: One creature/level
Duration: 1 round/level
Saving Throw: Will negates
Spell Resistance: Yes

Hissing and whispering softly, you stir feelings of confusion and madness in the targets' minds. You can choose to inflict one of the following conditions upon any creatures that fail their saving throws.

Hysteria: The subjects fall into fits of uncontrollable laughing or crying (equal chance for either). Hysterical creatures are unable to attack, cast spells, concentrate on spells, or do anything else requiring attention. The only action such a character can take is a single move action per turn.

Panic: The subjects become panicked. If cornered, a panicked creature cowers.

Violent Hallucinations: The subjects perceive any nearby creatures as dangerous enemies, attacking the nearest ones and fighting until the subjects are slain or until no more creatures are in sight.

Stupor: The subjects curl up on the floor and remain oblivious to events around them. Characters in a stupor are effectively stunned and prone.

Maddening whispers has no effect upon creatures that can see you, creatures that have already rolled saving throws against your frightful presence, or unconscious creatures.

Magic Fang, Superior

Transmutation
Level: Drd 5, Sor/Wiz 5
Components: V, S
Casting Time: 1 standard action
Range: Personal
Target: You
Duration: 1 round/level

Superior magic fang gives every natural weapon you possess an enhancement bonus on attack and damage rolls equal to +1 per four caster levels (maximum +5 at 20th level).

Mesmerizing Glare

Enchantment (Compulsion) [Mind-Affecting]
Level: Sor/Wiz 2
Components: S
Casting Time: 1 standard action
Range: Close (25 ft. + 5 ft./2 levels)
Targets: One living creature/level, no two of which may be more than 30 ft. apart
Duration: 1 round/level
Saving Throw: Will negates
Spell Resistance: Yes

Directing your gaze toward the target creatures, you cause them to stop and stare blankly at you, mesmerized. Creatures that fail their saving throws gaze at your eyes, heedless of all else. Affected creatures are dazed. Any potential threat (such as an armed opponent moving behind the mesmerized creature) allows the creature a new saving throw. Any obvious threat, such as casting a spell, drawing a sword, or aiming an arrow, automatically breaks the effect, as does shaking or slapping the creature. A mesmerized creature's ally may shake it free of the spell as a standard action.

Razorfangs

Transmutation
Level: Sor/Wiz 2
Components: V
Casting Time: 1 standard action
Range: Personal
Target: You
Duration: 1 round/level

Choose one of your natural weapons that deals slashing or piercing damage (your bite or a single claw). That natural weapon's threat range doubles (in most cases, becoming 19–20). This spell does not stack with any other effects that increase a weapon's threat range.

This spell's name derives from a marked preference among dragons for improving their bite attack with this spell, but it works equally well on a claw attack.

Rebuking Breath

Necromancy
Level: Sor/Wiz 4
Components: S, B
Casting Time: 1 standard action
Range: Personal
Target: Your breath weapon
Duration: Instantaneous

You imbue your breath weapon with negative energy that rebukes undead in its area. Undead within the area of your breath weapon that fail their saving throws against it are rebuked, and cower as if in awe for 10 rounds. The modification applies only to the breath produced as part of the casting.

Scintillating Scales

Abjuration
Level: Sor/Wiz 2
Components: V
Casting Time: 1 standard action
Range: Personal
Target: You
Duration: 1 round/level

Your hide glistens and shimmers with a protective magical aura, granting you a deflection bonus to your Armor Class equal to your Constitution modifier. Your natural armor bonus decreases by an amount equal to your Constitution modifier × 1/2.

This blue dragon's rebuking breath blasts wraiths from the sky.

Sharptooth

Transmutation
Level: Sor/Wiz 4
Components: V, S
Casting Time: 1 standard action
Range: Personal
Target: You
Duration: 1 round/level

Choose one of your natural weapons (your bite, a single claw, a wing, a crush, a tail slap, or a tail sweep). For the duration of the spell, that natural weapon deals damage as though you were one size larger than your actual size. You cannot gain additional attack forms (such as a tail slap) by using this spell; you can only improve attacks you already possess. This spell does not stack with itself.

This spell's name derives from a marked preference among dragons for improving their bite attacks with this spell, but it works equally well on claw, wing, tail, and crush attacks.

Stunning Breath

Transmutation
Level: Sor/Wiz 4
Components: S, B
Casting Time: 1 standard action
Range: Personal
Target: Your breath weapon
Duration: Instantaneous

You imbue your damaging breath weapon with concussive force that can stun those caught in its area. Creatures that take damage from the breath weapon must make successful Fortitude saves (DC equal to your breath weapon save DC) or be stunned for 1 round. The modification applies only to the breath produced as part of the casting.

Stunning Breath, Greater

Transmutation
Level: Sor/Wiz 7

As *stunning breath*, but creatures that fail their Fortitude saves are stunned for 2d4 rounds.

Wingbind

Evocation [Force]
Level: Sor/Wiz 4
Components: V, S
Casting Time: 1 standard action
Range: Close (25 ft. + 5 ft./2 levels)
Target: One creature
Duration: 1 round/level (D)
Saving Throw: Reflex negates
Spell Resistance: Yes

A web of force surrounds the target, entangling it like a net. If the target fails its saving throw, it is entangled. Perhaps most important, the creature cannot use wings to fly—hence the common name of this spell. A creature flying with wings falls immediately if it is entangled by *wingbind*.

An entangled creature can escape with a successful Escape Artist check against a DC equal to the saving throw DC of the spell. Like a *wall of force*, the web of force is impervious to most attacks: It is immune to damage of all kinds, cannot be burst with a Strength check, and is unaffected by most spells, including *dispel magic*. Also like *wall of force*, the web is immediately destroyed by *disintegrate*, a *rod of cancellation*, a *sphere of annihilation*, or *Mordenkainen's disjunction*.

Wings of Air

Transmutation
Level: Sor/Wiz 2
Components: V
Casting Time: 1 standard action
Range: Touch
Target: Winged creature touched
Duration: 1 minute/level
Saving Throw: None (harmless)
Spell Resistance: No (harmless)

The creature you touch becomes more agile in the air, able to make quicker turns, and more maneuverable when flying. The target must be capable of flight using wings. The creature's maneuverability improves by one step—from clumsy to poor, poor to average, average to good, or good to perfect.

A single creature cannot benefit from multiple applications of this spell at one time.

Wings of Air, Greater

Transmutation
Level: Sor/Wiz 5

As *wings of air*, but the creature's maneuverability improves by two steps—from clumsy to average, poor to good, or average to perfect.

DRAGON MAGIC ITEMS

This section describes magic items made particularly for use by dragons. Many of them can be used by other creatures as well.

Amulet of Supremacy (Minor Artifact): This stunning piece of jewelry is virtually priceless based simply on its artistic quality and the value of precious metal and gemstones it contains, but its magical abilities are even more valuable to a dragon. When worn by a dragon, an *amulet of supremacy* confers the benefits of the Maximize Breath feat on the dragon's breath weapon, and applies the effects of the Maximize Spell feat to the dragon's spells and spell-like abilities. These benefits come at no cost to the dragon: It need not wait extra rounds between uses of its breath weapon, and its maximized spells do not use higher-level spell slots.

An *amulet of supremacy* bestows two negative levels on any nondragon that dares to put it on. In addition, when a nondragon first dons the amulet, it immediately targets the offender with a *disintegrate* effect (caster level 20th, Fortitude DC 19 partial).

Strong (no school); CL 17th.

Claws of the Ripper: These metal, scythelike blades are designed to fit over one set of a dragon's claws, and they resize to fit any dragon of Large size or bigger. A dragon wearing *claws of the ripper* cannot also make use of a magic ring on that claw. When worn, *claws of the ripper* increase the damage dealt by the dragon's claws on a critical hit, giving them a ×4 multiplier (like that of a scythe).

Faint transmutation; CL 6th; Craft Ring; Price 2,000 gp; Weight 10 lb.

Dragonarmor of Invincibility: This is a set of *+5 half-plate armor* (barding) designed to fit a dragon of a specific size. It adjusts to fit any individual dragon within a specific size category, size Medium or bigger. In addition to its +12 armor bonus, the armor is fitted with spikes and blades designed to enhance the dragon's attacks, granting a +5 enhancement bonus to each of the dragon's natural weapon attacks (as if by use of the spell *superior magic fang*).

Strong transmutation; CL 15th; Craft Magic Arms and Armor, Craft Epic Magic Arms and Armor [an epic feat

Jaws of the Dragon

Illus. by W. England

available only to characters who have at least 28 ranks in both Knowledge (arcana) and Spellcraft], *superior magic fang*; Price 276,350 gp (Medium), 327,500 gp (Large), 379,950 gp (Huge), 434,750 gp (Gargantuan), 444,350 gp (Colossal); Cost 138,850 gp + 11,000 XP (Medium), 165,050 gp + 13,000 XP (Large), 192,450 gp + 15,000 XP (Huge), 222,250 gp + 17,000 XP (Gargantuan), 231,850 gp + 17,000 XP (Colossal);Weight 50 lb. (Medium), 100 lb. (Large), 250 lb. (Huge), 500 lb. (Gargantuan), 1,000 lb. (Colossal).

Draught of Metabreath Magic: These draughts are thick liquids, similar to potions, that bestow magical effects on a creature drinking them. The magical effects duplicate the metabreath spells described in the previous section, but the drinker must supply the breath component for the effect to take place. Drinking a draught is a standard action, and activates the magic of the draught for just over 1 round. After drinking, the drinker must use its breath weapon before the end of the next round. This use of the drinker's breath weapon is enhanced as if the drinker had cast the appropriate metabreath spell on itself.

Draughts of metabreath magic come in a number of different varieties, whose caster level and market price are listed on the table below.

Varies (no school); Craft Wondrous Item, appropriate metabreath spell; Weight 1/2 lb.

Draught Variety	Caster Level	Price
Blinding breath	5th	750 gp
Breath flare	1st	50 gp
Breath weapon admixture:		
acid	15th	6,000 gp
cold	15th	6,000 gp
electricity	15th	6,000 gp
fire	15th	6,000 gp
Breath weapon substitution:		
acid	7th	1,400 gp
cold	7th	1,400 gp
electricity	7th	1,400 gp
fire	7th	1,400 gp
Deafening breath	17th	7,650 gp
Dispelling breath	7th	1,400 gp
Enervating breath	15th	6,000 gp
Ethereal breath	9th	2,250 gp
Rebuking breath	7th	1,400 gp
Stunning breath	7th	1,400 gp
Greater stunning breath	13th	4,550 gp

Draught of Metallic Dragon Breath: A special variety of *draughts of metabreath magic,* this liquid comes in five varieties, corresponding to the five kinds of metallic dragons, and their color is the same: brass, bronze, copper, gold, and silver. When drunk, this draught alters the drinker's next use of its breath weapon, as long as that use occurs before the end of the next round. The breath weapon works just like the nondamaging effects of a metallic dragon. A brass draught creates a cone of *sleep,* a bronze draught creates a cone of *repulsion* gas, a copper draught creates a cone of *slow* gas, a gold draught creates a cone of weakening gas, and a silver draught creates a cone of paralyzing gas. The saving throw against the metallic breath weapon has the same DC as the drinker's natural breath weapon, and the effects are the same as if the drinker used the breath weapon normally. For example, an old red dragon that drank a gold *draught of metallic dragon breath* could breathe a cone of weakening gas that deals 8 points of Strength damage.

A character under the effects of a *potion of fire breath* or similar effect can use a *draught of metallic dragon breath* to alter the fiery blasts from that potion, using the caster level of the effect (3rd, in the case of a *potion of fire breath*) as the effective age category. A creature with no breath weapon ability is unaffected by drinking the draught.

Moderate transmutation; CL 7th; Craft Wondrous Item, *breath weapon substitution,* and one of the following: *sleep, repulsion, slow, ray of enfeeblement,* or *hold person*; Price 2,100 gp; Weight 1/2 lb.

Gemstone of Fortification: This large, faceted stone must be embedded in a creature's hide to function. True dragons can accomplish this with ease, since they routinely embed gems in among the scales of their bellies. Other creatures have a more difficult time of it, requiring at least a *limited wish,* at the DM's discretion.

When properly embedded, a *gemstone of fortification* protects the wearer's vital areas from lethal damage. When a critical hit or sneak attack is scored on the wearer, there is a chance that the critical hit or sneak attack is negated and damage is instead rolled normally. A *gemstone of light fortification* has a 25% chance to negate a critical hit or sneak attack, a *gemstone of moderate fortification* has a 75% chance, and a *gemstone of heavy fortification* has a 100% chance.

Strong universal or evocation; CL 13th; Craft Magic Arms and Armor, Craft Wondrous Item, *limited wish* or *miracle;* Price 3,000 gp (light), 15,000 gp (moderate), 35,000 gp (heavy).

Gorget of Tempest Breath: This metal collar bestows the benefit of the Tempest Breath feat upon its wearer. A creature wearing the gorget cannot also make use of a magic robe.

Strong (no school); CL 13th; Craft Wondrous Item, Tempest Breath; Price 10,000 gp; Weight 10 lb.

Jaws of the Dragon: This complex metal device is worn in the mouth, fitting over the teeth while allowing them to protrude. A row of metal teeth is set into the *jaws of the dragon* behind where the dragon's teeth emerge, increasing the damage dealt by the dragon's bite. The dragon gains the benefit of the *sharptooth* spell while the jaws are worn. The device resizes to fit any creature as normal for a magic item, but creatures with no natural bite attack gain no benefit from wearing it.

Moderate transmutation; CL 7th; Craft Wondrous Item, *sharptooth*; Price 40,000 gp; Weight 8 lb.

Pectoral of Maneuverability: This metal disk has straps that go over a dragon's forelimbs to hold the pectoral in place over its chest. A winged creature wearing a *pectoral of maneuverability* has its flying maneuverability improved by one step. A *greater pectoral of maneuverability* improves maneuverability by two steps. A humanoid can wear a pectoral as if it were a vest.

Faint (ordinary) or moderate (greater) transmutation; CL 3rd (ordinary) or 9th (greater); Craft Wondrous Item, *wings of air* (ordinary) or *greater wings of air* (greater); Price 12,000 gp (ordinary) or 90,000 (greater); Weight 5 lb.

LAIR WARDS

Lair wards are a special kind of wondrous item that dragons often use to protect their lairs and hoards. They are identical to certain kinds of wondrous architecture used in humanoid-built strongholds and dungeons, as detailed in the *Stronghold Builder's Guidebook*. Essentially, lair wards are immobile (or practically immobile) magic items, and they follow all the normal rules for the use of magic items. See the *Stronghold Builder's Guidebook* for information on creating these items and determining the market price for new items.

Most lair wards affect an area defined as a "single cavern." This need not be an actual cavern; such an effect wards an area of approximately 400 square feet.

Disabling a Lair Ward: As a stationary magic item, a lair ward is essentially identical to a magic trap (even though some have beneficial rather than harmful effects). A character with the trapfinding ability (including rogues and characters affected by a *find traps* spell) can use Search to find lair wards and Disable Device to deactivate them. The DC for both checks is 25 + the spell level of the highest-level spell used in the lair ward's construction. A successful Disable Device check suppresses the ward's magical properties for 1d4 rounds, just as if the character had cast *dispel magic* on it. If the character beats the DC by 10 or more, she suppresses its magical properties for 1d4 minutes instead.

Black Luminary: This 3-foot-wide steel half-orb sheds *darkness* in a 20-foot radius around itself. Not even creatures who can normally see in the dark can see through it, and it cancels out any normal light, as well as magical light of 1st level or lower. If magical light of 2nd level (such as *continual flame*) is brought into or cast in the area, it and the *black luminary* cancel each other out until the light spell expires or is removed from the area. Higher-level light spells, such as the *daylight* spell, are unaffected by a *black luminary*'s darkness.

The orb has a shutter that enables a person standing beneath a ceiling-mounted *black luminary* to conceal or reveal the item (and the resulting darkness) with a move action.

Faint evocation; CL 3rd; Craft Wondrous Item, *darkness*; Price 6,000 gp.

Black Luminary, Pitch: This 4-foot-wide steel half-orb sheds *deeper darkness* in a 60-foot radius around itself. Not even creatures that can normally see in the dark can see in this darkness, and it cancels out any normal light as well as any magical light of 2nd level or lower. If a *daylight* spell is brought into or cast in the area, it and the *pitch black luminary* cancel each other out until the light spell expires or is removed from the area.

The orb has a shutter that enables a person standing beneath a ceiling-mounted *pitch black luminary* to conceal or reveal the item (and the resulting darkness) with a move action.

Faint evocation; CL 5th; Craft Wondrous Item, *deeper darkness*; Price 15,000 gp.

Bright Luminary: This 4-foot-wide steel half-orb sheds *daylight* in a 60-foot radius around itself. Creatures affected by normal daylight are affected by a *bright luminary* as well. If magical darkness is brought into or cast in the area, it and the *bright luminary* cancel each other out until the magical darkness expires or is removed from the area.

The orb has a shutter that enables a person standing beneath a ceiling-mounted *bright luminary* to conceal or reveal the item with a move action.

Faint evocation; CL 5th; Craft Wondrous Item, *daylight*; Price 15,000 gp.

Cavern of the Earthbound: Within the walls of this cavern, the *fly* spell does not function. Characters who are flying when they enter the cavern float to the ground as if the spell's duration had expired. When they leave the cavern, any *fly* spells whose durations have not expired return to normal efficacy.

Moderate abjuration; CL 7th; Craft Wondrous Item, *spell immunity*; Price 14,000 gp.

Cloudgathering Orb: This 4-foot-wide crystal orb keeps the weather nasty (thunderstorms in spring, torrential rain in summer, sleet in autumn, and blizzards in winter) around a lair for a 2-mile radius. Anyone attempting to magically alter the weather in this area must make an opposed caster level check against the *cloudgathering orb's* power to succeed.

See pages 93–95 of the *Dungeon Master's Guide* for information on weather effects.

Moderate transmutation; CL 11th; Craft Wondrous Item, *control weather*; Price 33,000 gp.

Cavern of Babble: Anyone who enters this cavern must make a DC 14 Will save or have any words that she speaks come out as unintelligible gibberish. The exact nature of the transmuted sounds is determined by the creator of this magic item at the time of creation.

This effect makes it impossible for anyone in the cavern to communicate verbally with anyone else. Additionally, it prevents a spellcaster from casting a spell that requires a verbal component.

Faint transmutation; CL 5th; Craft Wondrous Item, *sculpt sound*; Price 7,500 gp.

Cavern of Silence: All sounds made within this cavern are negated (as if by a *silence* spell). Making a DC 13 Will save allows a character to speak normally (including casting spells with vocal components), though other sounds remain dampened.

This property doesn't affect sounds created outside this cavern.

Faint illusion; CL 3rd; Craft Wondrous Item, *silence*; Price 3,000 gp.

Hurricane's Eye: This 5-foot-wide crystal orb maintains hurricane-force winds (see page 95 of the *Dungeon Master's Guide*) around the outside of the lair at all times. The eye of the hurricane (the safe, calm part) is a cylinder with a diameter of up to 80 feet. If the lair is larger than this, multiple orbs can be linked together by overlapping the eyes. Any section that is surrounded by eyes on all sides automatically becomes a part of the eye, turning the whole region into one massive, continuously operating eye, keeping the raging winds of the hurricane entirely outside of the affected regions.

The winds circle the eye in a clockwise or counterclockwise fashion, as you prefer. However, if there are more orbs than one, they must all force the wind to circle in the same direction. If you join this item up with a *tornado's eye* or a *windstorm's eye*, they can each only function at the level of the weakest item.

Strong transmutation; CL 15th; Craft Wondrous Item, *control winds;* Price 75,000 gp.

Inscriptions of Privacy: This form of wondrous architecture places arcane sigils throughout the walls and ceiling of a cavern. They can be as subtle or outlandish as the creator likes. However, when anyone tries to spy upon anyone in the cavern by means of *clairaudience/clairvoyance* or *scrying* or a *crystal ball* or any other magic scrying device, the inscriptions glow softly. If the scrying attempt originates from within the cavern, the person making the attempt begins glowing as well.

Anyone scried upon can attempt an opposed caster level check (using the caster level of the *inscriptions of privacy*). If the target of the scrying attempt wins the opposed check, she immediately gets a mental image of the scrier, along with a sense of the direction and distance of the scrier, accurate to within one-tenth of the distance.

Moderate divination; CL 7th; Craft Wondrous Item, *detect scrying;* Price 14,000 gp.

Inscriptions of Vacancy: Everyone within a cavern adorned with these inscriptions becomes undetectable to scrying. In fact, to someone casting a *scrying* spell it appears as if the cavern is entirely empty of people and devoid of activity, no matter how many people are in it or what they are doing.

Moderate illusion; CL 9th; Craft Wondrous Item, *false vision;* Price 22,500 gp.

Missing Chamber: This cavern—and everyone and everything inside it—is difficult to detect by divination spells and detection spells and magic items. For such a spell or item to work, the caster or user must succeed on a caster level check (1d20 + caster level) against DC 16.

Faint abjuration; CL 5th; Craft Wondrous Item, *nondetection;* Price 7,500 gp.

Orb of Pleasant Breezes: This 4-foot-wide crystal orb keeps the weather in a 2-mile radius around the lair mild and pleasant no matter the time of year. Anyone attempting to magically alter the weather in this area must make an opposed caster level check against the orb's power to succeed.

Moderate transmutation; CL 11th; Craft Wondrous Item, *control weather;* Price 33,000 gp.

Platform of Healing: Any time an injured creature is placed on this 10-foot-round platform—which is affixed to the floor—the creature recieves the benefits of a *heal* spell.

If an undead creature somehow ends up on the platform, treat it as if a *harm* spell had been cast upon it instead.

Strong conjuration; CL 17th; Craft Wondrous Item, *mass heal;* Price 76,500 gp.

Pool of Scrying: This shallow pool forms a reflective surface in which the user can scry on others. This works just like the standard *scrying* spell. Spellcasters can cast certain spells through the *pool of scrying* at creatures or things they are scrying upon, as per the *scrying* spell.

While the pool can be shallow, it must be at least 2 feet by 4 feet. It can be formed into the top of a large pedestal, but these items are just as often found in a room's floor. If the water is ever entirely emptied from the pool, the item loses its magic.

Faint divination; CL 5th; Craft Wondrous Item, *scrying;* Price 7,500 gp.

Pool of Scrying, Greater: This magic item works just like the standard *pool of scrying*, with one exception. You can reliably cast any spells through it that you could use with the *greater scrying* spell.

Moderate divination; CL 11th; Craft Wondrous Item, *greater scrying;* Price 33,000 gp.

Secure Cavern: The entire cavern is affected by a *mind blank* spell. No one in the cavern can be affected by devices and spells that detect, influence, or read emotions and thoughts, up to and including *miracle* or *wish*. Even a scrying attempt that scans an area does not work.

Strong abjuration; CL 15th; Craft Wondrous Item, *mind blank;* Price 60,000 gp.

Sigils of Suppression: A *globe of invulnerability* fills the entire cavern, as represented by the arcane sigils that are inscribed upon the walls. No spell effects of 4th level or lower function within this cavern. Such spells cannot be cast within the cavern, nor can their effects extend to within the cavern.

A targeted *dispel magic* can temporarily suppress *sigils of suppression*, just like any other magic item.

Moderate abjuration; CL 11th; Craft Wondrous Item, *globe of invulnerability;* Price 33,000 gp.

Sigils of Suppression, Lesser: These are identical to *sigils of suppression*, except that they only block spell effects of 3rd level or lower (as per *lesser globe of invulnerability*).

Moderate abjuration; CL 7th; Craft Wondrous Item, *lesser globe of invulnerability;* Price 14,000 gp.

Tornado's Eye: This 6-foot-wide crystal orb maintains tornado-force winds (see page 95 of the *Dungeon Master's Guide*) around the outside of the lair at all times. See the description of the *hurricane's eye* for how this works.

If this item is joined with a *hurricane's eye* or a *windstorm's eye*, each item functions at the level of the weakest item.

Strong transmutation; CL 18th; Craft Wondrous Item, *control winds;* Price 90,000 gp.

Veil of Obscurity: This lair ward disguises up to 8,000 contiguous square feet of caverns with a *mirage arcana* effect, making the lair appear as something other than it is. It includes audible, visual, tactile, and olfactory elements, though it can't disguise, conceal, or add creatures.

Moderate illusion; CL 10th; Craft Wondrous Item, *mirage arcana;* Price 25,000 gp.

Windstorm's Eye: This 4-foot-wide crystal orb maintains windstorm-force winds (see page 95 of the *Dungeon Master's Guide*) around the outside of the lair at all times. See the description of the *hurricane's eye* for details.

If this item is joined with a *hurricane's eye* or a *tornado's eye*, each item functions at the level of the weakest item.

Moderate transmutation; CL 12th; Craft Wondrous Item, *control winds*; Price 60,000 gp.

Wondrous Absence: This ward conceals all magical auras in a single cavern, just as if *Nystul's magic aura* had been cast.

Faint illusion; CL 3rd; Craft Wondrous Item, *Nystul's magic aura*; Price 3,000 gp.

DRAGON PRESTIGE CLASSES

Dragons rarely adopt character classes. Their perspective on the passing of time, their enormous natural abilities, and their essentially bestial nature together incline them to a patient stance of allowing time to advance their abilities, rather than the sort of frantic adventuring and training typical of creatures with character classes.

That said, a not insignificant number of dragons, when they reach an age of some maturity (often mature adult or later), move directly into prestige classes, or adopt prestige classes after a relatively short stint in one of the standard classes described in Chapter 3 of the *Player's Handbook*. While the standard classes offer little benefit to most dragons, a dragon prestige class can give a dragon access to power that other dragons can only imagine.

Dragons are sometimes motivated to adopt prestige classes for religious reasons. Dragons who devote themselves to the service of the primary dragon deities frequently advance as sacred watchers of Bahamut or unholy ravagers of Tiamat. A number of lesser dragons (and a scattered handful of true dragons) become dispassionate watchers of Chronepsis, the draconic deity of fate, death, and judgment. The legendary evil dragon Ashardalon inspired a cult of draconic followers who emulate him by binding demonic spirits to their own hearts. Other dragons seek divine status for themselves, and their advancement through the dragon ascendant prestige class measures their progress toward that goal.

Other dragons pursue a prestige class to increase their power by perfecting their innate abilities. The bloodscaled fury is a destructive force of nature, a creature of unbridled chaos, while the hidecarved dragon takes a more disciplined approach to its advancement, carving protective runes into its own scales. The elemental master seeks a greater attunement to the natural forces that are a part of all true dragons' physical makeup, mastering the elements and energies that flow through its veins.

BLOODSCALED FURY

An angry dragon is fearsome indeed. A dragon in a frothing rage, with its eyes shot red, great gobbets of spittle foaming from its mouth, and a sheen of blood coating its scales, is a terror few can withstand. A bloodscaled fury is a dragon whose rage surpasses that of a human barbarian as the barbarian's rage surpasses a child's tantrum.

Most bloodscaled furies are dragons of at least juvenile age with several levels of barbarian. A very few dragons come to the prestige class along a more unusual path, such as the sohei class or Singh rager prestige class from *Oriental Adventures*. Few bloodscaled furies have levels in classes that do not feature a rage ability.

A bloodscaled fury

Bloodscaled furies are solitary dragons and rather akin to destructive forces of nature. Their tendency toward chaos means that no one can predict when a bloodscaled fury might descend upon a human settlement or wilderness outpost and level the place, leaving a blasted crater in its wake.

Hit Die: d12.

Requirements

To qualify to become a bloodscaled fury, a dragon must fulfill all the following criteria.

Race: Any dragon.

Alignment: Any chaotic.

Base Attack Bonus: +22.

Skills: Intimidate 14 ranks.

Feats: Power Attack, Shock Wave, Windstorm.

Special: *Rage:* The dragon must have some sort of rage ability, most commonly derived from levels in the barbarian class, and must be able to enter this rage at least three times per day.

Frightful Presence: The dragon must have the frightful presence ability.

Class Skills

The bloodscaled fury's class skills (and the key ability for each skill) are Climb (Str), Intimidate (Cha), Jump (Str), Listen (Wis), Swim (Str), Spot (Wis), and Survival (Wis). See Chapter 4: Skills in the *Player's Handbook* for skill descriptions.

Skill Points at Each Level: 2 + Int modifier.

TABLE 2–4: THE BLOODSCALED FURY

Class Level	Base Attack Bonus	Fort Save	Ref Save	Will Save	Special
1st	+1	+2	+0	+0	Fearsome presence
2nd	+2	+3	+0	+0	Draconic fury +2/+1
3rd	+3	+3	+1	+1	Scales of blood (spell resistance, damage reduction +5)
4th	+4	+4	+1	+1	Rend
5th	+5	+4	+1	+1	Extended fury
6th	+6	+5	+2	+2	Draconic fury +4/+2
7th	+7	+5	+2	+2	Scales of blood (damage reduction +0/magic and cold iron)
8th	+8	+6	+2	+2	Incite rage
9th	+9	+6	+3	+3	Tireless fury
10th	+10	+7	+3	+3	Draconic fury +6/+3
11th	+11	+7	+3	+3	Scales of blood (damage reduction +0/epic and cold iron)
12th	+12	+8	+4	+4	Blinding speed

Class Features

The following are class features of the bloodscaled fury prestige class.

Weapon and Armor Proficiency: A bloodscaled fury gains no proficiency with any weapons, armor, or shields.

Fearsome Presence (Ex): A bloodscaled fury is a terror to behold, and the seething fury that churns in its heart inspires terror in all who lay eyes on it. The dragon's frightful presence becomes more powerful: The saving throw DC to resist the ability is increased by the dragon's class level. Creatures with Hit Dice equal to or less than 1/2 the dragon's class level + 4 are panicked if they fail their saving throws, while creatures with more Hit Dice are shaken. Both fear effects last for 6d6 rounds (rather than the usual 4d6).

Draconic Fury (Ex): At 2nd level, a bloodscaled fury's rage becomes more fearsome. While raging, its Strength and Constitution scores increase by an additional 2 points and it gains an additional +1 morale bonus on its Will saves. Thus, an 11th-level barbarian/2nd-level bloodscaled fury gains +8 to its Strength and Constitution scores and +4 on its Will saves. (Its Armor Class penalty remains at –2.)

At 6th level, and again at 10th, these bonuses increase by a similar amount. An 11th-level barbarian/10th-level bloodscaled fury gains +12 to its Strength and Constitution scores and +6 on its Will saves.

Scales of Blood (Su): Beginning at 3rd level, a bloodscaled fury earns its name. When it enters a rage, small quantities of blood ooze out around its scales, lining their edges and adding to the dragon's fearsome appearance. More important, the blood supernaturally wards the dragon from spells and weapon damage. For the duration of the dragon's rage, its spell resistance increases by its class level, and its damage reduction improves as well. The number before the slash in the dragon's damage reduction increases by 5 at 3rd level. In addition, at 7th level a bloodscaled fury's damage reduction can be overcome only by magic cold iron weapons, and at 11th level only by epic cold iron weapons. For example, an old white dragon with damage reduction 10/magic who reaches 3rd level as a bloodscaled fury gains damage reduction 15/magic while raging. At 7th level, it gains damage reduction 15/magic and cold iron while raging, and at 11th level it gains damage reduction 15/epic and cold iron while raging.

Rend: At 4th level, a bloodscaled fury gains Rend (see page 73) as a bonus feat, even if it doesn't have the prerequisites.

Extended Fury (Ex): At 5th level, a bloodscaled fury can remain in a rage for a number of rounds equal to 6 + its Con modifier.

Incite Rage (Ex): At 8th level, a bloodscaled fury gains the ability to incite rage in its allies whenever it enters a rage. The dragon can affect all willing allies within 60 feet, granting them a +4 morale bonus to Strength, a +4 morale bonus to Constitution, a +2 morale bonus on Will saves, and a –2 penalty to Armor Class for as long as the dragon remains raging. This ability is otherwise identical to normal barbarian rage, including the fatigue at the end of the rage.

Tireless Fury (Ex): At 9th level, a bloodscaled fury no longer becomes fatigued at the end of its rage.

Blinding Speed (Ex): A 12th-level bloodscaled fury can act as if under the effects of a *haste* spell for a total of 12 rounds each day. The duration of the effect need not be consecutive rounds. Activating this power is a free action.

Ex-Bloodscaled Furies

A bloodscaled fury that becomes lawful loses all class features and cannot gain more levels as a bloodscaled fury.

DISCIPLE OF ASHARDALON

The ancient red dragon Ashardalon, when struck a mortal blow by a human druid, replaced his wounded heart with a living demon: a balor of enormous power named Ammet, the Eater of Souls. Inspired by this example, disciples of Ashardalon bind fiendish spirits to their own hearts, eventually taking on the characteristics of demonic spawn themselves. Disciples of Ashardalon do not really worship the ancient dragon, nor do they literally learn directly from him as the word "disciple" implies, but they regard Ashardalon as the great exemplar of their path and seek to emulate him in every way possible.

Dragons of any class or none can qualify for the disciple of Ashardalon prestige class. Those with a religious or arcane leaning who have pursued specialized knowledge are most likely to follow this course. Even the most martially minded evil dragons, though, often find enough to inspire them in Ashardalon's example that they adopt this class.

Disciples of Ashardalon are members of an organization, loose-knit and secretive though it may be. Of necessity, they have some contact with other members of the order, but their overwhelming personal ambition means they rarely cooperate with one another in pursuit of their various evil schemes. They are likely to make use of various minions, particularly those of a fiendish character, in pursuit of their plans, rather than rely on the cooperation of equals. Like their evil exemplar, they are often served by deluded cults made up of evil humanoids or even undead. Both they and their cultists contemplate plans of sweeping evil grandeur—seizing power, leveling kingdoms, reclaiming or destroying ancient artifacts, and the like. They are thus particularly well suited for use in campaigns of epic scope and, quite likely, epic level.

Hit Die: d8.

A disciple of Ashardalon

Illus. by S. Tappin

Requirements

To qualify to become a disciple of Ashardalon, a dragon must fulfill all the following criteria.

Race: Any dragon.

Alignment: Any evil.

Base Attack Bonus: +18.

Skills: Knowledge (religion) 18 ranks, Knowledge (the planes) 18 ranks.

Feats: Iron Will, Quicken Spell-Like Ability.

Special: *Initiation:* Before adopting the prestige class, a dragon must join the loose-knit cult of other disciples and undergo its initiation rites. This process includes the ritual scarring of the dragon's heart—an extremely dangerous practice that would claim the life of a dragon too weak to qualify for the class, and leaves even those that do robbed of 1 point of Constitution. (Dragons that progress to at least 6th level in this class regain the lost Constitution point eventually.)

Class Skills

The disciple of Ashardalon's class skills (and the key ability for each skill) are Concentration (Con), Hide (Dex), Intimidate (Cha), Knowledge (arcana) (Int), Knowledge (the planes) (Int), Knowledge (religion) (Int), Listen (Wis), Move Silently (Dex), Search (Int), Sense Motive (Wis), Spellcraft (Int), and Spot (Wis). See Chapter 4: Skills in the *Player's Handbook* for skill descriptions.

Skill Points at Each Level: 4 + Int modifier.

Class Features

The following are class features of the disciple of Ashardalon prestige class.

Weapon and Armor Proficiency: A disciple of Ashardalon gains no proficiency with any weapons, armor, or shields.

Fiendbond (Su): As part of its initiation, a disciple of Ashardalon binds a demonic spirit to its own heart, emulating the manner in which Ashardalon himself took a balor as his heart. The dragon's alignment changes to chaotic evil if it was not already of that alignment. The dragon gains bonus sorcerer spells as if its Charisma score were 2 points higher than actual.

Resistance (Ex): A disciple of Ashardalon gains resistance to acid, cold, electricity, and fire. This resistance is 5 at 1st level, and increases by 5 at 4th level and every four levels thereafter (10 at 4th level, 15 at 8th level, and 20 at 12th level).

Spell-Like Abilities: A disciple of Ashardalon gains spell-like abilities as it increases in level. Its caster level is equal to its class level, and its saving throw DCs are 10 + its Cha modifier + spell level. Once an ability is gained, the disciple can use it a certain number of times per day, as follows: 3/day—*darkness, poison, unholy aura;* 1/day—

Table 2–5: The Disciple of Ashardalon

Class Level	Base Attack Bonus	Fort Save	Ref Save	Will Save	Special
1st	+1	+2	+0	+2	Fiendbond, resistance 5, *darkness*
2nd	+2	+3	+0	+3	*Desecrate,* skill point increase
3rd	+3	+3	+1	+3	*Unholy blight,* ability increase (Str, Dex, Int)
4th	+4	+4	+1	+4	Resistance 10, *poison*
5th	+5	+4	+1	+4	*Contagion*
6th	+6	+5	+2	+5	Poison immunity, *blasphemy,* ability increase (Str, Dex, Con, Int, Cha)
7th	+7	+5	+2	+5	*Unhallow,* natural armor increase
8th	+8	+6	+2	+6	Resistance 15, *unholy aura*
9th	+9	+6	+3	+6	*Horrid wilting,* ability increase (Str, Dex, Int)
10th	+10	+7	+3	+7	Skill point increase
11th	+11	+7	+3	+7	*Destruction*
12th	+12	+8	+4	+8	Resistance 20, ability increase (Str, Dex, Con, Int, Cha), fiendish perfection

blasphemy, contagion, desecrate, destruction, horrid wilting, unhallow, unholy aura, unholy blight.

Skill Point Increase: At 2nd level, and again at 10th level, a disciple of Ashardalon gains a pool of bonus skill points equal to the number of dragon Hit Dice it possesses. This pool represents a gradual transition from being a creature of the dragon type (with 6 skill points per HD) to being an outsider (with 8 skill points per HD). These bonus skill points are in addition to the skill points gained at every level, and are not modified by the dragon's Intelligence score.

Ability Increase: Every three levels, a disciple of Ashardalon's ability scores increase automatically. At 3rd, 6th, 9th, and 12th level, its Strength, Dexterity, and Intelligence all increase by 1 point. At 6th and 12th level, its Constitution and Charisma also increase by 1 point. By 12th level, a disciple of Ashardalon has the ability score adjustments of the half-fiend template.

Poison Immunity (Ex): A disciple of Ashardalon of 6th level or higher is immune to all forms of poison.

Natural Armor Increase (Ex): At 7th level, a disciple of Ashardalon's natural armor bonus improves by 1.

Fiendish Perfection (Ex): At 12th level, a disciple of Ashardalon's bond with its demonic spirit is complete and perfect. The dragon now has the half-fiend template and becomes an outsider rather than a dragon.

DISPASSIONATE WATCHER OF CHRONEPSIS

The draconic deity of fate, death, and judgment, Chronepsis is silent, unconcerned, and dispassionate. Most dragons respect him, but few revere him or serve him as clerics because of his neutral alignment. Chromatic and metallic dragons are almost always too committed to philosophical extremes to become clerics of Chronepsis, and their passionate adherence to their alignment means they have little interest in the detached attitude of the watchers. Most dispassionate watchers are gem dragons, brown dragons, fang dragons, song dragons, dragon turtles, or wyverns.

True to their name, dispassionate watchers of Chronepsis remain aloof from the events of the world around them, taking the role of observers rather than active participants. They are excellent sources of information and advice, and dragons often appeal to them to judge disputes and complaints. They typically make their lairs in areas that other dragons use as graveyards, embodying their deity's aspect as a god of death and keeping the graves safe from robbers and defilers.

Hit Die: d8.

Requirements

To qualify to become a dispassionate watcher, a dragon must fulfill all the following criteria.

Race: Any dragon.

Alignment: Any neutral.

Skills: Knowledge (any two) 20 ranks.

Spells: Able to cast divine spells.

Domain: Knowledge (or able to cast at least three Knowledge domain spells as arcane spells).

Class Skills

The dispassionate watcher's class skills (and the key ability for each skill) are Concentration (Int), Decipher Script (Int), Knowledge (all skills, taken individually) (Int), and Spellcraft (Int). See Chapter 4: Skills in the *Player's Handbook* for skill descriptions.

Skill Points at Each Level: 2 + Int modifier.

Class Features

The following are class features of the dispassionate watcher of Chronepsis prestige class.

Weapon and Armor Proficiency: A dispassionate watcher gains no proficiency with any weapons, armor, or shields.

Divine Conversion: At 1st level, a dispassionate watcher loses any effective sorcerer level it had previously gained by virtue of its age and draconic variety. Its effective divine spellcasting level increases by the number of sorcerer levels it sacrificed. These effective levels apply only to the dragon's spellcasting, not to other class abilities (such as turning undead).

For example, a very old amethyst dragon/1st-level cleric adopts the dispassionate watcher of Chronepsis prestige class. Its sorcerer caster level of 11th converts into eleven effective cleric levels, giving the dragon the spellcasting ability of a 12th-level cleric.

A dispassionate watcher of Chronepsis

Illus. by D. Hudnut

Table 2–6: The Dispassionate Watcher of Chronepsis

Class Level	Base Attack Bonus	Fort Save	Ref Save	Will Save	Special	Spellcasting
1st	+0	+2	+0	+2	Divine conversion, calming aura, Draconic Knowledge	—
2nd	+1	+3	+0	+3	*Comprehend languages*	+1 level of existing class
3rd	+2	+3	+1	+3	—	+1 level of existing class
4th	+3	+4	+1	+4	Stunning rebuke	+1 level of existing class
5th	+3	+4	+1	+4	*Tongues*	+1 level of existing class
6th	+4	+5	+2	+5	*Discern lies*	+1 level of existing class
7th	+5	+5	+2	+5	—	+1 level of existing class
8th	+6	+6	+2	+6	—	+1 level of existing class
9th	+6	+6	+3	+6	Clearsight	+1 level of existing class
10th	+7	+7	+3	+7	*Vision*	+1 level of existing class
11th	+8	+7	+3	+7	—	+1 level of existing class
12th	+9	+8	+4	+8	*Analyze dweomer*	+1 level of existing class

Calming Aura (Su): At 1st level, a dispassionate watcher loses its frightful presence ability (if it had one), gaining instead an infectious aura of calm detachment. This aura has the same radius and Will save DC as the dragon's frightful presence ability, if it had one. If it did not possess frightful presence, the radius is equal to 5 feet per 2 HD the dragon possesses (counting only its base dragon Hit Dice, not any class levels). The Will saving throw to resist the effect has a DC of 10 + 1/2 dragon's base HD + its Cha modifier. The effect of the aura is the same as that of a *calm emotions* spell, but it lasts as long as the dispassionate watcher does not attack.

Draconic Knowledge: A dispassionate watcher gains Draconic Knowledge (see page 69) as a bonus feat. It uses its dispassionate watcher level as an additional modifier on its draconic knowledge checks.

Spellcasting: From 2nd level on, when a new dispassionate watcher level is gained, the dragon gains new spells per day as if it had also gained a level in a divine spellcasting class it belonged to before it added the prestige class. It does not, however, gain any other benefit a character of that class would have gained (an improved chance of turning or rebuking undead, wild shape, and so on). This essentially means that the dragon adds the level of dispassionate watcher to the level of whatever divine spellcasting class the dragon has, then determines spells per day and caster level accordingly.

If the dragon had more than one divine spellcasting class before becoming a dispassionate watcher, the dragon must decide to which class it adds each level of dispassionate watcher for the purpose of determining spells per day.

A very old amethyst dragon/1st-level cleric/2nd-level dispassionate watcher has the spellcasting ability of a 13th-level cleric: 11 from divine conversion of its sorcerer spellcasting levels, 1 from its single cleric level, and 1 from its two levels in the prestige class.

If a dragon advances an age category after taking levels in this class, the added levels of spellcasting ability are added to its effective divine spellcasting level. If the very old amethyst dragon in the example above lives to be ancient, its spellcasting level would increase by 2, so it would cast spells as a 15th-level cleric.

***Comprehend Languages* (Sp):** At 2nd level, a dispassionate watcher gains the ability to use *comprehend languages* at will.

Stunning Rebuke (Su): A 4th-level dispassionate watcher can deliver a thunderous rebuke that stuns one creature of its choice within 100 feet. If the target creature fails a Will saving throw (DC 10 + dispassionate watcher's class level + 1/2 its Cha modifier), it is stunned for 1d4+1 rounds. This is a sonic effect, but is not language-dependent.

***Tongues* (Sp):** A 5th-level dispassionate watcher can use *tongues* at will.

Discern Lies (Su): At 6th level, a dispassionate watcher knows when anyone (other than a deity) is deliberately lying. This ability is like the *discern lies* spell, except that it works continuously and applies to any creature the dragon can perceive.

Clearsight (Ex): A 9th-level dispassionate watcher can see illusions, transmuted creatures and objects, and disguised creatures and objects for what they really are, provided they are within 30 feet of the dragon. This ability is similar to the *true seeing* spell, except that it also foils mundane disguises.

***Vision* (Sp):** At 10th level, a dispassionate watcher gains the ability to use *vision* three times per day. Using this ability is only a standard action for the dragon.

***Analyze Dweomer* (Sp):** A 12th-level dispassionate watcher can use *analyze dweomer* at will.

DRAGON ASCENDANT

Easily the most powerful creatures native to the Material Plane, dragons hold a unique position in relation to the powers beyond that plane. Those who become dragon ascendants quest to transcend the limitations of material existence, rising above all other dragons to become nothing less than deities themselves. Their progress through the levels of this class represents their advancement toward their ultimate goal, and they become increasingly godlike as they advance.

Most dragon ascendants have not previously gained class levels, but all are dragons of considerable age and power. A few dragon clerics, paladins, and blackguards move into the dragon ascendant prestige class when they reach sufficient levels of power. Members of the divine prestige classes described in this chapter (the dispassionate watcher of Chronepsis, the sacred warder of Bahamut, and the unholy ravager of Tiamat) sometimes also choose the path of divine ascension to become more perfect servants of their deities.

Dragon ascendants are proud and typically aloof. They view travel along the path toward divine ascension as a race, and do not choose to share the road with others on the same course. On the other hand, they often have followers and allies who support them on their quest, and they work more freely with lesser dragons and nondragons than other dragons do.

Hit Die: d12.

Requirements

To qualify to become a dragon ascendant, a dragon must fulfill all the following criteria.

Race: Any true dragon.

Base Attack Bonus: +30.

Feats: Draconic Knowledge, Fast Healing, Great Fortitude, Improved Speed, Iron Will, Lightning Reflexes.

Special: *Consume Hoard:* A would-be dragon ascendant must eat its hoard to begin the process of divine ascension. Its hoard must have a value of at least 100,000 gp, but the dragon cannot choose to eat just 100,000 gp and leave the rest alone—it must consume its entire hoard.

Class Skills

The dragon ascendant's class skills (and the key ability for each skill) are Concentration (Con), Diplomacy (Cha), Heal (Wis), Intimidate (Cha), Jump (Str), Knowledge (arcana) (Int), Knowledge (the planes) (Int), Knowledge (religion) (Int), Listen (Wis), Search (Int), Sense Motive (Wis), Spellcraft (Int), and Spot (Wis). See Chapter 4: Skills in the *Player's Handbook* for skill descriptions.

A dragon ascendant

Skill Points at Each Level: 6 + Int modifier.

Class Features

The following are class features of the dragon ascendant prestige class.

Weapon and Armor Proficiency: A dragon ascendant gains no proficiency with any weapons, armor, or shields.

Awesome Aura (Ex): A dragon ascendant loses its innate frightful presence, replacing it with a special fear aura. This aura surrounds the dragon at any radius it chooses up to the extent of its frightful presence (30 feet × the dragon's age category), and is always active unless the dragon chooses to deactivate it. The dragon can choose to exclude its own allies from the effect of its aura. Creatures within the aura must make a Will save (DC equal to the dragon's frightful presence DC plus 1/2 its dragon ascendant levels). Creatures that fail their saving throws are shaken, while those that succeed are immune to the effect of that dragon's aura for 24 hours. If the dragon attacks or charges, shaken creatures must attempt a second Will save (same DC) or become frightened.

Illus. by J. Jarvis

Table 2–7: The Dragon Ascendant

Class Level	Base Attack Bonus	Fort Save	Ref Save	Will Save	Special
1st	+1	+2	+2	+2	Awesome aura (fear)
2nd	+2	+3	+3	+3	Hit point increase
3rd	+3	+3	+3	+3	Transmutation immunity
4th	+4	+4	+4	+4	Hit point increase, increased damage reduction
5th	+5	+4	+4	+4	Awesome aura (resolve)
6th	+6	+5	+5	+5	Hit point increase, lifewarding
7th	+7	+5	+5	+5	Deflection bonus
8th	+8	+6	+6	+6	Hit point increase, increased damage reduction
9th	+9	+6	+6	+6	Iron mind
10th	+10	+7	+7	+7	Awesome aura (daze), hit point increase
11th	+11	+7	+7	+7	Resistance to fire, spell resistance
12th	+12	+8	+8	+8	Hit point increase, immortality

When a dragon ascendant reaches 5th level, it can choose to modify its aura to inspire resolve in its allies and dread in its enemies. All allies of the dragon within the radius of its aura receive a +4 morale bonus on attack rolls, saves, and checks. The dragon's foes must succeed on a Will saving throw or take a –4 penalty on attack rolls, saves, and checks.

When a dragon ascendant reaches 10th level, it gains a third option for its aura. The dragon can cause affected creatures to become dazed, simply staring at the dragon in fascinated awe, if they fail their Will saves. As with the fear aspect of the aura, the dragon can choose to exclude its allies from the effects of the aura.

All uses of a dragon's awesome aura are mind-affecting effects.

Hit Point Increase (Ex): At 2nd level, and every two levels thereafter, a dragon ascendant gains 1 hit point per Hit Die it possesses, including all its dragon Hit Dice and those gained from class levels. This benefit can never increase a dragon's hit points above the maximum for its Hit Dice and Constitution bonus.

At 12th level, a dragon ascendant's hit points are equal to the maximum for its Hit Dice and Constitution bonus.

Transmutation Immunity (Ex): At 3rd level, a dragon ascendant gains immunity to polymorphing, petrification, and any other attack that would alter its form. Any shape-altering powers or spells the dragon has work normally on itself.

Increased Damage Reduction (Su): At 4th level, a dragon ascendant's damage reduction can be overcome only by epic weapons. At 8th level, the amount of the dragon's damage reduction (the number before the slash) is increased by 5. For example, an ancient black dragon/8th-level dragon ascendant has damage reduction 20/epic.

Lifewarding (Ex): At 6th level, a dragon ascendant is no longer vulnerable to attacks that cause energy drain, ability drain, or ability damage.

Deflection Bonus (Su): At 7th level, a dragon ascendant gains a deflection bonus to its Armor Class equal to its Charisma bonus, if any.

Iron Mind (Ex): At 9th level, a dragon ascendant becomes immune to mind-affecting effects (charms, compulsions, phantasms, patterns, and morale effects).

Resistance to Fire (Ex): At 11th level, a dragon ascendant gains resistance to fire 20, if it does not already possess immunity to fire.

Spell Resistance (Ex): At 11th level, a dragon ascendant's spell resistance increases to 33.

Immortality (Ex): A 12th-level dragon ascendant is actually a quasi-deity, and can no longer die from natural causes. It does not need to eat, sleep, or breathe. It can still be slain in physical or magical combat, and it is still subject to death from massive damage.

Code of Conduct: A dragon ascendant must be absolutely true to the principles of its alignment, whatever they may be. A dragon ascendant loses its awesome aura if it ever willingly commits an act opposed to its alignment (and it does not regain its frightful presence), and it cannot gain more levels as a dragon ascendant. The dragon can regain its awesome aura and once more advance in the dragon ascendant prestige class if it atones for its violations (see the *atonement* spell in the *Player's Handbook*), as appropriate.

ELEMENTAL MASTER

Dragons are creatures of raw elemental power. Two mighty forces rage within their veins: the energy that powers their breath weapons, and the elemental nature that forms the core of their being. Elemental masters strive to attain the purity of perfect attunement with both of these forces.

The path of the elemental master is almost exclusively pursued by true dragons, since the class requires a connection to elemental and energy forces. Some dragons have levels in other classes, commonly wizard or sorcerer, before adopting this prestige class, but many others do not.

Elemental masters are the most solitary and reclusive of dragons, spending their lives in communion with the natural forces of the universe rather than interacting with creatures they consider to be lesser life forms. When they do cooperate with other creatures, they choose elementals and outsiders from the elemental planes as their allies, and occasionally younger dragons of the same variety.

Hit Die: d12.

Requirements

To qualify to become an elemental master, a dragon must fulfill all the following criteria.

Race: Any dragon.

Base Attack Bonus: +20.

Feats: Any three metabreath feats.

Spells: Able to cast arcane spells.

Special: *Elemental Attunement:* The dragon must have an energy or elemental subtype, such as air, cold, earth, electricity, fire, or water.

Breath Weapon: The dragon must have a breath weapon that deals energy damage.

Class Skills

The elemental master's class skills (and the key ability for each skill) are Concentration (Con), Knowledge (arcana) (Int), Knowledge (geography) (Int), Knowledge (nature) (Int), Knowledge (the planes) (Int), Spellcraft (Int), and Survival (Wis). See Chapter 4: Skills in the *Player's Handbook* for skill descriptions.

Skill Points at Each Level: 2 + Int modifier.

Class Features

The following are class features of the elemental master prestige class.

Weapon and Armor Proficiency: An elemental master gains no proficiency with any weapons, armor, or shields.

Element Mastery (Ex): At 1st level, an elemental master gains an additional attunement to the element type that corresponds to its subtype.

Dragons with the air or electricity subtype (including emerald, green, crystal, fang, and song dragons) gain air mastery: Any airborne creature takes a –1 penalty on attack and damage rolls made against the dragon.

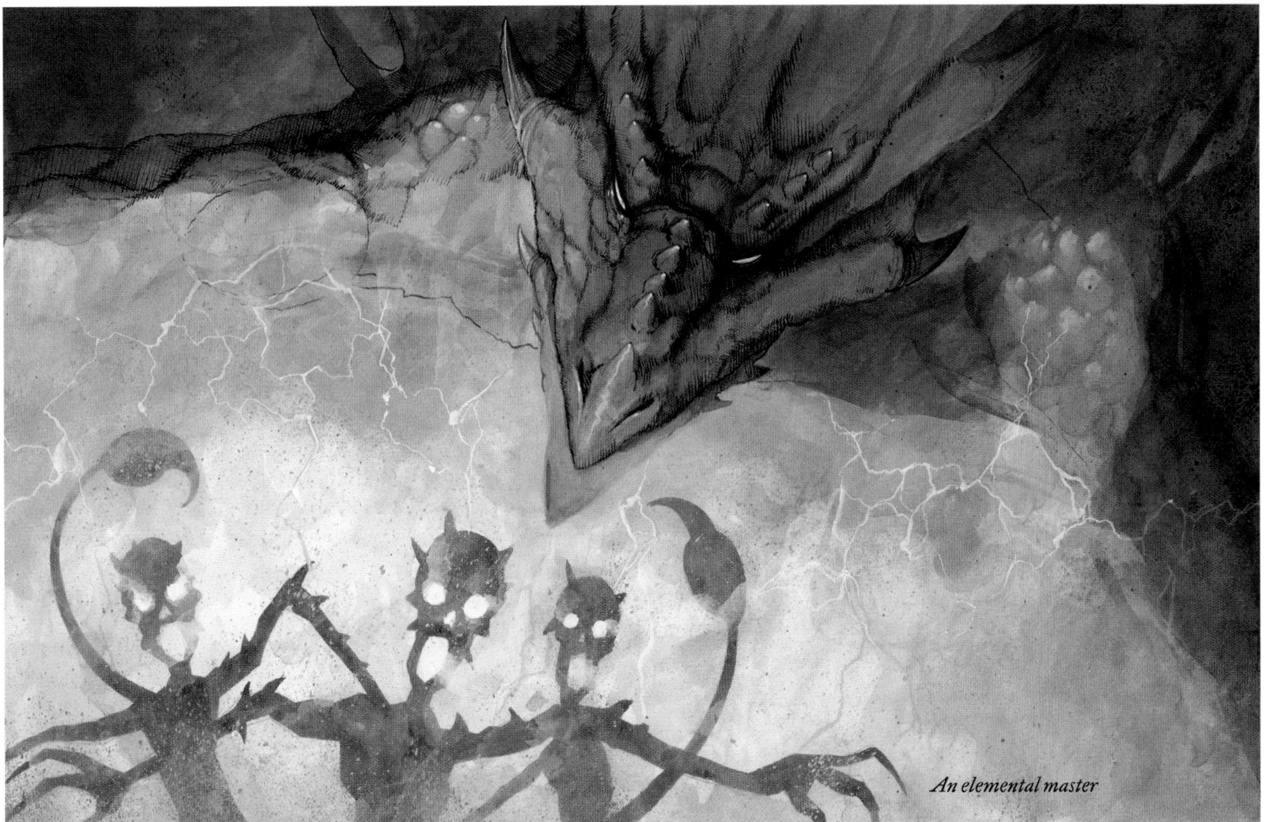
An elemental master

Dragons with the earth subtype (including blue, copper, amethyst, brown, deep, and sapphire dragons) gain earth mastery: The dragon gains a +1 bonus on attack and damage rolls if both it and its foe are touching the ground.

Dragons with the fire subtype (including red, gold, and brass dragons, as well as hellfire wyrms) gain fire mastery: The dragon gains a +1 bonus on attack and damage rolls if both it and its foe are touching fire or using weapons with the flaming or flaming burst special abilities.

Dragons with the water subtype (including black, bronze, and topaz dragons) gain water mastery: The dragon gains a +1 bonus on its attack and damage rolls if both it and its opponent are touching water.

Dragons with the cold subtype (silver and white dragons) gain cold mastery: The dragon gains a +1 bonus on attack and damage rolls if both it and its foe are touching ice or using weapons with the frost or icy burst special abilities.

Elemental Command (Su): An elemental master can turn or destroy creatures of the elemental subtype opposed to its own subtype, just as a good cleric turns undead. It can rebuke or command creatures of its own elemental subtype, as an evil cleric rebukes undead. The dragon can use these abilities a total number of times per day equal to 3 + its Charisma modifier.

Air and earth are opposed elemental subtypes; fire and water are opposed. Dragons with the cold subtype can rebuke cold creatures and turn fire creatures.

Energy Attunement (Ex): An elemental master is attuned to the energy type that powers its breath weapon. Dragons with more than one breath weapon gain attunement to the one that deals energy damage, usually acid, cold, electricity, fire, or sonic energy. A dragon with multiple energy breath weapons can choose a single energy type it is attuned to. This ability grants the dragon no special powers, but determines the form of powers it gains later, including energy substitution, energy focus, energy burst, and energy storm.

Energy Substitution (Ex): At 2nd level, an elemental master gains the ability to modify its spells that have an energy descriptor so that they use the dragon's attuned energy instead. The substituted spell works normally in all respects except the type of damage dealt.

***Summon Elemental* (Sp):** Once per day, starting at 2nd level, an elemental master can use its breath weapon to summon a Medium elemental corresponding to its elemental subtype. The dragon breathes as normal, but in the wake of its breath the elemental appears, attacking in the next round. If it chooses, the dragon can instead summon an adult arrowhawk (air or cold), average salamander (fire), adult tojanida (water), or average xorn (earth). This ability works like the *summon nature's ally V* spell, with the dragon's class level as its caster level. A dragon with the cold subtype can summon a Medium water elemental or an adult tojanida.

At 5th level, an elemental master can summon one Large elemental or two Medium elementals. This ability works like the *summon nature's ally VI* spell.

At 8th level, an elemental master can summon one Huge elemental, two Large elementals, or four Medium elementals. Instead, the dragon can summon one elder arrowhawk, noble salamander, elder tojanida, or elder xorn, or four

Illus. by W. England

Table 2–8: The Elemental Master

Class Level	Base Attack Bonus	Fort Save	Ref Save	Will Save	Special
1st	+1	+2	+2	+2	Element mastery, elemental command, energy attunement
2nd	+2	+3	+3	+3	Energy substitution, *summon elemental I*
3rd	+3	+3	+3	+3	Energy focus +1
4th	+4	+4	+4	+4	Energy burst
5th	+5	+4	+4	+4	*Summon elemental II*
6th	+6	+5	+5	+5	Energy focus +2
7th	+7	+5	+5	+5	Energy storm
8th	+8	+6	+6	+6	*Summon elemental III*
9th	+9	+6	+6	+6	Energy focus +3
10th	+10	+7	+7	+7	Spell-like ability
11th	+11	+7	+7	+7	*Summon elemental IV*
12th	+12	+8	+8	+8	Elemental qualities, energy focus +4

Medium creatures of the appropriate kind. This ability works like the *summon nature's ally VII* spell.

At 11th level, an elemental master can summon one greater elemental, two Huge elementals, or four Large or Medium elementals. This ability works like the *summon nature's ally VIII* spell.

Energy Focus (Ex): At 3rd level, an elemental master adds 1 to the save DC of spells it casts with an energy descriptor corresponding to the dragon's attuned energy type.

This bonus increases by +1 for every additional three levels the elemental master gains (+2 at 6th level, +3 at 9th level, and +4 at 12th level), and it stacks with the bonus from the Spell Focus feat.

Energy Burst (Su): A 4th-level elemental master can create a burst of damaging energy around its body. The burst consists of energy corresponding to the dragon's attuned energy type and has a radius of 5 feet per class level of the dragon. Anything in the area takes 1d8 points of damage per class level of the dragon. A successful Reflex save (DC 10 + dragon's class level + its Con modifier) reduces the damage by half.

Creating an energy burst counts as a use of the dragon's breath weapon. It cannot breathe or create another burst for 1d4 rounds after creating a burst.

Energy Storm (Su): A 7th-level elemental master can surround itself with a vortex of swirling energy corresponding to the dragon's attuned energy type. The vortex extends from the dragon in an emanation with a radius of 5 feet per class level. The effect stops attacks with thrown weapons and projectiles. Such attacks fail if made by creatures inside the area, or if targeted at creatures within the area, or if their paths take them through the area. The storm deals 2 points of damage per class level to every unprotected creature within its area each round. The storm lasts for 1 round per class level (though the dragon can dismiss it as a move action), and counts as two uses of the dragon's breath weapon. The dragon cannot use its breath weapon (or its energy burst ability) while the storm is in place and for 2d4 rounds after it subsides.

Spell-Like Ability: At 10th level, an elemental master gains a spell-like ability associated with its elemental subtype. An air dragon can use *whirlwind*, an earth dragon *earthquake*, a fire dragon *incendiary cloud*, a water dragon *horrid wilting*, and a cold dragon *polar ray*. The dragon can use this ability three times per day, with a caster level of 20th.

Elemental Qualities (Ex): A 12th-level elemental master is immune to poison, sleep effects, paralysis, and stunning. It is not subject to critical hits or flanking.

HIDECARVED DRAGON

Hidecarved dragons are members of an enigmatic order of dragons and half-dragons. Their name comes from the markings engraved on their scales, which grant them incredible mystical protection. Dragons of the hidecarved order resemble monks in their strict discipline, dedication to personal perfection, and mystical transcendence.

Most hidecarved dragons are true dragons, since many drakes, landwyrms, wyverns, and other creatures of the dragon type lack the thick, heavy scales necessary to receive the mystical engravings of the order. A half-dragon can become a hidecarved dragon only if its nondragon parent had very significant natural armor, although some half-dragon/half-giants have been known to use magic to thicken their hides sufficiently to qualify for the class. Some dragons advance in other classes—commonly monk, wizard, sorcerer, or cleric—before adopting this prestige class, primarily to meet the minimum base Will save requirement.

Hidecarved dragons do not build monasteries, but they do gather in small groups called "lauths." These tiny communities of three to five dragons share a large territory and come together only occasionally, but will gather quickly to help if one member of the lauth is threatened.

Hit Die: d10.

Requirements

To qualify to become a hidecarved dragon, a dragon must fulfill all the following criteria.

Race: Any dragon.

Alignment: Any lawful.

Natural Armor Bonus: +20.

Base Save Bonus: Will +12.

Feat: Iron Will.

Class Skills

The hidecarved dragon's class skills (and the key ability for each skill) are Balance (Dex), Climb (Str), Concentration

(Con), Diplomacy (Cha), Escape Artist (Dex), Hide (Dex), Jump (Str), Knowledge (arcana) (Int), Knowledge (religion) (Int), Listen (Wis), Move Silently (Dex), Sense Motive (Wis), Spot (Wis), Swim (Str), and Tumble (Dex). See Chapter 4: Skills in the *Player's Handbook* for skill descriptions.

Skill Points at Each Level: 4 + Int modifier.

Class Features

The following are class features of the hidecarved dragon prestige class.

Weapon and Armor Proficiency: A hidecarved dragon gains no proficiency with any weapons, armor, or shields.

Increased Spell Resistance (Ex): A hidecarved dragon adds its class level to its natural spell resistance. Dragons without natural spell resistance do not gain spell resistance when they adopt this class. However, if a hidecarved dragon with no natural spell resistance ages to the point where it gains spell resistance, it adds its class level to the natural spell resistance it gains at its new age category.

Suppress Weakness: At 2nd level, a hidecarved dragon gains Suppress Weakness (see page 74) as a bonus feat.

Poison Resistance (Ex): At 2nd level, a hidecarved dragon gains a +4 bonus on saving throws against poison.

Energy Resistance (Ex): At 3rd level, a hidecarved dragon gains resistance 10 to two energy types it is not already immune, vulnerable, or resistant to. The dragon can choose from resistance to acid, cold, electricity, fire, or sonic energy. For example, a gold hidecarved dragon could gain resistance to acid 10 and electricity 10.

A hidecarved dragon

Still Mind (Ex): At 4th level, a hidecarved dragon gains a +2 bonus on saving throws against spells and effects from the enchantment school.

Natural Armor (Ex): At 4th level, a hidecarved dragon's natural armor bonus increases by +2. At 8th level the increase becomes +4, and at 12th level it becomes +6.

Increased Damage Reduction (Su): At 5th level, the amount of a hidecarved dragon's natural damage reduction (the number before the slash) increases by 5, and its damage reduction can be overcome only by chaotic magic weapons. For example, a mature adult blue dragon/5th-level hidecarved dragon has damage reduction 15/magic and chaotic.

Extra Energy Immunity (Ex): At 6th level, a hidecarved dragon gains immunity to an energy type it was already resistant to. Its resistance to one other energy type it has resistance 10 against increases to 20, and it gains resistance 10 against a third energy type. For this third energy type, a dragon with the fire subtype cannot choose cold, and a dragon with the cold subtype cannot choose fire.

The gold hidecarved dragon from the earlier example could become immune to electricity at 6th level, increase its acid resistance to 20, and gain resistance to sonic 10.

At 12th level, a hidecarved dragon's energy resistances and immunities improve again. Its resistance 20 becomes immunity, its resistance 10 becomes resistance 20, and it gains resistance 10 to all other energy types

Table 2–9: The Hidecarved Dragon

Class Level	Base Attack Bonus	Fort Save	Ref Save	Will Save	Special
1st	+1	+2	+2	+2	Increased spell resistance
2nd	+2	+3	+3	+3	Suppress Weakness, poison resistance
3rd	+3	+3	+3	+3	Energy resistance
4th	+4	+4	+4	+4	Still mind, natural armor +2
5th	+5	+4	+4	+4	Increased damage reduction
6th	+6	+5	+5	+5	Extra energy immunity
7th	+7	+5	+5	+5	Overcome Weakness, *death ward*
8th	+8	+6	+6	+6	Natural armor +4
9th	+9	+6	+6	+6	Wholeness of body
10th	+10	+7	+7	+7	Poison immunity
11th	+11	+7	+7	+7	Superior damage reduction
12th	+12	+8	+8	+8	Natural armor +6, extra energy immunity

(acid, cold, electricity, fire, and sonic) that it is not already immune or resistant to.

The gold hidecarved dragon example, at 12th level, would have immunity to fire (naturally), electricity (since 6th level), and acid. It would have resistance to sonic 20 and cold 10.

Overcome Weakness: At 7th level, a hidecarved dragon gains Overcome Weakness (see page 72) as a bonus feat.

***Death Ward* (Sp):** At 7th level, a hidecarved dragon gains the ability to use *death ward* on itself once per day as a cleric of its class level.

Wholeness of Body (Su): At 9th level, a hidecarved dragon can cure its own wounds. It can cure up to three times its class level in hit points each day and can spread this healing out among several uses.

Poison Immunity (Ex): At 10th level, a hidecarved dragon gains immunity to poison of all kinds.

Superior Damage Reduction (Su): At 11th level, a hidecarved dragon's damage reduction can be overcome only by epic chaotic weapons. For example, a mature adult blue dragon/11th-level hidecarved dragon has damage reduction 15/epic and chaotic.

SACRED WARDER OF BAHAMUT

Among dragon clerics of Bahamut, some are moved primarily by compassion for those who suffer from the depredations of evil dragons. These clerics adopt the sacred warder of Bahamut prestige class, shaping their identities around the idea of protecting those who cannot hope to protect themselves from the awesome power of Tiamat's brood.

Sacred warders of Bahamut are usually gold or silver dragons with some levels in the cleric class. Good half-dragons are surprisingly common among the ranks of the sacred warders, and they find more acceptance there than in most other dragon groups and organizations. Sacred warders often possess some levels of paladin as well as cleric; other classes are rare.

Sacred warders can be found anywhere evil dragons threaten other creatures. Their usually lawful alignment inclines them to cooperate with other creatures. They sometimes operate in pairs, but more often work with groups of humanoids or other creatures drawn from the communities they try to protect.

Hit Die: d10.

Requirements

To qualify to become a sacred warder of Bahamut, a dragon must fulfill all the following criteria.

Race: Any dragon.

Alignment: Lawful good or neutral good.

Base Attack Bonus: +15.

Feats: Endure Blows, Power Attack.

Spells: Able to cast divine spells.

Domain: Protection.

Special: Damage reduction 5/magic.

Class Skills

The sacred warder's class skills (and the key ability for each skill) are Concentration (Con), Diplomacy (Cha), Heal (Wis), Knowledge (religion) (Int), and Sense Motive (Wis). See Chapter 4: Skills in the *Player's Handbook* for skill descriptions.

Skill Points at Each Level: 2 + Int modifier.

Class Features

The following are class features of the sacred warder of Bahamut prestige class.

Weapon and Armor Proficiency: A sacred warder gains no proficiency with any weapons, armor, or shields.

Divine Conversion: At 1st level, a sacred warder loses any effective sorcerer level it had previously gained by virtue of its age and draconic variety. Its effective divine spellcasting level increases by the number of sorcerer levels it sacrificed, allowing the dragon to cast cleric spells much more effectively. These effective levels apply only to the dragon's spellcasting, not to other class abilities (such as turning undead or wild shape).

For example, a very old gold dragon/1st-level cleric adopts the sacred warder of Bahamut prestige class. Its sorcerer caster level of 13th converts into thirteen effective cleric levels, giving the dragon the spellcasting ability of a 14th-level cleric.

Smite Evil Dragons (Su): Once per day, a sacred warder of Bahamut of at least 2nd level may attempt to smite an evil dragon with one normal melee attack. It adds its Charisma bonus to its attack roll and deals 1 extra point of damage per class level. If the sacred warder accidentally smites a dragon that is not evil, or a creature that is not a dragon, the smite

Table 2–10: The Sacred Warder of Bahamut

Class Level	Base Attack Bonus	Fort Save	Ref Save	Will Save	Special	Spellcasting
1st	+1	+2	+0	+2	Divine conversion	—
2nd	+2	+3	+0	+3	Smite evil dragons 1/day	+1 level of existing class
3rd	+3	+3	+1	+3	Aura of courage	+1 level of existing class
4th	+4	+4	+1	+4	—	+1 level of existing class
5th	+5	+4	+1	+4	—	+1 level of existing class
6th	+6	+5	+2	+5	Smite evil dragons 2/day	+1 level of existing class
7th	+7	+5	+2	+5	Sacred shield	+1 level of existing class
8th	+8	+6	+2	+6	—	+1 level of existing class
9th	+9	+6	+3	+6	—	+1 level of existing class
10th	+10	+7	+3	+7	Smite evil dragons 3/day	+1 level of existing class
11th	+11	+7	+3	+7	—	+1 level of existing class
12th	+12	+8	+4	+8	Area sacred shield	+1 level of existing class

has no effect but it is still used up for that day. A sacred warder can smite any creature of the dragon type that has an evil alignment.

At 6th level, a sacred warder may smite evil dragons twice per day, and at 10th level it can do so three times per day.

Spellcasting: From 2nd level on, when a new sacred warder level is gained, the dragon gains new spells per day as if it had also gained a level in a divine spellcasting class it belonged to before it added the prestige class. It does not, however, gain any other benefit a character of that class would have gained (an improved chance of turning or rebuking undead, wild shape, and so on). This essentially means that the dragon adds the level of sacred warder to the level of whatever divine spellcasting class the dragon has, then determines spells per day and caster level accordingly.

If the dragon had more than one divine spellcasting class before becoming a sacred warder, the dragon must decide to which class it adds each level of sacred warder for the purpose of determining spells per day.

A very old gold dragon/1st-level cleric/2nd-level sacred warder has the spellcasting ability of a 15th-level cleric: 13 from divine conversion of its sorcerer spellcasting levels, 1 from its single cleric level, and 1 from its two levels in the prestige class.

If a dragon advances an age category after taking levels in this class, the added levels of spellcasting ability are added to its effective divine spellcasting level. If the very old gold dragon in the example above lives to be ancient, its spellcasting level would increase by 2, so it would cast spells as a 17th-level cleric.

Aura of Courage (Ex): At 3rd level, a sacred warder becomes immune to fear effects. In addition, the dragon's frightful presence ability alters so that it inspires allies as well as striking terror into enemies. Allies within the radius of the dragon's aura (30 feet × its age category) are unaffected by the dragon's frightful presence and receive a morale bonus on their saving throws against fear equal to the dragon's class level + its Cha modifier. Allies within the aura cannot be panicked by an evil dragon's frightful presence, regardless of their Hit Dice.

Enemies within the aura are affected normally by the dragon's frightful presence.

Sacred Shield (Su): At 7th level, a sacred warder gains the ability to surround itself with a protective aura that lasts 10 minutes and protects the dragon's body and equipment from attacks. The shield absorbs 10 points of damage per class level. Once the shield absorbs that much damage, it collapses. The damage can be from any source—weapons, spells, any energy type, and so on. Damage the dragon would not take anyway (fire damage against a gold dragon, for example, or weapon damage blocked by the dragon's damage reduction) does not count against the damage absorbed by the shield. The dragon can use this ability three times per day.

Area Sacred Shield (Su): At 12th level, a sacred warder of Bahamut can extend its sacred shield to protect an area with a radius of 30 feet. The dragon can place the barrier anywhere within its line of sight, and can choose to make it mobile with respect to an unattended object or willing creature (including the dragon itself). The shield blocks incoming attacks, but creatures inside the shield can still attack out through the shield.

UNHOLY RAVAGER OF TIAMAT

The goddess of evil dragons and of conquest, Tiamat claims some allegiance from every evil dragon. Those who devote themselves entirely to her cause, however, are among the most fearsome forces of evil in the world, living embodiments of her destructive power. Unholy ravagers of Tiamat are dragon clerics that hope to attain a sliver of their deity's mighty power while aspiring to none of Tiamat's subtlety and sophistication. Unholy ravagers live only to destroy, and when they set their minds on destruction, no stone is left standing on another when they are finished.

Unholy ravagers of Tiamat are usually blue or green dragons with some levels of cleric. Though red dragons are born with a strong hereditary predisposition to chaos, a number of them stray from that alignment and end up as neutral evil unholy ravagers.

An unholy ravager typically works alone, but may drive marauding hordes of kobolds, lizardfolk, or hobgoblins ahead of itself to soften up the opposition—or lull its foes into overconfidence.

Hit Die: d10.

Requirements

To qualify to become an unholy ravager of Tiamat, a dragon must fulfill all the following criteria.

Race: Any dragon.

Alignment: Lawful evil or neutral evil.

Base Attack Bonus: +15.

Feats: Maximize Breath, Recover Breath, Tempest Breath.

Spells: Able to cast divine spells.

Domain: Destruction.

Class Skills

The unholy ravager's class skills (and the key ability for each skill) are Climb (Str), Concentration (Con), Intimidate (Cha), Jump (Str), Knowledge (arcana) (Int), Knowledge (religion) (Int), Spellcraft (Int), Survival (Wis), and Swim (Str). See Chapter 4: Skills in the *Player's Handbook* for skill descriptions.

Skill Points at Each Level: 2 + Int modifier.

Class Features

The following are class features of the unholy ravager of Tiamat prestige class.

Weapon and Armor Proficiency: An unholy ravager gains no proficiency with any weapons, armor, or shields.

Divine Conversion: At 1st level, an unholy ravager loses any effective sorcerer level it had previously gained by virtue of its age and draconic variety. Its effective divine spellcasting level increases by the number of sorcerer levels it sacrificed, allowing the dragon to cast cleric spells much more effectively. These effective levels apply only to the dragon's spellcasting, not to other class abilities (such as turning undead or wild shape).

A sacred warder of Bahamut protects innocents from an unholy ravager of Tiamat.

For example, a very old red dragon/1st-level cleric adopts the unholy ravager of Tiamat prestige class. Its sorcerer caster level of 13th converts into thirteen effective cleric levels in addition to its 1 level of cleric, giving the dragon the spellcasting ability of a 14th-level cleric.

Smite: An unholy ravager of Tiamat adds its class levels to its cleric levels to determine its bonus on damage when using its smite ability (the granted power of the Destruction domain).

At 4th level, 8th level, and 12th level, an unholy ravager can use its smite ability one additional time per day.

Spellcasting: From 2nd level on, when a new unholy ravager level is gained, the dragon gains new spells per day as if it had also gained a level in a divine spellcasting class it belonged to before it added the prestige class. It does not, however, gain any other benefit a character of that class would have gained (an improved chance of turning or rebuking undead, wild shape, and so on). This essentially means that the dragon adds the level of unholy ravager to the level of whatever divine spellcasting class the dragon has, then determines spells per day and caster level accordingly.

If the dragon had more than one divine spellcasting class before becoming an unholy ravager, the dragon must decide to which class it adds each level of unholy ravager for the purpose of determining spells per day.

A very old red dragon/1st-level cleric/2nd-level unholy ravager has the spellcasting ability of a 15th-level cleric: 13 from divine conversion of its sorcerer spellcasting levels, 1 from its single cleric level, and 1 from its two levels in the prestige class.

If a dragon advances an age category after taking levels in this class, the added levels of spellcasting ability are added to its effective divine spellcasting level. If the very old red dragon example above lives to be ancient, its spellcasting level would increase by 2, so it would cast spells as a 17th-level cleric.

***Breath Weapon Substitution* (Sp):** A 2nd-level unholy ravager of Tiamat can use *breath weapon substitution* at will. However, using this ability increases the number of rounds the dragon must wait before using its breath weapon again by 1 round, as if it were using a metabreath feat.

Aura of Despair (Su): At 3rd level, an unholy ravager's frightful presence alters slightly. In addition to the fear effect, creatures within the radius of the dragon's frightful

Table 2–11: The Unholy Ravager of Tiamat

Class Level	Base Attack Bonus	Fort Save	Ref Save	Will Save	Special	Spellcasting
1st	+1	+2	+0	+2	Divine conversion, smite	—
2nd	+2	+3	+0	+3	*Breath weapon substitution*	+1 level of existing class
3rd	+3	+3	+1	+3	Aura of despair	+1 level of existing class
4th	+4	+4	+1	+4	Smite 2/day	+1 level of existing class
5th	+5	+4	+1	+4		+1 level of existing class
6th	+6	+5	+2	+5		+1 level of existing class
7th	+7	+5	+2	+5	Profane blast	+1 level of existing class
8th	+8	+6	+2	+6	Smite 3/day	+1 level of existing class
9th	+9	+6	+3	+6		+1 level of existing class
10th	+10	+7	+3	+7		+1 level of existing class
11th	+11	+7	+3	+7		+1 level of existing class
12th	+12	+8	+4	+8	Mass profane blast, smite 4/day	+1 level of existing class

presence take a –2 penalty on all saving throws. This penalty is applied before creatures roll their saving throws against the frightful presence effect itself.

Profane Blast (Su): At 7th level, an unholy ravager of Tiamat can unleash a narrow blast of raw profane energy from its mouth three times per day. The blast is a ray, requiring a ranged touch attack, with a range of 400 feet + 40 feet per class level. The blast looks and feels like energy of the same type as the dragon's breath weapon. If it hits a target, it deals the same number of dice worth of damage as the dragon's breath weapon, but uses d12s. (So, a great wyrm blue dragon would deal 24d12 points of damage with its profane blast.) The damage it deals results directly from divine power and is therefore not subject to being reduced by *protection from energy* and similar magic. Each use of this ability counts as a use of the dragon's breath weapon, so it cannot use its breath weapon for 1d4 rounds after issuing a profane blast.

An unholy ravager can target a creature behind a *wall of force, prismatic wall,* or *prismatic sphere* with its profane blast. The dragon makes a special dispel check, rolling 1d20 + its age category + its class level against a DC of 11 + the effect's caster level. If this check is successful, the effect is instantly negated (all layers in a prismatic effect are destroyed) and the ray goes on to strike the intended target (if the ranged touch attack roll is successful). A profane blast is stopped normally by a sacred warder of Bahamut's sacred shield.

Mass Profane Blast (Su): At 12th level, an unholy ravager of Tiamat's profane blast occupies the same area as its breath weapon and affects all creatures within that area. The dragon can choose whether to use a ray profane blast or a mass profane blast, and can use both abilities no more than a total of three times per day.

If a *wall of force* or prismatic effect is within the area of a mass profane blast, the dragon makes a special dispel check as described above for each such effect within the area.

ADVANCED DRAGONS

The advancement rules in the *Monster Manual* allow dragons theoretically infinite progression even beyond the statistics of great wyrm. This book lets dragons improve more than their Hit Dice as they progress to unparalleled heights of power.

Age Category: A standard dragon gains one "virtual age category" for every 3 Hit Dice it gains beyond the great wyrm stage. A 61 HD red dragon, with 21 more Hit Dice than a standard great wyrm, has gained seven virtual age categories, meaning its effective age category is nineteen. Abilities that function once per day per age category or otherwise use the dragon's age category as part of a calculation use this adjusted number.

Size: One important element of dragon advancement is increasing size. The dragons that don't reach Colossal size by the great wyrm stage can never reach it according to the standard advancement rules. When advancing a dragon, consider its basic size group: smaller (black, brass, copper, and white dragons), normal (blue, bronze, and green dragons), or larger (gold, red, and silver dragons). A dragon that is Tiny as a wyrmling is in the smaller group, a dragon that is Small as a wyrmling and never reaches Colossal size is in the normal group, and a dragon that is Small to Large as a wyrmling and reaches Colossal by the great wyrm stage is in the larger group.

A smaller-sized dragon becomes Colossal when it gains two age categories (+6 HD) beyond great wyrm. It increases to Colossal+ (see below) when it gains an additional four age categories (+18 HD total). Thus, a white great wyrm reaches Colossal size at 42 HD and Colossal+ at 54 HD, while a brass great wyrm becomes Colossal at 43 HD and Colossal+ at 55 HD.

A normal-sized dragon becomes Colossal when it gains one age category (3 Hit Dice) beyond great wyrm. It increases to Colossal+ when it gains an additional four age categories (+15 HD total). Thus, a green great wyrm reaches Colossal size at 41 HD and Colossal+ size at 53 HD, while a bronze dragon becomes Colossal at 42 HD and Colossal+ at 54 HD.

A larger-sized dragon becomes Colossal+ when it gains four age categories (12 HD) more than it needed to reach the Colossal size. Thus, a silver or red dragon becomes Colossal+ at 52 HD, and a gold dragon becomes Colossal+ at 53 HD.

Colossal+ Size: Although there is no size category larger than Colossal, the largest advanced dragons have a greater reach and deal more damage with their attacks than other Colossal dragons. These dragons are said to be of Colossal+ ("Colossal plus") size.

A Colossal+ dragon has a space of 30 feet, like any other Colossal dragon, but its reach is 10 feet longer than normal with each attack form, and it has a proportionately longer tail slap and tail sweep. A Colossal+ dragon deals 6d6 points of damage with its bite attack, 4d8 with its claws, 4d6 with its wings, 4d8 with its tail slap, 6d6 with its crush, and 4d6 with its tail sweep.

A Colossal+ dragon's line-shaped breath weapon extends 160 feet (5 feet high and 5 feet wide, as normal). A Colossal+ dragon's cone-shaped breath weapon is 80 feet long, 80 feet high, and 80 feet wide. The size modifier for these dragons remains –8.

Armor Class: An advanced dragon's natural armor bonus increases by +1 for every Hit Die it gains beyond the great wyrm stage. (You can use this rule for lesser dragon advancement as well, since natural armor and Hit Dice always increase at the same rate.)

Breath Weapon: If an advanced dragon's breath weapon deals damage, the damage typically increases by 2 dice for every virtual age category the dragon gains. The two exceptions in the *Monster Manual* are the brass and white dragons, whose breath weapon damage increases by only 1 die per age category. The saving throw DC against the breath weapon remains 10 + 1/2 the dragon's HD + its Con modifier.

Spell Resistance: An advanced dragon's spell resistance increases by 2 per additional age category.

Speed: An advanced dragon's fly speed, maneuverability, land speed, and other special movement types (swim, burrow, and so on) do not change.

Ability Scores: A great wyrm's Strength and Constitution scores both increase by 2 points for every virtual age category the dragon gains. Its Dexterity remains unchanged. Its Intelligence, Wisdom, and Charisma increase by 2 points for every two virtual age categories the dragon gains.

Special Abilities: Dragons do not gain additional spell-like abilities. When a dragon gains one virtual age category beyond the great wyrm stage, its damage reduction improves to 20/epic.

Caster Level: A great wyrm's sorcerer caster level increases by 2 for every virtual age category the dragon gains.

Feats: Like ordinary dragons, advanced dragons receive one feat for every 4 Hit Dice they have. Any feats gained after the dragon reaches old age can be epic feats (see the descriptions earlier in this chapter).

Challenge Rating: An advanced dragon's Challenge Rating increases by 2 per additional virtual age category.

All other dragon statistics are as presented for dragons in general and specific dragon varieties in the *Monster Manual* and other sources.

SAMPLE ADVANCED DRAGON

This example uses a red dragon advanced to 61 Hit Dice. This advance represents an increase of 21 HD, or seven virtual age categories.

Advanced Red Great Wyrm: Male great wyrm red dragon; CR 40; Colossal+ dragon (fire); HD 61d12+1,037, hp 1,433; Init +3; Spd 40 ft., fly 200 ft. (clumsy); AC 70, touch 5, flat-footed 67; Base Atk +77; Grp +101; Atk +77 melee (6d6+24, bite); Full Atk +77 melee (6d6+24, bite), +72 melee (4d8+12, 2 claws), +72 melee (4d6+12, 2 wings), +72 melee (4d8+36, tail slap); Space/Reach 30 ft./30 ft.; SA breath weapon, crush, frightful presence, snatch, spell-like abilities, spells, tail sweep; SQ blindsense 60 ft., damage reduction 20/epic, darkvision 120 ft., immunity to fire, magic sleep effects, and paralysis, low-light vision, spell resistance 46, vulnerability to cold; AL CE; SV Fort +49, Ref +35, Will +43; Str 59, Dex 16 (with *gloves*), Con 45, Int 32, Wis 33, Cha 32.

Skills and Feats: Appraise +44, Balance +33, Bluff +75, Climb +54, Concentration +81, Diplomacy +79, Escape Artist +36, Heal +41, Intimidate +77, Jump +92, Knowledge (arcana) +75, Knowledge (history) +72, Knowledge (local) +72, Knowledge (nature) +72, Listen +72, Search +72, Sense Motive +72, Spellcraft +74, Spot +72, Survival +26, Swim +39; Blind-fight, Cleave, Combat Casting, Combat Reflexes, Dodge, Flyby Attack, Great Cleave, Hover, Improved Spell Capacity (10th), Improved Spell Capacity (11th), Improved Spell Capacity (12th), Improved Spell Capacity (13th), Mobility, Power Attack, Quicken Spell, Quicken Spell-Like Ability, Rend, Snatch, Spell Opportunity, Spellcasting Harrier, Wingover.

Breath Weapon (Su): 80-ft. cone, 38d10 fire, Reflex DC 57.

Crush (Ex): Area 30 ft. by 30 ft.; Huge or smaller opponents take 6d6+36 points of bludgeoning damage, and must succeed on a DC 57 Reflex save or be pinned.

Frightful Presence (Ex): 570-ft. radius, HD 60 or fewer, Will DC 51 negates.

Rend (Ex): Extra damage 8d8+36.

Snatch (Ex): Against Huge or smaller creatures, bite for 6d6+24/round or claw for 4d8+12/round.

Spell-Like Abilities: 19/day—*locate object*; 3/day—*suggestion*; 1/day—*discern location*. Caster level 33rd; save DC 21 + spell level.

Spells: As 33rd-level sorcerer.

Tail Sweep (Ex): Half-circle 40 ft. in diameter, Large or smaller opponents take 4d6+36 points of bludgeoning damage, Reflex DC 57 half.

Sorcerer Spells Known (6/9/9/9/8/8/8/8/7/7/2/2/1/1; save DC 21 + spell level): 0—*arcane mark, daze, detect magic, ghost sound, mage hand, prestidigitation, ray of frost, read magic, resistance;* 1st—*cause fear, expeditious retreat, magic missile, shield, ventriloquism;* 2nd—*darkness, detect thoughts, mirror image, see invisibility, web;* 3rd—*fireball, fly, haste, wind wall;* 4th—*confusion, polymorph, stoneskin;* 5th—*magic jar, passwall, teleport, wall of force;* 6th—*greater dispel magic, flesh to stone, true seeing;* 7th—*control undead, delayed blast fireball, prismatic spray;* 8th—*etherealness, horrid wilting, symbol of death;* 9th—*meteor swarm, power word kill, wish.*

Possessions: *Bracers of armor +5, gloves of Dexterity +6, ring of spell turning, major ring of elemental resistance (cold), chaos diamond,* 2,000 gp.

Illus. by J. Jarvis

A dragon is the player character's worst nightmare. It's likely the strongest foe he'll ever fight, as well as the smartest. The typical dragon has every conceivable advantage over an average group of adventurers, and then some. Any character who even thinks about fighting a dragon should have his head examined.

All of that is what dragons (and DMs) want players to think. They count on intimidating players (and their characters) before they even set out on the hunt. This chapter is designed for those characters brave enough to disregard the dire warnings, the lurid stories, and even common sense itself. This chapter is for *dragonslayers*.

This chapter also holds information for those who count a dragon among their allies—whether as cohort, mount, or familiar, as trusted ally or contact, or even as master.

FIGHTING A DRAGON

A dragon brings significant advantages to any combat—mobility, ranged attacks, keen senses, intelligence, durability, and, of course, the ability to deal out tremendous quantities of damage. Here are some tips for the would-be dragonslayer on how to even the odds.

FOREWARNED IS FOREARMED

Before you even think about fighting a dragon, do your research. Confirm the dragon's kind, age, and any other relevant factors before gearing up. Particularly if your DM utilizes dragons beyond those in the *Monster Manual*, it's not enough just to know that the dragon has "dark scales" or "breathes fire."

Start with mundane methods, such as Gather Information or bardic knowledge. Once you have a few good leads, divination magic is the way to go. Low-level dragonhunters can use *augury* or *clairaudience* to gain important clues, while more powerful characters can employ *divination* or *commune* to answer important questions and *arcane eye*, *scrying*, or even *ethereal jaunt* to scout out a dragon's lair before walking in. Sure, the dragon is likely to detect your spying attempt, but that doesn't mean it knows who's coming or when you'll arrive.

Once you know what you're up against, stock up on appropriate offensive and defensive items. Assuming such is an option, don't hesitate to pick up scrolls or potions of *resist energy* or *protection from energy* to help offset breath weapon effects. Throw in an appropriate wand or batch of scrolls with the right attack spells (*fireball*, *cone of cold*, and the like), and you're on your way to victory.

LIMIT THE BATTLEFIELD

If at all possible, you should never battle a dragon in any area where it can take full advantage of its flight (or swimming) capability. Fighting a dragon in a large cavern (or worse yet, outdoors) is a strategy destined to fail.

You can try to lure a dragon into cramped corridors or other small areas, but only the least intelligent will fall for this trick. Instead, use spells and common sense to alter the battlefield conditions as you go. Spells such as *slow* or *earthbind* (a new spell described on page 112) can limit a dragon's mobility. *Control water* takes away the black dragon's favorite hiding place. *Wall of stone*, *blade barrier*, and similar spells can drastically change the layout of a battle.

Alternatively, you can take the fight to the dragon with spells such as *fly*, *air walk*, or *water breathing*. But keep in mind that the dragon is more adept at moving in the air (or water) than you do.

The dragon's reach is closely connected to its mobility. Try to avoid charging through its threatened area and giving the dragon too many free attacks—the dragon doesn't need any more advantages. Use Mobility and Spring Attack to decrease or neutralize the effect of the dragon's reach; barring that, arm yourself with a longspear or some other reach weapon.

Even if you can't take advantage of any of these techniques, at least stay mobile during the fight. Assuming you're fighting in the dragon's lair, it knows the terrain much better than you do, and if you sit in the same place lobbing *fireball* after *fireball*, rest assured that the dragon will come to you. Use "shoot-and-scoot" techniques, such as those offered by Shot on the Run, so that the dragon can't plan its attack routines too far in advance. Movement-enhancing spells such as *expeditious retreat*, *longstrider*, and *haste* can help counteract the dragon's speed.

Since darkness is a dragon's best friend, don't hesitate to light up the battlefield. *Light* and *continual flame* work reasonably well, but there's no substitute for the *daylight* spell, with its 60-foot radius of bright light. If the dragon supplements darkness with fog or mist, a *gust of wind* spell can also negate its advantage.

THE ELEMENT OF SURPRISE

While it's extraordinarily difficult to sneak up on a dragon, thanks to its scent, darkvision, low-light vision, and blindsense abilities, it doesn't hurt to keep a low profile for as long as possible. Don't just trudge down the hallway, stand outside casting spells, then kick in the door—by now the dragon not only knows you and your companions are there, it has probably figured out your races, classes, and favorite breakfast foods.

Use *silence* or, if you're lucky enough to have a bard along, *sculpt sound* to muffle your approach. Though *invisibility* probably won't work against the dragon, it might protect you from any guardians it has stationed outside its lair (see below). *Hide from dragons* (a new spell described on page 113) can even help you defeat its blindsense.

Dragons are smart, and they often bargain with other creatures to guard their lairs or supplement their own defenses with traps or spells. Use that *augury* or *divination* scroll you've been carrying around to determine the best path of approach, with an eye toward bypassing rather than overcoming the dragon's defenses. If you have access to it, *find the path* is perfect for this job. Sure, you might be able to mow through the ogres at the cavern entrance without breaking a sweat, but once the carnage begins, the dragon knows you're coming.

SPREAD OUT, CONCENTRATE ATTACKS

Of course, one drawback to fighting a dragon in an enclosed area (hey, no plan is perfect) is that the dragon can probably target more characters with its breath weapon. Don't bunch up—to the dragon, three characters are a target, but one is probably a waste of a breath. When fighting dragons with line-shaped breath weapons (such as black or blue dragons), for Pelor's sake, don't all stand in the same corridor.

But it's not only the dragon's breath weapon that a group of characters must worry about. A dragon's full attack routine is devastating, and as tempting as it is to encourage a dragon to "split up" its attacks between multiple PCs, most dragons focus their physical attacks on a single target until that target is down. If your fighter is likely to be turned into dragon chow anyway, there's no point in standing nearby and letting the dragon use its Cleave feat, tail sweep, or any leftover attacks on you. That may sound a bit harsh, but healing fighters is what clerics are for.

That said, there may be reasons to

A ranger examines a dragon's footprint—unaware that he's partially in the shadow of the same dragon's wing.

stick together, at least for a while. Staying close to the paladin means you're more likely to resist the dragon's frightful presence, at the risk of being vulnerable to a breath weapon attack. If you're relying on a *magic circle against evil, antimagic field*, or similar emanation, don't go running off by yourself. If you plan to flank the dragon—and a rogue shouldn't be in the fight for any other reason—stay close enough to get into combat with a single move.

Spreading out your forces doesn't mean you can't concentrate your firepower. Once the battle begins, hit the dragon with everything you have, and don't hold back. Don't waste your time on the dragon's minions (unless they prevent you from targeting the dragon)—you can deal with them after the dragon is dead, assuming they stick around.

In following this tip, fighters often make the mistake of thinking that it's most important to use a full attack against the dragon. Chances are that the dragon's full attack is more devastating than yours, and anyway, your second, third, or fourth attack in the round may not even have much likelihood of hitting. There's no shame in making only a single attack and then falling back to a safe distance (particularly if you can do so without provoking attacks of opportunity). Just be sure to make that one attack count, with tactics such as a charge, the Power Attack feat, a smite ability, and the like.

DON'T STAY TOO LONG

Regardless of your good tactics, you may find yourself in a battle you simply can't win. Remember that, particularly against dragons, discretion is the better part of valor. If you've lost or are in imminent danger of losing a key party member (such as the cleric who's keeping you alive, the wizard who's blasting the dragon with spells, or the fighter who's keeping the dragon from munching the rest of the party), strongly consider falling back to return another day. Plus, you're now better informed about your foe, allowing you to prepare more effectively.

Don't waste too much time recuperating, though. The longer you stay away, the more rested and ready the dragon is likely to be when you return.

FEATS

Characters who find themselves interacting with dragons—whether as friend or foe—may find the feats in this section very useful. Some even let a character mimic the innate power of dragons.

These feats are described below in alphabetical order, using the format described on page 89 of the *Player's Handbook*. See Table 3–1 for a summary of these feats, their prerequisites, and their benefits.

CLEVER WRESTLING [GENERAL]

You have a better than normal chance to escape or wriggle free from a big creature's grapple or pin.

Prerequisites: Improved Unarmed Strike, size Small or Medium.

Benefit: When your opponent is larger than Medium, you gain a circumstance bonus on your grapple check to escape a grapple or pin. The size of the bonus depends on your opponent's size:

Opponent Size	Bonus
Colossal	+8
Gargantuan	+6
Huge	+4
Large	+2

CLOSE-QUARTERS FIGHTING [GENERAL]

You are skilled at fighting at very close range and in evading grappling attempts.

Prerequisite: Base attack bonus +3.

Benefit: You can make an attack of opportunity when someone tries to grapple you, provided that you are not flat-footed or already grappled, even if the attacker has the improved grab ability.

Any damage you deal with your attack of opportunity applies as a bonus to the ensuing grapple check you make to avoid becoming grappled. This feat does not grant you an additional attack of opportunity in a round, so the feat does not help you if you have no attacks of opportunity available.

Normal: A creature with the improved grab ability does not provoke an attack of opportunity when beginning a grapple.

CUNNING SIDESTEP [GENERAL]

You have a better than normal chance to avoid being bull rushed or tripped.

Prerequisites: Improved Unarmed Strike, Clever Wrestling, size Small or Medium.

Benefit: When your opponent is larger than Medium, you gain a circumstance bonus on any opposed check you make to avoid being bull rushed, tripped, knocked down, or pushed. The size of the bonus depends on your opponent's size:

Opponent Size	Bonus
Colossal	+8
Gargantuan	+6
Huge	+4
Large	+2

Special: This feat is effective against the Large and in Charge feat. The bonus from this feat does not stack with the Clever Wrestling feat.

DEFT STRIKE [GENERAL]

You can place attacks at weak points in your opponent's defenses.

Prerequisites: Int 13, Combat Expertise, Spot 10 ranks, sneak attack +1d6.

Benefit: As a standard action, you can attempt to find a weak point in a visible target's armor. This requires a Spot check against a DC equal to your target's Armor Class. If you succeed, your next attack against that target (which must be made no later than your next turn) ignores the target's armor bonus and natural armor bonus to AC (including any enhancement bonuses to armor or natural armor). Other AC bonuses still apply normally.

If you use a ranged weapon to deliver the attack, your

Table 3–1: Feats

General Feats	Prerequisites	Benefit
Clever Wrestling	Improved Unarmed Strike, size Small or Medium	Escape grapple or pin more easily
Cunning Sidestep	Improved Unarmed Strike, Clever Wrestling, size Small or Medium	Avoid a bull rush or trip attack more easily
Close-Quarters Fighting	Base attack bonus +3	Avoid being grappled more easily
Overhead Thrust	Close-Quarters Fighting, Power Attack, base attack bonus +6	Make attack of opportunity against foe attacking from above
Deft Strike	Int 13, Combat Expertise, Spot 10 ranks, sneak attack +1d6	Successful Spot check allows your next attack to ignore target's armor bonuses
Dragon Cohort	Character level 9th, Speak Language (Draconic)	Gain the service of a loyal dragon ally
Dragon Familiar	Cha 13, Speak Language (Draconic), arcane spellcaster level 7th, ability to acquire a new familiar, compatible alignment	Choose wyrmling dragon as new familiar
Dragon Hunter	Wis 13	Gain better defense against dragons' attacks
Dragon Hunter Bravery	Wis 13, Dragon Hunter	Dragons' frightful presence less effective against you and your allies
Dragon Hunter Defense	Wis 13, Dragon Hunter	Gain evasion aganst breath weapon plus save bonus against dragons' magical attacks
Dragon Steed	Cha 13, Ride 8 ranks, Speak Language (Draconic)	Dragonnel serves as loyal mount for you
Dragon Wild Shape	Wis 19, Knowledge (nature) 15 ranks, wild shape ability	You can take the form of a dragon
Dragoncrafter	Knowledge (arcana) 2 ranks	You can create dragoncraft items
Dragonfoe	Int 13	You are more adept at attacking dragons
Dragonbane	Int 13, Dragonfoe, base attack bonus +6	Single attack deals extra damage against dragons
Dragondoom	Int 13, Dragonfoe, Dragonbane, base attack bonus +10	Your critical hits against dragons deal tremendous damage
Dragonfriend	Cha 11, Speak Language (Draconic)	Good dragons regard you as an ally
Dragonsong	Cha 13, Knowledge (arcana) 4 ranks, Perform 6 ranks, Speak Language (Draconic).	Your verbal performances are enhanced
Dragonthrall	Speak Language (Draconic)	Evil dragons regard you as an ally
Frightful Presence	Cha 15, Intimidate 9 ranks	Gain frightful presence ability
Sense Weakness	Int 13, Combat Expertise, Weapon Focus	Your attacks more easily overcome damage reduction or hardness

opponent must be within 30 feet of you in order for you to benefit from this feat.

Dragon Cohort [General]

You gain the service of a loyal dragon ally.

Prerequisites: Character level 9th, Speak Language (Draconic).

Benefit: You gain a cohort selected from Table 3–14: Dragon Cohorts (page 139), just as you would by selecting the Leadership feat. However, you may treat the dragon's ECL as if it were 3 lower than indicated.

See Dragons as Cohorts, page 138, for more information.

Dragon Familiar [General]

When you are able to acquire a new familiar, you may select a wyrmling dragon as a familiar.

Prerequisites: Cha 13, Speak Language (Draconic), arcane spellcaster level 7th, ability to acquire a new familiar, compatible alignment.

Benefit: When acquiring a new familiar, you can choose a wyrmling dragon.See Dragons as Familiars, page 141, for more information.

Dragon Hunter [General]

You have made a special study of dragons and know how to defend against a dragon's attacks.

Prerequisite: Wis 13.

Benefit: You gain a +2 dodge bonus to Armor Class against attacks made by dragons and a +2 competence bonus on saving throws against the spells, attacks, and special abilities of dragons. Likewise, you gain a +2 competence bonus on any opposed check (such as a bull rush attempt or a grapple check) you make against a dragon.

Dragon Hunter Bravery [General]

You resist dragons' frightful presence, and your mere presence helps others resist as well.

Prerequisites: Wis 13, Dragon Hunter.

Benefit: You and all allies within 30 feet who can see you are treated as having +4 HD for the purposes of determining your resistance to the frightful presence of dragons. All creatures so affected also gain a +4 morale bonus on Will saves made to resist a dragon's frightful presence.

Your animal companion, familiar, or special mount automatically succeeds on its Will save to resist the dragon's frightful presence if you succeed on yours (or if your effective Hit Dice total makes you immune).

Dragon Hunter Defense [General]

Your insight into the tactics and abilities of dragons grants you awareness of how best to avoid their magical attacks.

Prerequisites: Wis 13, Dragon Hunter.

Benefit: You gain the evasion ability against the breath weapons of dragons. (If a dragon's breath weapon allows a Reflex save for half damage, a successful save indicates that you take no damage.)

Also, you gain a bonus equal to 1/2 your character level on all saving throws you make against the supernatural or spell-like abilities of dragons.

DRAGON STEED [GENERAL]

You have earned the service of a loyal draconic steed.

Prerequisites: Cha 13, Ride 8 ranks, Speak Language (Draconic).

Benefit: You gain the service of a dragonnel (see page 150) as a steed. It serves loyally as long as you treat it fairly, much like a cohort.

Special: If you have a special mount (such as from the paladin class feature), this dragonnel replaces your special mount. See Dragons as Special Mounts, page 139, for details.

DRAGON WILD SHAPE [GENERAL]

You can take the form of a dragon.

Prerequisites: Wis 19, Knowledge (nature) 15 ranks, wild shape ability.

Benefit: You can use your wild shape ability to change into a Small or Medium dragon. You gain all the extraordinary and supernatural abilities of the dragon whose form you take, but not any spell-like abilities or spellcasting powers.

DRAGONBANE [GENERAL]

You have made a special study of dragons and are adept at pulling off deliberate attacks that take advantage of a dragon's weak spots.

Prerequisites: Int 13, Dragonfoe, base attack bonus +6.

Benefit: You may use a full-round action to make a single attack (melee or ranged) against a dragon with a +4 bonus on the attack roll. Such an attack deals an extra 2d6 points of damage if it hits. For a ranged attack, the dragon must be within 30 feet to gain the bonus to hit and the extra damage.

Special: The bonus on the attack roll and the extra damage stack with the benefits provided by a weapon with the bane (dragons) special ability.

In the case of a critical hit, the extra damage dice aren't multiplied.

DRAGONCRAFTER [GENERAL]

You can make special weapons, armor, and other items using parts of dragons as materials.

Prerequisite: Knowledge (arcana) 2 ranks.

Benefit: You can create any dragoncraft item whose prerequisites you meet. Creating a dragoncraft item follows the normal rules for the Craft skill (see page 70 of the *Player's Handbook*).

See Dragoncraft Items, page 116, for details.

DRAGONDOOM [GENERAL]

You have learned how to place blows against a dragon that deal tremendous damage.

Prerequisites: Int 13, Dragonbane, Dragonfoe, base attack bonus +10.

Benefit: When you attack a dragon, the critical multiplier of your weapon improves as noted below.

Normal Multiplier	New Multiplier
×2	×3
×3	×5
×4	×7

Special: The benefit of this feat does not stack with any other ability or effect that alters a weapon's critical multiplier.

DRAGONFOE [GENERAL]

You have learned how to how to attack dragons more effectively than most other individuals.

Prerequisite: Int 13.

Benefit: You gain a +2 bonus on attack rolls against dragons and a +2 bonus on caster level checks made to overcome a dragon's spell resistance. Also, dragons take a –2 penalty on saving throws against your spells, spell-like abilities, and supernatural abilities.

DRAGONFRIEND [GENERAL]

You are a known and respected ally of dragons.

Prerequisites: Cha 11, Speak Language (Draconic).

Benefit: You gain a +4 bonus on Diplomacy checks made to adjust the attitude of a dragon, and a +2 bonus on Ride checks made when you are mounted on a dragon.

In addition, you gain a +4 bonus on saves against the frightful presence of good dragons.

Special: You can't select this feat if you have already taken the Dragonthrall feat.

DRAGONSONG [GENERAL]

Your song or poetics echo the power of the dragonsong, an ancient style of vocal performance created by dragons in the distant past.

Prerequisites: Cha 13, Knowledge (arcana) 4 ranks, Perform 6 ranks, Speak Language (Draconic).

Benefit: You gain a +2 bonus on Perform checks involving song, poetics, or any other verbal or spoken form of performance.

In addition, the DC of any saving throw required by mind-affecting effects based on your song or poetics (such as bardic music) is increased by +2.

DRAGONTHRALL [GENERAL]

You have pledged your life to the service of evil dragonkind.

Prerequisite: Speak Language (Draconic).

Benefit: You gain a +4 bonus on any Bluff check made against a dragon, and a +2 bonus on Ride checks made when you are mounted on a dragon.

You gain a +4 bonus on saves against the frightful presence of evil dragons.

You take a –2 penalty on saves against enchantment spells and effects cast by dragons.

Special: You can't select this feat if you have already taken the Dragonfriend feat.

FRIGHTFUL PRESENCE [GENERAL]

Like a dragon, your mere presence can terrify those around you.

Prerequisites: Cha 15, Intimidate 9 ranks.

Benefit: You gain the use of the frightful presence ability. Whenever you attack or charge, all opponents within a radius of 30 feet who have fewer levels or Hit Dice than you become shaken for a number of rounds equal to 1d6 + your Cha modifier. The effect is negated by a Will save (DC 10 + 1/2 your character level + your Cha modifier).

A successful save indicates that the opponent is immune to your frightful presence for 24 hours. This ability can't affect creatures with an Intelligence of 3 or lower, nor does it have any effect on dragons.

OVERHEAD THRUST [GENERAL]

You can deal a nasty attack to anything that tries to crush or run over you.

Prerequisites: Close-Quarters Fighting, Power Attack, base attack bonus +6.

Benefit: You can use a slashing or piercing weapon to make an attack of opportunity against a foe using an attack designed to batter you from above, such as an overrun, trample, power dive, or dragon crush attack. You cannot use this feat if you are flat-footed or already grappled. This feat does not grant you an additional attack of opportunity in a round, so the feat does not help you if you have no attacks of opportunity available.

You gain a special attack modifier based on your opponent's size, as shown below. If your attack hits, you deal triple damage.

Opponent Size	Bonus
Colossal	+16
Gargantuan	+12
Huge	+8
Large	+4
Medium or smaller	+0

Special: Any extra damage dice your attack deals (such as from a sneak attack ability or a weapon special ability) are not multiplied by this feat.

If you score a critical hit with your attack, the extra damage you deal stacks with the extra damage from this feat. Add the damage multipliers together according to the standard rule (see Multiplying, page 304 of the *Player's Handbook*). For example, if your weapon deals double damage on a critical hit, any critical hit you score while also using this feat deals quadruple damage.

SENSE WEAKNESS [GENERAL]

You can take advantage of subtle weaknesses in your opponents' defenses.

Prerequisites: Int 13, Combat Expertise, Weapon Focus.

Benefit: Whenever you attack with a weapon with which you have selected the Weapon Focus feat, you may ignore up to 5 points of the target's damage reduction (regardless of the material or enhancement bonus of your weapon) or hardness. This benefit can't reduce the effective damage reduction or hardness of a target to less than 0.

NEW SPELLS

This section presents a variety of dragon-related spells, as well as three new cleric domains. The following spell lists use the format and notational style described on page 181 of the *Player's Handbook*. Spell descriptions are presented alphabetically after the spell lists.

PRESTIGE DOMAINS

The two prestige domains described here, Domination and Glory, are available only to characters who have qualified to select the domains as a class feature (such as those who adopt the dracolyte prestige class; see page 122). They are not available to beginning characters.

ASSASSIN SPELLS

3rd-Level Assassin Spells

Fell the Greatest Foe: Deal extra damage to creatures larger than Medium.

Find the Gap: Your attacks ignore armor and natural armor.

4th-Level Assassin Spells

Hide from Dragons: Dragons can't perceive one subject/two levels.

Vulnerability: Reduces an opponent's damage reduction.

BARD SPELLS

1st-Level Bard Spell

Cheat: Caster rerolls when determining the success of a game of chance.

2nd-Level Bard Spell

Miser's Envy: Subject jealously covets a nearby object.

3rd-Level Bard Spell

Suppress Breath Weapon: Subject can't use breath weapon.

4th-Level Bard Spell

Voice of the Dragon: +10 on Bluff, Diplomacy, and Intimidate checks; can use one *suggestion.*

5th-Level Bard Spells

Hide from Dragons: Dragons can't perceive one subject/two levels.

Dragonsight: Gain low-light vision, darkvision, and blindsense.

CLERIC SPELLS

3rd-Level Cleric Spells

Cloak of Bravery: You and your allies gain a bonus on saves against fear.

Shield of Warding: Shield grants +1 bonus on Reflex saves per five levels (max. +5).

4th-Level Cleric Spells

Antidragon Aura [M]: Allies gain bonus to AC and saves against dragons.

Contingent Energy Resistance [M]: Energy damage triggers a *resist energy* spell.

Fell the Greatest Foe: Deal extra damage to creatures larger than Medium.

Lower Spell Resistance: Subject's spell resistance reduced.

5th-Level Cleric Spells

Aura of Evasion [M]: All within 10 ft. gain evasion against breath weapons.

Vulnerability: Reduces an opponent's damage reduction.

6th-Level Cleric Spells

Energy Immunity: Subject gains immunity to damage from one kind of energy.

7th-Level Cleric Spells

Death Dragon: You gain +4 enhancement bonus to natural armor, +4 deflection bonus to AC, and temporary hit points.

CLERIC DOMAINS

DOMINATION PRESTIGE DOMAIN

Deities: None (see the dracolyte prestige class, page 122).

Granted Power: You gain Spell Focus (enchantment) as a bonus feat.

Domination Domain Spells

1 **Command:** One subject obeys selected command for 1 round.
2 **Enthrall:** Captivates all within 100 ft. + 10 ft./level.
3 **Suggestion:** Compels subject to follow stated course of action.
4 **Dominate Person:** Controls humanoid telepathically.
5 **Command, Greater:** As *command*, but affects one subject/level.
6 **Geas/Quest:** As *lesser geas*, plus it affects any creature.
7 **Suggestion, Mass:** As *suggestion*, plus one/level subjects.
8 **True Domination:** As *dominate person*, but later saving throws at –4.
9 **Monstrous Thrall** [X]: As *true domination*, but permanent and affects any creature.

DRAGON DOMAIN

Deities: Aasterinian, Astilabor, Bahamut, Chronepsis, Falazure, Garyx, Hlal, Io, Lendys, Tamara, Tiamat.

Granted Power: Add Bluff and Intimidate to your list of cleric class skills.

Dragon Domain Spells

1 **Magic Fang:** One natural weapon of subject creature gets +1 on attack and damage rolls.
2 **Resist Energy:** Ignores 10 (or more) points of damage/attack from specified energy type.
3 **Magic Fang, Greater:** One natural weapon of subject creature gets +1/three levels on attack and damage rolls (max +5).
4 **Voice of the Dragon:** +10 on Bluff, Diplomacy, and Intimidate checks; can use one *suggestion*.
5 **True Seeing** [M]: Lets you see all things as they actually are.
6 **Stoneskin** [M]: Ignore 10 points of damage per attack.
7 **Dragon Ally** [X]: As *lesser dragon ally*, but up to 18 HD.
8 **Suggestion, Mass:** As *suggestion*, plus one/level subjects.
9 **Dominate Monster:** As *dominate person*, but any creature.

GLORY PRESTIGE DOMAIN

Deities: None (see the dracolyte prestige class, page 122).

Granted Power: You can turn undead with a +2 bonus on the turning check and +1d6 on the turning damage roll.

Glory Domain Spells

1 **Disrupt Undead:** Deals 1d6 damage to one undead.
2 **Bless Weapon:** Weapon strikes true against evil foes.
3 **Searing Light:** Ray deals 1d8/two levels damage, more against undead.
4 **Holy Smite:** Damages and blinds evil creatures.
5 **Holy Sword:** Weapon becomes +5, deals +2d6 damage against evil.
6 **Bolt of Glory:** Ray deals 1d6/two levels damage, more against undead and evil outsiders.
7 **Sunbeam:** Beam blinds and deals 4d6 damage.
8 **Crown of Glory** [M]: Gain +4 Cha and enthrall subjects.
9 **Gate** [X]: Connects two planes for travel or summoning.

GREED DOMAIN

Deity: Tiamat.

Granted Power: You gain a +2 competence bonus on Appraise, Open Lock, and Slight of Hand checks.

Greed Domain Spells

1 **Cheat:** Caster rerolls when determining the success of a game of chance.
2 **Entice Gift:** Subject gives caster what it's holding.
3 **Knock:** Opens locked or magically sealed door.
4 **Fire Trap** [M]: Opened object deals 1d4 damage +1/level.
5 **Fabricate:** Transforms raw materials into finished items.
6 **Guards and Wards:** Array of magic effects protects area.
7 **Teleport Object:** As *teleport*, but affects a touched object.
8 **Phantasmal Thief:** Creates an unseen force that steals from others.
9 **Sympathy** [F]: Object or location attracts certain creatures.

WEALTH DOMAIN

Deities: Astilabor, Io.

Granted Powers: Add Appraise to your list of cleric class skills.

You gain Skill Focus (Appraise) as a bonus feat.

Wealth Domain Spells

1 **Alarm:** Wards an area for 2 hours/level.
2 **Obscure Object:** Masks object against scrying.
3 **Glyph of Warding** [M]: Inscription harms those who pass it.
4 **Detect Scrying:** Alerts you of magical eavesdropping.
5 **Leomund's Secret Chest** [F]: Hides expensive chest on Ethereal Plane; you retrieve it at will.
6 **Forbiddance** [M]: Blocks planar travel, damages creatures of different alignment.
7 **Sequester:** Subject is invisible to sight and scrying; renders creature comatose.
8 **Discern Location:** Reveals exact location of creature or object.
9 **Antipathy:** Object or location affected by spell repels certain creatures.

DRUID SPELLS

2nd-Level Druid Spell

Earthbind: Subject creature can't fly.

4th-Level Druid Spell

Contingent Energy Resistance [M]: Energy damage triggers a *resist energy* spell.

6th-Level Druid Spell

Energy Immunity: Subject has immunity to damage from one kind of energy.

PALADIN SPELLS

2nd-Level Paladin Spells

Cloak of Bravery: You and your allies gain a bonus on saves against fear.
Shield of Warding: Shield grants +1 bonus on Reflex saves, +1 per five levels (max +5).

3rd-Level Paladin Spells

Fell the Greatest Foe: Deal extra damage to creatures larger than Medium.
Find the Gap: Your attacks ignore armor and natural armor.

4th-Level Paladin Spell

Draconic Might: Gain +5 to Str, Con, Cha; +4 natural armor; immunity to magic sleep effects and paralysis.

RANGER SPELLS

3rd-Level Ranger Spell

Find the Gap: Your attacks ignore armor and natural armor.

SORCERER/WIZARD SPELLS

1st-Level Sorcerer/Wizard Spell

Trans **Cheat:** Caster rerolls when determining the success of a game of chance.

2nd-Level Sorcerer/Wizard Spells

Ench **Entice Gift:** Subject gives caster what it's holding.
Trans **Earthbind:** Subject creature can't fly.
Scale Weakening: Subject's natural armor weakens.

3rd-Level Sorcerer/Wizard Spells

Ench **Miser's Envy:** Subject jealously covets nearby object.
Suppress Breath Weapon: Subject can't use its breath weapon.
Trans **Dragon Breath:** You gain a dragon's breath weapon for 1 hour.
Dragonskin: You gain +4 enhancement to natural armor, energy resistance 10.

4th-Level Sorcerer/Wizard Spells

Abjur **Antidragon Aura** [M]: Allies gain bonus to AC and saves against dragons.
Lower Spell Resistance: Subject's spell resistance reduced.
Voice of the Dragon: +10 on Bluff, Diplomacy, and Intimidate checks; can use one *suggestion*.

5th-Level Sorcerer/Wizard Spells

Abjur **Contingent Energy Resistance** [M]: Energy damage triggers a *resist energy* spell.
Conj **Lesser Dragon Ally** [X]: Exchange services with a 9 HD dragon.
Trans **Draconic Might:** Gain +5 to Str, Con, Cha; +4 natural armor; immunity to magic sleep and paralysis effects.
Dragonsight: Gain low-light vision, darkvision, and blindsense.
Flight of the Dragon: You grow dragon wings.
Vulnerability: Reduces an opponent's damage reduction.

6th-Level Sorcerer/Wizard Spell

Abjur **Aura of Evasion** [M]: All within 10 ft. gain evasion against breath weapons.

7th-Level Sorcerer/Wizard Spells

Abjur **Antimagic Ray** [M]: Target loses all magical powers.
Energy Immunity: Subject hss immunity to damage from one kind of energy.
Hide from Dragons: Dragons can't perceive one subject/two levels.
Conj **Dragon Ally** [X]: As *lesser dragon ally*, but up to 18 HD.

8th-Level Sorcerer/Wizard Spells

Conj **Phantasmal Thief:** Creates an unseen force that steals from others.

9th-Level Sorcerer/Wizard Spells

Conj **Greater Dragon Ally** [X]. As *lesser dragon ally*, but up to 27 HD.

SPELL DESCRIPTIONS

The spells herein are presented in alphabetical order (with the exception of those whose names begin with "greater" or "lesser"; see Order of Presentation, page 181 of the *Player's Handbook*).

Antidragon Aura

Abjuration
Level: Clr 4, Sor/Wiz 4
Components: V, S, M, DF
Casting Time: 1 standard action
Range: Close (25 ft. + 5 ft./2 levels)
Targets: 1 creature/two levels, no two of which can be more than 30 ft. apart
Duration: 1 minute/level
Saving Throw: Will negates (harmless)
Spell Resistance: Yes (harmless)

All targets gain a +2 luck bonus to Armor Class and on saving throws against the attacks, spells, and special attacks (extraordinary, supernatural, and spell-like) of dragons. This bonus increases by +1 for every four caster levels above 7th (to +3 at 11th, +4 at 15th, and a maximum of +5 at 19th).

Material Component: A chunk of platinum worth at least 25 gp (slightly less than 1 ounce).

Antimagic Ray

Abjuration
Level: Sor/Wiz 7
Components: V, S, M
Casting Time: 1 standard action
Range: Close (25 ft. + 5 ft./2 levels)
Target: One creature or object
Duration: 1 round/level
Saving Throw: Will negates (object)
Spell Resistance: Yes (object)

An invisible ray projects from your fingers. You must succeed on a ranged touch attack with the ray to strike a target. The target, if struck, functions as if it were inside an *antimagic field*.

If this spell is used against a creature, the target can't cast spells or can't use supernatural or spell-like abilities, nor do such abilities have any effect on the creature. However, the creature can still use spell completion items (such as scrolls) or spell trigger items (such as wands), even though it can't cast the spells required.

If this spell is usewd against an object, that object's magical powers are suppressed—including any spells previously cast and currently in effect on the item, as well as any spells or magical effects targeted on the object during the *antimagic ray*'s duration. Remember that an object struck by the ray only receives a saving throw if it is attended or if it is a magic item. An unattended item, even if currently under the effect of a spell (such as a torch with *continual flame* cast upon it), receives no save.

The spell doesn't affect any objects other than the target itself, even if those objects are worn, carried by, or in contact with the target. For instance, if a creature is the target, its equipment remains unaffected.

Material Component: A pinch of iron filings mixed with ruby dust worth 100 gp.

Aura of Evasion

Abjuration
Level: Clr 5, Sor/Wiz 6
Components: V, S, M, DF
Casting Time: 1 standard action
Area: 10-ft.-radius emanation centered on you
Duration: 1 minute/level
Saving Throw: No
Spell Resistance: No

You and all creatures within 10 feet of you gain evasion, but only against breath weapons. (If a breath weapon would normally allow a Reflex saving throw for half damage, a creature within an *aura of evasion* that successfully saves takes no damage instead.)

The effect of this spell doesn't stack with any existing evasion or improved evasion abilities.

Material Component: Powdered emerald worth 500 gp.

Bolt of Glory

Evocation [Good]
Level: Glory 6
Components: V, S, DF
Casting Time: 1 standard action
Range: Close (25 ft. + 5 ft./2 levels)
Effect: Ray
Duration: Instantaneous
Saving Throw: None
Spell Resistance: Yes

You project a bolt of positive energy at a single creature. You must make a successful ranged touch attack to strike your target. The bolt deals 1d6 points of damage per two caster levels (maximum 7d6). Against undead, evil outsiders, and creatures native to the Negative Energy Plane, the bolt instead deals 1d6 points of damage per caster level (maximum 15d6). The bolt deals no damage to good outsiders or creatures native to the Positive Energy Plane.

Cheat

Transmutation [Evil]
Level: Brd 1, Greed 1, Sor/Wiz 1
Components: V, S, F
Casting Time: 1 standard action
Range: Personal
Target: You
Duration: 1 minute/level or until used
Saving Throw: None
Spell Resistance: No

At one point during the duration of this spell, you can attempt to alter the outcome of a game of chance. This spell can only affect nonmagical games, such as those using cards or dice. It cannot affect a game involving magic, nor a magic item involved in a game of chance (such as a *deck of many things*). Whenever a roll is made to determine the outcome of the game, a character under the effect of this spell may demand a reroll and take the better of the two rolls.

For example, Darkon is playing a game that he has a 1 in 4 chance of winning. The DM secretly rolls 1d4 and tells the player that Darkon lost. Because Darkon is under the effect of a *cheat* spell, the player can have the DM reroll. The spell alters probability, so there is no subterfuge that another character could notice (except for the casting of the spell itself).

Focus: A pair of dice made from human bones.

Cloak of Bravery

Abjuration [Mind-Affecting]
Level: Clr 3, Pal 2
Components: V, S
Casting Time: 1 standard action
Range: 60 ft.
Area: 60-ft.-radius emanation centered on you
Duration: 10 minutes/level
Saving Throw: Will negates (harmless)
Spell Resistance: Yes (harmless)

All allies within the area (including you) gain a morale bonus on saving throws against fear effects equal to your caster level (max +10).

Contingent Energy Resistance

Abjuration
Level: Clr 4, Drd 4, Sor/Wiz 5
Components: V, S, M
Casting Time: 1 minute
Range: Personal
Target: You
Duration: 1 hour/level (D)

This spell functions similarly to *contingency*, but with a more limited scope. While *contingent energy resistance* is in effect, if you are dealt damage associated with one of the five types of energy (acid, cold, electricity, fire, or sonic), the spell automatically grants you resistance 10 against that type of energy for the remainder of the spell's duration (just as if you were under the effect of a *resist energy* spell of the appropriate type).

Once the energy type protected against by a particular casting of this spell is determined, it can't be changed. You can't have more than one *contingent energy resistance* in effect on yourself at the same time—if you cast the spell a second time while an earlier casting is still in effect, the earlier spell automatically expires.

The energy resistance granted by this spell does not stack with similar benefits against the same energy type (such as from the *resist energy* spell). However, it is possible to be simultaneously under the effect of *resist energy (fire)* and *contingent energy resistance (electricity)*, or any other two such spells that protect against different types of energy.

Material Component: A pearl worth at least 100 gp.

Crown of Glory

Evocation
Level: Glory 8
Components: V, S, M, DF
Casting Time: 1 standard action
Range: 120 ft.
Area: 120-ft.-radius emanation, centered on you
Duration: 1 minute/level
Saving Throw: Will negates
Spell Resistance: Yes

You are imbued with an aura of celestial authority, inspiring awe in all lesser creatures that behold your terrible perfection and righteousness. You gain a +4 enhancement bonus to Charisma for the duration of the spell.

All creatures in the spell's area with fewer than 8 Hit Dice or levels cease whatever they are doing and are compelled to pay attention to you. Any such creature that wants to take hostile action against you must succeed on a Will save to do so. Any creature that fails this save the first time it attempts a hostile action is enthralled for the duration of the spell (as the *enthrall* spell) as long as it is in the spell's area, and it will not try to leave the area on its own. Creatures with 8 or more Hit Dice are not affected by this spell.

When you speak, all listeners telepathically understand you, even if they do not understand your language. While the spell lasts, you can make up to three suggestions to creatures of fewer than 8 HD in range, as if using the *mass suggestion* spell (Will negates); creatures with 8 HD or more are not affected by this power.

Material Component: An opal worth at least 200 gp.

Death Dragon

Necromancy [Evil, Fear, Mind-Affecting]
Level: Clr 7
Components: V, S, DF
Casting Time: 1 round
Range: Personal
Effect: Dragon-shaped armor of energy and bones
Duration: 1 round/level (D)

You summon unholy power to gird yourself in a dragon-shaped cocoon of bones and negative energy. The cocoon gives you a +4 enhancement bonus to your natural armor and a +4 deflection bonus to Armor Class, plus 1 temporary hit point per caster level (maximum 20). You are treated as armed when you make unarmed attacks, and you deal damage as if your limbs were short swords of an appropriate size. You can use your off hand to attack, incurring the standard two-weapon fighting penalties (see page 160 of the *Player's Handbook*). The *death dragon* prevents you from casting spells with somatic, material, or focus (but not divine focus) components, but does not otherwise hinder your actions or movement.

As a standard action, you may project a cone of *fear* or make a melee touch attack to use *inflict critical wounds* on the creature touched. These effects are otherwise identical to the spells of the same names.

An evil cleric sheathes himself in a death dragon spell.

Draconic Might

Transmutation
Level: Pal 4, Sor/Wiz 5
Components: V, S, M
Casting Time: 1 standard action
Range: Touch
Target: Living creature touched
Duration: 1 minute/level (D)
Saving Throw: Fortitude negates (harmless)
Spell Resistance: Yes (harmless)

The subject of the spell gains a +5 enhancement bonus to Strength, Constitution, and Charisma. It also gains a +4 enhancement bonus to natural armor. Finally, it has immunity to magic sleep and paralysis effects.

Special: Sorcerers cast this spell at +1 caster level.

Dragon Ally

Conjuration (Summoning)
Level: Dragon 7, Sor/Wiz 7
Effect: Up to two summoned dragons, totaling no more than 18 HD, no two of which can be more than 30 ft. apart when they appear

As *lesser dragon ally*, except you may summon a single dragon of up to 18 HD or two dragons of the same kind whose HD total no more than 18. The dragons agree to help you and request your return payment together.

XP Cost: 250 XP.

Dragon Ally, Greater

Conjuration (Summoning)
Level: Sor/Wiz 9
Effect: Up to three summoned dragons, totaling no more than 27 HD, no two of which can be more than 30 ft. apart when they appear

As *lesser dragon ally*, except you may summon a single dragon of up to 27 HD or up to three dragons of the same kind whose HD total no more than 27. The dragons agree to help you and request your return payment together.

XP Cost: 500 XP.

Dragon Ally, Lesser

Conjuration (Summoning)
Level: Sor/Wiz 5
Components: V, XP
Casting Time: 10 minutes
Range: Close (25 ft. + 5 ft./2 levels)
Effect: One summoned dragon of up to 9 HD
Duration: Instantaneous
Saving Throw: None
Spell Resistance: No

This spell summons a dragon. You may ask the dragon to perform one task in exchange for a payment from you. Tasks might range from the simple (fly us across the chasm, help us fight a battle) to the complex (spy on our enemies, protect us on our foray into the dungeon). You must be able to communicate with the dragon to bargain for its services.

The summoned dragon requires payment for its services, which takes the form of coins, gems, or other precious objects the dragon can add to its hoard. This payment must be made before the dragon agrees to perform any services. The bargaining takes at least 1 round, so any actions by the creature begin in the round after it arrives.

Tasks requiring up to 1 minute per caster level require a payment of 100 gp per HD of the summoned dragon. For a task requiring up to 1 hour per caster level, the creature requires a payment of 500 gp per HD. Long-term tasks (those requiring up to 1 day per caster level) require a payment of 1,000 gp per HD.

Especially hazardous tasks require a greater gift, up to twice the given amount. A dragon never accepts less than the indicated amount, even for a nonhazardous task.

At the end of its task, or when the duration bargained for elapses, the creature returns to the place it was summoned from (after reporting back to you, if appropriate and possible).

XP Cost: 100 XP.

Special: Sorcerers cast this spell at +1 caster level.

Dragon Breath

Transmutation
Level: Sor/Wiz 3
Components: V, S
Casting Time: 1 standard action
Range: Personal
Target: You
Duration: 10 minutes/level (D)

You gain a breath weapon resembling that of a dragon. When you cast this spell, you choose both the shape and energy type of the breath weapon, from the following options: line (acid, electricity, or fire) or cone (acid, cold, or fire). A line is 5 feet high, 5 feet wide, and 60 feet long, while a cone is 30 feet long, 30 feet high, and 30 feet wide. Once you make the selection of shape and energy type, it is fixed for the duration of the spell.

Using your breath weapon is a standard action. The breath weapon deals 3d6 points of damage of the chosen energy type, plus an additional 1d6 points of damage for every two levels above 5th (to a maximum of 10d6 at 19th level). Targets in the area may attempt a Reflex save for half damage.

You can use this breath weapon up to three times during the spell's duration (plus one additional use per two levels above 5th). After using this breath weapon, you can't use it again for 1d4+1 rounds. (Using this breath weapon has no effect on your ability to use other breath weapons you might have, and vice versa.) You can't have more than one *dragon breath* spell active at the same time.

Even though using your breath weapon poses no danger to you, you don't gain any resistance or immunity to the energy type of the weapon.

Special: Sorcerers cast this spell at +1 caster level.

Dragonsight

Transmutation
Level: Brd 5, Sor/Wiz 5
Components: V, S, F
Casting Time: 1 standard action
Range: Personal
Target: You
Duration: 1 minute/level (D)

You gain the visual acuity of a dragon, including low-light vision, darkvision, and blindsense.

You can see four times as well as a normal human in low-light conditions and twice as well in normal light. (See the Dragon Sight sidebar, page 17.) Your darkvision has a range of 10 feet per caster level.

Your blindsense has a range of 5 feet per caster level. You do not need to make Spot or Listen checks to notice creatures within range of your blindsense.

None of these effects stack with any low-light vision, darkvision, or blindsense you may already have.

Focus: A dragon's eye.

Hennet uses the dragonskin spell to give himself scales like a red dragon.

Dragonskin

Transmutation
Level: Sor/Wiz 3
Components: S, M
Casting Time: 1 standard action
Range: Personal
Target: You
Duration: 10 minutes/level

Your skin toughens and becomes scaly like that of a chromatic dragon, of a color that you select. You gain an enhancement bonus to your natural armor equal to +3, +1 per two levels above 5th (to a maximum of +5 at 9th level), as well as energy resistance equal to twice your caster level (maximum of 20 at 10th level) against the type of energy appropriate to the color you select: acid (black or green), cold (white), electricity (blue), or fire (red).

Material Component: A dragon's scale.

Special: Sorcerers cast this spell at +1 caster level.

Earthbind

Transmutation
Level: Drd 2, Sor/Wiz 2
Components: V, S
Casting Time: 1 standard action
Range: Close (25 ft. + 5 ft./2 levels)
Targets: One creature
Duration: 1 minute/level (D)
Saving Throw: Fortitude partial
Spell Resistance: Yes

You hamper the subject creature's ability to fly (whether through natural or magical means) for the duration of the spell. If the target fails its saving throw, its fly speed (if any) becomes 0 feet. An airborne creature subjected to this spell falls to the ground as if under the effect of a *feather fall* spell. Even if a new effect would grant the creature the ability to fly, that effect is suppressed for the duration of the *earthbind* spell.

If the target makes a successful Fortitude save, its fly speed (including any new effect granted during the spell's duration) is reduced by 10 feet per caster level (maximum reduction 100 feet at 10th level). This reduction can't bring the creature's fly speed down to less than 10 feet.

Earthbind has no effect on other forms of movement, or even on effects that might grant airborne movement without granting a fly speed (such as jumping or *levitate* or *air walk* spells).

Energy Immunity
Abjuration
Level: Clr 6, Drd 6, Sor/Wiz 7
Components: V, S
Casting Time: 1 standard action
Range: Touch
Target: Creature touched
Duration: 24 hours
Saving Throw: None (harmless)
Spell Resistance: Yes (harmless)

This abjuration grants a creature complete protection against damage from whichever one of five energy types you select: acid, cold, electricity, fire, or sonic. The spell protects the recipient's equipment as well.

Energy immunity absorbs only damage. The recipient could still suffer unfortunate side effects, such as drowning in acid (since drowning results from a lack of oxygen), being deafened by a sonic attack, or becoming encased in ice.

The effect of this spell does not stack with similar effects, such as *resist energy* and *protection from energy*, that protect against the same energy type. If a character is warded with *energy immunity* (*fire*) and is also receiving resistance to fire from one or more of the other spells, the *energy immunity* makes the other spells irrelevant. However, it is possible to be simultaneously under the effect of *energy immunity* (*fire*) and *resist energy* (*electricity*), or any other two such spells that protect against different types of energy.

Entice Gift
Enchantment [Mind-Affecting]
Level: Greed 2, Sor/Wiz 2
Components: V, S
Casting Time: 1 standard action
Range: Close (25 ft. + 5 ft./2 levels)
Target: One creature
Duration: 1 round
Saving Throw: Will negates
Spell Resistance: Yes

You enchant a creature so that it feels suddenly compelled to give you what it is holding when you cast this spell. On the creature's next action, it moves as close to you as it can get in a single round and offers you the object as a standard action. This spell allows you to act out of turn and accept the "gift" if the creature reaches you to hand you the object (assuming you have a free hand and can accept it). The subject defends itself normally and acts as it wishes on subsequent rounds, including attempting to get the object back if desired. If the subject is prevented from doing as the spell compels, the spell is wasted. For example, if the subject is paralyzed and cannot move or drop the item, nothing happens.

Fell the Greatest Foe
Transmutation
Level: Asn 3, Clr 4, Pal 3
Components: V, S, M
Casting Time: 1 standard action
Range: Touch
Target: Large or larger creature touched
Duration: 1 round/level
Saving Throw: Fortitude negates (harmless)
Spell Resistance: Yes (harmless)

The subject gains the ability to deal greater damage against Large or larger creatures. For every size category of an opponent bigger than Medium, the subject deals an extra 1d6 points of damage on any successful melee attack (+1d6 against a Large creature, +2d6 against Huge, +3d6 against Gargantuan, or +4d6 against Colossal).

Material Component: A dragon's claw or a giant's fingernail.

Find the Gap
Divination
Level: Asn 3, Pal 3, Rgr 3
Components: V
Casting Time: 1 standard action
Range: Personal
Target: You
Duration: 1 round/level

You gain the ability to perceive weak points in your opponent's armor. Once per round, one of your melee or ranged attacks may disregard the target's armor, shield, and natural armor bonuses (including any enhancement bonuses) to Armor Class. Other AC bonuses, such as dodge bonuses, deflection bonuses, and luck bonuses, still apply.

Flight of the Dragon
Transmutation
Level: Sor/Wiz 5
Components: V, M
Casting Time: 1 standard action
Range: Personal
Target: You
Duration: 1 hour/level (D)

A pair of powerful draconic wings sprouts from your shoulders, granting you a fly speed of 100 feet (average). You can't carry aloft more than a light load.

When flying long distances, you can fly at 15 miles per hour (or 24 miles per hour at a hustle). In a day of normal flight, you can cover 120 miles.

Material Component: A dragon's wing-claw.

Special: Sorcerers cast this spell at +1 caster level.

Hide from Dragons
Abjuration
Level: Asn 4, Brd 5, Sor/Wiz 7, Hoardstealer 4 (see class description, page 130)
Components: S, M
Casting Time: 1 standard action
Range: Touch
Targets: One creature touched/two levels
Duration: 10 minutes/level (D)

Saving Throw: Will negates (harmless)
Spell Resistance: Yes

Dragons cannot see, hear, or smell the warded creatures, even with blindsense. They act as though the warded creatures are not there. Warded creatures could stand before the hungriest of red dragons and not be molested or even noticed. If a warded character touches or attacks a dragon, even with a spell, the spell ends for all recipients.

Material Component: A dragon scale.

Lower Spell Resistance

Transmutation
Level: Clr 4, Sor/Wiz 4
Components: V, S
Casting Time: 1 round
Range: Close (25 ft. + 5 ft./2 levels)
Target: One creature
Duration: 1 minute/level
Saving Throw: Fortitude negates (see text)
Spell Resistance: No

This spell reduces the subject's spell resistance by 1 per caster level (maximum reduction 15). This reduction can't lower a target's spell resistance below 0.

The target of the spell takes a penalty on its saving throw equal to your caster level.

Miser's Envy

Enchantment (Compulsion) [Mind-Affecting]
Level: Brd 2, Sor/Wiz 3
Components: V, S, M
Casting Time: 1 standard action
Range: Close (25 ft. + 5 ft./2 levels)
Target: One living creature and one object (see text)
Duration: 1 round/level
Saving Throw: Will negates and None (object)
Spell Resistance: Yes and No (object)

When you cast this spell, you designate a target creature and a target object, both of which must be within the spell's range. If the target creature fails its saving throw, it becomes consumed by a powerful desire for the object. For the duration of the spell, the creature seeks to obtain the object (going so far as to attack anyone holding or wearing it).

Once the creature gains possession of the object, it protects the item greedily, attacking anyone who approaches within 30 feet or who otherwise appears to be trying to take the object away.

Dragons, due to their greedy nature, take a –4 penalty on their saving throws against this spell.

Monstrous Thrall

Enchantment (Compulsion) [Mind-Affecting]
Level: Domination 9
Components: V, S, XP
Duration: Permanent

As *dominate monster* (see page 224 of the *Player's Handbook*), except the subject is permanently dominated if it fails its initial Will save. A subject ordered to take an action against its nature receives a Will save with a –4 penalty to resist taking that particular action. If the save succeeds, the subject still remains your thrall despite its minor mutiny. Once a subject makes a successful saving throw to resist a specific order, it makes all future saving throws to resist taking that specific action without a penalty.

XP Cost: 500 XP per Hit Die or level of the subject.

Phantasmal Thief

Conjuration (Creation)
Level: Greed 8, Sor/Wiz 8
Components: V, S, M
Casting Time: 1 standard action
Range: Close (25 ft. + 5 ft./2 levels)
Effect: One object
Duration: 1 round/level
Saving Throw: None
Spell Resistance: No

An invisible force, not unlike an *unseen servant,* comes into being where the caster wishes. On the caster's turn, this force steals objects from others as she inaudibly directs it to (a free action). A *phantasmal thief* can only steal from creatures. It cannot break into locked chests or steal unattended objects. A *phantasmal thief* has a Hide modifier of +20 (useful against those who can see invisible creatures) and a Move Silently modifier of +20.

If a *phantasmal thief* goes undetected, it can steal any object a creature possesses but is not holding or wearing. Even objects in a *bag of holding* can be stolen. It can only steal objects, bring objects to the caster, or put them back where they came from. It can take no other actions. A *phantasmal thief* needs 1 round to steal an object and another round to bring it to the caster.

A *phantasmal thief* can only hold one object at a time, and the object becomes invisible in its grasp.

The thief cannot take an item if it is detected by the creature it's trying to steal from (with a Listen or Spot check). However, the thief can repeat the attempt in the next round. It cannot be harmed in any way, although it can be dispelled.

A *phantasmal thief* can steal an object from a creature's hand by making a successful disarm attempt. It does this as if it had the Improved Disarm feat and a +20 Strength modifier. If a *phantasmal thief* is used in this way, it disappears after it brings the stolen object to the caster.

Material Component: A spool of green thread.

Scale Weakening

Transmutation
Level: Sor/Wiz 2
Components: V, S, M
Casting Time: 1 standard action
Range: Close (25 ft. + 5 ft./2 levels)
Effect: Ray

Duration: 10 minutes/level (D)
Saving Throw: None
Spell Resistance: Yes

A dull gray ray projects from your hand. You must succeed on a ranged touch attack to strike a target. The target's natural armor bonus is reduced by 4 points, +1 point per two caster levels above 3rd (maximum reduction 10 points at 15th level). This spell can't reduce a creature's natural armor bonus to less than 0, nor does it have any effect on an enhancement bonus to natural armor (such as that granted by the *barkskin* spell).

Material Component: A shed snakeskin.

Shield of Warding

Abjuration
Level: Clr 3, Pal 2
Components: V
Casting Time: 1 standard action
Range: Touch
Target: One shield or buckler
Duration: 1 minute/level
Saving Throw: Will negates (object, harmless)
Spell Resistance: No

The touched shield or buckler grants its wielder a +1 sacred bonus on Reflex saves, +1 per five caster levels (maximum +5 at 20th level). The bonus only applies when the shield is worn or carried normally (but not, for instance, if it is slung over the shoulder).

Suppress Breath Weapon

Enchantment (Compulsion) [Mind-Affecting]
Level: Brd 3, Sor/Wiz 3
Components: V
Casting Time: 1 standard action
Range: Close (25 ft. + 5 ft./2 levels)
Target: One creature
Duration: 1 minute/level
Saving Throw: Will negates
Spell Resistance: Yes

The target of this spell cannot choose to use its breath weapon unless "forced" to do so by an enchantment (compulsion) spell of higher level, such as *lesser geas*.

True Domination

Enchantment (Compulsion) [Mind-Affecting]
Level: Domination 8

As *dominate person* (see page 224 of the *Player's Handbook*), except that subjects forced to take actions against their nature receive a new saving throw with a –4 penalty.

Voice of the Dragon

Transmutation
Level: Brd 4, Dragon 4, Sor/Wiz 4
Components: V, S
Casting Time: 1 standard action
Range: Personal
Target: You
Duration: 10 minutes/level (D)

You gain a +10 enhancement bonus on your Bluff, Diplomacy, and Intimidate checks. You also gain the ability to speak and understand (but not read) Draconic.

At any time before the spell's duration expires, you can use a standard action to target a creature with a *suggestion* effect, which functions identically to the spell of that name (including range, duration, and other effects). Doing this causes the *voice of the dragon* spell to end, though the *suggestion* itself lasts for the normal duration thereafter.

Special: Sorcerers cast this spell at +1 caster level.

Vulnerability

Transmutation
Level: Asn 4, Clr 5, Sor/Wiz 5
Components: V, S
Casting Time: 1 standard action
Range: Touch
Target: Creature touched
Duration: 1 round/level
Saving Throw: Will negates
Spell Resistance: Yes

This spell lowers the subject's damage reduction by 5 points (to a minimum of 5). For instance, if you successfully cast *vulnerability* on a dragon with damage reduction 10/magic, its damage reduction becomes 5/magic.

For every four caster levels beyond 11th, the subject's damage reduction lowers by an additional 5 points: 10 at 15th and 15 at 19th.

DRAGONHIDE ARMOR

Armorsmiths can work with dragon hides to produce masterwork armor or shields for the normal cost (see Special Materials, page 283 of the *Dungeon Master's Guide*). The armor created has no special properties other than its masterwork quality. (An armorsmith who also has the Dragoncrafter feat can imbue even greater powers into the armor created; see Dragoncraft Items, below.)

Table 3–2: Dragonhide Armor shows the types and sizes of armor a dragon's body can supply. The terms on the table are defined below.

Armor Type and Size: These four columns show which kinds of armor can be made from dragonhide, and the largest size a single set of armor can be if made from a dragon of a certain size. For example, a Medium dragon's hide is large enough to make one suit of hide armor for a Small creature, or one suit of banded mail for a Tiny creature.

A single hide can yield more than one set of armor if the armor is sized for creatures smaller than the size given on the table. For each size category of the finished armor smaller than the size given on the table, double the number of sets of armor can be made. For instance, when making

Table 3–2: Dragonhide Armor

	Armor Type and Size				
Dragon Size	Hide	Banded Mail	Half-Plate	Full Plate or Breastplate	Shield?
Tiny	Diminutive	Fine	—	—	No
Small	Tiny	Diminutive	Fine	—	No
Medium	Small	Tiny	Diminutive	Fine	No
Large	Medium	Small	Tiny	Diminutive	Yes
Huge	Large	Medium	Small	Tiny	Yes
Gargantuan	Huge	Large	Medium	Small	Yes
Colossal	Gargantuan	Huge	Large	Medium	Yes

banded mail from the hide of a Colossal dragon, an armorsmith can make one suit of Huge armor (as the table indicates), two suits of Large armor, four suits of Medium armor, eight suits of Small armor, sixteen suits of Tiny armor, thirty-two suits of Diminutive armor, or sixty-four suits of Fine armor.

Shield?: A "Yes" entry in this column indicates that enough hide is left over after the armorsmithing process to create one heavy or light shield or a buckler sized for a character the same size as the dragon. An armorsmith can choose to make shields instead of armor out of all or part of a dragon's hide. Creating a tower shield uses up as much hide as a suit of hide armor. Creating two heavy shields or two light shields or two bucklers uses up as much hide as a suit of hide armor.

Special Properties of Dragonhide Armor: Many characters favor dragonhide armor simply because it looks good. In combat, dragonhide armor isn't any better than normal armor; however, the armor itself remains immune to energy damage of the same type as the breath weapon of the dragon that supplied the hide. For example, red dragon armor is impervious to fire. The character wearing the armor does not benefit from this property.

DRAGONCRAFT ITEMS

Dragoncraft items are nonmagical objects made from specific parts of a true dragon's body. Only a character with the Dragoncrafter feat (see page 105) can create dragoncraft items. They derive special powers from their origin, as well as from the skill of the person crafting them.

Creating a dragoncraft item is much like creating a masterwork weapon or similar item. In addition to the item itself (which may also include a masterwork component, if it is a weapon, shield, or suit of armor), the character must "create" the dragoncraft component.

A dragoncraft component has a price that varies based on the specific item (see item descriptions below). The Craft DC for creating a dragoncraft component is 25. Only after all components of a dragoncraft item are completed is the item considered finished.

Since dragoncraft items aren't magical, they don't lose their powers in an *antimagic field* or similar area. For those effects that require a caster level, treat the caster level as 3rd or the lowest level possible to cast the spell in question, whichever is higher. The powers of dragoncraft items don't stack with similar or identical effects, as noted in the specific item descriptions below. You can add magical qualities to a dragoncraft item (including enhancement bonuses for items such as weapons and armor) at the normal price, but only if you possess the Dragoncrafter feat (in addition to any other prerequisites).

Several dragoncraft items are described below. The description of each item gives a dragoncraft price, dragon part, and skill, as defined here.

Dragoncraft Price: This is the price of the dragoncraft component. Add the price of the item itself, as well as the price for masterwork quality (for armor, shields, and weapons), to find the item's full price.

Dragon Part: The portion of a dragon's body required to create the dragoncraft item. The cost of this part is included in the dragoncraft price. On average, the part has a value of approximately one-third of the dragoncraft price, since it represents the raw materials needed for the item. If the character crafting the item supplies the part himself (perhaps from a dragon he has slain), reduce the dragoncraft price for this item by one-third.

Skill: The Craft skill needed to create the dragoncraft component.

Dragoncraft Item Descriptions

Blood Elixir: A blood elixir is a concoction brewed from the concentrated blood of a true dragon. A blood elixir grants the drinker a +2 enhancement bonus to Strength (if brewed from a chromatic dragon) or Charisma (if brewed from a metallic dragon), as well as an additional effect as noted on the table below, based on the dragon's variety. You can consume a blood elixir as a full-round action (which provokes attacks of opportunity), and its effects last for 10 minutes. These effects are extraordinary, not magical.

Dragon Variety	Effect	Price
Black	darkvision 120 ft.	700 gp
Blue	sound imitation [1]	900 gp
Brass	*speak with animals*	400 gp
Bronze	*water breathing*	1,000 gp
Copper	*spider climb*	700 gp
Gold	*polymorph* [2]	1,700 gp
Green	*suggestion* [2]	1,200 gp
Red	*dragon breath* (fire) [2]	1,400 gp
Silver	cloudwalking [1]	1,400 gp
White	icewalking [1]	600 gp

1 Functions as the dragon ability of the same name.
2 This ability is usable only once during the elixir's duration. Its effect lasts until the end of the elixir's duration.

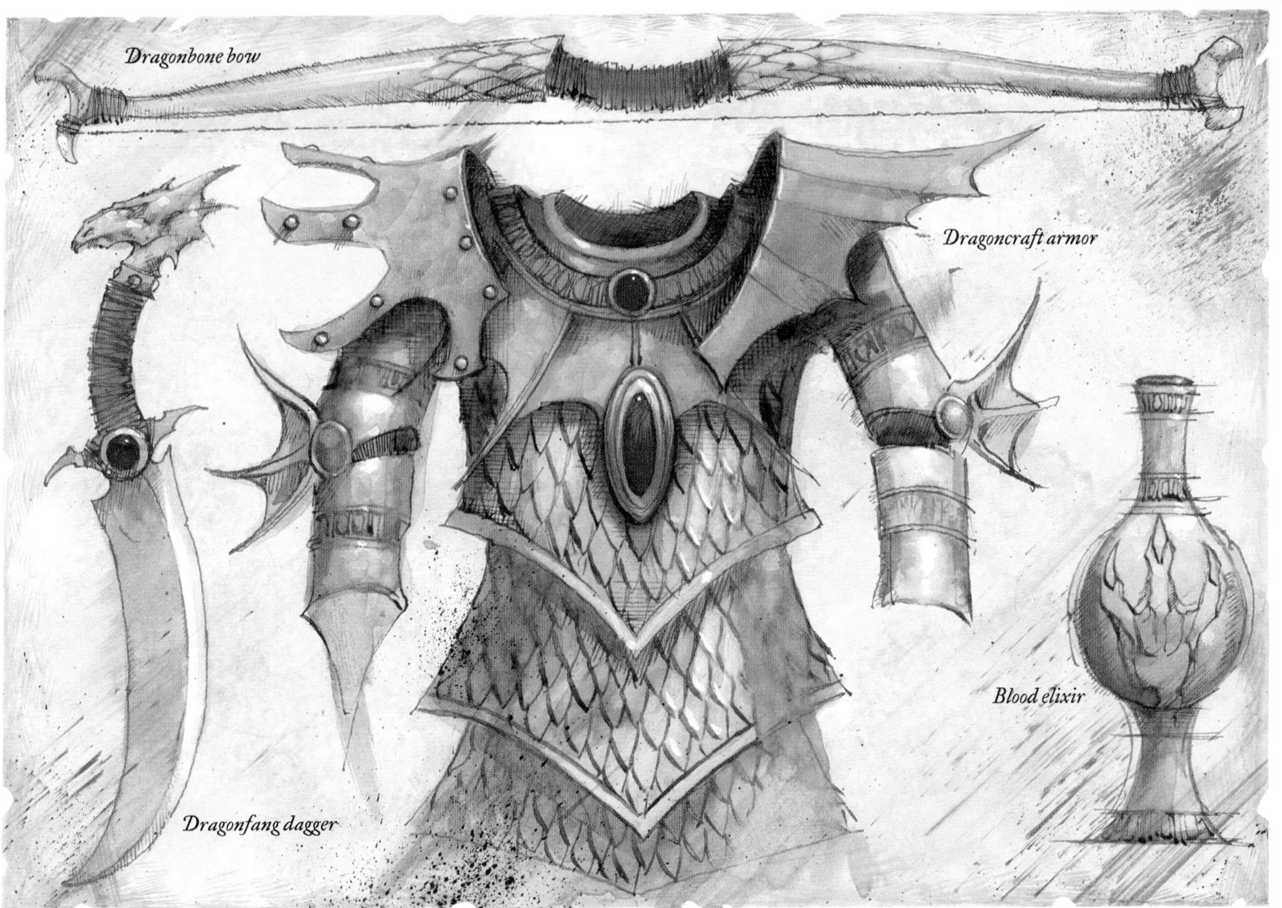

Illus. by W. England

Dragoncraft Price: see above; *Dragon Part:* dragon blood (1 gallon); *Skill:* Craft (alchemy); *Weight:* 1/2 lb.

Dragonbone Bow: A bow carved from a single bone of a dragon (a thigh bone or similarly large bone) displays superior tensile strength and power. Such a bow is considered a composite bow (short or long) with a strength rating set by the crafter. In addition, the bow's range increment is 20 feet longer than normal for the bow's type (90 feet for a composite shortbow or 130 feet for a composite longbow).

Dragoncraft Price: as composite bow +100 gp; *Dragon Part:* dragon bone; *Skill:* Craft (bowyer); Weight: 3 lb.

Dragoncraft Armor or Shield: Dragoncraft armor and shields are masterwork versions of armor and shields crafted from a dragon's hide that also grant energy resistance. A suit of dragoncraft armor or a dragoncraft shield grants the wearer resistance 5 against a specific type of energy, as appropriate to the dragon (acid for black, copper, or green; cold for silver or white; electricity for blue or bronze; fire for brass, gold, or red). This resistance is treated as an extraordinary (and thus nonmagical) feature of the armor. It doesn't stack with any other energy resistance (of the same type) possessed by the character.

In addition, dragoncraft armor is treated as one category lighter for purposes of movement and other determinations. Heavy dragoncraft armors are treated as medium, and medium and light armors are treated as light. Armor check penalties are reduced by 2 (including the 1-point reduction for masterwork armor or shield). Dragoncraft armor has the normal maximum Dexterity bonus.

Dragoncraft armor can be hide armor, scale mail, half-plate, or full plate armor. Dragoncraft shields can be light or heavy.

Dragoncraft Price: 3,000 gp (light armor); 6,000 gp (medium armor), 11,000 gp (heavy armor); *Dragon Part:* dragon hide; *Skill:* Craft (armorsmithing); *Weight:* same as ordinary armor or shield.

Dragonfang Weapon: Dragonfang weapons are masterwork weapons crafted from the claws and teeth of a dragon. In addition to the +1 nonmagical enhancement bonus on attack rolls granted by its masterwork quality, a dragonfang weapon deals 1 point of energy damage on each successful hit. The type of energy is the same as that of the dragon's breath weapon. If a dragon doesn't have a breath weapon that deals acid, cold, electricity, fire, or sonic damage, dragonfang weapons made from its remains do not deal any extra damage. This damage is treated as an extraordinary (and thus nonmagical) feature of the weapon. It doesn't stack with any other energy damage (of the same type) dealt by the weapon.

A single tooth or claw from a dragon can be crafted into a light weapon of the same size category as the dragon, a one-handed weapon of one size category smaller, or a two-handed weapon of two size categories smaller. A single dragon's body can provide enough material for up to twelve weapons.

Only piercing and slashing weapons may be created as dragonfang weapons.

Dragoncraft Price: 300 gp; *Dragon Part:* dragon tooth or claw; *Skill:* Craft (weaponsmithing); *Weight:* 2 lb.

Dragonhide Mantle: A dragon's hide can be rendered flexible enough to wear as a cloak. Crafting a dragonhide mantle requires as much hide as a suit of hide armor, and the mantle must be created to fit the wearer's size.

A dragonhide mantle grants the wearer resistance 5 against a specific type of energy, as appropriate to the dragon (acid for black, copper, or green; cold for silver or white; electricity for blue or bronze; fire for brass, gold, or red). This resistance is treated as an extraordinary (and thus nonmagical) feature of the mantle. It doesn't stack with any other energy resistance (of the same type) possessed by the character.

In addition, the wearer of a dragonhide mantle gains a +2 circumstance bonus on Intimidate checks against dragons.

Dragoncraft Price: 3,800 gp; *Dragon Part:* dragon hide; *Skill:* Craft (leatherworking); *Weight:* same as ordinary hide armor of appropriate size.

MAGIC ITEMS

The magic items introduced here are separated into armor, weapons, rings, rods, staffs, wondrous items, and artifacts, and presented alphabetically within each category.

ARMOR

Armor of Dragonshape: This suit of *+3 dragoncraft hide armor* grants its wearer resistance 5 against a specific type of energy, as appropriate to the dragon from whose scales it was crafted (acid for black, copper, or green; cold for silver or white; electricity for blue or bronze; or fire for brass, gold, or red). This resistance is treated as an extraordinary (and thus nonmagical) feature of the armor.

If the wearer has the wild shape ability, she may change into a Small or Medium dragon of the same color as the armor once per day, and may remain in that form for up to 7 hours. This change doesn't count against the character's normal limit of daily wild shape uses.

Moderate transmutation; CL 7th; Craft Magic Arms and Armor, Dragoncrafter, wild shape ability; Price 23,165 gp; Cost 14,665 gp + 680 XP; Weight 25 lb.

Armor of Mobility: This suit of *+2 leather armor* grants its wearer the Mobility feat, even if he doesn't have the prerequisites.

Faint transmutation; CL 5th; Craft Magic Arms and Armor, *cat's grace;* Price 16,160 gp; Cost 8,160 gp + 320 XP; Weight 15 lb.

Bulwark of Antimagic: Once per day, the wielder of this *+1 tower shield* can command it to radiate an *antimagic field.*

Moderate abjuration; CL 11th; Craft Magic Arms and Armor, *antimagic field;* Price 27,580 gp; Cost 14,380 gp + 575 XP; Weight 65 lb.

Dragondodger Armor: This suit of *+3 studded leather armor* grants its wearer the evasion ability, but only against breath weapons. (When a breath weapon would normally allow a Reflex save for half damage, the wearer of the armor takes no damage on a successful save.)

Moderate abjuration; CL 9th; Craft Magic Arms and Armor, *aura of evasion;* Price 15,675 gp; Cost 7,925 gp + 620 XP; Weight 20 lb.

Dragonrider Armor: This suit of *+1 full plate armor* is crafted from the cast-off scales of a dragon (rather than those harvested from a slain dragon). It grants resistance 10 to form of energy associated with the dragon from whose scales it is created (acid, cold, electricity, or fire, as appropriate). It also grants its wearer a +5 bonus on Ride checks whenever riding a dragon, and activates a *feather fall* spell whenever the rider falls more than 5 feet.

Faint abjuration; CL 3rd; Craft Magic Arms and Armor, *feather fall;* Price 26,150 gp; Cost 13,400 gp + 1,000 XP; Weight 50 lb.

WEAPONS

Blade of Dragondoom: The wielder of this *+3 greatsword* may, as a free action, choose to deliver a smite attack upon a dragon. For every size category of the dragon larger than Medium, the smite attack deals an extra 1d6 points of damage (+1d6 against a Large creature, +2d6 against Huge, +3d6 against Gargantuan, and +4d6 against Colossal). The smite function may be used three times per day, but no more than once per round. The wielder must declare the use of the smite before the attack is made, and if the attack misses, the smite is wasted.

Moderate transmutation; CL 7th; Craft Magic Arms and Armor, *fell the greatest foe;* Price 34,350 gp; Cost 17,305 gp + 1,360 XP; Weight 15 lb.

Bow of the Mighty Dragonhunter: This *+2 dragon bane composite longbow* (+4 Str bonus) is carved from the thigh bone of a Huge or larger dragon (and is thus considered a dragonbone bow; see Dragoncraft Items, above). If an arrow fired from this bow hits a dragon, the dragon takes 1 point of Strength damage. Furthermore, any critical hit inflicted on a dragon by an arrow fired from this bow deals ×5 damage, not ×3 (this benefit doesn't stack with any quality that improves the critical multiplier of a weapon). Thus, a critical hit deals normal arrow damage ×5 plus 5 points of Strength damage. (Other effects related to threatening or confirming critical hits, such as the *keen edge* or *bless weapon* spells, don't function if applied to this bow or the arrows it fires.)

Ring of dragon friendship

Moderate transmutation and necromancy; CL 9th; Craft Magic Arms and Armor, Dragoncrafter, *keen edge, ray of enfeeblement*; Price 36,900 gp; Cost 18,900 gp + 1,440 XP; Weight 3 lb.

Longspear of Piercing: Three times per day, the wielder of this +3 *longspear* may ignore the natural armor (including any enhancement bonuses) of a target he attacks with the weapon. The wielder decides to use this ability as a free action before the attack roll is made. Armor bonuses and all other bonuses to AC still apply normally.

Moderate divination; CL 9th; Craft Magic Arms and Armor, *find the gap*; Price 28,305 gp; Cost 14,305 gp + 1,120 XP; Weight 9 lb.

RINGS

Ring of Dragon Friendship: This ring is carved to look like a dragon coiled around the wearer's finger. The wearer gains a +5 enhancement bonus on Diplomacy checks made to influence the attitude of dragons. No dragon will voluntarily attack or otherwise attempt to harm the wearer.

Once per month, the wearer can use a *suggestion* effect on a dragon (heightened to 9th level; Will DC 23 negates).

If the wearer attacks a dragon in any way (including by the use of the ring's *suggestion* power), this ring loses its powers for 24 hours. (The *suggestion* effect can continue after the ring stops working.)

Strong enchantment; CL 17th; Forge Ring, Heighten Spell, *dominate monster, suggestion*; Price 28,750 gp.

Ring of Dragonshape: This ring is shaped like a hollowed dragon's claw. It is slipped over the length of the wearer's finger, but doesn't restrict manual dexterity in any way. Once per day, the wearer can activate the ring (as a standard action) to polymorph into a young red dragon (if the wearer is evil) or a young gold dragon (if the wearer is good). This effect functions as the *polymorph* spell, except that the duration is 1 hour. The effect can be dismissed by the wearer as a standard action.

Moderate transmutation; CL 7th; Forge Ring, *polymorph*; Price 23,000 gp.

RODS

Rod of Dragon Mastery: This scepter functions much like a *rod of rulership*, though it affects only dragons. The wielder can command the obedience and fealty of dragons within 500 feet when she activates the device (a standard action). Dragons totaling 300 Hit Dice can be ruled, but those with Intelligence scores of 16 or higher are entitled to a DC 22 Will save to negate the effect. Ruled dragons obey the wielder as if she were their absolute sovereign. Still, if the wielder gives a command that is contrary to the nature of the dragons commanded, the magic is broken. A *rod of dragon mastery* can be used for 500 minutes before it crumbles to dust. This duration need not be continuous.

There are two versions of this powerful magic item. The *crimson rod of dragon mastery* affects only evil and neutral dragons, while the *golden rod of dragon mastery* affects only good and neutral dragons.

Strong enchantment; CL 20th; Craft Rod, *mass charm monster*; Price 120,000 gp.

Rod of dragon mastery

Staff of draconic power

Ring of dragonshape

STAFFS

Staff of Draconic Power: This fire-blackened staff is studded with dragon's teeth. It allows use of the following spells:

- *Dragon breath* (30-ft. cone of fire, 5d6 damage; 1 charge)
- *Dragonskin* (1 charge)
- *Draconic might* (2 charges)

Moderate transmutation; CL 9th; Craft Staff, *draconic might, dragon breath, dragonskin*; Price 42,000 gp.

Staff of the Dragonslayer: This staff is carved from the thigh bone of a dragon of at least Huge size. It allows use of the following spells:

- *Scale weakening* (1 charge)
- *Suppress breath weapon* (1 charge)
- *Lower spell resistance* (1 charge)
- *Vulnerability* (2 charges)

Moderate enchantment and transmutation; CL 9th; Craft Staff, *lower spell resistance, scale weakening, suppress breath weapon, vulnerability*; Price 54,000 gp.

WONDROUS ITEMS

Boots of Dragonstriding: These scaled boots grant their wearer a +5 enhancement bonus on Climb and Jump checks. Once per day, the wearer can cast *jump* on himself.

Moderate transmutation; CL 9th; Craft Wondrous Item, *jump, spider climb*; Price 10,000 gp.

Crimson Dragonhide Bracers: These bracers, crafted from the armored hide of a red dragon, grant their wearer an enhancement bonus of +1 to +5 to his natural armor. They also grant resistance to fire 5.

Faint to strong abujuration and transmutation; CL 3rd (*bracers* +1), 6th (*bracers* +2), 9th (*bracers* +3), 12th (*bracers* +4), or 15th (*bracers* +5); Forge Ring, *barkskin*, *resist energy*, creator's caster level must be three times that of the bonus placed in the bracers; Price 5,000 gp (*bracers +1*), 11,000 gp (*bracers +2*), 21,000 gp (*bracers +3*), 35,000 gp (*bracers +4*), or 53,000 gp (*bracers +5*); Weight 1 lb.

Crimson dragonhide bracers

Dracolich Brew: This ingested poison (Fortitude DC 25; 2d6 Con/2d6 Con) is created specifically for a dragon who wishes to become a dracolich. It automatically slays the dragon for which it is prepared (no save allowed).

See the dracolich entry, page 146, for more information.

Moderate necromancy; CL 11th; Brew Potion, Knowledge (arcana) 14 ranks; Price 5,000 gp.

Dracolich Phylactery: A dracolich's phylactery is crafted from a solid, inanimate object of at least 2,000 gp value. Gemstones, particularly ruby, pearl, carbuncle, and jet, are commonly used for the phylactery, since they must be able to resist decay.

When a dracolich first dies, and any time its physical form is destroyed thereafter, its spirit instantly retreats to its phylactery regardless of the distance between that and its body. A dim light within the phylactery indicates the presence of the spirit. While so contained, the spirit cannot take any actions except to possess a suitable corpse; it cannot be contacted or attacked by magic. The spirit can remain in the phylactery indefinitely.

See the dracolich entry, page 146, for more information.

Strong necromancy; CL 13th; Craft Wondrous Item, *control undead*, gem or similar item of minimum value 2,000 gp; Price 50,000 gp plus value of gem; Cost 25,000 gp plus value of gem + 2,000 XP.

Dragon's Eye Amulet: This fist-sized orb resembles the eye of a dragon and dangles from a heavy gold chain. It grants its wearer a +10 enhancement bonus on Search and Spot checks, as well as blindsense with a 30-foot range.

Strong transmutation; CL 9th; Craft Wondrous Item, *dragonsight*; Price 85,000 gp.

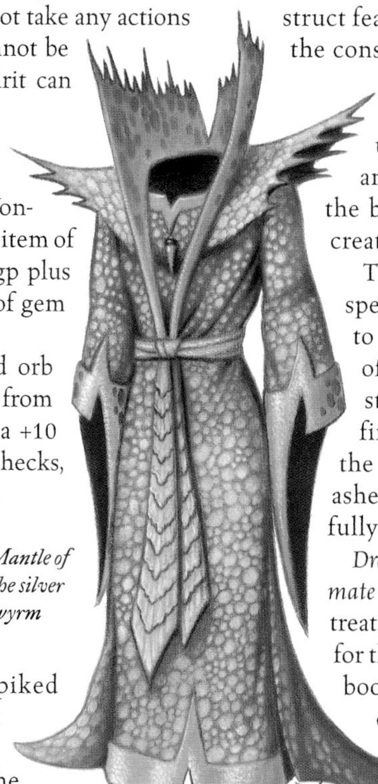

Mantle of the silver wyrm

Dragonfang Gauntlets: These leather gauntlets are studded with dragon teeth and deal damage as spiked gauntlets. They grant a +4 enhancement bonus to the wearer's Strength. Three times per day, the character may use the gauntlets to attack a weapon or shield as if she had the Improved Sunder feat (even if she doesn't have the prerequisites).

When worn by a character with the Improved Unarmed Strike feat, *dragonfang gauntlets* allow the wearer to overcome damage reduction with unarmed strikes as if she were wielding a magic weapon. In this case, the wielder deals her normal unarmed strike damage, rather than the damage for spiked gauntlets.

Moderate evocation and transmutation; CL 12th; Craft Wondrous Item, *bull's strength, greater magic fang, shatter*; Price 28,500 gp; Weight 1 lb.

Goggles of Draconic Vision: The wearer of these goggles gains a +10 bonus on Spot checks and enjoys low-light vision and 60-foot darkvision. Once per day, the wearer can command the goggles to grant him blindsense for 1 minute.

The goggles also protect the wearer from being blinded by the cloud created by a hovering dragon (though the cloud still provides concealment for all within it).

Moderate transmutation; CL 9th; Craft Wondrous Item, *dragonsight*; Price 46, 000 gp.

Golem Manual: A *golem manual* contains information, incantations, and magical power that help a character to craft a golem (see page 134 of the *Monster Manual*). The instructions therein grant a +5 competence bonus on skill checks made to craft the golem's body. Each manual also holds the prerequisite spells needed for a specific golem and effectively grants the builder use of the Craft Construct feat (see page 303 of the *Monster Manual*) during the construction of the golem, and grants the character an increase to her caster level for the purpose of crafting a golem. Any golem built using a *golem manual* does not cost the creator any XP, since the requisite XP are "contained" in the book and "expended" by the book during the creation process.

The spells included in a *golem manual* require a spell trigger activation and can be activated only to assist in the construction of a golem. The cost of the book does not include the cost of constructing the golem's body. Once the golem is finished, the writing in the manual fades and the book is consumed in flames. When the book's ashes are sprinkled upon the golem, it becomes fully animated.

Dragonbone Golem Manual: This book contains *animate dead, cause fear,* and *geas/quest*. The reader may treat her caster level as one level higher than normal for the purpose of crafting a dragonbone golem. The book supplies 4,400 XP for the creation of a dragonbone golem.

Strong enchantment and necromancy [evil]; CL 12th; Craft Construct, creator must be caster level 12th, *animate dead, cause fear, geas/quest*; Price 28,000 gp; Cost 3,000 gp + 4,640 XP; Weight 5 lb.

Drakestone Golem Manual: This book contains *animate objects, antimagic field, flesh to stone,* and *geas/quest.* The reader may treat her caster level as three levels higher than normal for the purpose of crafting a drakestone golem. The book supplies 6,400 XP for the creation of a drakestone golem.

Strong abjuration, enchantment, and transmutation; CL 16th; Craft Construct, creator must be caster level 16th, *animate objects, antimagic field, flesh to stone, geas/quest;* Price 40,000 gp; Cost 4,000 gp + 6,720 XP; Weight 5 lb.

Ironwyrm Golem Manual: This book contains *animate objects, antimagic field, geas/quest, incendiary cloud,* and *limited wish.* The reader may treat her caster level as four levels higher than normal for the purpose of crafting a ironwyrm golem. The book supplies 8,000 XP for the creation of a ironwyrm golem.

Strong abjuration, enchantment, evocation, and transmutation; CL 18th; Craft Construct, creator must be caster level 18th, *animate objects, antimagic field, geas/quest, incendiary cloud, limited wish;* Price 50,000 gp; Cost 5,000 gp + 8,400 XP; Weight 5 lb.

Horn of Dragons: This horn bears intricate carvings of dragons in flight. When blown (a full-round action), the horn summons an adult dragon 1 round later, to a location up to 100 feet away. The dragon remains for 1 hour and serves the user of the horn to the best of its ability. At the end of the duration, or if the dragon is slain or dispelled, the dragon disappears. The type of dragon depends on the user's alignment (see the table below). The horn may be blown once per month.

User's Alignment	Dragon Summoned
LG, NG, or LN	Bronze
CG, N, or CN	Copper
LE or NE	Green
CE	Black

Strong conjuration; CL: 17th; Craft Wondrous Item, *summon monster IX;* Price 75,000 gp.

Idol of the Dragon: Much like a *figurine of wondrous power,* an *idol of the dragon* is a miniature statuette (about 2 inches long) resembling a particular variety of dragon. The color and kind of the dragon is very apparent, even at a glance, due to the craftsmanship involved. The idol grants energy resistance (5 or 10) of the appropriate type to its owner while carried (but not while the idol is in dragon form).

Once per week, when the idol is tossed into the air and the proper command word spoken, it becomes a full-size dragon of the appropriate age (see the table below). The dragon is a living creature, not a construct, and has all the abilities and powers of an average dragon of its age. The dragon obeys and serves its owner for up to 1 hour. At the end of this duration, or if it is prematurely dismissed by its owner, the dragon returns to idol form. A targeted *dispel magic* on the full-size dragon can return it to idol form if successful. If the dragon is slain while at full size, the idol is destroyed.

Type	Age	Resistance	Price
White	wyrmling	cold 5	15,000 gp
Brass	wyrmling	fire 5	21,000 gp
Black	very young	acid 5	24,000 gp
Copper	very young	acid 5	32,000 gp
Green	young	acid 10	42,000 gp
Bronze	young	electricity 10	56,000 gp
Blue	juvenile	electricity 10	73,000 gp
Silver	juvenile	cold 10	93,000 gp
Red	young adult	fire 10	116,000 gp
Gold	young adult	fire 10	142,000 gp

Faint to strong conjuration; CL 3rd (white), 5th (black, brass), 7th (copper, green), 9th (bronze), 11th (blue), 13th (silver), 15th (red), or 17th (gold); Craft Wondrous Item, *resist energy,* and either *summon monster II* (white), *summon monster III* (black, brass), *summon monster IV* (copper, green), *summon monster V* (bronze), *summon monster VI* (blue), *summon monster VII* (silver), *summon monster VIII* (red), or *summon monster IX* (gold); Price as shown on table.

Mantle of the Silver Wyrm: This impressive cloak is fashioned from the hide of a silver dragon. It grants its wearer a +2 enhancement bonus to Charisma and resistance to cold 10. In addition, its wearer can use *fly* (as the spell) once per day.

Faint abjuration and transmutation; CL 5th; Craft Wondrous Item, *eagle's splendor, fly, resist energy;* Price 27,000 gp; Weight 3 lb.

Wyrmfang Amulet: This necklace of dragon teeth grants all of the wearer's natural attacks the ability to overcome damage reduction as if they were magic weapons. (The attacks don't actually gain an enhancement bonus, only the ability to ignore some creatures' damage reduction.)

Moderate transmutation; CL 12th; Craft Wondrous Item, *greater magic fang;* Price 2,500 gp.

MINOR ARTIFACT

Draco Mystere: This tome, known as "Mysteries of the Dragon" in Common, is a legendary book of lore regarding dragonkind. Some claim it was written by the first high priest of the Cult of Ashardalon, but others call this assertion nothing but an idle boast, believing the book to be far older than that. Over the centuries, it has been studied, copied, lost, and found again by dozens if not hundreds of readers. Many lesser versions of this book are known to exist, but none share its power.

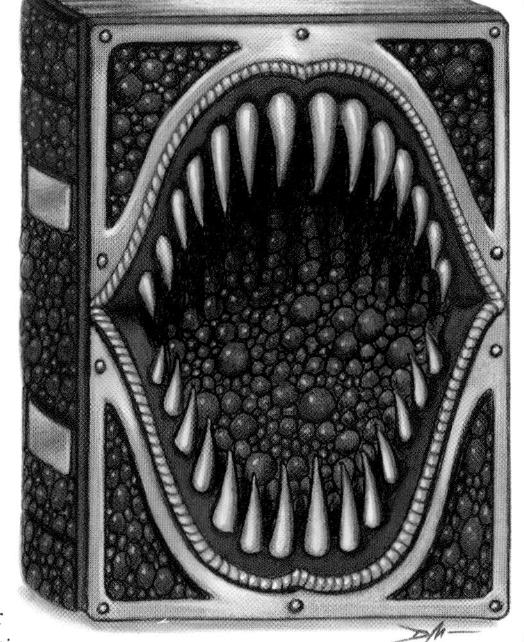

Draco Mystere

Reading *Draco Mystere* takes thirty consecutive 8-hour days of study. If the reader misses even a single day during this time, he must start again from the beginning. Completion of the study gives the reader a +5 inherent bonus on Knowledge (arcana) checks regarding dragons. The reader also gains low-light vision (if the character already has low-light vision, the effect is increased by one multiple, such as from double to triple) and immunity to magic sleep and paralysis effects.

In addition, a sorcerer who reads *Draco Mystere* gains 1 point of Charisma and sufficient XP to place him halfway into the next experience level (which must be used to increase his sorcerer level). Other characters who peruse the book do not receive these benefits.

Any individual can only receive the tome's benefits once in a lifetime.

Strong transmutation; CL 19th; Weight 3 lb.

PRESTIGE CLASSES

Each of the new prestige classes described here draws power, inspiration, or both from draconic sources.

DRACOLYTE

Only a few rare nondragons take up worship of the draconic gods. The dracolyte is the most dedicated of these rare individuals, a divine spellcaster who devotes his energy and support to the deities of dragonkind. As a dracolyte gains power and prestige, he receives abilities associated with the dragons themselves.

Clerics and druids are the most likely to become dracolytes. Some paladins and rangers, particularly those with metallic dragon allies, enter this prestige class. Most members of other classes don't have the religious bent to pursue this path.

A dracolyte

Dracolytes often congregate with others who share their respect and faith, including members of many of the other prestige classes presented here. They are outcasts in most cultures, except those that have innate respect for dragonkind (such as kobolds, lizardfolk, and troglodytes).

Hit Die: d8.

Requirements

To qualify to become a dracolyte, a character must fulfill all the following criteria.

Race: Any nondragon.

Feats: Dragonfriend, Toughness.

Skills: Concentration 8 ranks, Diplomacy 4 ranks, Knowledge (arcana) 4 ranks, Knowledge (religion) 8 ranks.

Languages: Draconic.

Spellcasting: Able to cast 2nd-level divine spells.

Class Skills

The dracolyte's class skills (and the key ability for each skill) are Bluff (Cha), Concentration (Con), Diplomacy (Cha), Heal (Wis), Jump (Str), Knowledge (arcana) (Int), Knowledge (religion) (Int), and Spellcraft (Int). See Chapter 4: Skills in the *Player's Handbook* for skill descriptions.

Skill Points at Each Level: 2 + Int modifier.

Class Features

All of the following are class features of the dracolyte prestige class.

Weapon and Armor Proficiency: A dracolyte gains no proficiency with any weapons, armor, or shields.

Spellcasting: When a new dracolyte level is gained, the character gains new spells per day as if he had also gained a level in a divine spellcasting class he belonged to before he added the prestige class. He does not, however, gain any other benefit a character of that class would have gained (improved chance of controlling or rebuking undead, and so on). This essentially means that the character adds the level

Table 3–3: The Dracolyte

Class Level	Base Attack Bonus	Fort Save	Ref Save	Will Save	Special	Spellcasting
1st	+0	+2	+0	+2	Prestige domain	+1 level of existing class
2nd	+1	+3	+0	+3	—	+1 level of existing class
3rd	+2	+3	+1	+3	Alertness	+1 level of existing class
4th	+3	+4	+1	+4	—	+1 level of existing class
5th	+3	+4	+1	+4	Foster dragon	+1 level of existing class
6th	+4	+5	+2	+5	—	+1 level of existing class
7th	+5	+5	+2	+5	Immunities	+1 level of existing class
8th	+6	+6	+2	+6	—	+1 level of existing class
9th	+6	+6	+3	+6	Keen senses	+1 level of existing class
10th	+7	+7	+3	+7	*Summon dragon*	+1 level of existing class

of dracolyte to the level of whatever divine spellcasting class the character has, then determines spells per day and caster level accordingly.

If a character had more than one divine spellcasting class before he became a dracolyte, he must decide to which class he adds each level of dracolyte for the purpose of determining spells per day.

Prestige Domain (Ex): At 1st level, a dracolyte gains access to a prestige domain based on his alignment. Good-aligned dracolytes (and neutral clerics who channel positive energy) gain access to the Glory prestige domain (and its granted power), while evil-aligned dracolytes (and neutral clerics who channel negative energy) gain access to the Domination prestige domain (and its granted power). Dracolytes who are neither good nor evil (and who don't channel positive or negative energy) can select either of these domains, but once made, the choice can never be altered.

The spells associated with the prestige domain can be selected to fill any domain spell slots the dracolyte has available. If the prestige domain is the character's only domain, he gains the ability to cast a domain spell of each spell level to which he has access once per day, in addition to those spells he already casts.

Prestige domains are presented and explained in the Cleric Domains section, beginning on page 107.

Alertness: At 3rd level, a dracolyte gains Alertness as a bonus feat.

Foster Dragon: At 5th level, a dracolyte is entrusted with the care of a wyrmling dragon. The kind of dragon is up to the DM, but the dragon's alignment should match the dracolyte's. The wyrmling dragon follows the dracolyte loyally, and will even accompany him on adventures (though it receives no XP and can't attain new levels).

If the wyrmling dies, the dracolyte cannot gain any additional dracolyte levels until he receives an *atonement* spell from another dracolyte or a cleric who worships a draconic deity.

Immunities (Ex): A 7th-level dracolyte gains immunity to magic sleep and paralysis effects.

Keen Senses (Ex): At 9th level, a dracolyte gains darkvision out to 60 feet and low-light vision.

***Summon Dragon* (Sp):** A 10th-level dracolyte can, as a full-round action, summon a dragon once per day. This ability is similar to a *summon monster* spell, except that the dracolyte summons an adult dragon of the same kind as the wyrmling dragon entrusted to his care (see above). The summoned dragon remains for 10 rounds and follows the dracolyte's commands.

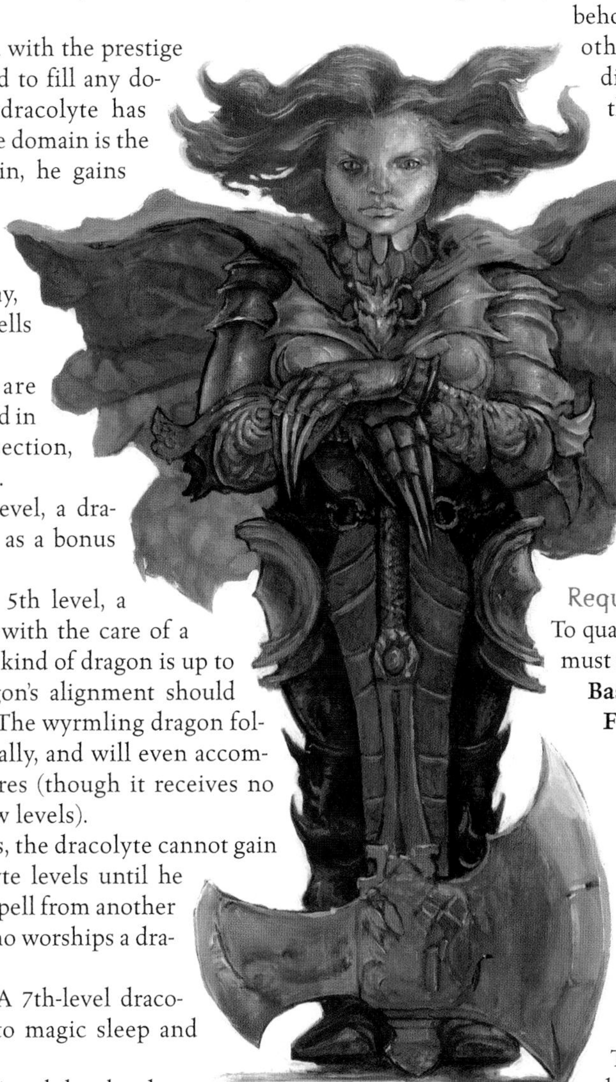

A dragonkith

DRAGONKITH

Dragonkith are creatures that serve and aid dragons. They live with or near a dragon or a group of dragons, acting as servants or peers (depending on the individual dragon and the dragonkith). In return for service, over time, the dragon bestows upon a dragonkith special abilities—and even physical changes—using complex rituals known only to their kind.

Although sometimes they are humans, elves, dwarves, halflings, or gnomes, dragonkith are just as often members of other intelligent species, such as lizardfolk, giants, troglodytes, lammasu, pseudodragons, titans, dragonnes, beholders, lamias, and others—even, rarely, other dragons. Thus, dragonkith are a diverse group; no one class is more likely than another to become one, and many dragonkith do not have classes at all (they are monsters). NPC dragonkith are usually found in the company of their dragon companion. Sometimes they are alone, completing some errand for the dragon. Occasionally they work in small, tight-knit groups of dragonkith, all pledged either to the same dragon or to allied dragons.

Hit Die: d8.

Requirements

To qualify to become a dragonkith, a character must fulfill all the following criteria.

Base Attack Bonus: +6.

Feats: Alertness, Endurance.

Skills: Knowledge (arcana) 4 ranks.

Language: Draconic.

Special: Must be chosen by a dragon of the same alignment. If a dragonkith ever ceases its relationship with the dragon, or the dragon dies, the character loses all special abilities gained from this prestige class.

Class Skills

The dragonkith's class skills (and the key ability for each skill) are Appraise (Int), Bluff (Cha), Craft (Int), Diplomacy (Cha), Intimidate (Cha), Knowledge (any) (Int), Profession (Wis), Search (Int), and Spot (Wis). See Chapter 4: Skills in the *Player's Handbook* for skill descriptions.

Skill Points at Each Level: 4 + Int modifier.

Illus. by M. Mitchell

Table 3–4: The Dragonkith

Class Level	Base Attack Bonus	Fort Save	Ref Save	Will Save	Special
1st	+1	+2	+0	+0	Scales (natural armor +1), telepathic plea
2nd	+2	+3	+0	+0	Mighty attack +1d6
3rd	+3	+3	+1	+1	*Detect treasure*, energy resistance 5
4th	+4	+4	+1	+1	Scales (natural armor +2), telepathic link
5th	+5	+4	+1	+1	Mighty attack +2d6
6th	+6	+5	+2	+2	*Sorcerous knack*
7th	+7	+5	+2	+2	Scales (natural armor +3), energy resistance 10
8th	+8	+6	+2	+2	Mighty attack +3d6
9th	+9	+6	+3	+3	Energy resistance 15, share spells
10th	+10	+7	+3	+3	Scales (natural armor +4)

Class Features

All of the following are class features of the dragonkith prestige class.

Weapon and Armor Proficiency: A dragonkith gains no proficiency with any weapons, armor, or shields.

Scales (Ex): A dragonkith, over time, develops crusty scales the same color as her dragon companion. At 1st level, this protection adds +1 to the natural armor bonus of the dragonkith, and its natural armor bonus improves by an additional +1 every three levels. If the dragonkith already has natural armor as an aspect of its creature kind (and not from a spell or magic item), this bonus stacks with its existing natural armor bonus.

Telepathic Plea (Su): Wherever a dragonkith is, its dragon companion can send an instantaneous, telepathic plea for help at any time. No details are provided in the message, other than that the dragon is in danger. This communication does not work both ways (the dragonkith cannot alert the dragon).

Mighty Attack (Su): At 2nd level, once per day, a dragonkith can call upon its dragon's might to deal an extra 1d6 points of damage on a single attack. The dragonkith must decide before an attack is resolved whether it will use this power. If the attack misses, that use of the mighty attack is wasted. For every three levels beyond 2nd, the damage increases by another 1d6.

***Detect Treasure* (Sp):** Once per day, a dragonkith of 3rd level or higher can use a *detect treasure* ability. This works like the *detect magic* spell, except that it senses Medium or smaller objects that are worth more than 100 gp. On the first round, the dragonkith detects the presence of such objects; on the second round, the power reveals the number of objects and the location of each. In each subsequent round, the dragonkith can make an Appraise check to estimate the value of one object.

Energy Resistance (Su): A dragonkith develops an ever stronger resistance to the energy associated with its dragon companion's breath weapon. Beginning at 3rd level, it can ignore some damage of the type generated by its dragon companion's breath weapon. This ability applies to sources of the energy type other than the dragon companion's breath weapon. Thus, a dragonkith with a red dragon companion gains resistance to fire 5 at 3rd level, effective against fire from any source. This resistance improves to 10 at 7th level and to 15 at 9th level. In the case of dragons with multiple breath weapons, the dragonkith gains resistance to one type of damaging breath.

Telepathic Link (Su): At 4th level, a dragonkith develops a telepathic link with its companion dragon out to a distance of up to 1 mile. The dragonkith and dragon can communicate telepathically. Because of this link, one has the same connection to an item or place that the other does. For instance, if the dragonkith has seen a room, its dragon companion can teleport into that room as if she had seen it too.

***Sorcerous Knack* (Sp):** At 6th level, a dragonkith acquires the ability to cast a single arcane spell once per day as a sorcerer of its class level. The dragonkith must choose a spell known to its dragon companion, and it must have a Charisma score of at least 10 + the spell's level to use the spell by means of the *sorcerous knack* ability. Once the spell is chosen, that decision can never be changed.

Share Spells (Su): At either the dragon's or the dragonkith's option, any spell one casts on itself also affects the other. The two must be touching at the time. If the spell has a duration other than instantaneous, the spell stops affecting them if they move farther than 100 feet apart. The spell's effect will not be restored even if they return to each other before the duration would otherwise have ended. The dragon and dragonkith can share spells even if the spells normally do not affect creatures of their respective types.

DRAGONRIDER

Some dream of soaring through the clouds atop a mighty draconic steed, feeling the wind on their faces, afraid of nothing. The dragonrider doesn't simply dream of this life—he leads it.

Characters of all classes may become dragonriders, though the most common are barbarians, fighters, paladins, and rangers. Other characters looking to follow this path often pick up a level of one of these classes first, to gain the riding talent necessary.

An NPC dragonrider might be encountered as a solitary ally of a family of dragons or as part of a larger fighting force, perhaps affiliated with a kingdom or city-state that uses dragons as part of its defenses.

Hit Die: d10.

Requirements

To qualify to become a dragonrider, a character must fulfill all the following criteria.

Base Attack Bonus: +5.

Feats: Mounted Combat, Skill Focus (Ride).

Skills: Diplomacy 4 ranks, Handle Animal 4 ranks, Ride 8 ranks.

Language: Draconic.

Class Skills

The dragonrider's class skills (and the key ability for each skill) are Balance (Dex), Concentration (Con), Diplomacy (Cha), Handle Animal (Cha), Jump (Str), Ride (Dex), Spot (Wis), and Tumble (Dex). See Chapter 4: Skills in the *Player's Handbook* for skill descriptions.

Skill Points at Each Level: 2 + Int modifier.

Class Features

All of the following are class features of the dragonrider prestige class.

Weapon and Armor Proficiency: A dragonrider gains proficiency with the lance, longspear, short bow, and all simple weapons. Dragonriders are proficient with light, medium, and heavy armor and with shields.

Dragonriding (Ex): A dragonrider may add his class level as a bonus to any Ride checks made in conjunction with riding a dragon.

In addition, any dragon ridden by a dragonrider enjoys maneuverability of one grade better than normal (maximum perfect maneuverability). For instance, an adult green dragon with a dragonrider astride it has average maneuverability rather than poor.

Immune to Frightful Presence (Su): While mounted on or within 10 feet of his dragon mount, a dragonrider is immune to the frightful presence of dragons.

Mounted Spellcasting (Ex): A dragonrider has a +5 bonus on Concentration checks made to cast a spell while riding a mount.

Bonus Feat: At 3rd level, a dragonrider gains a bonus feat drawn from the following list: Mounted Archery, Ride-By Attack, Spirited Charge, Trample, Weapon Focus (lance), Weapon Specialization (lance). He must meet all theprerequisites for this bonus feat.

Flyby Attack (Ex): Any dragon mount ridden by a dragonrider of at least 4th level is treated as having the Flyby Attack feat.

Spur Mount (Ex): A 5th-level dragonrider can make a DC 20 Ride check to spur his dragon mount to greater speed. Success on this check increases the dragon's speed (flying and otherwise) by 50% (round down to the nearest 5-foot increment), for 5 rounds.

A dragonrider

DRAGONSLAYER

They come from all walks of life, from all cultures and societies. They may be poor or wealthy, strong or wise, good or evil, skilled with blade or spell. But all dragonslayers share a singular courage and strength of heart—a necessary commodity in their line of work.

Characters of any class may pursue the path of the dragonslayer. Fighters, barbarians, and paladins enjoy the class's increased combat prowess against these powerful enemies. Sorcerers, clerics, wizards, and druids can continue to improve their spellcasting ability while gaining new powers suitable for use in battling dragons. Even bards, monks, rangers, and rogues have much to gain from this class, though the dragonstalker class (see below) is often more their style. Multiclass characters, such as fighter/sorcerers or barbarian/clerics, can make particularly good dragonslayers, bringing a variety of talents to the task.

NPC dragonslayers have few close associates who aren't as skilled as they are in the art of battling dragons. Unless a dragonslayer can trust you with his life, he isn't likely to spend much time in your company. This attitude can lead to a life of solitude, as the dragonslayer travels wherever

Table 3–5: The Dragonrider

Class Level	Base Attack Bonus	Fort Save	Ref Save	Will Save	Special
1st	+1	+2	+0	+2	Dragonriding, immune to frightful presence
2nd	+2	+3	+0	+3	Mounted spellcasting
3rd	+3	+3	+1	+3	Bonus feat
4th	+4	+4	+1	+4	Flyby attack
5th	+5	+4	+1	+4	Spur mount

the cause takes him. A few dragonslayers actively seek out others who share their bravery and dedication, even training those who show promise.

Hit Die: d10.

Requirements

To qualify to become a dragonslayer, a character must fulfill all the following criteria.

Base Attack Bonus: +5.

Feats: Dodge, Iron Will.

Skills: Tumble 2 ranks.

Class Skills

The dragonslayer's class skills (and the key ability for each skill) are Climb (Str), Craft (Wis), Intimidate (Cha), Knowledge (arcana), Jump (Str), Search (Int), and Tumble (Dex). See Chapter 4: Skills in the *Player's Handbook* for skill descriptions.

Skill Points at Each Level: 2 + Int modifier.

Class Features

All of the following are class features of the dragonslayer prestige class.

Weapon and Armor Proficiency: A dragonslayer gains proficiency with all simple and martial weapons, with all types of armor, and with shields and tower shields.

Spellcasting: Each time a character attains an odd-numbered dragonslayer level, the character gains new spells per day and spells known as if he had also gained a level in a spellcasting class he belonged to before he added the prestige class. He does not, however, gain any other benefit a character of that class would have gained (improved chance of controlling or rebuking undead, metamagic or item creation feats, and so on). This essentially means that the character adds the level of dragonslayer to the level of whatever spellcasting class the character has, then determines spells per day and caster level accordingly.

If a character takes one or more levels in this class before having any levels in a spellcasting class, he does not receive this spellcasting benefit. If he thereafter takes levels in one or more spellcasting classes, he becomes eligible to receive the spellcasting benefit for any level in the dragonslayer class that he has not already attained. For example, a 5th-level fighter/1st-level dragonslayer does not receive the spellcasting benefit for being a 1st-level dragonslayer because he did not belong to a spellcasting class before taking a level in the prestige class. If he then picks up one or more levels of wizard before advancing to 3rd level in the dragonslayer class, he receives the spellcasting benefit of a 3rd-level dragonslayer (when he attains that level) but does not receive the 1st-level benefit retroactively.

A dragonslayer

Aura of Courage (Su): At 1st level, a dragonslayer gains immunity to fear (magical or otherwise). Allies within 10 feet of the dragonslayer gain a +4 morale bonus on saving throws against fear effects.

Damage Bonus (Ex): A dragonslayer gains a bonus on weapon damage rolls against dragons equal to his class level.

Overcome Draconic Spell Resistance (Ex): Beginning at 2nd level, a dragonslayer may add his class level to any caster level checks made to overcome a dragon's spell resistance.

Damage Reduction (Ex): At 3rd level, a dragonslayer gains damage reduction 1/–. This improves to damage reduction 2/– at 6th level, and to damage reduction 3/– at 9th level.

Energy Resistance (Su): At 5th level, a dragonslayer gains resistance to acid 5, cold 5, electricity 5, fire 5, and sonic 5. These resistances improve to 10 at 10th level. These resistances don't stack with any other similar effects.

Table 3–6 The Dragonslayer

Class Level	Base Attack Bonus	Fort Save	Ref Save	Will Save	Special	Spellcasting
1st	+1	+2	+0	+2	Aura of courage, damage bonus	+1 level of existing class
2nd	+2	+3	+0	+3	Overcome draconic spell resistance	—
3rd	+3	+3	+1	+3	Damage reduction 1/—	+1 level of existing class
4th	+4	+4	+1	+4	—	—
5th	+5	+4	+1	+4	Energy resistance 5	+1 level of existing class
6th	+6	+5	+2	+5	Damage reduction 2/—, Lightning Reflexes	—
7th	+7	+5	+2	+5	Improved Critical	+1 level of existing class
8th	+8	+6	+2	+6	—	—
9th	+9	+6	+3	+6	Damage reduction 3/—	+1 level of existing class
10th	+10	+7	+3	+7	Energy resistance 10, *true strike*	—

Lightning Reflexes: A dragonslayer gains Lightning Reflexes as a bonus feat at 6th level.

Improved Critical (Ex): A 7th-level dragonslayer gains the effect of the Improved Critical feat for any weapon he uses against a dragon. This benefit does not stack with any other ability that increases the threat range of a weapon.

***True Strike* (Sp):** At 10th level, a dragonslayer may use *true strike* once per day as a move action.

DRAGONSONG LYRIST

The dragonsong lyrist taps into the power of dragonsong, an ancient form of performance that originated among the draconic races, to create strange and wondrous magical effects.

Many bards become dragonsong lyrists, though rogues and even a few monks have been known to pursue the class. Multiclass barbarian/bards and sorcerer/rogues also make good dragonsong lyrists.

Dragonsong lyrists are usually loners, though they occasionally congregate to share new songs or poems. They get along well with bards and sorcerers, and some occupy positions of great respect in barbarian tribes.

Hit Die: d6.

Requirements

To qualify to become a dragonsong lyrist, a character must fulfill all the following criteria.

Alignment: Any nonevil.

Feat: Dragonsong.

Skills: Concentration 5 ranks, Diplomacy 5 ranks, Knowledge (arcana) 5 ranks, Perform (oratory or sing) 10 ranks.

Languages: Draconic.

A dragonsong lyrist

Class Skills

The dragonsong lyrist's class skills (and the key ability for each skill) are Bluff (Cha), Concentration (Con), Craft (Int), Diplomacy (Cha), Knowledge (arcana) (Int), Listen (Wis), Perform (Cha), and Sense Motive (Wis). See Chapter 4: Skills in the *Player's Handbook* for skill descriptions.

Skill Points at Each Level: 4 + Int modifier.

Class Features

All of the following are class features of the dragonsong lyrist prestige class.

Weapon and Armor Proficiency: A dragonsong lyrist gains no proficiency with any weapons, armor, or shields.

Greater Dragonsong (Su): Once per day per class level, a dragonsong lyrist can use song or poetics to invoke the power of dragonsong. Invoking dragonsong requires a standard action. In the case of effects that require a saving throw, the DC is equal to 10 + lyrist' class level + lyrist's Cha modifier. The bonus from the Dragonsong feat also applies to this save DC.

In cases where the character continues a greater dragonsong effect over the course of multiple rounds (such as song of strength), the dragonsong lyrist can fight while using greater dragonsong but cannot cast spells, activate magic items by spell completion (such as scrolls), or activate magic items by command word (such as wands). Maintaining a greater dragonsong effect does not require concentration.

A deaf dragonsong lyrist has a 20% chance to fail when using greater dragonsong. If she fails, the attempt still counts against her daily limit.

Song of Strength: A 1st-level dragonsong lyrist can imbue herself and her allies with great physical power. The dragonsong lyrist and all allies within 30 feet who can hear her gain a +4 morale bonus to Strength for the duration of the lyrist's performance and for 5 rounds thereafter. This is a mind-affecting ability.

Song of Compulsion: At 2nd level, a dragonsong lyrist can use her greater dragonsong to make a *suggestion* to a single creature within 30 feet who can hear the lyrist. A Will save negates the effect. This is an enchantment (compulsion, mind-affecting, language-dependent effect. Dragons take a –2 penalty on this saving throw.

Song of Flight: A 3rd-level dragonsong lyrist can grant herself and her allies the ability to fly, as the spell

TABLE 3–7: THE DRAGONSONG LYRIST

Class Level	Base Attack Bonus	Fort Save	Ref Save	Will Save	Special	Spellcasting
1st	+0	+0	+2	+2	Greater dragonsong (song of strength)	—
2nd	+1	+0	+3	+3	Greater dragonsong (song of compulsion)	+1 level of existing class
3rd	+2	+1	+3	+3	Greater dragonsong (song of flight)	—
4th	+3	+1	+4	+4	Greater dragonsong (song of fear)	+1 level of existing class
5th	+3	+1	+4	+4	Greater dragonsong (song of healing)	—

of the same name. This song affects the character and a number of allies equal to her Charisma modifier (all of whom must be able to hear the lyrist) and lasts for 1 minute per level. This is a transmutation effect.

Song of Fear: At 4th level, a dragonsong lyrist can use her song or poetics to inspire fear in her foes. All enemies within a radius of 30 feet × class level are subject to the effect if they have fewer HD than the dragonsong lyrist. A potentially affected creature that succeeds on a Will save remains immune to that dragonsong lyrist's frightful presence ability for 24 hours. On a failure, creatures with fewer than half the dragonsong lyrist's HD become panicked for 2d6 rounds and those with HD equal to or greater than half the dragonsong lyrist's become shaken for 2d6 rounds. Dragons are immune to this ability, as are any creatures immune to fear. This is a mind-affecting effect.

Song of Healing: A 5th-level dragonsong lyrist can use her greater dragonsong to heal herself and her allies. Each ally within 30 feet who can hear the dragonsong lyrist regains hit points and ability points as if he or she had rested for a full day. No character may benefit from this ability more than once per hour. This is a conjuration (healing) effect.

Spellcasting: Each time an even-numbered dragonsong lyrist level is gained, the character gains new spells per day and spells known as if she had also gained a level in a spellcasting class she belonged to before she added the prestige class. She does not, however, gain any other benefit a character of that class would have gained (improved chance of controlling or rebuking undead, metamagic or item creation feats, and so on). This essentially means that the character adds 1/2 her dragonsong lyrist level to the level of whatever spellcasting class she has, then determines spells per day and caster level accordingly.

If a character takes two or more levels in this class before having any levels in a spellcasting class, she does not receive this spellcasting benefit. If she thereafter takes levels in one or more spellcasting classes, she becomes eligible to receive the spellcasting benefit for any level in the dragonsong lyrist class that she has not already attained. For example, a 6th-level monk/2nd-level dragonsong lyrist does not receive the spellcasting benefit for being a 2nd-level dragonsong lyrist because she did not belong to a spellcasting class before taking 2nd level in the prestige class. If she then picks up one or more levels of wizard before advancing to 4th level in the dragonsong lyrist class, she receives the spellcasting benefit of a 4th-level dragonsong lyrist (when she attains that level) but does not receive the 2nd-level benefit retroactively.

DRAGONSTALKER

"Dragonslayers? Pah, any fool can call himself a dragonslayer. Most get themselves killed within a few days, which is probably for the best. No, the real skill isn't in walking into the dragon's cave and challenging it to a duel—it's in tracking it across a hundred miles of wilderness, sneaking up close and killing it before it even knows you're there."

—Deirdre Firewalker, dragonstalker

The dragonstalker prefers a much more subtle approach than the dragonslayer. She uses stealth and guile to track her prey, striking with skill and uncanny accuracy when the time is right.

Rangers and rogues are the most common dragonstalkers, since the two classes share a predilection for the subtlety and patience the prestige class requires. Barbarians, particularly those from dragon-terrorized areas, often take up this class. Bards also make reasonable dragonstalkers—certainly, the profession makes for many great tales told around the fire. Most other classes are better off pursuing the path of the dragonslayer (see page 125).

NPC dragonstalkers are loners, since they rarely trust others to hold their own in a hunt. When tracking a particularly formidable foe, a dragonstalker might recruit other stealthy characters, such as rangers or rogues, for assistance. Once or twice in a generation, a hunt of great significance may arise that brings together a team of dragonstalkers from various backgrounds. In such a case, the dragon has little chance of escaping.

Hit Die: d8.

Requirements

To qualify to become a dragonstalker, a character must fulfill all the following criteria.

Base Attack Bonus: +5.

Feats: Blind-fight, Track.

Skills: Gather Information 4 ranks, Hide 6 ranks, Knowledge (arcana) 4 ranks, Move Silently 6 ranks, Search 6 ranks.

Language: Draconic.

Class Skills

The dragonstalker's class skills (and the key ability for each skill) are Bluff (Cha), Climb (Str), Craft (Wis), Diplomacy (Cha), Disguise (Cha), Gather Information (Cha), Hide (Dex), Jump (Str), Knowledge (arcana) (Int), Knowledge (local) (Int), Listen (Wis), Move Silently (Dex), Search (Int), Spot (Wis), and Survival (Wis). See Chapter 4: Skills in the *Player's Handbook* for skill descriptions.

Skill Points at Each Level: 4 + Int modifier.

Class Features

All of the following are class features of the dragonstalker prestige class.

Weapon and Armor Proficiency: A dragonstalker gains proficiency with the longbow, longspear, net, shortbow, and all simple weapons. Dragonstalkers are proficient with light armor and with shields.

Hunting Bonus (Ex): Starting at 1st level, a dragonstalker gains a bonus equal to her class level on Bluff, Listen, Search, Sense Motive, and Spot checks when using these skills against dragons.

Sneak Attack (Dragon): Beginning at 2nd level, if a dragonstalker catches a dragon when it is unable to defend itself effectively from her attack, she can strike a vital spot for extra damage. Basically, any time the dragonstalker's target would be denied its Dexterity bonus to AC (whether it actually has a Dexterity bonus or not), the dragonstalker's attack deals an extra 2d6 points of damage. This extra damage increases by 2d6 points every other level (4d6 at 4th level, 6d6 at 6th level, and so on). Should the dragonstalker score a critical hit with a sneak attack, this extra damage is not multiplied.

It takes precision and penetration to hit a vital spot, so ranged attacks can only count as sneak attacks if the dragon is 30 feet away or less.

With a sap or an unarmed strike, a dragonstalker can make a sneak attack that deals nonlethal damage instead of lethal damage. She cannot use a weapon that deals lethal damage to deal nonlethal damage in a sneak attack, not even with the usual –4 penalty, because she must make optimal use of her weapon to execute the sneak attack.

A dragonstalker can only sneak attack living dragons with discernible anatomies. Any dragon immune to critical hits is similarly immune to sneak attacks. Also, the dragonstalker must be able to see the target well enough to pick out a vital spot and must be able to reach a vital spot. A dragonstalker cannot sneak attack while striking at a dragon with concealment or by striking the limbs of a dragon whose vitals are beyond reach.

If a dragonstalker gets a sneak attack bonus from another source (such as rogue levels), the bonuses to damage stack when the ability is used against dragons.

Ignore Natural Armor (Ex): Once per day, a dragonstalker of 3rd level or higher can ignore a target's natural armor bonus (including any enhancement to that natural armor) for one attack (melee or ranged). You must declare that you are using this ability before you make the attack roll. At 7th level, a dragonstalker can use this ability twice per day.

Hide Scent (Ex): At 5th level, a dragonstalker can use the Disguise skill to hide her (or someone else's) scent. This requires a Disguise check (with a –10 penalty) opposed by a Wisdom check made by any creature attempting to use the scent ability to discover the dragonstalker's presence. Hiding one's scent requires twice as long as a typical Disguise check (1d3×20 minutes), and the effect lasts for 1 hour per class level. Magic that alters your form doesn't affect this Disguise check.

Foil Blindsense (Su): Once per day, a 9th-level dragonstalker can render herself completely imperceptible to blindsense. This requires a standard action, and the effect lasts for 10 minutes. This ability has no effect on other forms of vision (whether mundane or magical). For instance, it doesn't keep someone from spotting or hearing the dragonstalker with normal senses, or from noticing an invisible dragonstalker by means of a *true seeing* spell.

Dragonstrike (Su): At 10th level, the effective enhancement bonus of any weapon

A dragonstalker

Illus. by S. Tappin

Table 3–8: The Dragonstalker

Class Level	Base Attack Bonus	Fort Save	Ref Save	Will Save	Special
1st	+1	+0	+2	+2	Hunting bonus
2nd	+2	+0	+3	+3	Sneak attack (dragon) +2d6
3rd	+3	+1	+3	+3	Ignore natural armor (1/day)
4th	+4	+1	+4	+4	Sneak attack (dragon) +4d6
5th	+5	+1	+4	+4	Hide scent
6th	+6	+2	+5	+5	Sneak attack (dragon) +6d6
7th	+7	+2	+5	+5	Ignore natural armor (2/day)
8th	+8	+2	+6	+6	Sneak attack (dragon) +8d6
9th	+9	+3	+6	+6	Foil blindsense
10th	+10	+4	+7	+7	Dragonstrike, sneak attack (dragon) +10d6

wielded by a dragonstalker against a dragon is +2 better than normal, and the weapon deals an extra 2d6 points of damage against dragons. This benefit stacks with the enhancement bonus increase and bonus damage dice from a weapon with the bane (dragons) special ability.

HOARDSTEALER

"Don't call me a burglar. Burglars steal baubles and trinkets. If I wanted trinkets, I'd rob a dwarf. I want treasure."

—Liam Boldfingers, halfling hoardstealer

The hoardstealer specializes in relieving wealthy individuals from large amounts of said wealth. In most cases, these individuals are dragons, since few creatures keep so much wealth in one place. Stealing a dragon's hoard is a challenging task, to be sure, but if it were easy, it probably wouldn't be worth doing.

Most hoardstealers are rogues, though some bards and rangers can become hoardstealers with the right training. Other classes may fancy themselves treasure-finders, but they don't have the aptitudes to take up the art of hoardstealing.

By their very nature, most NPC hoardstealers work alone. Some may recruit assistance for tough jobs—such as rogues or other stealthy sorts—but a hoardstealer rarely sees such hired help as anything but expendable assets. The smart hoardstealer knows that he can only count on himself to get the job done—everyone else is just an amateur.

Hit Die: d6.

Requirements

To qualify to become a hoardstealer, a character must fulfill all the following criteria.

Alignment: Any nonlawful.

Skills: Appraise 8 ranks, Disable Device 4 ranks, Escape Artist 4 ranks, Hide 8 ranks, Move Silently 8 ranks, Open Lock 4 ranks, Search 8 ranks.

Special: The character must have participated in the location and recovery of a treasure hoard (dragon or otherwise) valued at 5,000 gp or more.

Class Skills

The hoardstealer's class skills (and the key ability for each skill) are Appraise (Int), Balance (Dex), Bluff (Cha), Climb (Str), Concentration (Con), Decipher Script (Int), Disable Device (Int), Disguise (Cha), Escape Artist (Dex), Gather Information (Cha), Jump (Str), Open Lock (Dex), Search (Int), Swim (Str), Use Magic Device (Cha), and Use Rope (Dex). See Chapter 4: Skills in the *Player's Handbook* for skill descriptions.

Skill Points at Each Level: 6 + Int modifier.

Class Features

All of the following are class features of the hoardstealer prestige class.

Weapon and Armor Proficiency: A hoardstealer is proficient with all simple weapons but gains no proficiency with armor or shields.

Spells: Beginning at 1st level, a hoardstealer gains the ability to cast a small number of arcane spells. To cast a spell,

A hoardstealer

Table 3–9: The Hoardstealer

Class Level	Base Attack Bonus	Fort Save	Ref Save	Will Save	Special	Spells per Day 1st	2nd	3rd	4th
1st	+0	+0	+2	+0	Darkvision +30 ft., trapfinding	0	—	—	—
2nd	+1	+0	+3	+0	*Hide from dragons* 1/day	1	—	—	—
3rd	+2	+1	+3	+1	Trap sense +2, deep pockets	1	0	—	—
4th	+3	+1	+4	+1	Treasure dowsing 1/day	1	1	—	—
5th	+3	+1	+4	+1	Darkvision +60 ft.	1	1	0	—
6th	+4	+2	+5	+2	Trap sense +4,*hide from dragons* 2/day	1	1	1	—
7th	+5	+2	+5	+2	Treasure dowsing 2/day	2	1	1	0
8th	+6	+2	+6	+2	Skill mastery	2	1	1	1
9th	+6	+3	+6	+3	Darkvision +90 ft., trap sense +6	2	2	1	1
10th	+7	+3	+7	+3	Treasure dowsing 3/day, *hide from dragons* 3/day	2	2	2	1

the hoardstealer must have an Intelligence score of at least 10 + the spell's level, so a hoardstealer with an Intelligence of 10 or lower cannot cast these spells. Hoardstealer bonus spells are based on Intelligence, and saving throws against these spells have a DC of 10 + spell level + the hoardstealer's Int modifier. When the hoardstealer gets 0 spells of a given level (for instance, 1st-level spells for a 1st-level hoardstealer), he gains only the bonus spells he would be entitled to based on his Intelligence score for that spell level. The hoardstealer's spell list appears below. A hoardstealer casts spells just as a wizard does.

Darkvision (Su): At 1st level, a hoardstealer gains darkvision with a range of 30 feet, or the range of his existing darkvision improves by 30 feet if he already has the ability.

At 5th level and at 9th level, the range of the hoardstealer's darkvision extends another 30 feet, to a maximum of +90 feet at 9th level.

Trapfinding (Ex): Like a rogue, a hoardstealer can use the Search skill to locate traps when the task has a DC higher than 20. He may also use the Disable Device skill to disarm a magic trap. A hoardstealer who beats a trap's DC by 10 or more can study a trap, figure out how it works, and bypass it (with his party) without disarming it.

***Hide from Dragons* (Sp):** A 2nd-level hoardstealer can cast *hide from dragons* on himself once per day. This functions as the spell of the same name (see page 113), except that it only affects the hoardstealer and lasts for only 1 round per level.

At 6th level, the hoardstealer may use this ability twice per day. At 10th level, he may use it three times per day.

Trap Sense (Ex): Starting at 3rd level, a hoardstealer gains an intuitive sense that alerts him to danger from traps, giving him a +2 bonus on Reflex saves made to avoid traps and a +2 dodge bonus to AC against attacks by traps. At 6th level these bonuses rise to +4, and at 9th level to +6. These bonuses stack with trap sense bonuses gained from other classes.

Deep Pockets (Su): Once per day, a 3rd-level hoardstealer can turn any container—from a waistcoat pocket to a backpack to a barrel—into the equivalent of a *bag of holding*. The container's weight remains the same, but it becomes capable of holding up to 10 cubic feet (or 100 pounds) of material per level. The duration of this effect is 1 hour per level. If the effect ends prematurely (such as by being dispelled), everything within the container spills out onto the floor.

Treasure Dowsing (Su): Once per day, a 4th-level hoardstealer can concentrate (a full-round action) to detect the location of the largest mass of metal or minerals within a range of 10 feet per level. If the hoardstealer concentrates on a specific metal or mineral (such as gold or diamonds), he detects the location of each such deposit within range. This is otherwise identical to the effect of a *rod of metal and mineral detection* (see page 236 of the *Dungeon Master's Guide*).

At 7th level, the hoardstealer may use this ability twice per day. At 10th level, he may use it three times per day.

Skill Mastery (Ex): At 8th level, a hoardstealer may select a number of skills equal to 3 + his Int modifier. When making a skill check with one of these skills, the hoardstealer may take 10 even if stress and distractions would normally prevent him from doing so. He becomes so certain in his ability that he can use his skill reliably under adverse conditions, such as when an angry dragon pursues him down a tunnel.

Hoardstealer Spell List

Hoardstealers choose their spells from the following list.

1st Level: *detect magic, detect secret doors, expeditious retreat, ghost sound, identify, Tenser's floating disk, Nystul's magic aura, read magic, unseen servant.*

2nd Level: *cat's grace, knock, invisibility, locate object, resist energy, spider climb.*

3rd Level: *arcane sight, clairaudience/clairvoyance, dispel magic, protection from energy, shrink item.*

4th Level: *arcane eye, dimension door, freedom of movement, hide from dragons*.*

*New spell detailed on page 106.

INITIATE OF THE DRACONIC MYSTERIES

Not all who explore the mysterious powers of dragons do so out of heritage or religious faith. Some become students of knowledge that leads to greater power.

Most initiates of the draconic mysteries are monks, though some fighters follow the path as well. In rare cases, barbarians, rangers, or rogues have been known to become initiates.

NPC initiates may gather in quiet places of study to share their learning and practice their techniques. Or they may test their powers in the field, either alone or with others who respect their ways. Regardless of her company, the initiate of the draconic mysteries remains a strange and wondrous individual, set apart from others of her race by her pursuit of ancient secrets.

Hit Die: d8.

Requirements

To qualify to become an initiate of the draconic mysteries, a character must fulfill all the following criteria.

Feats: Alertness, Improved Unarmed Strike, Power Attack.

Skills: Concentration 6 ranks, Jump 8 ranks, Knowledge (arcana) 6 ranks, Knowledge (religion) 4 ranks, Tumble 4 ranks.

Language: Draconic.

An initiate of the draconic mysteries

Class Skills

The initiate's class skills (and the key ability for each skill) are Balance (Dex), Concentration (Con), Diplomacy (Cha), Escape Artist (Dex), Heal (Wis), Listen (Wis), Knowledge (arcana) (Int), Knowledge (religion) (Int), Spot (Wis), and Tumble (Dex). See Chapter 4: Skills in the *Player's Handbook* for skill descriptions.

Skill Points at Each Level: 4 + Int modifier.

Class Features

All of the following are class features of the initiate of the draconic mysteries prestige class.

Weapon and Armor Proficiency: An initiate of the draconic mysteries gains no proficiency with any weapons, armor, or shields.

Evasion (Ex): An initiate of the draconic mysteries can avoid even magical and unusual attacks with great agility. If an initiate makes a successful Reflex saving throw against an attack that normally deals half damage on a save (such as a red dragon's fiery breath or a *fireball*), the initiate instead takes no damage. Evasion can only be used if the initiate is wearing light armor or no armor.

Claws of the Dragon (Su): At 2nd level, the unarmed strike of an initiate of the draconic mysteries is empowered with draconic might. The initiate's unarmed strike can overcome damage reduction as if it were a magic weapon.

In addition, the unarmed strikes of an initiate of the draconic mysteries may deal slashing damage, at her option. Such damage cannot be nonlethal damage.

Keen Senses (Ex): At 3rd level, an initiate gains darkvision out to 60 feet and low-light vision.

Increased Unarmed Damage (Ex): At 4th level, the damage dealt by an initiate's unarmed attacks increases by one die step (such as from 1d3 to 1d4, or from 1d8 to 1d10). At 8th level, it increases another die step.

Frightful Presence (Ex): A 5th-level initiate of the draconic mysteries can unsettle foes with her mere presence. The initiate can activate her frightful presence as a free action. Creatures within a radius of 30 feet per point of Charisma modifier (minimum 30 feet) are subject to the effect if they have fewer Hit Dice than the initiate (dragons are immune to the effect).

A potentially affected creature that succeeds on a Will save (DC 10 + initiate's class level + initiate's Cha modifier)

Table 3–10: The Initiate of the Draconic Mysteries

Class Level	Base Attack Bonus	Fort Save	Ref Save	Will Save	Special
1st	+0	+2	+2	+2	Evasion
2nd	+1	+3	+3	+3	Claws of the dragon
3rd	+2	+3	+3	+3	Keen senses
4th	+3	+4	+4	+4	Increased unarmed damage
5th	+3	+4	+4	+4	Frightful presence
6th	+4	+5	+5	+5	Improved evasion
7th	+5	+5	+5	+5	Spell resistance
8th	+6	+6	+6	+6	Increased unarmed damage
9th	+6	+6	+6	+6	Deadly strike, timeless body
10th	+7	+7	+7	+7	Dragon shape

remains immune to that initiate's frightful presence for 24 hours. On a failure, creatures with 4 or fewer HD become panicked for 2d6 rounds and those with 5 or more HD become shaken for 2d6 rounds.

Improved Evasion (Ex): At 6th level, an initiate's evasion ability improves. She still takes no damage on a successful Reflex saving throw against attacks such as a dragon's breath weapon or a *fireball*, but henceforth she only takes half damage on a failed save.

Spell Resistance (Su): Beginning at 7th level, an initiate of the draconic mysteries gains spell resistance equal to 15 + her class level.

Deadly Strike (Su): A 9th-level initiate deals triple damage on a critical hit inflicted by her unarmed strike, regardless of whether it dealt bludgeoning or slashing damage.

Timeless Body (Ex): After attaining 9th level, an initiate no longer takes ability score penalties for aging (see Table 6–5: Aging Effects, page 109 of the *Player's Handbook*) and cannot be magically aged. Any penalties she may have already taken, however, remain in place. Bonuses still accrue, and the initiate still dies of old age when her time is up.

Dragon Shape (Su): At 10th level, an initiate of the draconic mysteries gains the ability to use a *shapechange* ability once per day to take the form of a dragon, from Tiny to Huge size, for 1 hour. Once a form is assumed, it cannot be changed except to return to normal (which dismisses the effect). The effect is otherwise identical to the *shapechange* spell, including the HD limitation of the new form and the abilities of the form gained.

PLATINUM KNIGHT

The platinum knight protects good-aligned dragonkind from their natural enemies, the chromatic dragons, as well as any others who would prey upon these noble creatures. Bahamut, Lord of the Good Dragons, is his patron, while the minions of Tiamat are his mortal foes.

Paladins, clerics, and fighters are the most common platinum knights. Of course, any good-aligned character who counts himself an ally of dragonkind can pursue this class, and has much to gain from it.

NPC platinum knights often work with other good-aligned beings, including dragons, celestials, paladins, and, of course, characters of other classes who share their outlook. They do not hesitate to recruit assistance when facing powerful evil dragons, but voluntarily associate only with other good characters.

Hit Die: d8.

Requirements

To qualify to become a platinum knight, a character must fulfill all the following criteria.

Alignment: Any good.

Base Attack Bonus: +5.

Feats: Dragonfriend.

Skills: Diplomacy 4 ranks, Knowledge (arcana) 4 ranks.

Languages: Draconic.

Class Skills

The platinum knight's class skills (and the key ability for each skill) are Concentration (Con), Diplomacy (Cha), Heal (Wis), Intimidate (Cha), Knowledge (arcana) (Int), Ride (Dex), and Sense Motive (Wis). See Chapter 4: Skills in the *Player's Handbook* for skill descriptions.

Skill Points at Each Level: 2 + Int modifier.

Class Features

All of the following are class features of the platinum knight prestige class.

Weapon and Armor Proficiency: A platinum knight is proficient with all simple and martial weapons, with all types of armor, and with shields.

Smite Evil Dragon (Su): Once per day, a platinum knight may attempt to smite an evil dragon with one normal melee attack. He adds his Charisma modifier (if positive) to his attack roll and deals 2 extra points of damage per level. If a platinum knight accidentally smites a creature that is not an evil dragon, the smite has no effect but it is still used up for that day.

The bonuses from this ability don't stack with other smite abilities, such as the paladin's smite evil. Every three levels beyond 1st, the platinum knight gains one additional daily use of this ability.

Immune to Frightful Presence (Ex): Platinum knights are treated as dragons for the

A platinum knight

Illus. by S. Tappin

TABLE 3–11: THE PLATINUM KNIGHT

Class Level	Base Attack Bonus	Fort Save	Ref Save	Will Save	Special	Spellcasting
1st	+1	+2	+0	+2	Smite evil dragon 1/day, immune to frightful presence	—
2nd	+2	+3	+0	+3	—	+1 level of existing class
3rd	+3	+3	+1	+3	Platinum scales +1	—
4th	+4	+4	+1	+4	Smite evil dragon 2/day	+1 level of existing class
5th	+5	+4	+1	+4	Bahamut's grace	—
6th	+6	+5	+2	+5	—	+1 level of existing class
7th	+7	+5	+2	+5	Platinum scales +2, smite evil dragon 3/day	—
8th	+8	+6	+2	+6		+1 level of existing class
9th	+9	+6	+3	+6	Charisma increase	—
10th	+10	+7	+3	+7	Smite evil dragon 4/day, true seeing	+1 level of existing class

purpose of being immune to the frightful presence of dragons and similar creatures.

Spellcasting: When an even-numbered platinum knight level is gained, the character gains new spells per day as if he had also gained a level in a spellcasting class he belonged to before he added the prestige class. He does not, however, gain any other benefit a character of that class would have gained (improved chance of controlling or rebuking undead, metamagic or item creation feats, and so on). This essentially means that he adds 1/2 his platinum knight level to the level of some other spellcasting class he has, then determines spells per day and caster level accordingly.

If a character takes two or more levels in this class before having any levels in a spellcasting class, he does not receive this spellcasting benefit. If he thereafter takes levels in one or more spellcasting classes, he becomes eligible to receive the spellcasting benefit for any level in the platinum knight class that he has not already attained. For example, a 6th-level fighter/2nd-level platinum knight does not receive the spellcasting benefit for being a 2nd-level platinum knight because he did not belong to a spellcasting class before taking 2nd level in the prestige class. If he then picks up one or more levels of wizard before advancing to 4th level in the platinum knight class, he receives the spellcasting benefit of a 4th-level platinum knight (when he attains that level) but does not receive the 2nd-level benefit retroactively.

Platinum Scales (Ex): At 3rd level, a platinum knight's skin takes on a slightly metallic sheen. He gains a +1 increase to his natural armor bonus. At 7th level, this increase improves to +2.

Bahamut's Grace (Su): A 5th-level platinum knight adds his Charisma modifier (if positive) as a bonus on all saving throws against the attacks, special abilities, and spells cast by evil dragons. This effect stacks with the divine grace class feature of paladins and similar abilities.

Charisma Bonus (Ex): At 9th level, a platinum knight's Charisma increases by 2 points.

True Seeing (Su): At 10th level, a platinum knight gains the ability to see all things as they actually are. This ability is the equivalent of the *true seeing* spell and lasts for 1 hour. A platinum knight may use true seeing once per day.

TALON OF TIAMAT

The talon of Tiamat furthers the goals of evil dragonkind. He takes particular delight in causing harm to metallic dragons and their allies.

The talons of Tiamat welcome characters from any class or background, as long as they share a dedication to evil. Former fighters and barbarians rub shoulders with those who practice sorcery or divine magic. Even ex-paladins can find a home among the talons.

Talons of Tiamat may work individually or in groups, as befits their plans. They work well with evil characters of any stripe, and ally with evil dragons when possible.

Hit Die: d8.

Requirements

To qualify to become a talon of Tiamat, a character must fulfill all the following criteria.

Alignment: Any evil.

Base Attack Bonus: +4.

Feats: Dragonthrall.

Skills: Bluff 4 ranks, Intimidate 4 ranks, Knowledge (arcana) 4 ranks.

Languages: Draconic.

Class Skills

The talon of Tiamat's class skills (and the key ability for each skill) are Appraise (Int), Bluff (Cha), Concentration (Con), Intimidate (Cha), Knowledge (arcana) (Int), Ride (Dex), Search (Int), Sense Motive (Wis), and Spellcraft (Int). See Chapter 4: Skills in the *Player's Handbook* for skill descriptions.

Skill Points at Each Level: 2 + Int modifier.

Class Features

All of the following are class features of the talon of Tiamat prestige class.

Weapon and Armor Proficiency: A talon of Tiamat is proficient with all simple and martial weapons, with all types of armor, and with shields.

Breath Weapon (Su): At 1st level, a talon of Tiamat gains the ability to breathe out a cone of frost (size of the cone corresponds to the size of the character) that deals 3d6 points of cold damage.

As the talon gains levels, additional versions of his breath weapon become available to him. At 3rd level, the talon can breathe a line of acid (8d4 acid damage). At 5th level, he can breathe a cone of corrosive gas (10d6 acid damage). At 7th level, he can expel a line of lightning (12d8 electricity damage). At 9th level, he can breathe a cone of fire (14d8 fire damage).

In each case, a successful Reflex save halves the damage dealt. The DC for saves against the talon's breath weapon is 10 + talon class level + Con modifier. A talon of Tiamat can use each of his breath weapons once per day. Once a talon uses any of his breath weapons, he can't use any other breath weapon until 1d4 rounds have passed.

Spellcasting: When an even-numbered talon of Tiamat level is gained, the character gains new spells per day as if he had also gained a level in a spellcasting class he belonged to before he added the prestige class. He does not, however, gain any other benefit a character of that class would have gained (improved chance of controlling or rebuking undead, metamagic or item creation feats, and so on). This essentially means that he adds 1/2 his talon of Tiamat level to the level of some other spellcasting class he has, then determines spells per day and caster level accordingly.

If a character takes two or more levels in this class before having any levels in a spellcasting class, he does not receive this spellcasting benefit. If he thereafter takes levels in one or more spellcasting classes, he becomes eligible to receive the spellcasting benefit for any level in the talon of Tiamat class that he has not already attained. For example, a 7th-level fighter/2nd-level talon of Tiamat does not receive the spellcasting benefit for being a 2nd-level talon of Tiamat because he did not belong to a spellcasting class before taking 2nd level in the prestige class. If he then picks up one or more levels of wizard before advancing to 4th level in the talon of Tiamat class, he receives the spellcasting benefit of a 4th-level talon of Tiamat (when he attains that level) but does not receive the 2nd-level benefit retroactively.

A talon of Tiamat

Voice of the Dragon (Ex): At 2nd level, a talon of Tiamat gains a +2 bonus on Bluff and Intimidate checks. This bonus increases by +2 every four levels thereafter, to +4 at 6th level and +6 at 10th level.

Keen Senses (Ex): A talon of Tiamat gains low-light vision at 4th level. He gains darkvision out to 60 feet at 8th level.

Immunities (Ex): At 6th level, a talon of Tiamat gains immunity to magic sleep and paralysis effects. In addition, he gains immunity to one of the following forms of energy, at his option: acid, cold, electricity, or fire. Once an energy immunity is selected, the decision may never be changed.

Frightful Presence (Ex): An 8th-level talon of Tiamat can unsettle foes with his mere presence. The talon of Tiamat can activate his frightful presence as a free action. Creatures within a radius of 30 feet per point of Charisma modifier (minimum 30 feet) are subject to the effect if they have fewer Hit Dice than the talon of Tiamat (dragons are immune to the effect).

A potentially affected creature that succeeds on a Will save (DC 10 + talon's class level + talon's Cha modifier) remains immune to that talon's frightful presence for 24 hours. On a failure, creatures with 4 or fewer HD become panicked for 2d6 rounds and those with 5 or more HD become shaken for 2d6 rounds.

Dominate Dragon (Su): A 10th-level talon of Tiamat can attempt to dominate any dragon (as *dominate monster*, but it only applies to dragons) once per day. The target may attempt a Will save to negate the effect (DC 10 + talon's class level + talon's Cha modifier).

Table 3–12: The Talon of Tiamat

Class Level	Base Attack Bonus	Fort Save	Ref Save	Will Save	Special	Spellcasting
1st	+0	+2	+0	+0	Breath weapon (cone of cold)	—
2nd	+1	+3	+0	+0	Voice of the dragon +2	+1 level of existing class
3rd	+2	+3	+1	+1	Breath weapon (line of acid)	—
4th	+3	+4	+1	+1	Keen senses	+1 level of existing class
5th	+3	+4	+1	+1	Breath weapon (cone of corrosive gas)	—
6th	+4	+5	+2	+2	Immunities, voice of the dragon +4	+1 level of existing class
7th	+5	+5	+2	+2	Breath weapon (line of lightning)	—
8th	+6	+6	+2	+2	Keen senses, frightful presence	+1 level of existing class
9th	+6	+6	+3	+3	Breath weapon (cone of fire)	—
10th	+7	+7	+3	+3	Dominate dragon, voice of the dragon +6	+1 level of existing class

Illus. by W. England

DRAGONS IN THE PARTY

Adding a dragon to an adventuring party is an attractive option to most playing groups. Even the smallest dragon brings sharp senses and great mobility to the table, probably far beyond the capabilities of any of the other player characters.

While it's true that a dragon that adventures with PCs can change the game, with a few safeguards in place, the DM should be able to feel comfortable about this addition. This section details many of the most common methods of incorporating a dragon into a group of PCs, and provides the DM with guidelines to control the ramifications of that addition.

All of these options depend on your DM's permission. If you want to add a dragon to your group, work with your DM to ensure that this addition will fit smoothly into the campaign.

DRAGONS' ADVANTAGES AND DISADVANTAGES

While many players look at a dragon and see only its claws, teeth, and breath weapon, these abilities are among the least significant as far as "game balance" goes. After all, most characters can deal plenty of damage by means of attacks or magical effects.

Instead, it's the dragon's less spectacular abilities, such as blindsense and flight, that make it potentially "too powerful" as a member of an adventuring group. Here are some tips on how to handle those abilities in your game, as well as notes on some disadvantages that a draconic character might encounter.

Blindsense: True dragons possess blindsense, which threatens to remove a valuable tool from the DM's arsenal, because invisible foes aren't nearly as dire a threat to the partty anymore. Remember, though, that blindsense isn't the same thing as a true seeing effect—it merely allows the dragon to detect the presence of creatures within its blindsense range. The dragon can't automatically see through an illusion (though one without auditory and olfactory elements probably won't work), and disguises work perfectly well. Incorporeal, gaseous, and ethereal creatures also can give a dragon plenty of problems. A deafened dragon, or one inside a *silence* effect, also can't use its blindsense to full effect.

Equipment: Dragons can't easily use many items of equipment built for characters. While a dragon has little need for weapons and armor—its natural attacks and natural armor work well enough—it may be frustrated by its inability to wield or wear certain magic items. See the Dragons and Magic Items sidebar (page 24) for more information.

Keen Senses: All dragons have darkvision and low-light vision, making them at least the equal of any PC in the group in these regards. Lesser dragons can't see in the dark better than a dwarf or a half-orc, nor in low light better than an elf or a half-elf, but simply having both forms of vision makes them the best at spotting hidden foes and the like. Dragons also have good Spot and Listen skill modifiers, so a smart party will use the dragon as a lookout or scout.

Movement: Almost all dragons can fly at exceptional speed. A wyrmling dragon can cover 200 or 300 feet in a round, which is faster than most characters can run. Some dragons also have swim or burrow speeds, giving them even greater movement options.

Remember, though, that most dragons have average or worse maneuverability in flight. This hindrance can make the average dungeon corridor or cramped room all but impassable to a dragon in flight. Also, unless a dragon has the Hover feat, it probably must move a minimum distance each round, preventing it from making full attacks while airborne. See Fighting on the Wing (page 59) for more information on this topic.

Size: A dragon bigger than Medium has distinct difficulty accompanying characters into most buildings, and Huge or larger dragons probably can't even enter most dungeons. Only a very well-trained or otherwise loyal dragon will go along with characters into an area where it can't easily move around (see also Maneuverability, above).

Youth: In many cases when a dragon joins a party, it does so as a wyrmling or at a youthful age. But just because a wyrmling dragon has a decent Intelligence and more hit points than the average ogre doesn't make it adult in its outlook. Dragons mature slowly, meaning that even a 30-year-old juvenile dragon acts more like a child than an adult. This may mean that a youthful dragon doesn't always follow instructions well, and may even completely disobey the PC who "controls" it.

The DM should feel comfortable in occasionally having a juvenile or younger dragon "act up" in a manner appropriate to its alignment. A good dragon may simply sulk or pout, while an evil dragon might lash out at those upsetting it. Chaotic dragons are prone to tantrums in their youth, while lawful dragons are more likely to misbehave in a carefully plotted manner.

DRAGONS AS MOUNTS

The dream mount for many characters is a dragon. While other flying creatures might be cheaper or easier to train as mounts, nothing beats the look of awe from friends and foes when they see you swoop in astride a mighty draconic steed.

There are two methods of getting a dragon as your mount: raising the dragon from youth or negotiating with a full-grown dragon. The first may be easier and cheaper, but requires far more time. Each method is discussed later in this section

As strong, quadrupedal creatures, dragons can carry a lot of weight, even in flight. A dragon can carry a rider while swimming, but not while burrowing.

Table 3–13: Dragon Mounts, Overland Movement, and Carrying Capacity provides movement rates and carrying capacity for a great number of different dragons. The column headers on the table are defined below.

Dragon: The left-hand column lists a number of dragons that are suitable for use as mounts. The mounts are grouped according to the largest size of rider each dragon can accommodate. Just because a dragon can carry your weight doesn't necessarily mean that you can ride it as a mount. Even if a dragon is strong enough to carry a larger character than its grouping on the table would indicate, it can't accommodate such a character as a rider.

Table 3–13: Dragon Mounts, Overland Movement, and Carrying Capacity

	Light Load or No Load			Medium or Heavy Load	
Dragon	Miles per Hour	Miles per Day	Load Range	Miles per Hour	Miles per Day
Diminutive or Smaller Riders					
Pseudodragon	1.5, fly 6	12, fly 48	29–86 lb.	1	8
Tiny or Smaller Riders					
Black, very young	6, fly 20, swim 6	48, fly 160, swim 48	51–150 lb.	4, swim 4	32, swim 32
White, very young	6, fly 30, swim 6	48, fly 240, swim 48	51–150 lb.	4, swim 4	32, swim 32
Brass, very young	6, fly 30	48, fly 240	51–150 lb.	4	32
Copper, very young	4, fly 20	32, fly 160	51–150 lb.	3	24
Small or Smaller Riders					
Black, young	6, fly 20, swim 6	48, fly 160, swim 48	101–300 lb.	4, swim 4	32, swim 32
Black, juvenile	6, fly 20, swim 6	48, fly 160, swim 48	131–390 lb.	4, swim 4	32, swim 32
Blue, very young	4, fly 15	32, fly 120	101–300 lb.	3	24
Blue, young	4, fly 20	32, fly 160	131–390 lb.	3	24
Brass, young	6, fly 30	48, fly 240	101–300 lb.	4	32
Brass, juvenile	6, fly 30	48, fly 240	131–390 lb.	4	32
Bronze, very young	4, fly 15, swim 6	32, fly 120, swim 48	101–300 lb.	3, swim 4	24, swim 32
Bronze, young	4, fly 20, swim 6	32, fly 160, swim 48	131–390 lb.	3, swim 4	24, swim 32
Copper, young	4, fly 20	32, fly 160	101–300 lb.	3	24
Copper, juvenile	4, fly 20	32, fly 160	131–390 lb.	3	24
Green, very young	4, fly 15, swim 4	32, fly 120, swim 32	101–300 lb.	3, swim 3	24, swim 24
Green, young	4, fly 20, swim 4	32, fly 160, swim 32	131–390 lb.	3, swim 3	24, swim 24
Silver, very young	4, fly 15	32, fly 120	101–300 lb.	3	24
Silver, young	4, fly 20	32, fly 160	131–390 lb.	3	24
White, young	6, fly 30, swim 6	48, fly 240, swim 48	101–300 lb.	4, swim 4	32, swim 32
White, juvenile	6, fly 30, swim 6	48, fly 240, swim 48	131–390 lb.	4, swim 4	32, swim 32
Medium or Smaller Riders					
Black, young adult	6, fly 20, swim 6	48, fly 160, swim 48	351–1,050 lb.	4, swim 4	32, swim 32
Black, adult	6, fly 20, swim 6	48, fly 160, swim 48	461–1,380 lb.	4, swim 4	32, swim 32
Blue, juvenile	4, fly 20	32, fly 160	176–525 lb.	3	24
Blue, young adult	4, fly 20	32, fly 160	601–1,800 lb.	3	24
Brass, young adult	6, fly 30	48, fly 240	351–1,050 lb.	4	32
Brass, adult	6, fly 30	48, fly 240	601–1,800 lb.	4	32
Bronze, juvenile	4, fly 20, swim 6	32, fly 160, swim 48	351–1,050 lb.	3, swim 4	24, swim 32
Bronze, young adult	4, fly 20, swim 6	32, fly 160, swim 48	601–1,800 lb.	3, swim 4	24, swim 32
Copper, young adult	4, fly 20	32, fly 160	351–1,050 lb.	3	24
Copper, adult	4, fly 20	32, fly 160	601–1,800 lb.	3	24
Dragonnel	4, fly 9	32, fly 72	351–1,050 lb.	3	24
Gold, very young	6, fly 30, swim 6	48, fly 240, swim 48	461–1,380 lb.	4, swim 4	32, swim 32
Gold, young	6, fly 30, swim 6	48, fly 240, swim 48	801–2,400 lb.	4, swim 4	32, swim 32
Gold, juvenile	6, fly 30, swim 6	48, fly 240, swim 48	1,401–4,200 lb.	4, swim 4	32, swim 32
Green, juvenile	4, fly 20, swim 4	32, fly 160, swim 32	351–1,050 lb.	3, swim 3	24, swim 24
Green, young adult	4, fly 20, swim 4	32, fly 160, swim 32	601–1,800 lb.	3, swim 3	24, swim 24
Red, very young	4, fly 20	32, fly 160	461–1,380 lb.	3	24
Red, young	4, fly 20	32, fly 160	801–2,400 lb.	3	24
Red, juvenile	4, fly 20	32, fly 160	1,401–4,200 lb.	3	24
Silver, juvenile	4, fly 20	32, fly 160	351–1,050 lb.	3	24
Silver, young adult	4, fly 20	32, fly 160	601–1,800 lb.	3	24
White, young adult	6, fly 30, swim 6	48, fly 240, swim 48	351–1,050 lb.	4, swim 4	32, swim 32
Wyvern	2, fly 6	16, fly 48	233–700 lb.	1.5	12
Large or Smaller Riders					
Blue, adult	4, fly 20	32, fly 160	2,081–6,240 lb.	3	24
Bronze, adult	4, fly 20, swim 6	32, fly 160, swim 48	2,081–6,240 lb.	3, swim 4	24, swim 32
Dragon turtle	2, swim 3	16, swim 24	2,081–6,240 lb.	1.5, swim 2	12, swim 16
Gold, young adult	6, fly 30, swim 6	48, fly 240, swim 48	3,681–11,040 lb.	4, swim 4	32, swim 32
Gold, adult	6, fly 30, swim 6	48, fly 240, swim 48	4,161–12,480 lb.	4, swim 4	32, swim 32
Green, adult	4, fly 20, swim 4	32, fly 160, swim 32	2,081–6,240 lb.	3, swim 3	24, swim 24
Red, young adult	4, fly 20	32, fly 160	3,681–11,040 lb.	3	24
Red, adult	4, fly 20	32, fly 160	4,161–12,480 lb.	3	24
Silver, adult	4, fly 20	32, fly 160	2,081–6,240 lb.	3	24
White, adult	6, fly 30, swim 6	48, fly 240, swim 48	601–1,800 lb.	4, swim 4	32, swim 32

Light Load or No Load: Dragons, like other flying creatures, can only fly when carrying no more than a light load. The two columns beneath this line give the dragon's overland movement when it is not carrying enough weight to prevent it from flying.

Load Range: This column gives a pair of numbers representing the range from a medium load to a maximum load for the dragon. For example, the entry for a young black dragon is 101–300 lb. This means that when the dragon is carrying 101 pounds or more, it's hauling a medium load (and thus cannot fly); and it's not capable of moving at all while carrying more than 300 pounds, which is its maximum load.

Medium or Heavy Load: The two columns beneath this line give the dragon's overland movement when it is carrying enough weight to prevent it from flying. (An exception is the dragon turtle, which does not have a fly speed; its numbers in these columns simply represent the reduction in land speed and swim speed that any creature suffers if it carries more than a light load.)

Raising a Dragon

Raising a true dragon from an egg until it's large enough to use as a mount can take several years. Even lesser dragons, such as wyverns, mature at such a slow rate that most characters simply aren't willing to wait the necessary amount of time.

For rules on how to raise a newly hatched dragon, see the Rearing a Dragon sidebar, page 13. When you successfully complete the rearing process, you can begin to teach the domesticated dragon how to perform tasks.

Although intelligent, a dragon requires training before it can bear a rider in combat. Training a dragon you have reared to serve as a mount requires six weeks of work and a DC 25 Handle Animal check. Riding a dragon requires an exotic saddle. A dragon can fight while carrying a rider, but the rider cannot also attack unless he or she succeeds on a Ride check (see the Ride skill, page 80 of the *Player's Handbook*).

Even a trained or "tamed" dragon is still a dragon, not an ordinary domestic animal, with its own needs and desires. A young dragon is more like a very intelligent child than a simple animal (Intelligence score ranging from 8 to 18, depending on age and kind) and may well be smarter than its rider. With such a creature, patience and tact produce better results than harsh words and punishment. Expect a dragon to learn quickly, but allow for its inexperience to cause mistakes. Like children and pets, dragons get tired, and it's best to let them rest when they do.

Negotiating Service

It's likely that a character seeking a draconic mount can't or won't put in the time necessary to rear a dragon. In such a case, the best option is to bargain with your would-be mount. (Using magic such as *charm* spells is a mistake, since the magic eventually wears off, and such coercion angers the dragon.) These negotiations always require some form of payment or reward to the dragon, which should take a form appropriate to the dragon variety (such as pearls for a bronze dragon) and should amount to at least 500 gp per HD of the dragon per year of service—paid in advance, of course, generally as soon as the negotiations are over.

Most potential dragon mounts begin with an indifferent attitude toward a character who approaches them. A dragon whose attitude is changed to helpful (see Influencing NPC Attitudes, page 72 of the *Player's Handbook*) by a character can be trained to serve as a mount, but only as long as it is treated well and regularly rewarded. Promising an increased reward can help persuade a dragon to cooperate; each additional payment of 500 gp per HD provides a +2 circumstance bonus on any Diplomacy check made to change the dragon's attitude. You can't retry a failed Diplomacy check for the same purpose unless the DM decides that the circumstances merit giving you another chance (for instance, if you perform a great favor for the dragon).

A dragon whose alignment isn't within one step of its rider's isn't likely to serve for very long, even if the initial negotiations succeed.

Alternatively, you can select the Dragon Steed feat (see page 105) to gain the loyal service of a dragonnel. In this case, no payment or Diplomacy check is required.

Keeping a Dragon Mount

A dragon mount, although it may be loyal to you, is still an independent, intelligent creature with a mind of its own. Expect the DM to treat a dragon mount as an NPC, not as a passive participant. (A rider with only a modest Charisma score can expect to lose a lot of arguments with his or her mount.) A dragon mount ages normally, but does not gain experience points.

Regardless of how well you treat your dragon, a time will likely come when the dragon wants to leave. Because of a dragon's relatively slow growth rate during its extremely long life span, chances are you will gain experience (levels) faster than the dragon grows (and thereby increases its effective character level). At some point the dragon will realize it is being outpaced (when your level exceeds the dragon's ECL by 5 or more), and it will leave. Also, a dragon mount that reaches adult age often begins thinking about leaving to raise a family. Trying to keep a dragon from leaving, even if you manage to succeed, is a mistake. Whether or not a dragon discusses parting company before doing so depends on its alignment and its relationship with you. (This point doesn't apply if the dragon is your cohort or a special mount; see below.)

If you keep your promises to a dragon mount and let it leave when it chooses, usually it will remain friendly toward you. If it holds a grudge against you, it may attack openly, or it may plot secretly for years before striking.

DRAGONS AS COHORTS

If your DM is willing to allow it, you can use the Leadership feat to try attracting a dragon to be your cohort. To determine what sort of dragon will heed your call, first refer to the Leadership table on page 106 of the *Dungeon Master's Guide* to determine the highest level of cohort you can attract. Then consult Table 3–14: Dragon Cohorts to see what age and kind of dragon can be attracted based on the

TABLE 3–14: DRAGON COHORTS

Dragon	Alignment	Effective Character Level*
Pseudodragon	NG	4
White (wyrmling)	CE	5
Brass (wyrmling)	CG	6
Black (wyrmling)	CE	7
Copper (wyrmling)	CG	7
White (very young)	CE	9
Black (very young)	CE	10
Blue (wyrmling)	LE	10
Brass (very young)	CG	10
Bronze (wyrmling)	LG	10
Green (wyrmling)	LE	10
Copper (very young)	CG	11
Red (wyrmling)	CE	11
Silver (wyrmling)	LG	11
Gold (wyrmling)	LG	12
White (young)	CE	12
Wyvern	N	12
Black (young)	CE	13
Blue (very young)	LE	13
Bronze (very young)	LG	13
Green (very young)	LE	13
Brass (young)	CG	14
Silver (very young)	LG	14
Copper (young)	CG	15
Red (very young)	CE	15
Gold (very young)	LG	16
Green (young)	LE	16
Black (juvenile)	CE	17
Blue (young)	LE	17
Brass (juvenile)	CG	17
Dragon turtle	N	17
White (juvenile)	CE	17
Bronze (young)	LG	18
Copper (juvenile)	CG	18
Silver (young)	LG	18
Red (young)	CE	19
Gold (young)	LG	20
Green (juvenile)	LE	20

*Subtract 3 if using the Dragon Cohort feat.

level of cohort you can attract. Note that even though the table lists dragons with an ECL higher than 17, you can't use the Leadership feat to attract a cohort with a level higher than 17th.

Alternatively, the Dragon Cohort feat (see page 104) allows you to attract a draconic cohort. In this case, you can treat the dragon's ECL as if it were 3 lower than given, allowing you to gain a more powerful dragon than with the Leadership feat. (This adjustment to ECL is only for purposes of selecting an appropriate cohort, not for any other purpose.)

Regardless of which feat is used, the method by which the character attracts the dragon cohort should be decided by the player and DM together. Since most of the options listed on Table 3–14 are younger than adult, it's entirely possible that such a dragon was entrusted to the PC's care and training by its parents. The character might even have had the opportunity to raise his cohort from an egg! See Raising a Dragon, above, for more information on dealing with young dragons.

DRAGONS AS SPECIAL MOUNTS

Some paladins want more from a mount than loyalty. Some desire an intelligent companion who can share their adventures, a mighty ally against the forces of evil whose power can grow with the paladin's. For these paladins, only one choice exists: the dragon special mount.

Clearly, a dragon is a far more powerful special mount than any other a paladin could obtain. If a paladin can simply summon a dragon mount, a class feature designed primarily as flavor and secondarily as an actual power boost to the paladin becomes significant more useful to the character. Such a special mount threatens to become more special than the paladin herself.

Furthermore, most true dragons large enough to bear a rider have little interest in being at the beck and call of anyone, even a character as devoted to law and good as a paladin must be.

That said, few sights are more breathtaking than a paladin astride a mighty dragon, its scales glistening in the sunlight as it soars through the sky in search of evil to smite. If you (and your friends) are willing to put up with the headaches, this option might suit you.

Only a lawful good dragon should be allowed to serve as a paladin's special mount. The dragonnel (see Chapter 4) is a special exception to this guideline.

A paladin who wishes to be able to summon a dragon special mount must select the Dragon Steed feat (see page 105). She then selects an appropriate dragon from Table 3–15: Dragon Special Mount Availability based on her paladin level. She may select any dragon indicated as available at her level or lower. For instance, a 9th-level paladin could select only a dragonnel as her dragon special mount, while a 12th-level paladin could choose either a wyrmling gold dragon or a dragonnel. The paladin must choose a dragon capable of bearing her as a rider (which limits a Medium rider's selections).

TABLE 3–15: DRAGON SPECIAL MOUNT AVAILABILITY

Paladin Level	Dragon (Maximum Rider Size)
9th	Dragonnel (M)
11th	Spiked felldrake (M)
12th	Gold, wyrmling (S)
13th	Bronze, very young (S)
14th	Silver, very young (S)
16th	Gold, very young (M)
18th	Bronze, young (S)
19th	Silver, young (S)
20th	Gold, young (M)

A paladin must provide her special mount with a suitable lair; even a loyal silver dragon mount won't live in the stable with the other mounts. The *Monster Manual* describes what type of lair each kind of dragon prefers; any dragon denied the ability to build and reside in an appropriate lair will certainly rebel against its paladin.

The dragon must also be provided treasure to keep in its lair. A minimum hoard of 1,000 gp per Hit Die of the dragon is typical, with the exact makeup depending on the type and likes of the dragon. Bronze dragons, for instance, prefer pearls. (The dragon isn't just keeping the treasure safe for

Table 3–16: Special Dragon Mount Abilities

——— Paladin Level (by Mount's Availability)* ———				Bonus	Natural	Str		
9th	**10th–13th**	**14th–17th**	**18th–20th**	**HD**	**Armor Adj.**	**Adj.**	**Int**	**Special**
9th–10th	10th–14th	14th–18th	18th–20th	+2	+4	+1	6	Improved evasion, share spells, empathic link, share saving throws
11th–14th	15th–18th	19th–20th		+4	+6	+2	7	Improved speed
15th–18th	19th–20th			+6	+8	+3	8	Command creatures of its kind
19th–20th				+8	10	+4	9	Spell resistance

* The boldface column headers (9th, 10th–13th, etc.) represent the paladin level (or range of levels) at which a mount becomes available (as shown on Table 3–15). The number ranges below the header in each column are the paladin levels at which the special dragon mount has the characteristics indicated on the right-hand side of the table.

you, it belongs to the dragon, and it won't part with this treasure kindly).

Finally (and perhaps most important), the dragon must be treated with the respect that a creature of its intelligence, power, and stature commands. It is not a dumb beast to order around, nor is it merely a minion to command. Even lawful good dragons are willful creatures with their own desires and needs.

A dragon special mount gains abilities much as a typical special mount, though at a rate based on the level at which the mount first becomes available. This means that the most powerful special dragon mounts don't get all the typical abilities of a special mount. Table 3–16: Special Dragon Mount Abilities summarizes the details. For basic information about the terms on the table, see the sidebar The Paladin's Mount, page 45 of the *Player's Handbook*. Differences from that basic information are covered below.

Bonus HD: Treat the same as bonus HD for a regular paladin's mount, except that these are extra twelve-sided (d12) Hit Dice.

Int: The "Intelligence" column only applies to those dragons whose Intelligence score is lower than that value (that is, a dragon special mount with an Intelligence higher than the given value retains its normal Intelligence).

Improved Speed: This ability applies to all of the dragon's modes of movement, including land speed, fly speed, and even burrow speed or swim speed (if the dragon possesses one or both).

Share Spells: This ability applies only to spells that the paladin casts. The dragon can't elect for spells that it casts on itself to also affect the paladin.

Spell Resistance: The spell resistance gained by a dragon special mount doesn't stack with any natural spell resistance it might have. Only the higher value applies.

Dragons as Fiendish Servants

If your campaign includes blackguards, such a character can use these rules to recruit a dragon as his fiendish servant. Compare the blackguard's character and class level to Table 3–17: Dragon Fiendish Servant Availability. If the blackguard is of sufficient level, he may select an available dragon as his fiendish servant after taking the Dragon Cohort feat.

As with a dragon special mount, a dragon fiendish servant gains special abilities at a rate based on the level at which the servant first becomes available. This means that the most powerful dragon fiendish servants don't get all the typical abilities of a fiendish servant.

Table 3–17: Dragon Fiendish Servant Availability

Character Level*	Dragon (Maximum Rider Size)
9th (5th)	Dragonnel (M)
12th (6th)	White, young (S)
12th (6th)	Wyvern (L)
13th (7th)	Black, young (S)
16th (8th)	Green, young (S)
17th (9th)	Blue, young (S)
17th (9th)	Dragon turtle (L)
17th (9th)	White, juvenile (S)
18th (9th)	Black, juvenile (S)
19th (10th)	Red, young (M)
20th (10th)	Green, juvenile (M)

*The minimum blackguard level is in parentheses.

A dragon fiendish servant gains abilities much as a typical fiendish servant, though at a rate based on the blackguard character level level at which the mount first becomes available. This means that the most powerful dragon fiendish servants don't get all the typical abilities of a fiendish servent. Table 3–18: Dragon Fiendish Servant Abilities summarizes the details. For basic information about the terms on the table, see The Blackguard's Fiendish Servant, page 183 of the

Table 3–18: Dragon Fiendish Servant Abilities

— Blackguard Level (by Servant's Availability)* —				Bonus	Natural	Str		
9th	**10th–13th**	**14th–17th**	**18th–20th**	**HD**	**Armor**	**Adj.**	**Int**	**Special**
9th–10th	10th–14th	14th–18th	18th–20th	+2	4	+1	6	Improved evasion, share spells, empathic link, share saving throws
11th–14th	15th–18th	19th–20th		+4	6	+2	7	Improved speed
15th–18th	19th–20th			+6	8	+3	8	Blood bond
19th–20th				+8	10	+4	9	Spell resistance

* The boldface column headers (9th, 10th–13th, etc.) represent the character level (or a range of levels) at which a servant of a certain kind becomes available (as shown on Table 3–15). The number ranges below the header in each column are the blackguard levels at which the fiendish servant has the characteristics indicated on the right-hand side of the table.

Dungeon Master's Guide. Differences from that basic information are covered below.

Bonus HD: Treat the same as bonus HD for a regular fiendish servant, except that these are extra twelve-sided (d12) Hit Dice.

Int: The "Intelligence" column only applies to those dragons whose Intelligence score is lower than that value (that is, a dragon fiendish servant with an Intelligence higher than the given value retains its normal Intelligence).

Improved Speed: This ability applies to all of the dragon's modes of movement, including land speed, fly speed, and even burrow speed or swim speed (if the dragon possesses one or both).

Share Spells: This ability applies only to spells that the paladin casts. The dragon can't elect for spells that it casts on itself to also affect the blackguard.

Spell Resistance: The spell resistance gained by a dragon fiendish servant doesn't stack with any natural spell resistance it might have. Only the higher value applies.

DRAGONS AS FAMILIARS

By selecting the Dragon Familiar feat, an arcane spellcaster can gain a wyrmling dragon as a familiar. This option is most popular among sorcerers, though many wizards also understand the value of having a dragon on your side.

Your alignment must be one of the acceptable alignments indicated for the dragon kind on Table 3–19: Choosing a Dragon Familiar. In addition, your arcane spellcaster level must be at least as high as the value given for that dragon. For example, a 7th-level neutral sorcerer could select only a white dragon as his familiar, but a 10th-level neutral sorcerer could select a black, copper, green, or white dragon.

Table 3–19: Choosing a Dragon Familiar

Dragon Kind	Character Alignment	Arcane Spellcaster Level
White	N, CN, CE	7th
Black	N, NE, CE	8th
Brass	NG, CG, CN	9th
Green	N, LE, NE	9th
Copper	CG, N, CN	10th
Blue	LN, LE, NE	10th
Bronze	LG, LN, N	11th
Red	CN, CE, NE	12th
Silver	LG, NG, N	12th
Gold	LG, NG, LN	14th

A wyrmling copper dragon serves as a familiar.

A dragon familiar that becomes very young in age can no longer serve as a familiar. It loses its bond with you, including all special abilities granted to it or you because of this bond. Assuming you have treated it well, the dragon maintains a friendly relationship with you in the future.

The dragon familiar is magically linked to you like a normal familiar. The familiar uses the basic statistics for a creature of its kind, as given in the *Monster Manual,* with the following adjustments.

Hit Points: One-half the master's total or the familiar's normal total, whichever is higher.

Attacks: Use the master's base attack bonus or the familiar's, whichever is better. Damage equals that of a normal dragon of that kind and size.

Table 3–20: Dragon Familiar Special Abilities

Master Class Level	Natural Armor Adj.	Special
8th or lower	+1	Alertness, improved evasion, share spells, empathic link
9th–12th	+2	Deliver touch spells
13th–16th	+3	Spell resistance
17th–20th	+4	*Scry on familiar*

Familiar Ability Descriptions: All dragon familiars have special abilities (or impart abilities to their masters) depending on the level of the master. For full details about the abilities mentioned on Table 3–20, see the sidebar Familiars on pages 52–53 of the *Player's Handbook.*

DRAGONS AS PLAYER CHARACTERS

A very different campaign model features dragons most prominently in the game by allowing players to run dragon characters, either a single character in a party made up primarily of standard races, or in an entire party of dragons. Depending on the tone and level of the campaign, these powerful PCs can engage in traditional sorts of adventures, or they can concern themselves with epic quests, believing that more mundane tasks are beneath them.

In one effective campaign model, each player has two active characters in the campaign: a dragon and a member of a standard race who is bonded to the dragon as a kindred. Some adventures, particularly those involving treks into dungeons and cramped tunnels where a dragon can't bring

Illus. by G. Kubic

its full powers to bear, focus on the actions of the bonded kindred. Other adventures, especially those with a more epic sweep, bring the dragon PCs into the action.

If you adopt this campaign model, consider awarding experience points to both characters whenever either character adventures. Each time an active character gains XP, the inactive character receives an award equal to 25% of the award the active character gets.

Dragon kindred share a special emotional bond with the dragon character; this bond is best reflected by the dragonkith prestige class (see page 123). Kindred do not need to adopt this prestige class, but many advance at least a few levels in it, once they qualify.

A different way to focus on dragons as player characters is to use characters from the standard races, but with the half-dragon template applied. Such characters can make use of much of the material presented in this book, without straying so far from the boundaries of what "normal" D&D characters can do. See the half-dragon template on page 146 of the *Monster Manual* and the half-dragon entry in Chapter 4 of this book (page 166).

This wyrmling gold dragon adventures alongside a 13th-level paladin.

Advancement and Aging

A dragon PC begins at a specified age (in accordance with the current party level in the campaign) and gains character levels as the player wishes over the course of its adventures. As it ages from wyrmling to juvenile, a true dragon's level adjustment varies between +2 and +6, depending on the age and dragon variety. For a dragon PC, the dragon's Hit Dice and class levels plus this level adjustment is its effective character level (ECL). For a starting character of juvenile or younger age, this ECL is somewhere between 5 and 20.

As it ages, as shown on Table 3–21: Aging for Dragon PCs, the dragon is required to devote a level every few years to its dragon "class," reflecting the extra Hit Die or level adjustment it gains from aging. The character must add this dragon level as the first level it gains after reaching an age shown on the table. It gains no benefit from reaching a new age category until it attains this level.

Most of the time, a dragon character who advances a dragon level gains 1 Hit Die (1d12), 1 point of natural armor bonus, and 1 point of base attack bonus. Every two increased Hit Dice translate to an increased base save bonus and increased save DCs for the dragon's special abilities.

Once in a while, a dragon character must advance a dragon level without gaining a Hit Die, base attack bonus or save bonus increase, or any other tangible benefit. These levels are indicated on Table 3–21 by asterisks in the "Age in Years" column: When the dragon reaches the specified age, the next level the character attains must be used to advance its dragon level. When this occurs, its level adjustment increases (and its ECL rises accordingly) but the character receives no other benefits. These "extraneous levels" smooth the transitions between age categories, which are often accompanied by an increase in level adjustment to account for changes in size, ability scores, and other characteristics. In most cases on Table 3–21, a dragon PC that is close to reaching a new age category has a higher level adjustment than is specified for its age category and kind in the *Monster Manual*. This method of transitioning between age categories ensures that a dragon PC does not make rapid jumps in power out of proportion to its ECL by reaching a new age category and gaining the benefits of as many as three effective character levels at once (as, for example, a young white dragon with 11 HD and a level adjustment of +3 would do when advancing to the juvenile age category with 12 HD and a level adjustment of +5).

When a dragon reaches a new age category, its ability scores improve across the board. When a dragon's Intelligence score increases due to aging, it gains additional skill points for its new Intelligence score retroactively, in contrast to the standard rules governing character advancement. Each +2 increase in Intelligence gives the character an additional 1 skill point per dragon HD, which translates to a new skill at 1 rank per dragon HD (if it is a class skill) or 1/2 rank per dragon HD (for cross-class skills). The dragon does not get additional skill points for any class levels it possesses, nor does it gain retroactive skill points when its Intelligence increases through other means (such as a *headband of intellect* or an ability score increase gained as part of character advancement).

For example, Simon is creating a gold dragon PC to join a party of 13th-level characters. His character, Keryst, begins play as a newborn wyrmling dragon, with 8 dragon Hit Dice and a level adjustment of +4, plus one level of paladin, for a total effective character level (ECL) of 13th. Keryst has 8d12 Hit Dice from his dragon heritage plus 1d10 from his paladin level, has +7 natural armor, and possesses all the

TABLE 3–21: AGING FOR DRAGON PCs

Age in Years	Age Category	Dragon HD	Level Adj.	Base ECL
Black				
0	Wyrmling	4	+3	7
2	Wyrmling	5	+3	8
4	Wyrmling	6	+3	9
6	Very young	7	+3	10
9	Very young	8	+3	11
12	Very young	9	+3	12
16	Young	10	+3	13
18	Young	11	+3	14
21	Young	12	+3	15
24*	Young	12	+4	16
26	Juvenile	13	+4	17
32	Juvenile	14	+4	18
39	Juvenile	15	+4	19
45*	Juvenile	15	+5	20
Blue				
0	Wyrmling	6	+4	10
2	Wyrmling	7	+4	11
4	Wyrmling	8	+4	12
6	Very young	9	+4	13
8	Very young	10	+4	14
11	Very young	11	+4	15
14*	Very young	11	+5	16
16	Young	12	+5	17
18	Young	13	+5	18
21	Young	14	+5	19
24*	Young	14	+6	20
Green				
0	Wyrmling	5	+5	10
2	Wyrmling	6	+5	11
4	Wyrmling	7	+5	12
6	Very young	8	+5	13
9	Very young	9	+5	14
12	Very young	10	+5	15
16	Young	11	+5	16
18	Young	12	+5	17
21	Young	13	+5	18
24*	Young	13	+6	19
26	Juvenile	14	+6	20
Red				
0	Wyrmling	7	+4	11
2	Wyrmling	8	+4	12
3	Wyrmling	9	+4	13
5*	Wyrmling	9	+5	14
6	Very young	10	+5	15
8	Very young	11	+5	16
11	Very young	12	+5	17
14*	Very young	12	+6	18
16	Young	13	+6	19
19	Young	14	+6	20
White				
0	Wyrmling	3	+2	5
2	Wyrmling	4	+2	6
3	Wyrmling	5	+2	7
5*	Wyrmling	5	+3	8
6	Very young	6	+3	9
9	Very young	7	+3	10
12	Very young	8	+3	11
16	Young	9	+3	12
18	Young	10	+3	13
20*	Young	10	+4	14
22	Young	11	+4	15
24*	Young	11	+5	16
26	Juvenile	12	+5	17
32	Juvenile	13	+5	18
39	Juvenile	14	+5	19
45*	Juvenile	14	+6	20
Brass				
0	Wyrmling	4	+2	6
2	Wyrmling	5	+2	7
3	Wyrmling	6	+2	8
5*	Wyrmling	6	+3	9
6	Very young	7	+3	10
8	Very young	8	+3	11
11	Very young	9	+3	12
14*	Very young	9	+4	13
16	Young	10	+4	14
19	Young	11	+4	15
22	Young	12	+4	16
26	Juvenile	13	+4	17
32	Juvenile	14	+4	18
39	Juvenile	15	+4	19
45*	Juvenile	15	+5	20
Bronze				
0	Wyrmling	6	+4	10
2	Wyrmling	7	+4	11
4	Wyrmling	8	+4	12
6	Very young	9	+4	13
8*	Very young	9	+5	14
10	Very young	10	+5	15
12	Very young	11	+5	16
14*	Very young	11	+6	17
16	Young	12	+6	18
19	Young	13	+6	19
22	Young	14	+6	20
Copper				
0	Wyrmling	5	+2	7
2	Wyrmling	6	+2	8
3	Wyrmling	7	+2	9
5*	Wyrmling	7	+3	10
6	Very young	8	+3	11
8	Very young	9	+3	12
11	Very young	10	+3	13
14*	Very young	10	+4	14
16	Young	11	+4	15
19	Young	12	+4	16
22	Young	13	+4	17
26	Juvenile	14	+4	18
34	Juvenile	15	+4	19
42	Juvenile	16	+4	20
Gold				
0	Wyrmling	8	+4	12
2	Wyrmling	9	+4	13
3	Wyrmling	10	+4	14
5*	Wyrmling	10	+5	15
6	Very young	11	+5	16
8	Very young	12	+5	17
11	Very young	13	+5	18
14*	Very young	13	+6	19
16	Young	14	+6	20
Silver				
0	Wyrmling	7	+4	11
2	Wyrmling	8	+4	12
4	Wyrmling	9	+4	13
6	Very young	10	+4	14
8	Very young	11	+4	15
11	Very young	12	+4	16
14*	Very young	12	+5	17
16	Young	13	+5	18
19	Young	14	+5	19
22	Young	15	+5	20

* At these ages, a dragon must advance a dragon level without gaining a Hit Die (just an increased level adjustment).

other abilities typical of wyrmling gold dragons and 1st-level paladins. As a 13th-level character, he begins play with 78,000 XP (or whatever number the DM specifies between 78,000 and 90,999) and must accumulate a total of 91,000 XP to advance another level.

Keryst gains two levels as a paladin before reaching his second birthday. Before adding his next dragon level, he still has 8d12 dragon Hit Dice, and now has 3d10 paladin Hit Dice. His racial abilities are unchanged, but his paladin abilities have advanced according to his level. His ECL is 15. When he turns 2 years old, the next time he gains a level he must add a dragon Hit Die instead of a paladin level. He gains a 12-sided Hit Die, his natural armor bonus increases by +1, and his base attack bonus increases. Since he now has a total of 12 Hit Dice, he gains a feat and an ability score increase. His ECL increases by 1 just as if he had gained a paladin level, to 16.

After his 2nd birthday, Keryst gains only 1 more paladin level over the next year. Before turning 3, Keryst is a 4th-level paladin and a 17th-level character. After his 3rd birthday, he must again add a dragon level, giving him 10d12 dragon Hit Dice plus his 4d10 paladin Hit Dice. His base attack bonus, base save bonuses, and natural armor bonus all increase by +1, and the save DC against his breath weapon also increases to 15 + his Con modifier. His ECL is now 18.

Two more years pass and Keryst gains one more paladin level, making him a 5th-level paladin and a 19th-level character. Now he turns 5 and must add another dragon level—but this one does not gain him an additional Hit Die. He still has 10d12 dragon Hit Dice and 5d10 paladin Hit Dice, but his level adjustment is now +5, making him a 20th-level character.

When Keryst turns 6, he becomes a very young dragon and he must advance another dragon level. His dragon Hit Dice increase to 11d12, he is still a 5th-level paladin, and his level adjustment is still +5, so he is now a 21st-level character. In addition to the base attack bonus and natural armor bonus increases for his greater dragon Hit Dice, he gains the abilities of a very young dragon: His breath weapon damage increases to 4d10, and his ability scores increase as follows: Str +4, Con +2, Int +2, Wis +2, Cha +2. His increased Intelligence score grants him an additional 11 skill points, which he can use to gain a class skill (for his dragon "class") at 11 ranks or a cross-class skill at 5 1/2 ranks.

Other True Dragons

For true dragons other than those found in the *Monster Manual*, construct tables such as those above using the information on Table 3–22: Additional Level Adjustments.

Table 3–22: Additional Level Adjustments

Dragon Variety	Hit Dice	Level Adj.	Compare
Gem Dragons			
Sapphire	5/8/11/14	+2/+3/+4/+4	Copper
Crystal	5/8/11/14	+5/+5/+5/+6	Green
Amethyst	6/9/12	+4/+4/+5	Blue
Emerald	6/9/12	+4/+4/+6	Bronze
Topaz	7/10/13	+4/+4/+5	Silver
Faerûnian Dragons			
Fang	3/6/9/12	+3/+4/+5/+5	Brass
Shadow	4/7/10/13	+3/+3/+3/+4	Black
Song	5/8/11/14	+5/+5/+5/+6	Green
Brown	6/9/12/15	+2/+3/+4/+5	—
Deep	6/9/12	+4/+4/+5	Blue
Lung Dragons			
Yu lung	6/9/12	+1/+2/+3	Copper
Pan lung	13	+4	Black
Li lung	14	+6	Green
Fiendish Dragons			
Styx	5/8/11/14	+5/+5/+5/+6	Green
Rust	6/9/12	+4/+4/+5	Blue
Pyroclastic	7/10/13	+4/+5/+6	Red
Tarterian	8/11/14	+4/+5/+6	Gold
Howling	9/12	+4/+5	—
Planar Dragons			
Ethereal	4/7/10/13	+2/+3/+4/+4	Brass
Battle	5/8/11/14	+2/+3/+4/+4	Copper
Chaos	6/9/12	+4/+4/+6	Bronze
Oceanus	7/10/13	+4/+4/+5	Silver
Radiant	9/12	+4/+5	—

On the table, Hit Dice and Level Adjustment are given for wyrmling, very young, (usually) young, and (sometimes) juvenile dragons.

For example, a sapphire dragon has 5 HD and a level adjustment of +2 as a wyrmling, 8 HD and a level adjustment of +3 when it reaches the very young stage, 11 HD and a level adjustment of +4 at the young stage, and 15 HD and a level adjustment of +4 as a juvenile. Its progression is identical to that of a copper dragon.

If the sum of a dragon's Hit Dice and its level adjustment gives it an effective character level higher than 20, that dragon character is too powerful to fit into a party of PCs below epic level. For instance, a howling dragon has 9 HD and a level adjustment of +4 as a wyrmling and 12 HD and a level adjustment of +5 as a very young dragon. When it reaches young age, it has 15 HD and a +6 level adjustment, giving it an ECL of 21; thus, information on a young howling dragon as a PC is absent from Table 3–22.

Also, all lung dragons are yu lung for their first 25 years of life (through the young age category). When a yu lung reaches juvenile age, it transforms into a different variety of dragon. Because of their high juvenile Hit Dice and level adjustment, many lung dragons have ECLs higher than 20 at the juvenile stage and thus are not mentioned on this table. These varieties include the shen lung, chiang lung, tun mi lung, lung wang, and t'ien lung. The Hit Dice and level adjustment listings for the pan lung and li lung are for juveniles only.

Lesser Dragon PCs

Using another creature of the dragon type as a player character is rather less complicated than using a true dragon. Such a creature has a set level adjustment and no built-in progression due to age, so after the character begins play there is no reason to advance the character as a monster again. For example, a wyvern character, with a level adjustment of +4 and 7 Hit Dice, has an ECL of 11 and joins a party of 11th-level characters to adventure. The wyvern continues advancing as a character, just like the other characters in the party.

Many creatures of the dragon type have more than 20 Hit Dice, or their level adjustment would raise their ECL above 20. These monsters are not included in the following information.

Lesser Dragon	Level Adj.
Abyssal drake	+5
Air drake	+3
Dragon turtle	+5
Dragonnel	+3
Earth drake	+3
Faerie dragon	+2
Fire drake	+3
Forest landwyrm	+3
Ice drake	+3
Magma drake	+3
Ooze drake	+3
Plains landwyrm	+2
Pseudodragon	+3
Smoke drake	+3
Spiked felldrake	+2
Underdark landwyrm	+2
Water drake	+3
Wyvern	+4

Template	Level Adj.
Dracolich	+4
Draconic	+1
Ghostly dragon	+5
Half-dragon	+3
Vampiric dragon	+5

This chapter introduces a variety of dragon-related monsters for your campaign. A few are reproduced from previous sources; consider the versions presented here to be the official and correct ones.

ABYSSAL DRAKE

Huge Outsider (Chaotic, Evil, Extraplanar, Fire)
Hit Dice: 10d8+50 (95 hp)
Initiative: +1
Speed: 40 ft. (8 squares), fly 150 ft. (poor)
Armor Class: 21 (–2 size, +1 Dex, +12 natural), touch 9, flat-footed 20
Base Attack/Grapple: +10/+18
Attack: Sting +19 melee (1d6+9 plus poison)
Full Attack: Sting +19 melee (1d6+9 plus poison) and bite +14 melee (2d6+4); or 2 claws +19 melee (2d4+9)
Space/Reach: 15 ft./10 ft.
Special Attacks: Breath weapon, frightful presence, poison, rend
Special Qualities: Darkvision 60 ft., immunity to fire, magic sleep effects, and paralysis, low-light vision, outsider traits, scent, resistance to acid 20, cold 20, and electricity 20, vulnerability to cold
Saves: Fort +12, Ref +8, Will +9
Abilities: Str 29, Dex 12, Con 20, Int 6, Wis 15, Cha 15
Skills: Bluff +15, Diplomacy +5, Hide +12, Intimidate +5, Listen +17, Move Silently +14, Search +11, Spot +17
Feats: Alertness, Flyby Attack, Power Attack, Power Dive
Environment: Infinite Layers of the Abyss
Organization: Solitary, pair, or flight (3–6)
Challenge Rating: 9
Treasure: Standard
Alignment: Always chaotic evil
Advancement: 11–20 HD (Huge); 21–30 HD (Gargantuan)
Level Adjustment: +5

The abyssal drake is the horrific result of an ancient breeding program that combines the nastiest elements of demons, wyverns, and red dragons. Originally intended to serve as mounts for mighty demon princes, abyssal drakes proved too unruly for such service. Now they roam the wilds of the Abyss, preying on demons and visitors alike.

Abyssal drakes resemble their wyvern ancestors, but their dark red, scaled hides betray their fiendish heritage. They have powerful batlike wings, a serpentine neck, and razor-sharp claws.

Abyssal drakes speak Abyssal and Common.

COMBAT

An abyssal drake retains the aggressive nature of its wyvern ancestors, diving upon prey in a barely controlled descent, strafing its foes with its breath weapon and scattering them with its frightful presence, then picking off lone survivors.

When using the Flyby Attack feat, an abyssal drake can attack with sting, bite, or both claws. Its claws lack the dexterity to snatch up an opponent, so it contents itself with merely rending its foe.

An abyssal drake's natural weapons, as well as any weapons it wields, are treated as chaotic-aligned and evil-aligned for purpose of overcoming damage reduction.

Breath Weapon (Su): 60-ft. cone, every 1d4 rounds, 10d6 special, Reflex DC 20 half. Much like a *flame strike* spell, half of this damage is fire damage and the remainder is unholy damage (and thus not subject to resistance to fire and similar defenses). The save DC is Constitution-based.

Frightful Presence (Ex): When an abyssal drake charges, attacks, or flies overhead, it inspires terror in all creatures within 120 feet that have fewer Hit Dice or levels than it has. Each potential victim must attempt a DC 17 Will save. On a failure, a creature with 4 or fewer HD becomes panicked for 4d6 rounds, and one with 5 or more HD becomes shaken for 4d6 rounds. A successful save leaves that opponent immune to that abyssal drake's frightful presence for 24 hours. Dragons ignore the frightful presence of an abyssal drake, as do other abyssal drakes.

Abyssal drake

Illus. by S. Tappin

Poison (Ex): Sting, Fortitude DC 20; initial and secondary damage 2d6 Con.

Rend (Ex): If an abyssal drake hits with both claw attacks, it latches onto the opponent's body and tears the flesh. This rending attack automatically deals an extra 4d4+13 points of damage.

Outsider Traits: An abyssal drake cannot be raised, reincarnated, or resurrected (though a *limited wish, wish, miracle,* or *true resurrection* spell can restore life).

DRACOLICH

The dracolich is an undead creature resulting from the transformation of an evil dragon. The process usually involves a cooperative effort between an evil dragon and a powerful cleric, sorcerer, or wizard, but especially powerful spellcasters have been known to coerce an evil dragon to undergo the transformation against its will.

The dragon must first consume a lethal concoction known as a dracolich brew (see page 120). This act instantly slays the dragon, whereupon its spirit is transferred to its dracolich phylactery (also see page 120), regardless of the distance between the phylactery and the dragon's body.

A spirit contained in a phylactery can sense any reptilian or dragon corpse of Medium or larger size within 90 feet and attempt to possess it. Under no circumstances can the spirit possess a living body. The spirit's original body is an ideal vessel, and any attempt to possess it is automatically successful. To possess a suitable corpse other than its own, a dracolich must make a successful Charisma check (DC 10 for a true dragon,

MONSTERS BY TYPE (AND SUBTYPE)

Aberration: squamous spewer.

(Air): air drake, ice drake, smoke drake, storm drake.

(Aquatic): Oceanus dragon, ooze drake, Styx dragon, swamp landwyrm, water drake.

(Chaotic): chaos dragon.

(Cold): ice drake.

Construct: dragonbone golem, drakestone golem, ironwyrm golem.

Dragon: battle dragon, chaos dragon, dragonnel, elemental drakes, ethereal dragon, faerie dragon, half-dragon, howling dragon, landwyrms, Oceanus dragon, pyroclastic dragon, radiant dragon, rust dragon, shadow dragon, spiked felldrake, storm drake, Styx dragon, Tarterian dragon.

(Earth): earth drake, magma drake, ooze drake.

(Extraplanar): battle dragon, chaos dragon, ethereal dragon, howling dragon, Oceanus dragon, pyroclastic dragon, radiant dragon, rust dragon, Styx dragon, Tarterian dragon.

(Fire): abyssal drake, fire drake, magma drake, smoke drake.

Monstrous Humanoid: dragonkin.

Outsider (Chaotic): abyssal drake.

Outsider (Evil): abyssal drake.

(Reptilian): dragonkin.

(Swarm): hoard scarab swarm.

Undead: dracolich, ghostly dragon, skeletal dragon, vampiric dragon, zombie dragon.

Vermin: hoard scarab, hoard scarab swarm.

(Water): ice drake, ooze drake, water drake.

DC 15 for any other creature of the dragon type, or DC 20 for any other kind of reptilian creature, such as a giant snake or lizardfolk). If the check fails, the dracolich can never possess that particular corpse.

If the corpse accepts the spirit, the corpse becomes animated. If the animated corpse is the spirit's former body, it immediately becomes a dracolich. Otherwise, it becomes a proto-dracolich (see below).

A dracolich appears as a skeletal or semiskeletal version of its former self, with glowing points of light in its shadowy eye sockets.

SAMPLE DRACOLICH

This example uses an ancient blue dragon as the base creature.

Ancient Blue Dracolich
Gargantuan Undead
Hit Dice: 33d12 (214 hp)
Initiative: +0
Speed: 40 ft. (8 squares), burrow 20 ft., fly 200 ft. (clumsy)
Armor Class: 40 (–4 size, +34 natural), touch 8, flat-footed 42
Base Attack/Grapple: +33/+57
Attack: Bite +41 melee (4d6+12)
Full Attack: Bite +41 melee (4d6+12) and 2 claws +36 melee (2d8+6) and 2 wings +36 melee (2d6+6) and tail slap +36 melee (2d8+18)
Space/Reach: 20 ft./15 ft.
Special Attacks: Breath weapon, *control undead*, create/destroy water, crush, frightful presence, paralyzing gaze, paralyzing touch, rend, snatch, spell-like abilities, spells, tail sweep
Special Qualities: Blindsense 60 ft., damage reduction 15/magic and 5/bludgeoning, darkvision 120 ft., immunity to cold, electricity, magic sleep effects, *polymorph*, and paralysis, invulnerability, keen senses, low-light vision,spell resistance 30, undead traits
Saves: Fort +18, Ref +18, Will +23
Abilities: Str 35, Dex 10, Con —, Int 20, Wis 21, Cha 22
Skills: Bluff +42, Concentration +27, Disguise +6 (+8 acting), Diplomacy +46, Gather Information +8, Hide +19, Intimidate +44, Knowledge (arcana) +24, Knowledge (geography) +15, Knowledge (history) +15, Knowledge (local) +15, Knowledge (nature) +15, Knowledge (religion) +15, Listen +41, Search +41, Sense Motive +41, Spellcraft +43, Spot +41, Survival +5 (+7 aboveground natural environments, avoiding getting lost, following tracks)
Feats: Blind-Fight, Combat Expertise, Extend Spell, Flyby Attack, Hover, Improved Maneuverability, Large and in Charge, Power Attack, Recover Breath, Rend, Shape Breath, Snatch
Environment: Temperate deserts
Organization: Solitary
Challenge Rating: 23
Treasure: Triple standard
Alignment: Lawful evil
Advancement: 34–35 HD (Gargantuan)

This diabolical creature has turned an ancient tomb complex into its lair. Once a place of respect for the dead, the area has become a charnel house.

Combat

This dracolich uses its spells to warn of and spy on approaching enemies, ensuring that it knows enough to defend itself. It prefers hit-and-run tactics, using *dimension door* to come and go as it pleases. It separates targets with spells such as *solid fog* and *web*, and then picks off lone foes.

This dracolich also uses any magic items in its possession to best effect (generate its treasure according to the normal rules or use the sample CR 23 dragon hoard in Appendix 1).

This dracolich's natural weapons are treated as magic weapons for the purpose of overcoming damage reduction.

Breath Weapon (Su): 120-ft. line (60-ft. cone if shaped), 20d8 electricity, Reflex DC 32 half.

Frightful Presence (Ex): This dracolich can unsettle foes with its mere presence. The ability takes effect automatically whenever it attacks, charges, or flies overhead. Creatures within a radius of 180 feet are subject to the effect if they have fewer than 35 HD. A potentially affected creature that succeeds on a DC 32 Will save remains immune to its frightful presence for 24 hours. On a failure, creatures with 4 or fewer HD become panicked for 4d6 rounds and those with 5 or more HD become shaken for 4d6 rounds. Dracoliches ignore the frightful presence of other dracoliches.

Rend (Ex): Extra damage 4d8+18.

Snatch (Ex): Against Medium or smaller creatures, bite for 4d6+12/round or claw for 2d8+6/round.

Invulnerability: If a dracolich is slain, its spirit immediately returns to its phylactery, from where it may attempt to possess a suitable corpse.

Keen Senses (Ex): This dracolich sees four times as well as a human in low-light conditions and twice as well in normal light. It also has darkvision out to 120 feet.

Paralyzing Gaze (Su): The gaze of a dracolich's glowing eyes can paralyze victims within 40 feet if they fail a DC 24 Fortitude save. If the saving throw is successful, the character is forever immune to the gaze of that particular dracolich. If it fails, the victim is paralyzed for 2d6 rounds.

Paralyzing Touch (Su): A creature struck by any of this dracolich's physical attacks must make a DC 24 Fortitude save or be paralyzed for 2d6 rounds. A successful saving throw against this effect does not confer any immunity against subsequent attacks.

Spell-Like Abilities: 3/day—*create/destroy water* (Will DC 32 negates), *ventriloquism* (DC 17); 1/day—*hallucinatory terrain* (DC 20), *veil* (DC 22). Caster level 33rd.

Spells: As 13th-level sorcerer.

Tail Sweep (Ex): A dracolich can sweep with its tail as a standard action. The sweep affects a half-circle with a diameter of 30 feet. It deals 2d6+21 points of damage to Small or smaller creatures (Reflex DC 32 half).

Undead Traits: A dracolich is immune to mind-affecting effects, poison, magic sleep effects, paralysis, stunning, disease, death effects, and any effect that requires a Fortitude save unless it also works on objects or is harmless. It is not subject to critical hits, nonlethal damage, ability damage to its physical ability scores, ability drain, energy drain, fatigue, exhaustion, or death from massive damage. It cannot be raised, and resurrection works only if it is willing.

Spells Known (6/8/8/7/7/7/5; save DC 16 + spell level): 0—*arcane mark, dancing lights, daze, detect magic, ghost sound, mage hand, mending, ray of frost, read magic*; 1st—*alarm, comprehend languages, magic missile, shield, unseen servant*; 2nd—*blur, darkness, detect thoughts, resist energy, web*; 3rd—*blink, dispel magic, slow, vampiric touch*; 4th—*arcane eye, confusion, dimension door, solid fog*; 5th—*cloudkill, dispel good, dominate person*; 6th—*disintegrate, globe of invulnerability*.

CREATING A DRACOLICH

"Dracolich" is an acquired template that can be added to any evil dragon (hereafter referred to as the base creature), though dragons of old age or older, with spellcasting abilities, are preferred.

A dracolich uses all the base creature's statistics and special abilities except as noted here.

Size and Type: The creature's type changes to undead. Do not recalculate the creature's base attack bonus, saves, or skill points. Size is unchanged.

Speed: A dracolich's ability to fly becomes supernatural in nature.

Armor Class: A dracolich gains an additional +2 natural armor bonus (the hide toughens when the dragon becomes a dracolich).

Attacks: A dracolich cannot make crush attacks even if it was capable of doing so when the base creature was alive.

Damage: A dracolich deals an extra 1d6 points of cold damage on any successful hit. A successful attack may also paralyze the victim (see below).

Special Attacks: A dracolich retains all the special attack forms of the base creature, including breath weapon, spell use, and spell-like abilities. Some of these attack forms are enhanced, and it also gains some new abilities.

Breath Weapon (Su): Since a dracolich doesn't have a Constitution score, it uses its Charisma modifier to determine the save DC for its breath weapon instead.

Control Undead (Sp): Once every three days, a dracolich can use *control undead* as the spell (caster level 15th). The dracolich cannot cast other spells while this ability is in effect.

Frightful Presence (Ex): Since the creature's Charisma score increases by 2, the save DC for the dracolich's frightful presence ability increases by 1.

Paralyzing Gaze (Su): The gaze of a dracolich's glowing eyes can paralyze victims within 40 feet who fail a Fortitude save (DC 10 + 1/2 dracolich's HD + dracolich's Cha modifier). If the saving throw is successful, the character is forever immune to the gaze of that particular dracolich. If it fails, the victim is paralyzed for 2d6 rounds.

Paralyzing Touch (Su): A creature struck by any of a dracolich's physical attacks must make a Fortitude save (DC same as for the dracolich's paralyzing gaze) or be paralyzed for 2d6 rounds. A successful saving throw against this effect does not confer any immunity against subsequent attacks.

Dracolich

Special Qualities: A dracolich retains all the special qualities of the base creature. Again, some are enhanced, and a dracolich gains some new special qualities as well.

Damage Reduction: Like a skeleton, a dracolich has damage reduction 5/bludgeoning.

Immunities: In addition to the standard undead immunities (see below), a dracolich is immune to polymorph, cold, and electricity effects.

Invulnerability: If a dracolich is slain, its spirit immediately returns to its phylactery. If no dragon-type corpse lies within 90 feet for the spirit to possess, the dracolich is trapped in the phylactery until such a time—if ever—that a corpse becomes available. A dracolich is difficult to destroy. If its spirit is currently contained in its phylactery, destroying that item when a suitable corpse is not within range effectively destroys the dracolich. Likewise, an active dracolich is unable to attempt further possessions if its phylactery is destroyed. The fate of a disembodied dracolich spirit—that is, a spirit with no body or phylactery—is unknown, but presumably it is drawn to the Lower Planes.

Spell Resistance (Ex): Becoming a dracolich increases the dragon's spell resistance by +3. A dracolich has a minimum spell resistance of 16.

Undead Traits: A dracolich is immune to mind-affecting effects, poison, magic sleep effects, paralysis, stunning, disease, death effects, and any effect that requires a Fortitude save unless it also works on objects or is harmless. It is not subject to critical hits, nonlethal damage, ability damage to its physical ability scores, ability drain, energy drain, fatigue, exhaustion, or death from massive damage. It cannot be raised, and resurrection works only if it is willing. It has darkvision out to 60 feet (unless the base creature had a greater range).

Saves: As undead, dracoliches are immune to anything that requires a Fortitude save unless it affects objects.

Abilities: Being undead, the dracolich has no Constitution score (use its Charisma modifier to determine save DC against its breath weapon, tail sweep, and similar special attacks). Its Charisma score is increased by 2, which increases the DC of the save against its frightful presence and other special abilities. Otherwise, the dracolich's ability scores remain the same as the base creature's scores.

Organization: Solitary.
Challenge Rating: Same as base creature +3.
Alignment: Always evil.
Advancement: Up to +2 HD.
Level Adjustment: Same as base creature +4.

PROTO-DRACOLICHES

A proto-dracolich comes into being when a dracolich's spirit possesses any body other than the corpse that was created when the dragon consumed its dose of dracolich brew. A proto-dracolich has the mind and memories of its original form but the hit points and immunities of a dracolich. A proto-dracolich can neither speak nor cast spells. Further, it cannot deal extra cold damage, use a breath weapon, or use frightful presence as a dracolich. Its Strength, speed, and Armor Class are those of the possessed body.

A proto-dracolich transforms into a full-fledged dracolich in 2d4 days. When the transformation is complete, the dracolich's form resembles that of its original body. It can now speak, cast spells, and employ the breath weapon it originally had, in addition to gaining all the abilities of a dracolich. A dracolich typically keeps a few "spare" bodies of a suitable size near the hiding place of its phylactery, so that if its current form is destroyed, it can possess and transform a new body within a few days.

DRACONIC CREATURE

A draconic creature is descended from a dragon ancestor, though that ancestor may be many generations removed. Draconic creatures often bear hints of their heritage, such as slitted pupils or talonlike nails. They are sometimes mistaken for half-dragons.

It isn't necessary to determine the source of a draconic creature's heritage (unlike with half-dragons), since the creature doesn't gain any abilities directly related to its dragon ancestor (such as resistance to a certain type of energy).

SAMPLE DRACONIC CREATURE

This example uses a fire giant as the base creature.

Draconic Fire Giant
Large Giant (Fire)
Hit Dice: 15d8+90 (157 hp)
Initiative: –1
Speed: 30 ft. in half-plate armor (6 squares); base speed 40 ft.
Armor Class: 24 (–1 size, –1 Dex, +9 natural, +7 half-plate armor), touch 8, flat-footed 24
Base Attack/Grapple: +11/+26
Attack: Greatsword +21 melee (3d6+16) or slam +21 melee (1d4+11) or rock +10 ranged (2d6+11 plus 2d6 fire) or claw +21 melee (1d4+11)
Full Attack: Greatsword +21/+16/+11 melee (3d6+16) or 2 slams +21 melee (1d4+11) or rock +10 ranged (2d6+11 plus 2d6 fire) or 2 claws +21 melee (1d4+11)
Space/Reach: 10 ft./10 ft.
Special Attacks: Rock throwing
Special Qualities: Darkvision 60 ft., immunity to fire, low-light vision, rock catching, save bonuses, vulnerability to cold
Saves: Fort +15, Ref +4, Will +9
Abilities: Str 33, Dex 9, Con 23, Int 10, Wis 14, Cha 13
Skills: Climb +10, Craft (weaponsmithing) +6, Intimidate +7, Jump +10, Spot +14
Feats: Cleave, Great Cleave, Improved Overrun, Improved Sunder, Iron Will, Power Attack
Environment: Warm mountains
Organization: Solitary, gang (2–5), band (6–9 plus 35% noncombatants plus 1 adept or cleric of 1st or 2nd level), hunting/raiding party (6–9 plus 1 adept or sorcerer of 3rd–5th level plus 2–4 hell hounds and 2–3 trolls or ettins), or tribe (21–30 plus 1 adept, cleric, or sorcerer of 6th or 7th level plus 12–30 hell hounds, 12–22 trolls, 5–12 ettins, and 1–2 young red dragons)
Challenge Rating: 11
Treasure: Standard
Alignment: Lawful evil
Advancement: By character class
Level Adjustment: +5

Most likely the descendant of a union between a fire giant and a red dragon, this draconic fire giant uses his superior personality and physical power to lead a tribe of fire giants.

Combat

Draconic fire giants fight much like their giant brethren, relying either on a greatsword or on thrown boulders heated by volcanic fire.

Rock Throwing (Ex): The range increment is 120 feet for this draconic fire giant's thrown rocks. The creature can hurl rocks weighing 40 to 50 pounds each (Small objects) up to five range increments.

Rock Catching (Ex): This giant can catch Small, Medium, or Large rocks (or projectiles of similar shape). Once per round, if the creature would normally be hit by a rock, it can make a Reflex save to catch the projectile as a free action. The DC is 15 for a Small rock, 20 for a Medium one, and 25 for a Large one. (If the projectile has a magical bonus on attack rolls, the DC increases by that amount.) The giant must be ready for and aware of the attack.

Save Bonuses (Ex): This draconic fire giant has a +4 bonus on saves against magic sleep and paralysis effects.

CREATING A DRACONIC CREATURE

"Draconic" is an inherited template that can be added to any living corporeal creature (referred to hereafter as the base creature) except a dragon.

A draconic creature uses all the base creature's statistics and special abilities except as noted here.

Size and Type: Animals with this template become magical beasts, but otherwise the creature type is unchanged. Size is unchanged.

Armor Class: Natural armor improves by 1.

Damage: Draconic creatures have two claw attacks. If the base creature does not have this attack form, use the damage values in the table below. Otherwise, use the values below or the base creature's damage, whichever is greater.

Size	Claw Damage
Up to Tiny	1
Small	1d2
Medium	1d3
Large	1d4
Huge	1d6
Gargantuan	1d8
Colossal	1d10

Draconic fire giant

Illus. by S. Tappin

Special Qualities: A draconic creature has all the special qualities of the base creature, plus darkvision out to 60 feet and low-light vision.

Saves: A draconic creature has a +4 racial bonus on saves against magic sleep effects and paralysis, thanks to its heritage.

Abilities: Increase from the base creature as follows: Str +2, Dex +0, Con +2, Int +0, Wis +0, Cha +2.

Skills: Draconic creatures have a +2 racial bonus on Intimidate and Spot checks.

Organization: Solitary or as base creature.

Challenge Rating: Same as base creature +1.

Level Adjustment: Same as base creature +1.

Draconic Characters

Draconic creatures with Charisma scores of 12 or higher are often sorcerers.

DRAGONKIN

Large Monstrous Humanoid (Reptilian)
Hit Dice: 7d8+7 (38 hp)
Initiative: +5
Speed: 20 ft. (4 squares), fly 40 ft. (good)
Armor Class: 17 (+1 Dex, –1 size, +7 natural), touch 10, flat-footed 16
Base Attack/Grapple: +7/+15
Attack: Foreclaw +10 melee (1d6+4) or longspear +10/+5 melee (1d10+6)
Full Attack: 2 foreclaws +10 melee (1d6+4) or longspear +10/+5 melee (1d10+6)
Space/Reach: 10 ft./10 ft. (20 ft. with longspear)
Special Attacks: Rake 1d6+2
Special Qualities: Darkvision 60 ft., detect magic
Saves: Fort +5, Ref +6, Will +7
Abilities: Str 19, Dex 12, Con 13, Int 10, Wis 14, Cha 13
Skills: Listen +12, Spot +12
Feats: Flyby Attack, Great Fortitude, Improved Initiative
Environment: Warm hills
Organization: Solitary, clutch (2–8), or squad (4–16 plus 1 human necromancer of 7th–11th-level)
Challenge Rating: 3
Treasure: Standard coins; no goods; double items
Alignment: Usually chaotic evil
Advancement: By character class
Level Adjustment: +2

Dragonkin are humanoid creatures believed to be distant cousins of dragons. Found in wild tribes or serving human masters, their brute strength and sharp claws make them a deadly threat.

Dragonkin are humanoids of 8 to 9 feet in height with draconic features. Their scaled hides range from dark yellow ocher to reddish brown with darker spots or bands. Their faces are decidedly dragonlike, with a long snout, a mane of thick hair, and small horns swept back behind their heads. They have green wings that lighten to gold or yellow, or sometimes wings that match the color of their bodies.

Dragonkin speak Draconic.

COMBAT

Dragonkin prefer to fight in the air, swooping down to slash earthbound opponents with their foreclaws. If forced to bring combat to the ground, dragonkin move in and use their claws or weapons (they favor longspears and other reach weapons).

Most dragonkin have a strong desire to acquire magic items (perhaps inherited from their ancestors) and tend to attack characters possessing such items in preference to others. If possible, a dragonkin grabs a magic item from its opponent and flees with it, taking the item back to its cave. (Resolve this as a disarm attempt; since the dragonkin is unarmed, it holds the item if it wins the opposed check.)

Rake (Ex): Dragonkin make two additional attacks (+10 melee) with their rear claws for 1d6+2 points of damage each when attacking from the air.

Detect Magic (Su): Dragonkin have the innate ability to use *detect magic* as a free action, once per round.

DRAGONKIN AS CHARACTERS

Most dragonkin with character classes are barbarians, and barbarian is their favored class. However, a handful of dragonkin sorcerers have been reported, and their number seems to be slowly increasing.

DRAGONKIN PLAYER CHARACTERS

Dragonkin characters possess the following racial traits.

—+8 Strength, +2 Dexterity, +2 Constitution, +4 Wisdom, +2 Charisma. Dragonkin are powerful creatures that derive great abilities from their ancestral tie with the dragons.

—Large size: –1 penalty to Armor Class, –1 penalty on attack rolls, –4 penalty on Hide checks, lifting and carrying limits twice those of Medium characters.

—A dragonkin's base land speed is 20 feet. It has a fly speed of 40 feet (good).

—Natural Attacks: A dragonkin is proficient with its claw attacks, which deal 1d6 points of damage each. If it uses a claw as a secondary weapon (along with a weapon held in the other hand), it takes the normal penalties for two-weapon fighting.

When making a full attack while airborne, a dragonkin character may also make two additional attacks with its rear claws at its full base attack bonus (with a –5 penalty if also attacking with a weapon).

—Dragonkin can use *detect magic* at will as a supernatural ability, as a sorcerer whose level is equal to the dragonkin's HD.

—Racial Hit Dice: A dragonkin begins with seven levels of monstrous humanoid, which provide 7d8 Hit Dice, a base attack bonus of +7, and base saving throw bonuses of Fort +2, Ref +5, and Will +5.

—Racial Skills: A dragonkin's monstrous humanoid levels give it skill points equal to 10 × (2 + Int modifier). Its class skills are Spot and Listen.

—Racial Feats: A dragonkin's monstrous humanoid levels give it three feats.

—+7 natural armor bonus.

—Automatic Languages: Draconic. Bonus Languages: Common, Dwarf, Gnoll, Goblin, Orc.

—Favored Class: Barbarian.

—Level adjustment +2.

Dragonkin

DRAGONNEL

Large Dragon
Hit Dice: 6d12+6 (45 hp)
Initiative: +5
Speed: 40 ft. (8 squares), fly 90 ft. (average)
Armor Class: 16 (–1 size, +1 Dex, +6 natural), touch 10, flat-footed 15
Base Attack/Grapple: +7/+15
Attack: Bite +9 melee (2d6+4) or claw +4 melee (1d8+2)
Full Attack: Bite +9 melee (2d6+4) and 2 claws +4 melee (1d8+2)
Space/Reach: 10 ft./5 ft.
Special Attacks: Roar
Special Qualities: Darkvision 60 ft., immunity to magic sleep effects and paralysis, low-light vision, scent
Saves: Fort +6, Ref +6, Will +6
Abilities: Str 19, Dex 13, Con 12, Int 6, Wis 12, Cha 10
Skills: Hide +6, Listen +12, Move Silently +10, Spot +12
Feats: Ability Focus (roar), Alertness, Improved Initiative
Environment: Temperate hills
Organization: Solitary, pair, family (2–5), or pack (5–20)
Challenge Rating: 4
Treasure: Standard
Alignment: Always neutral
Advancement: 7–12 HD (Large); 13–18 HD (Huge)
Level Adjustment: +3

Dragonnels are powerful, graceful creatures often bred and trained as steeds for mighty paladins and knights. Though relatively simpleminded for dragons, they are fiercely loyal to their masters.

A dragonnel stands about 5 feet tall at the shoulder and measures nearly 10 feet from nose to tail. Its scales range from red-brown to a brilliant gold. A pair of muscled wings sprouts from its shoulders, spanning up to 30 feet in flight.

In the wild, dragonnels typically lair in hidden caves located far from civilization. Occasionally, a group of up to four families settles in nearby locations, sharing hunting and protection duties among the various adults.

Dragonnels speak Draconic.

COMBAT

A dragonnel opens combat with its roar, hoping to frighten would-be opponents. Once engaged in battle, it fights fearlessly, using its claws and bite to shred its enemies.

Roar (Ex): Once per day, a dragonnel can unleash a mighty roar. All enemies within a 30-foot-radius spread who can hear the dragonnel must succeed on a DC 14 Will save or become shaken for 1d6 rounds.

Training a Dragonnel

Although intelligent, a dragonnel requires training before it can bear a rider in combat. To be trained, a dragonnel must have a friendly attitude toward the trainer (this can be achieved through a successful Diplomacy check). Training a friendly dragonnel requires six weeks of work and a successful Handle Animal check (DC 30 for a young creature, or DC 35 for a mature creature of three or more years in age).

Dragonnel eggs are worth 5,000 gp apiece on the open market, while young are worth 7,500 gp each. Professional trainers charge 2,500 gp to rear or train a dragonnel. Riding a trained dragonnel requires an exotic saddle. A dragonnel can fight while carrying a rider, but the rider cannot also attack unless he or she succeeds on a Ride check (see the Ride skill, page 80 of the *Player's Handbook*).

Carrying Capacity: A light load for a dragonnel is up to 400 pounds; a medium load, 401–800 pounds; and a heavy load, 801–1200 pounds. A dragonnel can carry up to a light load (such as an armored Medium creature) while flying.

Dragonnel

Illus. by J. Jarvis

Dragonnels as Special Mounts

At the DM's option, a paladin of 9th level or higher can call a dragonnel instead of a horse as her special mount. For the purposes of the mount's bonus Hit Dice, natural armor, Strength adjustment, Intelligence score, and special powers, treat the paladin as if she were four levels lower than normal.

ELEMENTAL DRAKE

Elemental drakes are fierce creatures distantly related to wyverns, but with a heritage that derives from the Elemental Planes.

They resemble lithe, sinuous dragons with scale colorations and textures appropriate to their elemental legacy. Most measure about 12 feet from nose to tail.

Some jann breed and train elemental drakes as steeds.

COMBAT

All elemental drakes share certain tendencies and tactics. They are all difficult to surprise. Once encountered, they use Flyby Attack to remain out of reach of their opponents as long as possible. Once engaged, they unleash deadly melee attacks without mercy. Their sinuous bodies allow them to focus all their attacks (including the tail slap) on any creature within their reach, even while airborne.

AIR DRAKE

Large Dragon (Air)
Hit Dice: 8d12+24 (78 hp)
Initiative: +2
Speed: 30 ft. (6 squares), fly 120 ft. (good)
Armor Class: 17 (–1 size, +2 Dex, +6 natural), touch 11, flat-footed 15
Base Attack/Grapple: +8/+16
Attack: Bite +11 melee (2d6+4)
Full Attack: Bite +11 melee (2d6+4) and 2 claws +9 melee (1d8+2) and tail slap +9 melee (1d8+6)
Space/Reach: 10 ft./5 ft.
Special Attacks: Air mastery, blinding sandstorm
Special Qualities: Blindsense 60 ft., darkvision 60 ft., gaseous form, immunity to magic sleep effects and paralysis, low-light vision
Saves: Fort +9, Ref +8, Will +8
Abilities: Str 19, Dex 14, Con 17, Int 8, Wis 14, Cha 11
Skills: Bluff +11, Diplomacy +2, Escape Artist +13, Hide +17*, Intimidate +2, Listen +14, Move Silently +13, Spot +15
Feats: Alertness, Blind-Fight[B], Flyby Attack, Multiattack
Environment: Temperate deserts
Organization: Solitary, pair, or flight (3–6)
Challenge Rating: 6
Treasure: Standard
Alignment: Usually chaotic neutral
Advancement: 9–19 HD (Large); 20–24 HD (Huge)
Level Adjustment: +3

Air drakes are temperamental and cowardly, lording over those weaker than themselves but fleeing more powerful threats.

An air drake's scales are sandy brown, the better to blend in with the desert below. Its underbelly shades to a light blue, making it difficult to spot by viewers on the ground. The drake's teeth are needle-sharp, as are its claws.

Air drakes often clash with dragonnes, since the two prefer similar lairs and often fight over territory. Air drakes generally flee from copper dragons or blue dragons unless they can ambush a small one or poach eggs from an unguarded nest.

Air drakes speak Draconic and Auran in a susurrant tone, often slurring words together or mixing the languages unintentionally.

Combat

Air drakes use their airborne speed and maneuverability to their advantage, employing Flyby Attack to strike at slower-moving opponents. They prefer to sneak up on targets that appear weak, injured, or defenseless. They can also hover in place, kicking up a blinding sandstorm to hamper their foes.

Air Mastery (Ex): Airborne creatures take a –1 penalty on attack and damage rolls against an air drake.

Blinding Sandstorm (Ex): If an air drake hovers close to the ground in an area with lots of loose debris (such as a sandy desert), the draft from its wings creates a hemispherical cloud with a radius of 30 feet. The winds so generated can snuff torches, small campfires, exposed lanterns, and other small, open flames of nonmagical origin. The cloud obscures vision, and creatures caught within are blinded while inside it and for 1 round after emerging. Those caught in the cloud must succeed on a DC 14 Concentration check to cast a spell. The air drake is not immune to this effect, though its Blind-Fight feat compensates somewhat.

Gaseous Form (Su): Once per day, an air drake can assume *gaseous form* as the spell (caster level equals drake's HD).

Skills: Air drakes have a +4 racial bonus on Move Silently checks. *They have a +4 racial bonus on Hide checks when airborne in temperate or warm desert environments.

EARTH DRAKE

Large Dragon (Earth)
Hit Dice: 12d12+48 (129 hp)
Initiative: +0
Speed: 20 ft. (4 squares), burrow 20 ft., fly 60 ft. (poor)
Armor Class: 21 (–1 size, +12 natural), touch 9, flat-footed 21
Base Attack/Grapple: +12/+22
Attack: Bite +17 melee (2d6+6)
Full Attack: Bite +17 melee (2d6+6) and 2 claws +15 melee (1d8+3) and tail slap +15 melee (1d8+9)
Space/Reach: 10 ft./5 ft.
Special Attacks: Tremor, earth mastery
Special Qualities: Darkvision 60 ft., immunity to magic sleep effects and paralysis, low-light vision, tremorsense 60 ft.
Saves: Fort +12, Ref +10, Will +9
Abilities: Str 23, Dex 10, Con 19, Int 6, Wis 12, Cha 9
Skills: Bluff + 15, Climb +21, Diplomacy +1, Hide +15*, Intimidate +1, Listen +18, Search +13, Spot +18
Feats: Alertness, Flyby Attack, Lightning Reflexes, Multiattack, Power Attack
Environment: Temperate mountains
Organization: Solitary, pair, or cluster (3–6)
Challenge Rating: 11
Treasure: Standard
Alignment: Usually lawful neutral
Advancement: 13–19 HD (Large); 20–29 HD (Huge); 30–36 HD (Gargantuan)
Level Adjustment: +3

Earth drakes are ponderous creatures, slow of speech and action. When roused, though, they are fearsome to behold.

An earth drake's hide is brownish gray and craggy in texture, helping it to blend with its natural surroundings. Its claws are short and sturdy, helping it to burrow through the earth. Its green eyes glisten like emeralds.

Earth drakes lair underground, often in vaulted caverns that allow them to spread their wings when desired. They prefer gems as treasure, and their low Intelligence occasionally leaves them susceptible to crafty characters who attempt to trade relatively low-value gemstones for valuable items or information.

Earth drakes speak both Draconic and Terran, but slowly, with occasional pauses in speech that give evidence of their low intellect.

Combat

Unlike other drakes, earth drakes prefer to remain landbound, only using flight to escape from danger. When faced with multiple opponents, an earth drake begins combat with its tremor ability, and then attacks fallen targets. Because of its poor eyesight (compared to other drakes), it relies on tremorsense to keep track of opponents.

Earth Mastery (Ex): An earth drake gains a +1 bonus on attack and damage rolls if both it and its foe are touching the ground. If an opponent is airborne or waterborne, the drake takes a –4 penalty on attack and damage rolls. (These modifiers are not included in the statistics block.)

Tremor (Su): Once per day, an earth drake can cause a tremor at a point where it touches the ground. All creatures standing on the ground within 60 feet of the drake must make a DC 20 Reflex save or fall down. Airborne or waterborne creatures don't suffer any ill effects, and the tremor doesn't deal any structural damage.

Skills: Earth drakes have a +4 racial bonus on Hide checks. *They have an additional +4 racial bonus on Hide checks when in rocky environments (such as mountain terrain or underground).

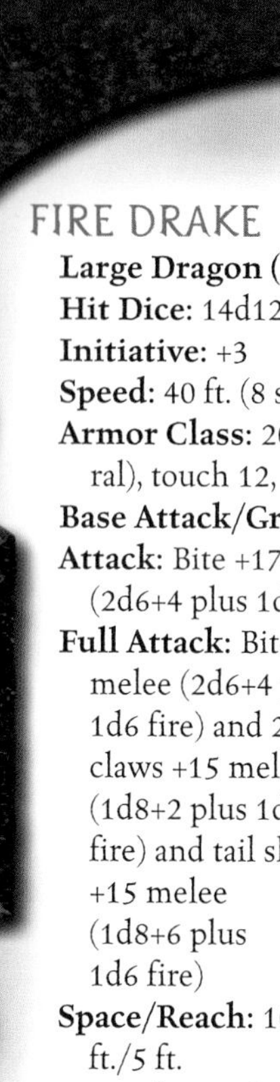

FIRE DRAKE

Large Dragon (Fire)
Hit Dice: 14d12+28 (122 hp)
Initiative: +3
Speed: 40 ft. (8 squares), fly 90 ft. (average)
Armor Class: 20 (–1 size, +3 Dex, +8 natural), touch 12, flat-footed 17
Base Attack/Grapple: +14/+22
Attack: Bite +17 melee (2d6+4 plus 1d6 fire)
Full Attack: Bite +17 melee (2d6+4 plus 1d6 fire) and 2 claws +15 melee (1d8+2 plus 1d6 fire) and tail slap +15 melee (1d8+6 plus 1d6 fire)
Space/Reach: 10 ft./5 ft.
Special Attacks: Heat
Special Qualities: Darkvision 60 ft., immunity to fire, magic sleep effects, and paralysis, low-light vision, vulnerability to cold
Saves: Fort +11, Ref +14, Will +10
Abilities: Str 19, Dex 16, Con 15, Int 8, Wis 12, Cha 11
Skills: Bluff +17, Climb +23, Diplomacy +2, Intimidate +2, Jump +21, Listen +20, Search +20, Spot +20
Feats: Alertness, Combat Reflexes, Flyby Attack, Lightning Reflexes, Multiattack
Environment: Warm hills
Organization: Solitary, pair, or brood (3–6)
Challenge Rating: 10
Treasure: Standard
Alignment: Usually neutral evil
Advancement: 15–19 HD (Large); 20–29 HD (Huge); 30–39 HD (Gargantuan); 40–42 HD (Colossal)
Level Adjustment: +3

The fire drake is a cunning predator, one of the most powerful of its kind. It is also among the most evil of the elemental drakes.

Fire drakes range in color from blood red to a dazzling vermilion and are often mistaken for young red dragons, aided by the fact that the two creatures share similar territories. They enjoy capitalizing on this mistaken identity, bargaining that most people would do anything to avoid angering a red dragon. The eyes of a fire drake are fiery yellow.

Most fire drakes avoid direct contact with red dragons. Fire giants occasionally tame these drakes as pets or guardians, though the drakes have no love for the giants.

Fire drakes speak both Draconic and Ignan in a screeching tone.

Fire drake
Air drake
Ice drake
Earth drake

Combat

A fire drake often feigns surprise when encountered, attempting to draw opponents into range of its attacks of opportunity. Thanks to its Combat Reflexes feat, it may make four such attacks each round.

Heat (Ex): A fire drake's red-hot body deals 1d6 points of extra fire damage whenever it hits in melee or, when grappling, during each round that it maintains a hold.

Creatures or weapons that strike a fire drake also take this damage (no save allowed).

Skills: Fire drakes have a +4 racial bonus on Search checks.

ICE DRAKE

Large Dragon (Air, Cold, Water)
Hit Dice: 8d12+32 (86 hp)
Initiative: +2
Speed: 30 ft. (6 squares), fly 110 ft. (average), swim 20 ft.
Armor Class: 19 (–1 size, +2 Dex, +8 natural), touch 11, flat-footed 17
Base Attack/Grapple: +8/+17
Attack: Bite +12 melee (2d6+5)

Full Attack: Bite +12 melee (2d6+5) and 2 claws +10 melee (1d8+2 plus 1d6 cold) and tail slap +10 melee (1d8+7)
Space/Reach: 10 ft./5 ft.
Special Attacks: Freezing touch
Special Qualities: Darkvision 60 ft., immunity to cold, magic sleep effects, and paralysis, low-light vision, vulnerability to fire
Saves: Fort +10, Ref +8, Will +9
Abilities: Str 21, Dex 14, Con 19, Int 10, Wis 16, Cha 13
Skills: Balance +15, Climb +15, Escape Artist +12, Hide +9*, Listen +13, Search +8, Spot +15, Swim +5
Feats: Alertness, Flyby Attack, Multiattack
Environment: Cold deserts
Organization: Solitary, pair, or cluster (3–6)
Challenge Rating: 7
Treasure: Standard
Alignment: Usually chaotic evil
Advancement: 9–19 HD (Large); 20–24 HD (Huge)
Level Adjustment: +3

Ice drakes are vicious scavengers that lair in cold or arctic lands.

The scales of an ice drake are ivory in color, with occasional tinges of ice-blue. Ice drakes have short, stocky limbs and a wide, flat tail that helps them climb on icy surfaces.

Ice drakes give large predators a wide berth, preferring to wait until after such creatures have finished feasting to move in on the remains. They aren't afraid to chase off smaller predators such as wolves.

An ice drake speaks Draconic and either Auran or Aquan (50% chance of either). The creatures speak haltingly, but woe to any who mistake this trait for lack of intelligence.

Combat

Unless it is desperate, an ice drake only takes on living opponents smaller than itself, and preferably from hiding. It focuses its attacks on an individual, using its freezing touch to weaken that opponent to the point where it can grapple it and fly away.

Freezing Touch (Su): Anyone hit by an ice drake's claw attack takes an extra 1d6 points of cold damage and must succeed on a DC 18 Reflex save or also take 1 point of Strength damage.

Skills: An ice drake has a +8 racial bonus on any Swim check to perform some special action or avoid a hazard. It can always choose to take 10 on a Swim check, even if distracted or endangered. It can use the run action while swimming, provided it swims in a straight line. Ice drakes have a +2 racial bonus on Balance checks and on Climb checks. *They have a +4 racial bonus on Hide checks in icy environments.

MAGMA DRAKE

Large Dragon (Earth, Fire)
Hit Dice: 16d12+64 (172 hp)
Initiative: +6
Speed: 30 ft. (6 squares), burrow 10 ft., fly 60 ft. (poor)
Armor Class: 23 (–1 size, +2 Dex, +12 natural), touch 11, flat-footed 21
Base Attack/Grapple: +16/+26
Attack: Bite +21 melee (2d6+6); or claw +19 melee (1d8+3)
Full Attack: Bite +21 melee (2d6+6) and 2 claws +19 melee (1d8+3) and tail slap +19 melee (1d8+9)
Space/Reach: 10 ft./5 ft.
Special Attacks: Improved grab, burn
Special Qualities: Darkvision 60 ft., immunity to fire, magic sleep effects, and paralysis, low-light vision, tremorsense 60 ft., vulnerability to cold
Saves: Fort +14, Ref +14, Will +11
Abilities: Str 23, Dex 14, Con 19, Int 8, Wis 12, Cha 11
Skills: Bluff +19, Climb +27, Diplomacy +2, Hide +19, Intimidate +2, Listen +22, Search +18, Spot +22
Feats: Alertness, Flyby Attack Improved Initiative, Lightning Reflexes, Multiattack, Power Attack
Environment: Warm mountains
Organization: Solitary, pair, or cluster (3–6)
Challenge Rating: 13
Treasure: Standard
Alignment: Usually lawful evil
Advancement: 17–19 HD (Large); 20–29 HD (Huge); 30–39 HD (Gargantuan); 40–51 HD (Colossal)
Level Adjustment: +3

The mightiest of the elemental drakes, the magma drake smolders with evil power.

The thick, scaled hide of a magma drake resembles cooling lava, with obsidian claws and gleaming crimson eyes. Though these creatures appear slow and clumsy, they move with surprising agility.

Magma drakes generally live in deep caves or in volcanic craters, particularly those with nearby lakes or rivers or molten rock. They often ally with efreet or salamanders.

A magma drake speaks Draconic and either Ignan or Terran (50% chance of either). The creatures' voices rumble with power, suggestive of their volcanic heritage.

Combat

A magma drake wastes no time toying with its prey, preferring to pin a grappled target and watch it burn to death. If it has room to fly, it uses Flyby Attack to grapple an opponent and bring it somewhere where it can dispatch it at its leisure.

Burn (Ex): Those grappled by a magma drake must succeed on a DC 22 Reflex save or catch fire. The fire burns for 1d4 rounds (see Catching on Fire, page 303 of the *Dungeon Master's Guide*). A burning creature can take a move action to put out the flame (but not while grappled).

Improved Grab (Ex): To use this ability, a magma drake must hit a creature of its size or smaller with a claw attack. It can then attempt to start a grapple as a free action without provoking an attack of opportunity.

Skills: Magma drakes have a +2 racial bonus on Climb checks and on Hide checks.

OOZE DRAKE

Large Dragon (Aquatic, Earth, Water)
Hit Dice: 12d12+60 (141 hp)
Initiative: +0
Speed: 20 ft. (4 squares), burrow 10 ft., fly 50 ft. (clumsy), swim 20 ft.
Armor Class: 21 (–1 size, +12 natural), touch 9, flat-footed 21
Base Attack/Grapple: +12/+22
Attack: Bite +23 melee (2d6+7 plus 1d6 acid); or claw +21 melee (1d8+3 plus 1d6 acid)
Full Attack: Bite +23 melee (2d6+7 plus 1d6 acid) and 2 claws +21 melee (1d8+3 plus 1d6 acid) and tail slap +21 melee (1d8+10 plus 1d6 acid)
Space/Reach: 10 ft./5 ft.
Special Attacks: Acid, improved grab
Special Qualities: Amphibious, darkvision 60 ft., immunity to magic sleep effects and paralysis, low-light vision
Saves: Fort +13, Ref +10, Will +10
Abilities: Str 25, Dex 10, Con 21, Int 8, Wis 14, Cha 11
Skills: Bluff +15, Diplomacy +2, Hide +13*, Intimidate +2, Listen +19, Move Silently +17, Search +14, Spot +19, Swim +7
Feats: Alertness, Flyby Attack Lightning Reflexes, Multiattack, Power Attack
Environment: Cold marshes
Organization: Solitary, pair, or clutch (3–6)
Challenge Rating: 12
Treasure: Standard
Alignment: Usually lawful evil
Advancement: 13–19 HD (Large); 20–29 HD (Huge); 30–36 HD (Gargantuan)
Level Adjustment: +3

The ooze drake is a disgusting and vile creature that relies on stealth and cunning to defeat its prey.

The slimy, gray-green scales of an ooze drake drip with caustic goo. The creature's claws and teeth are dirty gray, and its eyes are a pale, watery yellow.

Ooze drakes live in dank swamps and stinking marshes, or in dark caverns beneath the earth. They occasionally take bands of lizardfolk or troglodytes under their wing, though their patience with such lesser beings is limited.

An ooze drake speaks Draconic and either Aquan or Terran (50% chance of either). Its speech is slow and slurred, as if it is speaking with a mouth half full of water.

Combat

Thanks to their vision abilities, ooze drakes can detect potential prey from some distance away. They approach either by air or underwater, as appropriate, grab a target, and either take flight or pull it underwater with them. They disdain anything resembling a fair fight.

Acid (Ex): An ooze drake's body exudes acid at all times. This acid deals 1d6 points of extra acid damage whenever it hits in melee or, when grappling, during each round when maintains a hold. Only stone is unaffected by this acid.

Creatures or weapons striking an ooze drake also take this damage (no save allowed).

Improved Grab (Ex): To use this ability, an ooze drake must hit a creature of its size or smaller with a claw attack. It can then attempt to start a grapple as a free action without provoking an attack of opportunity.

Amphibious (Ex): Although ooze drakes are aquatic, they can survive indefinitely on land.

Skills: An ooze drake has a +8 racial bonus on any Swim check to perform some special action or avoid a hazard. It can always choose to take 10 on a Swim check, even if distracted or endangered. It can use the run action while swimming, provided it swims in a straight line. Ooze drakes have a +2 racial bonus on Hide and Move Silently checks. *The racial bonus on Hide checks improves to +4 when in marsh terrain.

SMOKE DRAKE

Large Dragon (Air, Fire)
Hit Dice: 12d12+36 (117 hp)
Initiative: +4
Speed: 40 ft. (8 squares), fly 120 ft. (good)
Armor Class: 19 (–1 size, +4 Dex, +6 natural), touch 13, flat-footed 15
Base Attack/Grapple: +12/20
Attack: Bite +15 melee (2d6+4)
Full Attack: Bite +15 melee (2d6+4) and 2 claws +13 melee (1d8+2) and tail slap +13 melee (1d8+6)
Space/Reach: 10 ft./5 ft.
Special Attacks: Breath weapon
Special Qualities: Darkvision 60 ft., immunity to fire, magic sleep effects, and paralysis, low-light vision, vulnerability to cold
Saves: Fort +11, Ref +14, Will +10
Abilities: Str 19, Dex 18, Con 17, Int 10, Wis 14, Cha 13
Skills: Escape Artist +19, Hide +15*, Listen +19, Move Silently +21, Search +15, Spot +19
Feats: Alertness, Flyby Attack, Lightning Reflexes, Multiattack, Track
Environment: Underground
Organization: Solitary, pair, or pack (3–6)
Challenge Rating: 9
Treasure: Standard
Alignment: Usually chaotic evil
Advancement: 13–19 HD (Large); 20–29 HD (Huge); 30–36 HD (Gargantuan)
Level Adjustment: +3

Smoke drakes are patient, cunning predators that follow prey for miles before striking with surprise.

A smoke drake's smooth scales are charcoal gray in color, with occasional highlights of dark red and a dorsal ridge of ebony. Its eyes glow like red-hot embers, particularly when the creature is angry or in battle.

The most territorial of the drakes, the smoke drake is known to hold a grudge against those who wrong it. The creatures are skilled trackers, able to follow prey for long distances if necessary.

A smoke drake speaks Draconic and either Auran or Ignan (50% chance of either). The creature rarely raises its voice above a hissing whisper, even when angered.

Combat

Once a smoke drake has tracked down its prey, it opens combat with its smoky breath, blinding its targets. It then attacks a lone or separated individual, focusing its strikes on that creature until it is incapacitated or the drake must flee. If faced with a foe it can't easily defeat, it retreats to safety, only to follow and strike again later.

Breath Weapon (Su): As a standard action once every 1d4 rounds, a smoke drake can breathe a hazy cloud of smoke in a 30-ft.-radius spread that provides concealment (20% miss chance) to all creatures within. Thanks to its blindsense, the drake ignores this miss chance. The haze lasts for 1 minute, but can be blown away by a moderate wind (11+ mph) in 4 rounds or a strong wind (21+ mph) in 1 round. This breath weapon is not usable underwater.

Once per day, a smoke drake can exhale an incendiary cloud rather than a hazy cloud. The cloud provides concealment as the hazy cloud does, but the white-hot embers suspended within the incendiary cloud deal 2d6 points of fire damage to everything within it each round (Reflex DC 19 half). The incendiary breath is otherwise identical to the haze breath.

Skills: Smoke drakes have a +2 racial bonus on Move Silently checks and on Search checks. *They have a +4 racial bonus on Hide checks in areas of shadow or darkness.

WATER DRAKE

Large Dragon (Aquatic, Water)
Hit Dice: 10d12+30 (97 hp)
Initiative: +1
Speed: 30 ft. (6 squares), fly 80 ft. (poor), swim 30 ft.
Armor Class: 20 (–1 size, +1 Dex, +10 natural), touch 10, flat-footed 19
Base Attack/Grapple: +10/+19
Attack: Bite +14 melee (2d6+5)
Full Attack: Bite +14 melee (2d6+5) and 2 claws +12 melee (1d8+2) and tail slap +12 melee (1d8+7)
Space/Reach: 10 ft./5 ft.
Special Attacks: Drench, water mastery
Special Qualities: Amphibious, darkvision 60 ft., immunity to magic sleep effects and paralysis, low-light vision
Saves: Fort +10, Ref +10, Will +8
Abilities: Str 21, Dex 12, Con 17, Int 8, Wis 14, Cha 11
Skills: Escape Artist +14, Hide +10*, Listen +17, Search +12, Sense Motive +15, Spot +19, Swim +5
Feats: Alertness, Flyby Attack, Lightning Reflexes, Multiattack
Environment: Temperate aquatic
Organization: Solitary, pair, or cete (3–6)
Challenge Rating: 8
Treasure: Standard
Alignment: Usually neutral
Advancement: 11–19 HD (Large); 20–29 HD (Huge); 30 HD (Gargantuan)
Level Adjustment: +3

Water drakes lay claim to areas of coastline or island chains, preying on sailors and any other creatures foolish enough to enter their territory.

A water drake's silver-blue scales appear more like those of a fish than a reptile, smooth and shimmering. Its sleek body cuts through the water with decent speed; however, it can't keep up with most other aquatic creatures, so it tends to remain at shallow depths so it can take to the air as needed.

Dragon turtles and water drakes often share similar territory, though a lone drake is no match for such an opponent. Only groups of water drakes are brave enough to face a foe of such power. Water drakes hate bronze dragons, but fear them even more.

Water drakes speak Draconic and Aquan. Their speech is burbling and pleasant to the ear.

Combat

Water drakes prefer to fight their battles beneath the waves, to take advantage of their combat prowess there. They take wing only to snatch victims (such as off the deck of a ship), using Flyby Attack to grab a target and return to the water in a single swoop.

Drench (Ex): A water drake's touch puts out torches, campfires, exposed lanterns, and other open flames of nonmagical origin if these are Large or smaller. The drake can dispel magical fire it touches as by a *dispel magic* spell cast by a sorcerer whose level equals the drake's HD.

Water Mastery (Ex): A water drake gains a +1 bonus on attack and damage rolls if both it and its opponent are touching water. If the opponent or the drake is landbound, the drake takes a –4 penalty on attack and damage rolls. (These modifiers are not included in the statistics block.)

Amphibious (Ex): Although water drakes are aquatic, they can survive indefinitely on land.

Skills: A water drake has a +8 racial bonus on any Swim check to perform some special action or avoid a hazard. It can always choose to take 10 on a Swim check, even if distracted or endangered. It can use the run action while swimming, provided it swims in a straight line. Water drakes have a +4 racial bonus on Spot checks. *They have a +4 racial bonus on Hide checks when submerged.

FAERIE DRAGON

Small Dragon
Hit Dice: 8d12+6 (58 hp)
Initiative: +8
Speed: 30 ft. (6 squares), fly 100 ft. (perfect), swim 30 ft.
Armor Class: 19 (+1 size, +4 Dex, +4 natural), touch 15, flat-footed 15
Base Attack/Grapple: +8/+5
Attack: Bite +13 melee (1d6+1)
Full Attack: Bite +13 melee (1d6+1) and 2 claws +8 melee (1d4)
Space/Reach: 5 ft./5 ft.
Special Attacks: Breath weapon, spell-like abilities
Special Qualities: Darkvision 60 ft., immunity to magic sleep effects and paralysis, low-light vision, scent, spell resistance 18, water breathing
Saves: Fort +7, Ref +10, Will +9
Abilities: Str 13, Dex 18, Con 12, Int 15, Wis 17, Cha 16
Skills: Bluff +14, Diplomacy +7, Disguise +3 (+5 acting), Hide +19, Intimidate +5, Knowledge (nature) +13, Listen +14, Move Silently +15, Sense Motive + 14, Sleight of Hand +17, Spot +14, Survival +3 (+5 in aboveground natural environments), Swim +1
Feats: Flyby Attack, Improved Initiative, Weapon Finesse
Environment: Temperate forests
Organization: Solitary or pair
Challenge Rating: 6
Treasure: Standard
Alignment: Always chaotic good
Advancement: 9 HD (Small); 10–13 HD (Medium); 14–19 HD (Large); 20–24 HD (Huge)
Level Adjustment: +2

The faerie dragon is a mischievous creature that often allies with fey creatures such as pixies.

A faerie dragon's scales are iridescent, reflecting all the colors of the rainbow. Its butterflylike wings are a beautiful platinum. It bears a sharp-toothed grin at all times except when attacked in anger. It has a long, prehensile tail that constantly flicks and twitches, particularly when the creature is happy or excited.

Faerie dragon

Illus. by G. Kubic

Faerie dragons generally keep their distance from intruders into their forest homes, preferring to lead such creatures away rather than confront them directly. It is not uncommon to encounter them near the tree of a dryad, the lake of a nymph, or the lair of a tribe of sprites, since such creatures get along well with one another.

Faerie dragons speak Draconic and Sylvan. They can converse with any animal. Some also learn Common, Elven, or Gnome.

COMBAT

A faerie dragon prefers to deal with enemies from afar, using its spell-like abilities to confuse and bewilder opponents. If this tactic doesn't work, it summons one or more allies or animates nearby objects to fight for it. It uses *charm monster, entangle,* and *glitterdust* to neutralize dangerous foes. If seriously pressed, a faerie dragon reluctantly enters melee, and then only after using its breath weapon to daze its opponents.

Breath Weapon (Su): A faerie dragon has one type of breath weapon, a 20-foot cone of euphoria gas. Any creature within the area of the gas must succeed on a DC 15 Will save or become dazed for 1d6 rounds.

Spell-Like Abilities: At will—*dancing lights, detect magic, ghost sound* (DC 13); 3/day—*charm monster* (DC 17), *entangle* (DC 14), *glitterdust* (DC 15), *invisibility* (DC 15), *major image* (DC 16), *obscuring mist*; 1/day—*animate objects, mind fog* (DC 18), *project image* (DC 20), *summon nature's ally* IV; 1/month—*commune with nature.* Caster level 12th.

Skills: A faerie dragon has a +8 racial bonus on any Swim check to perform some special action or avoid a hazard. It can always choose to take 10 on a Swim check, even if distracted or endangered. It can use the run action while swimming, provided it swims in a straight line.

FANG DRAGON

Dragon

Environment: Temperate mountains

Organization: Wyrmling, very young, young, juvenile, or young adult: solitary or clutch (2–5); adult, mature adult, old, very old, ancient, wyrm, or great wyrm: solitary, pair, or family (1–2 and 2–5 offspring)

Challenge Rating: Wyrmling 2; very young 3; young 4; juvenile 6; young adult 8; adult 10; mature adult 12; old 15; very old 17; ancient 18; wyrm 19; great wyrm 21

Treasure: Double standard

Alignment: Always chaotic neutral

Advancement: Wyrmling 4–5 HD; very young 7–8 HD; young 10–11 HD; juvenile 13–14 HD; young adult 16–17 HD; adult 19–20 HD; mature adult 22–23 HD; old 25–26 HD; very old 28–29 HD; ancient 31–32 HD; wyrm 34–35 HD; great wyrm 37+ HD

Level Adjustment: Wyrmling +3; very young +4; young +5; juvenile +5; others —

Fang dragon

Fang dragons are greedy, rapacious, and cunning creatures.

Their bodies are armored with bony plates that rise into projecting spurs at limb joints and end in long, forked tails tipped with a pair of scythelike bone blades. They fly poorly, but can rise with a single clap of their wings to lunge forward. Their body plates are a mottled gray and brown, their wings are small but muscled, and their eyes tend to be glittering red or orange. Fang dragons' heads are adorned with many small horns or spikes.

Fang dragons prefer to seek food far from their lairs, typically walling up their residences with huge boulders to keep out intruders in their absence. They speak snippets of many languages and bargain to avoid hopeless or hard battles. They are prone to random violence and outbursts of rage.

Fang dragons eat all manner of fresh meat. They especially enjoy the flesh of intelligent mammals.

Combat

Fang dragons are masters of physical combat, and every part of their body is lethal. They have a tendency to play with their food in a cruel way.

Young adult and older fang dragons' natural weapons are treated as magic weapons for the purpose of overcoming damage reduction.

Ability Drain (Su): A fang dragon does not have a breath weapon, but its bite drains Constitution if the victim fails a Fortitude save. The number of Constitution points drained and the saving throw DC are given on the accompanying table.

Increased Damage (Ex): Because of their sharp claws, teeth, and scales, fang dragons deal damage as if they were

Fang Dragons by Age

Age	Size	Hit Dice (hp)	Str	Dex	Con	Int	Wis	Cha	Base Attack/ Grapple	Attack	Fort Save	Ref Save	Will Save	Breath Weapon (DC)	Frightful Presence DC
Wyrmling	T	3d12+3 (22)	11	10	13	8	13	8	+3/–5	5	4	3	4	1d2 (DC 10)	—
Very young	S	6d12+6 (45)	13	10	13	8	13	8	+6/+3	8	6	5	6	1d3 (DC 12)	—
Young	M	9d12+18 (76)	15	10	15	10	15	10	+9/+11	11	8	6	8	1d4 (DC 14)	—
Juvenile	L	12d12+36 (114)	19	10	17	10	15	10	+12/+20	15	11	8	10	1d4 (DC 16)	—
Young adult	L	15d12+45 (142)	21	10	17	12	17	12	+15/+24	19	12	9	12	1d6 (DC 18)	18
Adult	L	18d12+72 (189)	23	10	19	12	17	12	+18/+28	23	15	11	14	1d6 (DC 20)	20
Mature adult	H	21d12+84 (220)	27	10	19	14	19	14	+21/+37	27	16	12	16	1d8 (DC 22)	22
Old	H	24d12+120 (276)	29	10	21	14	19	14	+24/+41	31	19	14	18	1d8 (DC 24)	24
Very old	G	27d12+135 (310)	31	10	21	16	21	16	+27/+49	33	20	15	20	2d4 (DC 26)	26
Ancient	G	30d12+180 (375)	33	10	23	16	21	16	+30/+53	37	23	17	22	2d4 (DC 28)	28
Wyrm	G	33d12+198 (412)	35	10	23	18	23	18	+33/+57	41	24	18	24	2d6 (DC 30)	30
Great wyrm	G	36d12+252 (486)	37	10	25	20	23	20	+36/+61	45	27	20	26	2d6 (DC 33)	33

Fang Dragon Abilities by Age

Age	Speed	Initiative	AC	Special Abilities	Caster Level	SR
Wyrmling	60 ft., fly 90 ft. (average)	+0	14 (+2 size, +2 natural)	Increased damage, trip, sound imitation, *detect magic, read magic*	—	—
Very young	60 ft., fly 120 ft. (poor)	+0	16 (+1 size, +5 natural)	—	—	—
Young	60 ft., fly 120 ft. (poor)	+0	18 (+8 natural)	*Shield*	—	—
Juvenile	60 ft., fly 120 ft. (poor)	+0	20 (–1 size, +11 natural)	*Dispel magic*	—	16
Young adult	60 ft., fly 120 ft. (poor)	+0	23 (–1 size, +14 natural)	Damage reduction 5/magic	1st	18
Adult	60 ft., fly 120 ft. (poor)	+0	26 (–1 size, +17 natural	*Spell turning*	3rd	20
Mature adult	60 ft., fly 120 ft. (poor)	+0	28 (–2 size, +20 natural)	Damage reduction 10/magic	5th	22
Old	60 ft., fly 120 ft. (poor)	+0	31 (–2 size, +23 natural)	*Telekinesis*	7th	25
Very old	60 ft., fly 150 ft. (clumsy)	+0	32 (–4 size, +26 natural)	Damage reduction 15/magic	9th	27
Ancient	60 ft., fly 150 ft. (clumsy)	+0	35 (–4 size, +29 natural)	Fast healing 2	11th	28
Wyrm	60 ft., fly 150 ft. (clumsy)	+0	38 (–4 size, +32 natural)	Damage reduction 20/magic	13th	29
Great wyrm	60 ft., fly 150 ft. (clumsy)	+0	41 (–4 size, +35 natural)	*Globe of invulnerability*	15th	31

* Can also cast cleric spells and those from the Chaos, Death, Magic, and Protection domains as arcane spells.

one size category larger. This ability does not enable the dragon to use attack forms normally not allowed to a dragon of its size. Thus, a very young (Small) fang dragon deals 1d8 points of damage on a bite attack and 1d6 points of damage on a claw attack (as if it were Medium), but cannot make wing attacks.

Trip (Ex): A fang dragon that hits with a claw or tail attack can attempt to trip the opponent as a free action (see page 158 of the *Player's Handbook*). If the attempt fails, the opponent cannot react to trip the dragon.

Sound Imitation (Ex): A fang dragon can mimic any voice or sound it has heard, anytime it likes. Listeners must succeed on a Will save (DC equal to that of the dragon's frightful presence) to detect the ruse.

Spell-Like Abilities: At will—*detect magic, read magic;* 2/day—*shield, telekinesis;* 1/day—*dispel magic, spell turning, globe of invulnerability.*

FELLDRAKE, SPIKED

Large Dragon
Hit Dice: 6d12+12 (51 hp)
Initiative: +2
Speed: 40 ft. (8 squares)
Armor Class: 19 (–1 size, +2 Dex, +8 natural), touch 11, flat-footed 17
Base Attack/Grapple: +6/+15
Attack: Bite +10 melee (2d6+5)
Full Attack: Bite +10 melee (2d6+5) and 2 claws +5 melee (1d8+2); or spikes +7 ranged (1d8+5)
Space/Reach: 10 ft./5 ft.
Special Qualities: Darkvision 60 ft., immunity to magic sleep effects and paralysis, low-light vision, scent
Saves: Fort +7, Ref +7, Will +8
Abilities: Str 20, Dex 14, Con 15, Int 10, Wis 12, Cha 8
Skills: Climb +14, Intimidate +8, Listen +12, Search +9, Spot +12, Survival +10
Feats: Alertness, Iron Will, Point Blank Shot
Environment: Temperate plains
Organization: Solitary or clutch (2–4)
Challenge Rating: 4
Treasure: None
Alignment: Always neutral good
Advancement: 7–9 HD (Large); 10–18 HD (Huge)
Level Adjustment: +2

The felldrakes trace their origin to Bahamut the Platinum Dragon. After helping a group of powerful elf wizards turn back a demonic invasion, Bahamut created the felldrakes to guard the elves against future incursions. All felldrakes have the blood of Bahamut in their veins and are fierce, loyal, and good at heart.

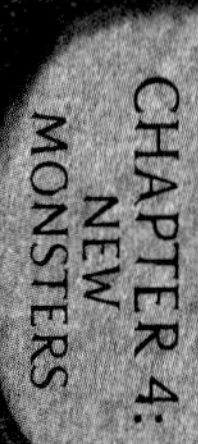

Spiked felldrake

Of the many kinds of felldrakes, few are as powerful as the spiked felldrake. Its size and strength place it in the front line of important battles, and some mighty knights or paladins employ the spiked felldrake as a steed.

Felldrakes speak Draconic and Sylvan.

Combat

A spiked felldrake can stand up to terrible punishment while dealing out plenty of its own with swordlike claws. The spikes on its tail are not just for show—it can project them in a hail of deadly fire at approaching enemies. With its scent and vision abilities, a spiked felldrake can root out even hidden enemies reliably.

Spiked Felldrakes as Special Mounts

At the DM's option, a paladin of 11th level or higher can call a spiked felldrake as her special mount. For the purposes of the mount's bonus Hit Dice, natural armor, Strength adjustment, Intelligence score, and special powers, treat the paladin as if she were six levels lower than actual.

GHOSTLY DRAGON

A ghost template is found in the *Monster Manual*. The ghostly dragon template presented here provides an alternative method of creating ghostly dragons to have them retain more of their innate draconic power and deadliness.

Ghostly dragons are most often created when a powerful dragon is slain and its hoard looted. In such a case, the ghostly dragon can only be laid to rest by returning its lost treasure (or the equivalent value) to the creature's lair. (You can estimate the ghostly dragon's hoard by using the average treasure value for an encounter with the dragon, were it still alive.) Should this occur, the ghostly dragon settles upon the new hoard and disappears into nothingness, taking the hoard with it to the afterlife.

SAMPLE GHOSTLY DRAGON

This example uses an adult green dragon as the base dragon.

Ghostly Adult Green Dragon
Huge Undead (Incorporeal)
Hit Dice: 20d12+40 (170 hp)
Initiative: +4
Speed: Fly 150 ft. (perfect)
Armor Class: 13 (–2 size, +5 deflection), touch 13, flat-footed 13; or 27 (–2 size, +19 natural), touch 8, flat-footed 27
Base Attack/Grapple: +20/+36
Attack: Incorporeal touch +20 melee (1d4 corruption plus 1d4 Str plus 1d4 Con plus energy drain); or bite +26 melee (2d8+8)
Full Attack: Incorporeal touch +20 melee (1d4 corruption plus 1d4 Str plus 1d4 Con plus energy drain); or bite +26 melee (2d8+8) and 2 claws +21 melee (2d6+4) and 2 wings +21 melee (1d8+4) and tail slap +21 melee (2d6+12)
Space/Reach: 15 ft./10 ft.
Special Attacks: Breath weapon, energy drain, frightful presence, manifestation, snatch, spellcasting, spell-like abilities, withering
Special Qualities: Blindsense 60 ft., damage reduction 5/magic, darkvision 120 ft., immunity to acid, magic sleep effects, and paralysis, keen senses, low-light vision, rejuvenation, spell resistance 21, turn resistance +4, undead traits
Saves: Fort +12, Ref +12, Will +15
Abilities: Str 27, Dex 10, Con —, Int 16, Wis 17, Cha 20
Skills: Bluff +22, Concentration +15, Diplomacy +15, Hide +8, Intimidate +27, Knowledge (arcana) +18, Knowledge (nature) +18, Listen +31, Move Silently +20, Search +31, Sense Motive +11, Spellcraft +25, Spot +31, Swim +16
Feats: Clinging Breath, Flyby Attack, Hover, Improved Initiative, Power Attack, Snatch, Wingover
Environment: Temperate forests
Organization: Solitary
Challenge Rating: 14
Treasure: None
Alignment: Lawful evil
Advancement: 21–22 HD (Huge)
Level Adjustment: —

This ghostly green dragon still haunts its dark underground or forest lair, longing for the return of the hoard it guarded in life. Tormented by its inability to seek out additional treasure, it waits . . . and plots.

Combat

Should intruders enter its lair, the ghostly green dragon learns as much as it can about them before commencing the attack. When it finally manifests, it uses frightful presence to terrify its opponents, then unleashes its ability-draining breath weapon before moving in to finish off the survivors.

This ghostly green dragon's natural weapons are treated as magic weapons for the purpose of overcoming damage reduction.

Breath Weapon (Su): 50-ft. cone, 12d6 acid, Reflex DC 25 half; or 50-ft. cone, 6 points of Strength, Dexterity, and Constitution drain, Fortitude DC 25 negates.

Frightful Presence (Ex): 60-ft. radius, HD 19 or fewer, Will DC 25 negates.

Snatch (Ex): Against Small or smaller creatures, bite for 2d8+8/round or claw for 2d6+4/round.

Spell-Like Abilities: 3/day—*suggestion* (DC 18). Caster level 6th.

Spells: As 5th-level sorcerer.

Keen Senses (Ex): This ghostly dragon sees four times as well as a human in low-light conditions and twice as well in normal light. It also has darkvision out to 120 feet.

Water Breathing (Ex): This ghostly dragon can breathe underwater indefinitely and can freely use its breath weapon, spells, and other abilities while submerged.

Sorcerer Spells Known (6/8/5; save DC 15 + spell level): 0—*dancing lights, detect magic, ghost sound, mending, open/close, read magic*; 1st—*alarm, shield, true strike, unseen servant*; 2nd—*darkness, detect thoughts.*

CREATING A GHOSTLY DRAGON

"Ghostly" is an acquired template that can be added to any dragon. The creature (referred to hereafter as the base dragon) must have a Charisma score of at least 8.

A ghostly dragon uses all the base dragon's statistics and special abilities except as noted here.

Size and Type: The creature's type changes to undead. It gains the incorporeal subtype. Size is unchanged.

Hit Dice: The base dragon's Hit Dice remain the same, but it loses any Constitution bonus to its hit points (see Abilities, below). However, a ghostly dragon gains bonus hit points equal to twice its HD.

Speed: A ghostly dragon has a fly speed of 30 feet, unless the base dragon has a higher fly speed. Regardless of its fly speed, the ghostly dragon has perfect maneuverability.

Armor Class: A ghostly dragon's natural armor bonus is the same as the base dragon but applies only to ethereal encounters. When a ghostly dragon manifests (see below), its natural armor bonus is +0, but it gains a deflection bonus equal to its Charisma modifier or +1, whichever is higher.

Attacks: A ghostly dragon retains all the attacks of the base dragon, although those relying on physical contact do not affect nonethereal creatures. It also gains an incorporeal touch attack, which it can use with any body part normally capable of attacking (which may include the bite, a claw, a wing, or a tail). Apply a ghostly dragon's Dexterity modifier, not its Strength modifier, to its incorporeal touch attack roll.

Damage: Against ethereal creatures, a ghostly dragon uses the base dragon's damage ratings. Against nonethereal creatures, a ghostly dragon usually cannot deal physical damage but can use its special attacks, if any, when it manifests (see below).

Special Attacks: A ghostly dragon retains all the special attacks of the base creature, although those relying on physical contact do not affect nonethereal creatures. The ghost gains the manifestation ability plus other special attacks described below. Saves against a ghostly dragon's special attacks (including those of the base dragon) have a DC of 10 + 1/2 ghostly dragon's HD + ghostly dragon's Cha modifier unless otherwise noted.

Breath Weapon (Su): In addition to any breath weapons it had in life, a ghostly dragon gains a breath weapon that creates a cone-shaped cloud of gray mist. Any creature caught within is affected by a catastrophic ability drain, permanently losing a number of points of Strength, Dexterity, and Constitution equal to the base dragon's age category (Fortitude negates). A creature that successfully saves against this effect cannot be affected by this breath weapon from the same ghostly dragon for 24 hours (though it can be affected by the ghostly dragon's other breath weapons as normal). This breath weapon can be used once every 1d4 rounds and a maximum of three times per day.

Energy Drain (Su): With a successful touch attack, a ghostly dragon bestows two negative levels on the target. A ghostly dragon does not bestow negative levels with any of its natural attacks (claws, bite, wing, tail, and so on).

Ghostly green dragon

Manifestation (Su): A ghostly dragon dwells on the Ethereal Plane and, as an ethereal creature, it cannot affect or be affected by anything in the material world. When a ghostly dragon manifests, it partly enters the Material Plane and becomes visible but incorporeal on the Material Plane. A manifested ghostly dragon can be harmed only by other incorporeal creatures, magic weapons, or spells, with a 50% chance to ignore any damage from a corporeal

source. A manifested ghostly dragon can pass through solid objects at will, and its own attacks pass through armor. A manifested ghostly dragon always moves silently.

A manifested ghostly dragon can strike with its touch attack or with a ghost touch weapon. A manifested ghostly dragon remains partially on the Ethereal Plane, where is it not incorporeal. The creature can be attacked by opponents on either the Material Plane or the Ethereal Plane. The ghostly dragon's incorporeality helps protect it from foes on the Material Plane, but not from foes on the Ethereal Plane.

When a spellcasting ghostly dragon is not manifested and is on the Ethereal Plane, its spells cannot affect targets on the Material Plane, but they work normally against ethereal targets. When a spellcasting ghostly dragon manifests, its spells continue to affect ethereal targets and can affect targets on the Material Plane normally unless the spells rely on touch. A manifested ghostly dragon's touch spells don't work on nonethereal targets.

A ghostly dragon has two home planes, the Material Plane and the Ethereal Plane. It is not considered extraplanar when on either of these planes.

Withering (Su): A ghostly dragon's touch acts as a *rod of withering*, dealing 1d4 points of Strength damage and 1d4 points of Constitution damage with a successful touch attack (Fortitude negates). If a ghostly dragon scores a critical hit, the damage is ability drain instead.

Special Qualities: A ghostly dragon has all the special qualities of the base dragon (except for any subtypes possessed). If the base dragon had any immunities based on its subtype (such as immunity to fire for the fire subtype), it keeps those immunities despite losing the subtype. It also gains the incorporeal subtype (see page 310 of the *Monster Manual*) and the special qualities described below.

Rejuvenation (Su): In most cases, it's difficult to destroy a ghostly dragon through simple combat: The "destroyed" spirit will often restore itself in 2d4 days. Even the most powerful spells are usually only temporary solutions. A ghostly dragon that would otherwise be destroyed returns to its old haunts with a successful level check (1d20 + ghost's HD) against DC 16. As a rule, the only way to get rid of a ghostly dragon for sure is to determine the reason for its existence and set right whatever prevents it from resting in peace. The exact means varies with each spirit and may require a good deal of research.

Turn Resistance (Ex): A ghostly dragon has +4 turn resistance (see page 317 of the *Monster Manual*).

Undead Traits: A ghostly dragon is immune to mind-affecting effects, poison, magic sleep effects, paralysis, stunning, disease, death effects, and any effect that requires a Fortitude save unless it also works on objects or is harmless. It is not subject to critical hits, nonlethal damage, ability damage to its physical ability scores, ability drain, energy drain, fatigue, exhaustion, or death from massive damage. It cannot be raised, and resurrection works only if it is willing. It has darkvision out to 60 feet (unless the base creature had a greater range).

Saves: As undead, ghostly dragons are immune to anything that requires a Fortitude save unless it affects objects.

Abilities: As the base dragon, except that the ghostly dragon has no Constitution score, and its Charisma score increases by 4.

Skills: Ghostly dragons have a +8 racial bonus on Hide, Listen, Search, and Spot checks.

Organization: Solitary.

Challenge Rating: Same as the base dragon +2.

Treasure: None.

Alignment: Usually same as the base dragon.

Advancement: Up to +2 HD.

Level Adjustment: Same as the base dragon +5.

GOLEM

Golems are magically created automatons of great power. Constructing one involves the use of mighty magic and elemental forces.

Normally, the animating force for a golem is a spirit from the Elemental Plane of Earth. However, the three golems presented here—the dragonbone golem, the drakestone golem, and the ironwyrm golem—are instead imbued with the life force of a mighty dragon. The process of creation binds the unwilling spirit to the artificial body and subjects it to the will of the golem's creator.

In all three cases, these golems are constructed in forms traditionally associated with dragons—quadrupedal creatures with long necks and tails, claws, and wings. Though these constructs are built with wings, they are incapable of flight (but the golems can use their wings for attacks).

Golems have no language of their own, but they can understand simple instructions from their creators.

COMBAT

Golems are tenacious in combat and prodigiously strong as well. Despite their former existence as highly intelligent dragons, these golems are mindless and thus can do nothing in the absence of orders from their creators. They always follow instructions explicitly and are incapable of any strategy or tactics. They are emotionless in combat and cannot be provoked.

If a golem's creator is within 60 feet of it and both visible and audible to it, he or she can command the creature directly. An uncommanded golem usually follows its last instruction to the best of its ability, though it returns any attacks made against it. The creator can give the golem a simple program (such as "Remain in this area and attack all creatures or creatures of a specific kind that enter," or "Ring a gong and attack," or the like) to govern its actions in his or her absence.

Since golems do not need to breathe and are immune to most forms of energy, they can press an attack against an opponent almost anywhere, from the bottom of the sea to the frigid top of the tallest mountain.

Construct Traits: A golem has immunity to poison, magic sleep effects, paralysis, stunning, disease, death effects, necromancy effects, mind-affecting effects (charms, compulsions, phantasms, patterns, and morale effects), and any effect that requires a Fortitude save unless it also works on objects or is harmless. It is not subject to critical hits, nonlethal damage, ability damage, ability drain, fatigue, exhaustion, or energy drain. It cannot heal damage, but it can be repaired. It has darkvision out to 60 feet and low-light vision.

Immunity to Magic (Ex): Golems have immunity to magical and supernatural effects, except when otherwise noted.

DRAGONBONE GOLEM

Large Construct
Hit Dice: 20d10 (110 hp)
Initiative: +0
Speed: 40 ft. (8 squares)
Armor Class: 17 (–1 size, +8 natural), touch 9, flat-footed 17
Base Attack/Grapple: +15/+23
Attack: Bite +18 melee (1d10+4)
Full Attack: Bite +18 melee (1d10+4) and 2 claws +13 melee (1d8+2) and 2 wings +13 melee (1d6+2) and tail slap +13 melee (1d8+6)
Space/Reach: 10 ft./5 ft.
Special Attacks: Fear aura
Special Qualities: Construct traits, damage reduction 5/magic and adamantine, immunity to magic
Saves: Fort +7, Ref +7, Will +7
Abilities: Str 19, Dex 10, Con —, Int —, Wis 11, Cha 10
Environment: Any
Organization: Solitary
Challenge Rating: 12
Treasure: None
Alignment: Always neutral
Advancement: 21–30 HD (Large); 31–60 HD (Huge)
Level Adjustment: —

A dragonbone golem is crafted from the skeletons of one or more dragons, wired together into a gruesome whole. It typically measures about 10 feet in length and stands 5 feet tall at the shoulder. It is easily mistaken for a skeletal dragon or a dracolich (see those entries in this chapter)—and, in fact, is often built by necromancers—but it is a construct, not an undead creature.

Combat

A dragonbone golem wades into combat without hesitation, weakening opponents' resolve with its fear aura.

Fear Aura (Su): A dragonbone golem radiates an aura of fear in a 60-foot-radius burst. Any creature with fewer HD than the dragonbone golem is shaken (Will DC 20 negates). The effect lasts for as long as the creature remains within range and for 2d6 rounds afterward. A creature that succeeds on the Will save to resist is immune to that dragonbone golem's fear aura for 24 hours.

Magic Immunity (Ex): A dragonbone golem has immunity to all spells, spell-like abilities, and supernatural effects and abilities.

Construction

A dragonbone golem's body must be crafted from the skeletons of one or more dragons, strung together with adamantine wire worth 5,000 gp. Creating the body requires a DC 20 Heal check.

CL 13th; Craft Construct (see page 303 of the *Monster Manual*), *animate dead, cause fear, geas/quest*, caster must be at least 13th level; Price 115,000 gp; Cost 60,000 gp + 4,400 XP.

DRAKESTONE GOLEM

Large Construct
Hit Dice: 35d10 (192 hp)
Initiative: –1
Speed: 30 ft. (6 squares)
Armor Class: 36 (–1 size, –1 Dex, +28 natural), touch 8, flat-footed 36
Base Attack/Grapple: +26/+41
Attack: Bite +36 melee (2d8+11)
Full Attack: Bite +36 melee (2d8+11) and 2 claws +31 melee (2d6+5) and 2 wings +31 melee (1d10+5) and tail slap +31 melee (2d6+16)
Space/Reach: 10 ft./5 ft.
Special Attacks: Petrifying breath
Special Qualities: Construct traits, damage reduction 10/magic and adamantine, immunity to magic
Saves: Fort +12, Ref +11, Will +13
Abilities: Str 33, Dex 8, Con —, Int —, Wis 13, Cha 15
Environment: Any
Organization: Solitary
Challenge Rating: 15
Treasure: None
Alignment: Always neutral
Advancement: 36–50 HD (Large); 51–70 HD (Huge)
Level Adjustment: —

A drakestone golem appears at first glance to be a beautifully crafted statue of a dragon, 12 feet long and 6 feet tall at the shoulder. Only when it animates, its stone scales rippling like muscled flesh and its eyes gleaming with amber light, do its enemies realize their danger.

Combat

A drakestone golem opens any combat with its petrifying breath, but otherwise relies on its devastating physical attacks to reduce foes to a pulp.

Petrifying Breath (Su): Once every 1d4 rounds, a drakestone golem can exhale a 30-foot cone of petrifying gas (Fortitude DC 27 negates).

Immunity to Magic (Ex): A drakestone golem is immune to all spells, spell-like abilities, and supernatural effects, except as follows. A *transmute rock to mud* spell slows it (as the *slow* spell) for 2d6 rounds, with no saving throw, while *transmute mud to rock* heals all its lost hit points.

Construction

A drakestone golem's body is intricately chiseled from a single block of high-quality stone, usually granite, weighing at least 3,000 pounds and costing 5,000 gp. It must also be polished with rare oils worth 10,000 gp. Assembling the body requires a DC 25 Craft (sculpting or masonry) check.

Illus. by M. Nelson

CL 16th; Craft Construct (see page 303 of the *Monster Manual*), *animate objects, antimagic field, flesh to stone, geas/quest*, caster must be at least 16th level; Price 175,000 gp; Cost 95,000 gp + 6,400 XP.

IRONWYRM GOLEM

Large Construct
Hit Dice: 40d10 (220 hp)
Initiative: –1
Speed: 30 ft. (6 squares)
Armor Class: 40 (–1 size, –1 Dex, +32 natural), touch 8, flat-footed 40
Base Attack/Grapple: +30/+49
Attack: Bite +44 melee (2d10+15)
Full Attack: Bite +44 melee (2d10+15) and 2 claws +39 melee (2d8+7) and 2 wings +39 melee (2d6+7) and tail slap +39 melee (2d8+22)
Space/Reach: 10 ft./5 ft.
Special Attacks: Breath weapon
Special Qualities: Construct traits, damage reduction 15/magic and adamantine, immunity to magic, immunity to rust
Saves: Fort +13, Ref +12, Will +14
Abilities: Str 41, Dex 8, Con —, Int —, Wis 13, Cha 19
Environment: Any
Organization: Solitary
Challenge Rating: 17
Treasure: None
Alignment: Always neutral
Advancement: 41–60 HD (Large); 61–80 HD (Huge)
Level Adjustment: —

An ironwyrm golem is an animated, self-contained furnace built into the shape of a dragon. It measures up to 15 feet in length and typically stands 7 to 8 feet high at the shoulder. Smoke trails from its nostrils except when the creature is at rest, and when animate, it exudes a palpable heat.

Combat

The ironwyrm golem softens up foes with its fiery breath and then uses its formidable strength to destroy its foes in melee. It can even use this breath weapon on itself, in order to restore hit points or negate *slow* effects.

Breath Weapon (Su): 60-ft. cone, every 1d4 rounds, 20d10 fire, Reflex DC 30 half. The breath weapon type remains the same regardless of the dragon spirit contained within.

Immunity to Magic (Ex): An ironwyrm golem is immune to all spells, spell-like abilities, and supernatural effects, except as follows. A cold effect slows it (as the *slow* spell) for 3 rounds, with no saving throw. A fire effect breaks any slow effect on the golem and cures 1 point of damage for each 3 points of damage it would otherwise deal. For example, an ironwyrm golem hit by a *delayed blast fireball* cast by a 15th-level wizard that would normally deal 52 points of damage instead gains back 17 hit points. The golem gets no saving throw against fire effects.

Immunity to Rust (Ex): An ironwyrm golem is immune to rust attacks, whether magical or not.

Construction

An ironwyrm golem is sculpted from 5,000 pounds of pure iron, smelted with other rare components and elixirs costing at least 25,000 gp. Assembling the body requires a DC 30 Craft (armorsmithing or weaponsmithing) check.

CL 18th; Craft Construct (see page 303 of the *Monster Manual*), *animate objects, antimagic field, geas/quest, incendiary cloud, limited wish,* caster must be at least 18th level; Price 225,000 gp; Cost 125,000 gp + 8,000 XP.

An elf half-li lung

Cause Rain (Su): A half-chiang lung can breathe storm clouds three times per day, causing rain. The rain lasts for 2d4 hours and extends in a 2-mile radius centered on the half-dragon.

Roar (Ex): A half-li lung can roar three times per day, creating a sound resembling metal scraping against stone. All creatures within 60 feet are automatically deafened for 1 round (no saving throw).

Water Fire (Su): Three times per day, a half-pan lung or half-shen lung touching or submerged in water can surround itself in an aura of ghostly, flickering, multicolored flames that cause damage to any creature touching it. Any creature striking the half-dragon with a natural weapon or a melee weapon deals normal damage, but at the same time the attacker takes 1d6 points of fire damage. Lung dragons and half-lung dragons are immune to water fire. The water fire lasts for 1 minute or until it comes in contact with normal or magical fire. If

HALF-DRAGON

The half-dragon template on page 146 of the *Monster Manual* presents special attacks and special qualities for half-dragon versions of the ten varieties of true dragons described in that book. The information here expands that list to include all true dragons published in DUNGEONS & DRAGONS products to date.

The Half-Dragon Breath Weapons table below presents the breath weapon type for each half-dragon derived from one of the various true dragons that have appeared in *Monsters of Faerûn, Monster Manual II, Fiend Folio,* and this book. A half-dragon's line-shaped breath weapon is always 5 feet high, 5 feet wide, and 60 feet long. A half-dragon's cone-shaped breath weapon is always 30 feet long, 30 feet high, and 30 feet wide.

The Half-Dragon Immunities and Resistances table below presents the immunities and/or resistances possessed by half-dragons descended from these true dragons.

The lung dragons, presented in *Oriental Adventures*, are a special case. Many either don't have breath weapons or lack immunities (or both), so half-dragons descended from these parents gain special attacks and special qualities as noted on the Lung Half-Dragons table below.

Half-Dragon Breath Weapons

Dragon Variety	Breath Weapon
Amethyst[3]	Line of force
Battle[1]	Cone of sonic energy
Brown[2]	Line of acid
Chaos[1]	Line of random energy
Crystal[3]	Cone of light
Deep[2]	Cone of flesh-corrosive gas
Emerald[3]	Cone of sonic energy
Ethereal[1]	Cone of force
Fang[1,2]	None*
Howling[1]	Cone of sonic energy
Oceanus[1]	Line of electricity
Pyroclastic[1]	Cone of fire and sonic energy**
Radiant[1]	Line of force
Rust[1]	Line of acid
Sapphire[3]	Cone of sonic energy
Shadow[1,2]	Cone of shadows (bestows one negative level)
Song[2]	Cone of electrically charged gas
Styx[1]	Line of acid
Tarterian[1]	Line of force
Topaz[3]	Cone of dehydration

*Three times per day, a fang half-dragon can choose to deal 1d4 points of Constitution drain with its bite attack (Fort DC 14 negates).

**Half of the indicated damage is fire and the other half is sonic energy.

1 Described elsewhere in this chapter.

2 First published in *Monsters of Faerûn*.

3 First published in *Monster Manual II*.

Half-Dragon Immunities and Resistances

Dragon Variety	Immunity or Resistance
Amethyst	Immunity to poison
Battle	Immunity to sonic
Brown	Immunity to acid
Chaos	Immunity to *confusion*/insanity
Crystal	Immunity to cold
Deep	Immunity to charms, resistance to cold 10 and fire 10
Emerald	Immunity to sonic
Ethereal	None
Fang	None
Howling	Immunity to sonic
Oceanus	Immunity to electricity
Pyroclastic	Immunity to fire or sonic (50% chance for either)
Radiant	None
Rust	None
Sapphire	Immunity to electricity
Shadow	Immunity to energy drain
Song	Immunity to electricity and poison
Styx	Immunity to disease and poison
Tarterian	None
Topaz	Immunity to cold

Lung Half-Dragons

Dragon Variety	Special Abilities
Chiang lung	Water breathing, cause rain (see text)
Li lung	Roar (see text), burrow 10 ft.
Lung wang	Water breathing, immunity to fire, cone of steam (fire) breath weapon (6d10, DC 18)
Pan lung	Water breathing, water fire (see text)
Shen lung	Water breathing, immunity to electricity and poison, water fire (see text)
T'ien lung	Water breathing, cone of fire breath weapon (6d10; DC 18)
Tun mi lung	Water breathing, air and water immunity
Yu lung	Water breathing

the water fire is dispelled by fire, the half-dragon can't activate the ability again for 2d6 minutes.

HOARD SCARAB

A hoard scarab is an eyeless, beetlelike creature that hides in piles of treasure. Thanks to its size and its silver or golden shell, it looks much like a coin when dormant (though close observation reveals its nature). A swarm resembles a pile of gold and silver pieces.

Hoard scarabs are often found hidden among the treasure of a dragon (hence their name). They often live in a symbiotic relationship with a dragon, keeping the wyrm's scales clean of troublesome vermin (the dragon's natural armor keeps it safe from the scarab's burrow ability).

Hoard scarabs are unintelligent and cannot speak or understand any languages.

COMBAT

An individual hoard scarab seeks to burrow into its target's flesh. However, hoard scarabs prefer to attack en masse, swarming over a target and chewing it apart.

Burrow (Ex): If a hoard scarab hits a Small or larger living creature with a bite attack (or if a hoard scarab swarm hits with its swarm attack), on its next turn it can attempt to burrow into the target's flesh. The target may attempt a Reflex save (DC 11 for an individual scarab, or DC 14 for a swarm) to prevent the hoard scarab from burrowing in (a helpless creature can't prevent the burrowing). If the save fails, each round thereafter the target takes 1d2 points of Constitution damage (from an individual scarab) or 2d4 points of Constitution damage (from a swarm of scarabs).

A hoard scarab doesn't leave a target until the target is dead. Once a hoard scarab has burrowed into its target, it can be destroyed by any effect that would cure a disease, such as *remove disease* or *heal*. (A single spell eliminates all burrowing hoard scarabs, though it gives no protection against further burrowings.)

Creatures with immunity to disease, as well as those with a natural armor bonus (including enhancement) of +3 or better, are immune to a hoard scarab's burrowing attack.

Distraction (Ex): Any living creature vulnerable to the swarm's damage that begins its turn with a swarm in its square is nauseated for 1 round (Fortitude DC 14 negates). Even with a successful save, spellcasting or concentrating on spells within the area of a swarm requires a Concentration check (DC 20 + spell level). Using any skill involving patience and concentration requires a DC 20 Concentration check. The save DC is Constitution-based.

Swarm Traits: A swarm has no clear front or back and no discernible anatomy, so it is not subject to critical hits or flanking. A hoard scarab swarm is immune to all weapon damage.

Reducing a swarm to 0 hit points or fewer causes the swarm to break up, though damage taken until that point does not degrade its

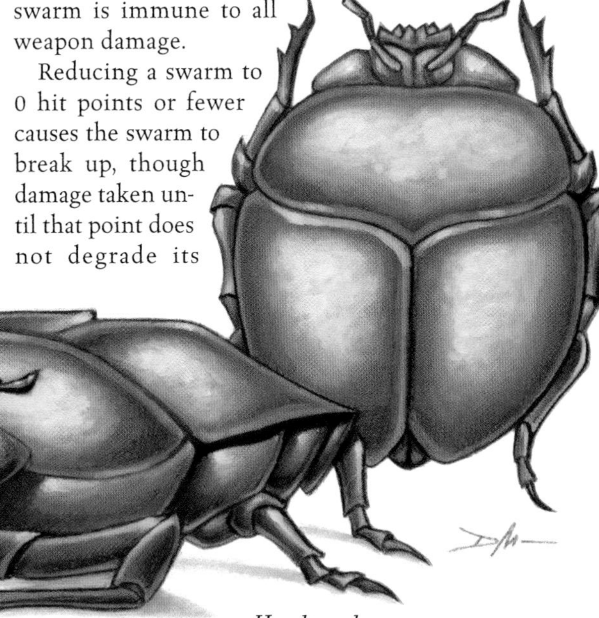

Hoard scarab

	Hoard Scarab Fine Vermin	Hoard Scarab Swarm Fine Vermin (Swarm)
Hit Dice:	1/8 d8+1 (2 hp)	6d8+6 (33 hp)
Initiative:	+1	+1
Speed:	20 ft. (4 squares), climb 20 ft.	20 ft. (4 squares), climb 20 ft.
Armor Class:	21 (+8 size, +1 Dex, +2 natural), touch 19, flat-footed 20	13 (+1 Dex, +2 natural), touch 11, flat-footed 12
Base Attack/Grapple:	+0/–21	+4./—
Attack:	Bite +3 melee (1d2–5)	Swarm (2d6)
Full Attack:	Bite +3 melee (1d2–5)	Swarm (2d6)
Space/Reach:	1 ft./0 ft.	10 ft./—
Special Attacks:	Burrowing	Burrowing, distraction
Special Qualities:	Tremorsense 20 ft., vermin traits	Tremorsense 20 ft., swarm traits, vermin traits
Saves:	Fort +3, Ref +1, Will +1	Fort +6, Ref +3, Will +3
Abilities:	Str 1, Dex 13, Con 13, Int —, Wis 12, Cha 2	Str 11, Dex 13, Con 13, Int —, Wis 12, Cha 2
Skills:	Hide +13*, Listen +5	Hide +13*, Listen +5
Environment:	Warm deserts	Warm deserts
Organization:	Solitary or cluster (2–5)	Individual swarm or cluster of swarms (2–5)
Challenge Rating:	1/2	5
Treasure:	None	None
Alignment:	Always neutral	Always neutral
Advancement:	None	None
Level Adjustment:	—	—

ability to attack or resist attack. Swarms are never staggered or reduced to a dying state by damage. Also, they cannot be tripped, grappled, or bull rushed, and they cannot grapple an opponent.

A hoard scarab swarm is immune to any spell or effect that targets a specific number of creatures (including single-target spells such as *disintegrate*). A swarm takes a –10 penalty on saving throws against spells or effects that affect an area, such as many evocation spells or splash weapons. If such as attack does not allow a saving throw, the swarm takes double damage instead.

Hoard scarab swarms are susceptible to high winds such as that created by a *gust of wind* spell. For purposes of determining the effects of wind on a hoard scarab swarm, treat the swarm as a creature of Fine size. Wind effects deal 1d6 points of nonlethal damage to the swarm per spell level (or Hit Die of the originating creature, in the case of effects such as an air elemental's whirlwind). A swarm rendered unconscious by means of nonlethal damage becomes disorganized and dispersed, and does not re-form until its hit points exceed its nonlethal damage.

For full information about the swarm subtype, see pages 315 and 316 of the *Monster Manual.*

Vermin Traits: A hoard scarab is immune to all mind-affecting effects (charms, compulsions, phantasms, patterns, and morale effects). It also has darkvision out to 60 feet.

Skills: Hoard scarabs have a +4 racial bonus on Listen checks. Hoard scarabs have a +4 racial bonus on Hide checks when they are concealed among coins (at least 10 coins for an individual scarab, or at least 10,000 coins for a swarm). A hoard scarab has a +8 racial bonus on Climb checks and can always choose to take 10 on Climb checks, even if rushed or threatened.

LANDWYRM

Landwyrms are cunning, wingless predatory dragons who ruthlessly scour their environment for prey. While some claim they represent a primitive, ancestral form of the true dragons, most dismiss such claims. Regardless of its origin, each variety of landwyrm is singularly adapted to its natural environment.

All landwyrms lack wings, but their body shapes vary by type, from serpentine (desert landwyrms) to craggy (mountain landwyrms). They have large, powerful jaws, clawed fore and hind limbs, and thick scales whose coloration matches that of their natural environment.

Landwyrms have stores of great knowledge about their environment, and if approached peacefully and respectfully, they can be sources of great wisdom.

Landwyrms can make excellent steeds, though they are strong-willed and independent, so even the least intelligent must be treated with great respect, or it will turn on its rider.

COMBAT

Each type of landwyrm has different combat tactics, though most rely on stealth to surprise their opponents. They are skilled trackers, and they see nothing wrong with fleeing a battle only to follow their prey and attack again later.

Frightful Presence (Ex): Much like the chromatic and metallic dragons, landwyrms can unsettle their foes with their mere presence. This ability takes effect automatically whenever the landwyrm attacks or charges. Creatures within the specified radius are subject to the effect if they are at least one size category smaller than the landwyrm and have fewer HD than the landwyrm.

A potentially affected creature that succeeds on a Will save (DC 10 + 1/2 landwyrm's HD + landwyrm's Cha modifier)

Illus. by W. England

remains immune to that landwyrm's frightful presence for 24 hours. On a failure, creatures whose HD are less than half the landwyrm's HD become panicked for 2d6 rounds and those whose HD are equal to or more than half the landwyrm's HD become shaken for 2d6 rounds. Other dragons (whether landwyrms or not) are immune to a landwyrm's frightful presence.

DESERT LANDWYRM

Gargantuan Dragon
Hit Dice: 32d12+224 (432 hp)
Initiative: +4
Speed: 40 ft. (8 squares), burrow 20 ft.
Armor Class: 33 (–4 size, +27 natural), touch 6, flat-footed 33
Base Attack/Grapple: +32/+56
Attack: Bite +40 melee (4d6+12/19–20)
Full Attack: Bite +40 melee (4d6+12/19–20) and 2 claws +38 melee (2d8+6)
Space/Reach: 20 ft./15 ft.
Special Attacks: Frightful presence, sandstorm
Special Qualities: Desert adaptation
Saves: Fort +25, Ref +18, Will +21
Abilities: Str 35, Dex 10, Con 24, Int 21, Wis 17, Cha 20
Skills: Bluff +35, Concentration +37, Diplomacy +39, Escape Artist +30, Gather Information +7, Hide +20*, Intimidate +7, Knowledge (arcana) +35, Knowledge (local) +35, Knowledge (nature) +35, Listen +34, Move Silently +31, Sense Motive +31, Spot +38*, Survival +32
Feats: Alertness, Blind-Fight, Cleave, Great Cleave, Improved Critical (bite), Improved Initiative, Improved Overrun, Multiattack, Power Attack, Stealthy, Track
Environment: Warm deserts
Organization: Solitary, pair, or flight (3–6)
Challenge Rating: 18
Treasure: Standard
Alignment: Usually neutral evil
Advancement: 33–39 HD (Gargantuan); 40–48 HD (Colossal)
Level Adjustment: —

The heart of a desert landwyrm burns with a patient evil as it lies in wait for victims.

A desert landwyrm's yellow-brown scales perfectly blend with its arid surroundings. Their sinuous bodies make them look like enormous serpents, until one notices the powerful front and rear claws normally held tight against the body.

Desert landwyrms often lair in ancient tombs or other ruined buildings, which leads to their nickname of "tomb dragon." They are quite capable of defending their lairs from any but the largest blue dragons, with whom they often clash over territory. They respond best when offered valuables.

Desert landwyrms speak Draconic and Common.

Combat

Thanks to its hardy nature, a desert landwyrm can lie buried in the sand for weeks at a time waiting for prey, with only its rocky eye-ridge protruding. When potential victims approach, the landwyrm bursts forth, creating a sandstorm to blind its prey. It ignores panicked opponents, knowing that it can track them down later if needed.

Desert Adaptation (Ex): Desert landwyrms can go without water for a number of days equal to their Constitution score. Even after this point, they need only make a Constitution check each day (rather than each hour, as noted in Starvation and Thirst, page 304 of the *Dungeon Master's Guide*) to avoid taking nonlethal damage from thirst. They take no nonlethal damage from heat exposure (though they take damage from fire normally). They suffer no ill effects from being caught in dust storms or sandstorms (including their own sandstorm attack; see below).

Frightful Presence (Ex): 160-ft. radius, HD 31 or fewer, Will DC 31 negates.

Sandstorm (Ex): As a standard action, a desert landwyrm can create a small sandstorm by kicking up sand, dust, and debris in a 120-foot-radius spread centered on itself. Any creature in the affected area must succeed on a DC 33 Fortitude save or be blinded for 1d6 rounds. This ability only functions in deserts or areas with similar quantities of dust or sand.

Skills: Desert landwyrms have a +4 racial bonus on Spot checks. *They have a +4 racial bonus on Hide checks when in temperate or warm desert environments. This bonus on Hide checks increases to +8 when the landwyrm is immobile.

FOREST LANDWYRM

Large Dragon
Hit Dice: 16d12+48 (152 hp)
Initiative: +5
Speed: 60 ft. (12 squares), burrow 10 ft.
Armor Class: 19 (–1 size, +1 Dex, +9 natural), touch 10, flat-footed 18
Base Attack/Grapple: +16/+23
Attack: Bite +21 melee (2d6+6/19–20)
Full Attack: Bite +21 melee (2d6+6/19–20) and 2 claws +19 melee (1d8+3)
Space/Reach: 10 ft./5 ft.
Special Attacks: Frightful presence
Special Qualities: Forest adaptation, commune with nature
Saves: Fort +13, Ref +11, Will +15
Abilities: Str 23, Dex 12, Con 16, Int 13, Wis 21, Cha 16
Skills: Climb +22*, Concentration +11, Diplomacy +19, Gather Information +5, Hide +13*, Knowledge (local) +9, Knowledge (nature) +9, Listen +13, Move Silently +17, Sense Motive +11, Spot +13, Survival +9
Feats: Improved Critical (bite), Improved Initiative, Multiattack, Power Attack, Stealthy, Track
Environment: Temperate forests
Organization: Solitary, pair, or cluster (3–6)
Challenge Rating: 10
Treasure: Standard
Alignment: Usually lawful neutral
Advancement: 17–19 HD (Large); 20–31 HD (Huge); 32–39 HD (Gargantuan); 40–48 HD (Colossal)
Level Adjustment: +3

The noblest of the landwyrms, the forest landwyrm sees itself as a protector of its woodland territory. It takes only what it needs to survive, and ruthlessly hunts down enemy predators.

The hide of a forest landwyrm bears a mottled pattern of green and brown, although in autumn it takes on aspects of yellow or even red to blend in. When threatened, a forest landwyrm expands a leafy frill of scales from its neck, making it appear even larger than it is.

Forest landwyrms brook no competitors within their territory, chasing out animals, vermin, and even humanoids who encroach therein. However, they are open to peaceful discussions with those who convince the landwyrm they do not pose a threat. In rare instances, a forest landwyrm may befriend local gnomes, serving as the unofficial protector of a nearby village.

Forest landwyrms speak Draconic, Gnome, Sylvan, and Common.

Combat

Forest landwyrms prefer to strike from hiding, attacking unwary opponents with its claws and bite. Such attacks may come from below (thanks to the landwyrm's burrowing ability) or above (as they are quite capable of climbing large trees).

***Commune with Nature* (Sp):** Once per day a forest landwyrm can use *commune with nature*. Caster level 16th.

Forest Adaptation (Ex): Forest landwyrms can ignore any concealment provided by foliage.

Frightful Presence (Ex): 80-ft. radius, HD 15 or fewer, Will DC 21 negates.

Skills: Forest landwyrms have a +4 racial bonus on Climb checks. *They have a +4 racial bonus on Hide checks when in cold or temperate forest environments. This bonus on Hide checks increases to +8 when the landwyrm is immobile.

HILL LANDWYRM

Huge Dragon
Hit Dice: 20d12+100 (230 hp)
Initiative: +4
Speed: 50 ft. (10 squares), burrow 10 ft.
Armor Class: 23 (–2 size, +15 natural), touch 8, flat-footed 23
Base Attack/Grapple: +20/36
Attack: Bite +27 melee (2d8+9/19–20); or claw +25 melee (2d6+4)
Full Attack: Bite +27 melee (2d8+9/19–20) and 2 claws +25 melee (2d6+4)
Space/Reach: 15 ft./10 ft.
Special Attacks: Frightful presence, improved grab
Special Qualities: —
Saves: Fort +17, Ref +10, Will +11
Abilities: Str 29, Dex 10, Con 20, Int 9, Wis 13, Cha 12
Skills: Hide +12*, Intimidate +21, Knowledge (local) +9, Knowledge (nature) +9, Listen +19, Sense Motive +19, Spot +11, Survival +9

Feats: Improved Critical (bite), Improved Initiative, Improved Overrun, Multiattack, Power Attack, Stealthy, Track
Environment: Temperate hills
Organization: Solitary, pair, or brood (3–6)
Challenge Rating: 12
Treasure: Standard
Alignment: Usually chaotic evil
Advancement: 21–31 HD (Huge); 32–39 HD (Gargantuan); 40–48 HD (Colossal)
Level Adjustment: —

Hill landwyrms are slow-witted bullies who rely on intimidation and displays of physical prowess to subdue their enemies.

A hill landwyrm's coloration varies with its surroundings. Some are slate-gray, while others have brown, red-brown, or tan scales. They appear bulky and muscular, with long, daggerlike claws.

Despite their might, hill landwyrms prefer to pick on opponents clearly weaker than themselves. While a single hill giant is a tempting target, a hunting party of giants sends a hill landwyrm into hiding. Some giants capture hill landwyrms to use as guardians or steeds, though the dragons hate this and escape as soon as possible. It is possible for a suitably intimidating individual to humble a hill landwyrm without striking a blow.

Hill landwyrms speak Draconic, Goblin, and Common.

Combat

A hill landwyrm likes to open combat with an overrun attack against the weakest-looking target. Once an opponent is prone, it focuses its attacks on that individual, using improved grab to neutralize the target and crush it to death. If reduced to half its hit points or fewer, a hill landwyrm begins looking for an escape route.

Frightful Presence (Ex): 100-ft. radius, HD 19 or fewer, Will DC 21 negates.

Improved Grab (Ex): To use this ability, a hill landwyrm must hit a creature of its size or smaller with a claw attack. It can then attempt to start a grapple as a free action without provoking an attack of opportunity.

Skills: *Hill landwyrms have a +4 racial bonus on Hide checks when in hills terrain. This bonus on Hide checks increases to +8 when the landwyrm is immobile.

JUNGLE LANDWYRM

Huge Dragon
Hit Dice: 28d12+168 (350 hp)
Initiative: +4
Speed: 50 ft. (10 squares), burrow 10 ft.
Armor Class: 23 (–2 size, +15 natural), touch 8, flat-footed 23
Base Attack/Grapple: +28/+46
Attack: Bite +36 melee (2d8+10/19–20)
Full Attack: Bite +36 melee (2d8+10/19–20) and 2 claws +34 melee (2d6+5)
Space/Reach: 15 ft./10 ft.
Special Attacks: Disease, frightful presence, rend, snatch
Special Qualities: Jungle adaptation
Saves: Fort +22, Ref +16, Will +21
Abilities: Str 31, Dex 10, Con 22, Int 17, Wis 21, Cha 16
Skills: Bluff +31, Climb +38, Concentration +30, Diplomacy +5, Gather Information +5, Hide +22*, Intimidate +24, Knowledge (local) +24, Knowledge (nature) +24, Listen +26, Move Silently +30, Sense Motive +35, Spot +19, Survival +31
Feats: Blind-Fight, Cleave, Combat Expertise, Improved Critical (bite), Improved Initiative, Multiattack, Power Attack, Rend[B], Snatch, Stealthy, Track
Environment: Warm forests
Organization: Solitary, pair, or cluster (3–6)
Challenge Rating: 16
Treasure: Standard
Alignment: Usually neutral evil
Advancement: 29–31 HD (Huge); 32–39 HD (Gargantuan); 40–48 HD (Colossal)
Level Adjustment: —

Among its kind, the jungle landwyrm is considered the most purely sinister and evil. It knows no emotion except hate, which it holds for all other living creatures.

A jungle landwyrm's scaled hide is deep green in color, with occasional splotches of bright red or yellow that blend in with its tropical environment. Despite their size, jungle landwyrms have lithe forms that slide easily through foliage and between trees. Some unwitting individuals mistake the jungle landwyrm for an enormous dinosaur and think they can treat it as they would a mere animal. Such fools don't live long after making this mistake.

A jungle landwyrm eats anything it can, though it prefers living prey to carrion or plants. It has few rivals for power, although it avoids older green dragons. Even in rare instances when the landwyrm seems willing to negotiate, it inevitably tricks its prey and attacks it later.

Jungle landwyrms speak Draconic and Common.

Combat

Like others of its kind, a jungle landwyrm relies on its natural camouflage to surprise enemies. However, it is also willing to follow potential prey for great distances, choosing just the right circumstances to strike. If faced with multiple opponents, it spreads out its early attacks and doesn't hesitate to flee if overmatched, knowing it can return days later to pick off those weakened by its disease-bearing claws.

Disease (Ex): The wounds caused by a jungle landwyrm's claws may become infected with red ache disease (DC 15; incubation 1d3 days; damage 1d6 Strength).

Frightful Presence (Ex): 140-ft. radius, HD 27 or fewer, Will DC 27 negates.

Rend (Ex): Extra damage 2d10+15.

Snatch (Ex): Against Small or smaller creatures, bite for 2d8+10/round or claw for 2d6+5/round.

Jungle Adaptation (Ex): Jungle landwyrms can ignore any concealment provided by foliage.

Skills: *Jungle landwyrms have a +4 racial bonus on Hide checks when in warm forest (or jungle) environments. This bonus on Hide checks increases to +8 when the landwyrm is immobile.

MOUNTAIN LANDWYRM

Colossal Dragon
Hit Dice: 40d12+440 (700 hp)
Initiative: +3
Speed: 30 ft. (6 squares), burrow 10 ft.
Armor Class: 31 (–8 size, –1 Dex, +30 natural), touch 1, flat-footed 31
Base Attack/Grapple: +40/+72
Attack: Bite +48 melee (4d18+16/19–20)
Full Attack: Bite +48 melee (4d18+16/19–20) and 2 claws +46 melee (4d6+8)
Space/Reach: 30 ft./20 ft.
Special Attacks: Frightful presence, snatch, thunderous roar
Special Qualities: —
Saves: Fort +33, Ref +21, Will +29
Abilities: Str 43, Dex 8, Con 32, Int 13, Wis 25, Cha 20
Skills: Climb +46, Concentration +31, Diplomacy +45, Gather Information +7, Hide +23*, Intimidate +25, Knowledge (local) +21, Knowledge (nature) +21, Listen +27, Sense Motive +27, Spot +47, Survival +31
Feats: Awesome Blow, Blind-Fight, Cleave, Great Cleave, Improved Bull Rush, Improved Critical (bite), Improved Initiative, Improved Overrun, Improved Sunder, Multiattack, Power Attack, Snatch, Stealthy, Track
Environment: Temperate mountains
Organization: Solitary, pair, or cluster (3–6)
Challenge Rating: 22
Treasure: Standard
Alignment: Usually lawful evil
Advancement: 41–48 HD (Colossal)
Level Adjustment: —

The mountain landwyrm spends most of its days in slumber, hidden away in a secret cave in the heart of a great peak. But when awake, it is one of the fiercest creatures to walk the planet.

At first glance, a mountain landwyrm appears to be a craggy mass of rock. In fact, it is possible to walk right past one (despite its size) and never suspect it was there. However, once it is awakened, its tread shakes the ground.

Mountain landwyrms subsist primarily on a diet of stone, occasionally venturing forth for a meal of a few dire bears or stone giants. They have no true enemies, since even the eldest red dragon knows better than to pick a fight with such a creature. Still, they have been known to interact peacefully with creatures that offer the proper gifts and obeisance.

Mountain landwyrms speak Draconic, Dwarven, Giant, and Common.

Combat

A mountain landwyrm opens combat with its thunderous roar and frightful presence, and then picks off injured opponents with patient skill. Once angered, a mountain landwyrm does not rest until it has destroyed its foes, tracking them for days if necessary.

Frightful Presence (Ex): 200-ft. radius, HD 39 or fewer, Will DC 35 negates.

Snatch (Ex): Against Large or smaller creatures, bite for 4d8+16/round or claw for 4d6+8/round.

Thunderous Roar (Su): Once per day a mountain landwyrm can emit a thunderous roar. This is the equivalent of a *greater shout* spell. Caster level 20th.

Skills: *Mountain landwyrms have a +4 racial bonus on Hide checks when in mountain terrain. This bonus on Hide checks increases to +8 when the landwyrm is immobile.

PLAINS LANDWYRM

Medium Dragon
Hit Dice: 8d12+16 (68 hp)
Initiative: +2
Speed: 60 ft. (12 squares), burrow 10 ft.
Armor Class: 18 (+2 Dex, +6 natural), touch 12, flat-footed 16
Base Attack/Grapple: +8/+10
Attack: Bite +13 melee (1d8+5/19–20)
Full Attack: Bite +13 melee (1d8+5/19–20) and 2 claws +11 melee (1d6+2)
Space/Reach: 5 ft./5 ft.
Special Attacks: Burst of speed, frightful presence, poison
Special Qualities: —
Saves: Fort +8, Ref +8, Will +7
Abilities: Str 15, Dex 14, Con 14, Int 9, Wis 13, Cha 12
Skills: Bluff +9, Diplomacy +3, Gather Information +3, Hide +10*, Intimidate +3, Knowledge (local) +10, Knowledge (nature) +10, Listen +12, Spot +12, Survival +7
Feats: Improved Critical (bite), Multiattack, Track
Environment: Temperate plains
Organization: Solitary, pair, or clutch (3–6)
Challenge Rating: 6
Treasure: Standard
Alignment: Usually chaotic neutral
Advancement: 9–11 HD (Medium); 12–19 HD (Large); 20–24 HD (Huge)
Level Adjustment: +2

The plains landwyrm would be a pitiful beast if it weren't so dangerous. Despite its general cowardice, this scavenger occasionally attacks living creatures when it is hungry or desperate.

A plains landwyrm has scales that bear stripes of tan or light green, allowing it to blend in with its surroundings. It is sometimes mistaken for a raptorlike dinosaur, since it often stands up on its hind legs.

Most plains landwyrms wander their environment, since they aren't courageous enough to fight other creatures for territory. The creature is capable of bluffing when in a crisis, though it rarely has the patience for such tactics. Some particularly brave halflings tame these creatures as mounts, though it takes an attentive rider to keep them on task.

Plains landwyrms speak Draconic and Common.

Combat

Whether lying in wait in the tall grass or hiding under a thin layer of earth, a plains landwyrm favors a quick strike against an unwary foe.

Burst of Speed (Ex): Once per day, a plains landwyrm may activate a burst of speed as a free action. This doubles its

Plains landwyrm

Mountain landwyrm

Jungle landwyrm

Illus. by M. nelson

speed for 5 rounds, after which it is fatigued for 10 minutes. It usually uses this ability to escape from danger.

Frightful Presence (Ex): 40-ft. radius, HD 7 or fewer, Will DC 15 negates.

Poison (Ex): The bite of a plains landwyrm delivers a toxic venom (Fort DC 16; 1d6 Str/2d6 Str).

Skills: *Plains landwyrms have a +4 racial bonus on Hide checks when in temperate or warm plains environments. This bonus on Hide checks increases to +8 when the landwyrm is immobile.

SWAMP LANDWYRM

Gargantuan Dragon (Aquatic)
Hit Dice: 36d12+288 (522 hp)
Initiative: +4
Speed: 30 ft. (6 squares), swim 20 ft.
Armor Class: 30 (–4 size, +24 natural), touch 6, flat-footed 30
Base Attack/Grapple: +36/+62
Attack: Bite +46 melee (4d6+14/19–20)
Full Attack: Bite +46 melee (4d6+14/19–20) and 2 claws +44 melee (2d8+7)
Space/Reach: 20 ft./15 ft.
Special Attacks: Frightful presence, hypnotizing gaze, snatch
Special Qualities: Amphibious, resistance to acid 30
Saves: Fort +28, Ref +20, Will +23
Abilities: Str 39, Dex 10, Con 26, Int 17, Wis 17, Cha 24
Skills: Bluff +43, Concentration +26, Diplomacy +50, Gather Information +9, Hide +12*, Intimidate +25, Jump +32, Knowledge (local) +21, Knowledge (nature) +21, Listen +30, Move Silently +36, Sense Motive +39, Spot +37, Survival +39, Swim +14
Feats: Alertness, Blind-Fight, Cleave, Combat Reflexes, Great Cleave, Improved Critical (bite), Improved Initiative, Multiattack, Persuasive, Power Attack, Snatch, Stealthy, Track
Environment: Warm marshes
Organization: Solitary, pair, or cluster (3–6)
Challenge Rating: 20
Treasure: Standard
Alignment: Usually chaotic evil
Advancement: 37–39 HD (Gargantuan); 40–48 HD (Colossal)
Level Adjustment: —

The foul, murderous swamp landwyrm takes pleasure in dealing maximum agony upon its prey.

Its mottled brown and green hide is constantly covered in slime and algae. It has webbed toes to help it swim. When it is angry, its eyes shine like pale yellow lanterns.

Swamp landwyrms fear nothing, not even the largest tyrannosaurus or black dragon. From time to time, foolish lizardfolk attempt to trade valuables with swamp landwyrms in exchange for protection. Such deals always end badly for the "protected" creatures.

Swamp landwyrms speak Draconic and Common.

Combat

If facing a large group of foes, a swamp landwyrm employs its frightful presence to reduce the number of capable opponents. Otherwise, it opens by targeting a single individual with its hypnotizing gaze, drawing it in close for a deadly attack.

Frightful Presence (Ex): 180-ft. radius, HD 35 or fewer, Will DC 35 negates.

Hypnotizing Gaze (Su): A swamp landwyrm can hypnotize its prey just by looking into its eyes. This is similar to a gaze attack, except that the landwyrm must use a standard action, and those merely looking at the creature are not affected. Anyone the landwyrm targets must succeed on a DC 35 Will save or be hypnotized (as the *hypnotism* spell, except it affects a single target whose Hit Dice do not exceed the landwyrm's). If a landwyrm uses this ability in combat, the target gains a +2 bonus on the save. The effect has a range of 60 feet and lasts for 10 rounds.

Snatch (Ex): Against Medium or smaller creatures, bite for 4d6+14/round or claw for 2d8+7/round.

Amphibious (Ex): Although swamp landwyrms are aquatic, they can survive indefinitely on land.

Skills: A swamp landwyrm has a +8 racial bonus on any Swim check to perform some special action or avoid a hazard. It can always choose to take 10 on a Swim check, even if distracted or endangered. It can use the run action while swimming, provided it swims in a straight line. *Swamp landwyrms have a +4 racial bonus on Hide checks when in swamp environments. This bonus on Hide checks increases to +8 when the landwyrm is immobile.

TUNDRA LANDWYRM

Huge Dragon
Hit Dice: 24d12+144 (300 hp)
Initiative: +4
Speed: 50 ft. (10 squares), burrow 20 ft.
Armor Class: 26 (–2 size, +18 natural), touch 8, flat-footed 26
Base Attack/Grapple: +24/+40
Attack: Bite +30 melee (2d8+8/19–20); or claw +28 melee (2d6+4)
Full Attack: Bite +30 melee (2d8+8/19–20) and 2 claws +28 melee (2d6+4)
Space/Reach: 15 ft./10 ft.
Special Attacks: Blood drain, frightful presence, improved grab, snatch
Special Qualities: Cold adaptation, resistance to cold 20, tremorsense 60 ft.
Saves: Fort +20, Ref +14, Will +15

Tundra landwyrm
Swamp landwyrm
Underdark landwyrm

Abilities: Str 27, Dex 10, Con 22, Int 9, Wis 13, Cha 12
Skills: Diplomacy +13, Gather Information +3, Hide +16*, Knowledge (local) +21, Knowledge (nature) +21, Listen +31, Sense Motive +9, Spot +17, Survival +23
Feats: Blind-Fight, Cleave, Improved Critical (bite), Improved Initiative, Multiattack, Power Attack, Snatch, Stealthy, Track
Environment: Cold plains
Organization: Solitary, pair, or cluster (3–6)
Challenge Rating: 14
Treasure: Standard
Alignment: Usually neutral
Advancement: 25–31 HD (Huge); 32–39 HD (Gargantuan); 40–48 HD (Colossal)
Level Adjustment: —

The blood-drinking tundra landwyrm spends much of its life in semihibernation, burrowed under the icy ground in wait for prey to happen by.

The scales of a tundra landwyrm are dirty ivory. It has short, stubby claws that help it dig through the frozen earth. Its roar sounds like the bark of an angry sea lion.

A tundra landwyrm prefers mammalian prey, such as caribou or even polar bears. The creatures occasionally tangle with white dragons or frost worms. Any offering of live or recently killed animals can sway a tundra landwyrm's opinion.

Tundra landwyrms speak Draconic and Common.

Combat

A tundra landwyrm lies motionless a few feet beneath the surface of the ground, relying on its tremorsense to warn it of prey. It scatters targets with its frightful presence, then grapples a single creature and attempts to drain its blood.

Blood Drain (Ex): If a tundra landwyrm gets a hold on a living foe, it can drain blood with a successful grapple check. Each successful grapple check deals 1d6 points of Constitution damage to its target. A single landwyrm can deal as many points of Constitution damage in a day as it has Hit Dice.

Frightful Presence (Ex): 120-ft. radius, HD 23 or fewer, Will DC 23 negates.

Improved Grab (Ex): To use this ability, a tundra landwyrm must hit a creature of its size or smaller with a claw attack. If it gets a hold, it can attempt to draw blood. It can also attempt to start a grapple as a free action without provoking an attack of opportunity.

Snatch (Ex): Against Small or smaller creatures, bite for 2d8+8/round or claw for 2d6+4/round.

Cold Adaptation (Ex): Tundra landwyrms take no nonlethal damage from exposure to low temperatures (though this ability doesn't affect normal cold-based damage). They suffer no ill effects (such as penalties on Spot checks) from snow or sleet and can walk across icy surfaces without needing to make a Balance check.

Skills: *Tundra landwyrms have a +4 racial bonus on Hide checks when in cold desert or plains environments. This bonus on Hide checks increases to +8 when the landwyrm is immobile.

UNDERDARK LANDWYRM

Large Dragon
Hit Dice: 12d12+48 (126 hp)
Initiative: +5
Speed: 60 ft., swim 30 ft.
Armor Class: 22 (–1 size, +1 Dex, +12 natural), touch 10, flat-footed 21
Base Attack/Grapple: +12/+20
Attack: Bite +15 melee (2d6+4/19–20); or claw +13 melee (1d8+2 plus 1 Con)
Full Attack: Bite +15 melee (2d6+4/19–20) and 2 claws +13 melee (1d8+2 plus 1 Con)
Space/Reach: 10 ft./5 ft.
Special Attacks: Frightful presence, *obscuring mist*, wounding
Special Qualities: Blindsense 60 ft.
Saves: Fort +12, Ref +9, Will +11
Abilities: Str 19, Dex 12, Con 18, Int 13, Wis 17, Cha 16
Skills: Bluff +14, Diplomacy +5, Escape Artist +12, Gather Information +5, Hide +9*, Intimidate +15, Jump +16, Knowledge (local) +7, Knowledge (Underdark) +12, Move Silently +20*, Sense Motive +14, Survival +13, Swim +4
Feats: Improved Critical (bite), Improved Initiative, Multiattack, Stealthy, Track
Environment: Underground
Organization: Solitary, pair, or clutch (3–6)
Challenge Rating: 8
Treasure: Standard
Alignment: Usually lawful evil
Advancement: 13–19 HD (Large); 20–31 HD (Huge); 31–36 HD (Gargantuan)
Level Adjustment: +2

The Underdark landwyrm, or cave dragon, spends its entire existence in darkness, making evil plans and sowing death.

The creature's hide is dark gray, to match its subterranean environment. Its vision and hearing are extraordinarily poor, though it makes up for this disadvantage with other sensory capabilities.

Underdark landwyrms often keep elaborate lairs that take advantage of their natural surroundings, such as chasms or lakes. They can sometimes be swayed by gifts of magic.

Underdark landwyrms speak Draconic, Undercommon, and Common.

Combat

An Underdark landwyrm relies on its blindsense to sense nearby prey. Once it detects a victim, it uses *obscuring mist* to cloak its quiet approach, and then bursts into view with frightful presence. It often retreats from battle after injuring opponents, relying on the wounds inflicted upon its prey to further weaken them.

Blindsense (Ex): An Underdark landwyrm's extraordinary powers of scent and echolocation allow it to pinpoint the location of any living creature within 60 feet.

Frightful Presence (Ex): 60-ft. radius, HD 11 or fewer, Will DC 19 negates.

Obscuring Mist (Su): Three times per day, an Underdark landwyrm can exhale a cloud of obscuring mist (as the spell, caster level equals landwyrm's HD).

Wounding (Ex): An Underdark landwyrm's claws deal bleeding wounds, similar to those caused by a wounding weapon. In addition to hit point damage, a claw attack deals 1 point of Constitution damage when it hits a creature. A critical hit does not multiply the Constitution damage. Creatures immune to critical hits are immune to this Constitution damage.

Skills: An underdark landwyrm has a +8 racial bonus on any Swim check to perform some special action or avoid a hazard. It can always choose to take 10 on a Swim check, even if distracted or endangered. It can use the run action while swimming, provided it swims in a straight line. Underdark landwyrms have a +4 racial bonus on Move Silently checks. *They have a +4 racial bonus on Hide checks when in rocky, underground environments. This bonus on Hide checks increases to +8 when the landwyrm is immobile.

PLANAR DRAGONS

In addition to the many dragon species native to the Material Plane, a number of dragons hail from other planes, particularly the Outer Planes. Collectively referred to as planar dragons, these creatures hail from planes as diverse as Limbo, Acheron, Ysgard, and even the Ethereal Plane.

Unlike most other true dragons, planar dragons are not innate spellcasters; though they have a variety of spell-like powers, they don't have the natural affinity for sorcery that their Material Plane relatives have. A planar dragon uses its age category as its caster level for all spell-like abilities.

Though native to planes other than the Material, these creatures are nonetheless of the dragon type and are not outsiders. Instead, they all possess the extraplanar subtype.

BATTLE DRAGON

Dragon (Extraplanar)
Environment: Heroic Domains of Ysgard
Organization: Solitary (1 dragon, any age), clutch (1d4+1 wyrmlings, very young, young, or juveniles or young adults), family (pair of mature adults and 1d4+1 offspring)
Challenge Rating: Wyrmling 3; very young 4; young 6; juvenile 8; young adult 10; adult 12; mature adult 14; old 17; very old 18; ancient 19; wyrm 20; great wyrm 22
Treasure: Triple standard
Alignment: Always neutral good
Advancement: Wyrmling 6–7 HD; very young 9–10 HD; young 12–13 HD; juvenile 15–16 HD; young adult 18–19 HD; adult 21–22 HD; mature adult 24–25 HD; old 27–28 HD; very old 30–31 HD; ancient 33–34 HD; wyrm 36–37 HD; great wyrm 39+ HD
Level Adjustment: Wyrmling +2; very young +3; young +4; juvenile +4; others —

Battle dragons are glorious creature that exult in valorous combat. They often serve as steeds for powerful warriors.

A battle dragon at rest has a dull brown sheen to its scales. However, as soon as it takes wing, allowing the sun to strike its armored skin, it gleams like the finest gold.

Battle dragons are notorious optimists, and always seem to find the silver lining to any cloud. This emotion is often contagious, as they inspire others to bravery and valor in battle.

By juvenile age, battle dragons may find use as steeds for Small riders. Young adult and older dragons can serve Medium riders. Some cities or knightly orders have reached mutual protection and assistance accords with nearby battle dragon families, as generation after generation of rider finds an ally within the same line of dragons.

Battle dragons speak Common, Draconic, and Celestial.

Battle dragon

Battle Dragons by Age

Age	Size	Hit Dice (hp)	Str	Dex	Con	Int	Wis	Cha	Base Attack/ Grapple	Attack	Fort Save	Ref Save	Will Save	Breath Weapon (DC)	Frightful Presence DC
Wyrmling	T	5d12+10 (43)	13	10	15	10	11	12	+5/-2	+8	+6	+4	+4	2d6 (14)	—
Very young	S	8d12+16 (68)	15	10	15	10	11	12	+8/+6	+11	+8	+6	+6	4d6 (16)	—
Young	M	11d12+33 (105)	17	10	17	12	13	14	+11/+14	+14	+10	+7	+8	6d6 (18)	—
Juvenile	M	14d12+42 (133)	19	10	17	12	13	14	+14/+18	+18	+12	+9	+10	8d6 (20)	—
Young adult	L	17d12+68 (169)	21	10	19	14	15	16	+17/+26	+21	+14	+10	+12	10d6 (22)	21
Adult	L	20d12+100 (230)	25	10	21	14	15	16	+20/+31	+26	+17	+12	+14	12d6 (25)	23
Mature adult	H	23d12+138 (288)	29	10	23	16	17	18	+23/+40	+30	+19	+13	+16	14d6 (28)	25
Old	H	26d12+156 (325)	31	10	23	16	17	18	+26/+44	+34	+21	+15	+18	16d6 (29)	27
Very old	H	29d12+203 (392)	33	10	25	18	19	20	+29/+48	+38	+23	+16	+20	18d6 (31)	29
Ancient	H	32d12+224 (432)	35	10	25	18	19	20	+32/+52	+42	+25	+18	+22	20d6 (33)	31
Wyrm	G	35d12+280 (508)	37	10	27	20	21	22	+35/+60	+44	+27	+19	+24	22d6 (35)	33
Great wyrm	G	38d12+342 (589)	39	10	29	20	21	22	+38/+64	+48	+30	+21	+26	24d6 (38)	35

Battle Dragon Abilities by Age

Age	Speed	Initiative	AC	Special Abilities	SR
Wyrmling	40 ft., fly 100 ft. (average)	+0	17 (+2 size, +5 natural)	Immunity to sonic	—
Very young	40 ft., fly 100 ft. (average)	+0	19 (+1 size, +8 natural)	*Protection from evil*	—
Young	40 ft., fly 150 ft. (poor)	+0	21 (+11 natural)	Damage reduction 5/magic	—
Juvenile	40 ft., fly 150 ft. (poor)	+0	24 (+14 natural)	*Aid, shield other*	—
Young adult	40 ft., fly 150 ft. (poor)	+0	26 (–1 size, +17 natural)	Damage reduction 10/magic	21
Adult	40 ft., fly 150 ft. (poor)	+0	29 (–1 size, +20 natural)	Inspire courage	24
Mature adult	40 ft., fly 150 ft. (poor)	+0	31 (–2 size, +23 natural)	Damage reduction 15/magic	26
Old	40 ft., fly 150 ft. (poor)	+0	34 (–2 size, +26 natural)	Fast healing 2	29
Very old	40 ft., fly 150 ft. (poor)	+0	37 (–2 size, +29 natural)	Damage reduction 20/magic and 5/evil	30
Ancient	40 ft., fly 150 ft. (poor)	+0	40 (–2 size, +32 natural)	Battle fury	32
Wyrm	40 ft., fly 200 ft. (clumsy)	+0	41 (–4 size, +35 natural)	Damage reduction 20/magic and 10/evil	33
Great wyrm	40 ft., fly 200 ft. (clumsy)	+0	44 (–4 size, +38 natural)	*Heroes' feast*	35

Combat

A battle dragon is a fearless combatant, raised from birth to take joy in the simple act of conflict. It uses its special abilities to fortify the prowess of its allies, while striking fear into foes with its breath weapon, frightful presence, and battle fury.

Young and older battle dragons' natural weapons are treated as magic weapons for the purpose of overcoming damage reduction.

Battle Fury (Ex): Once per day, an ancient or older battle dragon may enter a battle fury, which grants it a +2 morale bonus to Strength and Constitution and a +1 morale bonus on Will saves, but a –2 penalty to AC. This battle fury lasts for a number of rounds equal to the dragon's (new) Constitution modifier +3, at the end of which the dragon loses the indicated bonuses but suffers no fatigue or other ill effects. This ability is otherwise identical to the barbarian's rage class feature.

Breath Weapon (Su): A battle dragon has two types of breath weapon, a cone of sonic energy and a cone of fear gas. Creatures within the cone of fear gas must succeed on a Will save or become shaken for 4d6 rounds. Multiple exposures are not cumulative, but if an affected creature is already shaken (for instance, from the dragon's frightful presence), it becomes frightened instead.

Inspire Courage (Su): Once per day, an adult or older battle dragon can inspire courage in itself and its allies, granting them a +2 morale bonus on saving throws against charm or fear effects and a +1 morale bonus on attack rolls and weapon damage rolls. This is identical with the bardic ability of the same name, and requires the dragon to speak, sing, or roar for 1 full round.

Spell-Like Abilities: 3/day—*aid, protection from evil*; 1/day—*heroes' feast, shield other.*

Skills: Perform is a class skill for battle dragons. Their preferred modes of performance include oratory and singing.

CHAOS DRAGON

Dragon (Chaos, Extraplanar)

Environment: Ever-Changing Chaos of Limbo

Organization: Solitary (1 dragon, any age), clutch (1d4+1 wyrmlings, very young, young, or juveniles or young adults), family (pair of mature adults and 1d4+1 offspring)

Challenge Rating: Wyrmling 3; very young 4; young 6; juvenile 8; young adult 11; adult 13; mature adult 15; old 16; very old 17; ancient 19; wyrm 20; great wyrm 22

Treasure: Triple standard

Alignment: Always chaotic (good, neutral, or evil)

Advancement: Wyrmling 7–8 HD; very young 10–11 HD; young 13–14 HD; juvenile 16–17 HD; young adult 19–20 HD; adult 22–23 HD; mature adult 25–26 HD; old 28–29 HD; very old 31–32 HD; ancient 34–35 HD; wyrm 37–38 HD; great wyrm 40+ HD

Level Adjustment: Wyrmling +4; very young +4; young +6; others —

The very personification of unpredictability, a chaos dragon is a whirling cyclone of barely controlled power.

Chaos Dragons by Age

Age	Size	Hit Dice (hp)	Str	Dex	Con	Int	Wis	Cha	Base Attack/ Grapple	Attack	Fort Save	Ref Save	Will Save	Breath Weapon (DC)	Frightful Presence DC
Wyrmling	S	6d12+12 (51)	11	10	15	12	15	16	+6/+2	+7	+7	+5	+7	2d4 (15)	—
Very young	M	9d12+27 (86)	13	10	17	12	15	16	+9/+10	+10	+9	+6	+8	4d4 (17)	—
Young	M	12d12+36 (114)	15	10	17	14	17	18	+12/+14	+14	+11	+8	+11	6d4 (19)	—
Juvenile	L	15d12+60 (158)	17	10	19	16	19	20	+15/+22	+17	+13	+9	+13	8d4 (21)	—
Young adult	L	18d12+90 (207)	19	10	21	16	19	20	+18/+26	+21	+16	+11	+15	10d4 (24)	24
Adult	H	21d12+105 (242)	21	10	21	18	21	22	+21/+34	+24	+17	+12	+17	12d4 (25)	26
Mature adult	H	24d12+144 (300)	23	10	23	18	21	22	+24/+38	+28	+20	+14	+19	14d4 (28)	28
Old	H	27d12+189 (365)	25	10	25	20	23	24	+27/+42	+32	+22	+15	+21	16d4 (30)	30
Very old	H	30d12+240 (435)	27	10	27	20	23	24	+30/+46	+36	+25	+17	+23	18d4 (33)	32
Ancient	G	33d12+297 (512)	29	10	29	22	25	26	+33/+54	+38	+27	+18	+25	20d4 (35)	34
Wyrm	G	36d12+360 (594)	31	10	31	24	27	28	+36/+58	+42	+30	+20	+28	22d4 (38)	37
Great wyrm	G	39d12+429 (683)	33	10	33	24	27	28	+39/+62	+46	+32	+21	+29	24d4 (40)	38

Chaos Dragon Abilities by Age

Age	Speed	Initiative	AC	Special Abilities	SR
Wyrmling	60 ft., fly 150 ft. (poor)	+0	16 (+1 size, +5 natural)	Immunity to compulsion effects	—
Very young	60 ft., fly 150 ft. (poor)	+0	18 (+8 natural)	*Protection from law*	—
Young	60 ft., fly 150 ft. (poor)	+0	21 (+11 natural)	Damage reduction 5/magic	—
Juvenile	60 ft., fly 150 ft. (poor)	+0	23 (–1 size, +14 natural)	*Chaos hammer, entropic shield*	—
Young adult	60 ft., fly 150 ft. (poor)	+0	26 (–1 size, +17 natural)	Damage reduction 10/magic	24
Adult	60 ft., fly 150 ft. (poor)	+0	28 (–2 size, +20 natural)	*Dispel law, mind fog*	26
Mature adult	60 ft., fly 150 ft. (poor)	+0	31 (–2 size, +23 natural)	Damage reduction 15/magic	28
Old	60 ft., fly 200 ft. (clumsy)	+0	34 (–2 size, +26 natural)	*Word of chaos*	30
Very old	60 ft., fly 200 ft. (clumsy)	+0	37 (–2 size, +29 natural)	Damage reduction 20/magic and 5/law	32
Ancient	60 ft., fly 200 ft. (clumsy)	+0	38 (–4 size, +32 natural)	*Mislead*	34
Wyrm	60 ft., fly 200 ft. (clumsy)	+0	41 (–4 size, +35 natural)	Damage reduction 20/magic and 10/law	37
Great wyrm	60 ft., fly 200 ft. (clumsy)	+0	44 (–4 size, +38 natural)	*Cloak of chaos*	38

No two chaos dragons look exactly alike, and some people claim that even the same chaos dragon changes its form over time. While all chaos dragons are roughly the same in appearance—four powerful clawed limbs, mighty wings, long serpentine neck topped by a mouth full of dagger-sharp teeth, jagged-edged tail—each has unique markings and scale patterns that differentiate it from others of its kind.

In general, chaos dragons seek to tear down structured societies and civilizations. Those that tend toward good might use positive means to effect change, but those tending to evil are merely violent and murderous.

For a brief period of time, a sect of githzerai attempted to make a pact with the chaos dragons, thinking that they could use them just as their enemies, the githyanki, employed red dragons. The chaos dragons' innate unpredictability and disloyalty ensured the failure of this effort, though the two kinds of creatures may still be encountered side by side in rare instances.

A chaos dragon speaks Draconic and either Celestial (chaotic good and some chaotic neutral dragons only) or Abyssal (chaotic evil and some chaotic neutral dragons only).

Chaos dragon

Combat

A chaos dragon opens combat with its *confusion* breath weapon, seeking to send its opponents into disarray. It uses its spell-like abilities against particularly vexing foes.

Young and older chaos dragons' natural weapons are treated as magic weapons for the purpose of overcoming damage reduction.

Breath Weapon (Su): A chaos dragon has two types of breath weapon, a line of energy and a cone of *confusion* gas. The energy type of its breath weapon is determined randomly each time it uses the breath weapon by rolling d%: 01–20 acid, 21–40 cold, 41–60 electricity, 61–80 fire, 81–100 sonic. Even the dragon itself doesn't know which type of energy it will emit before it actually breathes. Creatures within the cone of *confusion* gas must succeed on a Will save or be *confused* for 1d6 rounds plus 1 round per age category of the dragon.

Spell-Like Abilities: 3/day—*entropic shield, protection from law, chaos hammer;* 1/day—*cloak of chaos, dispel law, mind fog, mislead, word of chaos.*

ETHEREAL DRAGON

Dragon (Extraplanar)
Environment: Ethereal Plane
Organization: Solitary (1 dragon, any age), clutch (1d4+1 wyrmlings, very young, young, or juveniles or young adults), family (pair of mature adults and 1d4+1 offspring)
Challenge Rating: Wyrmling 3; very young 4; young 6; juvenile 7; young adult 9; adult 10; mature adult 13; old 15; very old 16; ancient 17; wyrm 18; great wyrm 19
Treasure: Triple standard
Alignment: Always neutral
Advancement: Wyrmling 5–6 HD; very young 8–9 HD; young 11–12 HD; juvenile 14–15 HD; young adult 17–18 HD; adult 20–21 HD; mature adult 23–24 HD; old 26–27 HD; very old 29–30 HD; ancient 32–33 HD; wyrm 35–36 HD; great wyrm 38+ HD
Level Adjustment: Wyrmling +2; very young +3; young +4, juvenile +4; others —

Ethereal dragons spend most of their lives floating through the Ethereal Plane, spying into the Material Plane for valuable treasure.

Ethereal dragons' natural coloration is a pearlescent brown-gray, which accounts for their nickname of "moonstone dragon." They have needlelike claws and teeth.

Ethereal dragons are naturally curious and inquisitive, and often spy on those "stuck" on the Material Plane. They are also greedy, and may come to covet the valuables carried by those they spy upon. In such cases, an ethereal dragon might visit the Material Plane only to appropriate such items, returning to its native Ethereal Plane as soon as possible.

Ethereal dragons speak Draconic.

Combat

Most ethereal dragons prefer escape over battle, heading either to the Ethereal Plane or the Material Plane to avoid conflict. If forced into a fight, or if the ethereal dragon feels combat is necessary, it uses its powers to frustrate its

Ethereal Dragons by Age

Age	Size	Hit Dice (hp)	Str	Dex	Con	Int	Wis	Cha	Base Attack/ Grapple	Attack	Fort Save	Ref Save	Will Save	Breath Weapon (DC)	Frightful Presence DC
Wyrmling	T	4d12+18 (44)	9	10	13	10	13	10	+4/-5	+5	+5	+4	+5	2d6 (13)	—
Very young	S	7d12+36 (82)	11	10	13	10	13	10	+7/+3	+8	+6	+5	+6	4d6 (14)	—
Young	M	10d12+45 (110)	13	10	15	12	15	12	+10/+11	+11	+9	+7	+9	6d6 (17)	—
Juvenile	M	13d12+72 (157)	15	10	15	12	15	12	+13/+15	+15	+10	+8	+10	8d6 (18)	—
Young adult	L	16d12+105 (209)	17	10	17	14	17	14	+16/+23	+18	+13	+10	+13	10d6 (21)	20
Adult	L	19d12+120 (244)	19	10	19	14	17	14	+19/+27	+22	+15	+11	+14	12d6 (23)	21
Mature adult	H	22d12+162 (305)	23	10	21	16	19	16	+22/+36	+26	+18	+13	+17	14d6 (26)	24
Old	H	25d12+210 (373)	25	10	21	16	19	16	+25/+40	+30	+19	+14	+18	16d6 (27)	25
Very old	H	28d12+264 (446)	27	10	23	18	21	18	+28/+44	+34	+22	+16	+21	18d6 (30)	28
Ancient	H	31d12+324 (526)	29	10	23	18	21	18	+31/+48	+38	+23	+17	+22	20d6 (31)	29
Wyrm	G	34d12+390 (611)	31	10	25	20	23	20	+34/+56	+40	+26	+19	+25	22d6 (34)	32
Great wyrm	G	37d12+462 (703)	33	10	27	20	23	20	+37/+60	+44	+28	+20	+26	24d6 (36)	33

Ethereal Dragon Abilities by Age

Age	Speed	Initiative	AC	Special Abilities	SR
Wyrmling	60 ft., fly 60 ft. (poor)	+0	15 (+2 size, +3 natural)	Immune to ether cyclones	—
Very young	60 ft., fly 60 ft. (poor)	+0	17 (+1 size, +6 natural)	Ethereal vision	—
Young	60 ft., fly 40 ft. (clumsy)	+0	19 (+9 natural)	Damage reduction 5/magic	—
Juvenile	60 ft., fly 40 ft. (clumsy)	+0	22 (+12 natural)	*Blink*	—
Young adult	60 ft., fly 40 ft. (clumsy)	+0	24 (–1 size, +15 natural)	Damage reduction 10/magic	20
Adult	60 ft., fly 40 ft. (clumsy)	+0	27 (–1 size, +18 natural)	*Dimensional anchor, ethereal jaunt*	21
Mature adult	60 ft., fly 40 ft. (clumsy)	+0	29 (–2 size, +21 natural)	Damage reduction 15/magic	24
Old	60 ft., fly 40 ft. (clumsy)	+0	32 (–2 size, +24 natural)	*Etherealness*	25
Very old	60 ft., fly 40 ft. (clumsy)	+0	35 (–2 size, +27 natural)	Damage reduction 20/magic and 5/cold iron	28
Ancient	60 ft., fly 40 ft. (clumsy)	+0	38 (–2 size, +30 natural)	Strike ethereal creatures	29
Wyrm	60 ft., fly 30 ft. (clumsy)	+0	39 (–4 size, +33 natural)	Damage reduction 20/magic and 10/cold iron	32
Great wyrm	60 ft., fly 30 ft. (clumsy)	+0	42 (–4 size, +36 natural)	Summon ethereal cyclone	33

foes. An adult or older ethereal dragon relies on *dimensional anchor* to trap opponents on one plane while it escapes to the other.

Young and older ethereal dragons' natural weapons are treated as magic weapons for the purpose of overcoming damage reduction.

Breath Weapon (Su): An ethereal dragon has one type of breath weapon, a cone of force. Like all force effects, this breath weapon affects ethereal creatures when the ethereal dragon is on the Material Plane.

Ethereal Vision (Ex): While on the Material Plane, a very young or older ethereal dragon can see ethereal creatures as if they were visible. While on the Ethereal Plane, an ethereal dragon can see normally out to the range of its darkvision (normally, creatures on the Ethereal Plane have a visual limit of 60 feet). Note that blindsense functions normally even on the Ethereal Plane, regardless of visual limits.

See Ethereal (Su): A very young or older ethereal dragon can see ethereal creatures as if they were visible.

Strike Ethereal Creatures (Ex): An ancient or older ethereal dragon can strike ethereal creatures as if they were material. This ability does not allow an ethereal dragon on the Ethereal Plane to affect creatures on the Material Plane.

Summon Ethereal Cyclone (Su): Once per day, a great wyrm ethereal dragon on the Ethereal Plane can summon an ethereal cyclone. This requires a full-round action, and the storm lasts for 1 minute. All creatures (except undead) within 120 feet of the ethereal dragon are affected as described in Chapter 5 of *Manual of the Planes*. (If you don't have access to *Manual of the Planes*, you can simply rule that each creature within the cyclone is thrown 1d10 miles in a random direction.) This power has no effect anywhere other than on the Ethereal Plane

Ethereal dragon

Spell-Like Abilities: 3/day—*dimensional anchor, ethereal jaunt**; 1/day—*blink, etherealness.*

*An ethereal dragon on the Ethereal Plane can instead use this spell-like ability to become material, with the same duration as normal for the spell.

Skills: An ethereal dragon has a +8 racial bonus on Hide checks when on the Ethereal Plane.

HOWLING DRAGON

Dragon (Extraplanar)

Environment: Windswept Depths of Pandemonium

Organization: Solitary (1 dragon, any age), clutch (1d4+1 wyrmlings, very young, young, or juveniles or young adults), family (pair of mature adults and 1d4+1 offspring)

Challenge Rating: Wyrmling 5; very young 6; young 8; juvenile 10; young adult 13; adult 14; mature adult 17; old 19; very old 20; ancient 21; wyrm 22; great wyrm 23

Treasure: Triple standard

Alignment: Always chaotic evil or chaotic neutral

Advancement: Wyrmling 10–11 HD; very young 13–14 HD; young 16–17 HD; juvenile 19–20 HD; young adult 22–23 HD; adult 25–26 HD; mature adult 28–29 HD; old 31–32 HD; very old 34–35 HD; ancient 37–38 HD; wyrm 40–41 HD; great wyrm 43+ HD

Level Adjustment: Wyrmling +4; very young +5; others —

Howling Dragons by Age

Age	Size	Hit Dice (hp)	Str	Dex	Con	Int	Wis	Cha	Base Attack/ Grapple	Attack	Fort Save	Ref Save	Will Save	Breath Weapon (DC)	Frightful Presence DC
Wyrmling	M	9d12+18 (76)	17	10	15	14	9	14	+9/+12	+12	+8	+6	+5	2d10 (16)	16
Very young	L	12d12+36 (114)	21	10	17	14	9	14	+12/+21	+16	+11	+8	+7	4d10 (19)	18
Young	L	15d12+45 (142)	25	10	17	16	11	16	+15/+26	+21	+12	+9	+9	6d10 (20)	20
Juvenile	L	18d12+72 (189)	29	10	19	18	13	18	+18/+31	+26	+15	+11	+12	8d10 (23)	23
Young adult	H	21d12+105 (241)	31	10	21	18	13	18	+21/+39	+29	+17	+12	+13	10d10 (25)	24
Adult	H	24d12+120 (276)	33	10	21	20	15	20	+24/+43	+33	+19	+14	+16	12d10 (27)	27
Mature adult	H	27d12+162 (337)	35	10	23	20	15	20	+27/+47	+37	+21	+15	+17	14d10 (29)	28
Old	G	30d12+210 (405)	39	10	25	22	17	22	+30/+56	+40	+24	+17	+20	16d10 (32)	31
Very old	G	33d12+264 (478)	41	10	27	24	19	24	+33/+60	+44	+26	+18	+22	18d10 (34)	33
Ancient	G	36d12+324 (558)	43	10	29	26	21	26	+36/+64	+48	+29	+20	+25	20d10 (37)	36
Wyrm	C	39d12+390 (643)	45	10	31	28	23	28	+39/+72	+48	+31	+21	+27	22d10 (39)	38
Great wyrm	C	42d12+462 (735)	47	10	33	30	25	30	+42/+76	+52	+34	+23	+30	24d10 (42)	41

Howling Dragon Abilities by Age

Age	Speed	Initiative	AC	Special Abilities	SR
Wyrmling	60 ft., fly 150 ft. (poor)	+0	18 (+8 natural)	Immunity to sonic	15
Very young	60 ft., fly 150 ft. (poor)	+0	20 (–1 size, +11 natural)	*Shatter, sound burst*	18
Young	60 ft., fly 150 ft. (poor)	+0	23 (–1 size, +14 natural)	Damage reduction 5/magic	20
Juvenile	60 ft., fly 150 ft. (poor)	+0	26 (–1 size, +17 natural)	*Gust of wind, Tasha's hideous laughter*	22
Young adult	60 ft., fly 150 ft. (poor)	+0	28 (–2 size, +20 natural)	Damage reduction 10/magic	24
Adult	60 ft., fly 150 ft. (poor)	+0	31 (–2 size, +23 natural)	*Confusion, wind wall*	26
Mature adult	60 ft., fly 150 ft. (poor)	+0	34 (–2 size, +26 natural)	Damage reduction 15/magic	28
Old	60 ft., fly 200 ft. (clumsy)	+0	35 (–4 size, +29 natural)	*Phantasmal killer, shout*	30
Very old	60 ft., fly 200 ft. (clumsy)	+0	38 (–4 size, +32 natural)	Damage reduction 20/magic and 5/law	32
Ancient	60 ft., fly 200 ft. (clumsy)	+0	41 (–4 size, +35 natural)	*Insanity, whirlwind*	33
Wyrm	60 ft., fly 200 ft. (clumsy)	+0	40 (–8 size, +38 natural)	Damage reduction 20/magic and 10/law	35
Great wyrm	60 ft., fly 200 ft. (clumsy)	+0	43 (–8 size, +41 natural)	*Symbol of insanity, weird*	36

Native to the windswept plane of Pandemonium, howling dragons are brilliant, scheming, and quite insane.

A howling dragon is long and slender, with short, thin legs and narrow wings. Long spines form a frill behind its head, and twin clusters of similar spines sprout from its shoulders. Its scales are mottled purple and black, darkening as the dragon ages. Its yellow eyes are large and feral-looking, with tiny pupils.

Howling dragons make their lairs in isolated caverns amid the twisting tunnels of their native plane. When they find their way to the Material Plane, they seek out similar terrain, and are thus usually encountered far underground. They roam widely in the territory surrounding their lair, exploring every narrow crevice and tunnel.

Howling dragons feed on any creatures they can catch—living, undead, or even construct. They enjoy the sensation of biting into a still-moving morsel.

Howling dragon

Combat

Howling dragons attack with primal ferocity, battering their foes with every power at their disposal. They breathe as often as possible, switching between breath forms apparently at random.

Young and older howling dragons' natural weapons are treated as magic weapons for the purpose of overcoming damage reduction.

Breath Weapon (Su): A howling dragon has two types of breath weapon, a cone of howling sound that deals sonic damage, or a cone of maddening wails. Creatures within the area of the maddening wails effect must succeed on a Fortitude save or take 1 point of Wisdom damage per age category of the dragon. On the plane of Pandemonium, where screaming winds restrict sound and hearing, both effects are limited to a 10-foot cone.

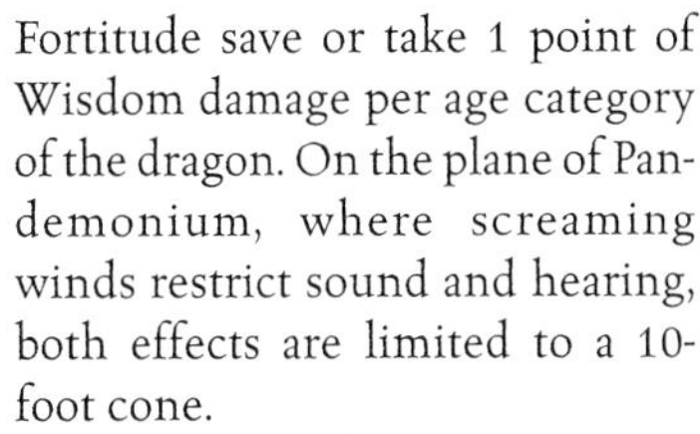

Spell-Like Abilities: 3/day—*Tasha's hideous laughter, wind wall;* 1/day—*confusion, gust of wind, insanity, phantasmal killer, shatter, shout, sound burst, symbol of insanity, weird, whirlwind.*

OCEANUS DRAGON

Dragon (Aquatic, Extraplanar)

Environment: Any Upper Plane

Organization: Solitary (1 dragon, any age), clutch (1d4+1 wyrmlings, very young, young, or juveniles or young adults), family (pair of mature adults and 1d4+1 offspring)

Challenge Rating: Wyrmling 4; very young 5; young 6; juvenile 9; young adult 12; adult 13; mature adult 16; old 18; very old 19; ancient 20; wyrm 21; great wyrm 22

Treasure: Triple standard

Alignment: Always neutral good

Advancement: Wyrmling 8–9 HD; very young 11–12 HD; young 14–15 HD; juvenile 17–18 HD; young adult 20–21 HD; adult 23–24 HD; mature adult 26–27 HD; old 29–30 HD; very old 32–33 HD; ancient 35–36 HD; wyrm 38–39 HD; great wyrm 41+ HD

Level Adjustment: Wyrmling +4; very young +4; young +5; others —

The Oceanus dragon protects travelers along the River Oceanus, which connects the Upper Planes in the same manner that the River Styx links the Lower Planes, while

Oceanus Dragons by Age

Age	Size	Hit Dice (hp)	Str	Dex	Con	Int	Wis	Cha	Base Attack/ Grapple	Attack	Fort Save	Ref Save	Will Save	Breath Weapon (DC)	Frightful Presence DC
Wyrmling	S	7d12+14 (60)	15	10	15	14	11	14	+7/+5	+10	+7	+5	+5	2d8 (15)	—
Very young	M	10d12+30 (95)	17	10	17	14	11	14	+10/+13	+13	+10	+7	+7	4d8 (18)	—
Young	M	13d12+39 (124)	19	10	17	16	13	16	+13/+17	+17	+11	+8	+9	6d8 (19)	—
Juvenile	L	16d12+64 (168)	21	10	19	18	15	18	+16/+25	+20	+14	+10	+12	8d8 (22)	—
Young adult	L	19d12+95 (219)	25	10	21	18	17	18	+19/+30	+25	+16	+11	+14	10d8 (24)	23
Adult	H	22d12+132 (275)	29	10	23	20	17	20	+22/+39	+29	+19	+13	+16	12d8 (27)	26
Mature adult	H	25d12+150 (313)	31	10	23	20	19	20	+25/+43	+33	+20	+14	+18	14d8 (28)	27
Old	H	28d12+196 (378)	33	10	25	22	19	22	+28/+47	+37	+23	+16	+20	16d8 (31)	30
Very old	H	31d12+217 (419)	35	10	25	24	21	24	+31/+51	+41	+24	+17	+22	18d8 (32)	32
Ancient	G	34d12+272 (493)	39	10	27	26	23	26	+34/+60	+44	+27	+19	+25	20d8 (35)	35
Wyrm	G	37d12+370 (611)	41	10	31	28	25	28	+37/+64	+48	+30	+20	+27	22d8 (38)	37
Great wyrm	C	40d12+440 (700)	45	10	33	30	27	30	+40/+73	+49	+33	+22	+30	24d8 (41)	40

jealously guarding its domain against evil creatures of all kinds.

Oceanus dragons appear much like great winged eels, with relatively short limbs ending in webbed fingers. Though capable of flight, most Oceanus dragons prefer life in the water to that in the air.

The typical lair of an Oceanus dragon is a hidden cave, either along a riverbank or completely underwater. Most Oceanus dragons spend little time in their lairs, instead patrolling a stretch of river in search of good-aligned creatures in need of assistance or evil creatures in need of punishment.

Oceanus dragons speak Celestial, Draconic, and Aquan.

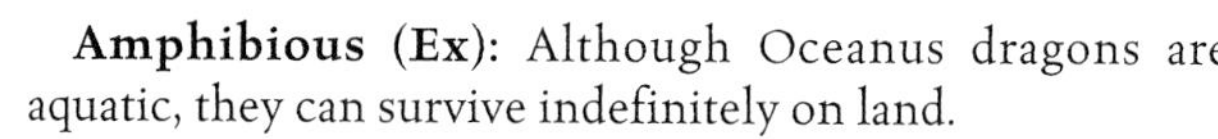

Oceanus dragon

Combat

Oceanus dragons prefer to end fights quickly, using their tranquility breath weapon and spell-like abilities to neutralize foes. However, they aren't afraid to go toe-to-toe with particularly resistant opponents, using their lightning breath weapon, smite evil ability, and prodigious melee attacks to make short work of their enemies.

Young and older Oceanus dragons' natural weapons are treated as magic weapons for the purpose of overcoming damage reduction.

Breath Weapon (Su): An Oceanus dragon has two types of breath weapon, a line of lightning or a cone of tranquility gas. Creatures within the cone must succeed on a Will save or become dazed for 1d6 rounds plus 1 round per age category of the dragon. Both breath weapons function normally underwater.

Smite Evil (Su): Once per day an Oceanus dragon can make a normal attack to deal extra damage equal to its HD total against an evil foe.

Spell-Like Abilities: At will—*detect evil;* 3/day—*control water, holy smite, water breathing;* 1/day—*control winds, dispel evil, holy word.*

Amphibious (Ex): Although Oceanus dragons are aquatic, they can survive indefinitely on land.

Water Breathing (Ex): An Oceanus dragon can breathe underwater indefinitely and can freely use its breath weapon, spell-like abilities, and other abilities while submerged.

PYROCLASTIC DRAGON

Dragon (Extraplanar)

Environment: Bleak Eternity of Gehenna

Organization: Solitary (1 dragon, any age), clutch (1d4+1 wyrmlings, very young, young, or juveniles or young adults), family (pair of mature adults and 1d4+1 offspring)

Challenge Rating: Wyrmling 4; very young 5; young 6; juvenile 9; young adult 12; adult 13; mature adult 16; old 18; very old 19; ancient 20; wyrm 21; great wyrm 22

Oceanus Dragon Abilities by Age

Age	Speed	Initiative	AC	Special Abilities	SR
Wyrmling	40 ft., fly 100 ft. (average), swim 60 ft.	+0	18 (+1 size, +7 natural)	Amphibious, immunity to electricity	—
Very young	40 ft., fly 100 ft. (poor), swim 60 ft.	+0	20 (+10 natural)	*Detect evil*	—
Young	40 ft., fly 100 ft. (poor), swim 60 ft.	+0	23 (+13 natural)	Damage reduction 5/magic	—
Juvenile	40 ft., fly 100 ft. (poor), swim 60 ft.	+0	25 (–1 size, +16 natural)	*Control water*	—
Young adult	40 ft., fly 100 ft. (poor), swim 60 ft.	+0	28 (–1 size, +19 natural)	Damage reduction 10/magic	23
Adult	40 ft., fly 150 ft. (poor), swim 90 ft.	+0	30 (–2 size, +22 natural)	Smite evil	26
Mature adult	40 ft., fly 150 ft. (poor), swim 90 ft.	+0	33 (–2 size, +25 natural)	Damage reduction 15/magic	27
Old	40 ft., fly 150 ft. (poor), swim 90 ft.	+0	36 (–2 size, +28 natural)	*Holy smite*	30
Very old	40 ft., fly 150 ft. (poor), swim 90 ft.	+0	39 (–2 size, +31 natural)	Damage reduction 20/magic and 5/evil	32
Ancient	40 ft., fly 150 ft. (clumsy), swim 90 ft.	+0	40 (–4 size, +34 natural)	*Control winds, dispel evil*	35
Wyrm	40 ft., fly 150 ft. (clumsy), swim 90 ft.	+0	43 (–4 size, +37 natural)	Damage reduction 20/magic and 10/evil	37
Great wyrm	40 ft., fly 150 ft. (clumsy), swim 60 ft.	+0	42 (–8 size, +40 natural)	*Holy word*	40

Pyroclastic dragon

Illus. by J. Jarvis

Treasure: Triple standard
Alignment: Always lawful evil or neutral evil
Advancement: Wyrmling 8–9 HD; very young 11–12 HD; young 14–15 HD; juvenile 17–18 HD; young adult 20–21 HD; adult 23–24 HD; mature adult 26–27 HD; old 29–30 HD; very old 32–33 HD; ancient 35–36 HD; wyrm 38–39 HD; great wyrm 41+ HD
Level Adjustment: Wyrmling +4; very young +5; young +6; others —

Pyroclastic dragons are creatures of elemental fury, embodying the forces of fire, earth, and rumbling

Pyroclastic Dragons by Age

Age	Size	Hit Dice (hp)	Str	Dex	Con	Int	Wis	Cha	Base Attack/ Grapple	Attack	Fort Save	Ref Save	Will Save	Breath Weapon (DC)	Frightful Presence DC
Wyrmling	M	7d12+14 (59)	17	10	15	10	11	10	+7/+10	+10	+7	+5	+5	2d6 (15)	13
Very young	L	10d12+30 (95)	21	10	17	10	11	10	+10/+19	+14	+10	+7	+7	4d6 (18)	15
Young	L	13d12+39 (123)	25	10	17	12	13	12	+13/+24	+19	+11	+8	+9	6d6 (19)	17
Juvenile	L	16d12+64 (168)	29	10	19	12	13	12	+16/+29	+24	+14	+10	+11	8d6 (22)	19
Young adult	H	19d12+95 (218)	31	10	21	14	15	14	+19/+37	+27	+16	+11	+13	10d6 (24)	21
Adult	H	22d12+110 (253)	33	10	21	14	15	14	+22/+41	+31	+18	+13	+15	12d6 (26)	23
Mature adult	H	25d12+150 (312)	33	10	23	16	17	16	+25/+44	+34	+20	+14	+17	14d6 (28)	25
Old	G	28d12+196 (378)	35	10	25	16	17	16	+28/+52	+36	+23	+16	+19	16d6 (31)	27
Very old	G	31d12+248 (449)	37	10	27	18	19	18	+31/+56	+40	+25	+17	+21	18d6 (33)	29
Ancient	G	34d12+306 (527)	39	10	29	18	19	18	+34/+60	+44	+28	+19	+23	20d6 (36)	31
Wyrm	G	37d12+370 (610)	41	10	31	20	21	20	+37/+64	+48	+30	+20	+25	22d6 (38)	33
Great wyrm	C	40d12+400 (660)	45	10	31	20	21	20	+40/+73	+49	+32	+22	+27	24d6 (40)	35

Pyroclastic Dragon Abilities by Age

Age	Speed	Initiative	AC	Special Abilities	SR
Wyrmling	60 ft., fly 100 ft. (poor), climb 40 ft., burrow 45 ft.	+0	16 (+6 natural)	Immunity to fire and sonic	14
Very young	60 ft., fly 100 (poor), climb 40 ft., burrow 45 ft.	+0	18 (–1 size, +9 natural)	*Pyrotechnics, sound burst*	15
Young	60 ft., fly 100 (poor), climb 40 ft., burrow 45 ft.	+0	21 (–1 size, +12 natural)	Damage reduction 5/magic	17
Juvenile	60 ft., fly 100 (poor), climb 40 ft., burrow 45 ft.	+0	24 (–1 size, +15 natural)	*Produce flame, shatter*	20
Young adult	60 ft., fly 100 (poor), climb 40 ft., burrow 45 ft.	+0	26 (–2 size, +18 natural)	Damage reduction 10/magic	22
Adult	60 ft., fly 100 (poor), climb 40 ft., burrow 45 ft.	+0	29 (–2 size, +21 natural)	*Shout, wall of fire*	24
Mature adult	60 ft., fly 100 (poor), climb 40 ft., burrow 45 ft.	+0	32 (–2 size, +24 natural)	Damage reduction 15/magic	26
Old	60 ft., fly 150 (clumsy), climb 40 ft., burrow 45 ft.	+0	33 (–4 size, +27 natural)	*Fire storm, wall of stone*	28
Very old	60 ft., fly 150 (clumsy), climb 40 ft., burrow 45 ft.	+0	36 (–4 size, +30 natural)	Damage reduction 20/magic and 5/good	29
Ancient	60 ft., fly 150 (clumsy), climb 40 ft., burrow 45 ft.	+0	39 (–4 size, +33 natural)	*Incendiary cloud, power word stun*	31
Wyrm	60 ft., fly 150 (clumsy), climb 40 ft., burrow 45 ft.	+0	42 (–4 size, +36 natural)	Damage reduction 20/magic and 10/good	32
Great wyrm	60 ft., fly 150 (clumsy), climb 40 ft., burrow 45 ft.	+0	41 (–8 size, +39 natural)	*Meteor swarm*	34

thunder that move earth and shape continents. They are native to the Bleak Eternity of Gehenna, an infinite plane of volcanic earthbergs and infernal lava.

A pyroclastic dragon is solidly built and powerfully muscled, conveying a sense of immovability. Its scales resemble fractured obsidian and glowing magma, forming a mottled pattern of reds, oranges, blacks, and grays over its entire body. Its large wings seem almost to be made of ash, but despite their flimsy appearance they are quite capable of bearing the dragon's great weight aloft.

Pyroclastic dragons enjoy swimming through magma, but they make their lairs in caves carved out of volcanic rock. When they venture to the Material Plane, they live only in volcanic regions.

These dragons enjoy the taste of meat but can also subsist on a purely mineral diet.

Combat

Pyroclastic dragons have all the subtlety of a volcanic eruption—they may simmer and hiss for a time, but when they erupt at last their fury is unmatched.

Young and older pyroclastic dragons' natural weapons are treated as magic weapons for the purpose of overcoming damage reduction.

Breath Weapon (Su): A pyroclastic dragon has two types of breath weapon, a cone of superheated ash accompanied by crushing waves of sonic force (dealing half fire damage and half sonic damage) or a disintegrating line. Creatures within the area of the line must succeed on a Fortitude save or crumble to ash. (Creatures that successfully save do not take any damage.)

Spell-Like Abilities: 3/day—*produce flame, sound burst;* 1/day—*fire storm, incendiary cloud, meteor swarm, power word, stun, pyrotechnics, shatter, shout, wall of fire, wall of stone.*

Radiant Dragons by Age

Age	Size	Hit Dice (hp)	Str	Dex	Con	Int	Wis	Cha	Base Attack/ Grapple	Attack	Fort Save	Ref Save	Will Save	Breath Weapon (DC)	Frightful Presence DC
Wyrmling	M	9d12+18 (76)	17	14	15	14	17	16	+9/+12	+12	+8	+8	+9	2d10 (16)	—
Very young	L	12d12+36 (114)	21	12	17	14	19	16	+12/+21	+16	+11	+9	+12	4d10 (19)	—
Young	L	15d12+45 (142)	25	12	17	16	19	18	+15/+26	+21	+12	+10	+13	6d10 (20)	—
Juvenile	L	18d12+72 (189)	27	12	19	18	21	20	+18/+30	+25	+15	+12	+16	8d10 (23)	—
Young adult	H	21d12+105 (241)	31	12	21	18	21	20	+21/+39	+29	+17	+13	+17	10d10 (25)	25
Adult	H	24d12+120 (276)	33	12	21	20	23	22	+24/+43	+33	+19	+15	+20	12d10 (27)	28
Mature adult	H	27d12+162 (337)	35	12	23	20	23	22	+27/+47	+37	+21	+16	+21	14d10 (29)	29
Old	G	30d12+210 (405)	39	12	25	22	25	24	+30/+56	+40	+24	+18	+24	16d10 (32)	32
Very old	G	33d12+264 (478)	41	12	27	24	27	26	+33/+60	+44	+26	+19	+26	18d10 (34)	34
Ancient	G	36d12+324 (558)	43	10	29	26	29	28	+36/+64	+48	+29	+20	+29	20d10 (37)	37
Wyrm	C	39d12+390 (643)	47	10	31	28	31	30	+39/+73	+49	+31	+21	+31	22d10 (39)	39
Great wyrm	C	42d12+462 (735)	49	10	33	30	33	32	+42/+77	+53	+34	+23	+34	24d10 (42)	42

RADIANT DRAGON

Dragon (Extraplanar)
Environment: Seven Mounting Heavens of Celestia
Organization: Solitary (1 dragon, any age), clutch (1d4+1 wyrmlings, very young, young, or juveniles or young adults), family (pair of mature adults and 1d4+1 offspring)
Challenge Rating: Wyrmling 5; very young 6; young 8; juvenile 10; young adult 13; adult 14; mature adult 17; old 19; very old 20; ancient 21; wyrm 22; great wyrm 23
Treasure: Triple standard
Alignment: Always lawful good
Advancement: Wyrmling 10–11 HD; very young 13–14 HD; young 16–17 HD; juvenile 19–20 HD; young adult 22–23 HD; adult 25–26 HD; mature adult 28–29 HD; old 31–32 HD; very old 34–35 HD; ancient 37–38 HD; wyrm 40–41 HD; great wyrm 43+ HD
Level Adjustment: Wyrmling +4; very young +5; others —

Radiant dragons are simultaneously wonderful and terrible, awesome in their righteousness and fearsome in their dedication to destroying evil.

Radiant dragon

A radiant dragon seems to shine with a heavenly glow, though it can douse this brightness as desired. If you can bear to look upon its grandeur, you can make out that its perfectly shaped scales glisten like molten white gold. Its proud, regal bearing is unmistakable, and its voice rings like heavenly thunder.

Radiant dragons prefer lairs that allow plenty of sunlight, and often place gems and other bright valuables in places where they catch and refract the light, creating marvelous displays of color and radiance. To creatures that display nobility and justice, they are the staunchest of allies, offering succor and healing to any in need. But when faced by those who foster chaos or evil, a radiant dragon becomes a furious whirl of color and light, destroying all who oppose it.

Radiant dragons speak Common, Celestial, and Draconic.

Combat

A radiant dragon relies on its blinding breath weapon primarily in situations when it wishes to defuse a difficult situation without causing unnecessary injury. Against true enemies it unleashes its

Illus. by R. Spencer

RADIANT DRAGON ABILITIES BY AGE

Age	Speed	Initiative	AC	Special Abilities	SR
Wyrmling	60 ft., fly 150 ft. (poor)	+2	19 (+5 natural, +1 deflection, +2 Dex)	Immunity to light effects	—
Very young	60 ft., fly 150 ft. (poor)	+1	20 (–1 size, +8 natural) +2 deflection, +1 Dex)	*Daylight*	—
Young	60 ft., fly 150 ft. (poor)	+1	24 (–1 size, +11 natural) +3 deflection, +1 Dex)	Damage reduction 5/magic	—
Juvenile	60 ft., fly 150 ft. (poor)	+1	28 (–1 size, +14 natural) +4 deflection, +1 Dex)	Dispel darkness	—
Young adult	60 ft., fly 150 ft. (poor)	+1	31 (–2 size, +17 natural) +5 deflection, +1 Dex)	Damage reduction 10/magic	25
Adult	60 ft., fly 150 ft. (poor)	+1	35 (–2 size, +20 natural) +6 deflection, +1 Dex)	*Searing light*	28
Mature adult	60 ft., fly 150 ft. (poor)	+1	39 (–2 size, +23 natural) +7 deflection, +1 Dex)	Damage reduction 15/magic	29
Old	60 ft., fly 200 ft. (clumsy)	+1	41 (–4 size, +26 natural) +8 deflection, +1 Dex)	Healing touch	32
Very old	60 ft., fly 200 ft. (clumsy)	+1	45 (–4 size, +29 natural) +9 deflection, +1 Dex)	Damage reduction 20/magic and 5/evil	34
Ancient	60 ft., fly 200 ft. (clumsy)	+0	49 (–4 size, +32 natural) +10 deflection, +1 Dex)	*Sunburst*	37
Wyrm	60 ft., fly 200 ft. (clumsy)	+0	49 (–8 size, +35 natural) +11 deflection, +1 Dex)	Damage reduction 20/magic and 10/evil	39
Great wyrm	60 ft., fly 200 ft. (clumsy)	+0	53 (–8 size, +38 natural) +12 deflection, +1 Dex)	*Prismatic sphere*	42

force breath and spell-like abilities, showing no mercy to those who do not deserve it.

Young and older radiant dragons' natural weapons are treated as magic weapons for the purpose of overcoming damage reduction.

Breath Weapon (Su): A radiant dragon has two types of breath weapons, a line of force or a cone of light. Creatures caught within the cone must make Fortitude saves or be blinded for 1d6 rounds plus 1 round per age category of the dragon. A successful save means the creature is merely dazzled for the same duration. Sightless creatures are immune to the cone of light breath weapon.

Dispel Darkness (Su): A juvenile or older radiant dragon automatically dispels any darkness spell (whose level is equal to or less than his age category) within 60 feet.

Healing Touch (Su): An old or older radiant dragon can generate any one of the following effects with its touch: *cure critical wounds, regenerate, remove blindness/deafness, remove disease, remove paralysis,* or *restoration.* It may use its healing touch a number of times per day equal to its age category.

Spell-Like Abilities: At will—*daylight;* 3/day—*searing light;* 1/day—*prismatic sphere, sunburst.*

RUST DRAGON

Dragon (Extraplanar)

Environment: Infernal Battlefield of Acheron

Organization: Solitary (1 dragon, any age), clutch (1d4+1 wyrmlings, very young, young, or juveniles or young adults), family (pair of mature adults and 1d4+1 offspring)

Challenge Rating: Wyrmling 3; very young 4; young 6; juvenile 8; young adult 11; adult 13; mature adult 15; old 16; very old 17; ancient 19; wyrm 20; great wyrm 22

Treasure: Triple standard

Alignment: Always lawful evil or lawful neutral

Advancement: Wyrmling 7–8 HD; very young 10–11 HD;

Rust Dragons by Age

Age	Size	Hit Dice (hp)	Str	Dex	Con	Int	Wis	Cha	Base Attack/ Grapple	Attack	Fort Save	Ref Save	Will Save	Breath Weapon (DC)	Frightful Presence DC
Wyrmling	S	6d12+6 (45)	13	10	13	6	11	6	+6/+3	+8	+6	+5	+5	2d4 (14)	—
Very young	M	9d12+18 (76)	15	10	15	6	11	6	+9/+11	+11	+8	+6	+6	4d4 (16)	12
Young	M	12d12+24 (102)	17	10	15	6	11	6	+12/+15	+15	+10	+8	+8	6d4 (18)	14
Juvenile	L	15d12+45 (142)	19	10	17	8	11	8	+15/+23	+18	+12	+9	+9	8d4 (20)	16
Young adult	L	18d12+72 (189)	23	10	19	8	11	8	+18/+28	+23	+15	+11	+11	10d4 (23)	18
Adult	H	21d12+105 (241)	27	10	21	10	11	10	+21/+37	+27	+17	+12	+12	12d4 (25)	20
Mature adult	H	24d12+120 (276)	29	10	21	12	13	12	+24/+41	+31	+19	+14	+15	14d4 (27)	23
Old	H	27d12+162 (337)	31	10	23	12	13	12	+27/+45	+35	+21	+15	+16	16d4 (29)	24
Very old	H	30d12+180 (375)	33	10	23	14	15	14	+33/+53	+39	+23	+17	+19	18d4 (31)	27
Ancient	G	33d12+231 (445)	35	10	25	14	15	14	+33/61	+41	+25	+18	+20	20d4 (33)	28
Wyrm	G	36d12+288 (522)	37	10	27	14	15	14	+36/+65	+45	+28	+20	+22	22d4 (36)	30
Great wyrm	G	39d12+312 (565)	39	10	27	18	19	18	+39/+69	+49	+29	+21	+25	24d4 (37)	33

Rust Dragon Abilities by Age

Age	Speed	Initiative	AC	Special Abilities	SR
Wyrmling	60 ft., fly 100 ft. (average), burrow 45 ft.	+0	17 (+1 size, +6 natural)	Metal resistance, rusting bite	13
Very young	60 ft., fly 150 ft. (poor), burrow 45 ft.	+0	19 (+9 natural)	—	14
Young	60 ft., fly 150 ft. (poor), burrow 45 ft.	+0	22 (+12 natural)	Damage reduction 5/magic	16
Juvenile	60 ft., fly 150 ft. (poor), burrow 45 ft.	+0	24 (–1 size, +15 natural)	—	18
Young adult	60ft., fly 150 ft. (poor), burrow 45 ft.	+0	27 (–1 size, +18 natural)	Damage reduction 10/magic	20
Adult	60 ft., fly 150 ft. (poor), burrow 45 ft.	+0	29 (–2 size, +21 natural)	*Wall of iron*	23
Mature adult	60 ft., fly 150 ft. (poor), burrow 45 ft.	+0	32 (–2 size, +24 natural)	Damage reduction 15/magic	25
Old	60 ft., fly 150 ft. (poor), burrow 45 ft.	+0	35 (–2 size, +27 natural)	*Acid fog*	27
Very old	60 ft., fly 150 ft. (poor), burrow 45 ft.	+0	38 (–2 size, +30 natural)	Damage reduction 20/magic and 5/chaotic	28
Ancient	60 ft., fly 200 ft. (clumsy), burrow 45 ft.	+0	39 (–4 size, +33 natural)	*Repel metal or stone*	30
Wyrm	60 ft., fly 200 ft. (clumsy), burrow 45 ft.	+0	42 (–4 size, +36 natural)	Damage reduction 20/magic and 10/chaotic, rusting scales	32
Great wyrm	60 ft., fly 200 ft. (clumsy), burrow 45 ft.	+0	45 (–4 size, +39 natural)	—	34

young 13–14 HD; juvenile 16–17 HD; young adult 19–20 HD; adult 22–23 HD; mature adult 25–26 HD; old 28–29 HD; very old 31–32 HD; ancient 34–35 HD; wyrm 37–38 HD; great wyrm 40+ HD
Level Adjustment: Wyrmling +4; very young +4; young +5; others —

Native to the Infernal Battlefield of Acheron, rust dragons are creatures of tarnished metal, embodying forces of decay and corruption. Some Material Plane sages posit some connection between these fiendish monstrosities and the relatively innocuous rust monster, but the rational mind correctly sees these claims as the ravings of deranged lunatics.

Rust dragons bear a strong resemblance to the metallic dragons of the Material Plane, but appear covered in rust, tarnish, or verdigris. Though some rust dragons resemble copper dragons and others silver or brass, individual rust dragons' abilities do not differ. Their scales appear pitted and lined with corrosive color, and the membranes of their wings are very thin and iridescent.

On their native plane of Acheron, rust dragons have an ample food supply in the endless iron cubes the size of continents floating in the void. When drawn to the Material Plane, rust dragons seek out veins of metal in underground caverns, making them particularly loathed by miners.

Rust dragons feed on corroded metal, but enjoy fresh meat (particularly vermin) to cleanse the palate between ores.

Rust dragon

Combat

Rust dragons are not the furious forces of nature that pyroclastic dragons are, nor are they violently insane like howling dragons. Rather, they are simply hungry, and they attack carefully with their goal clearly fixed in mind. They do not tolerate too much interference in pursuit of that goal, and readily break off from combat if a meal proves to be more trouble than it's worth.

Young and older rust dragons' natural weapons are treated as magic weapons for the purpose of overcoming damage reduction.

Breath Weapon (Su): A rust dragon has two breath weapons: a line of acid or a cone of reddish-brown liquid that instantly corrodes and destroys any metal it touches. Attended and magical metals receive Reflex saves to avoid this effect, but any metal is susceptible: iron, steel, silver, gold, even mithral and adamantine.

Metal Resistance (Ex): A rust dragon is resistant to attacks from metal weapons. Against weapons whose damage-dealing part is metal (a blade, metal point, arrowhead, or even mace head), a rust dragon has damage reduction equal to what a rust dragon two age categories older than itself has. Wyrm and great wyrm rust dragons have damage reduction 20/magic and 10/chaotic against metal weapons, and lesser weapons corrode when used against them (see Rusting Scales, below).

Rusting Bite (Ex): A rust dragon that makes a successful bite attack causes metal armor worn by the target creature to corrode, falling to pieces and becoming useless immediately. A dragon can also use its bite attack to target a weapon or other metal object, of course. The size of the object is immaterial—a full suit of armor rusts away as quickly as a sword. Magic metal items are allowed Reflex saves against a DC equal to the dragon's breath weapon save DC.

Rusting Scales (Ex): A metal weapon with less than a +5 enhancement bonus that hits a wyrm or great wyrm rust dragon corrodes and is destroyed immediately, with no saving throw. A +5 weapon deals damage normally, but then must succeed on a Reflex save (DC equal to the dragon's breath weapon save DC) or rust away.

Spell-Like Abilities: 3/day—*wall of iron*; 1/day—*acid fog*, *repel metal or stone*.

STYX DRAGON

Dragon (Aquatic, Extraplanar)
Environment: Any Lower Plane
Organization: Solitary (1 dragon, any age), clutch (1d4+1 wyrmlings, very young, young, or juveniles or young adults), family (pair of mature adults and 1d4+1 offspring)
Challenge Rating: Wyrmling 3; very young 4; young 6; juvenile 8; young adult 10; adult 12; mature adult 14; old 17; very old 18; ancient 19; wyrm 20; great wyrm 22
Treasure: Triple standard
Alignment: Always neutral evil
Advancement: Wyrmling 6–7 HD; very young 9–10 HD; young 12–13 HD; juvenile 15–16 HD; young adult 18–19 HD; adult 21–22 HD; mature adult 24–25 HD; old 27–28 HD; very old 30–31 HD; ancient 33–34 HD; wyrm 36–37 HD; great wyrm 39+ HD

Styx Dragons by Age

Age	Size	Hit Dice (hp)	Str	Dex	Con	Int	Wis	Cha	Base Attack/ Grapple	Attack	Fort Save	Ref Save	Will Save	Breath Weapon (DC)	Frightful Presence DC
Wyrmling	S	5d12+5 (37)	13	10	13	10	11	10	+5/+2	+7	+5	+4	+4	1d6 (13)	—
Very young	M	8 d12+16 (68)	15	10	15	12	13	12	+8/+10	+10	+8	+6	+7	2d6 (16)	15
Young	M	11 d12+22 (93)	17	10	15	12	13	12	+11/+14	+14	+9	+7	+8	3d6 (17)	16
Juvenile	L	14 d12+42 (133)	19	10	17	14	15	14	+14/+22	+17	+12	+9	+11	4d6 (20)	19
Young adult	L	17 d12+68 (178)	23	10	19	14	15	14	+17/+27	+22	+14	+10	+12	5d6 (22)	20
Adult	H	20 d12+100 (230)	27	10	21	16	17	16	+20/+36	+26	+17	+12	+15	6d6 (25)	23
Mature adult	H	23 d12+115 (264)	29	10	21	18	19	18	+23/+40	+30	+18	+13	+17	7d6 (26)	25
Old	H	26 d12+156 (325)	31	10	23	20	21	20	+26/+44	+34	+21	+15	+20	8d6 (29)	28
Very old	H	29 d12+174 (362)	33	10	23	22	23	22	+29/+48	+38	+22	+16	+22	9d6 (30)	30
Ancient	G	32 d12+224 (432)	35	10	25	24	25	24	+32/+56	+40	+25	+18	+25	10d6 (33)	33
Wyrm	G	35 d12+280 (507)	37	10	27	24	25	24	+35/+60	+44	+27	+19	+26	11d6 (35)	34
Great wyrm	G	38 d12+304 (551)	39	10	27	26	27	26	+38/+64	+48	+29	+21	+29	12d6 (37)	37

Level Adjustment: Wyrmling +5; very young +5; young +5; juvenile +6; others —

Also known as shadowdrakes or darkwyrms, Styx dragons haunt the putrid waters of the River Styx throughout its nearly infinite length. One of the few creatures immune to the harmful effects of the river, Styx dragons swim with impunity across the top layers of all the Lower Planes, feasting on fiends and any other creature they can find and catch.

A Styx dragon has a long, serpentine body with tiny, flipperlike claws that are useless on land and in combat. Its wings are too small to carry it aloft, but help to propel it through the water. Its tail splits into two long, bladed whips that it can use to slash and grab its prey. A Styx dragon's scales are slimy and range from dark brown to rusty red in color. Its eyes glow with a lurid yellow light.

Styx dragons make their lairs by burrowing into the mud on the banks of the Styx. They do not like to leave their native plane, but if one is forcibly brought to the Material Plane, it will thrive in fetid water.

Styx dragons normally subsist on the flesh of fiends, but enjoy eating any meat—particularly rotting carrion.

Styx dragon

Combat

A Styx dragon's physical attacks are limited: It attacks with the twin blades of its tail instead of claws, it cannot use its wings effectively, and it does not gain tail slap attacks in addition to its tail blades. Its tail blades deal damage as if the dragon were one size category larger than actual, however, as does its tail sweep.

Young and older Styx dragons' natural weapons are treated as magic weapons for the purpose of overcoming damage reduction.

Breath Weapon (Su): A Styx dragon has two types of breath weapon, a line of acid that persists for 3 rounds (dealing half damage on the second round and one-quarter damage on the third round), or a cone of stupefying gas. Creatures within the cone must succeed on a Fortitude save or take 1 point of Intelligence damage per age category of the dragon.

Amphibious (Ex): Although Styx dragons are aquatic, they can survive indefinitely on land.

Constrict (Ex): With a successful grapple check, a Styx dragon can crush a grabbed opponent, dealing twice its tail blade damage as bludgeoning damage.

Disease (Ex): Any creature hit by a Styx dragon's bite or tail attack must succeed on a Fortitude save (DC equal to that of the dragon's breath weapon save DC) or contract Stygian wasting. The symptoms of the disease include flesh rotting away and hair falling out. The incubation period is 1 day, and the disease deals 1d6 points of Charisma damage. A victim must make three successful Fortitude saves in a row to recover from Stygian wasting (see Disease, page 292 of the *Dungeon Master's Guide*).

Improved Grab (Ex): To use this ability, a Styx dragon must hit a creature that is at least one size category

Styx Dragon Abilities by Age

Age	Speed	Initiative	AC	Special Abilities	SR
Wyrmling	60 ft., swim 60 ft., burrow 20 ft.	+0	15 (+1 size, +4 natural)	Amphibious, constrict, improved grab, immunity to poison and disease, Styx adaptation	13
Very young	60 ft., swim 60 ft., burrow 20 ft.	+0	17 (+7 natural)	—	14
Young	60 ft., swim 60 ft., burrow 20 ft.	+0	20 (+10 natural)	Damage reduction 5/magic	15
Juvenile	60 ft., swim 60 ft., burrow 20 ft.	+0	22 (–1 size, +13 natural)	*Curse water, fog cloud*	18
Young adult	60 ft., swim 60 ft., burrow 20 ft.	+0	25 (–1 size, +16 natural)	Damage reduction 10/magic	20
Adult	60 ft., swim 60 ft., burrow 20 ft.	+0	27 (–2 size, +19 natural)	*Deeper darkness, stinking cloud*	22
Mature adult	60 ft., swim 60 ft., burrow 20 ft.	+0	30 (–2 size, +22 natural)	Damage reduction 15/magic	25
Old	60 ft., swim 60 ft., burrow 20 ft.	+0	33 (–2 size, +25 natural)	*Hold monster, mind fog*	27
Very old	60 ft., swim 60 ft., burrow 20 ft.	+0	36 (–2 size, +28 natural)	Damage reduction 20/magic and 5/good	28
Ancient	60 ft., swim 60 ft., burrow 20 ft.	+0	37 (–4 size, +31 natural)	*Control water, feeblemind*	30
Wyrm	60 ft., swim 60 ft., burrow 20 ft.	+0	40 (–4 size, +34 natural)	Damage reduction 20/magic and 10/good	31
Great wyrm	60 ft., swim 60 ft., burrow 20 ft.	+0	43 (–4 size, +37 natural)	*Horrid wilting, summon monster VIII*	33

smaller than itself with its tail blade attack. If it gets a hold, it can constrict in the same round. It can also attempt to start a grapple as a free action without provoking an attack of opportunity.

Spell-Like Abilities: At will—*curse water;* 3/day—*control water, deeper darkness, fog cloud;* 1/day—*feeblemind, hold monster, horrid wilting, mind fog, stinking cloud.*

Styx Adaptation (Ex): Styx dragons are immune to the harmful effects of the River Styx, and they can breathe water.

***Summon Monster VIII* (Sp):** Once per day, a great wyrm Styx dragon can summon a fiendish giant squid, 1d3 fiendish giant octopi or Large tojanidas, or 1d4+1 Large water elementals, Huge fiendish sharks, or fiendish giant crocodiles. Aside from the monsters available, this ability is identical to *summon monster* VIII. Caster level 15th.

TARTERIAN DRAGON

Dragon (Extraplanar)
Environment: Tarterian Depths of Carceri
Organization: Solitary (1 dragon, any age), clutch (1d4+1 wyrmlings, very young, young, or juveniles or young adults), family (pair of mature adults and 1d4+1 offspring)
Challenge Rating: Wyrmling 5; very young 6; young 8; juvenile 10; young adult 13; adult 14; mature adult 17; old 19; very old 20; ancient 21; wyrm 22; great wyrm 23
Treasure: Triple standard
Alignment: Always neutral evil or chaotic evil
Advancement: Wyrmling 9–10 HD; very young 12–13 HD; young 15–16 HD; juvenile 18–19 HD; young adult 21–22 HD; adult 24–25 HD; mature adult 27–28 HD; old 30–31 HD; very old 33–34 HD; ancient 36–37 HD; wyrm 39–40 HD; great wyrm 42+ HD

Tarterian Dragons by Age

Age	Size	Hit Dice (hp)	Str	Dex	Con	Int	Wis	Cha	Base Attack/ Grapple	Attack	Fort Save	Ref Save	Will Save	Breath Weapon (DC)	Frightful Presence DC
Wyrmling	M	8d12+16 (68)	17	10	15	14	15	14	+8/+11	+11	+8	+6	+8	2d8 (16)	16
Very young	L	11d12+33 (104)	21	10	17	14	15	14	+11/+20	+15	+10	+7	+9	4d8 (18)	17
Young	L	14d12+42 (133)	25	10	17	16	17	16	+14/+25	+20	+12	+9	+12	6d8 (20)	20
Juvenile	L	17d12+68 (178)	29	10	19	18	19	18	+17/+30	+25	+14	+10	+14	8d8 (22)	22
Young adult	H	20d12+100 (230)	31	10	21	18	19	18	+20/+38	+28	+17	+12	+16	10d8 (25)	24
Adult	H	23d12+115 (264)	33	10	21	20	21	20	+23/+42	+32	+18	+13	+18	12d8 (26)	26
Mature adult	H	26d12+156 (325)	35	10	23	20	21	20	+26/+46	+36	+21	+15	+20	14d8 (29)	28
Old	G	29d12+203 (391)	39	10	25	22	23	22	+29/+55	+39	+23	+16	+22	16d8 (31)	30
Very old	G	32d12+256 (464)	41	10	27	22	23	22	+32/+59	+43	+26	+18	+24	18d8 (34)	32
Ancient	G	35d12+315 (542)	43	10	29	24	25	24	+35/+63	+47	+28	+19	+26	20d8 (36)	34
Wyrm	C	38d12+380 (627)	45	10	31	26	27	26	+38/+71	+47	+31	+21	+29	22d8 (39)	37
Great wyrm	C	41d12+451 (717)	47	10	33	26	27	26	+41/+75	+51	+33	+22	+30	24d8 (41)	38

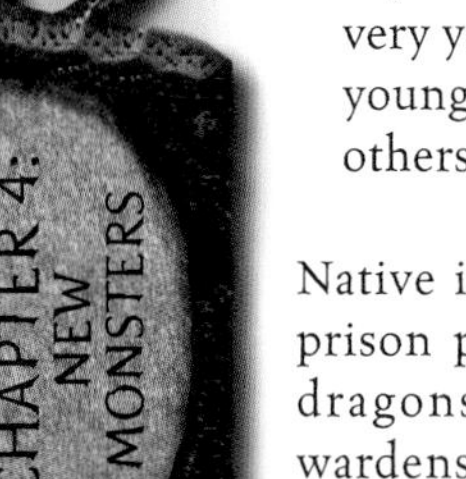

Tarterian dragon

Level Adjustment: Wyrmling +4; very young +5; young +6; others —

Native inhabitants of a prison plane, Tarterian dragons are at once wardens and prisoners themselves, preying on weaker denizens than themselves.

Tarterian dragons are skeletally gaunt, with leathery scales stretched tight over withered-looking flesh. Their wings have a tattered appearance, though they can fly fast and ably. Their teeth and claws are long and black, while their scales form a striped pattern of black, gray, and olive green. Ghostly green light flickers in their black eyes, and their faces seem to wear a perpetual sneering grin.

Tarterian dragons inhabit a wide range of habitats on their native plane of Carceri, from the steaming jungles of Cathrys (the second layer) to the cruel mountains of Colothys (the fourth). Similarly, when they make their way to the Material Plane they can dwell comfortably in a variety of locales, both above and under the ground. They delight in reproducing the jailhouse atmosphere of Carceri whenever they find themselves on the Material Plane.

Tarterian dragons are accustomed to a diet of fiendish flesh and condemned souls. They do not enjoy other food, but can live on literally anything.

Combat

Tarterian dragons use their spell-like abilities to divide and constrain their opponents, trying to face each one individually when possible. They use their gas breath weapon to weaken foes at the start of combat, then their force breath to take out the strongest foes.

Young and older Tarterian dragons' natural weapons are treated as magic weapons for the purpose of overcoming damage reduction.

Breath Weapon (Su): A Tarterian dragon has two types of breath weapon, a line of disruptive force or a cone of will-sapping gas. Creatures within the cone must succeed on a Will save or be affected by a *crushing despair* effect, taking a –2 penalty on saving throws, attack rolls, ability checks, skill checks, and weapon damage rolls for 1 round per age category of the dragon.

Force Resistance (Ex): Tarterian dragons have a +4 racial bonus on saving throws against force-based spells and effects.

Freedom of Movement (Su): Tarterian dragons can move and attack normally despite any magic that usually impedes movement, such as *hold monster*, paralysis effects, *solid fog*, *slow*, and *web* spells.

Strength of Will (Ex): Tarterian dragons have a +4 morale bonus on saving throws against charm and compulsion effects.

Spell-Like Abilities: 1/day—*forcecage, imprisonment, maze, Otiluke's resilient sphere.*

Tarterian Dragon Abilities by Age

Age	Speed	Initiative	AC	Special Abilities	SR
Wyrmling	60 ft., fly 150 ft. (poor)	+0	17 (+7 natural)	Force resistance, strength of will, freedom of movement	15
Very young	60 ft., fly 150 ft. (poor)	+0	19 (–1 size, +10 natural)		17
Young	60 ft., fly 150 ft. (poor)	+0	22 (–1 size, +13 natural)	Damage reduction 5/magic	19
Juvenile	60 ft., fly 150 ft. (poor)	+0	25 (–1 size, +16 natural)		21
Young adult	60 ft., fly 150 ft. (poor)	+0	27 (–2 size, +19 natural)	Damage reduction 10/magic	23
Adult	60 ft., fly 150 ft. (poor)	+0	30 (–2 size, +22 natural)	*Otiluke's resilient sphere*	25
Mature adult	60 ft., fly 150 ft. (poor)	+0	33 (–2 size, +25 natural)	Damage reduction 15/magic	27
Old	60 ft., fly 200 ft. (clumsy)	+0	34 (–4 size, +28 natural)	*Maze*	29
Very old	60 ft., fly 200 ft. (clumsy)	+0	37 (–4 size, +31 natural)	Damage reduction 20/magic and 5/good	30
Ancient	60 ft., fly 200 ft. (clumsy)	+0	40 (–4 size, +34 natural)	*Forcecage*	32
Wyrm	60 ft., fly 200 ft. (clumsy)	+0	39 (–8 size, +37 natural)	Damage reduction 20/magic and 10/good	33
Great wyrm	60 ft., fly 200 ft. (clumsy)	+0	42 (–8 size, +40 natural)	*Imprisonment*	35

Shadow Dragons by Age

Age	Size	Hit Dice (hp)	Str	Dex	Con	Int	Wis	Cha	Base Attack/ Grapple	Attack	Fort Save	Ref Save	Will Save	Breath Weapon (DC)	Frightful Presence DC
Wyrmling	T	4d12+4 (30)	11	10	13	14	14	15	+4/-4	+6	+5	+4	+6	1 (14)	—
Very young	S	7d12+7 (52)	13	10	13	16	16	17	+7/+4	+9	+6	+5	+8	1 (16)	—
Young	S	10d12+10 (75)	13	10	13	16	16	17	+10/+7	+12	+8	+7	+10	1 (18)	—
Juvenile	M	13d12+26 (110)	15	10	15	18	18	19	+13/+15	+15	+10	+8	+12	2 (20)	—
Young adult	M	16d12+32 (136)	17	10	15	18	18	19	+16/+19	+19	+12	+10	+14	2 (22)	22
Adult	L	19d12+57 (180)	19	10	17	20	20	21	+19/+27	+22	+14	+11	+16	3 (24)	24
Mature adult	L	22d12+88 (231)	23	10	19	20	20	21	+22/+32	+27	+17	+13	+18	4 (26)	26
Old	H	25d12+125 (287)	27	10	21	24	24	25	+25/+41	+31	+19	+14	+21	5 (29)	29
Very old	H	28d12+140 (322)	29	10	21	26	26	27	+28/+45	+35	+21	+16	+24	5 (32)	32
Ancient	H	31d12+186 (387)	31	10	23	28	28	29	+31/+49	+39	+22	+17	+26	6 (34)	34
Wyrm	G	34d12+238 (459)	33	10	25	30	30	31	+34/+57	+41	+26	+19	+29	7 (37)	37
Great wyrm	G	37d12+296 (536)	35	10	27	32	32	33	+37/+61	+45	+29	+21	+32	8 (39)	39

SHADOW DRAGON

Dragon
Environment: Underground
Organization: Wyrmling, very young, young, juvenile, and young adult: solitary or clutch (2–5); adult, mature adult, old, very old, ancient, wyrm, or great wyrm: solitary, pair, or family (1–2 and 2–5 offspring)
Challenge Rating: Wyrmling 3; very young 4; young 6; juvenile 8; young adult 11; adult 13; mature adult 16; old 18; very old 19; ancient 21; wyrm 22; great wyrm 24
Treasure: Triple standard
Alignment: Always chaotic evil
Advancement: Wyrmling 5–6 HD; very young 8–9 HD; young 11–12 HD; juvenile 14–15 HD; young adult 17–18 HD; adult 20–21 HD; mature adult 23–24 HD; old 26–27 HD; very old 29–30 HD; ancient 32–33 HD; wyrm 35–36 HD; great wyrm 38+ HD
Level Adjustment: Wyrmling +3; very young +3; young +3, juvenile +4; others —

Shadow dragon

Shadow dragons are sly and devious creatures with ties to the Plane of Shadow.

Shadow dragons have translucent scales and dark bodies, giving them an indistinct appearance; from a distance, they seem to be nothing but a foreboding mass of shadows.

COMBAT

Shadow dragons prefer to attack from hiding, employing their shadow blend ability. They use illusion spells to confuse and misdirect their foes.

Young adult and older shadow dragons' natural weapons are treated as magic weapons for purpose of overcoming damage reduction.

Breath Weapon (Su): A shadow dragon's breath weapon is a cone of billowing, smoky shadows with an energy drain effect. Creatures within the cone gain the number of negative levels indicated on the Shadow Dragons by Age table; the saving throw to remove the negative level is given on the table as well. A successful Reflex save (against the same DC) reduces the number of negative levels by half (round down).

Shadow Blend (Su): In any condition of illumination other than full daylight, a very young or older shadow dragon can disappear into the shadows, giving it total concealment. Artificial illumination, even a *light* or *continual flame* spell, does not negate this ability. A *daylight* spell, however, does.

Create Shadows (Su): Three times per day, a great wyrm shadow dragon can conjure a mass of leaping shadows with a radius of 100 yards and a duration of 1 hour (this is a creation effect). All normal and magical light sources are negated within this radius. All characters and creatures gain a +4 bonus on their Hide checks within the shadows, and can hide even if directly observed. Shadow dragons and other creatures with ties to the Plane of Shadow gain total concealment within the shadows, though they can move and attack normally. Their attacks gain a +2 bonus and deny their opponents any Dexterity bonus to AC, because they are considered invisible.

Shadow Dragon Abilities by Age

Age	Speed	Initiative	AC	Special Abilities	Caster Level	SR
Wyrmling	80 ft., fly 150 ft. (average)	+0	19 (+2 size, +7 natural)	Energy drain immunity	—	12
Very young	80 ft., fly 150 ft. (average)	+0	21 (+1 size, +10 natural)	Shadow blend	—	13
Young	80 ft., fly 150 ft. (average)	+0	24 (+1 size, +13 natural)	—	—	15
Juvenile	80 ft., fly 150 ft. (poor)	+0	26 (+16 natural)	*Mirror image*	1st	17
Young adult	80 ft., fly 150 ft. (poor)	+0	29 (+19 natural)	Damage reduction 5/magic	3rd	20
Adult	80 ft., fly 150 ft. (poor)	+0	31 (–1 size, +22 natural	*Dimension door*	5th	22
Mature adult	80 ft., fly 150 ft. (poor)	+0	34 (–1 size, +25 natural)	Damage reduction 10/magic	7th	25
Old	80 ft., fly 150 ft. (poor)	+0	36 (–2 size, +28 natural)	*Nondetection*	9th	27
Very old	80 ft., fly 150 ft. (poor)	+0	39 (–2 size, +31 natural)	Damage reduction 15/magic	11th	28
Ancient	80 ft., fly 150 ft. (poor)	+0	42 (–2 size, +34 natural)	*Shadow walk*	13th	30
Wyrm	80 ft., fly 150 ft. (clumsy)	+0	43 (–4 size, +37 natural)	Damage reduction 20/magic	15th	31
Great wyrm	80 ft., fly 150 ft. (clumsy)	+0	46 (–4 size, +40 natural)	Create shadows	17th	33

*Can also cast cleric spells and those from the Chaos, Evil, and Trickery domains as arcane spells.

Spell-Like Abilities: 3/day—*mirror image, nondetection;* 2/day—*dimension door;* 1/day—*shadow walk.*

SKELETAL DRAGON

Skeletal dragons are created via the *animate dead* spell and function as normal skeletons in most ways, though they retain a few of their draconic abilities and qualities even after death. Despite a skeletal dragon's loss of sentience, the pinpoints of red light smoldering in its eye sockets betray the spark of unlife that still exists.

Like typical skeletons, skeletal dragons do only what they are ordered to do. They can draw no conclusions of their own and take no initiative. Necromancers particularly prize skeletal dragons, because they make formidable guardians. They are sturdier than a typical skeleton of their size, and their added qualities strike terror into would-be intruders.

Powerful draconic spellcasters have even been known to animate the skeletons of their fallen rivals or, in the case of particularly vile dragons, family members who have passed away.

Skeletal black dragon

SAMPLE SKELETAL DRAGON

This example uses a mature adult black dragon as the base dragon.

Skeletal Mature Adult Black Dragon
Huge Undead
Hit Dice: 22d12+22 (165 hp)
Initiative: +4
Speed: 60 ft. (12 squares)
Armor Class: 12 (–2 size, +4 natural), touch 8, flat-footed 12
Base Attack/Grapple: +22/+38
Attack: Bite +28 melee (2d8+8)
Full Attack: Bite +28 melee (2d8+8) and 2 claws +23 melee (2d6+4) and 2 wings +23 melee (1d8+4) and tail slap +23 melee (2d6+12)
Space/Reach: 15 ft./10 ft. (15 ft. with bite)
Special Attacks: Frightful presence
Special Qualities: Blindsense 60 ft., damage reduction 5/bludgeoning, immunity to acid and cold, keen senses, spell resistance 21, undead traits
Saves: Fort +13, Ref +13, Will +13
Abilities: Str 27, Dex 10, Con —, Int —, Wis 10, Cha 14
Feats: Improved Initiative
Environment: Warm mountains
Organization: Any
Challenge Rating: 7
Treasure: None
Alignment: Always neutral
Advancement: 23–24 HD (Huge)
Level Adjustment: —

A skeletal black dragon takes on a new level of horror in undeath. Lizardfolk adepts and clerics often animate skeletal black dragons to protect their tribes.

Combat

A skeletal black dragon possesses none of the craftiness it had in life. It merely attacks as its master has ordered. Its blindsense and keen senses make it an excellent guardian.

Frightful Presence (Ex): This skeletal black dragon can unsettle foes within 210 feet with its mere presence, whenever it attacks, charges, or flies overhead. Creatures with 4 or fewer HD become panicked for 4d6 rounds, while those with 5 to 21 HD become shaken for 4d6 rounds. A DC 23 Will save negates the effect and makes the creature immune to that dragon's frightful presence for 24 hours.

Keen Senses (Ex): A skeletal dragon sees four times as well as a human in low-light conditions and twice as well in normal light.

CREATING A SKELETAL DRAGON

"Skeletal" is an acquired template that can be applied to any dragon (referred to hereafter as the base dragon). A skeletal dragon uses all the base dragon's statistics and special abilities except as noted here.

Size and Type: The creature's type changes to undead. Do not recalculate the creature's base attack bonus, saves, or skill points. Size is unchanged.

Hit Dice: The base dragon's Hit Dice remain the same, but it loses any Constitution bonus to its hit points (see Abilities, below). However, a skeletal dragon gains bonus hit points equal to its HD.

Speed: The creature retains its land speed, but loses fly and swim speeds. If it had a burrow or climb speed, it retains that as well.

Armor Class: Replace the base dragon's existing natural armor bonus to AC with a new natural armor bonus based on its size.

Size	Natural Armor
Up to Tiny	+0
Small	+1
Medium	+2
Large	+3
Huge	+4
Gargantuan	+6
Colossal	+10

Attacks: Same as the base dragon, except that skeletal dragons cannot make crush attacks.

Special Attacks: A skeletal dragon loses all supernatural and spell-like special attacks possessed by the base dragon. It retains any exceptional special attacks (such as frightful presence or improved grab).

Special Qualities: A skeletal dragon loses all supernatural and spell-like special qualities possessed by the base dragon. It retains any exceptional special qualities (such as immunities or blindsense). It loses any subtypes it had, though if the base dragon had any immunities based on its subtype (such as immunity to fire for the fire subtype), it keeps those immunities despite losing the subtype. It also gains additional special qualities as noted below.

Damage Reduction (Ex): Skeletal dragons have damage reduction 5/bludgeoning.

Immunity to Cold (Ex): Skeletal dragons have immunity to cold.

Undead Traits: A skeletal dragon is immune to mind-affecting effects, poison, magic sleep effects, paralysis, stunning, disease, death effects, and any effect that requires a Fortitude save unless it also works on objects or is harmless. It is not subject to critical hits, nonlethal damage, ability damage to its physical ability scores, ability drain, energy drain, fatigue, exhaustion, or death from massive damage. It cannot be raised, and resurrection works only if it is willing. It has darkvision out to 60 feet (unless the base dragon had a greater range).

Saves: As undead, skeletal dragons are immune to anything that requires a Fortitude save unless it affects objects.

Abilities: A skeletal dragon retains the base dragon's Strength, Dexterity, and Charisma scores. Being undead, a skeletal dragon has no Constitution score. It also has no Intelligence score. Its Wisdom score becomes 10.

Skills: A skeletal dragon loses all skill ranks and racial skill bonuses possessed by the base dragon.

Feats: A skeletal dragon loses all feats possessed by the base dragon. It gains Improved Initiative as a bonus feat.

Environment: Any.
Organization: Any.
Challenge Rating: Base dragon's CR × 1/2 (minimum 1).
Treasure: None.
Alignment: Always neutral.
Advancement: Up to +2 HD.
Level Adjustment: —.

SQUAMOUS SPEWER

Large Aberration
Hit Dice: 8d8+24 (60 hp)
Initiative: +1
Speed: 20 ft. (4 squares)
Armor Class: 22 (–1 size, +1 Dex, +12 natural), touch 10, flat-footed 21
Base Attack/Grapple: +6/+14
Attack: 1 bite +10 melee (1d10+4)
Full Attack: 6 bites +10 melee (1d10+4)
Space/Reach: 10 ft./5 ft.
Special Attacks: Breath weapon, roar
Special Qualities: Amorphous, blindsense 60 ft., darkvision 60 ft., immunity to magic sleep effects and paralysis, low-light vision, resistance to acid 10, cold 10, electricity 10, and fire 10
Saves: Fort +7, Ref +3, Will +9
Abilities: Str 19, Dex 13, Con 17, Int 10, Wis 16, Cha 16
Skills: Hide +12, Listen +14, Spot +18
Feats: Ability Focus (roar), Combat Reflexes, Great Fortitude
Environment: Underground
Organization: Solitary
Challenge Rating: 7
Treasure: Standard
Alignment: Usually neutral evil
Advancement: 9–15 HD (Huge); 16–24 HD (Gargantuan)
Level Adjustment: —

A squamous spewer is an evil, amorphous mass of scales, mouths, fangs, and reptilian eyes. Sages guess that it has some connection to the gibbering mouther, but it is more hideous and deadly than that creature.

A typical squamous spewer—if such a thing can be said to exist—has scales of many different colors and lusters, sometimes both chromatic and metallic in nature. It has no allegiance to dragons, and in fact, the two species generally despise one another.

Squamous spewers speak Draconic.

COMBAT

A squamous spewer prefers to hide from enemies until they are within range of its roar. After dispersing weaker foes, the creature uses its breath weapons until targets close within melee range (using Combat Reflexes if the opportunity presents itself).

Breath Weapon (Su): Despite its large number of mouths, a squamous spewer can only use one type of breath weapon in a given round, though it may spew it from up to three mouths simultaneously in up to three different areas. The energy type is determined randomly by rolling d% before each use: 01–25 acid, 26–50 cold, 51–75 electricity, 76–100 fire. The area of the breath weapon in any given round is either a 30-foot cone or a 60-foot line (50% chance of either). Regardless of the type of energy it uses or the area it affects, the breath weapon deals 3d6 points of damage (Reflex DC 17 half). Once a squamous spewer uses its breath weapon, it cannot use it again until 1d4 rounds have passed.

Some squamous spewers may have breath weapon varieties that differ from these options—the DM can select a breath weapon possessed by another type of dragon if he or she so wishes.

Roar (Ex): Three times per day, a squamous spewer can let loose a frightening roar from its many mouths. All creatures within a 60-foot-radius spread with fewer Hit Dice than the squamous spewer become panicked if they fail a DC 19 Fortitude save. Creatures with HD equal to or greater than the squamous spewer are shaken on a failed save rather than panicked.

Amorphous (Ex): Squamous spewers are not subject to critical hits. They have no clear front or back, so they cannot be flanked.

Blindsense (Ex): A squamous spewer's extraordinary powers of scent and echolocation allow it to pinpoint the location of any living creature within 60 feet.

Dragon Traits: Despite their aberrant nature, squamous spewers share certain traits with creatures of the dragon type, including darkvision out to 60 feet, immunity to paralysis and magic sleep effects, and low-light vision.

Skills: Thanks to its multiple eyes, a squamous spewer has a +4 racial bonus on Spot checks. Its natural camouflage gives it a +4 racial bonus on Hide checks.

Squamous spewer

Illus. by S. Tappin

STORM DRAKE

Gargantuan Dragon (Air)
Hit Dice: 30d12+210 (405 hp)
Initiative: +5
Speed: 60 ft. (12 squares), fly 200 ft. (poor); or fly 60 ft. (perfect)
Armor Class: 31 (–4 size, +1 Dex, +24 natural), touch 7, flat-footed 30
Base Attack/Grapple: +30/+54
Attack: Bite +42 melee (4d6+12)
Full Attack: Bite +42 melee (4d6+12) and 2 claws +37 melee (2d8+6) and tail slap +37 melee (2d8+18)
Space/Reach: 20 ft./15 ft.
Special Attacks: Breath weapon, snatch, spell-like abilities
Special Qualities: Darkvision 60 ft., gaseous form, immunity to magic sleep effects and paralysis, low-light vision, resistance to cold 30 and electricity 30
Saves: Fort +24, Ref +20, Will +21
Abilities: Str 35, Dex 13, Con 24, Int 15, Wis 19, Cha 20
Skills: Bluff +38, Concentration +40, Diplomacy +7, Hide +22, Intimidate +40, Knowledge (nature) +36, Listen +39, Spot +39, Tumble +34
Feats: Alertness, Blind-Fight, Cleave, Combat Reflexes, Dodge, Flyby Attack, Hover, Lightning Reflexes, Power Attack, Snatch, Wingover
Environment: Cold hills
Organization: Solitary or pair
Challenge Rating: 17
Treasure: Standard
Alignment: Always neutral
Advancement: 31–38 HD (Gargantuan); 39–45 HD (Colossal)
Level Adjustment: —

Also called cloud dragons or wind dragons, these enormous creatures live in the clouds themselves.

When the creature is at rest, a storm drake's scales have a pearlescent sheen. A happy cloud dragon shimmers with golden highlights, while an angered one turns dark gray, like a thundercloud. The drake's silver wings are nearly translucent.

A storm drake spends most of its life soaring through the clouds, enjoying weather in all its variable forms. It typically makes its lair on a misty mountain peak.

Storm drakes speak Draconic and Auran. Some also learn Common or Giant to converse with creatures living near their lair.

COMBAT

A storm drake picks its fights carefully. Assuming it is confident of victory, it begins by using its breath weapon to separate the combatants from one another, then softens up the remaining opponents with *call lightning*, *ice storm*, and *shout*. If it has time to prepare, it may use *control winds* or *control weather* to create a setting more conducive to its victory. It doesn't hesitate to flee if outmatched, using either gaseous form or (if pursued) *wind walk* to escape.

Breath Weapon (Su): A storm drake has one type of breath weapon, a 60-foot cone of wind usable once every 1d4 rounds. This attack produces the equivalent of tornado-strength winds (see Table 3–24 on page 95 of the *Dungeon Master's Guide*). Those in the cone may attempt DC 30 Fortitude saves to resist the effect.

Gaseous Form (Su): A storm drake can assume gaseous form at will as a standard action. While gaseous, the drake has a fly speed of 60 feet (perfect) and is unaffected by wind of any kind. It can't attack or use its breath weapon while gaseous, but it can use spell-like abilities normally. This ability is otherwise identical with the *gaseous form* spell.

Snatch (Ex): Against Medium or smaller creatures, bite for 4d6+12/round or claw for 2d8+6/round.

Spell-Like Abilities: At will—*fog cloud* (DC 17), 3/day—*call lightning* (DC 18), *sleet storm* (DC 18), *stinking cloud* (DC 18), *wind wall* (DC 18); 1/day—*control weather* (DC 21), *control winds* (DC 20), *ice storm* (DC 19), *shout* (DC 19), *wind walk* (DC 22). Caster level 20th.

Storm drake

VAMPIRIC DRAGON

A vampiric dragon is forever anchored to its hoard, much like a normal vampire craves its coffin. It appears much as it did as a living dragon, though its eyes gleam with a feral and predatory glint. It dreams only of death and evil, spreading legends of its treasure to draw in unwitting adventurers in order to create vampire spawn.

Thankfully, such creatures are rare in the extreme, most often created by energy draining effects or unique confluences of negative energy.

Like normal vampires, vampiric dragons cast no shadows and throw no reflections in mirrors. They speak any languages they knew in life.

SAMPLE VAMPIRIC DRAGON

This example uses a mature adult red dragon as the base dragon.

Vampiric Mature Adult Red Dragon
Huge Undead
Hit Dice: 25d12+100 (262 hp)
Initiative: +3
Speed: 40 ft. (8 squares), fly 150 ft. (poor)
Armor Class: 37 (–2 size, +3 Dex, +26 natural), touch 11, flat-footed 34
Base Attack/Grapple: +25/+46
Attack: Bite +38 melee (2d8+13)
Full Attack: Bite +36 melee (2d8+13) and 2 claws +31 melee (2d6+6) and 2 wings +31 melee (1d8+6) and tail slap +31 melee (2d6+19)
Space/Reach: 15 ft./10 ft. (15 ft. with bite)
Special Attacks: Blood drain, breath weapon, charm, create spawn, domination, energy drain, improved snatch, spells, spell-like abilities
Special Qualities: Blindsense 60 ft., damage reduction 10/magic, darkvision 120 ft., fast healing 5, immunity to fire, keen senses, resistance to cold 20 and electricity 20, spell resistance 23, turn resistance +4, undead traits, vampiric weaknesses
Saves: Fort +14, Ref +17, Will +16
Abilities: Str 37, Dex 16, Con —, Int 20, Wis 21, Cha 22
Skills: Appraise +30, Bluff +19, Concentration +24, Diplomacy +24, Hide +3, Intimidate +32, Jump +38, Knowledge (arcana) +22, Knowledge (geography) +16, Knowledge (history) +16, Knowledge (nature) +13, Knowledge (the planes) +13, Knowledge (religion) +16, Listen +40, Move Silently +11, Search +38, Sense Motive +23, Spellcraft +30, Spot +35
Feats: Alertness, Cleave, Combat Reflexes, Dodge, Flyby Attack, Hover, Improved Initiative, Improved Snatch, Lightning Reflexes, Multisnatch, Power Attack, Quicken Breath, Snatch, Wingover
Environment: Warm mountains
Organization: Solitary or guarded (1 plus 2–5 vampire spawn)
Challenge Rating: 20
Treasure: Triple standard
Alignment: Always chaotic evil
Advancement: 26–27 HD (Huge)
Level Adjustment: —

This vampiric red dragon lurks in a dark cave deep beneath the earth, guarding its life-preserving hoard and awaiting new victims to add to its tally of death.

Combat

This vampiric red dragon casts *desecrate* upon its lair each day, granting combat bonuses to it and its vampire spawn minions, if any. When it first senses intruders, it listens from a distance to learn more about them, sending vampire spawn forward to battle if available. If it can employ its charming voice before revealing its presence, it does so. In battle, it prefers to target lone opponents, using Flyby Attack and Snatch to grapple the target and then carry it to a safe location to employ its blood drain.

The DC is 28 for the Will save against this vampiric dragon's charm, domination, and frightful presence, and for the Fortitude save to regain levels lost to its energy drain.

This vampiric red dragon's natural weapons are treated as magic weapons for purpose of overcoming damage reduction.

Breath Weapon (Su): 50-ft. cone, 14d10 fire, Reflex DC 28 half.

Improved Snatch (Ex): Against Medium or smaller creatures, bite for 2d8+13/round or claw for 2d6+6/round.

Spell-Like Abilities: 7/day—*locate object*. Caster level 9th.

Spells: As 9th-level sorcerer.

Keen Senses (Ex): This vampiric red dragon sees four times as well as a human in low-light conditions and twice as well in normal light.

Sorcerer Spells Known (6/8/8/7/5; save DC 16 + spell level): 0—*arcane mark, dancing lights, detect magic, ghost sound, guidance, mage hand, read magic, resistance*; 1st—*alarm, magic missile, protection from good, shield, shocking grasp*; 2nd—*cat's grace, cure moderate wounds, darkness, sound burst*; 3rd—*dispel magic, protection from energy, stinking cloud*; 4th—*fire shield, greater invisibility*.

Vampiric red dragon

CREATING A VAMPIRIC DRAGON

"Vampiric" is a template that can be added to any dragon of at least adult age (referred to hereafter as the base dragon). The creature uses all the base dragon's statistics and special abilities except as noted here.

Size and Type: The creature's type changes to undead, and it loses any subtypes it had in life. Do not recalculate the creature's base attack bonus, saves, or skill points. Size is unchanged.

Hit Dice: The base dragon's Hit Dice remain the same, but it loses any Constitution bonus to its hit points (see Abilities, below). However, a vampiric dragon gains bonus hit points equal to four times its HD.

Armor Class: The base dragon's natural armor bonus improves by 2.

Attacks: A vampiric dragon retains all the attacks of the base dragon. Unlike typical vampires, a vampiric dragon does not gain slam attacks.

Special Attacks: A vampiric dragon retains all the special attacks of the base dragon and also gains those noted below. Saves have a DC of 10 + 1/2 vampiric dragon's HD + vampiric dragon's Cha modifier unless noted otherwise.

Blood Drain (Ex): A vampiric dragon can suck blood from a living victim one size category smaller than itself or larger. If it pins the foe with whom it is grappling, it drains blood, dealing 1d4 points of Constitution drain each round the pin is maintained.

Charm (Su): The voice of a vampiric dragon can bewitch listeners. This requires a full-round action by the vampiric dragon, but any creatures within 30 feet per age category of the base dragon who can hear its voice must make a Will save or become charmed (as *charm monster*). The charm is immediately broken if the vampiric dragon uses its frightful presence within range of the charmed individual or makes any attack against the charmed individual. A vampiric dragon need not see its targets to use this power.

Create Spawn (Su): A humanoid or monstrous humanoid slain by a vampiric dragon's energy drain attack rises as a vampire spawn (see page 253 of the *Monster Manual*) 1d4 days after death.

If a vampiric dragon instead drains its victim's Constitution to 0, the victim returns as a spawn if it had 4 or fewer Hit Dice and as a vampire if it had 5 or more HD. In either case, the new vampire or spawn is under the command of the vampiric dragon that created it and remains enslaved until its master's death.

An adult or older dragon slain by a vampiric dragon's blood drain returns as a vampiric dragon under the command of the vampiric dragon that created it, as noted above. Young adult or younger dragons slain by its blood drain attack, or any dragons slain by its energy drain attack, rise instead as mindless zombie dragons (see page 197).

Domination (Su): A vampiric dragon can crush an opponent's will just by looking into its eyes. This ability works similarly to a gaze attack, except that the vampiric dragon must use a standard action, and those merely looking at the creature are not affected. Anyone the vampiric dragon targets must succeed on a Will save or fall instantly under the vampiric dragon's influence as though by a *dominate monster* spell (caster level 18th). The ability has a range of 30 feet plus 10 feet per age category of the base dragon.

Energy Drain (Su): A living creature hit by a vampiric dragon's claw attack gains one negative level.

Special Qualities: A vampiric dragon retains all the special qualities of the base dragon (except for any subtypes it possessed) and gains those noted below. If the base dragon had any immunities based on its subtype (such as immunity to fire for the fire subtype), it keeps those immunities despite losing the subtype.

Fast Healing (Ex): A vampiric dragon heals 5 hit points of damage each round so long as it has at least 1 hit point. If reduced to 0 hit points or lower, a vampiric dragon automatically assumes *gaseous form* (fly speed 40 feet, otherwise as the spell) and attempts to escape. It must reach its hoard within 2 hours or be utterly destroyed. (It can travel up to 18 miles in 2 hours.) Once at rest upon its hoard, it rises to 1 hit point after 1 hour, then resumes healing at the rate of 5 hit points per round. For obvious reasons, a vampiric dragon prefers to keep its hoard well concealed from adventurers and would-be thieves.

Resistance (Ex): A vampiric dragon has resistance to cold 20 and electricity 20.

Turn Resistance (Ex): A vampiric dragon has +4 turn resistance (see page 317 of the *Monster Manual*).

Undead Traits: A vampiric dragon is immune to mind-affecting effects, poison, magic sleep effects, paralysis, stunning, disease, death effects, and any effect that requires a Fortitude save unless it also works on objects or is harmless. It is not subject to critical hits, nonlethal damage, ability damage to its physical ability scores, ability drain, energy drain, fatigue, exhaustion, or death from massive damage. It cannot be raised, and resurrection works only if it is willing. It has darkvision out to 60 feet (unless the base creature had a greater range).

Vampiric Weaknesses: Vampiric dragons share the typical vampire's vulnerability to sunlight. Direct sunlight slows a vampiric dragon, allowing it only a single standard action or move action each round. A vampiric dragon can survive exposure to direct sunlight for a number of consecutive rounds equal to its age category, after which it is utterly destroyed. Driving a wooden stake through a vampiric dragon's heart slays it, just as with a normal vampire (though for larger dragons, you'll need a stake the size of a spear).

Unlike other vampires, vampiric dragons are not injured by immersion in water. Vampiric dragons are not repelled by garlic or mirrors (though they don't keep mirrors in their hoards), and they can freely cross running water. They can't enter a home unless invited, but most simply destroy the home and then pick through the rubble for their victims.

Saves: As undead, vampiric dragons are immune to anything that requires a Fortitude save unless it affects objects.

Abilities: Increase from the base dragon as follows: Str +4, Dex +6, Int +2, Wis +2, Cha +4. As undead creatures, vampiric dragons have no Constitution score.

Skills: Vampiric dragons have a +8 racial bonus on Bluff, Hide, Listen, Move Silently, Search, Sense Motive, and Spot checks.

Feats: Vampiric dragons gain Alertness, Combat Reflexes, Dodge, Improved Initiative, and Lightning Reflexes, assuming the base dragon meets the prerequisites and doesn't already have the feats.

Organization: Solitary or guarded (1 plus 2–5 vampire spawn).

Challenge Rating: Same as the base dragon +2.

Treasure: Triple standard.

Alignment: Always chaotic evil.

Advancement: Up to +2 HD.

Level Adjustment: +5.

ZOMBIE DRAGON

A zombie dragon is created by use of the *animate dead* spell or by a vampiric dragon (see above). It functions as a normal zombie in most ways, though it retains a few of its draconic abilities and qualities even after death

A zombie dragon stinks of death, and its once glorious scaled hide sports gaping holes chewed by worms. Because of the creature's utter lack of intelligence, the instructions given to a newly created zombie dragon must be very simple, such as "Destroy anything that comes within sight."

Zombie dragons are often used as sentries (although they aren't capable of calling for help, the sounds of the battle usually serve to raise the alarm) or guardians. Draconic spellcasters capable of creating such creatures may use the bodies of dead rivals or, in the case of particularly vile necromancers, deceased family members.

CREATING A ZOMBIE DRAGON

"Zombie" is a template that can be added to any dragon of at least adult age (referred to hereafter as the base dragon). The creature uses all the base dragon's statistics and special abilities except as noted here.

Size and Type: The creature's type changes to undead, and it loses any subtypes it had in life. Do not recalculate the creature's base attack bonus, saves, or skill points. Size is unchanged.

Hit Dice: The base dragon's Hit Dice remain the same, but it loses any Constitution bonus to its hit points (see Abilities, below). However, a zombie dragon gains bonus hit points equal to twice its HD.

Speed: Reduce flight maneuverability by one category (to a minimum of clumsy).

Armor Class: Reduce natural armor bonus to one-half the base dragon's value (rounding down).

Special Attacks: A zombie dragon retains any exceptional special attacks of the base dragon (such as improved grab), except for special attacks with a save DC based on the base dragon's Charisma (such as frightful presence). It loses all supernatural and spell-like special attacks possessed by the base dragon, except for any breath weapon attack, which is altered as noted below.

Breath Weapon (Su): A zombie dragon keeps the base dragon's breath weapon (if any), though it deals only half the listed damage. Breath weapons that don't deal damage (such as the brass dragon's *sleep* breath weapon) are unchanged. The save DC to resist the dragon's breath weapon is 10 + 1/2 zombie dragon's HD + zombie dragon's Cha modifier.

Special Qualities: A zombie dragon loses all supernatural and spell-like special qualities possessed by the base dragon. It retains any exceptional special qualities (such as immunities or blindsense). It loses any subtypes it had, though if the base dragon had any immunities based on its subtype (such as immunity to fire for the fire subtype), it keeps those immunities despite losing the subtype. It also gains additional special qualities as noted below.

Damage Reduction (Ex): Zombie dragons gain damage reduction 5/slashing.

Slow (Ex): Like zombies, zombie dragons have poor reflexes and can perform only a single standard action or move action each round.

Undead Traits: A zombie dragon is immune to mind-affecting effects, poison, magic sleep effects, paralysis, stunning, disease, death effects, and any effect that requires a Fortitude save unless it also works on objects or is harmless. It is not subject to critical hits, nonlethal damage, ability damage to its physical ability scores, ability drain, energy drain, fatigue, exhaustion, or death from massive damage. It cannot be raised, and resurrection works only if it is willing. It has darkvision out to 60 feet (unless the base dragon had a greater range).

Saves: As undead, zombie dragons are immune to anything that requires a Fortitude save unless it affects objects.

Abilities: Adjust from the base dragon as follows: Str +0, Dex –2, Cha –6. Being undead, a zombie dragon has no Constitution score. It also has no Intelligence score. Its Wisdom score becomes 10 (regardless of the base dragon's Wisdom).

Skills: A zombie dragon loses all skill ranks and racial skill bonuses possessed by the base dragon.

Feats: A zombie dragon loses all feats possessed by the base dragon. It gains Toughness as a bonus feat.

Environment: Any.

Organization: Any.

Challenge Rating: Base dragon's CR × 1/2 +1 (minimum 2).

Treasure: None.

Alignment: Always neutral.

Advancement: Up to +2 HD.

Level Adjustment: —.

SAMPLE ZOMBIE DRAGON

This example uses a young adult white dragon as the base dragon.

Zombie Young Adult White Dragon
Large Undead
Hit Dice: 15d12+33 (130 hp)
Initiative: +4
Speed: 60 ft. (12 squares), burrow 30 ft., fly 200 ft. (clumsy), swim 60 ft.
Armor Class: 15 (–1 size, –1 Dex, +7 natural), touch 8, flat-footed 15
Base Attack/Grapple: +15/+23
Attack: Bite +18 melee (2d6+4)
Full Attack: Bite +18 melee (2d6+4) and 2 claws +13 melee (1d8+2) and 2 wings +13 melee (1d6+2)
Space/Reach: 10 ft./5 ft. (10 ft. with bite)
Special Attacks: Breath weapon, frightful presence
Special Qualities: Blindsense 60 ft., damage reduction 5/slashing, darkvision 120 ft., icewalking, immunity to cold, keen senses, slow, spell resistance 16, undead traits
Saves: Fort +9, Ref +8, Will +9
Abilities: Str 19, Dex 8, Con —, Int —, Wis 11, Cha 2
Skills: Swim +4
Feats: Toughness
Environment: Cold mountains
Organization: Any
Challenge Rating: 5
Treasure: None
Alignment: Always neutral
Advancement: Up to +2 HD
Level Adjustment: —

A zombie white dragon can often be found guarding the lairs of frost giant adepts or clerics. Colder climates also slow the rotting process, keeping the zombie white dragon intact for a longer time.

Zombie white dragon

Illus. by S. Tappin

Combat

The zombie white dragon possesses none of the animalistic ferocity it had in life. It merely acts according to the (simple) orders given it by its master. Its blindsense and keen senses make it an excellent guardian, and its icewalking ability allows it to perch in difficult-to-reach places.

Breath Weapon (Su): 40-ft. cone, 2d6 cold, Reflex DC 13 halves.

Frightful Presence (Ex): 150-ft. radius, HD 14 or fewer, Will DC 14 negates.

Icewalking (Ex): This ability works like the *spider climb* spell, but the surfaces the dragon climbs must be icy. It is always in effect.

Keen Senses (Ex): A zombie dragon sees four times as well as a human in shadowy illumination and twice as well in normal light. It also has darkvision out to 120 feet.

Skills: This zombie dragon has a +8 racial bonus on any Swim check to perform some special action or avoid a hazard. It can always choose to take 10 on a Swim check, even if distracted or endangered. It can use the run action while swimming, provided it swims in a straight line.

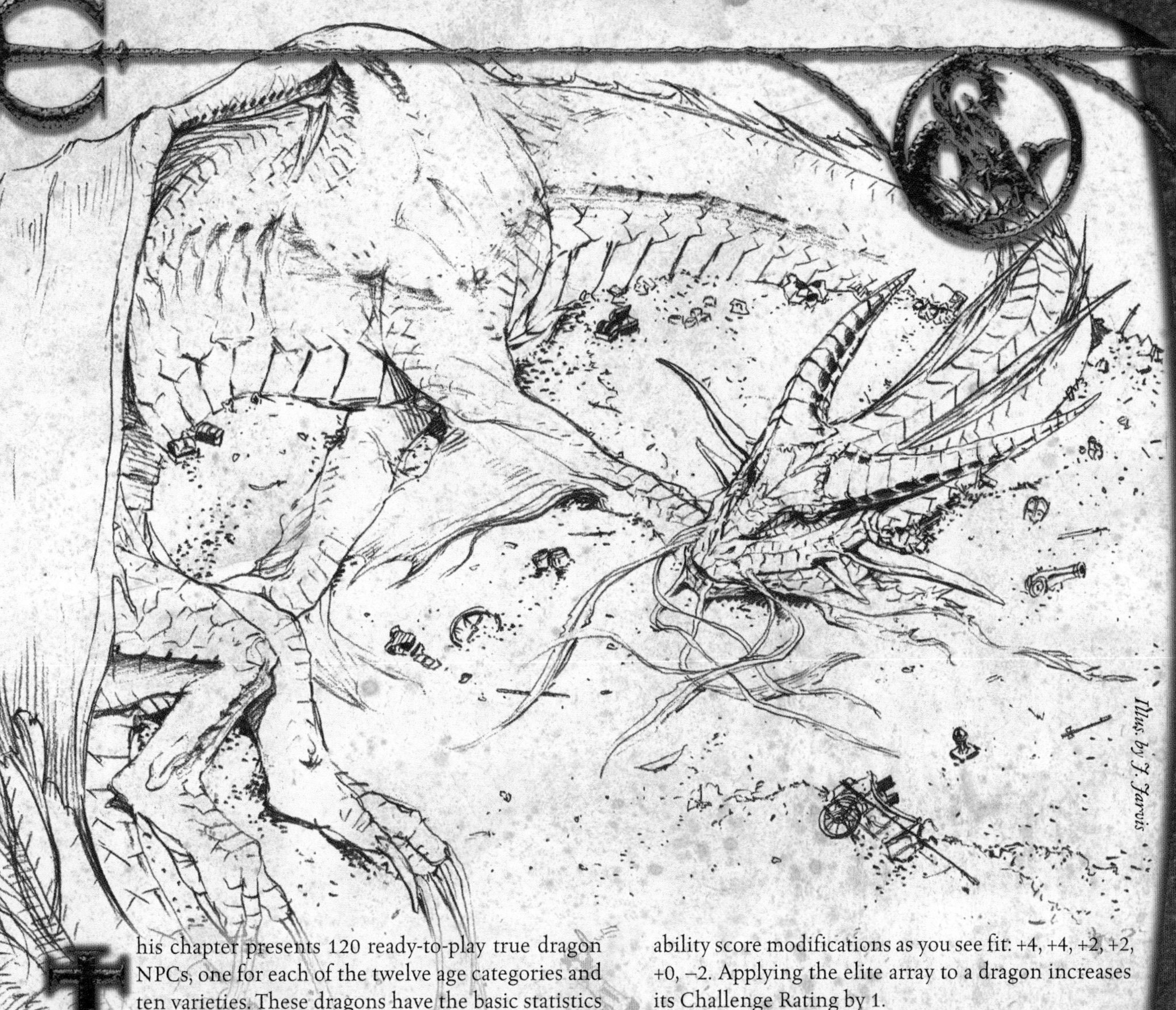

This chapter presents 120 ready-to-play true dragon NPCs, one for each of the twelve age categories and ten varieties. These dragons have the basic statistics given in the *Monster Manual*. Each entry includes notes about the dragon's personality, combat tactics, and other details of its life and habits. Some entries differ slightly from their *Monster Manual* counterparts because the skills and feats for some of them have been adjusted.

Though the dragons are presented here as individuals, nearly any dragon described in this chapter could serve as a member of a dragon family, or in the case of younger dragons, the leader of a clutch. A clutch or family led by one of these dragons tends to reflect the leader's personality and tastes.

CUSTOMIZING THE DRAGONS

You can customize any sample dragon by altering its ability scores. As presented here, each dragon's ability scores (as given in the *Monster Manual* or another source) assume the standard array (all 11s and 10s), modified to take into account the dragon's racial ability adjustments. See Ability Score Arrays, page 290 of the *Monster Manual*, for more information.

To create an elite dragon, you could apply the elite array typically used for NPC ability scores: 15, 14, 13, 12, 10, 8. To apply the elite array to any dragon, assign the following ability score modifications as you see fit: +4, +4, +2, +2, +0, –2. Applying the elite array to a dragon increases its Challenge Rating by 1.

For a slightly less powerful dragon, use the nonelite array: 13, 12, 11, 10, 9, 8. To apply this array to any dragon, assign the following ability score modifications as you see fit: +2, +2, +0, +0, –2, –2. Applying the nonelite array to a dragon has no effect on its Challenge Rating.

EXAMPLE

Rime, the white wyrmling described on page 270, would have the following ability scores using the elite array: Str 15, Dex 14, Con 15, Int 8, Wis 11, Cha 4.

Changing a dragon's ability scores requires making several adjustments to its statistics block, as detailed below.

Strength: Adjust the dragon's attack bonus, damage values, and skill modifiers according to its new Strength modifier. In the example, Rime gained 4 points of Strength, increasing his Strength modifier from +0 to +2. Rime doesn't have the Snatch feat or a crush attack, but if he did, his +2 Strength modifier would apply to the grapple check bonus he would use for those abilities.

BLACK DRAGON
Never assume an exposed nest is unguarded
Ventral view (note distinctive horns)
Egg
Tiny
Small
Juvenile
Adult
Tail barb
There are two acid glands located inside the mouth on either side of the tongue
Don't bother trying to chop at the horns...
Illus. by L. Grant-West

Dexterity: Adjust the dragon's initiative modifier, Armor Class, Reflex save bonus, and skill modifiers according to its new Dexterity modifier. In the example, Rime gained 4 points of Dexterity, which increased his Dexterity modifier from +0 to +2.

Constitution: Adjust the dragon's hit points, breath weapon save DC, Fortitude save bonus, and skill modifiers according to its new Constitution modifier. In the example, Rime gained 2 points of Constitution, which increased his Constitution modifier from +1 to +2. Rime doesn't have a crush attack or tail sweep attack, but if he did, the save DCs against those attacks also would increase by 1.

Intelligence: Adjust the dragon's total skill points and skill modifiers according to its new Intelligence modifier. In the example, Rime gained 2 points of Intelligence, which increased his Intelligence modifier from +0 to +1 and gave him 3 extra skill points (1 point per Hit Die).

Wisdom: Adjust the dragon's Will save bonus and skill modifiers according to its new Wisdom modifier. In the example, Rime gained 0 points of Wisdom, leaving his Wisdom modifier unchanged.

Charisma: Adjust the dragon's frightful presence save DC, spell-like ability save DCs, and skill modifiers according to its new Charisma modifier. In the example, Rime lost 2 points of Charisma, which lowers his Charisma modifier from –2 to –3. If the dragon is a spellcaster, a change in Charisma also affects the save DCs for its spells and the number of bonus spells it gets. A dragon needs a Charisma score of at least 10 to cast any spells. Since Rime has no spellcasting ability, spell-like abilities, frightful presence, or Charisma-based skills, his reduced Charisma score has no real impact.

Assuming Rime spent his extra 3 skill points from his Intelligence increase on Hide, Listen, and Spot, his new statistics would be as follows:

Rime: Male wyrmling white dragon; CR 2; Tiny dragon (cold); HD 3d12+6; hp 25; Init +6; Spd 60 ft., burrow 30 ft., fly 150 ft. (average), swim 60 ft.; AC 16, touch 14, flat-footed 14; Base Atk +7; Grp –3; Atk +7 melee (1d4+2, bite); Full Atk +7 melee (1d4+2, bite), +2 melee (1d3+1, 2 claws); Space/Reach 2-1/2 ft./0 ft. (5 ft. with bite); SA breath weapon; SQ blindsense 60 ft., darkvision 120 ft., icewalking, immunity to cold, magic sleep effects, and paralysis, low-light vision, vulnerability to fire; AL CE; SV Fort +5, Ref +5, Will +3; Str 15, Dex 14, Con 15, Int 8, Wis 10, Cha 4.

Skills and Feats: Hide +16, Listen +8, Search +2, Sense Motive +3, Spot +8, Swim +16; Improved Initiative, Power Attack.

Breath Weapon (Su): 15-ft. cone, 1d6 cold, Reflex DC 13 half.

SAMPLE BLACK DRAGONS

Described below are twelve sample black dragons, one of each age category. The descriptions include basic personality and encounter notes that the DM will want to flesh out for his campaign, along with a set of statistics that make the dragon ready to play.

Water Breathing (Ex): All black dragons can breathe underwater indefinitely and can freely use their breath weapons, spells, and other abilities underwater.

Skills: A black dragon can move through water at its swim speed without making Swim checks. It has a +8 racial bonus on any Swim check to perform some special action or avoid a hazard. The dragon can always can choose to take 10 on a Swim check, even if distracted or endangered. The dragon can use the run action while swimming, provided it swims in a straight line.

Blight
Wyrmling Black Dragon

Mean as the proverbial polecat, fiercely territorial, vain, and perpetually hungry, Blight tends to breathe acid first and consider the consequences later. Blight thinks of herself as the most dangerous creature in her patch of swamp. She is queen of all she surveys; however, she is a Tiny dragon and doesn't actually survey very much. The mere sight of any creature more attractive than herself (and that's most creatures) fills Blight with rage. She delights in destroying beautiful things, especially birds and small animals. Likewise, she scars small plants, trees, and even rocks just for the fun of it.

Blight: Female wyrmling black dragon; CR 3; Tiny dragon (water); HD 4d12+4; hp 30; Init +4; Spd 60 ft., fly 100 ft. (average), swim 60 ft.; AC 15, touch 12, flat-footed 15; Base Atk +6; Grp –4; Atk +6 melee (1d4, bite); Full Atk +6 melee (1d4, bite), +1 melee (1d3, 2 claws); Space/Reach 2-1/2 ft./0 ft. (5 ft. with bite); SA breath weapon; SQ blindsense 60 ft., darkvision 120 ft., immunity to acid, magic sleep effects, and paralysis, low-light vision, water breathing; AL CE; SV Fort +5, Ref +4, Will +4; Str 11, Dex 10, Con 13, Int 8, Wis 11, Cha 8.

Skills and Feats: Hide +14, Listen +6, Move Silently +6, Search +2, Sense Motive +2, Spot +6, Swim +14; Alertness, Improved Initiative.

DRAGONS AND LANGUAGES

All dragons speak Draconic. With their high degree of intelligence, most dragons have an affinity for language and speak additional languages as well. Many even study the science of language, developing a wide range of tongues.

As with all intelligent creatures, a dragon speaks a number of additional languages equal to its Intelligence bonus. Dragons with ranks in the Speak Language skill can speak a number of additional languages equal to those ranks.

Additional languages commonly spoken by dragons include Auran, Celestial, Common, Dwarven, Elven, Gnome, Ignan, Infernal, Orc, Terran, and Undercommon.

Breath Weapon (Su): 30-ft. line, 2d4 acid, Reflex DC 13 half.

Kurnoc
Very Young Black Dragon

Kurnoc likes to prowl around his home swamp and congratulate himself on how nasty and tough and excellent he is. Kurnoc takes special delight in stealing kills from other predators. (Such victories seem more like conquests than simply collecting food.)

Kurnoc likes to announce his presence before attacking, usually by bellowing a challenge. His favorite topic of conversation is the party's ultimate demise at the fangs and claws of Kurnoc. If a party decides to retreat in response to Kurnoc's bluster, the dragon attacks the moment their backs are turned.

When facing one opponent in battle, Kurnoc usually charges, snarling and spitting like an angry cat. This display often sends the foe running, and the dragon gleefully pursues. When facing a group of intelligent foes, Kurnoc taunts and threatens for a short while, then attacks by using his breath weapon on as many enemies as possible before charging into melee.

Kurnoc: Male very young black dragon; CR 4; Small dragon (water); HD 7d12+7; hp 52; Init +0; Spd 60 ft., fly 100 ft. (average), swim 60 ft.; AC 17, touch 11, flat-footed 17; Base Atk +9; Grp +4; Atk +9 melee (1d6+1, bite); Full Atk +9 melee (1d6+1, bite), +7 melee (1d4, 2 claws); Space/Reach 5 ft./5 ft.; SA breath weapon, water breathing; SQ blindsense 60 ft., darkvision 120 ft., immunity to acid, magic sleep effects and paralysis, low-light vision; AL CE; SV Fort +6, Ref +5, Will +5; Str 13, Dex 10, Con 13, Int 8, Wis 11, Cha 8.

Skills and Feats: Hide +8, Intimidate +7, Listen +6, Move Silently +6, Search +5, Sense Motive +6, Spot +8, Swim +15; Multiattack, Enlarge Breath, Power Attack.

Breath Weapon (Su): 40-ft. line (60-ft. line if enlarged), 4d4 acid, Reflex DC 14 half.

Jurlfalud
Young Black Dragon

Jurlfalud craves darkness, solitude, and piles of coins to make a comfortable bed for herself. She spends most of her days lurking silently in her lair. She receives tribute from a tribe of kobolds whose leader she killed a few years ago. Occasionally, she feels the need to remind the kobolds of the fear they should hold for her, or to scout the area around her lair for intruders. She is careful to remain unseen as she comes and goes.

Jurlfalud prefers to begin combat with a melee attack. She lies in hiding and chooses a lightly armored foe for her first attack.

Jurlfalud: Female young black dragon; CR 5; Medium dragon (water); HD 10d12+20; hp 85; Init +4; Spd 60 ft., fly 150 ft. (poor), swim 60 ft.; AC 19, touch 10, flat-footed 19; Base Atk +12; Grp +12; Atk +12 melee (1d8+2, bite); Full Atk +12 melee (1d8+2, bite), +7 melee (1d6+1, 2 claws), +7 melee (1d4+1, 2 wings); Space/Reach 5 ft./5 ft.; SA breath weapon; SQ blindsense 60 ft., darkvision 120 ft., immunity to acid, magic sleep effects, and paralysis, low-light vision, water breathing; AL CE; SV Fort +9, Ref +7, Will +7; Str 15, Dex 10, Con 15, Int 10, Wis 11, Cha 10.

Skills and Feats: Bluff +3, Diplomacy +3, Hide +10, Intimidate +13, Knowledge (arcana) +3, Listen +12, Search +10, Spot +15, Swim +23; Alertness, Improved Initiative, Power Attack, Shape Breath.

Breath Weapon (Su): 60-ft. line (30-ft. cone if shaped), 6d4 acid, Reflex DC 17 half.

Myastanaklon
Juvenile Black Dragon

Dwelling at the bottom of a fetid lake, Myastanaklon rarely surfaces or sees the sun. In fact, when the sun shines unusually brightly upon the lake surface and the water becomes unusually clear, he swathes himself in magical *darkness* so he can continue to enjoy the watery gloom. He never speaks and only rarely fights, preferring to float slowly through the water, brooding while he consumes fish, crocodiles, and lizardfolk that come too near.

Myastanaklon: Male juvenile black dragon; CR 7; Medium dragon (water); HD 13d12+26; hp 110; Init +0; Spd 60 ft., fly 150 ft. (poor), swim 60 ft.; AC 22, touch 10, flat-footed 22; Base Atk +16; Grp +16; Atk +16 melee (1d8+3, bite); Full Atk +16 melee (1d8+3, bite), +14 melee (1d6+1, 2 claws), +14 melee (1d4+1, 2 wings); Space/Reach 5 ft./5 ft.; SA breath weapon, *darkness;* SQ blindsense 60 ft., darkvision 120 ft., immunity to acid, magic sleep effects, and paralysis, low-light vision, water breathing; AL CE; SV Fort +10, Ref +8, Will +8; Str 17, Dex 10, Con 15, Int 10, Wis 11, Cha 10.

Skills and Feats: Bluff +4, Concentration +18, Diplomacy +4, Intimidate +16, Knowledge (arcana) +4, Knowledge (nature) +4, Listen +12, Search +12, Spot +12, Swim +23; Clinging Breath, Enlarge Breath, Flyby Attack, Multiattack, Wingover.

Breath Weapon (Su): 60-ft. line (90-ft. line if enlarged), 8d4 acid, Reflex DC 18 half.

***Darkness* (Sp):** 3/day—as *darkness*, but 40-ft. radius. Caster level 4th.

Munwithurix
Young Adult Black Dragon

Bloodthirsty, ill-humored, and rapacious, Munwithurix proves as treacherous and unforgiving as the fens she calls home. She has utterly cowed several gangs of scrags, who live in terror of her. Munwithurix has become increasingly dissatisfied with her position at the top of the local pecking order and now delights in the sparkle of gold, which does not tarnish even in the silty waters of her lair. She has also begun thinking about finding a mate.

Munwithurix has a taste for close combat; still, she is no fool. She usually observes foes for a few minutes, either by hiding and watching them approach or by stalking them for a time, before committing herself to combat.

Munwithurix: Female young adult black dragon; CR 9; Large dragon (water); HD 16d12+48, hp 152; Init +0; Spd 60 ft., fly 150 ft. (poor), swim 60 ft.; AC 24, touch 9, flat-footed 24; Base Atk +19; Grp +24; Atk +19 melee (2d6+4, bite); Full Atk +19 melee (2d6+4, bite), +17 melee (1d8+2, 2 claws), +17 melee (1d6+2, 2 wings), +17 melee (1d8+6, tail slap); Space/Reach 10 ft./5 ft. (10 ft. with bite); SA breath weapon, *darkness*, frightful presence, spells; SQ blindsense 60 ft., damage reduction 5/magic, darkvision 120 ft., immunity to acid, magic sleep effects, and paralysis, low-light vision, spell resistance 17, water breathing; AL CE; SV Fort +13, Ref +10, Will +11; Str 19, Dex 10, Con 17, Int 12, Wis 13, Cha 12.

Skills and Feats: Bluff +9, Climb +12, Diplomacy +10, Hide +4, Intimidate +19, Listen +17, Move Silently +16, Search +17, Speak Language 3 ranks, Spot +17, Swim +20; Cleave, Clinging Breath, Combat Reflexes, Multiattack, Power Attack, Wingover.

Breath Weapon (Su): 80-ft. line, 10d4 acid, Reflex DC 21 half.

Darkness **(Sp):** 3/day—as *darkness*, but 50-ft. radius. Caster level 5th.

Frightful Presence (Ex): 150-ft. radius, HD 15 or fewer, Will DC 19 negates.

Spells: As 1st-level sorcerer.

Sorcerer Spells Known (5/4; save DC 11 + spell level): 0—*daze, detect magic, ray of frost, resistance;* 1st—*grease, protection from good.*

Haldulfvinemmonis
Adult Black Dragon

Haldulfvinemmonis is a bully. He enjoys his physical strength for its own sake, but enjoys it even more for what he can do with it. He views the entire world as his buffet, and the other creatures in it as either objects of fun or annoyances to be eliminated. In the latter category is his mother, Bluutsvilvarrt, who tormented him mercilessly when he was younger and now commands all the hatred he can muster. Haldulfvinemmonis lives for the day he can wreak his revenge.

Haldulfvinemmonis: Male adult black dragon; CR 11; Large dragon (water); HD 19d12+76, hp 199; Init +4; Spd 60 ft., fly 150 ft. (poor), swim 60 ft.; AC 27, touch 9, flat-footed 27; Base Atk +24; Grp +29; Atk +24 melee (2d6+6, bite); Full Atk +24 melee (2d6+6, bite), +19 melee (1d8+3, 2 claws), +19 melee (1d6+3, 2 wings), +19 melee (1d8+9, tail slap); Space/Reach 5 ft./5 ft. (10 ft. with bite); SA breath weapon, *corrupt water, darkness,* frightful presence, spells; SQ blindsense 60 ft., damage reduction 5/magic, darkvision 120 ft., immunity to acid, magic sleep effects, and paralysis, low-light vision, spell resistance 18, water breathing; AL CE; SV Fort +15, Ref +11, Will +12; Str 23, Dex 10, Con 19, Int 12, Wis 13, Cha 12.

Skills and Feats: Bluff +9, Diplomacy +9, Hide +2, Intimidate +20, Knowledge (arcana) +9, Knowledge (nature) +7, Listen +18, Move Silently +20, Search +21, Spellcraft +13, Spot +21, Swim +20; Flyby Attack, Improved Initiative, Power Attack, Quicken Spell-Like Ability, Recover Breath, Shape Breath, Wingover.

Breath Weapon (Su): 80-ft. line (40-ft. cone if shaped), 12d4 acid, Reflex DC 23 half.

Corrupt Water **(Sp):** 1/day—spoil up to 10 cubic ft. of water or liquids containing water; range 180 ft.; Will DC 20 negates.

Darkness **(Sp):** 3/day—as *darkness*, but 60-ft. radius. Caster level 6th.

Frightful Presence (Ex): 180-ft. radius, HD 18 or fewer, Will DC 20 negates.

Spells: As 3rd-level sorcerer.

Sorcerer Spells Known (6/6; save DC 11 + spell level): 0—*daze, detect magic, ghost sound, ray of frost, resistance;* 1st—*protection from good, shield, true strike.*

Eliinwyluwyther
Mature Adult Black Dragon

Eliinwyluwyther is a leader, a diplomat, and a ruthless tyrant. She rules a small empire of several lizardfolk tribes, an enslaved clan of barbaric wild elves, and several chuuls. She makes her lair in an ancient ruin at the heart of a vast swampland, built by a long-forgotten race to honor their bizarre and alien deities. In her innermost sanctum, these deities whisper to her while she sleeps, planting the seeds of madness in her mind. Her behavior now is unpredictable—she can change in a heartbeat from smooth diplomacy to uncontrolled savagery, and her subjects have grown to dread any audience with her.

Eliinwyluwyther: Female mature adult black dragon; CR 14; Huge dragon (water); HD 22d12+110, hp 253; Init +0; Spd 60 ft., fly 150 ft. (poor), swim 60 ft.; AC 29, touch 8, flat-footed 29; Base Atk +28; Grp +38; Atk +28 melee (2d8+8, bite); Full Atk +28 melee (2d8+8, bite), +23 melee (2d6+4, 2 claws), +23 melee (1d8+4, 2 wings), +23 melee (2d6+12, tail slap); Space/Reach 15 ft./10 ft. (15 ft. with bite); SA breath weapon, *corrupt water,* crush, *darkness,* frightful presence, spells; SQ blindsense 60 ft., damage reduction 10/magic, darkvision 120 ft., immunity to acid, magic sleep effects, and paralysis, low-light vision, spell resistance 23, water breathing; AL CE; SV Fort +18, Ref +13, Will +15; Str 27, Dex 10, Con 21, Int 14, Wis 15, Cha 14.

Skills and Feats: Bluff +9, Concentration +27, Diplomacy +26, Hide –1, Intimidate +26, Knowledge (local) +7, Listen +24, Move Silently +22, Search +24, Spellcraft +13, Spot +24, Swim +21; Awaken Spell Resistance, Clinging Breath, Flyby Attack, Power Attack, Quicken Breath, Shape Breath, Split Breath, Wingover.

Breath Weapon (Su): 100-ft. line (50-ft. cone if shaped), 14d4 acid, Reflex DC 26 half.

Corrupt Water **(Sp):** 1/day—spoil up to 10 cubic ft. of water or liquids containing water; range 210 ft.; Will DC 23 negates.

Crush (Ex): Area 15 ft. by 15 ft.; Small or smaller opponents take 2d8+12 points of bludgeoning damage, and must succeed on a DC 26 Reflex save or be pinned.

Darkness **(Sp):** 3/day—as *darkness*, but 70-ft. radius. Caster level 7th.

Black Dragon

Typical Black Dragon Lair

[Size of lair varies with size of dragon]

ABOVE WATER LEVEL

BELOW WATER LEVEL

main water entry [front view]

Front View

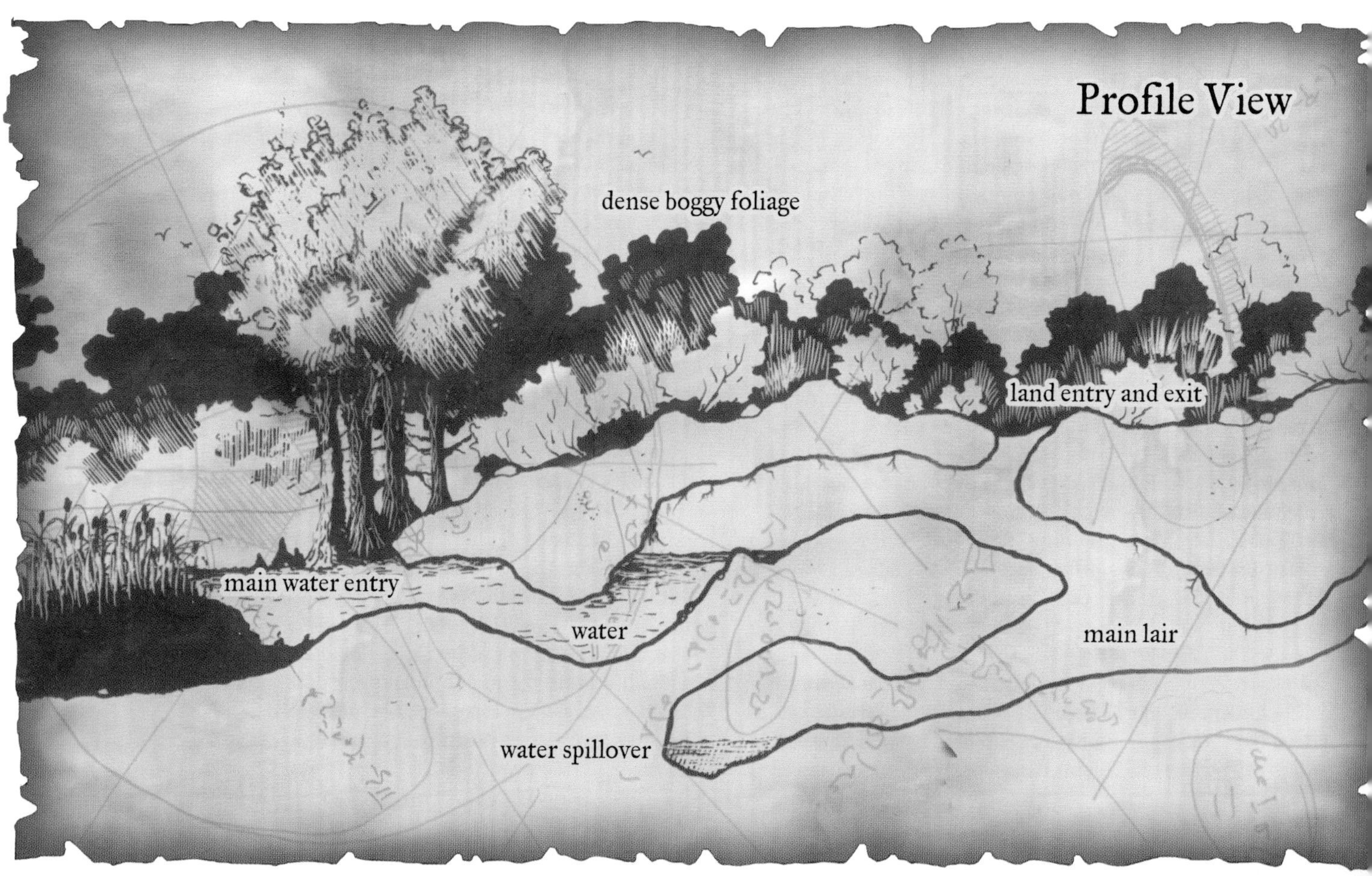

Profile View

dense boggy foliage

land entry and exit

main water entry

water

main lair

water spillover

Frightful Presence (Ex): 210-ft. radius, HD 21 or fewer, Will DC 23 negates.

Spells: As 5th-level sorcerer.

Sorcerer Spells Known (6/7/5; save DC 12 + spell level): 0—*arcane mark, dancing lights, detect magic, ghost sound, ray of frost, resistance*; 1st—*magic missile, ray of enfeeblement, shield, true strike*; 2nd—*fog cloud, web.*

Twohvritturnuroth
Old Black Dragon

Twohvritturnuroth likes snakes. He hisses when he speaks, and he samples the air with his tongue more than strictly necessary. Even his enormous pride doesn't prevent him from slithering on his belly when it suits him. In the dense jungle around his lair, where the trees seem to drip with snakes, it is an effective form of movement. Twohvritturnuroth has no magical control over snakes, but he is served by a number of yuan-ti (he favors abominations). He thinks of himself as sneaky, even seductive, but he is most effective when he descends to raw savagery.

Twohvritturnuroth: Male old black dragon; CR 16; Huge dragon (water); HD 25d12+125, hp 287; Init +0; Spd 60 ft., fly 150 ft. (poor), swim 60 ft.; AC 32, touch 8, flat-footed 32; Base Atk +32; Grp +42; Atk +32 melee (2d8+9, bite); Full Atk +32 melee (2d8+9, bite), +27 melee (2d6+4, 2 claws), +27 melee (1d8+4, 2 wings), +27 melee (2d6+13, tail slap); Space/Reach 15 ft./10 ft. (15 ft. with bite); SA breath weapon, *corrupt water,* crush, *darkness,* frightful presence, improved snatch, spell-like abilities, spells; SQ blindsense 60 ft., damage reduction 10/magic, darkvision 120 ft., immunity to acid, magic sleep effects, and paralysis, low-light vision, spell resistance 22, water breathing; AL CE; SV Fort +19, Ref +14, Will +16; Str 29, Dex 10, Con 21, Int 14, Wis 15, Cha 14.

Skills and Feats: Bluff +10, Climb +13, Concentration +13, Diplomacy +12, Hide +0, Intimidate +32, Knowledge (local) +10, Listen +30, Move Silently +28, Search +30, Spellcraft +16, Spot +30, Swim +25; Blind-Fight, Flyby Attack, Improved Snatch, Power Attack, Quicken Breath, Shape Breath, Snatch, Tail Constrict, Wingover.

Breath Weapon (Su): 100-ft. line (50-ft. cone if shaped), 16d4 acid, Reflex DC 27 half.

***Corrupt Water* (Sp):** 1/day—spoil up to 10 cubic ft. of water or liquids containing water; range 240 ft.; Will DC 24 negates.

Crush (Ex): Area 15 ft. by 15 ft.; Small or smaller opponents take 2d8+13 points of bludgeoning damage, and must succeed on a DC 27 Reflex save or be pinned.

***Darkness* (Sp):** 3/day—as *darkness,* but 80-ft. radius. Caster level 8th.

Frightful Presence (Ex): 240-ft. radius, HD 24 or fewer, Will DC 24 negates.

Improved Snatch (Ex): Against Medium or smaller creatures, bite for 2d8+9/round or claw for 2d6+4/round.

Spell-Like Abilities: 1/day—*plant growth.* Caster level 8th.

Spells: As 7th-level sorcerer.

Sorcerer Spells Known (6/7/7/4; save DC 12 + spell level): 0—*arcane mark, dancing lights, detect magic, ghost sound, mage hand, ray of frost, resistance*; 1st—*chill touch, magic missile, shield, shocking grasp, true strike*; 2nd—*darkness, fog cloud, hypnotic pattern*; 3rd—*stinking cloud, suggestion.*

Iyriddelmirev
Very Old Black Dragon

On the edge of a vast swamp stands a small city of humans and their kind, a river port where herbs and woods from the marshlands are shipped to a nearby seaport and out to other lands. The brackish water of the river flows through the sewers beneath the city, and this is where Iyriddelmirev makes her lair. Most often, however, she is found in the city above, polymorphed into the form of a black-skinned human woman. She leads a gang of thieves, most of them human and almost none of them aware of her true identity. The gang benefits greatly from their leader's knowledge of the city sewer system, and its members often make their escapes through water-filled passages the city authorities believe to be impassable.

Iyriddelmirev: Female very old black dragon; CR 18; Huge dragon (water); HD 28d12+168, hp 350; Init +4; Spd 60 ft., fly 150 ft. (poor), swim 60 ft.; AC 35, touch 8, flat-footed 35; Base Atk +36; Grp +46; Atk +36 melee (2d8+10, bite); Full Atk +36 melee (2d8+10, bite), +34 melee (2d6+5, 2 claws), +34 melee (1d8+5, 2 wings), +34 melee (2d6+15, tail slap); Space/Reach 15 ft./10 ft. (15 ft. with bite); SA breath weapon, *corrupt water,* crush, *darkness,* frightful presence, spell-like abilities, spells; SQ blindsense 60 ft., damage reduction 15/magic, darkvision 120 ft., immunity to acid, magic sleep effects, and paralysis, low-light vision, spell resistance 23, water breathing; AL CE; SV Fort +22, Ref +16, Will +19; Str 31, Dex 10, Con 23, Int 16, Wis 17, Cha 16.

Skills and Feats: Bluff +13, Concentration +16, Diplomacy +15, Hide +2, Intimidate +36, Knowledge (arcana) +16, Knowledge (geography) +13, Knowledge (local) +13, Knowledge (nature) +13, Listen +36, Move Silently +31, Search +34, Spellcraft +20, Spot +36, Swim +28; Alertness, Combat Reflexes, Dire Charge, Flyby Attack, Improved Initiative, Multiattack, Power Attack, Quicken Breath, Spellcasting Harrier, Wingover.

Breath Weapon (Su): 100-ft. line, 18d4 acid, Reflex DC 30 half.

***Corrupt Water* (Sp):** 1/day—spoil up to 10 cubic ft. of water or liquids containing water; range 270 ft.; Will DC 27 negates.

Crush (Ex): Area 15 ft. by 15 ft.; Small or smaller opponents take 2d8+15 points of bludgeoning damage, and must succeed on a DC 30 Reflex save or be pinned.

***Darkness* (Sp):** 3/day—as *darkness,* but 90-ft. radius. Caster level 9th.

Frightful Presence (Ex): 270-ft. radius, HD 27 or fewer, Will DC 27 negates.

Spell-Like Abilities: 1/day—*plant growth.* Caster level 9th.

Spells: As 9th-level sorcerer.

Sorcerer Spells Known (6/7/7/7/4; save DC 13 + spell level): 0—*arcane mark, dancing lights, detect magic, ghost sound, mage hand, ray of frost, read magic, resistance*; 1st—*burning hands, magic missile, shield, shocking grasp, true strike*; 2nd—*detect thoughts, false life, fog cloud, summon swarm*; 3rd—*dispel magic, nondetection, slow*; 4th—*Evard's black tentacles, polymorph.*

Keygrodekkerrhylon
Ancient Black Dragon

Keygrodekkerrhylon has mellowed somewhat with age. In his youth, he was hot-tempered and extremely violent. He sought out confrontation even with older and more powerful dragons, and triumphed through sheer tenacity—or fled with his life. Having survived to celebrate his 800th birthday, he has slowed down and no longer seeks out conflict. Neither does he shy away from it, however, and many young upstarts who assume his retreat is a sign of weakness have learned the truth to their dismay.

Keygrodekkerrhylon wants nothing more now than to be left alone, but his reputation for savagery draws a procession of those who seek glory and wealth by slaying the fearsome monster. He has recently abandoned the lair he held for five centuries, and seeks greater seclusion in a new subterranean abode at the bottom of a large dungeon complex.

Keygrodekkerrhylon: Male ancient black dragon; CR 19; Huge dragon (water); HD 31d12+186, hp 387; Init +4; Spd 60 ft., fly 150 ft. (poor), swim 60 ft.; AC 38, touch 8, flat-footed 38; Base Atk +40; Grp +50; Atk +40 melee (2d8+11, bite); Full Atk +40 melee (2d8+11, bite), +36 melee (2d6+5, 2 claws), +35 melee (1d8+5, 2 wings), +35 melee (2d6+16, tail slap); Space/Reach 15 ft./10 ft. (15 ft. with bite); SA breath weapon, *corrupt water,* crush, *darkness,* frightful presence, improved snatch, rend, spell-like abilities, spells; SQ blindsense 60 ft., damage reduction 15/magic, darkvision 120 ft., immunity to acid, magic sleep effects, and paralysis, low-light vision, spell resistance 25, water breathing; AL CE; SV Fort +23, Ref +17, Will +20; Str 33, Dex 10, Con 23, Int 16, Wis 17, Cha 16.

Skills and Feats: Bluff +14, Concentration +19, Diplomacy +18, Hide +5, Intimidate +39, Knowledge (arcana) +16, Knowledge (local) +16, Knowledge (nature) +16, Listen +37, Move Silently +34, Search +37, Spellcraft +22, Spot +37, Swim +32; Clinging Breath, Combat Reflexes, Flyby Attack, Improved Initiative, Improved Snatch, Power Attack, Rend, Snatch, Snatch and Swallow, Weapon Focus (claw), Wingover.

Breath Weapon (Su): 100-ft. line, 20d4 acid, Reflex DC 31 half.

***Corrupt Water* (Sp):** 1/day—spoil up to 10 cubic ft. of water or liquids containing water; range 300 ft.; Will DC 28 negates.

Crush (Ex): Area 15 ft. by 15 ft.; Small or smaller opponents take 2d8+16 points of bludgeoning damage, and must succeed on a DC 31 Reflex save or be pinned.

***Darkness* (Sp):** 3/day—as *darkness,* but 100-ft. radius. Caster level 11th.

Frightful Presence (Ex): 300-ft. radius, HD 30 or fewer, Will DC 28 negates.

Improved Snatch (Ex): Against Medium or smaller creatures, bite for 4d6+14/round or claw for 2d8+7/round.

Rend (Ex): Extra damage 4d6+16.

Spell-Like Abilities: 3/day—*insect plague;* 1/day—*plant growth.* Caster level 11th; save DC 13 + spell level.

Spells: As 11th-level sorcerer.

Sorcerer Spells Known (6/7/7/7/6/4; save DC 13 + spell level): 0—*arcane mark, dancing lights, detect magic, ghost sound, mage hand, ray of frost, read magic, resistance*; 1st—*burning hands, magic missile, shield, shocking grasp, true strike*; 2nd—*darkness, detect thoughts, fog cloud, summon swarm*; 3rd—*dispel magic, gust of wind, vampiric touch*; 4th—*Evard's black tentacles, polymorph*; 5th—*cloudkill, hold monster.*

Bluutsvilvarrt
Wyrm Black Dragon

Bluutsvilvarrt is a sadistic tyrant whose greatest pleasure in life is inflicting as much suffering as possible on any creature that dares to enter her sight. Her deepest contempt is reserved for younger black dragons, including her own offspring. Several of her brood, including Haldulfvinemmonis (page 203), nurse centuries-old grudges against her because of this.

Bluutsvilvarrt loves to inspire terror, stalking intruders in her swampy domain and allowing them glimpses of her wing, tail, or eyes before disappearing. When the intruders are properly terrorized, she separates the members of the group and toys with each one before dispatching it. She discontinues these playful tactics if her life is threatened, shifting to full offensive mode or escaping invisibly if need be.

Bluutsvilvarrt: Female wyrm black dragon; CR 20; Gargantuan dragon (water); HD 34d12+238, hp 459; Init +4; Spd 60 ft., fly 200 ft. (clumsy), swim 60 ft.; AC 39, touch 6, flat-footed 39; Base Atk +42; Grp +58; Atk +42 melee (4d6+12, bite); Full Atk +42 melee (4d6+12, bite), +40 melee (2d8+6, 2 claws), +40 melee (2d6+6, 2 wings), +40 melee (2d8+18, tail slap); Space/Reach 20 ft./15 ft. (20 ft. with bite); SA breath weapon, *corrupt water,* crush, *darkness,* frightful presence, snatch, spell-like abilities, spells, tail sweep; SQ blindsense 60 ft., damage reduction 20/magic, darkvision 120 ft., immunity to acid, magic sleep effects, and paralysis, low-light vision, spell resistance 26, water breathing; AL CE; SV Fort +26, Ref +19, Will +27; Str 35, Dex 10, Con 25, Int 18, Wis 19, Cha 18.

Skills and Feats: Bluff +24, Concentration +27, Diplomacy +23, Hide +8, Intimidate +43, Knowledge (arcana) +24, Knowledge (geography) +21, Knowledge (nature) +21, Listen +41, Move Silently +37, Search +41, Spellcraft +24, Spot +41, Swim +37; Blind-Fight, Dire Charge, Epic Will, Fast Healing, Flyby Attack, Improved Initiative, Maximize Breath, Multiattack, Power Attack, Shape Breath, Snatch, Wingover.

Breath Weapon (Su): 120-ft. line (60-ft. cone if shaped), 22d4 acid, Reflex DC 34 half.

Corrupt Water **(Sp)**: 1/day—spoil up to 10 cubic ft. of water or liquids containing water; range 330 ft.; Will DC 31 negates.

Crush (Ex): Area 20 ft. by 20 ft.; Medium or smaller opponents take 4d6+18 points of bludgeoning damage, and must succeed on a DC 34 Reflex save or be pinned.

Darkness **(Sp)**: 3/day—as *darkness*, but 110-ft. radius. Caster level 13th.

Frightful Presence (Ex): 330-ft. radius, HD 33 or fewer, Will DC 31 negates.

Snatch (Ex): Against Medium or smaller creatures, bite for 4d6+12/round or claw for 2d8+6/round.

Spell-Like Abilities: 3/day—*insect plague*; 1/day—*plant growth*. Caster level 13th; save DC 14 + spell level.

Spells: As 13th-level sorcerer.

Tail Sweep (Ex): Half-circle 30 ft. in diameter, Small or smaller opponents take 2d6+18 points of bludgeoning damage, Reflex DC 34 half.

Sorcerer Spells Known (6/7/7/7/7/6/4; save DC 14 + spell level): 0—*arcane mark, dancing lights, detect magic, ghost sound, mage hand, prestidigitation, ray of frost, read magic, resistance*; 1st—*burning hands, magic missile, shield, shocking grasp, true strike*; 2nd—*cat's grace, darkness, fog cloud, minor image, shatter*; 3rd—*dispel magic, haste, stinking cloud, vampiric touch*; 4th—*bestow curse, enervation, greater invisibility, phantasmal killer*; 5th—*cloudkill, feeblemind, hold monster*; 6th—*control water, greater dispel magic*.

Eribonyxtaliff
Great Wyrm Black Dragon

Eribonyxtaliff fancies himself the new Ashardalon: the greatest black dragon that has ever lived and the progenitor of an entirely new race. He is a mighty dragon, to be sure, but his half-dragon offspring never live up to their father's expectations. His children include bestial half-crocodiles and half-dinosaurs, a small tribe of half-lizardfolk, a scattering of half-merrows, and even a few half-shambling mounds and half-tendriculoses. He uses this small army of half-dragons as minions and agents in his swamp domain and beyond. In keeping with his conceit, Eribonyxtaliff is currently seeking membership in the loose-knit cult called the disciples of Ashardalon (see page 87).

Eribonyxtaliff: Male great wyrm black dragon; CR 22; Gargantuan dragon (water); HD 37d12+296, hp 536; Init +0; Spd 60 ft., fly 200 ft. (poor), swim 60 ft.; AC 42, touch 6, flat-footed 42; Base Atk +46; Grp +62; Atk +46 melee (4d6+13, bite); Full Atk +46 melee (4d6+13, bite), +45 melee (2d8+6, 2 claws), +44 melee (2d6+6, 2 wings), +44 melee (2d8+19, tail slap); Space/Reach 20 ft./15 ft. (20 ft. with bite); SA breath weapon, *charm reptiles, corrupt water*, crush, *darkness*, frightful presence, rend, snatch, spell-like abilities, spells, tail sweep; SQ blindsense 60 ft., damage reduction 20/magic, darkvision 120 ft., immunity to acid, magic sleep effects, and paralysis, low-light vision, spell resistance 30, water breathing; AL CE; SV Fort +28, Ref +20, Will +29; Str 37, Dex 10, Con 27, Int 20, Wis 21, Cha 20.

Skills and Feats: Bluff +45, Concentration +24, Diplomacy +49, Hide +4, Intimidate +47, Knowledge (arcana) +45, Knowledge (nature) +45, Listen +21, Move Silently +40, Search +45, Sense Motive +21, Spellcraft +27, Spot +45, Swim +37; Awaken Spell Resistance, Blind-Fight, Epic Will, Flyby Attack, Improved Maneuverability, Multiattack, Power Attack, Quicken Breath, Rend, Shape Breath, Snatch, Weapon Focus (claw), Wingover.

Breath Weapon (Su): 120-ft. line (60-ft. cone if shaped), 24d4 acid, Reflex DC 36 half.

Charm Reptiles **(Sp)**: 3/day—as *mass charm monster*, but works only on reptilian animals; the dragon can communicate with *charmed* reptiles as if using *speak with animals*. Caster level 15th.

Corrupt Water **(Sp)**: 1/day—spoil up to 10 cubic ft. of water or liquids containing water; range 360 ft.; Will DC 33 negates.

Crush (Ex): Area 20 ft. by 20 ft.; Medium or smaller opponents take 4d6+19 points of bludgeoning damage, and must succeed on a DC 36 Reflex save or be pinned.

Darkness **(Sp)**: 3/day—as *darkness*, but 120-ft. radius. Caster level 15th.

Frightful Presence (Ex): 360-ft. radius, HD 36 or fewer, Will DC 33 negates.

Rend (Ex): Extra damage 4d8+19.

Snatch (Ex): Against Medium or smaller creatures, bite for 4d6+13/round or claw for 2d8+6/round.

Spell-Like Abilities: 3/day—*insect plague*; 1/day—*plant growth*. Caster level 15th; save DC 15 + spell level.

Spells: As 15th-level sorcerer.

Tail Sweep (Ex): Half-circle 30 ft. in diameter, Small or smaller opponents take 2d6+19 points of bludgeoning damage, Reflex DC 36 half.

Sorcerer Spells Known (6/8/7/7/7/7/6/4; save DC 15 + spell level): 0—*arcane mark, dancing lights, detect magic, ghost sound, mage hand, prestidigitation, ray of frost, read magic, resistance*; 1st—*burning hands, magic missile, shield, shocking grasp, true strike*; 2nd—*cat's grace, darkness, fog cloud, minor image, shatter*; 3rd—*dispel magic, haste, stinking cloud, vampiric touch*; 4th—*bestow curse, enervation, greater invisibility, phantasmal killer*; 5th—*animal growth, cloudkill, feeblemind, hold monster*; 6th—*acid fog, circle of death, greater dispel magic*; 7th—*insanity, power word stun*.

SAMPLE BLUE DRAGONS

Listed below are twelve sample blue dragons, one of each age category. The descriptions include basic personality and encounter notes that the DM will want to flesh out for his campaign, along with a set of statistics that make the dragon ready to play.

Dazzle
Wyrmling Blue Dragon

Dazzle spends his days soaring over his desert home like a big, blue hawk—and most of his nights flapping through the darkness like some malevolent bat. He delights in stealing kills from weaker predators. When on the hunt, he pursues

Blue
Dragon
Lawful Evil
Earth Subtype
Desert
Underground
Flight
Old
24 ft.
Vain and territorial, blue dragons are well equipped for burrowing in sand in which they often lie with just the tops of their heads exposed.
Hallucinatory terrain
Destroy water
Ventriloquism
Mirage arcana
Mimicry
Detail of upper and lower jaw fragment showing supporting substructure of heavy bone.
Specimen found at alchemy shop, the rest of the skull having already been ground for potions.
Sub-adult
12 ft.
Young
6 ft.
Wyrmling
3 feet

his quarry any way he can, even if it means digging his prey out of a burrow. Dazzle is almost always on the hunt, but he's smart enough to attempt the occasional parley. His version of a parley, however, usually involves trying to bully someone into giving up treasure, a mount, or even a companion.

Dazzle: Male wyrmling blue dragon; CR 3; Small dragon (earth); HD 6d12+6; hp 45; Init +0; Spd 40 ft., burrow 20 ft., fly 100 ft. (average); AC 16, touch 11, flat-footed 16; Base Atk +8; Grp +3; Atk +8 melee (1d6+1, bite); Full Atk +8 melee (1d6+1, bite), +3 melee (1d4, 2 claws); Space/Reach 5 ft./5 ft.; SA breath weapon, *create/destroy water;* SQ blindsense 60 ft., darkvision 120 ft., immunity to electricity, magic sleep effects, and paralysis, low-light vision; AL LE; SV Fort +6, Ref +7, Will +5; Str 13, Dex 10, Con 13, Int 10, Wis 11, Cha 10.

Skills and Feats: Diplomacy +5, Hide +7, Intimidate +8, Knowledge (nature) +8, Listen +8, Search +8, Sense Motive +8, Spot +8; Clinging Breath, Lightning Reflexes, Hover.

Breath Weapon (Su): 40-ft. line, 2d8 electricity, Reflex DC 14 half.

***Create/Destroy Water* (Sp):** 3/day—as *create water,* but can also be used to destroy water. Caster level 1st; Will DC 13 negates.

Jalnur

Very Young Blue Dragon

Jalnur loves the feel of the hot desert sun. When not basking on a sun-warmed rock, she's skimming low over desert sands shimmering with heat. She tolerates no interlopers in her territory, especially humanoids, whom she regards as inferior and too uppity to admit it. Her blood boils whenever she sees a humanoid traveling with a domestic animal, because she believes that no humanoid should have mastery of anything else, except perhaps, another humanoid. She never hesitates to attack caravans, even when they are far too large for her to handle. In theses cases, she settles for a few passes with her breath weapon, then retreats to attack again another day.

Jalnur: Female very young blue dragon; CR 4; Medium dragon (earth); HD 9d12+18; hp 76; Init +4; Spd 40 ft., burrow 20 ft., fly 150 ft. (poor); AC 18, touch 10, flat-footed 18; Base Atk +11; Grp +11; Atk +11 melee (1d8+2, bite); Full Atk +11 melee (1d8+2, bite), +6 melee (1d6+1, 2 claws), +6 melee (1d4+1, 2 wings); Space/Reach 5 ft./5 ft.; SA breath weapon, *create/destroy water;* SQ blindsense 60 ft., darkvision 120 ft., immunity to electricity, magic sleep effects, and paralysis, low-light vision; AL LE; SV Fort +8, Ref +8, Will +6; Str 15, Dex 10, Con 15, Int 10, Wis 11, Cha 10.

Skills and Feats: Bluff +11, Diplomacy +10, Intimidate +13, Listen +11, Search +11, Sense Motive +11, Spot +11; Flyby Attack, Hover, Improved Initiative, Lightning Reflexes.

Breath Weapon (Su): 60-ft. line, 4d8 electricity, Reflex DC 16 half.

***Create/Destroy Water* (Sp):** 3/day—as *create water,* but can also be used to destroy water. Caster level 2nd; Will DC 14 negates.

Ysauraithus

Young Blue Dragon

Ysauraithus lives on a wide, dry steppe populated by horse-riding nomads. She has quite an appetite for horseflesh, but tries to limit her ravenous cravings in order to avoid drawing the full wrath of the nomadic population upon herself. Some of the nomadic clans make regular offerings of weak or injured horses to appease her, while others suffer occasional raids in which Ysauraithus makes a meal of a horse or two.

Ysauraithus loves to fly, and soars for hours over her domain. As a result, she knows every knoll and gulch on the steppe, and recognizes most of the creatures that dwell there. Newcomers and strangers can count on a visit from the self-appointed queen of the steppe, but as long as they fawn and grovel appropriately she usually lets them live—particularly if they offer her a horse.

Ysauraithus: Female young blue dragon; CR 6; Medium dragon (earth); HD 12d12+24; hp 102; Init +0; Spd 50 ft., burrow 30 ft., fly 170 ft. (poor); AC 21, touch 10, flat-footed 21; Base Atk +15; Grp +15; Atk +15 melee (1d8+3, bite); Full Atk +15 melee (1d8+3, bite), +10 melee (1d6+1, 2 claws), +10 melee (1d4+1, 2 wings); Space/Reach 5 ft./5 ft.; SA breath weapon, *create/destroy water,* frightful presence; SQ blindsense 60 ft., darkvision 120 ft., immunity to electricity, magic sleep effects, and paralysis, low-light vision; AL LE; SV Fort +10, Ref +8, Will +9; Str 17, Dex 10, Con 15, Int 12, Wis 13, Cha 12.

Skills and Feats: Bluff +7, Diplomacy +18, Intimidate +18, Knowledge (arcana) +7, Knowledge (geography) +7, Knowledge (local) +7, Knowledge (nature) +7, Listen +16, Search +16, Spot +16; Awaken Frightful Presence, Flyby Attack, Hover, Improved Speed, Power Climb.

Breath Weapon (Su): 60-ft. line, 6d8 electricity, Reflex DC 18 half.

***Create/Destroy Water* (Sp):** 3/day—as *create water,* but can also be used to destroy water. Caster level 3rd; Will DC 17 negates.

Frightful Presence (Ex): 50-ft. radius, HD 11 or fewer, Will DC 17 negates.

Daudhir

Juvenile Blue Dragon

Daudhir lives in a stretch of desert dotted with several oases, and rules over several bands of jann in that area. He leads the jann in raids on other caravans and settlements, taking the choicest treasures for his own hoard and distributing the rest among his followers. Though thoroughly evil, he is fair, and tries to ensure that the jann profit as much from the association as he does. He does not subject them to unnecessary risks, and rewards those who perform exceptionally well.

Daudhir: Male juvenile blue dragon; CR 8; Large dragon (earth); HD 15d12+45, hp 142; Init +4; Spd 40 ft., burrow 20 ft., fly 150 ft. (poor); AC 23, touch 9, flat-footed 23; Base Atk +18; Grp +23; Atk +18 melee (2d6+4, bite);

Full Atk +18 melee (2d6+4, bite), +13 melee (1d8+2, 2 claws), +13 melee (1d6+2, 2 wings), +13 melee (1d8+6, tail slap); Space/Reach 5 ft./5 ft. (10 ft. with bite); SA breath weapon, *create/destroy water,* sound imitation, spells; SQ blindsense 60 ft., darkvision 120 ft., immunity to electricity, magic sleep effects, and paralysis, low-light vision; AL LE; SV Fort +12, Ref +9, Will +11; Str 19, Dex 10, Con 17, Int 14, Wis 15, Cha 14.

Skills and Feats: Bluff +18, Concentration +19, Diplomacy +11, Hide +3, Intimidate +20, Knowledge (arcana) +12, Knowledge (local) +9, Listen +20, Move Silently +3, Search +18, Speak Language 5 ranks, Spot +20; Alertness, Combat Expertise, Hover, Improved Initiative, Power Attack, Shape Breath.

Breath Weapon (Su): 80-ft. line (40-ft. cone if shaped), 8d8 electricity, Reflex DC 20 half.

***Create/Destroy Water* (Sp):** 3/day—as *create water,* but can also be used to destroy water. Caster level 4th; Will DC 19 negates.

Sound Imitation (Ex): Can mimic any voice or sound it has heard, anytime it likes. Listeners must succeed on DC 19 Will saves to detect the ruse.

Spells: As 1st-level sorcerer.

Sorcerer Spells Known (5/4; save DC 12 + spell level): 0—detect magic, ghost sound, light, mage hand; 1st—bane, magic missile.

Acophisinian
Young Adult Blue Dragon

The bane of Acophisinian's existence is a nest of guardian nagas that "share" her territory. The three nagas have so far been unable to force the dragon out of their region of badlands, and the dragon for her part has honed her combat skills for years, preparing to wipe out the nagas once and for all. She is insecure about her magical ability, however, and wants to improve that—probably by adding levels of sorcerer—before challenging them. She believes the nagas are guarding a priceless treasure and she covets it—in addition to simply wanting them out of her rightful dominion, as she considers it. Acophisinian has an intense personality, and even without the aid of her frightful presence or a *hypnotism* spell other creatures tend to find her either enthralling or terrifying.

Acophisinian: Female young adult blue dragon; CR 11; Large dragon (earth); HD 18d12+72, hp 189; Init +0; Spd 40 ft., burrow 20 ft., fly 150 ft. (poor); AC 26, touch 9, flat-footed 26; Base Atk +23; Grp +28; Atk +23 melee (2d6+6, bite); Full Atk +23 melee (2d6+6, bite), +22 melee (1d8+3, 2 claws), +17 melee (1d8+3, 2 claws), +21 melee (1d6+3, 2 wings), +21 melee (1d8+9, tail slap); Space/Reach 5 ft./5 ft. (15 ft. with bite); SA breath weapon, *create/destroy water,* frightful presence, sound imitation, spells; SQ blindsense 60 ft., damage reduction 5/magic, darkvision 120 ft., immunity to electricity, magic sleep effects, and paralysis, low-light vision, spell resistance 19; AL LE; SV Fort +15, Ref +11, Will +13; Str 23, Dex 10, Con 19, Int 14, Wis 15, Cha 14.

Skills and Feats: Bluff +22, Concentration +13, Diplomacy +15, Hide +5, Intimidate +16, Knowledge (geography) +11, Listen +22, Search +22, Sense Motive +22, Spellcraft +22, Spot +22; Hover, Multiattack, Power Attack, Rapidstrike (claws), Quicken Breath, Recover Breath, Weapon Focus (claw).

Breath Weapon (Su): 80-ft. line, 10d8 electricity, Reflex DC 23 half.

***Create/Destroy Water* (Sp):** 3/day—as *create water,* but can also be used to destroy water. Caster level 5th; Will DC 21 negates.

Frightful Presence (Ex): 150-ft. radius, HD 17 or fewer, Will DC 21 negates.

Sound Imitation (Ex): Can mimic any voice or sound it has heard, anytime it likes. Listeners must succeed on DC 21 Will saves to detect the ruse.

Spells: As 3rd-level sorcerer.

Sorcerer Spells Known (6/6; save DC 12 + spell level): 0—*dancing lights, detect magic, ghost sound, ray of frost, resistance;* 1st—*bane, doom, hypnotism.*

Jabidakimbatuul
Adult Blue Dragon

Young for a suzerain, Jabidakimbatuul has let the power go to his head. By virtue of dwelling in an area that not many blue dragons find appealing—a temperate desert on the leeward side of a high, cold mountain range—he is the oldest of perhaps a half-dozen blue dragons within hundreds of miles, and thus holds the title of suzerain. He enjoys commanding the younger dragons, meddling overmuch in their affairs, and disciplining any misstep or challenge on their part with violent retribution. He considers himself so superior to these younger dragons that non-dragons hardly even merit his notice—which will likely be the death of him.

Jabidakimbatuul: Male adult blue dragon; CR 14; Huge dragon (earth); HD 21d12+105, hp 241; Init +0; Spd 40 ft., burrow 20 ft., fly 150 ft. (average); AC 28, touch 8, flat-footed 28; Base Atk +27; Grp +37; Atk +27 melee (2d8+8, bite); Full Atk +27 melee (2d8+8, bite), +25 melee (2d6+4, 2 claws), +25 melee (1d8+4, 2 wings), +25 melee (2d6+12, tail slap); Space/Reach 15 ft./10 ft. (15 ft. with bite); SA breath weapon, *create/destroy water,* crush, frightful presence, sound imitation, spell-like abilities, spells; SQ blindsense 60 ft., damage reduction 5/magic, darkvision 120 ft., immunity to electricity, magic sleep effects, and paralysis, low-light vision, spell resistance 21; AL LE; SV Fort +17, Ref +12, Will +15; Str 27, Dex 10, Con 21, Int 16, Wis 17, Cha 16.

Skills and Feats: Bluff +26, Concentration +14, Diplomacy +16, Hide +1, Intimidate +28, Knowledge (arcana) +13, Knowledge (geography) +12, Knowledge (local) +12, Listen +26, Search +26, Sense Motive +26, Spellcraft +28, Spot +26; Blind-Fight, Flyby Attack, Hover, Improved Maneuverability, Multiattack, Power Attack, Shape Breath, Spreading Breath.

Breath Weapon (Su): 100-ft. line (50-ft. cone if shaped, 25-ft. spread if spreading), 12d8 electricity, Reflex DC 25 half.

Blue Dragon

Profile View

Typical Blue Dragon Lair

[Size of lair varies with size of dragon]

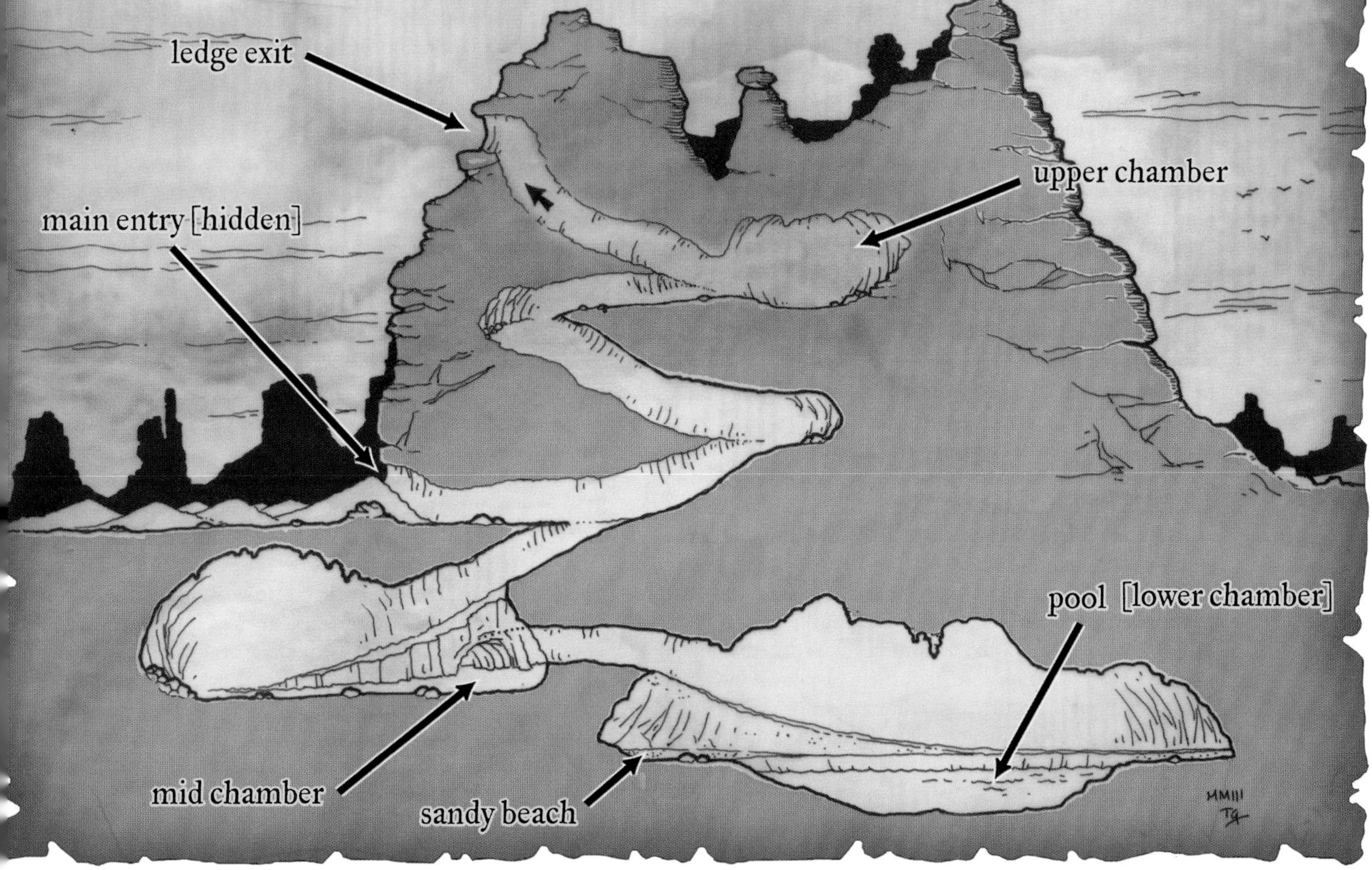

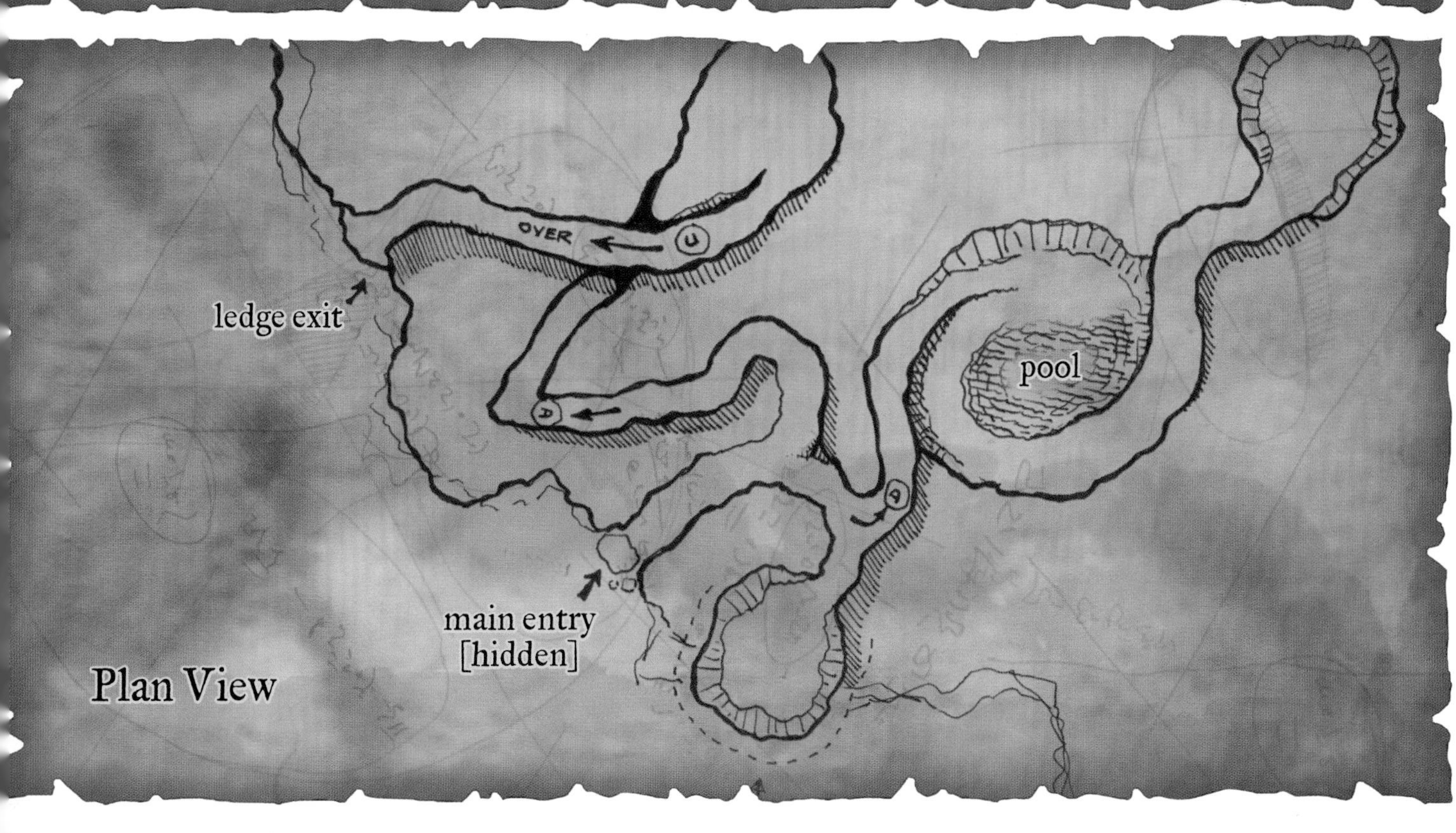

ledge exit

upper chamber

main entry [hidden]

pool [lower chamber]

mid chamber

sandy beach

MMIII

Plan View

OVER

ledge exit

pool

main entry
[hidden]

Create/Destroy Water **(Sp)**: 3/day—as *create water*, but can also be used to destroy water. Caster level 6th; Will DC 21 negates.

Crush (Ex): Area 15 ft. by 15 ft.; Small or smaller opponents take 2d8+12 points of bludgeoning damage, and must succeed on a DC 25 Reflex save or be pinned.

Frightful Presence (Ex): 180-ft. radius, HD 20 or fewer, Will DC 23 negates.

Sound Imitation (Ex): Can mimic any voice or sound it has heard, anytime it likes. Listeners must succeed on DC 23 Will saves to detect the ruse.

Spell-Like Abilities: 3/day—*ventriloquism*. Caster level 6th; save DC 14 + spell level.

Spells: As 5th-level sorcerer.

Sorcerer Spells Known (6/7/5; save DC 13 + spell level): 0—*dancing lights, detect magic, ghost sound, ray of frost, read magic, resistance*; 1st—*bane, chill touch, command, shield*; 2nd—*darkness, sound burst*.

Trundrachedandion
Mature Adult Blue Dragon

A devout worshiper of Tiamat, Trundrachedandion is wantonly destructive and intentionally cruel. She fancies herself a cleric of the Chromatic Dragon, and counts a handful of cleric spells among her spells known. She is not actually a cleric, though someday she might aspire to the unholy ravager of Tiamat prestige class (see Dragon Prestige Classes in the Chapter ???). In the meantime, she contents herself with wreaking as much destruction as possible on the world around her, with a particular emphasis on hunting down every brass or copper dragon that comes within a hundred miles of her lair.

Trundrachedandion: Female mature adult blue dragon; CR 16; Huge dragon (earth); HD 24d12+120, hp 276; Init +4; Spd 40 ft., burrow 20 ft., fly 150 ft. (poor); AC 31, touch 8, flat-footed 31; Base Atk +31; Grp +41; Atk +31 melee (2d8+9, bite); Full Atk +31 melee (2d8+9, bite), +29 melee (2d6+4, 2 claws), +29 melee (1d8+4, 2 wings), +29 melee (2d6+13, tail slap); Space/Reach 15 ft./10 ft. (15 ft. with bite); SA breath weapon, *create/destroy water*, crush, frightful presence, sound imitation, spell-like abilities, spells; SQ blindsense 60 ft., damage reduction 10/magic, darkvision 120 ft., immunity to electricity, magic sleep effects, and paralysis, low-light vision, spell resistance 22; AL LE; SV Fort +19, Ref +14, Will +17; Str 29, Dex 10, Con 21, Int 16, Wis 17, Cha 16.

Skills and Feats: Bluff +28, Concentration +16, Diplomacy +32, Hide +3, Intimidate +30, Knowledge (arcana) +14, Knowledge (nature) +13, Listen +28, Search +28, Sense Motive +28, Spellcraft +30, Spot +28; Combat Expertise, Flyby Attack, Hover, Improved Initiative, Large and in Charge, Multiattack, Power Attack, Recover Breath, Shape Breath.

Breath Weapon (Su): 100-ft. line (50-ft. cone if shaped), 14d8 electricity, Reflex DC 27 half.

Create/Destroy Water **(Sp)**: 3/day—as *create water*, but can also be used to destroy water. Caster level 7th; Will DC 25 negates.

Crush (Ex): Area 15 ft. by 15 ft.; Small or smaller opponents take 2d8+13 points of bludgeoning damage, and must succeed on a DC 27 Reflex save or be pinned.

Frightful Presence (Ex): 210-ft. radius, HD 23 or fewer, Will DC 25 negates.

Sound Imitation (Ex): Can mimic any voice or sound it has heard, anytime it likes. Listeners must succeed on DC 25 Will saves to detect the ruse.

Spell-Like Abilities: 3/day—*ventriloquism*. Caster level 7th; save DC 13 + spell level.

Spells: As 7th-level sorcerer.

Sorcerer Spells Known (6/7/7/5; save DC 13 + spell level): 0—*dancing lights, detect magic, ghost sound, mage hand, ray of frost, read magic, resistance*; 1st—*alarm, command, magic missile, Nystul's magic aura, shield of faith*; 2nd—*darkness, invisibility, shatter*; 3rd—*cure serious wounds, flame arrow*.

Vurlymakipvearox
Old Blue Dragon

Vurlymakipvearox is loud, boisterous, and obnoxious. Silence annoys him; even when soaring a mile above the earth he roars, bellows, and laughs raucously to himself. His prey inevitably hear him coming before they see him—but even such advance warning is seldom enough, for he is as persistent and rapacious as he is noisy. A rushing river runs through the caves at the bottom of his subterranean lair, filling the entire lair with echoes of its splashing and roaring. For obvious reasons, *shout* and *sound burst* are among his favorite spells, but he casts every spell in a thunderous voice.

Vurlymakipvearox: Male old blue dragon; CR 18; Huge dragon (earth); HD 27d12+162, hp 337; Init +4; Spd 40 ft., burrow 20 ft., fly 150 ft. (poor); AC 34, touch 8, flat-footed 34; Base Atk +35; Grp +45; Atk +35 melee (2d8+10, bite); Full Atk +35 melee (2d8+10, bite), +30 melee (2d6+5, 2 claws), +30 melee (1d8+5, 2 wings), +30 melee (2d6+15, tail slap); Space/Reach 15 ft./10 ft. (15 ft. with bite); SA breath weapon, *create/destroy water*, crush, frightful presence, sound imitation, spell-like abilities, spells; SQ blindsense 60 ft., damage reduction 10/magic, darkvision 120 ft., immunity to electricity, magic sleep effects, and paralysis, low-light vision, spell resistance 24; AL LE; SV Fort +21, Ref +15, Will +19; Str 31, Dex 10, Con 23, Int 18, Wis 19, Cha 18.

Skills and Feats: Bluff +32, Concentration +22, Diplomacy +34, Hide +4, Intimidate +34, Knowledge (arcana) +16, Knowledge (geography) +16, Knowledge (local) +16, Knowledge (nature) +16, Listen +32, Search +32, Sense Motive +32, Spellcraft +34, Spot +32; Blind-Fight, Combat Reflexes, Dire Charge, Flyby Attack, Hover, Improved Initiative, Power Attack, Quicken Breath, Recover Breath, Shape Breath.

Breath Weapon (Su): 100-ft. line (50-ft. cone if shaped), 16d8 electricity, Reflex DC 29 half.

Create/Destroy Water **(Sp)**: 3/day—as *create water*, but can also be used to destroy water. Caster level 9th; Will DC 27 negates.

Crush (Ex): Area 15 ft. by 15 ft.; Small or smaller opponents take 2d8+15 points of bludgeoning damage, and must succeed on a DC 29 Reflex save or be pinned.

Frightful Presence (Ex): 240-ft. radius, HD 26 or fewer, Will DC 27 negates.

Sound Imitation (Ex): Can mimic any voice or sound it has heard, anytime it likes. Listeners must succeed on DC 27 Will saves to detect the ruse.

Spell-Like Abilities: 3/day—*ventriloquism;* 1/day—*hallucinatory terrain.* Caster level 9th; save DC 14 + spell level.

Spells: As 9th-level sorcerer.

Sorcerer Spells Known (6/7/7/7/5; save DC 14 + spell level): 0—*arcane mark, dancing lights, detect magic, ghost sound, mage hand, ray of frost, read magic, resistance;* 1st—*command, magic missile, Nystul's magic aura, shield, shield of faith;* 2nd—*detect thoughts, fog cloud, minor image, sound burst;* 3rd—*clairaudience/clairvoyance, deeper darkness, dispel magic;* 4th—*crushing despair, shout.*

Renveshalhiarisv
Very Old Blue Dragon

A straggling line of barren peaks winds along one edge of a great desert, as dry and desolate as the windswept sand far below. Atop the highest of these peaks is the cavernous lair of Renveshalhiarisv. To the troglodytes that live in smaller caves on the lower slopes of the range, she is a raging force of nature, a living embodiment of violent storms of wind and hail. They offer regular sacrifices to appease the dragon's wrath, and tremble at the sound of her approach. Renveshalhiarisv considers herself more a philosopher than a destroyer, however—a student of subjects natural and arcane, a repository of local gossip from every settlement and tribe near her lair, and a keen judge of character. For all her scholarly pretension, however, nothing survives for long if it gets in her way when she is hungry.

Renveshalhiarisv: Female very old blue dragon; CR 19; Huge dragon (earth); HD 30d12+180, hp 375; Init +0; Spd 40 ft., burrow 20 ft., fly 150 ft. (average); AC 37, touch 8, flat-footed 37; Base Atk +39; Grp +49; Atk +39 melee (2d8+11, bite); Full Atk +39 melee (2d8+11, bite), +37 melee (2d6+5, 2 claws), +37 melee (1d8+5, 2 wings), +37 melee (2d6+16, tail slap); Space/Reach 15 ft./10 ft. (15 ft. with bite); SA breath weapon, *create/destroy water,* crush, frightful presence, sound imitation, spell-like abilities, spells; SQ blindsense 60 ft., damage reduction 15/magic, darkvision 120 ft., immunity to electricity, magic sleep effects, and paralysis, low-light vision, spell resistance 25; AL LE; SV Fort +23, Ref +17, Will +21; Str 33, Dex 10, Con 23, Int 18, Wis 19, Cha 18.

Skills and Feats: Bluff +35, Concentration +22, Diplomacy +39, Hide +6, Intimidate +37, Knowledge (arcana) +20, Knowledge (geography) +16, Knowledge (local) +16, Knowledge (nature) +16, Listen +35, Search +35, Sense Motive +35, Spellcraft +37, Spot +35; Combat Reflexes, Flyby Attack, Hover, Improved Maneuverability, Multiattack, Power Attack, Quicken Breath, Recover Breath, Shape Breath, Spreading Breath, Wingstorm.

Breath Weapon (Su): 100-ft. line (50-ft. cone if shaped, 25-ft. spread if spreading), 18d8 electricity, Reflex DC 31 half.

***Create/Destroy Water* (Sp):** 3/day—as *create water,* but can also be used to destroy water. Caster level 11th; Will DC 29 negates.

Crush (Ex): Area 15 ft. by 15 ft.; Small or smaller opponents take 2d8+16 points of bludgeoning damage, and must succeed on a DC 31 Reflex save or be pinned.

Frightful Presence (Ex): 270-ft. radius, HD 29 or fewer, Will DC 29 negates.

Sound Imitation (Ex): Can mimic any voice or sound it has heard, anytime it likes. Listeners must succeed on DC 29 Will saves to detect the ruse.

Spell-Like Abilities: 3/day—*ventriloquism;* 1/day—*hallucinatory terrain.* Caster level 11th; save DC 14 + spell level.

Spells: As 11th-level sorcerer.

Sorcerer Spells Known (6/7/7/7/7/4; save DC 14 + spell level): 0—*arcane mark, dancing lights, detect magic, ghost sound, guidance, mage hand, ray of frost, read magic, resistance;* 1st—*alarm, bane, protection from good, shield, shield of faith;* 2nd—*cat's grace, cure moderate wounds, detect thoughts, fog cloud, shatter;* 3rd—*deeper darkness, dispel magic, haste, suggestion;* 4th—*charm monster, freedom of movement, ice storm;* 5th—*cone of cold, greater command.*

Dreargakaduayrte
Ancient Blue Dragon

His eyes grown milky and blind with age, Dreargakaduayrte shrouds himself with darkness at all times. His cavern lair is draped with *deeper darkness* (cast using the Extend Spell feat so he only needs to renew a given spell every 26 days) and infested with shadows he made with *create undead.* (The shadows are intelligent enough to leave Dreargakaduayrte alone, though he has no magical control over them.) He spends much time sleeping, and seems to be preparing to enter his twilight. However, he is a simmering cauldron of anger and resentment, lashing out violently at any living creature that comes too near his lair while he happens to be awake. He has no interest in conversation or negotiation, only in death—other creatures' first, but he is fascinated with the concept of his own inevitable demise, after having lived so long.

Dreargakaduayrte: Male ancient blue dragon; CR 21; Gargantuan dragon (earth); HD 33d12+231, hp 445; Init +0; Spd 40 ft., burrow 20 ft., fly 200 ft. (poor); AC 38, touch 6, flat-footed 38; Base Atk +41; Grp +57; Atk +41 melee (4d6+12, bite); Full Atk +41 melee (4d6+12, bite), +36 melee (2d8+6, 2 claws), +36 melee (2d6+6, 2 wings), +36 melee (2d8+18, tail slap); Space/Reach 20 ft./15 ft. (20 ft. with bite); SA breath weapon, *create/destroy water,* crush, frightful presence, rend, snatch, sound imitation, spell-like abilities, spells, tail sweep; SQ blind, blindsense 60 ft., damage reduction 15/magic, darkvision 120 ft., immunity to electricity, magic sleep effects, and paralysis, low-light vision, spell resistance 27; AL LE; SV Fort +25, Ref +18, Will +23; Str 35, Dex 10, Con 25, Int 20, Wis 21, Cha 20.

Skills and Feats: Bluff +41, Concentration +27, Diplomacy +45, Hide +7, Intimidate +43, Knowledge (arcana) +24, Knowledge (geography) +15, Knowledge (history) +15, Knowledge (local) +15, Knowledge (nature) +15, Knowledge (religion) +15, Listen +41, Search +41, Sense Motive +41, Spellcraft +43, Spot +41; Blind-Fight, Combat Expertise, Extend Spell, Flyby Attack, Hover, Improved Maneuverability, Large and in Charge, Power Attack, Recover Breath, Rend, Shape Breath, Snatch.

Blind (Ex): Dreargakaduayrte is blind and relies completely on his blindsense. He is immune to gaze attacks and blinding attacks.

Breath Weapon (Su): 120-ft. line (60-ft. cone if shaped), 20d8 electricity, Reflex DC 33 half.

Create/Destroy Water **(Sp):** 3/day—as *create water*, but can also be used to destroy water. Caster level 13th; Will DC 31 negates.

Crush (Ex): Area 20 ft. by 20 ft.; Medium or smaller opponents take 4d6+18 points of bludgeoning damage, and must succeed on a DC 33 Reflex save or be pinned.

Frightful Presence (Ex): 300-ft. radius, HD 32 or fewer, Will DC 31 negates.

Rend (Ex): Extra damage 4d8+18.

Snatch (Ex): Against Medium or smaller creatures, bite for 4d6+12/round or claw for 2d8+6/round.

Sound Imitation (Ex): Can mimic any voice or sound it has heard, anytime it likes. Listeners must succeed on DC 31 Will saves to detect the ruse.

Spell-Like Abilities: 3/day—*ventriloquism;* 1/day—*hallucinatory terrain, veil.* Caster level 13th; save DC 15 + spell level.

Spells: As 13th-level sorcerer.

Tail Sweep (Ex): Half-circle 30 ft. in diameter, Small or smaller opponents take 2d6+18 points of bludgeoning damage, Reflex DC 33 half.

Sorcerer Spells Known (6/8/7/7/7/7/4; save DC 15 + spell level): 0—*arcane mark, dancing lights, detect magic, ghost sound, guidance, mage hand, ray of frost, read magic, resistance;* 1st—*alarm, bane, protection from good, shield, shield of faith;* 2nd—*cat's grace, cure moderate wounds, detect thoughts, fog cloud, shatter;* 3rd—*deeper darkness, dispel magic, haste, suggestion;* 4th—*charm monster, freedom of movement, ice storm;* 5th—*cone of cold, greater command;* 6th—*create undead, greater dispel magic.*

Aarazthoorus
Wyrm Blue Dragon

Many evil dragons never aspire for more than selfishness and cruelty, random destruction, or cold-blooded killing. Aarazthoorus, however, is filled with as much unmitigated malevolence as a fiend from Hell, and has the power to wreak her evil upon the world. Her heart is untarnished by any shred of mercy or compassion, any sentiment whatsoever, and every word out of her mouth is utter blasphemy to those of good alignment. Domination and tyranny are her life, and she seeks to expunge every trace of goodness from her domain. She consorts with devils and traffics with their lords as a near-equal. Her deep subterranean lair holds a permanent *gate* to one of the layers of Hell, and she spends nearly as much time there as on the Material Plane.

Aarazthoorus: Female wyrm blue dragon; CR 23; Gargantuan dragon (earth); HD 36d12+288, hp 522; Init +4; Spd 40 ft., burrow 20 ft., fly 200 ft. (poor); AC 41, touch 6, flat-footed 41; Base Atk +45; Grp +61; Atk +45 melee (4d6+13, bite); Full Atk +45 melee (4d6+13, bite), +43 melee (2d8+6, 2 claws), +43 melee (2d6+6, 2 wings), +43 melee (2d8+19, tail slap); Space/Reach 20 ft./15 ft. (20 ft. with bite); SA breath weapon, *create/destroy water*, crush, frightful presence, sound imitation, spell-like abilities, spells, tail sweep; SQ blindsense 60 ft., damage reduction 20/magic, darkvision 120 ft., immunity to electricity, magic sleep effects, and paralysis, low-light vision, spell resistance 29; AL LE; SV Fort +28, Ref +20, Will +25; Str 37, Dex 10, Con 27, Int 20, Wis 21, Cha 20.

Skills and Feats: Appraise +15, Bluff +44, Concentration +30, Diplomacy +48, Hide +10, Intimidate +46, Knowledge (arcana) +24, Knowledge (nature) +20, Listen +44, Search +44, Sense Motive +44, Spellcraft +46, Spot +44, Survival +14; Dire Charge, Flyby Attack, Hover, Improved Initiative, Improved Maneuverability, Multiattack, Power Attack, Power Climb, Quicken Breath, Recover Breath, Shape Breath, Snatch, Spreading Breath.

Breath Weapon (Su): 120-ft. line (60-ft. cone if shaped, 30-ft. spread if spreading), 22d8 electricity, Reflex DC 36 half.

Create/Destroy Water **(Sp):** 3/day—as *create water*, but can also be used to destroy water. Caster level 15th; Will DC 33 negates.

Crush (Ex): Area 20 ft. by 20 ft.; Medium or smaller opponents take 4d6+19 points of bludgeoning damage, and must succeed on a DC 36 Reflex save or be pinned.

Frightful Presence (Ex): 330-ft. radius, HD 35 or fewer, Will DC 33 negates.

Snatch (Ex): Against Medium or smaller creatures, bite for 4d6+13/round or claw for 2d8+6/round.

Sound Imitation (Ex): Can mimic any voice or sound it has heard, anytime it likes. Listeners must succeed on DC 33 Will saves to detect the ruse.

Spell-Like Abilities: 3/day—*ventriloquism;* 1/day—*hallucinatory terrain, veil.* Caster level 15th; save DC 15 + spell level.

Spells: As 15th-level sorcerer.

Tail Sweep (Ex): Half-circle 30 ft. in diameter, Small or smaller opponents take 2d6+19 points of bludgeoning damage, Reflex DC 36 half.

Sorcerer Spells Known (6/8/7/7/7/7/6/4; save DC 15 + spell level): 0—*arcane mark, dancing lights, detect magic, ghost sound, guidance, mage hand, ray of frost, read magic, resistance;* 1st—*alarm, bane, protection from good, shield, shield of faith;* 2nd—*cat's grace, cure moderate wounds, detect thoughts, fog cloud, shatter;* 3rd—*deeper darkness, dispel magic, haste, suggestion;* 4th—*dimension door, enervation, freedom of movement, unholy blight;* 5th—*dominate person, greater command, hold monster, persistent image;* 6th—*circle of death, greater dispel magic, heal;* 7th—*blasphemy, prismatic spray.*

Lothaenorixius
Great Wyrm Blue Dragon

Lothaenorixius is a dragon possessed. For decades, he preyed on salt caravans crossing his desert territory. The people who operated the caravans and the mines that supplied them constantly sought to eliminate the dragon. One day, a group of adventurers hired by a mine owner located Lothaenorixius's lair and nearly succeeded in slaying him. Enraged, the dragon assaulted the mine itself, destroying the owners and taking over the entire mine.

Lothaenorixius was quick to realize that the mine was a source of wealth. Rather than destroy it, he kept it in operation. The dragon now spends his days and nights trying to extract the maximum profit from his mine.

Lothaenorixius knows he must spend something on food and lodgings for his workers and draft animals, but in his greed he begrudges every copper spent. He constantly tries to produce the maximum profit for the minimum investment. He makes extensive use of undead labor, but undead creatures do not work quickly enough to satisfy him. As a result, he finds some living workers a necessity, especially for transporting salt to market.

Every three months, Lothaenorixius reviews production and income, then makes adjustments to his workforce. This usually entails killing and eating some workers (though he always saves some bodies for later animation as undead). If he's particularly displeased with the results, even his followers and cohorts feel his wrath.

In spite of his management methods, Lothaenorixius tries to keep a low profile. He has circulated a tale of his defeat at the hands of the party who unsuccessfully assaulted him in his lair. He runs the mine through his special cohort Lilanab (currently his 8th, the previous seven having been slain as examples to the rest of the workforce). Lilanab is an erinyes devil who masquerades as a human and poses as the leader of the group that "killed" Lothaenorixius.

Parties are more likely to encounter Lothaenorixius's servants that the dragon himself, unless they attack and loot the mine. Lothaenorixius comes forth to defend his holding if he perceives any threat. He also occasionally takes wing just to feel and breathe the hot desert air, or to disrupt a competitor's trade.

Lothaenorixius spends most of each day keeping tabs on business at the mine. He uses *prying eyes* spells and a *crystal ball* to monitor activities throughout the place. This surveillance usually gives him ample warning of any attempts to invade his lair.

Lothaenorixius usually tries to disguise himself before entering combat. He uses his *veil* ability to appear as some other big, flying creature. A gynosphinx or a brass dragon are two of his favorite guises.

Lothaenorixius stays hidden in a vast, secret chamber in the salt mine he has taken over. The mine and the complex of buildings that support it are home to more than 300 beings. These include Lilanab and more than 50 clerics with access to the Evil and Earth domains, dozens of mummies, and about 100 zombies. The remainder (around 150 individuals) consists of overworked slaves of various kinds (mostly humans). Every resident with an Intelligence score is aware that an unseen master controls the mine, but only Lilanab and the clerics know their overlord is the great blue wyrm Lothaenorixius.

Lothaenorixius: Male great wyrm blue dragon; CR 25; Gargantuan dragon (earth); HD 39d12+312, hp 565; Init +0; Spd 40 ft., burrow 20 ft., fly 200 ft. (poor); AC 44, touch 6, flat-footed 44; Base Atk +49; Grp +65; Atk +49 melee (4d6+14, bite); Full Atk +49 melee (4d6+14, bite), +47 melee (2d8+7, 2 claws), +47 melee (2d6+7, 2 wings), +47 melee (2d8+21, tail slap); Space/Reach 20 ft./15 ft. (20 ft. with bite); SA breath weapon, *create/destroy water*, crush, frightful presence, snatch, sound imitation, spell-like abilities, spells, tail sweep; SQ blindsense 60 ft., damage reduction 20/magic, darkvision 120 ft., immunity to electricity, magic sleep effects, and paralysis, low-light vision, spell resistance 31; AL LE; SV Fort +29, Ref +21, Will +27; Str 39, Dex 10, Con 27, Int 22, Wis 23, Cha 22.

Skills and Feats: Bluff +48, Concentration +29, Diplomacy +52, Hide +9, Intimidate +50, Knowledge (arcana) +27, Knowledge (history) +27, Knowledge (nature) +27, Knowledge (religion) +27, Listen +48, Move Silently +10, Search +48, Sense Motive +48, Spellcraft +50, Spot +48, Survival +16; Blind-Fight, Combat Expertise, Epic Will, Flyby Attack, Hover, Improved Maneuverability, Leadership, Multiattack, Power Attack, Recover Breath, Shape Breath, Shock Wave, Snatch, Spreading Breath.

Breath Weapon (Su): 120-ft. line (60-ft. cone if shaped, 30-ft. spread if spreading), 24d8 electricity, Reflex DC 37 half.

***Create/Destroy Water* (Sp):** 3/day—as *create water*, but can also be used to destroy water. Caster level 17th; Will DC 35 negates.

Crush (Ex): Area 20 ft. by 20 ft.; Medium or smaller opponents take 4d6+21 points of bludgeoning damage, and must succeed on a DC 37 Reflex save or be pinned.

Frightful Presence (Ex): 360-ft. radius, HD 38 or fewer, Will DC 35 negates.

Snatch (Ex): Against Medium or smaller creatures, bite for 4d6+14/round or claw for 2d8+7/round.

Sound Imitation (Ex): Can mimic any voice or sound it has heard, anytime it likes. Listeners must succeed on DC 35 Will saves to detect the ruse.

Spell-Like Abilities: 3/day—*ventriloquism*; 1/day—*hallucinatory terrain, mirage arcana, veil.* Caster level 17th; save DC 16 + spell level.

Spells: As 17th-level sorcerer.

LOTHAENORIXIUS'S LEADERSHIP FEAT

Lothaenorixius's base leadership score is 61. However, his score with respect to cohorts is only 47, mostly because he has killed 7 of them. With respect to followers, his leadership score is 62.

Tail Sweep (Ex): Half-circle 30 ft. in diameter, Small or smaller opponents take 2d6+21 points of bludgeoning damage, Reflex DC 37 half.

Sorcerer Spells Known (6/8/8/7/7/7/7/6/4; save DC 16 + spell level): 0—*arcane mark, dancing lights, detect magic, ghost sound, guidance, mage hand, ray of frost, read magic, resistance;* 1st—*alarm, command, protection from good, shield, shield of faith;* 2nd—*cat's grace, cure moderate wounds, detect thoughts, touch of idiocy, whispering wind;* 3rd—*animate dead, deeper darkness, haste, suggestion;* 4th—*dimension door, cure critical wounds, freedom of movement, unholy blight;* 5th—*dominate person, greater command, prying eyes, symbol of pain;* 6th—*circle of death, create undead, greater dispel magic;* 7th—*blasphemy, destruction, prismatic spray;* 8th—*horrid wilting, whirlwind.*

SAMPLE BRASS DRAGONS

Listed below are twelve sample brass dragons, one of each age category. The descriptions include basic personality and encounter notes that the DM will want to flesh out for his campaign, along with a set of statistics that make the dragon ready to play.

Mychasi
Wyrmling Brass Dragon

Mychasi loves to talk—nonstop—about anything, but tends to steer any conversation toward topics he knows, even when doing so forces him into a non sequitur. When unable to converse with a sapient creature, Mychasi happily converses with passing animals, or simply talks to himself. Adventurers can often get useful information about local events from him, but only after engaging in an extended chat in which the little dragon relates a seemingly endless stream of superfluous details.

Mychasi: Male wyrmling brass dragon; CR 3; Tiny dragon (fire); HD 4d12+4; hp 30; Init +0; Spd 60 ft., burrow 30 ft., fly 150 ft. (average); AC 15, touch 12, flat-footed 15; Base Atk +6; Grp –4; Atk +6 melee (1d4, bite); Full Atk +6 melee (1d4, bite), +1 melee (1d3, 2 claws); Space/Reach 2-1/2 ft./0 ft. (5 ft. with bite); SA breath weapon, spell-like abilities; SQ blindsense 60 ft., darkvision 120 ft., immunity to fire, magic sleep effects, and paralysis, low-light vision, vulnerability to cold; AL CG; SV Fort +5, Ref +4, Will +4; Str 11, Dex 10, Con 13, Int 10, Wis 11, Cha 10.

Skills and Feats: Hide +11, Knowledge (history) +6, Knowledge (local) +6, Knowledge (nature) +5, Listen +6, Search +6, Spot +6; Enlarge Breath, Flyby Attack.

Breath Weapon (Su): 30-ft. line (45-ft. line if enlarged), 1d6 fire, Reflex DC 13 half; or 15-ft. cone (20-ft. cone if enlarged), *sleep* 1d6+1 rounds, Will DC 13 negates.

Spell-Like Abilities: At will—*speak with animals.* Caster level 1st.

Poccri
Very Young Brass Dragon

Poccri is a dragon on the run. Forced out of her lair by a marauding band of gnolls, she now finds herself hunted throughout her territory. Strangely, the gnolls seem protected against her frightful presence, uncowed by her combat prowess, and not satisfied by just taking over her lair and stealing her hoard. The reason behind this uncharacteristic behavior is a gnoll cleric who has taken Poccri's destruction as a personal quest in honor of Erythnul.

Poccri never stays in the same place for long, rarely curling up in the same crevice for more than one night. She expends all her energy fighting the gnolls where she can and seeking allies in the desolate land of her territory.

Poccri: Female very young brass dragon; CR 4; Small dragon (fire); HD 7d12+7; hp 52; Init +4; Spd 60 ft., burrow 30 ft., fly 150 ft. (average); AC 17, touch 11, flat-footed 17; Base Atk +9; Grp +4; Atk +9 melee (1d6+1, bite); Full Atk +9 melee (1d6+1, bite), +4 melee (1d4, 2 claws); Space/Reach 5 ft./5 ft.; SA breath weapon, spell-like abilities; SQ blindsense 60 ft., darkvision 120 ft., immunity to fire, magic sleep effects, and paralysis, low-light vision, spell resistance 7, vulnerability to cold; AL CG; SV Fort +6, Ref +5, Will +5; Str 13, Dex 10, Con 13, Int 10, Wis 11, Cha 10.

Skills and Feats: Bluff +8, Diplomacy +8, Hide +6, Intimidate +6, Knowledge (local) +8, Listen +8, Search +8, Sense Motive +8, Spot +8; Awaken Spell Resistance, Improved Initiative, Wingover.

Breath Weapon (Su): 40-ft. line, 2d6 fire, Reflex DC 14 half; or 20-ft. cone, *sleep* 1d6+2 rounds, Will DC 14 negates.

Spell-Like Abilities: At will—*speak with animals.* Caster level 2nd.

Vultsubai
Young Brass Dragon

Unlike many of his kind, Vultsubai enjoys the fine art of conversation—not simply the sound of his own voice. He lairs near a large city, and his favorite topic of conversation is local gossip about the humans and dwarves who live in the city. He knows intimate secrets about people he has never met, simply finding their quirks, habits, and misadventures a source of endless fascination. He finds the dwarves especially interesting, since their personalities are generally so different from his own. He can eagerly listen to the most long-winded dwarf recite a lengthy clan history in Dwarven without showing a trace of boredom.

Vultsubai: Male young brass dragon; CR 6; Medium dragon (fire); HD 10d12+20; hp 85; Init +4; Spd 60 ft., burrow 30 ft., fly 200 ft. (poor); AC 19, touch 10, flat-footed 19; Base Atk +12; Grp +2; Atk +12 melee (1d8+2, bite); Full Atk +12 melee (1d8+2, bite), +7 melee (1d6+1, 2 claws), +7 melee (1d4+1, 2 wings); Space/Reach 5 ft./5 ft.; SA breath weapon, spell-like abilities, spells; SQ blindsense 60 ft., darkvision 120 ft., immunity to fire, magic sleep effects, and paralysis, low-light vision, vulnerability to cold; AL CG; SV Fort +9, Ref +7, Will +8; Str 15, Dex 10, Con 15, Int 12, Wis 13, Cha 12.

Skills and Feats: Bluff +14, Diplomacy +11, Gather Information +8, Intimidate +8, Knowledge (local) +14, Listen +14, Search +13, Sense Motive +13, Spot +13; Heighten Breath, Hover, Improved Initiative, Power Attack.

Breath Weapon (Su): 60-ft. line, 3d6 fire, Reflex DC 17 half (or higher if heightened); or 30-ft. cone, *sleep* 1d6+3 rounds, Will DC 17 negates (or higher if heightened).

Spell-Like Abilities: At will—*speak with animals.* Caster level 3rd.

Spells: As 1st-level sorcerer.

Sorcerer Spells Known: (5/4; save DC 11 + spell level): 0—*dancing lights, guidance, prestidigitation, read magic;* 1st—*command, magic missile.*

Amnehodenphinix
Juvenile Brass Dragon

Amnehodenphinix has a friend and mentor from whom she is virtually inseparable: a gynosphinx named Taerhanna. The dragon imitates the sphinx's mannerisms and shares her love of puzzles and riddles. The two engage in witty banter during nearly every waking moment, weaving complex multilingual puns in an unending contest of cleverness and ingenuity. While Amnehodenphinix remains so young, the sphinx is clearly her superior in this match of wits. The dragon's greatest fear is that Taeranna will die—of old age if not from violence—before Amnehodenphinix can best her intellect (quite likely, since Amnehodenphinix will not attain an 18 Intelligence for over 5 centuries).

Amnehodenphinix: Female juvenile brass dragon; CR 8; Medium dragon (fire); HD 13d12+26, hp 110; Init +0; Spd 60 ft., burrow 30 ft., fly 200 ft. (poor); AC 22, touch 10, flat-footed 22; Base Atk +16; Grp +16; Atk +16 melee (1d8+3, bite); Full Atk +16 melee (1d8+3, bite), +11 melee (1d6+1, 2 claws), +11 melee (1d4+1, 2 wings); Space/Reach 5 ft./5 ft.; SA breath weapon, spell-like abilities, spells; SQ blindsense 60 ft., darkvision 120 ft., *endure elements,* immunity to fire, magic sleep effects, and paralysis, low-light vision, vulnerability to cold; AL CG; SV Fort +10, Ref +8, Will +9; Str 17, Dex 10, Con 15, Int 12, Wis 13, Cha 12.

Skills and Feats: Bluff +16, Concentration +17, Diplomacy +9, Gather Information +9, Hide +3, Intimidate +8, Knowledge (local) +7, Listen +18, Search +16, Sense Motive +5, Spellcraft +8, Spot +7; Alertness, Flyby Attack, Heighten Breath, Heighten Spell, Hover.

Breath Weapon (Su): 60-ft. line, 4d6 fire, Reflex DC 18 half (or higher if heightened); or 30-ft. cone, *sleep* 1d6+4 rounds, Will DC 18 negates (or higher if heightened).

***Endure Elements* (Sp):** 3/day—as *endure elements,* but 40-ft. radius. Caster level 4th.

Spell-Like Abilities: At will—*speak with animals.* Caster level 4th.

Spells: As 3rd-level sorcerer.

Sorcerer Spells Known (6/6; save DC 11 + spell level): 0—*detect magic, mage hand, prestidigitation, read magic, resistance;* 1st—*chill touch, expeditious retreat, hypnotism.*

Alazphraxion
Young Adult Brass Dragon

Alazphraxion likes to set things on fire. He is not destructive, he simply finds fire beautiful—and sometimes loses track of what is burning. He tends to toy with fire while talking (which he does as much as any brass dragon), which can have an unnerving effect on his conversation partners, but he is oblivious to their discomfort.

Alazphraxion makes his lair in a series of volcanic caverns in a mountain range at the edge of a great desert. When he has no one to talk to in his lair, he enjoys splashing lava around and observing its effects on various other substances.

Alazphraxion: Young adult male brass dragon; CR 10; Large dragon (fire); HD 16d12+48, hp 152; Init +0; Spd 60 ft., burrow 30 ft., fly 200 ft. (poor); AC 24, touch 9, flat-footed 24; Base Atk +19; Grp +24; Atk +19 melee (2d6+4, bite); Full Atk +19 melee (2d6+4, bite), +14 melee (1d8+2, 2 claws), +14 melee (1d6+2, 2 wings), +14 melee (1d8+6, tail slap); Space/Reach 10 ft./5 ft. (10 ft. with bite); SA breath weapon, frightful presence, spell-like abilities, spells; SQ blindsense 60 ft., damage reduction 5/magic, darkvision 120 ft., *endure elements,* immunity to fire, magic sleep effects, and paralysis, low-light vision, spell resistance 18, vulnerability to cold; AL CG; SV Fort +13, Ref +10, Will +12; Str 19, Dex 10, Con 17, Int 14, Wis 15, Cha 14.

Skills and Feats: Bluff +21, Concentration +22, Diplomacy +16, Gather Information +10, Hide –1, Intimidate +9, Knowledge (local) +7, Listen +21, Search +21, Sense Motive +8, Spellcraft +11, Spot +21; Combat Expertise, Hover, Multiattack, Power Attack, Recover Breath, Shape Breath.

Breath Weapon (Su): 80-ft. line (40-ft. cone if shaped), 5d6 fire, Reflex DC 21 half; or 40-ft. cone (80-ft. line if shaped), *sleep* 1d6+5 rounds, Will DC 21 negates.

***Endure Elements* (Sp):** 3/day—as *endure elements,* but 50-ft. radius. Caster level 5th.

Frightful Presence (Ex): 150-ft. radius, HD 15 or fewer, Will DC 20 negates.

Spell-Like Abilities: At will—*speak with animals.* Caster level 5th.

Spells: As 5th-level sorcerer.

Sorcerer Spells Known (6/7/5; save DC 12 + spell level): 0—*detect magic, ghost sound, mage hand, prestidigitation, read magic, resistance;* 1st—*entropic shield, hypnotism, shield, true strike;* 2nd—*flaming sphere, pyrotechnics.*

Iksagyarjerit
Adult Brass Dragon

Iksagyarjerit considers herself a peerless judge of talent and character. In her earlier years, she befriended a young human named Erjanus who had unwillingly become a wizard because his parents wished it. But Iksagyarjerit could see that the human's heart yearned to fight for truth and justice, so she eventually persuaded him to become a paladin. Though he died soon afterward fighting for truth, she is convinced that he was truly happy. Since then, Iksagyarjerit has dedicated herself to aiding as many other beings as possible in finding their true professions—for their own good, of course.

Iksagyarjerit: Female adult brass dragon; CR 12; Large dragon (fire); HD 19d12+76, hp 199; Init +4; Spd 60 ft.,

Brass
DRAGON
Flight
Chaotic Good
Fire Subtype
Warm Desert
Underground
Adult
12 ft.
Talkative with supple expressive lips, brass dragons may relinquish useful information but only after much rambling and hinting at gifts.
Speak with animals
Summon djinni
Control weather
Control winds
Suggestion
Detail of heavily damaged skull showing span of head crest.
Specimen found atop wilderness cairn. Left at site.
Juvenile
6 ft.
Very young
3 ft.
Wyrmling
18 inches

burrow 30 ft., fly 200 ft. (poor); AC 27, touch 9, flat-footed 27; Base Atk +24; Grp +29; Atk +24 melee (2d6+6, bite); Full Atk +24 melee (2d6+6, bite), +19 melee (1d8+3, 2 claws), +19 melee (1d6+3, 2 wings), +19 melee (1d8+9, tail slap); Space/Reach 10 ft./5 ft. (10 ft. with bite); SA breath weapon, frightful presence, spell-like abilities, spells; SQ blindsense 60 ft., damage reduction 5/magic, darkvision 120 ft., *endure elements*, immunity to fire, magic sleep effects, and paralysis, low-light vision, spell resistance 20, vulnerability to cold; AL CG; SV Fort +15, Ref +11, Will +13; Str 23, Dex 10, Con 19, Int 14, Wis 15, Cha 14.

Skills and Feats: Bluff +20, Concentration +24, Diplomacy +16, Gather Information +22, Hide –2, Intimidate +7, Knowledge (local) +17, Listen +20, Search +17, Sense Motive +22, Spellcraft +12, Spot +17; Blind-Fight, Heighten Breath, Hover, Improved Initiative, Power Attack, Recover Breath, Shape Breath.

Breath Weapon (Su): 80-ft. line (40-ft. cone if shaped), 6d6 fire, Reflex DC 23 half (or higher if heightened); or 40-ft. cone (80-ft. line if shaped), *sleep* 1d6+6 rounds, Will DC 23 negates (or higher if heightened).

***Endure Elements* (Sp):** 3/day—as *endure elements*, but 60-ft. radius. Caster level 7th.

Frightful Presence (Ex): 180-ft. radius, HD 18 or fewer, Will DC 21 negates.

Spell-Like Abilities: At will—*speak with animals*; 1/day—*suggestion*. Caster level 7th; save DC 12 + spell level.

Spells: As 7th-level sorcerer.

Sorcerer Spells Known (6/7/7/4; save DC 12 + spell level): 0—*detect magic, ghost sound, guidance, mage hand, prestidigitation, read magic, resistance*; 1st—*alarm, command, magic missile, random action, shield*; 2nd—*enthrall, pyrotechnics, shatter*; 3rd—*cure serious wounds, dispel magic*.

Urevhocymkearsus
Mature Adult Brass Dragon

Urevhocymkearsus is full of questions. He finds the workings of other creatures' minds endlessly fascinating, and seeks to learn how they think. Beyond benign interest, however, Urevhocymkearsus enjoys manipulating the thoughts, emotions, and actions of other creatures—through both magical and mundane means. He is particularly interested in what makes creatures such as humanoids—beings not born to evil the way evil dragons or demons are, choose evil. She has been known to tempt such creatures to commit evil acts in order to learn what motivates them to abandon what they believe is the right path. As a result of this whole fascination, he is extremely forgiving of evil humanoids, though he has no tolerance for creatures of utter evil.

Urevhocymkearsus: Male mature adult brass dragon; CR 15; Huge dragon (fire); HD 22d12+110, hp 253; Init +0; Spd 60 ft., burrow 30 ft., fly 200 ft. (average); AC 29, touch 8, flat-footed 29; Base Atk +28; Grp +38; Atk +28 melee (2d8+8, bite); Full Atk +28 melee (2d8+8, bite), +26 melee (2d6+4, 2 claws), +26 melee (1d8+4, 2 wings), +26 melee (2d6+12, tail slap); Space/Reach 15 ft./10 ft. (15 ft. with bite); SA breath weapon, crush, frightful presence, spell-like abilities, spells; SQ blindsense 60 ft., damage reduction 10/magic, darkvision 120 ft., *endure elements*, immunity to fire, magic sleep effects, and paralysis, low-light vision, spell resistance 22, vulnerability to cold; AL CG; SV Fort +18, Ref +13, Will +16; Str 27, Dex 10, Con 21, Int 16, Wis 17, Cha 16.

Skills and Feats: Bluff +13, Concentration +29, Diplomacy +17, Gather Information +29, Hide –3, Intimidate +15, Knowledge (arcana) +13, Knowledge (local) +13, Listen +27, Search +27, Sense Motive +27, Spellcraft +17, Spot +24; Heighten Breath, Hover, Improved Maneuverability, Multiattack, Power Attack, Quicken Breath, Recover Breath, Shape Breath.

Breath Weapon (Su): 100-ft. line (50-ft. cone if shaped), 7d6 fire, Reflex DC 26 half (or higher if heightened); or 50-ft. cone (100-ft. line if shaped), *sleep* 1d6+7 rounds, Will DC 26 negates (or higher if heightened).

Crush (Ex): Area 15 ft. by 15 ft.; Small or smaller opponents take 2d8+12 points of bludgeoning damage, and must succeed on a DC 26 Reflex save or be pinned.

***Endure Elements* (Sp):** 3/day—as *endure elements*, but 70-ft. radius. Caster level 9th.

Frightful Presence (Ex): 210-ft. radius, HD 21 or fewer, Will DC 24 negates.

Spell-Like Abilities: At will—*speak with animals*; 1/day—*suggestion*. Caster level 9th; save DC 13 + spell level.

Spells: As 9th-level sorcerer.

Sorcerer Spells Known (6/7/7/7/4; save DC 13 + spell level): 0—*cure minor wounds, detect magic, ghost sound, guidance, mage hand, prestidigitation, read magic, resistance*; 1st—*change self, shield of faith, magic missile, shield, true strike*; 2nd—*cat's grace, darkness, enthrall, pyrotechnics*; 3rd—*clairaudience/clairvoyance, cure serious wounds, dispel magic*; 4th—*confusion, spell immunity*.

Livoxdrinacepsek
Old Brass Dragon

Livoxdrinacepsek is a Huge dragon with a Colossal personality. Every movement of his enormous body is exaggerated—he punctuates his loud, loquacious speech with flamboyant gestures, paces back and forth when he speaks, and brings his gigantic face deafeningly close to his audience to really drive a point home. His speech is melodramatic and histrionic, and he expects appreciation if not applause for his every action. Some creatures—particularly humans of a similar temperament—find his company delightfully entertaining, while many others find him overwhelming or terribly irritating.

Livoxdrinacepsek: Male old brass dragon; CR 17; Huge dragon (fire); HD 25d12+125, hp 287; Init +0; Spd 60 ft., burrow 30 ft., fly 200 ft. (average); AC 32, touch 8, flat-footed 32; Base Atk +32; Grp +42; Atk +32 melee (2d8+9, bite); Full Atk +32 melee (2d8+9, bite), +27 melee (2d6+4, 2 claws), +27 melee (1d8+4, 2 wings), +27 melee (2d6+13, tail slap); Space/Reach 15 ft./10 ft. (15 ft. with bite); SA breath weapon, crush, frightful presence, spell-like abilities, spells; SQ blindsense 60 ft., damage reduction 10/magic, darkvision 120 ft., *endure elements*, immunity to fire, magic sleep effects, and paralysis, low-light vision, spell resistance 24, vulnerability to cold; AL CG; SV Fort +19, Ref +18, Will +17; Str 29, Dex 10, Con 21, Int 16, Wis 17, Cha 16.

Skills and Feats: Bluff +12, Concentration +28, Diplomacy +30, Gather Information +28, Hide –4, Intimidate +20, Knowledge (arcana) +15, Knowledge (local) +26, Listen +26, Search +26, Sense Motive +26, Spellcraft +16, Spot +26; Empower Spell, Enlarge Breath, Epic Reflexes, Heighten Breath, Hover, Improved Maneuverability, Power Attack, Recover Breath, Shape Breath.

Breath Weapon (Su): 100-ft. line (150-ft. line if enlarged, 50-ft. cone if shaped, 75-ft. cone if shaped and enlarged), 8d6 fire, Reflex DC 27 half (or higher if heightened); or 50-ft. cone (75-ft. cone if enlarged, 100-ft. line if shaped, 150-ft. line if shaped and enlarged), *sleep* 1d6+8 rounds, Will DC 27 negates (or higher if heightened).

Crush (Ex): Area 15 ft. by 15 ft.; Small or smaller opponents take 2d8+13 points of bludgeoning damage, and must succeed on a DC 27 Reflex save or be pinned.

***Endure Elements* (Sp):** 3/day—as *endure elements*, but 80-ft. radius. Caster level 11th.

Frightful Presence (Ex): 240-ft. radius, HD 24 or fewer, Will DC 25 negates.

Spell-Like Abilities: At will—*speak with animals;* 1/day—*control winds, suggestion.* Caster level 11th; save DC 13 + spell level.

Spells: As 11th-level sorcerer.

Sorcerer Spells Known (6/7/7/7/6/4; save DC 13 + spell level): 0—*cure minor wounds, dancing lights, detect magic, ghost sound, guidance, mage hand, prestidigitation, read magic, resistance;* 1st—*command, disguise self, magic missile, shield, shield of faith;* 2nd—*cat's grace, enthrall, fog cloud, pyrotechnics, Tasha's hideous laughter;* 3rd—*clairaudience/clairvoyance, cure serious wounds, dispel magic, protection from energy;* 4th—*confusion, freedom of movement, rainbow pattern;* 5th—*greater command, mind fog.*

Suncamilahsundi
Very Old Brass Dragon

Suncamilahsundi has seen enough: All these humans are just ruining the world; that's all there is to it. The days of her youth, some seven centuries ago, were the best years the world has ever known, and it's been all downhill from there. Not that she's bitter—she certainly doesn't hate humanity, but she can't keep from shaking her head and clucking her tongue every time she sees a human, remembering what it was like before they built that city too close to her lair and started messing everything up. She keeps up with all the news of the area, but none of it pleases her, and she's equally sour about the state of the natural world. Like most brass dragons, she shares her opinions with anyone who will listen, and is more than willing to make people listen if she feels they really need a talking-to.

Suncamilahsundi: Female very old brass dragon; CR 19; Huge dragon (fire); HD 28d12+168, hp 350; Init +0; Spd 60 ft., burrow 30 ft., fly 200 ft. (poor); AC 35, touch 8, flat-footed 35; Base Atk +36; Grp +46; Atk +36 melee (2d8+10, bite); Full Atk +36 melee (2d8+10, bite), +34 melee (2d6+5, 2 claws), +34 melee (1d8+5, 2 wings), +34 melee (2d6+15, tail slap Space/Reach 15 ft./10 ft. (15 ft. with bite); SA breath weapon, crush, frightful presence, spell-like abilities, spells; SQ blindsense 60 ft., damage reduction 15/magic, darkvision 120 ft., *endure elements,* immunity to fire, magic sleep effects, and paralysis, low-light vision, spell resistance 25, vulnerability to cold; AL CG; SV Fort +22, Ref +20, Will +22; Str 31, Dex 10, Con 23, Int 18, Wis 19, Cha 18.

Skills and Feats: Bluff +16, Concentration +32, Diplomacy +34, Gather Information +32, Hide –2, Intimidate +18, Knowledge (arcana) +19, Knowledge (geography) +16, Knowledge (local) +19, Knowledge (nature) +16, Listen +30, Search +30, Sense Motive +30, Spellcraft +19, Spot +30, Survival +16; Blind-Fight, Epic Reflexes, Heighten Breath, Hover, Iron Will, Multiattack, Power Attack, Quicken Breath, Recover Breath, Suppress Weakness.

Breath Weapon (Su): 100-ft. line, 9d6 fire, Reflex DC 30 half (or higher if heightened); or 50-ft. cone, *sleep* 1d6+9 rounds, Will DC 30 negates (or higher if heightened).

Crush (Ex): Area 15 ft. by 15 ft.; Small or smaller opponents take 2d8+15 points of bludgeoning damage, and must succeed on a DC 30 Reflex save or be pinned.

***Endure Elements* (Sp):** 3/day—as *endure elements*, but 90-ft. radius. Caster level 13th.

Frightful Presence (Ex): 270-ft. radius, HD 27 or fewer, Will DC 28 negates.

Spell-Like Abilities: At will—*speak with animals;* 1/day—*control winds, suggestion.* Caster level 13th; save DC 14 + spell level.

Spells: As 13th-level sorcerer.

Sorcerer Spells Known (6/7/7/7/7/6/4; save DC 14 + spell level): 0—*cure minor wounds, dancing lights, detect magic, ghost sound, guidance, mage hand, prestidigitation, read magic, resistance;* 1st—*command, disguise self, magic missile, shield, shield of faith;* 2nd—*cat's grace, enthrall, fog cloud, pyrotechnics, Tasha's hideous laughter;* 3rd—*clairaudience/clairvoyance, cure serious wounds, dispel magic, protection from energy;* 4th—*confusion, fire shield, freedom of movement, rainbow pattern;* 5th—*greater command, hold monster, mind fog;* 6th—*heal, Otiluke's freezing sphere.*

Ariikdasadakuundax
Ancient Brass Dragon

Other good dragons worry about Ariikdasadakuundax, while evil dragons laugh at him. He is all too willing to part with his treasure, always making sizable donations to worthy causes. Every good-aligned temple within 100 miles of his lair has the name of Ariikdasadakuundax inscribed on a lintel or a cornerstone in honor of his generous gifts, and there are countless stories of people, once down on their luck, who have the dragon to thank for their present improved circumstances. The reason for his unusual generosity is as straightforward as it is tragic: in his youth, Ariikdasadakuundax was even more avaricious than most dragons. Through a complicated series of events his greed caused the death of his lifelong mate. In her memory, he

Brass Dragon

Typical Brass Dragon Lair

[Size of lair varies with size of dragon]

Oblique View

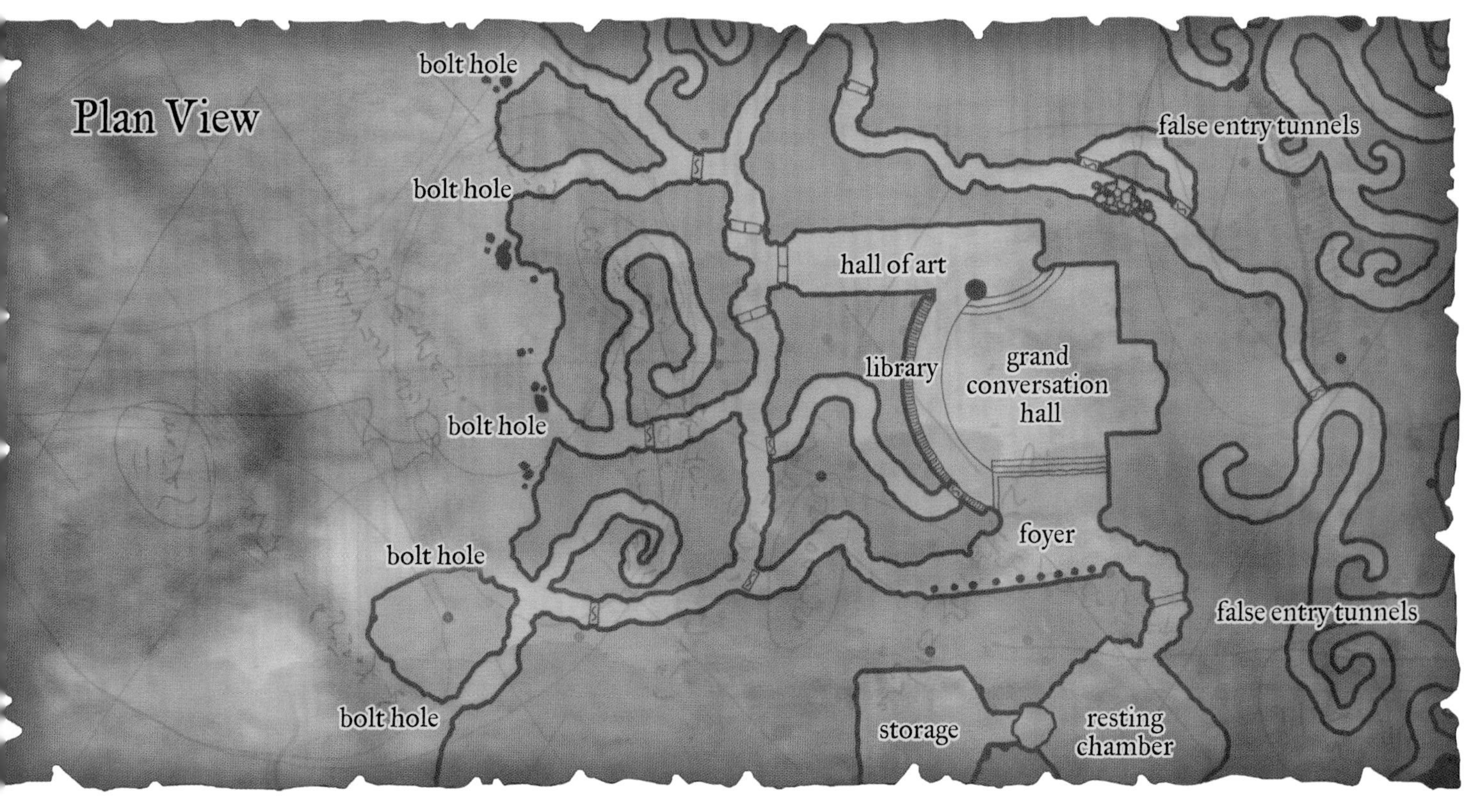

Plan View

now gives as much as he hoards, believing that somehow he can atone for his error in this way.

Ariikdasadakuundax: Male ancient brass dragon; CR 20; Huge dragon (fire); HD 31d12+186, hp 387; Init +4; Spd 60 ft., burrow 30 ft., fly 200 ft. (poor); AC 38, touch 8, flat-footed 38; Base Atk +40; Grp +50; Atk +40 melee (2d8+11, bite); Full Atk +40 melee (2d8+11, bite), +38 melee (2d6+5, 2 claws), +38 melee (1d8+5, 2 wings), +38 melee (2d6+16, tail slap); Space/Reach 15 ft./10 ft. (15 ft. with bite); SA breath weapon, crush, frightful presence, spell-like abilities, spells; SQ blindsense 60 ft., damage reduction 15/magic, darkvision 120 ft., *endure elements,* immunity to fire, magic sleep effects, and paralysis, low-light vision, spell resistance 27, vulnerability to cold; AL CG; SV Fort +23, Ref +17, Will +23; Str 33, Dex 10, Con 23, Int 18, Wis 19, Cha 18.

Skills and Feats: Bluff +33, Concentration +19, Diplomacy +37, Gather Information +35, Hide –2, Intimidate +19, Knowledge (arcana) +17, Knowledge (geography) +17, Knowledge (local) +17, Knowledge (nature) +17, Knowledge (the planes) +17, Knowledge (religion) +17, Listen +33, Search +24, Sense Motive +33, Spellcraft +20, Spot +33; Empower Spell, Enlarge Breath, Heighten Breath, Hover, Improved Initiative, Iron Will, Multiattack, Power Attack, Recover Breath, Shape Breath, Suppress Weakness.

Breath Weapon (Su): 100-ft. line (150-ft. line if enlarged, 50-ft. cone if shaped, 75-ft. cone if shaped and enlarged), 10d6 fire, Reflex DC 31 half (or higher if heightened); or 50-ft. cone (75-ft. cone if enlarged, 100-ft. line if shaped, 150-ft. line if shaped and enlarged), *sleep* 1d6+10 rounds, Will DC 31 negates (or higher if heightened).

Crush (Ex): Area 15 ft. by 15 ft.; Small or smaller opponents take 2d8+16 points of bludgeoning damage, and must succeed on a DC 31 Reflex save or be pinned.

***Endure Elements* (Sp):** 3/day—as *endure elements,* but 100-ft. radius. Caster level 15th.

Frightful Presence (Ex): 300-ft. radius, HD 30 or fewer, Will DC 29 negates.

Spell-Like Abilities: At will—*speak with animals;* 1/day—*control weather, control winds, suggestion.* Caster level 15th; save DC 14 + spell level.

Spells: As 15th-level sorcerer.

Sorcerer Spells Known (6/7/7/7/7/6/6/4; save DC 14 + spell level): 0—*cure minor wounds, dancing lights, detect magic, ghost sound, guidance, mage hand, prestidigitation, read magic, resistance;* 1st—*command, disguise self, divine favor, magic missile, shield;* 2nd—*cat's grace, enthrall, fog cloud, pyrotechnics, Tasha's hideous laughter;* 3rd—*clairaudience/clairvoyance, cure serious wounds, dispel magic, protection from energy;* 4th—*bestow curse, confusion, freedom of movement, good hope;* 5th—*greater command, hold monster, mirage arcana, telekinesis;* 6th—*animate objects, Bigby's forceful hand, heal;* 7th—*insanity, holy word*

Conjazmynabryte
Wyrm Brass Dragon

In the center of a great desert, a narrow pillar rises impossibly high into the sky, a remnant of or monument to some long-lost civilization. High on its apex, Conjazmynabryte basks in the hot desert sun and bathes in the cool night air. Among nearby communities, legend holds that she will answer any question put to her by someone who climbs the pillar to reach her, but she attacks anyone who flies to the height.

She has lost much of the love of conversation she had in her youth, mainly because she is tired of answering insipid questions from idiots who happen to be strong enough to scale the pillar. She no longer couches unpleasant truths in soft language, instead being painfully blunt with advice and criticism, in an attempt to bring any conversation to a hasty end. The only thing known to have brought her down from her pillar-lair is the sight of a blue dragon entering her territory. Most blues know better.

Conjazmynabryte: Female wyrm brass dragon; CR 21; Gargantuan dragon (fire); HD 34d12+238, hp 459; Init +4; Spd 60 ft., burrow 30 ft., fly 250 ft. (poor); AC 39, touch 6, flat-footed 39; Base Atk +42; Grp +58; Atk +42 melee (4d6+12, bite); Full Atk +42 melee (4d6+12, bite), +37 melee (2d8+6, 2 claws), +37 melee (2d6+6, 2 wings), +37 melee (2d8+18, tail slap); Space/Reach 20 ft./15 ft. (20 ft. with bite); SA breath weapon, crush, frightful presence, spell-like abilities, spells, tail sweep; SQ blindsense 60 ft., damage reduction 20/magic, darkvision 120 ft., *endure elements,* immunity to fire, magic sleep effects, and paralysis, low-light vision, spell resistance 28, vulnerability to cold; AL CG; SV Fort +26, Ref +19, Will +26; Str 35, Dex 10, Con 25, Int 20, Wis 21, Cha 20.

Skills and Feats: Bluff +41, Concentration +22, Diplomacy +45, Gather Information +43, Hide –5, Intimidate +22, Knowledge (arcana) +20, Knowledge (geography) +20, Knowledge (local) +20, Knowledge (nature) +20, Listen +41, Search +41, Sense Motive +41, Spellcraft +25, Spot +41, Survival +19; Empower Spell, Extend Spell, Heighten Breath, Hover, Improved Initiative, Improved Maneuverability, Iron Will, Overcome Weakness, Power Attack, Recover Breath, Shape Breath, Suppress Weakness.

Breath Weapon (Su): 120-ft. line (60-ft. cone if shaped), 11d6 fire, Reflex DC 34 half (or higher if heightened); or 60-ft. cone (120-ft. line if shaped), *sleep* 1d6+11 rounds, Will DC 34 negates (or higher if heightened).

Crush (Ex): Area 20 ft. by 20 ft.; Medium or smaller opponents take 4d6+18 points of bludgeoning damage, and must succeed on a DC 34 Reflex save or be pinned.

***Endure Elements* (Sp):** 3/day—as *endure elements,* but 110-ft. radius. Caster level 17th.

Frightful Presence (Ex): 330-ft. radius, HD 33 or fewer, Will DC 32 negates.

Spell-Like Abilities: At will—*speak with animals;* 1/day—*control weather, control winds, suggestion.* Caster level 17th; save DC 15 + spell level.

Spells: As 17th-level sorcerer.

Tail Sweep (Ex): Half-circle 30 ft. in diameter, Small or smaller opponents take 2d6+18 points of bludgeoning damage, Reflex DC 34 half.

Sorcerer Spells Known (6/8/7/7/7/7/6/6/4; save DC 15 + spell level): 0—*cure minor wounds, dancing lights, detect* *magic, ghost sound, guidance, mage hand, prestidigitation, read magic, resistance;* 1st—*command, divine favor, magic missile, protection from evil, shield;* 2nd—*cat's grace, enthrall, fog cloud, pyrotechnics, Tasha's hideous laughter;* 3rd—*clairaudience/clairvoyance, cure serious wounds, haste, protection from energy;* 4th—*bestow curse, confusion, freedom of movement, good hope;* 5th—*greater command, hold monster, mirage arcana, telekinesis;* 6th—*animate objects, Bigby's forceful hand, heal;* 7th—*insanity, prismatic spray, spell turning;* 8th—*maze, symbol of insanity.*

Fellithysaar
Great Wyrm Brass Dragon

As old as his desert home, Fellithysaar speaks with the wisdom of ages in his low, rumbling voice. Unlike Conjazmynabryte, he gladly shares his thoughts with anyone who will listen, hoping thereby to make the world better for his having been in it. Scarred from literally hundreds of past battles, Fellithysaar knows his end is near, and meets every possible threat wondering, "Will this be my doom at last?" An aura of resigned melancholy surrounds him, yet his endless stories are full of heroism, virtue, and hope. He has an acute appreciation of tragedy, and loves tales of valiant self-sacrifice and painful struggles against overwhelming odds.

Fellithysaar: Male great wyrm brass dragon; CR 23; Gargantuan dragon (fire); HD 37d12+296, hp 536; Init +0; Spd 60 ft., burrow 30 ft., fly 250 ft. (poor); AC 42, touch 6, flat-footed 42; Base Atk +46; Grp +62; Atk +46 melee (4d6+13, bite); Full Atk +46 melee (4d6+13, bite), +41 melee (2d8+6, 2 claws), +41 melee (2d6+6, 2 wings), +41 melee (2d8+19, tail slap); Space/Reach 20 ft./15 ft. (20 ft. with bite); SA breath weapon, crush, frightful presence, spell-like abilities, spells; SQ blindsense 60 ft., damage reduction 20/magic, darkvision 120 ft., *endure elements*, immunity to fire, magic sleep effects, and paralysis, low-light vision, spell resistance 30, summon djinni, vulnerability to cold; AL CG; SV Fort +28, Ref +20, Will +31; Str 37, Dex 10, Con 27, Int 20, Wis 21, Cha 20.

Skills and Feats: Bluff +45, Concentration +32, Diplomacy +49, Gather Information +25, Hide –1, Intimidate +27, Knowledge (arcana) +27, Knowledge (geography) +21, Knowledge (local) +23, Knowledge (nature) +25, Listen +45, Search +45, Sense Motive +45, Spellcraft +27, Spot +45; Adroit Flyby Attack, Blind-Fight, Empower Spell, Epic Will, Flyby Attack, Heighten Breath, Hover, Improved Maneuverability, Iron Will, Power Attack, Recover Breath, Shape Breath, Suppress Weakness.

Breath Weapon (Su): 120-ft. line (60-ft. cone if shaped), 12d6 fire, Reflex DC 36 half (or higher if heightened); or 60-ft. cone (120-ft. line if shaped), *sleep* 1d6+12 rounds, Will DC 36 negates (or higher if heightened).

Crush (Ex): Area 20 ft. by 20 ft.; Medium or smaller opponents take 4d6+19 points of bludgeoning damage, and must succeed on a DC 36 Reflex save or be pinned.

***Endure Elements* (Sp):** 3/day—as *endure elements*, but 120-ft. radius. Caster level 19th.

Frightful Presence (Ex): 360-ft. radius, HD 36 or fewer, Will DC 33 negates.

Spell-Like Abilities: At will—*speak with animals;* 1/day—*control weather, control winds, suggestion.* Caster level 19th; save DC 15 + spell level.

Spells: As 19th-level sorcerer.

***Summon Djinni* (Sp):** 1/day—as *summon monster* VII, but summons 1 djinni; 19th-level caster.

Tail Sweep (Ex): Half-circle 30 ft. in diameter, Small or smaller opponents take 2d6+19 points of bludgeoning damage, Reflex DC 36 half.

Sorcerer Spells Known (6/8/7/7/7/7/6/6/6/4; save DC 15 + spell level): 0—*cure minor wounds, dancing lights, detect magic, ghost sound, guidance, mage hand, prestidigitation, read magic, resistance;* 1st—*command, divine favor, magic missile, protection from evil, shield;* 2nd—*cat's grace, enthrall, fog cloud, pyrotechnics, Tasha's hideous laughter;* 3rd—*clairaudience/clairvoyance, cure serious wounds, haste, protection from energy;* 4th—*bestow curse, confusion, freedom of movement, good hope;* 5th—*greater command, hold monster, mirage arcana, telekinesis;* 6th—*animate objects, Bigby's forceful hand, heal;* 7th—*insanity, prismatic spray, spell turning;* 8th—*mass charm monster, maze, symbol of death;* 9th—*foresight, time stop.*

SAMPLE BRONZE DRAGONS

Listed below are twelve sample bronze dragons, one of each age category. The descriptions include basic personality and encounter notes that the DM will want to flesh out for his campaign, along with a set of statistics that make the dragon ready to play.

Water Breathing (Ex): All bronze dragons can breathe underwater indefinitely and can freely use their breath weapons, spells, and other abilities underwater.

Skills: A bronze dragon can move through water at its swim speed without making Swim checks. It has a +8 racial bonus on any Swim check to perform some special action or avoid a hazard. The dragon can always can choose to take 10 on a Swim check, even if distracted or endangered. The dragon can use the run action while swimming, provided it swims in a straight line.

Immersa
Wyrmling Bronze Dragon

Immersa is as playful as a dolphin and curious as a cat. She seldom sits still. Immersa loves animals, and makes frequent use of her *speak with animals* ability. She has befriended almost every creature that swims, flies, or crawls along her section of rocky seacoast. She finds humanoid fishers and hunters somewhat distasteful. While she would never deny a being sustenance or a means of making a livelihood, she remains alert for signs of over harvesting, killing for sport, or cruelty. From time to time, Immersa aids shipwrecked sailors, helping them to shore and sending them inland toward civilization. This gives her a good reputation among the local sailors even if the hunters and fishers don't care for her much.

Bronze
DRAGON
Flight
Lawful Good
Water Subtype
Warm Aquatic
Underground
Old
24 ft.
Inquisitive and oddly fascinated with warfare, bronze dragons eagerly join armies with just causes and good pay.
Speak with animals
Detect thoughts
Polymorph self
Control water
Fog cloud
Detail of skull horn arrangement.
Specimen obtained from nomadic dwarven raiders in exchange for 6 casks of ale and 3 live pigs.
Sub-adult
12 ft.
Young
6 ft.
Wyrmling
3 feet

Immersa: Female wyrmling bronze dragon; CR 3; Small dragon (water); HD 6d12+6; hp 45; Init +4; Spd 40 ft., fly 100 ft. (average), swim 60 ft.; AC 16, touch 11, flat-footed 16; Base Atk +8; Grp +3; Atk +8 melee (1d6+1, bite); Full Atk +8 melee (1d6+1, bite), +3 melee (1d4, 2 claws); Space/Reach 5 ft./5 ft.; SA breath weapon, spell-like abilities; SQ blindsense 60 ft., darkvision 120 ft., immunity to electricity, magic sleep effects, and paralysis, low-light vision, water breathing; AL LG; SV Fort +6, Ref +5, Will +7; Str 13, Dex 10, Con 13, Int 14, Wis 15, Cha 14.

Skills and Feats: Diplomacy +13, Hide +6, Knowledge (nature) +8, Listen +11, Search +10, Sense Motive +11, Spot +11, Swim +18, Survival +11; Combat Expertise, Improved Initiative, Power Attack.

Breath Weapon (Su): 40-ft. line, 2d6 electricity, Reflex DC 14 half; or 20-ft. cone, *repulsion* 1d6+1 rounds, Will DC 14 negates.

Spell-Like Abilities: At will—*speak with animals.* Caster level 1st.

Eyruaad
Very Young Bronze Dragon

Older bronze dragons shake their heads and write him off as another youthful idealist, but Eyruaad sees himself as something more like a paladin. While other bronzes may be content to let evil dragons make their lairs nearby and hatch who knows what evil plans, Eyruaad believes in taking the fight right to evil's front door. He does not tolerate any evil creature's presence anywhere near his (rather small) territory, especially evil dragons. He uses a wide network of animals and humanoids to keep him informed of attacks by evil creatures, and personally investigates each such report in order to protect the innocents in his care. His major failing is an eagerness to do battle, with little regard for his actual chance of success. So far, his luck has not failed him, but it might not be long before Eyruaad needs protection himself.

Eyruaad: Male very young bronze dragon; CR 5; Medium dragon (water); HD 9d12+18; hp 76; Init +0; Spd 40 ft., fly 150 ft. (poor), swim 60 ft.; AC 18, touch 10, flat-footed 18; Base Atk +11; Grp +11; Atk +11 melee (1d8+2, bite); Full Atk +11 melee (1d8+2, bite), +9 melee (1d6+1, 2 claws), +9 melee (1d4+1, 2 wings); Space/Reach 5 ft./5 ft.; SA breath weapon, spell-like abilities; SQ blindsense 60 ft., darkvision 120 ft., immunity to electricity, magic sleep effects, and paralysis, low-light vision, water breathing; AL LG; SV Fort +8, Ref +6, Will +8; Str 15, Dex 10, Con 15, Int 14, Wis 15, Cha 14.

Skills and Feats: Bluff +8, Diplomacy +16, Intimidate +14, Knowledge (geography) +7, Knowledge (history) +7, Knowledge (local) +7, Listen +14, Move Silently +3, Search +12, Sense Motive +12, Spot +14, Swim +19; Alertness, Hover, Multiattack, Power Attack.

Breath Weapon (Su): 60-ft. line, 4d6 electricity, Reflex DC 16 half; or 30-ft. cone, *repulsion* 1d6+2 rounds, Will DC 16 negates.

Spell-Like Abilities: At will—*speak with animals.* Caster level 2nd.

Louteah
Young Bronze Dragon

Though she would never admit it or accept anyone saying it of her, Louteah is a coward. All bluster, she puts on a good show, and is quite capable of sending weaker enemies—or gullible ones—fleeing in fear. However, when she can't avert a fight through intimidation, frightful presence, or *repulsion* gas, she tends to fly away, usually with a comment such as, "You're not a worthy challenge!" She saves her belligerence for evil creatures, of course, and is quite kind among friends and like-minded allies—as long as no one calls her bravery into question.

Louteah: Female young bronze dragon; CR 7; Medium dragon (water); HD 12d12+24; hp 102; Init +0; Spd 40 ft., fly 150 ft. (average), swim 60 ft.; AC 21, touch 10, flat-footed 21; Base Atk +15; Grp +15; Atk +15 melee (1d8+3, bite); Full Atk +15 melee (1d8+3, bite), +10 melee (1d6+1, 2 claws), +10 melee (1d4+1, 2 wings); Space/Reach 5 ft./5 ft.; SA breath weapon, spell-like abilities, spells; SQ alternate form, blindsense 60 ft., darkvision 120 ft., immunity to electricity, magic sleep effects, and paralysis, low-light vision, water breathing; AL LG; SV Fort +10, Ref +8, Will +11; Str 17, Dex 10, Con 15, Int 16, Wis 17, Cha 16.

Skills and Feats: Bluff +9, Concentration +16, Diplomacy +21, Disguise +15, Intimidate +19, Knowledge (local) +9, Listen +17, Search +17, Sense Motive +17, Spellcraft +6, Spot +17, Swim +17; Awaken Frightful Presence, Combat Expertise, Improved Maneuverability, Power Attack, Wingover.

Alternate Form (Su): Can assume any humanoid form of Medium size or smaller as a standard action three times per day. This ability functions as a *polymorph* spell cast on itself by a 3rd-level sorcerer, except that the dragon does not regain hit points for changing form and can only assume the form of a humanoid. The dragon can remain in its humanoid from until it chooses to assume a new one or return to its natural form.

Breath Weapon (Su): 60-ft. line, 6d6 electricity, Reflex DC 18 half; or 30-ft. cone, *repulsion* 1d6+3 rounds, Will DC 18 negates.

Frightful Presence (Ex): 60-ft. radius, HD 11 or fewer, Will DC 19 negates.

Spell-Like Abilities: At will—*speak with animals.* Caster level 3rd.

Spells: As 1st-level sorcerer.

Sorcerer Spells Known (5/4; save DC 13 + spell level): 0—*detect magic, ghost sound, read magic, resistance;* 1st—*shield of faith, shocking grasp.*

Plantagonox
Juvenile Bronze Dragon

Plantagonox is a spy. When evil forces threaten the human kingdom near his lair, he uses a combination of his alternate form ability and his Disguise skill to infiltrate their ranks, learn their plans, and bring about their undoing. The nature of his work makes him somewhat grim and rather morbid. He has a wry sense of humor few others can appreciate, focusing largely on the various forms of death and dismemberment he has been forced to witness and, often, only narrowly escaped himself. He never tries to paint himself as a hero, however, and actually avoids any direct conversation about his missions. Having spent so much time undercover, living a lie, he finds it almost impossible to trust anybody. As a result, though he is as gregarious as most bronze dragons, he is extremely private and avoids revealing anything about himself that might give an enemy an advantage.

Plantagonox: Juvenile male bronze dragon; CR 9; Large dragon (water); HD 15d12+45, hp 142; Init +4; Spd 40 ft., fly 150 ft. (poor), swim 60 ft.; AC 23, touch 9, flat-footed 23; Base Atk +18; Grp +23; Atk +18 melee (2d6+4, bite); Full Atk +18 melee (2d6+4, bite), +16 melee (1d8+2, 2 claws), +16 melee (1d6+2, 2 wings), +16 melee (1d8+6, tail slap); Space/Reach 10 ft./5 ft. (10 ft. with bite); SA breath weapon, spell-like abilities, spells; SQ alternate form, blindsense 60 ft., darkvision 120 ft., immunity to electricity, magic sleep effects, and paralysis, low-light vision, water breathing; AL LG; SV Fort +12, Ref +9, Will +13; Str 19, Dex 10, Con 17, Int 18, Wis 19, Cha 18.

Skills and Feats: Appraise +6, Bluff +9, Concentration +20, Diplomacy +25, Disguise +21, Hide –2, Intimidate +11, Knowledge (arcana) +9, Knowledge (local) +9, Knowledge (nature) +9, Listen +21, Search +21, Sense Motive +21, Spellcraft +14, Spot +21, Swim +16, Survival +9; Improved Initiative, Multiattack, Recover Breath, Shape Breath, Weapon Focus (claw), Wingover.

Alternate Form (Su): Can assume any humanoid form of Medium size or smaller as a standard action three times per day. This ability functions as a *polymorph* spell cast on itself by a 4th-level sorcerer, except that the dragon does not regain hit points for changing form and can only assume the form of a humanoid. The dragon can remain in its humanoid from until it chooses to assume a new one or return to its natural form.

Breath Weapon (Su): 60-ft. line (30-ft. cone if shaped), 8d6 electricity, Reflex DC 20 half; or 40-ft. cone (80-ft. line if shaped), *repulsion* 1d6+4 rounds, Will DC 20 negates.

Spell-Like Abilities: At will—*speak with animals.* Caster level 4th.

Spells: As 3rd-level sorcerer.

Sorcerer Spells Known (6/6; save DC 14 + spell level): 0—*dancing lights, detect magic, mage hand, ray of frost, read magic;* 1st—*animate rope, magic missile, shield.*

Cybilenemarea
Young Adult Bronze Dragon

Cybilenemarea has dedicated her life to fighting the widespread piracy near her home. In human form (or occasionally a different humanoid form), she hires herself out as a sailor on merchant ships, touting her "minor spellcasting ability" as a selling point if necessary. She has spent so much time in this guise that she is actually quite a competent sailor. Being on ships has brought her into contact with dozens of pirate vessels—including some that hired her without initially revealing their true mission—and allowed her to protect her fellow sailors while bringing quite a number of pirate captains to justice. She is something of a local legend, though she tries not to reveal her own true nature even in the midst of a pirate attack. She never takes the same human form twice, using Disguise to alter her appearance beyond what even alternate form allows, in order to avoid attracting unwanted attention—positive or negative.

Cybilenemarea: Female young adult bronze dragon; CR 12; Large dragon (water); HD 18d12+72, hp 189; Init +4; Spd 40 ft., fly 150 ft. (poor), swim 60 ft.; AC 26, touch 9, flat-footed 26; Base Atk +23; Grp +28; Atk +23 melee (2d6+6, bite); Full Atk +23 melee (2d6+6, bite), +18 melee (1d8+3, 2 claws), +18 melee (1d6+3, 2 wings), +18 melee (1d8+9, tail slap); Space/Reach 10 ft./5 ft. (10 ft. with bite); SA breath weapon, frightful presence, spell-like abilities, spells; SQ alternate form, blindsense 60 ft., damage reduction 5/magic, darkvision 120 ft., immunity to electricity, magic sleep effects, and paralysis, low-light vision, spell resistance 20, water breathing; AL LG; SV Fort +15, Ref +11, Will +15; Str 23, Dex 10, Con 19, Int 18, Wis 19, Cha 18.

Skills and Feats: Bluff +11, Concentration +23, Craft (ropemaking) +6, Diplomacy +27, Disguise +23, Hide –2, Intimidate +14, Knowledge (arcana) +14, Knowledge (local) +10, Listen +23, Profession (sailor) +6, Search +23, Sense Motive +23, Spellcraft +15, Spot +23, Swim +23, Use Rope +2; Flyby Attack, Heighten Breath, Improved Initiative, Power Attack, Recover Breath, Shape Breath, Wingover.

Alternate Form (Su): Can assume any humanoid form of Medium size or smaller as a standard action three times per day. This ability functions as a *polymorph* spell cast on itself by a 5th-level sorcerer, except that the dragon does not regain hit points for changing form and can only assume the form of a humanoid. The dragon can remain in its humanoid from until it chooses to assume a new one or return to its natural form.

Breath Weapon (Su): 80-ft. line (40-ft. cone if shaped), 10d6 electricity, Reflex DC 23 half (or higher if heightened); or 40-ft. cone (80-ft. line if shaped), *repulsion* 1d6+5 rounds, Will DC 23 negates (or higher if heightened).

Frightful Presence (Ex): 150-ft. radius, HD 17 or fewer, Will DC 23 negates.

Spell-Like Abilities: At will—*speak with animals.* Caster level 5th.

Spells: As 5th-level sorcerer.

Sorcerer Spells Known (6/7/5; save DC 14 + spell level): 0—*dancing lights, detect magic, mage hand, mending, ray of frost, read magic;* 1st—*burning hands, divine favor, shield, true strike;* 2nd—*mirror image, summon swarm.*

Kepsektokiversvex
Adult Bronze Dragon

Kepsektokiversvex is often mistaken for a ranger, since he spends much of his time in human form stalking the wild coastlands near his lair, hunting sahuagin. The humans of the area call him Darkblade and regard him with a mixture of gratitude, awe, and fear. The nearby elves, likely suspecting more of his true nature, call him *Aisveraen*, which translates as "Noble Eyes." Among humans, Kepsektokiversvex tends to be gruff and taciturn, but he opens up and laughs freely in elven company. In battle with sahuagin, he is relentless, deadly, and absolutely silent, for his hatred of those foul creatures is all-consuming.

Kepsektokiversvex: Male adult bronze dragon; CR 15; Huge dragon (water); HD 21d12+105, hp 241; Init +0; Spd 40 ft., fly 150 ft. (poor), swim 60 ft.; AC 28, touch 8, flat-footed 28; Base Atk +27; Grp +37; Atk +27 melee (2d8+8, bite); Full Atk +27 melee (2d8+8, bite), +25 melee (2d6+4, 2 claws), +25 melee (1d8+4, 2 wings), +25 melee (2d6+12, tail slap); Space/Reach 15 ft./10 ft. (15 ft. with bite); SA breath weapon, crush, frightful presence, spell-like abilities, spells; SQ alternate form, blindsense 60 ft., darkvision 120 ft., immunity to electricity, magic sleep effects, and paralysis, low-light vision, damage reduction 5/magic, spell resistance 22, water breathing; AL LG; SV Fort +17, Ref +12, Will +17; Str 27, Dex 10, Con 21, Int 20, Wis 21, Cha 20.

Skills and Feats: Balance +4, Bluff +14, Concentration +26, Diplomacy +30, Disguise +23, Escape Artist +6, Hide –4, Intimidate +15, Knowledge (arcana) +15, Knowledge (history) +13, Knowledge (nature) +11, Listen +26, Search +26, Sense Motive +26, Spellcraft +17, Spot +26, Swim +34, Survival +22; Flyby Attack, Heighten Breath, Multiattack, Recover Breath, Shape Breath, Spreading Breath, Track, Wingover.

Alternate Form (Su): Can assume any humanoid form of Medium size or smaller as a standard action three times per day. This ability functions as a *polymorph* spell cast on itself by a 7th-level sorcerer, except that the dragon does not regain hit points for changing form and can only assume the form of a humanoid. The dragon can remain in its humanoid from until it chooses to assume a new one or return to its natural form.

Breath Weapon (Su): 100-ft. line (50-ft. cone if shaped, 25-ft. spread if spreading), 12d6 electricity, Reflex DC 25 half (or higher if heightened); or 50-ft. cone (100-ft. line if shaped, 25-ft. spread if spreading), *repulsion* 1d6+6 rounds, Will DC 25 negates (or higher if heightened).

Crush (Ex): Area 15 ft. by 15 ft.; Small or smaller opponents take 2d8+12 points of bludgeoning damage, and must succeed on a DC 25 Reflex save or be pinned.

Frightful Presence (Ex): 180-ft. radius, HD 20 or fewer, Will DC 25 negates.

Spell-Like Abilities: At will—*speak with animals;* 3/day—*create food and water, fog cloud.* Caster level 7th.

Spells: As 7th-level sorcerer.

Sorcerer Spells Known (6/8/7/5; save DC 15 + spell level): 0—*dancing lights, detect magic, mage hand, mending, prestidigitation, ray of frost, read magic;* 1st—*alarm, burning hands, magic missile, shield, shield of faith;* 2nd—*cat's grace, cure moderate wounds, darkness;* 3rd—*haste, keenness.*

Hezjinglahjonan
Mature Adult Bronze Dragon

Hezjinglahjonan is an eccentric. Her seaside lair is filled with items better described as knick-knacks than treasure, though she defends them as vociferously as any dragon guards its hoard. She wanders the beach near her lair, often in human form, collecting odd-shaped pieces of driftwood, interesting shells, and flotsam from the shipwrecks that are all too common along that stretch of coast. If she happens to see a ship foundering off shore, she immediately swims out (in her natural form) to rescue as many sailors as she can, bringing them to shore and abandoning them there. Humans who interact with her in dragon form tend to come away with the impression of a doddering old woman, but she chooses young, attractive, and frequently male alternate forms.

Hezjinglahjonan: Female mature adult bronze dragon; CR 17; Huge dragon (water); HD 24d12+120, hp 276; Init +4; Spd 40 ft., fly 150 ft. (poor), swim 60 ft.; AC 31, touch 8, flat-footed 31; Base Atk +31; Grp +41; Atk +31 melee (2d8+9, bite); Full Atk +31 melee (2d8+9, bite), +26 melee (2d6+4, 2 claws), +26 melee (1d8+4, 2 wings), +26 melee (2d6+13, tail slap); Space/Reach 15 ft./10 ft. (15 ft. with bite); SA breath weapon, crush, frightful presence, spell-like abilities, spells; SQ alternate form, blindsense 60 ft., damage reduction 10/magic, darkvision 120 ft., immunity to electricity, magic sleep effects, and paralysis, low-light vision, spell resistance 23, water breathing; AL LG; SV Fort +19, Ref +14, Will +19; Str 29, Dex 10, Con 21, Int 20, Wis 21, Cha 20.

Skills and Feats: Bluff +31, Concentration +15, Diplomacy +19, Disguise +31, Hide –3, Intimidate +19, Knowledge (geography) +15, Knowledge (nature) +13, Knowledge (religion) +14, Listen +31, Search +31, Sense Motive +31, Spellcraft +18, Spot +31, Swim +39, Survival +29; Adroit Flyby Attack, Clinging Breath, Flyby Attack, Heighten Breath, Improved Initiative, Lingering Breath, Power Attack, Shape Breath, Wingover.

Alternate Form (Su): Can assume any humanoid form of Medium size or smaller as a standard action three times per day. This ability functions as a *polymorph* spell cast on itself by a 9th-level sorcerer, except that the dragon does not regain hit points for changing form and can only assume the form of a humanoid. The dragon can remain in its humanoid from until it chooses to assume a new one or return to its natural form.

Breath Weapon (Su): 100-ft. line (50-ft. cone if shaped), 14d6 electricity, Reflex DC 27 half (or higher if heightened); or 50-ft. cone (100-ft. line if shaped), *repulsion* 1d6+7 rounds, Will DC 27 negates (or higher if heightened).

Crush (Ex): Area 15 ft. by 15 ft.; Small or smaller opponents take 2d8+13 points of bludgeoning damage, and must succeed on a DC 27 Reflex save or be pinned.

Frightful Presence (Ex): 210-ft. radius, HD 23 or fewer, Will DC 27 negates.

Spell-Like Abilities: At will—*speak with animals;* 3/day—*create food and water, fog cloud.* Caster level 9th.

Spells: As 9th-level sorcerer.

Sorcerer Spells Known (6/8/7/7/5; save DC 15 + spell level): 0—*dancing lights, detect magic, mage hand, mending, open/close, prestidigitation, ray of frost, read magic;* 1st—*alarm, cure light wounds, divine favor, magic missile, shield;* 2nd—*cat's grace, darkness, detect thoughts, spiritual weapon;* 3rd—*haste, nondetection, suggestion;* 4th—*good hope, wall of ice.*

Kepesksippiolosnin
Old Bronze Dragon

Kepesksippiolosnin considers himself a connoisseur of beauty. He does not tolerate simple gold coins in his hoard—he much prefers platinum for its shine, but accepts gold if the coins are artistically minted or extremely old. He is far more interested in objects of art than in coins anyway, and particularly admires masterwork musical instruments and items of sculpted glass. His lair is an abandoned human temple—large and spacious, with grand columns, high ceilings, and fine sculpture. He delights in quality music, but has no tolerance for second-rate bards (he will not listen to a Perform check result less than 20). He often invites bards who manage to impress him (with a check result of 30 or better) to entertain him further by playing one of his many magic instruments.

Kepesksippiolosnin: Male old bronze dragon; CR 19; Huge dragon (water); HD 27d12+162, hp 337; Init +4; Spd 40 ft., fly 150 ft. (poor), swim 60 ft.; AC 34, touch 8, flat-footed 34; Base Atk +35; Grp +45; Atk +35 melee (2d8+10, bite); Full Atk +35 melee (2d8+10, bite), +33 melee (2d6+5, 2 claws), +33 melee (1d8+5, 2 wings), +33 melee (2d6+15, tail slap); Space/Reach 15 ft./10 ft. (15 ft. with bite); SA breath weapon, crush, frightful presence, spell-like abilities, spells; SQ alternate form, blindsense 60 ft., damage reduction 10/magic, darkvision 120 ft., immunity to electricity, magic sleep effects, and paralysis, low-light vision, spell resistance 25, water breathing; AL LG; SV Fort +21, Ref +15, Will +21; Str 31, Dex 10, Con 23, Int 22, Wis 23, Cha 22.

Skills and Feats: Bluff +34, Concentration +19, Diplomacy +38, Disguise +32, Hide –2, Intimidate +22, Knowledge (arcana) +24, Knowledge (geography) +22, Knowledge (nature) +16, Knowledge (the planes) +20, Listen +34, Profession (scribe) +10, Search +34, Sense Motive +34, Spellcraft +22, Spot +34, Swim +28, Survival +28; Blind-Fight, Dire Charge, Empower Spell, Flyby Attack, Heighten Breath, Improved Initiative, Multiattack, Power Attack, Recover Breath, Wingover.

Alternate Form (Su): Can assume any humanoid form of Medium size or smaller as a standard action three times per day. This ability functions as a *polymorph* spell cast on itself by a 11th-level sorcerer, except that the dragon does not regain hit points for changing form and can only assume the form of a humanoid. The dragon can remain in its humanoid from until it chooses to assume a new one or return to its natural form.

Breath Weapon (Su): 100-ft. line, 16d6 electricity, Reflex DC 29 half (or higher if heightened); or 50-ft. cone, *repulsion* 1d6+8 rounds, Will DC 29 negates (or higher if heightened).

Crush (Ex): Area 15 ft. by 15 ft.; Small or smaller opponents take 2d8+15 points of bludgeoning damage, and must succeed on a DC 29 Reflex save or be pinned.

Frightful Presence (Ex): 240-ft. radius, HD 26 or fewer, Will DC 29 negates.

Spell-Like Abilities: At will—*speak with animals;* 3/day—*create food and water, detect thoughts, fog cloud.* Caster level 11th; save DC 16 + spell level.

Spells: As 11th-level sorcerer.

Water Breathing (Ex): Can breathe underwater indefinitely and can freely use breath weapon, spells, and other abilities underwater.

Sorcerer Spells Known (6/8/8/7/7/5; save DC 16 + spell level): 0—*dancing lights, detect magic, guidance, mage hand, mending, open/close, prestidigitation, ray of frost, read magic;* 1st—*alarm, comprehend languages, divine favor, magic missile, shield;* 2nd—*cat's grace, cure moderate wounds, darkness, sound burst, summon swarm;* 3rd—*dispel magic, gust of wind, sleet storm, suggestion;* 4th—*confusion, ice storm, polymorph;* 5th—*cloudkill, telekinesis.*

Ofkrysantemiselni
Very Old Bronze Dragon

The self-appointed guardian of the wharves in a major coastal metropolis, Ofkrysantemiselni spends most of her time in the form of an old dwarf with a knack for carpentry. While not a shipwright, she makes cabinetry, rudders, oars, chests, and other wooden objects used on ships, as well as building and repairing docks. This pastime keeps her aware of activity in the dockside area, and she has made herself the nemesis of a criminal organization running a protection racket there. She is a fascinating conversation partner, knowledgeable about many subjects and stunningly intelligent, while possessing an unusual amount of humility and graciousness for a dragon.

Ofkrysantemiselni: Female very old bronze dragon; CR 20; Huge dragon (water); HD 30d12+180, hp 375; Init +4; Spd 40 ft., fly 150 ft. (poor), swim 60 ft.; AC 37, touch 8, flat-footed 37; Base Atk +39; Grp +49; Atk +39 melee (2d8+11, bite); Full Atk +39 melee (2d8+11, bite), +34 melee (2d6+5, 2 claws), +34 melee (1d8+5, 2 wings), +34 melee (2d6+16, tail slap); Space/Reach 15 ft./10 ft. (15 ft. with bite); SA breath weapon, crush, frightful presence, snatch, spell-like abilities, spells; SQ alternate form, blindsense 60 ft., damage reduction 15/magic,darkvision 120 ft., immunity to electricity, magic sleep effects, and paralysis, low-light vision, spell resistance 26, water breathing; AL LG; SV Fort +23, Ref +17, Will +23; Str 33, Dex 10, Con 23, Int 22, Wis 23, Cha 22.

Skills and Feats: Bluff +22, Concentration +24, Craft (carpentry) +11, Diplomacy +42, Disguise +34, Hide +1, Intimidate +28, Knowledge (arcana) +24, Knowledge (history) +15, Knowledge (local) +20, Knowledge (nature) +11, Knowledge (religion) +13, Listen +36, Search +35, Sense Motive +38, Spellcraft +23, Spot +38, Swim +39, Survival +34; Adroit Flyby Attack, Combat Expertise, Dire Charge, Empower Spell, Flyby Attack, Heighten Breath, Improved Initiative, Power Attack, Shape Breath, Snatch, Wingover.

Bronze Dragon

Typical Bronze Dragon Lair

[Size of lair varies with size of dragon]

direction of slow-moving lava flow into ocean

main entry [coral reef]

coral reef protecting island beach

CORAL REEF

N

Overland View

MMIII TA

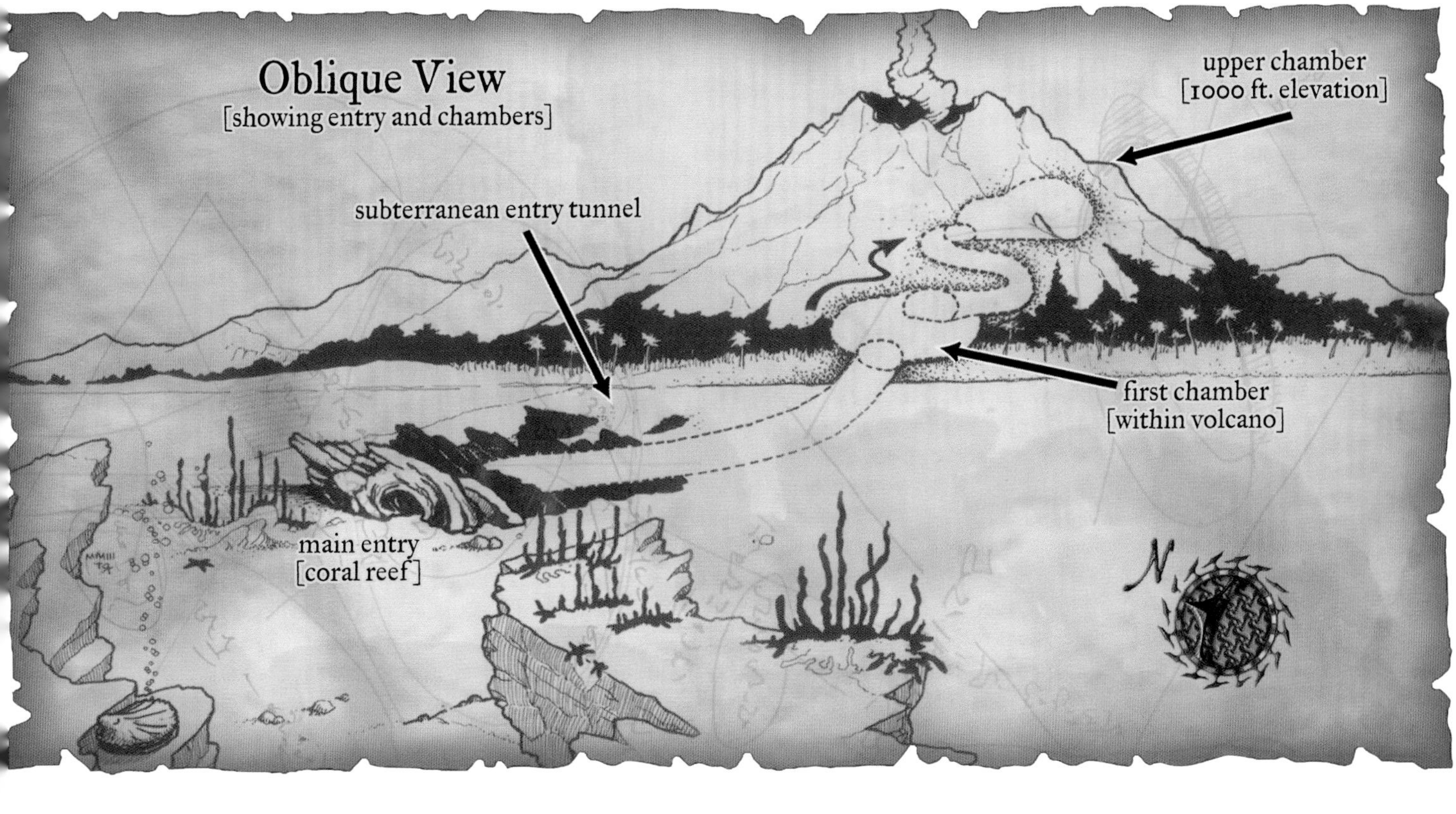

Oblique View

[showing entry and chambers]

upper chamber [1000 ft. elevation]

subterranean entry tunnel

first chamber [within volcano]

main entry [coral reef]

N

Alternate Form (Su): Can assume any humanoid form of Medium size or smaller as a standard action three times per day. This ability functions as a *polymorph* spell cast on itself by a 13th-level sorcerer, except that the dragon does not regain hit points for changing form and can only assume the form of a humanoid. The dragon can remain in its humanoid from until it chooses to assume a new one or return to its natural form.

Breath Weapon (Su): 100-ft. line (50-ft. cone if shaped), 18d6 electricity, Reflex DC 31 half (or higher if heightened); or 50-ft. cone (100-ft. line if shaped), *repulsion* 1d6+9 rounds, Will DC 31 negates (or higher if heightened).

Crush (Ex): Area 15 ft. by 15 ft.; Small or smaller opponents take 2d8+16 points of bludgeoning damage, and must succeed on a DC 31 Reflex save or be pinned.

Frightful Presence (Ex): 270-ft. radius, HD 29 or fewer, Will DC 31 negates.

Snatch (Ex): Against Small or smaller creatures, bite for 2d8+11/round or claw for 2d6+5/round.

Spell-Like Abilities: At will—*speak with animals;* 3/day—*create food and water, detect thoughts, fog cloud.* Caster level 13th; save DC 16 + spell level.

Spells: As 13th-level sorcerer.

Sorcerer Spells Known (6/8/8/7/7/7/5; save DC 16 + spell level): 0—*arcane mark, dancing lights, detect magic, guidance, mage hand, mending, prestidigitation, ray of frost, read magic;* 1st—*alarm, burning hands, magic missile, shield, shield of faith;* 2nd—*cat's grace, cure moderate wounds, darkness, locate object, summon swarm;* 3rd—*dispel magic, haste, searing light, suggestion;* 4th—*charm monster, greater invisibility, solid fog, tongues;* 5th—*cone of cold, fabricate, wall of force;* 6th—*acid fog, heal.*

Aujigweybermanoth
Ancient Bronze Dragon

Aujigweybermanoth lives near a small fishing village, and spends a great deal of time in the form of a wizened old fisherman, mending nets and sharing stories with the folk of the village. Unlike many dragons, he makes no attempt to conceal his true nature; he simply takes human form because it is easier for the humans to talk with him that way. The villagers think of Aujigweybermanoth as their protector and champion, and even attribute the abundance of fish in their waters to his care, which is one thing he has nothing to do with. He laughs frequently, shares long sagas and anecdotes readily, and loves "his people" deeply.

Aujigweybermanoth: Male ancient bronze dragon; CR 22; Gargantuan dragon (water); HD 33d12+231, hp 445; Init +0; Spd 40 ft., fly 200 ft. (poor), swim 60 ft.; AC 38, touch 6, flat-footed 38; Base Atk +41; Grp +57; Atk +41 melee (4d6+12, bite); Full Atk +41 melee (4d6+12, bite), +39 melee (2d8+6, 2 claws), +39 melee (2d6+6, 2 wings), +39 melee (2d8+18, tail slap); Space/Reach 20 ft./15 ft. (20 ft. with bite); SA breath weapon, crush, frightful presence, improved snatch, spell-like abilities, spells, tail sweep; SQ alternate form, blindsense 60 ft., damage reduction 15/magic, darkvision 120 ft., immunity to electricity, magic sleep effects, and paralysis, low-light vision, spell resistance 28, water breathing; AL LG; SV Fort +25, Ref +18, Will +25; Str 35, Dex 10, Con 25, Int 24, Wis 25, Cha 24.

Skills and Feats: Bluff +43, Concentration +28, Craft (netmaking) +10, Diplomacy +31, Disguise +29, Hide –2, Intimidate +33, Knowledge (arcana) +33, Knowledge (geography) +21, Knowledge (local) +32, Knowledge (nature) +27, Knowledge (the planes) +19, Knowledge (religion) +22, Listen +43, Profession (fisher) +11, Search +43, Sense Motive +43, Spot +43, Swim +42, Survival +39; Awaken Frightful Presence, Combat Reflexes, Flyby Attack, Heighten Breath, Improved Maneuverability, Improved Snatch, Multiattack, Power Attack, Recover Breath, Shape Breath, Snatch, Wingover.

Alternate Form (Su): Can assume any humanoid form of Medium size or smaller as a standard action three times per day. This ability functions as a *polymorph* spell cast on itself by a 15th-level sorcerer, except that the dragon does not regain hit points for changing form and can only assume the form of a humanoid. The dragon can remain in its humanoid from until it chooses to assume a new one or return to its natural form.

Breath Weapon (Su): 120-ft. line (60-ft. cone if shaped), 20d6 electricity, Reflex DC 33 half (or higher if heightened); or 60-ft. cone (120-ft. line if shaped), *repulsion* 1d6+10 rounds, Will DC 33 negates (or higher if heightened).

Crush (Ex): Area 20 ft. by 20 ft.; Medium or smaller opponents take 4d6+18 points of bludgeoning damage, and must succeed on a DC 33 Reflex save or be pinned.

Frightful Presence (Ex): 450-ft. radius, HD 32 or fewer, Will DC 35 negates.

Improved Snatch (Ex): Against Large or smaller creatures, bite for 4d6+12/round or claw for 2d8+6/round.

Spell-Like Abilities: At will—*speak with animals;* 3/day—*control water, create food and water, detect thoughts, fog cloud.* Caster level 15th; save DC 15 + spell level.

Spells: As 15th-level sorcerer.

Tail Sweep (Ex): Half-circle 30 ft. in diameter, Small or smaller opponents take 2d6+18 points of bludgeoning damage, Reflex DC 31 half.

Sorcerer Spells Known (6/8/8/8/7/7/7/5; save DC 17 + spell level): 0—*arcane mark, dancing lights, detect magic, guidance, mage hand, mending, prestidigitation, ray of frost, read magic;* 1st—*alarm, burning hands, divine favor, magic missile, shield;* 2nd—*cat's grace, cure moderate wounds, darkness, locate object, summon swarm;* 3rd—*dispel magic, haste, searing light, suggestion;* 4th—*charm monster, divination, greater invisibility, solid fog;* 5th—*cone of cold, feeblemind, flame strike, hold monster;* 6th—*acid fog, greater dispelling, heal;* 7th—*dictum, delayed blast fireball.*

Saluraropicrusa
Wyrm Bronze Dragon

In her youth, Saluraropicrusa was much like Ofkrysantemiselni—a skilled carpenter and sailor who lived in a city, worked her trades, and protected the humans in her care. With her increasing age and magical power, however, she has been drawn more and more into the study and practice of the arcane arts. A human wizard in the city where she lived shared some of his theoretical explorations of magical principles with her, and she was hooked—she studied with him until he died, then carried on her studies of arcana and spellcraft for decades more. She travels widely now, visiting libraries, universities, and renowned sages and scholars of magic in order to increase her knowledge. Like all bronze dragons, she hates chaos and evil, but her greatest hatred is reserved for those who, as she puts it, pervert magic to the service of evil—particularly necromancers and evil conjurers.

Saluraropicrusa: Female wyrm bronze dragon; CR 23; Gargantuan dragon (water); HD 36d12+288, hp 522; Init +0; Spd 40 ft., fly 200 ft. (poor), swim 60 ft.; AC 41, touch 6, flat-footed 41; Base Atk +45; Grp +61; Atk +45 melee (4d6+13, bite); Full Atk +45 melee (4d6+13, bite), +40 melee (2d8+6, 2 claws), +40 melee (2d6+6, 2 wings), +40 melee (2d8+19, tail slap); Space/Reach 20 ft./15 ft. (20 ft. with bite); SA breath weapon, crush, frightful presence, improved snatch, snatch, spell-like abilities, spells, tail sweep; SQ alternate form, blindsense 60 ft., damage reduction 20/magic, darkvision 120 ft., immunity to electricity, magic sleep effects, and paralysis, low-light vision, spell resistance 29, water breathing; AL LG; SV Fort +28, Ref +20, Will +32; Str 37, Dex 10, Con 27, Int 26, Wis 27, Cha 26.

Skills and Feats: Balance +6, Bluff +47, Climb +18, Concentration +32, Craft (carpentry) +12, Diplomacy +51, Disguise +40, Hide +3, Intimidate +26, Knowledge (arcana) +34, Knowledge (geography) +24, Knowledge (local) +32, Knowledge (nature) +26, Listen +47, Profession (sailor) +13, Search +43, Sense Motive +47, Spellcraft +27, Spot +44, Survival +40, Swim +45, Use Rope +7; Blind-Fight, Empower Spell, Epic Will, Flyby Attack, Heighten Breath, Heighten Spell, Improved Snatch, Improved Maneuverability, Power Attack, Shape Breath, Snatch, Tail Constrict, Wingover.

Alternate Form (Su): Can assume any humanoid form of Medium size or smaller as a standard action three times per day. This ability functions as a *polymorph* spell cast on itself by a 17th-level sorcerer, except that the dragon does not regain hit points for changing form and can only assume the form of a humanoid. The dragon can remain in its humanoid from until it chooses to assume a new one or return to its natural form.

Breath Weapon (Su): 120-ft. line (60-ft. cone if shaped), 22d6 electricity, Reflex DC 36 half (or higher if heightened); or 60-ft. cone (120-ft. line if shaped), *repulsion* 1d6+11 rounds, Will DC 36 negates (or higher if heightened).

Crush (Ex): Area 20 ft. by 20 ft.; Medium or smaller opponents take 4d6+19 points of bludgeoning damage, and must succeed on a DC 36 Reflex save or be pinned.

Frightful Presence (Ex): 330-ft. radius, HD 35 or fewer, Will DC 36 negates.

Improved Snatch (Ex): Against Large or smaller creatures, bite for 4d6+13/round or claw for 2d8+6/round.

Spell-Like Abilities: At will—*speak with animals;* 3/day—*control water, create food and water, detect thoughts, fog cloud.* Caster level 17th; save DC 18 + spell level.

Spells: As 17th-level sorcerer.

Tail Sweep (Ex): Half-circle 30 ft. in diameter, Small or smaller opponents take 2d6+19 points of bludgeoning damage, Reflex DC 36 half.

Sorcerer Spells Known (6/8/8/8/8/7/7/7/5; save DC 18 + spell level): 0—*arcane mark, dancing lights, detect magic, guidance, mage hand, mending, prestidigitation, ray of frost, read magic;* 1st—*alarm, burning hands, magic missile, shield, shield of faith;* 2nd—*cat's grace, cure moderate wounds, darkness, locate object, summon swarm;* 3rd—*dispel magic, haste, searing light, suggestion;* 4th—*charm monster, divination, greater invisibility, solid fog;* 5th—*cone of cold, feeblemind, flame strike, hold monster;* 6th—*acid fog, greater dispel magic, heal;* 7th—*dictum, Mordenkainen's sword, spell turning;* 8th—*mass charm monster, mind blank.*

Kielistanilopais
Great Wyrm Bronze Dragon

Kielistanilopais has had a full life—many lives, one might say. She has lived extensively among humans, including a lengthy period serving as a cohort and mount to a mighty paladin who only recently died in battle. She has lived in more humble disguise in human villages and towns, hunted evil dragons in coastal forests and mountains, raised three wyrmlings to young adulthood, and sought enlightenment in a solitary undersea retreat. Now, her grief over her epic paladin companion still fresh, she devotes all her energy to hunting the blackguard who caused her loss. She has left her hoard guarded by her three children (now adults), and travels far and wide in search of the villain.

Kielistanilopais: Female great wyrm bronze dragon; CR 25; Gargantuan dragon (water); HD 39d12+312, hp 565; Init +4; Spd 40 ft., fly 200 ft. (poor), swim 60 ft.; AC 44, touch 6, flat-footed 44; Base Atk +49; Grp +65; Atk +49 melee (4d6+14, bite); Full Atk +49 melee (4d6+14, bite), +44 melee (2d8+7, 2 claws), +44 melee (2d6+7, 2 wings), +44 melee (2d8+21, tail slap); Space/Reach 20 ft./15 ft. (20 ft. with bite); SA breath weapon, crush, frightful presence, snatch, spell-like abilities, spells, tail sweep; SQ alternate form, blindsense 60 ft., damage reduction 20/magic, darkvision 120 ft., immunity to electricity, magic sleep effects, and paralysis, low-light vision, spell resistance 31, water breathing; AL LG; SV Fort +29, Ref +21, Will +33; Str 39, Dex 10, Con 27, Int 26, Wis 27, Cha 26.

Skills and Feats: Bluff +48, Concentration +44, Craft (blacksmithing) +13, Diplomacy +52, Disguise +40, Handle Animal +13, Hide +5, Intimidate +43, Knowledge (arcana) +42, Knowledge (local) +38, Knowledge (nature) +34, Knowledge (the planes) +34, Listen +48, Profession (teamster) +12, Ride +8, Search +48, Sense Motive +50, Spellcraft +29, Survival +44, Swim +42; Empower Spell, Epic Will, Flyby Attack, Heighten Breath, Heighten Spell, Improved Initiative, Improved Maneuverability, Power Attack, Recover Breath, Shape Breath, Snatch, Tempest Breath, Wingover, Wingstorm.

Alternate Form (Su): Can assume any humanoid form of Medium size or smaller as a standard action three times

Copper
Dragon
Chaotic Good
Earth Subtype
Dry Mountains
Underground
Flight
Adult
12 ft.
Incorrigible pranksters, joke tellers and riddlers, copper dragons are mostly good-natured but with a covetous miserly streak.
Transmute rock to mud
Stone shape
Move earth
Spider climb
Wall of stone
Detail of skull showing horn boss and zygomatic wing plate arrangement.
Specimen retrieved from deserted red dragon lair.
Juvenile
6 ft.
Very Young
3 ft.
Wyrmling
18 inches
SARDINHA

per day. This ability functions as a *polymorph* spell cast on itself by a 19th-level sorcerer, except that the dragon does not regain hit points for changing form and can only assume the form of a humanoid. The dragon can remain in its humanoid from until it chooses to assume a new one or return to its natural form.

Breath Weapon (Su): 120-ft. line (60-ft. cone if shaped), 24d6 electricity, Reflex DC 37 half (or higher if heightened); or 60-ft. cone (120-ft. line if shaped), *repulsion* 1d6+12 rounds, Will DC 37 negates (or higher if heightened).

Crush (Ex): Area 20 ft. by 20 ft.; Medium or smaller opponents take 4d6+21 points of bludgeoning damage, and must succeed on a DC 37 Reflex save or be pinned.

Frightful Presence (Ex): 360-ft. radius, HD 38 or fewer, Will DC 37 negates.

Snatch (Ex): Against Medium or smaller creatures, bite for 4d6+14/round or claw for 2d8+7/round.

Spell-Like Abilities: At will—*speak with animals*; 3/day—*control water, create food and water, detect thoughts, fog cloud*; 1/day—*control weather*. Caster level 19th; save DC 18 + spell level.

Spells: As 19th-level sorcerer.

Tail Sweep (Ex): Half-circle 30 ft. in diameter, Small or smaller opponents take 2d6+21 points of bludgeoning damage, Reflex DC 37 half.

Sorcerer Spells Known (6/8/8/8/8/7/7/7/7/4; save DC 18 + spell level): 0—*arcane mark, dancing lights, detect magic, guidance, mage hand, mending, prestidigitation, ray of frost, read magic*; 1st—*alarm, burning hands, divine favor, magic missile, shield*; 2nd—*cat's grace, cure moderate wounds, darkness, locate object, summon swarm*; 3rd—*dispel magic, haste, searing light, suggestion*; 4th—*charm monster, divination, greater invisibility, solid fog*; 5th—*cone of cold, feeblemind, flame strike, hold monster*; 6th—*acid fog, greater dispel magic, heal*; 7th—*dictum, Mordenkainen's sword, spell turning*; 8th—*horrid wilting, mass charm monster, mind blank*; 9th—*meteor swarm, elemental swarm*.

SAMPLE COPPER DRAGONS

Detailed below are twelve sample copper dragons, one of each age category. The descriptions include basic personality and encounter notes that the DM can flesh out for his campaign, along with a set of statistics that make the dragon ready to play.

Spider Climb (Ex): All copper dragons can use *spider climb* (as the spell) when moving on stone surfaces.

Acydiphul
Wyrmling Copper Dragon

Acydiphul has a penchant for wordplay and seldom can resist plying any intelligent creature he meets with riddles, limericks, puns, and even the occasional double entendre. When not practicing the art of verbal offense, he spends his time crawling all over the local rocks hunting for spiders, centipedes, and scorpions to eat. He sticks his nose into every nook and cranny.

Acydiphul: Male wyrmling copper dragon; CR 3; Tiny dragon (earth); HD 5d12+5; hp 37; Init +0; Spd 40 ft., fly 100 ft. (average); AC 16, touch 12, flat-footed 16; Base Atk +5; Grp –3; Atk +7 melee (1d4, bite); Full Atk +7 melee (1d4, bite), +5 melee (1d3, 2 claws); Space/Reach 2-1/2 ft./0 ft. (5 ft. with bite); SA breath weapon; SQ blindsense 60 ft., darkvision 120 ft., immunity to acid, magic sleep effects, and paralysis, low-light vision, spider climb; AL CG; SV Fort +5, Ref +4, Will +5; Str 11, Dex 10, Con 13, Int 12, Wis 13, Cha 12.

Skills and Feats: Bluff +7, Diplomacy +9, Hide +8, Intimidate +11, Jump +9, Knowledge (geography) +5, Listen +6, Search +6, Sense Motive +5, Spot +6; Multiattack, Power Attack, Wingover.

Breath Weapon (Su): 30-ft. line, 2d4 acid, Reflex DC 13 half; or 15-ft. cone, *slow* 1d6+1 rounds, Fortitude DC 13 negates.

Rhindani
Very Young Copper Dragon

Rhindani fancies herself a comic lyricist. She hums constantly and loudly sings amusing little ditties as she thinks of them, which is quite often. She lives in a narrow gully where a stream emerges from a hillside, babbling along with the water. A young red dragon, Fylokkipyron, lives uncomfortably close, and the two have a long history of conflict—which invariably ends with Rhindani fleeing for her life, but shouting some humorous song about the encounter as she goes.

Rhindani: Female very young copper dragon; CR 5; Small dragon (earth); HD 8d12+8; hp 60; Init +0; Spd 40 ft., fly 100 ft. (average); AC 18, touch 11, flat-footed 18; Base Atk +8; Grp +5; Atk +10 melee (1d6+1, bite); Full Atk +10 melee (1d6+1, bite), +5 melee (1d4, 2 claws); Space/Reach 5 ft./5 ft.; SA breath weapon; SQ blindsense 60 ft., darkvision 120 ft., immunity to acid, magic sleep effects, and paralysis, low-light vision, spider climb; AL CG; SV Fort +7, Ref +6, Will +7; Str 13, Dex 10, Con 13, Int 12, Wis 13, Cha 12.

Skills and Feats: Bluff +12, Diplomacy +5, Hide +4, Intimidate +7, Jump +16, Knowledge (geography) +9, Listen +12, Perform (sing) +5, Search +9, Sense Motive +9, Spot +9; Cleave, Flyby Attack, Power Attack, Wingover.

Breath Weapon (Su): 40-ft. line, 4d4 acid, Reflex DC 15 half; or 20-ft. cone, *slow* 1d6+2 rounds, Fortitude DC 15 negates.

Snydil
Young Copper Dragon

Snydil has an abiding fascination with magic items, and enjoys using those he finds rather than stockpiling them in his hoard. In fact, he often uses coins and gemstones he acquires to purchase magic items he can carry and use, and he keeps only a few items in his lair. Without a hoard to protect, Snydil roams widely, often staying away from his lair for weeks at a time. He is an accomplished prankster, and purchases magic items that facilitate his trickery. He is considering saving up for a *ring of invisibility*.

Snydil: Male young copper dragon; CR 7; Medium dragon (earth); HD 11d12+22; hp 93; Init +0; Spd 40 ft., fly 150 ft. (poor); AC 20, touch 10, flat-footed 20; Base Atk +11; Grp +13; Atk +13 melee (1d8+2, bite); Full Atk +13 melee (1d8+2, bite), +11 melee (1d6+1, 2 claws), +11 melee (1d4+1, 2 wings); Space/Reach 5 ft./5 ft.; SA breath weapon, spells; SQ blindsense 60 ft., darkvision 120 ft., immunity to acid, magic sleep effects, and paralysis, low-light vision, spider climb; AL CG; SV Fort +9, Ref +7, Will +9; Str 15, Dex 10, Con 15, Int 14, Wis 15, Cha 14.

Skills and Feats: Bluff +10, Concentration +13, Diplomacy +6, Intimidate +4, Jump +17, Knowledge (geography) +10, Knowledge (nature) +9, Listen +13, Perform (comedy) +9, Search +13, Sense Motive +13, Spellcraft +7, Spot +13, Use Magic Device +14; Combat Expertise, Flyby Attack, Multiattack, Wingover.

Breath Weapon (Su): 60-ft. line, 6d4 acid, Reflex DC 17 half; or 30-ft. cone, *slow* 1d6+3 rounds, Fortitude DC 17 negates.

Spells: As 1st-level sorcerer.

Sorcerer Spells Known (5/4; save DC 12 + spell level): 0—*dancing lights, daze, detect magic, ghost sound;* 1st—*command, grease.*

Possessions: *Potion of blur, potion of Charisma, potion of invisibility, rust bag of tricks.*

Ladunappindon
Juvenile Copper Dragon

A large town of gnomes nestled in a rocky valley has a guardian few such communities can boast. Ladunappindon makes her lair in a large house carved into a cliff side in the midst of the town. She is not by any means an accomplished illusionist, but she entertains young gnomes greatly with comic presentations created with *silent image* and narrated by the dragon through *ventriloquism.* She contributes her modest magic and significant combat prowess to the defense of the town from a neighboring tribe of goblins who still occasionally dare to make raids on the gnomes.

Ladunappindon: Female juvenile copper dragon; CR 9; Medium dragon (earth); HD 14d12+28, hp 119; Init +0; Spd 40 ft., fly 150 ft. (average), AC 23, touch 10, flat-footed 23; Base Atk +14; Grp +17; Atk +17 melee (1d8+3, bite); Full Atk +17 melee (1d8+3, bite), +12 melee (1d6+1, 2 claws), +12 melee (1d4+1, 2 wings); Space/Reach 5 ft./5 ft.; SA breath weapon, spells; SQ blindsense 60 ft., darkvision 120 ft., immunity to acid, magic sleep effects, and paralysis, low-light vision, spider climb; AL CG; SV Fort +11, Ref +9, Will +11; Str 17, Dex 10, Con 15, Int 14, Wis 15, Cha 14.

Skills and Feats: Bluff +16, Concentration +13, Diplomacy +6, Intimidate +4, Jump +21, Knowledge (arcana) +7, Knowledge (geography) +7, Knowledge (local) +12, Listen +16, Perform (comedy) +10, Search +16, Sense Motive +16, Spellcraft +10, Spot +16; Flyby Attack, Improved Maneuverability, Power Attack, Spell Focus (Illusion), Wingover.

Breath Weapon (Su): 60-ft. line, 8d4 acid, Reflex DC 19 half; or 30-ft. cone, *slow* 1d6+4 rounds, Fortitude DC 19 negates.

Spells: As 3rd-level sorcerer.

Sorcerer Spells Known (6/6; save DC 12 + spell level or 14 + spell level for illusion spells): 0—*dancing lights**, *ghost sound**, *prestidigitation, ray of frost, read magic;* 1st—*color spray**, *silent image**, *ventriloquism**.

*illusion spell.

Vijaylommaxius
Young Adult Copper Dragon

No less a prankster than other copper dragons, Vijaylommaxius at least plays his pranks in service of a greater cause. His lair lies at the edge of a tyrant's domain, whose people are heavily burdened with taxes and oppressive regulations. Vijaylommaxius's pranks are usually directed toward the tyrant's soldiers and tax collectors—he takes every opportunity to humiliate them and foil their errands for the king. Unfortunately, each time the king's agents are hindered in their duties, the king orders reprisals against the common folk. Spurred by this injustice, Vijaylommaxius is growing increasingly angry, and his pranks are getting much more serious—and deadly.

Vijaylommaxius: Male young adult copper dragon; CR 11; Large dragon (earth); HD 17d12+51, hp 161; Init +0; Spd 40 ft., fly 150 ft. (poor); AC 25, touch 9, flat-footed 25; Base Atk +17; Grp +25; Atk +20 melee (2d6+4, bite); Full Atk +20 melee (2d6+4, bite), +15 melee (1d8+2, 2 claws), +15 melee (1d6+2, 2 wings), +15 melee (1d8+6, tail slap); Space/Reach 10 ft./5 ft. (10 ft. with bite); SA breath weapon, frightful presence, spells; SQ blindsense 60 ft., damage reduction 5/magic, darkvision 120 ft., immunity to acid, magic sleep effects, and paralysis, low-light vision, spell resistance 19, spider climb; AL CG; SV Fort +13, Ref +10, Will +13; Str 19, Dex 10, Con 17, Int 16, Wis 17, Cha 16.

Skills and Feats: Bluff +20, Concentration +18, Diplomacy +7, Hide –4, Intimidate +5, Jump +20, Knowledge (arcana) +15, Knowledge (geography) +15, Knowledge (nature) +15, Listen +20, Perform (comedy) +13, Search +20, Sense Motive +20, Spellcraft +12, Spot +20; Clinging Breath, Flyby Attack, Power Attack, Shock Wave, Spell Focus (Enchantment), Wingover.

Breath Weapon (Su): 80-ft. line, 10d4 acid, Reflex DC 21 half; or 40-ft. cone, *slow* 1d6+5 rounds, Fortitude DC 21 negates.

Frightful Presence (Ex): 150-ft. radius, HD 16 or fewer, Will DC 21 negates.

Spells: As 5th-level sorcerer.

Sorcerer Spells Known (6/7/5; save DC 13 + spell level): 0—*dancing lights, detect magic, ghost sound, mage hand, prestidigitation, read magic;* 1st—*grease, random action, ray of enfeeblement, shocking grasp;* 2nd—*minor image, Tasha's hideous laughter.*

Kearidilonshar
Adult Copper Dragon

Kearidilonshar is fascinated by elementals, particularly earth elementals (as well as xorn and other outsiders from the Plane of Earth). She lairs in a deep cavern near a permanent portal to that plane, and seeks out the conversation of its natives above all others. Her knowledge of other planes in general is quite extensive, thanks to her good relationship with a number of renowned dwarf and deep gnome scholars. She tries to mimic the mannerisms of earth creatures, straining to keep her voice slow and low, searching for just the right rumble in her throat, but she quickly loses patience for that affectation in an extended conversation and resumes her normal rapid, higher-pitched voice.

Kearidilonshar: Female adult copper dragon; CR 14; Large dragon (earth); HD 20d12+80, hp 210; Init +0; Spd 40 ft., fly 150 ft. (average); AC 28, touch 9, flat-footed 28; Base Atk +20; Grp +30; Atk +25 melee (2d6+6, bite); Full Atk +25 melee (2d6+6, bite), +20 melee (1d8+3, 2 claws), +20 melee (1d6+3, 2 wings), +20 melee (1d8+9, tail slap); Space/Reach 10 ft./5 ft. (10 ft. with bite); SA breath weapon, frightful presence, spell-like abilities, spells; SQ blindsense 60 ft., damage reduction 5/magic, darkvision 120 ft., immunity to acid, magic sleep effects, and paralysis, low-light vision, spell resistance 21, spider climb; AL CG; SV Fort +16, Ref +12, Will +15; Str 23, Dex 10, Con 19, Int 16, Wis 17, Cha 16.

Skills and Feats: Bluff +20, Concentration +21, Diplomacy +7, Hide –4, Intimidate +5, Jump +30, Knowledge (arcana) +15, Knowledge (geography) +14, Knowledge (the planes) +15, Listen +23, Perform (oratory) +14, Search +23, Sense Motive +23, Spellcraft +14, Spot +23; Flyby Attack, Hover, Improved Maneuverability, Power Attack, Shape Breath, Split Breath, Wingover.

Breath Weapon (Su): 80-ft. line (40-ft. cone if shaped), 12d4 acid, Reflex DC 24 half; or 40-ft. cone (80-ft. line if shaped), *slow* 1d6+6 rounds, Fortitude DC 24 negates.

Frightful Presence (Ex): 180-ft. radius, HD 19 or fewer, Will DC 21 negates.

Spell-Like Abilities: 2/day—*stone shape.* Caster level 7th.

Spells: As 7th-level sorcerer.

Sorcerer Spells Known (6/7/7/5; save DC 13 + spell level): 0—*arcane mark, dancing lights, detect magic, ghost sound, mage hand, prestidigitation, read magic;* 1st—*hypnotism, magic missile, random action, shield of faith, true strike;* 2nd—*fog cloud, Tasha's hideous laughter, web;* 3rd—*cure serious wounds, stinking cloud.*

Hypvaliidedarix
Mature Adult Copper Dragon

Hypvaliidedarix is most often found in the company of a band of wood elves, and his taste in music and humor is somewhat elevated above the copper dragon norm as a result. His humor relies on elaborate word plays (often in Elvish) and goes over the heads of most other creatures, and he doesn't care for what he calls the "gnome pranks" of other copper dragons. He enjoys flying at top speed through the light forests around his canyon home, racing fleet-footed elves who certainly have the edge in maneuverability. Even more, he enjoys their evening feasts, where they share fine food, song, and dance. In his mind, the life of these simple people, the plain beauty of their folk melodies, and their lusty enjoyment of life are the finest things in the world.

Hypvaliidedarix: Male mature adult copper dragon; CR 16; Huge dragon (earth); HD 23d12+115, hp 264; Init +0; Spd 40 ft., fly 150 ft. (poor); AC 30, touch 8, flat-footed 30; Base Atk +23; Grp +39; Atk +29 melee (2d8+8, bite); Full Atk +29 melee (2d8+8, bite), +24 melee (2d6+4, 2 claws), +24 melee (1d8+4, 2 wings), +24 melee (2d6+12, tail slap); Space/Reach 15 ft./10 ft. (15 ft. with bite); SA breath weapon, crush, frightful presence, spell-like abilities, spells; SQ blindsense 60 ft., damage reduction 10/magic, darkvision 120 ft., immunity to acid, magic sleep effects, and paralysis, low-light vision, spell resistance 23, spider climb; AL CG; SV Fort +18, Ref +13, Will +17; Str 27, Dex 10, Con 21, Int 18, Wis 19, Cha 18.

Skills and Feats: Bluff +30, Concentration +22, Diplomacy +19, Hide –8, Intimidate +18, Jump +35, Knowledge (arcana) +19, Knowledge (geography) +19, Knowledge (nature) +17, Listen +30, Perform (oratory) +17, Search +30, Sense Motive +30, Spellcraft +16, Spot +30; Flyby Attack, Heighten Breath, Heighten Spell, Hover, Power Attack, Shape Breath, Skill Focus (Perform [oratory]), Wingover.

Breath Weapon (Su): 100-ft. line (50-ft. cone if shaped), 14d4 acid, Reflex DC 27 half (or higher if heightened); or 50-ft. cone (100-ft. line if shaped), *slow* 1d6+7 rounds, Fortitude DC 27 negates (or higher if heightened).

Crush (Ex): Area 15 ft. by 15 ft.; Small or smaller opponents take 2d8+12 points of bludgeoning damage, and must succeed on a DC 27 Reflex save or be pinned.

Frightful Presence (Ex): 210-ft. radius, HD 22 or fewer, Will DC 25 negates.

Spell-Like Abilities: 2/day—*stone shape.* Caster level 9th.

Spells: As 9th-level sorcerer.

Sorcerer Spells Known (6/7/7/7/5; save DC 14 + spell level): 0—*arcane mark, dancing lights, detect magic, ghost sound, guidance, mage hand, prestidigitation, read magic;* 1st—*command, magic missile, random action, shield of faith, true strike;* 2nd—*cat's grace, fog cloud, Tasha's hideous laughter, web;* 3rd—*bestow curse, cure serious wounds, stinking cloud;* 4th—*greater invisibility, summon monster IV.*

Turuntmenkajanki
Old Copper Dragon

Sworn to hunt devils for the rest of her days, Turuntmenkajanki is rather more serious and intense than most copper dragons. Though she often regrets what she now recognizes as an oath sworn in haste without due consideration of its repercussions, her own personal sense of honor compels her to obey it, and so she is an old dragon without a home or hoard, with no children, and who is haunted by the taint of evil's touch in her very soul. When she was a juvenile, Turuntmenkajanki's parents and a close friend of theirs, a human bard, were all slain by a trio of pit fiends. When Turuntmenkajanki found their bodies, she had to tell the bard's husband what had happened, and his grief so moved the dragon that she swore an oath on the spot—not just to avenge their deaths, but to make war on

Copper Dragon

Typical Copper Dragon Lair

[Size of lair varies with size of dragon]

rocks to conceal entry to lair

Oblique View

lairs usually found in
dry, rocky uplands and mountains

Plan View

secret escape tunnel
[500 ft. elevation]

secret door for
escape tunnel

main entry
[concealed with stones]

main
foyer

main entertaining
chamber

prankster designed
entrance for guests

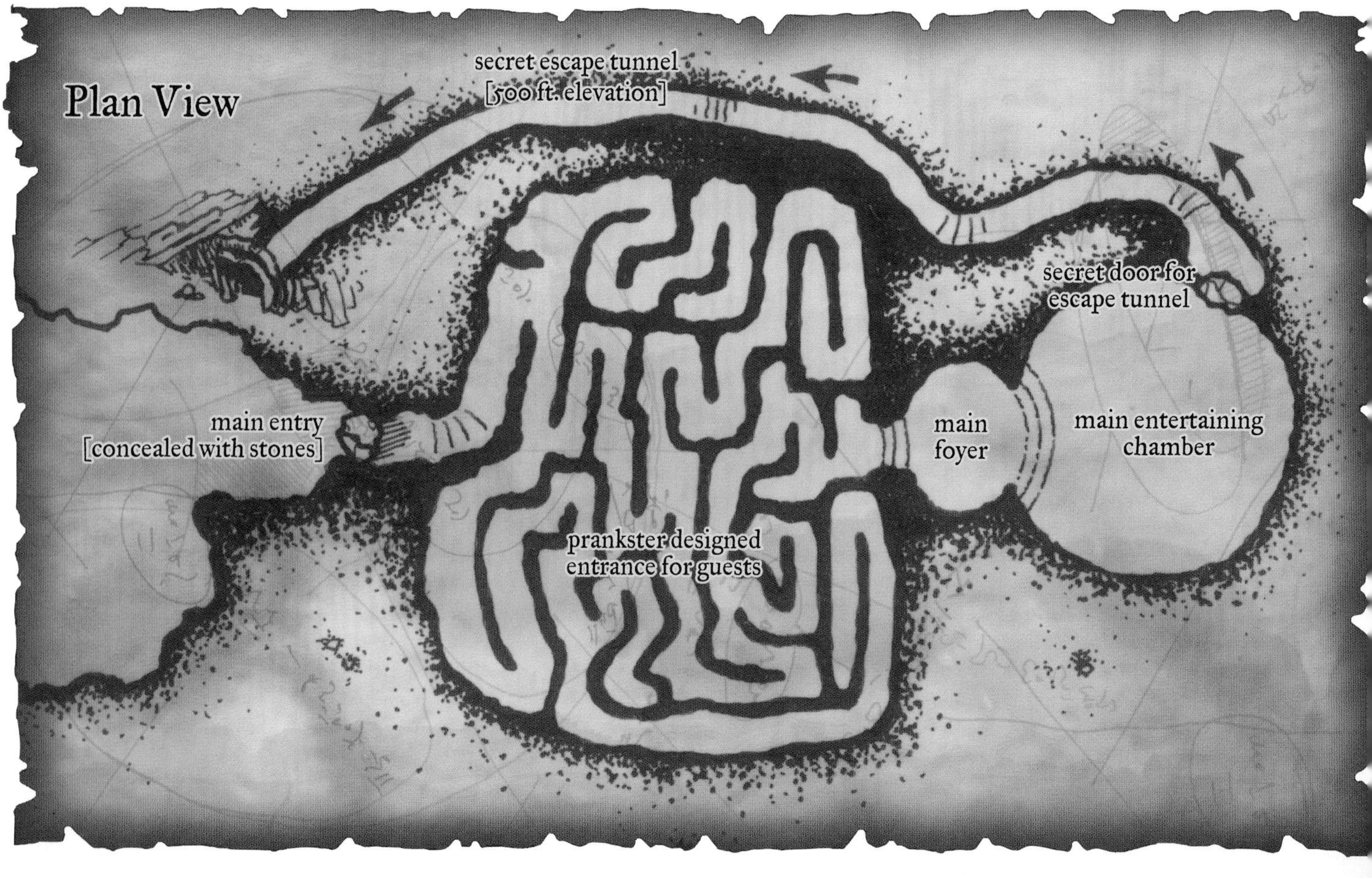

all devils until the day of her death. There can be no denying that, as much as her rash oath has cost her personally, it has removed great evil from the world and helped many creatures in need.

Turuntmenkajanki: Female old copper dragon; CR 19; Huge dragon (earth); HD 26d12+130, hp 299; Init +0; Spd 40 ft., fly 150 ft. (poor); AC 33, touch 8, flat-footed 33; Base Atk +26; Grp +43; Atk +33 melee (2d8+9, bite); Full Atk +33 melee (2d8+9, bite), +28 melee (2d6+4, 2 claws), +28 melee (1d8+4, 2 wings), +28 melee (2d6+13, tail slap); Space/Reach 15 ft./10 ft. (15 ft. with bite); SA breath weapon, crush, frightful presence, spell-like abilities, spells; SQ blindsense 60 ft., damage reduction 10/magic, darkvision 120 ft., immunity to acid, magic sleep effects, and paralysis, low-light vision, spell resistance 25, spider climb; AL CG; SV Fort +20, Ref +15, Will +21; Str 29, Dex 10, Con 21, Int 18, Wis 19, Cha 18.

Skills and Feats: Bluff +33, Concentration +15, Diplomacy +18, Hide –8, Intimidate +22, Jump +39, Knowledge (arcana) +15, Knowledge (geography) +15, Knowledge (nature) +15, Knowledge (the planes) +15, Listen +30, Perform (act) +18, Search +30, Sense Motive +33, Spellcraft +18, Spot +30; Enlarge Breath, Flyby Attack, Heighten Breath, Heighten Spell, Hover, Iron Will, Power Attack, Shape Breath, Wingover.

Breath Weapon (Su): 100-ft. line (150-ft. line if enlarged, 50-ft. cone if shaped, 75-ft. cone if shaped and enlarged), 16d4 acid, Reflex DC 28 half (or higher if heightened); or 50-ft. cone (75-ft. cone if enlarged, 100-ft. line if shaped, 150-ft. line if shaped and enlarged), *slow* 1d6+8 rounds, Fortitude DC 28 negates (or higher if heightened).

Crush (Ex): Area 15 ft. by 15 ft.; Small or smaller opponents take 2d8+13 points of bludgeoning damage, and must succeed on a DC 28 Reflex save or be pinned.

Frightful Presence (Ex): 240-ft. radius, HD 25 or fewer, Will DC 27 negates.

Spell-Like Abilities: 2/day—*stone shape.* 1/day—*transmute rock to mud/mud to rock.* Caster level 11th.

Spells: As 11th-level sorcerer.

Sorcerer Spells Known (6/7/7/7/7/4; save DC 14 + spell level): 0—*arcane mark, dancing lights, detect magic, ghost sound, guidance, light, mage hand, prestidigitation, read magic;* 1st—*animate rope, magic missile, random action, shield of faith, true strike;* 2nd—*cat's grace, fog cloud, shatter, summon swarm, web;* 3rd—*cure serious wounds, dispel magic, stinking cloud, suggestion;* 4th—*giant vermin, ice storm, solid fog;* 5th—*mirage arcana, wall of force.*

Drumduruhullwix
Very Old Copper Dragon

Incorrigible is perhaps the best word to describe Drumduruhullwix, and he would hasten to add, "So don't encourage me!" Puns are his meat and drink, and he hasn't given a straight answer to any question in over three hundred years. (And yes, he is keeping track.) Engaging in conversation with him is like fencing with a vastly superior foe: Every sentence, every word means what he wants it to mean, regardless of the speaker's intent, and he usually wants everything to mean something that embarrasses or demeans the speaker. Most creatures just give up on talking to him after a matter of minutes, which leaves him in fits of laughter at what he considers success.

Drumduruhullwix: Male very old copper dragon; CR 20; Huge dragon (earth); HD 29d12+174, hp 362; Init +0; Spd 40 ft., fly 150 ft. (poor); AC 36, touch 8, flat-footed 36; Base Atk +29; Grp +47; Atk +37 melee (2d8+10, bite); Full Atk +37 melee (2d8+10, bite), +35 melee (2d6+5, 2 claws), +35 melee (1d8+5, 2 wings), +35 melee (2d6+15, tail slap); Space/Reach 15 ft./10 ft. (15 ft. with bite); SA breath weapon, crush, frightful presence, spell-like abilities, spells; SQ blindsense 60 ft., damage reduction 15/magic, darkvision 120 ft., immunity to acid, magic sleep effects, and paralysis, low-light vision, spell resistance 26, spider climb; AL CG; SV Fort +22, Ref +16, Will +21; Str 31, Dex 10, Con 23, Int 20, Wis 21, Cha 20.

Skills and Feats: Bluff +34, Concentration +23, Diplomacy +34, Hide –8, Intimidate +29, Jump +24, Knowledge (arcana) +24, Knowledge (geography) +24, Knowledge (local) +24, Knowledge (nature) +24, Knowledge (religion) +24, Listen +34, Perform (oratory) +21, Search +34, Sense Motive +34, Spellcraft +20, Spot +34; Cleave, Clinging Breath, Flyby Attack, Heighten Breath, Hover, Multiattack, Power Attack, Recover Breath, Shape Breath, Wingover.

Breath Weapon (Su): 100-ft. line (50-ft. cone if shaped), 18d4 acid, Reflex DC 30 half (or higher if heightened); or 50-ft. cone (100-ft. line if shaped), *slow* 1d6+9 rounds, Fortitude DC 30 negates (or higher if heightened).

Crush (Ex): Area 15 ft. by 15 ft.; Small or smaller opponents take 2d8+15 points of bludgeoning damage, and must succeed on a DC 30 Reflex save or be pinned.

Frightful Presence (Ex): 270-ft. radius, HD 28 or lower, Will DC 29 negates.

Spell-Like Abilities: 2/day—*stone shape.* 1/day—*transmute rock to mud/mud to rock.* Caster level 13th.

Spells: As 13th-level sorcerer.

Sorcerer Spells Known (6/8/7/7/7/7/4; save DC 15 + spell level): 0—*arcane mark, cure minor wounds, dancing lights, detect magic, ghost sound, guidance, mage hand, prestidigitation, read magic;* 1st—*command, magic missile, random action, shield of faith, true strike;* 2nd—*cat's grace, fog cloud, summon swarm, Tasha's hideous laughter, web;* 3rd—*bestow curse, cure serious wounds, stinking cloud, suggestion;* 4th—*chaos hammer, crushing despair, enervation, lesser geas;* 5th—*cloudkill, mirage arcana, telekinesis;* 6th—*Bigby's forceful hand, heal.*

Keicjannicarayas
Ancient Copper Dragon

At the bottom of a vast, yawning chasm in the midst of a wild mountain range, Keicjannicarayas makes her lair. There, where the clear blue sky is just a sliver shining between the towering walls of rock, she passes years lost in conversation with her one companion: a titan named Parakoursos, imprisoned here eons ago for a crime against the deities that he does not reveal. The titan's knowledge and wisdom are a match for the dragon's, and the two never tire of probing each others' minds and hearts to learn more about the universe and about each other. Keicjannicarayas brings the titan food and water, tells him what she sees in the world above, and cares for him tenderly. Parakoursos, for his part, would do anything for her, but his imprisonment makes him virtually helpless. In the last year or so, however, Keicjannicarayas has come to believe that Parakoursos holds some piece of information that is vital to the survival of the cosmos, one item of knowledge he does not share even with her that is somehow related to his imprisonment. This suspicion is beginning to cast a pall over their conversations, and now they sit together in silence at times, often for days at a time.

Keicjannicarayas: Female ancient copper dragon; CR 22; Huge dragon (earth); HD 32d12+192, hp 400; Init +0; Spd 40 ft., fly 150 ft. (poor); AC 39, touch 8, flat-footed 39; Base Atk +32; Grp +51; Atk +41 melee (2d8+11, bite); Full Atk +41 melee (2d8+11, bite), +36 melee (2d6+5, 2 claws), +36 melee (1d8+5, 2 wings), +36 melee (2d6+16, tail slap); Space/Reach 15 ft./10 ft. (15 ft. with bite); SA breath weapon, crush, frightful presence, spell-like abilities, spells; SQ blindsense 60 ft., damage reduction 15/magic, darkvision 120 ft., immunity to acid, magic sleep effects, and paralysis, low-light vision, spell resistance 28, spider climb; AL CG; SV Fort +24, Ref +18, Will +23; Str 33, Dex 10, Con 23, Int 20, Wis 21, Cha 20.

Skills and Feats: Bluff +37, Concentration +23, Diplomacy +38, Gather Information +39, Hide –8, Intimidate +34, Jump +28, Knowledge (arcana) +25, Knowledge (geography) +25, Knowledge (local) +25, Knowledge (nature) +25, Knowledge (religion) +25, Listen +37, Perform (sing) +15, Search +37, Sense Motive +37, Spellcraft +22, Spot +34; Cleave, Clinging Breath, Combat Reflexes, Flyby Attack, Heighten Breath, Hover, Large and in Charge, Power Attack, Recover Breath, Shape Breath, Wingover.

Breath Weapon (Su): 100-ft. line (50-ft. cone if shaped), 20d4 acid, Reflex DC 32 half (or higher if heightened); or 50-ft. cone (100-ft. line if shaped), *slow* 1d6+10 rounds, Fortitude DC 32 negates (or higher if heightened).

Crush (Ex): Area 15 ft. by 15 ft.; Small or smaller opponents take 2d8+16 points of bludgeoning damage, and must succeed on a DC 32 Reflex save or be pinned.

Frightful Presence (Ex): 300-ft. radius, HD 31 or fewer, Will DC 31 negates.

Spell-Like Abilities: 2/day—*stone shape.* 1/day—*transmute rock to mud/mud to rock, wall of stone.* Caster level 15th.

Spells: As 15th-level sorcerer.

Sorcerer Spells Known (6/8/7/7/7/7/6/4; save DC 15 + spell level): 0—*arcane mark, cure minor wounds, dancing lights, detect magic, ghost sound, guidance, mage hand, prestidigitation, read magic;* 1st—*command, magic missile, random action, shield of faith, true strike;* 2nd—*cat's grace, fog cloud, summon swarm, Tasha's hideous laughter, web;* 3rd—*bestow curse, cure serious wounds, stinking cloud, suggestion;* 4th—*chaos hammer, crushing despair, enervation, lesser geas;* 5th—*cloudkill, feeblemind, mirage arcana, telekinesis;* 6th—*Bigby's forceful hand, heal, mislead;* 7th—*earthquake, forcecage.*

Bruntutalephion
Wyrm Copper Dragon

Like a plague of vermin, young red dragons seem to keep cropping up in Bruntutalephion's territory. His current working theory is that an extremely prolific female seeded the highly volcanic region with eggs over a period of decades, and the hatched young are reaching young adulthood, worming their way from their underground nests to the surface, and emerging to spread chaos and destruction through his precious lands. It can take as long as a year for Bruntutalephion to hunt down and exterminate a single red, and he increasingly finds himself facing packs of canny juveniles and young adults. Three or four young reds at a time is enough to give even a mighty copper such as Bruntutalephion some difficulty, and he is growing tired of the endless war.

Bruntutalephion: Male wyrm copper dragon; CR 23; Gargantuan dragon (earth); HD 35d12+245, hp 472; Init +0; Spd 40 ft., fly 200 ft. (clumsy); AC 40, touch 6, flat-footed 40; Base Atk +35; Grp +59; Atk +44 melee (4d6+12/19–20, bite); Full Atk +44 melee (4d6+12/19–20, bite), +41 melee (2d8+6, 2 claws), +41 melee (2d6+6, 2 wings), +41 melee (2d8+18, tail slap); Space/Reach 20 ft./15 ft. (20 ft. with bite); SA breath weapon, crush, frightful presence, spell-like abilities, spells; SQ blindsense 60 ft., damage reduction 20/magic, darkvision 120 ft., immunity to acid, magic sleep effects, and paralysis, low-light vision, spell resistance 29, spider climb; AL CG; SV Fort +26, Ref +19, Will +25; Str 35, Dex 10, Con 25, Int 22, Wis 23, Cha 22.

Skills and Feats: Bluff +37, Concentration +29, Diplomacy +48, Hide –12, Intimidate +46, Jump +28, Knowledge (arcana) +32, Knowledge (geography) +32, Knowledge (local) +32, Knowledge (nature) +32, Knowledge (religion) +32, Listen +41, Perform (act) +18, Search +41, Sense Motive +41, Spellcraft +24, Spot +41; Cleave, Combat Reflexes, Flyby Attack, Great Cleave, Hover, Improved Critical (bite), Improved Sunder, Multiattack, Power Attack, Recover Breath, Weapon Focus (bite), Wingover.

Breath Weapon (Su): 120-ft. line, 22d4 acid, Reflex DC 34 half; or 60-ft. cone, *slow* 1d6+11 rounds, Fortitude DC 34 negates.

Crush (Ex): Area 20 ft. by 20 ft.; Medium or smaller opponents take 4d6+18 points of bludgeoning damage, and must succeed on a DC 34 Reflex save or be pinned.

Frightful Presence (Ex): 330-ft. radius, HD 34 or fewer, Will DC 33 negates.

Spell-Like Abilities: 2/day—*stone shape.* 1/day—*transmute rock to mud/mud to rock, wall of stone.* Caster level 17th.

Spells: As 17th-level sorcerer.

Sorcerer Spells Known (6/8/8/7/7/7/7/6/4; save DC 16 + spell level): 0—*arcane mark, cure minor wounds, dancing lights, daze, detect magic, ghost sound, mage hand, prestidigitation, read magic;* 1st—*alarm, grease, magic missile, ray of fatigue, shield of faith;* 2nd—*blur, cat's grace, shatter, summon swarm, web;* 3rd—*bestow curse, cure serious wounds, dispel magic, stinking cloud;* 4th—*chaos hammer, crushing despair, dimension door, ice storm;* 5th—*baleful polymorph, cone of cold, feeblemind,* *telekinesis;* 6th—*chain lightning, globe of invulnerability, heal;* 7th—*ethereal jaunt, earthquake, forcecage;* 8th—*horrid wilting, power word stun.*

Ugilanistorda
Great Wyrm Copper Dragon

Ugilanistorda is the laughing ruler of a quiet sylvan domain populated with all manner of fey. Like a faerie queen, she presides over unceasing banquets in a quiet glen, surrounded by sprites and satyrs, nymphs and dryads, centaurs and unicorns, wild elves and a handful of treants. She is so ancient that she seems to be almost a part of the earth where she lies—rock and earth are embedded in her hide, and grass and leaves sprout from her shoulders and tail. She and her assembly have little tolerance for intrusion: Creatures that enter her domain are usually trapped by the wild elves and brought blindfolded before Ugilanistorda. She slays creatures her pixies tell her are evil, and generally sends away good or neutral creatures unless they greatly impress or amuse her.

Ugilanistorda: Female great wyrm copper dragon; CR 25; Gargantuan dragon (earth); HD 38d12+304, hp 551; Init +4; Spd 40 ft., fly 200 ft. (clumsy); AC 43, touch 6, flat-footed 43; Base Atk +38; Grp +63; Atk +47 melee (4d6+13, bite); Full Atk +47 melee (4d6+13, bite), +42 melee (2d8+6, 2 claws), +42 melee (2d6+6, 2 wings), +42 melee (2d8+19, tail slap); Space/Reach 20 ft./15 ft. (20 ft. with bite); SA breath weapon, crush, frightful presence, spell-like abilities, spells; SQ blindsense 60 ft., damage reduction 20/magic, darkvision 120 ft., immunity to acid, magic sleep effects, and paralysis, low-light vision, spell resistance 31, spider climb; AL CG; SV Fort +29, Ref +21, Will +27; Str 37, Dex 10, Con 27, Int 22, Wis 23, Cha 22.

Skills and Feats: Bluff +40, Concentration +30, Diplomacy +51, Hide –12, Intimidate +45, Jump +55, Knowledge (arcana) +36, Knowledge (geography) +34, Knowledge (local) +34, Knowledge (nature) +34, Knowledge (religion) +34, Listen +47, Perform (sing) +26, Search +44, Sense Motive +47, Spellcraft +28, Spot +47; Cleave, Clinging Breath, Flyby Attack, Great Cleave, Heighten Breath, Hover, Improved Initiative, Lingering Breath, Power Attack, Recover Breath, Shape Breath, Shock Wave, Wingover.

Breath Weapon (Su): 120-ft. line (60-ft. cone if shaped), 24d4 acid, Reflex DC 37 half (or higher if heightened); or 60-ft. cone (120-ft. line if shaped), *slow* 1d6+12 rounds, Fortitude DC 37 negates (or higher if heightened).

Crush (Ex): Area 20 ft. by 20 ft.; Medium or smaller opponents take 4d6+19 points of bludgeoning damage, and must succeed on a DC 37 Reflex save or be pinned.

Frightful Presence (Ex): 360-ft. radius, HD 37 or fewer, Will DC 35 negates.

Spell-Like Abilities: 2/day—*stone shape.* 1/day—*transmute rock to mud/mud to rock, move earth, wall of stone.* Caster level 19th.

Spells: As 19th-level sorcerer.

Sorcerer Spells Known (6/8/8/7/7/7/7/6/6/4; save DC 16 + spell level): 0—*arcane mark, cure minor wounds, dancing lights, detect magic, ghost sound, guidance, mage hand, open/close, read magic;* 1st—*command, magic missile, shield, true strike, ventriloquism;* 2nd—*cat's grace, detect thoughts, fog cloud, mirror image, Tasha's hideous laughter;* 3rd—*blink, magic circle against evil, major image, suggestion;* 4th—*cure critical wounds, enervation, Evard's black tentacles, lesser geas;* 5th—*cloudkill, hold monster, mirage arcana, transmute rock to mud;* 6th—*dispel magic, greater, mislead, permanent image;* 7th—*Bigby's grasping hand, mass cure critical wounds, summon monster VII;* 8th—*Otiluke's telekinetic sphere, Otto's irresistible dance, polymorph any object;* 9th—*dominate monster, elemental swarm.*

SAMPLE GOLD DRAGONS

Detailed below are twelve sample gold dragons, one of each age category. The descriptions include basic personality and encounter notes that the DM can flesh out for his campaign, along with a set of statistics that make the dragon ready to play.

Alternate Form (Su): A gold dragon can assume any animal or humanoid form of Medium size or smaller as a standard action three times per day. This ability functions as a *polymorph* spell cast on itself at its caster level, except that the dragon does not regain hit points for changing form and can only assume the form of an animal or humanoid. The dragon can remain in its animal or humanoid form until it chooses to assume a new one or return to its natural form.

Water Breathing (Ex): All gold dragons can breathe underwater indefinitely and can freely use their breath weapons, spells, and other abilities underwater.

Skills: A gold dragon can move through water at its swim speed without making Swim checks. It has a +8 racial bonus on any Swim check to perform some special action or avoid a hazard. The dragon can always can choose to take 10 on a Swim check, even if distracted or endangered. The dragon can use the run action while swimming, provided it swims in a straight line.

Luminia
Wyrmling Gold Dragon

Luminia is practically a newborn, currently being fostered in the house of a wise and good king. She lives in human form, appearing as a girl about 7 years of age. Visitors and members of the household are quite taken aback when they address her as a child and find themselves confronting the formidable intellect of a gold wyrmling! Despite her youth, she has full access to the king as well as his most trusted and sagacious advisers. She frequently rides with a paladin attached to the king's house, an exemplary woman named Nhalia (LG female human Pal8). She is allowed to assume her normal form only once each day, for no more than 1 hour. She uses this time to practice flying.

Luminia: Female wyrmling gold dragon; CR 5; Medium dragon (fire); HD 8d12+16; hp 68; Init +0; Spd 60 ft., swim 60 ft., fly 200 ft. (poor); AC 17, touch 10, flat-footed 17; Base Atk +8; Grp +11; Atk +11 melee (1d8+3, bite); Full Atk +11 melee (1d8+3, bite), +9 melee (1d6+1, 2 claws), +9 melee (1d4+1, 2 wings); Space/Reach 5 ft./5 ft.; SA breath weapon; SQ alternate form, blindsense 60 ft., darkvision 120 ft., immunity to fire, magic sleep effects, and paralysis, low-light vision, vulnerability to cold, water breathing; AL LG; SV Fort +8, Ref +6, Will +8; Str 17, Dex 10, Con 15, Int 14, Wis 15, Cha 14.

Skills and Feats: Bluff +6, Diplomacy +14, Disguise +10, Escape Artist +8, Intimidate +4, Jump +19, Knowledge (arcana) +10, Knowledge (nobility and royalty) +10, Listen +10, Search +10, Spot +10, Swim +27; Cleave, Multiattack, Power Attack.

Breath Weapon (Su): 30-ft. cone, 2d10 fire, Reflex DC 16 half; or 30-ft. cone, 1 Str, Fortitude DC 16 negates.

Tekumu Nho
Very Young Gold Dragon

Tekumu Nho has grown quite attached to a half-elf man he regards as something between his pet and his child, a ranger called Thoran (LG male half-elf Rgr12). The two stalk the wilderness together, hunting Thoran's favored enemies (giants, goblinoids, and gnolls). The ranger puts up with Tekumu Nho's relative clumsiness for the sake of his invaluable aid in combat. Most of the time, Tekumu Nho travels in the form of a halfling, in order to get the benefits of Small size and above-average Dexterity, or a ferret (same statistics as a weasel) when stealth is essential.

Tekumu Nho: Male very young gold dragon; CR 7; Large dragon (fire); HD 11d12+33; hp 104; Init +0; Spd 60 ft., swim 60 ft., fly 200 ft. (poor); AC 19, touch 9, flat-footed 19; Base Atk +11; Grp +20; Atk +15 melee (2d6+5, bite); Full Atk +15 melee (2d6+5, bite), +13 melee (1d8+2, 2 claws), +13 melee (1d6+2, 2 wings), +13 melee (1d8+7, tail slap); Space/Reach 10 ft./5 ft. (10 ft. with bite); SA alternate form, breath weapon; SQ blindsense 60 ft., darkvision 120 ft., immunity to fire, magic sleep effects, and paralysis, low-light vision, vulnerability to cold, water breathing; AL LG; SV Fort +10, Ref +7, Will +10; Str 21, Dex 10, Con 17, Int 16, Wis 17, Cha 16.

Skills and Feats: Bluff +8, Diplomacy +16, Disguise +14, Hide –4, Intimidate +18, Jump +22, Knowledge (nature) +9, Knowledge (religion) +14, Listen +14, Search +14, Sense Motive +14, Spot +14, Swim +22; Flyby Attack, Multiattack, Power Attack, Shock Wave.

Breath Weapon (Su): 40-ft. cone, 4d10 fire, Reflex DC 19 half; or 40-ft. cone, 2 Str, Fortitude DC 19 negates.

Possessions: *+1 ring of protection, brooch of shielding* (90 points).

Natintrapa
Young Gold Dragon

For such a young dragon, Natintrapa has endured events that granted her a depth of faith and wisdom coveted by dragons five times her age. Her parents were renowned champions of Bahamut, instrumental in purging the earth of countless evil dragons. By the time they neared their twilight, they had earned the unmitigated loathing of Tiamat, who finally took it upon herself to eliminate them when they threatened one of her greatest champions, sending an avatar to kill both great wyrms. Natintrapa was caught in the struggle, and though both of her parents perished, she herself was rescued—by none other than an avatar of Bahamut. Before leaving her, the Platinum Dragon bestowed his special blessing on her, and she has devoted her life to following in her parents' footsteps.

Natintrapa: Female young gold dragon; CR 9; Large dragon (fire); HD 14d12+42; hp 133; Init +0; Spd 60 ft., swim 60 ft., fly 200 ft. (poor); AC 22, touch 9, flat-footed 22; Base Atk +14; Grp +26; Atk +20 melee (2d6+7, bite); Full Atk +20 melee (2d6+7, bite), +16 melee (1d8+3, 2 claws), +15 melee (1d6+3, 2 wings), +15 melee (1d8+10, tail slap); Space/Reach 10 ft./5 ft. (10 ft. with bite); SA breath weapon, spells; SQ alternate form, blindsense 60 ft., darkvision 120 ft., immunity to fire, magic sleep effects, and paralysis, low-light vision, vulnerability to cold, water breathing; AL LG; SV Fort +12, Ref +9, Will +12; Str 25, Dex 10, Con 17, Int 16, Wis 17, Cha 16.

Skills and Feats: Bluff +7, Concentration +17, Diplomacy +19, Disguise +17, Heal +19, Hide –4, Intimidate +15, Jump +26, Knowledge (nobility and royalty) +12, Knowledge (religion) +11, Listen +17, Search +17, Sense Motive +16, Spot +17, Swim +23; Combat Expertise, Extend Spell, Hover, Power Attack, Weapon Focus (claw).

Breath Weapon (Su): 40-ft. cone, 6d10 fire, Reflex DC 20 half; or 40-ft. cone, 3 Str, Fortitude DC 20 negates.

Spells: As 1st-level sorcerer.

Sorcerer Spells Known (5/4; save DC 13 + spell level): 0—*dancing lights, detect magic, mage hand, prestidigitation;* 1st—*expeditious retreat, true strike.*

Yunshenunomei
Juvenile Gold Dragon

A large atrium ringed with exquisite statuary, a cascading fountain in the center, is the entry to Yunshenunomei's lair, and the rest of the mountaintop lair is no less beautifully appointed. The other rooms are spacious and airy, admitting plenty of sunlight through open windows and skylights. He is a passionate collector of art, with a particular fondness for sculpture depicting religious subjects, which appears in every room. He typically greets visitors (and intruders) in the atrium in human form, wearing a silk robe and sandals. He kneels on the floor while talking, and offers no better seat to his guests.

Yunshenunomei: Male juvenile gold dragon; CR 11; Large dragon (fire); HD 17d12+68, hp 178; Init +0; Spd 60 ft., swim 60 ft., fly 200 ft. (poor); AC 25, touch 9, flat-footed 25; Base Atk +17; Grp +30; Atk +25 melee (2d6+9, bite); Full Atk +25 melee (2d6+9, bite), +20 melee (1d8+4, 2 claws), +20 melee (1d6+4, 2 wings), +20 melee (1d8+13, tail slap); Space/Reach 10 ft./5 ft. (10 ft. with bite); SA breath weapon, spell-like abilities, spells; SQ alternate form, blindsense 60 ft., darkvision 120 ft., immunity to fire, magic sleep effects, and paralysis, low-light vision, vulnerability to cold, water

Habitat/Lair
GOLD DRAGON
Gargantuan
Huge
Large
Medium
Stomach
Back
Leg
Wing
SCALES
Blast Radius
Wing movement in flight

breathing; AL LG; SV Fort +14, Ref +10, Will +14; Str 29, Dex 10, Con 19, Int 18, Wis 19, Cha 18

Skills and Feats: Bluff +6, Concentration +19, Diplomacy +13, Disguise +21, Heal +24, Hide –4, Intimidate +26, Jump +29, Knowledge (arcana) +14, Knowledge (nobility and royalty) +14, Knowledge (religion) +14, Listen +24, Search +24, Sense Motive +23, Spellcraft +13, Spot +24, Swim +29; Cleave, Combat Expertise, Flyby Attack, Improved Sunder, Power Attack, Wingover.

Breath Weapon (Su): 40-ft. cone, 8d10 fire, Reflex DC 22 half; or 40-ft. cone, 4 Str, Fortitude DC 22 negates.

Spell-Like Abilities: 3/day—*bless*. Caster level 4th.

Spells: As 3rd-level sorcerer.

Sorcerer Spells Known (6/6; save DC 14 + spell level): 0—*arcane mark, detect magic, disrupt undead, mending, prestidigitation;* 1st—*chill touch, command, doom.*

Kacdaninymila
Young Adult Gold Dragon

Kacdaninymila lives the life of a wealthy urban merchant, without actually engaging in trade. She maintains an impeccable, luxurious townhouse with enormous stables, rides extensively in the surrounding lands with a small entourage of admirers and sycophants, and squanders her considerable wealth on fine horses to add to her collection. Beneath the appearance of a spoiled petty noble, however, is the heart of a paladin. She displays her wealth largely in order to lure thieves she can then capture and bring to justice, and rides outside the city on guard against evil creatures—and her "sycophantic" followers include a number of paladins as well as good clerics, fighters, and others, a veritable adventuring troupe protecting the city from harm without reward or recognition.

Kacdaninymila: Female young adult gold dragon; CR 14; Huge dragon (fire); HD 20d12+100, hp 230; Init +0; Spd 60 ft., swim 60 ft., fly 200 ft. (poor); AC 27, touch 8, flat-footed 27; Base Atk +20; Grp +38; Atk +28 melee (2d8+10, bite); Full Atk +28 melee (2d8+10, bite), +23 melee (2d6+5, 2 claws), +23 melee (1d8+5, 2 wings), +23 melee (2d6+15, tail slap); Space/Reach 15 ft./10 ft. (15 ft. with bite); SA breath weapon, crush, frightful presence, spell-like abilities, spells; SQ alternate form, blindsense 60 ft., damage reduction 5/magic, darkvision 120 ft., immunity to fire, magic sleep effects, and paralysis, low-light vision, spell resistance 21, vulnerability to cold, water breathing; AL LG; SV Fort +17, Ref +12, Will +16; Str 31, Dex 10, Con 21, Int 18, Wis 19, Cha 18.

Skills and Feats: Bluff +8, Concentration +23, Diplomacy +15, Disguise +14, Escape Artist +20, Handle Animal +14, Heal +15, Hide –8, Intimidate +22, Jump +32, Knowledge (local) +17, Listen +24, Ride +12, Search +24, Sense Motive +24, Spellcraft +14, Spot +24, Swim +34; Flyby Attack, Heighten Breath, Hover, Power Attack, Recover Breath, Tempest Breath, Wingover.

Breath Weapon (Su): 50-ft. cone, 10d10 fire, Reflex DC 25 half (or higher if heightened); or 50-ft. cone, 5 Str, Fortitude DC 25 negates (or higher if heightened).

Crush (Ex): Area 15 ft. by 15 ft.; Small or smaller opponents take 2d8+15 points of bludgeoning damage, and must succeed on a DC 25 Reflex save or be pinned.

Frightful Presence (Ex): 150-ft. radius, HD 19 or fewer, Will DC 24 negates.

Spell-Like Abilities: 3/day—*bless*. Caster level 5th.

Spells: As 5th-level sorcerer.

Sorcerer Spells Known (6/7/5; save DC 14 + spell level): 0—*detect magic, flare, light, mending, prestidigitation, read magic;* 1st—*magic missile, protection from evil, shield of faith, true strike;* 2nd—*darkness, resist energy.*

Clytanmoorninyx
Adult Gold Dragon

An older gold dragon once told Clytanmoorninyx, "The fire runs too hot in your veins. Master it, or it masters you." So far, Clytanmoorninyx has failed to master it. He is easily angered by the slightest insult (and his impeccable sense of good manners makes him oversensitive to even minor violations of etiquette), and he considers the existence of evil creatures in the world a personal insult. Though he has been known to associate with royalty, offering counsel particularly in times of war, he chooses to spend most of his time in isolated wilderness regions, away from the intrigue and machinations that so infuriate him.

Clytanmoorninyx: Male adult gold dragon; CR 16; Huge dragon (fire); HD 23d12+115, hp 264; Init +0; Spd 60 ft., swim 60 ft., fly 200 ft. (poor); AC 30, touch 8, flat-footed 30; Base Atk +23; Grp +42; Atk +32 melee (2d8+11, bite); Full Atk +32 melee (2d8+11, bite), +27 melee (2d6+5, 2 claws), +27 melee (1d8+5, 2 wings), +27 melee (2d6+16, tail slap); Space/Reach 15 ft./10 ft. (15 ft. with bite); SA breath weapon, crush, frightful presence, spell-like abilities, spells; SQ alternate form, blindsense 60 ft., damage reduction 5/magic, darkvision 120 ft., immunity to fire, magic sleep effects, and paralysis, low-light vision, *luck bonus*, spell resistance 23, vulnerability to cold, water breathing; AL LG; SV Fort +18, Ref +13, Will +18; Str 33, Dex 10, Con 21, Int 20, Wis 21, Cha 20.

Skills and Feats: Bluff +9, Concentration +20, Diplomacy +28, Disguise +28 (30 acting), Hide –3, Intimidate +24, Jump +35, Knowledge (arcana) +20, Knowledge (local) +25, Knowledge (nobility and royalty) +15, Listen +28, Move Silently +5, Search +28, Sense Motive +25, Spellcraft +17, Spot +28, Swim +35, Survival +15; Cleave, Flyby Attack, Heighten Breath, Hover, Leadership, Power Attack, Recover Breath, Wingover.

Breath Weapon (Su): 50-ft. cone, 12d10 fire, Reflex DC 26 half (or higher if heightened); or 50-ft. cone, 6 Str, Fortitude DC 26 negates (or higher if heightened).

Crush (Ex): Area 15 ft. by 15 ft.; Small or smaller opponents take 2d8+16 points of bludgeoning damage, and must succeed on a DC 26 Reflex save or be pinned.

Frightful Presence (Ex): 180-ft. radius, HD 22 or fewer, Will DC 26 negates.

Spell-Like Abilities: 3/day—*bless*. Caster level 7th.

Spells: As 7th-level sorcerer.

Luck Bonus **(Sp):** 1/day—good creatures within a 60-ft. radius of the dragon gain a +1 luck bonus on all saving throws, ability checks, and skill checks for 1d3+18 hours. Caster level 2nd.

Sorcerer Spells Known (6/8/7/5; save DC 15 + spell level): 0—*arcane mark, detect magic, flare, light, mage hand, prestidigitation, read magic;* 1st—*charm person, magic missile, protection from evil, shield of faith, true strike;* 2nd—*cure moderate wounds, fog cloud, resist energy;* 3rd—*searing light, suggestion.*

Zudinmulamshius
Mature Adult Gold Dragon

Zudinmulamshius has found what she considers to be the best use of her considerable hoard: She has taken up residence in a bustling metropolis, where she lives the life of a wealthy noble, acting as a patron of adventurers. She offers substantial bounties for the heads of evil creatures that threaten the city or its outlying areas, and spends much of her time researching valuable artifacts that might be useful in fighting evil, then commissioning adventurers to locate and recover them.

Zudinmulamshius: Female mature adult gold dragon; CR 19; Huge dragon (fire); HD 26d12+156, hp 325; Init +0; Spd 60 ft., swim 60 ft., fly 200 ft. (poor); AC 33, touch 8, flat-footed 33; Base Atk +26; Grp +46; Atk +36 melee (2d8+12, bite); Full Atk +36 melee (2d8+12, bite), +31 melee (2d6+6, 2 claws), +31 melee (1d8+6, 2 wings), +31 melee (2d6+18, tail slap); Space/Reach 15 ft./10 ft. (15 ft. with bite); SA breath weapon, crush, frightful presence, spell-like abilities, spells; SQ alternate form, blindsense 60 ft., damage reduction 10/magic, darkvision 120 ft., immunity to fire, magic sleep effects, and paralysis, low-light vision, *luck bonus,* spell resistance 25, vulnerability to cold, water breathing; AL LG; SV Fort +21, Ref +15, Will +22; Str 35, Dex 10, Con 23, Int 20, Wis 21, Cha 20.

Skills and Feats: Appraise +12, Bluff +9, Concentration +25, Diplomacy +28, Disguise +31, Hide –8, Intimidate +22, Jump +36, Knowledge (arcana) +18, Knowledge (geography) +18, Knowledge (local) +18, Knowledge (nobility and royalty) +18, Knowledge (religion) +18, Listen +31, Profession (metalworking) +15, Search +31, Sense Motive +31, Spellcraft +19, Spot +30, Swim +20; Cleave, Heighten Breath, Flyby Attack, Hover, Iron Will, Power Attack, Recover Breath, Suppress Weakness, Wingover.

Breath Weapon (Su): 50-ft. cone, 14d10 fire, Reflex DC 29 half (or higher if heightened); or 50-ft. cone, 7 Str, Fortitude DC 29 negates (or higher if heightened).

Crush (Ex): Area 15 ft. by 15 ft.; Small or smaller opponents take 2d8+18 points of bludgeoning damage, and must succeed on a DC 29 Reflex save or be pinned.

Frightful Presence (Ex): 210-ft. radius, HD 25 or fewer, Will DC 31 negates.

Spell-Like Abilities: 3/day—*bless.* Caster level 9th.

Spells: As 9th-level sorcerer.

Luck Bonus **(Sp):** 1/day—good creatures within a 70-ft. radius of the dragon gain a +1 luck bonus on all saving throws, ability checks, and skill checks for 1d3+21 hours. Caster level 2nd.

Sorcerer Spells Known (6/8/7/7/5; save DC 15 + spell level): 0—*arcane mark, detect magic, flare, light, mage hand, mending, prestidigitation, read magic;* 1st—*magic missile, protection from evil, shield of faith, true strike, unseen servant;* 2nd—*cat's grace, cure moderate wounds, fog cloud, whispering wind;* 3rd—*protection from energy, searing light, suggestion;* 4th—*greater invisibility, Otiluke's resilient sphere.*

Shimanyo-Kocoi
Old Gold Dragon

Though his scales are covered with gouges and scars and he walks with a pronounced limp thanks to a poorly healed injury, Shimanyo-Kocoi prefers his natural form to any other. He wears his scars proudly, for they are the trophies of many hard victories against countless evil foes. He generally assumes other forms only so that he can more easily practice the art of pottery, a creative endeavor that he finds relaxing. Though he is grim and relentless in the pursuit of evil, Shimanyo-Kocoi is generally well mannered and quietly cheerful, and laughs loudly and deeply when amused.

Shimanyo-Kocoi: Male old gold dragon; CR 21; Gargantuan dragon (fire); HD 29d12+203, hp 391; Init +0; Spd 60 ft., swim 60 ft., fly 250 ft. (poor); AC 34, touch 6, flat-footed 34; Base Atk +29; Grp +55; Atk +39 melee (4d6+14, bite); Full Atk +39 melee (4d6+14, bite), +34 melee (2d8+7, 2 claws), +34 melee (2d6+7, 2 wings), +34 melee (2d8+21, tail slap); Space/Reach 20 ft./15 ft. (20 ft. with bite); SA breath weapon, crush, frightful presence, spell-like abilities, spells; SQ alternate form, blindsense 60 ft., damage reduction 10/magic, darkvision 120 ft., *detect gems,* immunity to fire, magic sleep effects, and paralysis, low-light vision, *luck bonus,* spell resistance 27, vulnerability to cold, water breathing; AL LG; SV Fort +23, Ref +20, Will +25; Str 39, Dex 10, Con 25, Int 24, Wis 25, Cha 24.

Skills and Feats: Appraise +15, Bluff +12, Concentration +26, Craft (potter) +18, Diplomacy +36, Disguise +36, Hide –12, Intimidate +37, Jump +40, Knowledge (arcana) +27, Knowledge (geography) +27, Knowledge (local) +27, Knowledge (nature) +27, Knowledge (nobility and royalty) +27, Knowledge (religion) +27, Listen +36, Search +36, Sense Motive +36, Spellcraft +22, Spot +32, Swim +22; Cleave, Flyby Attack, Hover, Improved Maneuverability, Iron Will, Legendary Reflexes, Power Attack, Recover Breath, Suppress Weakness, Wingover.

Breath Weapon (Su): 60-ft. cone, 16d10 fire, Reflex DC 31 half; or 60-ft. cone, 8 Str, Fortitude DC 31 negates.

Crush (Ex): Area 20 ft. by 20 ft.; Medium or smaller opponents take 4d6+21 points of bludgeoning damage, and must succeed on a DC 31 Reflex save or be pinned.

Frightful Presence (Ex): 240-ft. radius, HD 28 or fewer, Will DC 30 negates.

Spell-Like Abilities: 3/day—*bless;* 1/day—*geas/quest.* Caster level 11th; save DC 17 + spell level.

Spells: As 11th-level sorcerer.

Gold Dragon

Typical Gold Dragon Lair

[Size of lair varies with size of dragon]

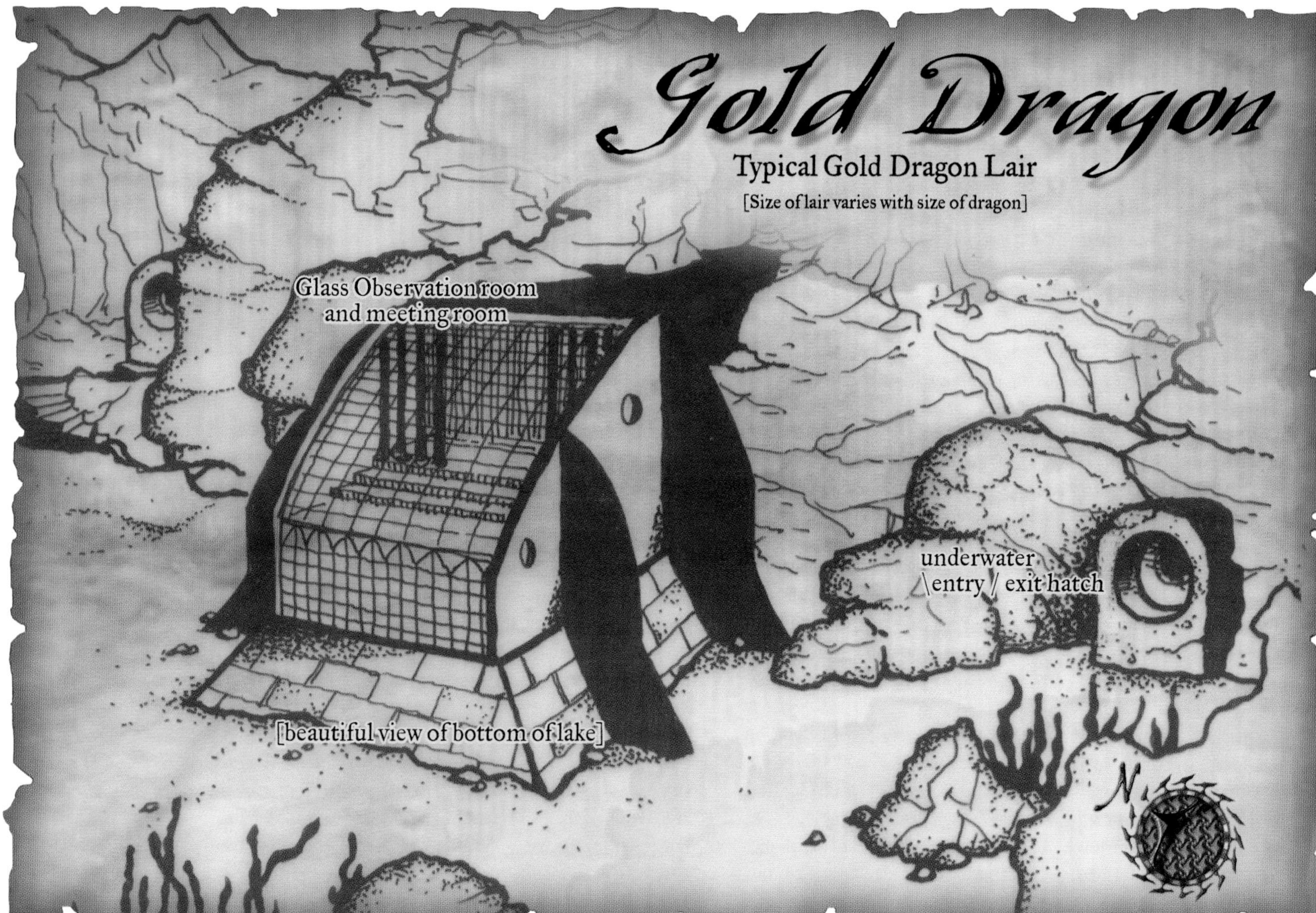

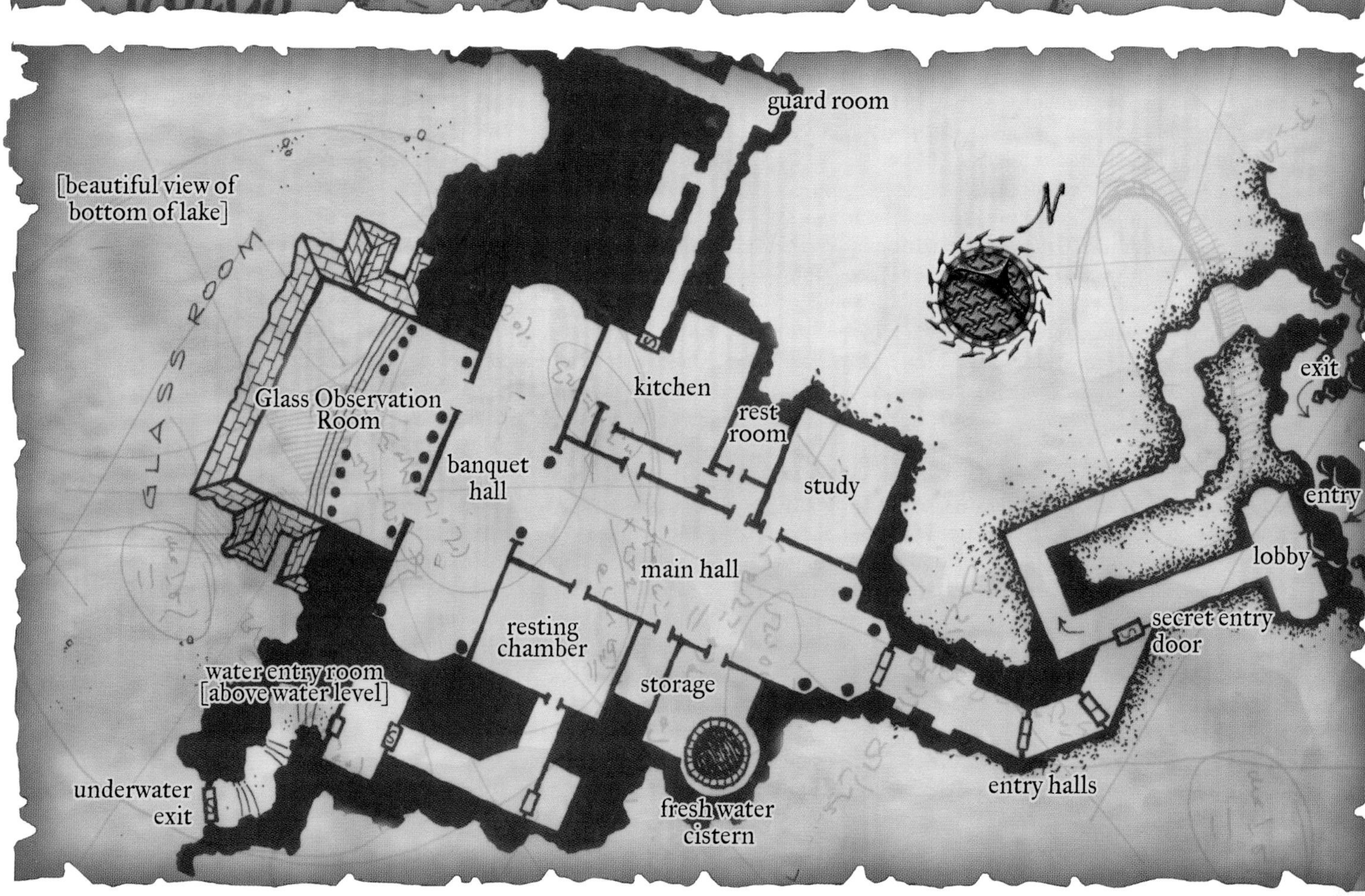

Glass Observation room
and meeting room

underwater
\entry / exit hatch

[beautiful view of bottom of lake]

N

guard room

[beautiful view of
bottom of lake]

N

GLASS ROOM

Glass Observation
Room

kitchen

rest
room

exit

banquet
hall

study

entry

lobby

main hall

resting
chamber

secret entry
door

water entry room
[above water level]

storage

underwater
exit

entry halls

fresh water
cistern

Detect Gems (**Sp**): 3/day—as *detect magic* (caster level 11th), except that the power only detects gems.

Luck Bonus (**Sp**): 1/day—good creatures within an 80-ft. radius of the dragon gain a +1 luck bonus on all saving throws, ability checks, and skill checks for 1d3+24 hours. Caster level 2nd.

Sorcerer Spells Known (6/8/8/8/7/5; save DC 17 + spell level): 0—*arcane mark, detect magic, flare, guidance, light, mage hand, mending, prestidigitation, read magic;* 1st—*magic missile, protection from evil, shield of faith, true strike, unseen servant;* 2nd—*augury, cat's grace, cure moderate wounds, fog cloud, whispering wind;* 3rd—*dispel magic, protection from energy, searing light, suggestion;* 4th—*dismissal, ice storm, greater invisibility;* 5th—*cone of cold, true seeing.*

Fuunharkaspirinon
Very Old Gold Dragon

"Fiends walk among us," warns an old woman in simple clothes. Fuunharkaspirinon should know, for she has dedicated herself to hunting and banishing or destroying infernal creatures who dare to insinuate themselves into human society and tempt mortals to evil. She has spent several human lifetimes living among mortals—posing as an aristocrat, a scholar, a cleric, a soldier—searching for signs of fiendish influence and tracking it to its source. She is currently wrestling with persuasive evidence that someone has managed to bring a Tarterian dragon (see page 189) to the Material Plane.

Fuunharkaspirinon: Female very old gold dragon; CR 22; Gargantuan dragon (fire); HD 32d12+256, hp 464; Init +0; Spd 60 ft., swim 60 ft., fly 250 ft. (poor); AC 37, touch 6, flat-footed 37; Base Atk +32; Grp +59; Atk +43 melee (4d6+15, bite); Full Atk +43 melee (4d6+15, bite), +38 melee (2d8+7, 2 claws), +38 melee (2d6+7, 2 wings), +38 melee (2d8+22, tail slap); Space/Reach 20 ft./15 ft. (20 ft. with bite); SA breath weapon, crush, frightful presence, spell-like abilities, spells; SQ alternate form, blindsense 60 ft., damage reduction 15/magic, darkvision 120 ft., *detect gems*, immunity to fire, magic sleep effects, and paralysis, low-light vision, *luck bonus*, spell resistance 28, vulnerability to cold, water breathing; AL LG; SV Fort +26, Ref +18, Will +28; Str 41, Dex 10, Con 27, Int 26, Wis 27, Cha 26.

Skills and Feats: Appraise +18, Bluff +16, Concentration +28, Craft (alchemy) +18, Diplomacy +41, Disguise +40, Escape Artist +15, Heal +33, Hide –12, Intimidate +30, Jump +38, Knowledge (arcana) +28, Knowledge (geography) +28, Knowledge (local) +28, Knowledge (nobility and royalty) +28, Knowledge (the planes) +28, Knowledge (religion) +28, Listen +38, Search +38, Sense Motive +38, Spellcraft +24, Spot +38; Survival +18, Swim +59; Enlarge Breath, Flyby Attack, Heighten Breath, Hover, Improved Maneuverability, Iron Will, Power Attack, Recover Breath, Spell Focus (Enchantment), Suppress Weakness, Wingover.

Breath Weapon (Su): 60-ft. cone (90-ft. cone if enlarged), 18d10 fire, Reflex DC 34 half (or higher if heightened); or 60-ft. cone (90-ft. cone if enlarged), 9 Str, Fortitude DC 34 negates (or higher if heightened).

Crush (Ex): Area 20 ft. by 20 ft.; Medium or smaller opponents take 4d6+22 points of bludgeoning damage, and must succeed on a DC 34 Reflex save or be pinned.

Frightful Presence (Ex): 270-ft. radius, HD 31 or fewer, Will DC 34 negates.

Spell-Like Abilities: 3/day—*bless;* 1/day—*geas/quest.* Caster level 13th; save DC 18 + spell level.

Spells: As 13th-level sorcerer.

Detect Gems (**Sp**): 3/day—as *detect magic* (caster level 13th), except that the power only detects gems.

Luck Bonus (**Sp**): 1/day—good creatures within a 90-ft. radius of the dragon gain a +1 luck bonus on all saving throws, ability checks, and skill checks for 1d3+27 hours. Caster level 2nd.

Sorcerer Spells Known (6/8/8/8/8/7/5; save DC 18 + spell level): 0—*arcane mark, detect magic, flare, guidance, light, mage hand, mending, prestidigitation, read magic;* 1st—*magic missile, protection from evil, shield of faith, true strike, unseen servant;* 2nd—*cat's grace, cure moderate wounds, fog cloud, shatter, zone of truth;* 3rd—*haste, protection from energy, remove curse, remove disease;* 4th—*charm monster, dimensional anchor, freedom of movement, greater invisibility;* 5th—*dispel evil, true seeing, hold monster;* 6th—*disintegrate, mass suggestion.*

Ayunken-vanzan
Ancient Gold Dragon

Ayunken-vanzan is a well-rounded dragon, with many interests and areas of expertise. He is sophisticated, polite, and charming, and speaks with authority on dozens of subjects. He is a connoisseur of fine jewelry, and a master jeweler in his own right. His particular area of interest, at least at present, is theology, and he actively seeks out the company of celestials in order to discuss matters concerning good deities and the planes they call home. He enjoys adopting the guise of a humanoid sage in order to visit universities and other places of learning and consult with other experts in his fields of interest.

Ayunken-vanzan: Male ancient gold dragon; CR 24; Gargantuan dragon (fire); HD 35d12+315, hp 542; Init +0; Spd 60 ft., swim 60 ft., fly 250 ft. (poor); AC 40, touch 6, flat-footed 40; Base Atk +35; Grp +63; Atk +47 melee (4d6+16, bite); Full Atk +47 melee (4d6+16, bite), +42 melee (2d8+8, 2 claws), +42 melee (2d6+8, 2 wings), +42 melee (2d8+24, tail slap); Space/Reach 20 ft./15 ft. (20 ft. with bite); SA breath weapon, crush, frightful presence, spell-like abilities, spells, tail sweep; SQ alternate form, blindsense 60 ft., damage reduction 15/magic, darkvision 120 ft., *detect gems*, immunity to fire, magic sleep effects, and paralysis, low-light vision, *luck bonus*, spell resistance 30, vulnerability to cold, water breathing; AL LG; SV Fort +28, Ref +19, Will +30; Str 43, Dex 10, Con 29, Int 28, Wis 29, Cha 28.

Skills and Feats: Appraise +19, Bluff +21, Concentration +29, Craft (jeweler) +19, Diplomacy +47, Disguise +44, Escape Artist +10, Hide –12, Intimidate +40, Jump +45, Knowledge (arcana) +34, Knowledge (geography) +34, Knowledge (history) +34, Knowledge (local) +34, Knowledge (nobility and royalty) +34, Knowledge (the planes)

+29, Knowledge (religion) +34, Listen +44, Search +44, Sense Motive +44, Spellcraft +28, Spot +44, Survival +28; Cleave, Enlarge Breath, Flyby Attack, Heighten Breath, Hover, Improved Maneuverability, Iron Will, Power Attack, Recover Breath, Shock Wave, Suppress Weakness, Wingover.

Breath Weapon (Su): 60-ft. cone (90-ft. cone if enlarged), 20d10 fire, Reflex DC 36 half (or higher if heightened); or 60-ft. cone (90-ft. cone if enlarged), 10 Str, Fortitude DC 36 negates (or higher if heightened).

Crush (Ex): Area 20 ft. by 20 ft.; Medium or smaller opponents take 4d6+24 points of bludgeoning damage, and must succeed on a DC 34 Reflex save or be pinned.

Frightful Presence (Ex): 300-ft. radius, HD 34 or fewer, Will DC 36 negates.

Spell-Like Abilities: 3/day—*bless;* 1/day—*geas/quest, sunburst.* Caster level 15th; save DC 19 + spell level.

Spells: As 15th-level sorcerer.

Tail Sweep (Ex): Half-circle 30 ft. in diameter, Small or smaller opponents take 2d6+24 points of bludgeoning damage, Reflex DC 36 half.

***Detect Gems* (Sp):** 3/day—as *detect magic* (caster level 15th), except that the power only detects gems.

***Luck Bonus* (Sp):** 1/day—good creatures within a 100-ft. radius of the dragon gain a +1 luck bonus on all saving throws, ability checks, and skill checks for 1d3+30 hours. Caster level 2nd.

Sorcerer Spells Known (6/9/8/8/8/8/7/5; save DC 19 + spell level): 0—*arcane mark, detect magic, flare, guidance, light, mage hand, mending, prestidigitation, read magic;* 1st—*magic missile, protection from evil, shield of faith, true strike, unseen servant;* 2nd—*cat's grace, cure moderate wounds, fog cloud, shatter, zone of truth;* 3rd—*haste, protection from energy, remove curse, remove disease;* 4th—*charm monster, dimensional anchor, freedom of movement, greater invisibility;* 5th—*dispel evil, feeblemind, hold monster, Mordenkainen's faithful hound;* 6th—*blade barrier, mass suggestion, summon monster VI;* 7th—*limited wish, prismatic spray.*

Sheeredni-vaktar
Wyrm Gold Dragon

As if the abundance of evil in the world weren't bad enough, Sheeredni-vaktar is fond of saying, just look at the way supposedly good people behave. She has no tolerance whatsoever for poor manners, bad grooming, offensive language, or—worst of all—anything she defines as immorality. Her definition goes far beyond any objective definitions of evil, including such sins as impiety and irreverence, disrespect for one's elders, the use of alcohol and other drugs, and sexual promiscuity. Perhaps surprisingly, she does not take issue with the prevalence of violence, and, in fact, quickly resorts to violent measures to discipline those who offend her sense of propriety—even if that violence is just a backhanded swat with her tail for nonlethal damage, accompanied by a sharp-tongued admonition.

Sheeredni-vaktar: Female wyrm gold dragon; CR 25; Colossal dragon (fire); HD 38d12+380, hp 627; Init +0; Spd 60 ft., swim 60 ft., fly 250 ft. (poor); AC 39, touch 2, flat-footed 39; Base Atk +38; Grp +71; Atk +47 melee (4d8+17, bite); Full Atk +47 melee (4d8+17, bite), +45 melee (4d6+8, 2 claws), +45 melee (2d8+8, 2 wings), +45 melee (4d6+25, tail slap); Space/Reach 30 ft./20 ft. (30 ft. with bite); SA breath weapon, crush, frightful presence, spell-like abilities, spells, tail sweep; SQ alternate form, blindsense 60 ft., damage reduction 20/magic, darkvision 120 ft., *detect gems,* immunity to fire, magic sleep effects, and paralysis, low-light vision, *luck bonus,* spell resistance 31, vulnerability to cold, water breathing; AL LG; SV Fort +31, Ref +23, Will +33; Str 45, Dex 10, Con 31, Int 30, Wis 31, Cha 30.

Skills and Feats: Bluff +25, Concentration +32, Craft (cobbler) +24, Diplomacy +56, Disguise +48, Escape Artist +10, Hide –16, Intimidate +46, Jump +48, Knowledge (arcana) +40, Knowledge (geography) +40, Knowledge (history) +40, Knowledge (local) +40, Knowledge (nobility and royalty) +40, Knowledge (the planes) +40, Knowledge (religion) +40, Listen +48, Profession (tanner) +20, Search +48, Sense Motive +48, Spellcraft +31, Spot +48, Survival +30; Cleave, Flyby Attack, Great Cleave, Heighten Breath, Hover, Improved Maneuverability, Iron Will, Lightning Reflexes, Multiattack, Power Attack, Recover Breath, Suppress Weakness, Wingover.

Breath Weapon (Su): 70-ft. cone, 22d10 fire, Reflex DC 39 half (or higher if heightened); or 70-ft. cone, 11 Str, Fortitude DC 39 negates (or higher if heightened).

Crush (Ex): Area 30 ft. by 30 ft.; Large or smaller opponents take 4d8+25 points of bludgeoning damage, and must succeed on a DC 39 Reflex save or be pinned.

Frightful Presence (Ex): 330-ft. radius, HD 37 or fewer, Will DC 39 negates.

Spell-Like Abilities: 3/day—*bless;* 1/day—*geas/quest, sunburst.* Caster level 17th; save DC 20 + spell level.

Spells: As 17th-level sorcerer.

Tail Sweep (Ex): Half-circle 40 ft. in diameter, Large or smaller opponents take 2d8+25 points of bludgeoning damage, Reflex DC 39 half.

***Detect Gems* (Sp):** 3/day—as *detect magic* (caster level 17th), except that the power only detects gems.

***Luck Bonus* (Sp):** 1/day—good creatures within a 110-ft. radius of the dragon gain a +1 luck bonus on all saving throws, ability checks, and skill checks for 1d3+33 hours. Caster level 2nd.

Sorcerer Spells Known (6/9/9/8/8/8/8/7/5; save DC 20 + spell level): 0—*arcane mark, detect magic, flare, guidance, light, mage hand, mending, prestidigitation, read magic;* 1st—*magic missile, protection from evil, shield of faith, true strike, unseen servant;* 2nd—*cat's grace, cure moderate wounds, fog cloud, shatter, zone of truth;* 3rd—*haste, protection from energy, remove curse, remove disease;* 4th—*charm monster, dimensional anchor, freedom of movement, greater invisibility;* 5th—*dispel evil, feeblemind, hold monster, Mordenkainen's faithful hound;* 6th—*blade barrier, disintegrate, mass suggestion;* 7th—*holy word, limited wish, prismatic spray;* 8th—*polymorph any object, symbol of death.*

Riikano-alinaris
Great Wyrm Gold Dragon

The library of Riikano-alinaris, to those who know of its existence, is considered one of the finest in the world. The dragon has amassed a collection of books from lands known and unknown, purchasing, trading for, and even copying himself every book he can find. He does not bother with the traditional wealth of a dragon's hoard—"You can't learn anything from gold," he often says with a snort—valuing currency only insofar as it can be used to acquire more books. His breadth of knowledge is astonishing, accumulated over a period of four millennia. As his twilight approaches, Riikano-alinaris is searching for an appropriate heir to his collection. He has many children, but none of them have proven to his satisfaction that their love of knowledge, and of books in particular, is great enough to deserve such a monumental inheritance.

Riikano-alinaris: Male great wyrm gold dragon; CR 27; Colossal dragon (fire); HD 41d12+451, hp 717; Init +0; Spd 60 ft., swim 60 ft., fly 250 ft. (poor); AC 42, touch 2, flat-footed 42; Base Atk +41; Grp +75; Atk +51 melee (4d8+18, bite); Full Atk +51 melee (4d8+18, bite), +46 melee (4d6+9, 2 claws), +46 melee (2d8+9, 2 wings), +46 melee (4d6+27, tail slap); Space/Reach 30 ft./20 ft. (30 ft. with bite); SA breath weapon, crush, frightful presence, snatch, spell-like abilities, spells, tail sweep; SQ alternate form, blindsense 60 ft., damage reduction 20/magic, darkvision 120 ft., *detect gems*, immunity to fire, magic sleep effects, and paralysis, low-light vision, *luck bonus*, spell resistance 33, vulnerability to cold, water breathing; AL LG; SV Fort +33, Ref +22, Will +35; Str 47, Dex 10, Con 33, Int 32, Wis 33, Cha 32.

Skills and Feats: Bluff +28, Concentration +36, Craft (bookbinding) +21, Craft (calligraphy) +22, Diplomacy +59, Disguise +52, Escape Artist +15, Gather Information +23, Hide –16, Intimidate +55, Jump +50, Knowledge (arcana) +51, Knowledge (geography) +51, Knowledge (history) +51, Knowledge (local) +51, Knowledge (nobility and royalty) +51, Knowledge (religion) +51, Listen +52, Profession (scribe) +21, Search +52, Sense Motive +52, Spellcraft +33, Spot +52, Swim +47; Cleave, Draconic Knowledge, Flyby Attack, Great Cleave, Heighten Breath, Hover, Improved Maneuverability, Iron Will, Large and in Charge, Power Attack, Recover Breath, Snatch, Suppress Weakness, Wingover.

Breath Weapon (Su): 70-ft. cone, 24d10 fire, Reflex DC 41 half (or higher if heightened); or 70-ft. cone, 12 Str, Fortitude DC 41 negates (or higher if heightened).

Crush (Ex): Area 30 ft. by 30 ft.; Large or smaller opponents take 4d8+27 points of bludgeoning damage, and must succeed on a DC 41 Reflex save or be pinned.

Frightful Presence (Ex): 360-ft. radius, HD 40 or fewer, Will DC 41 negates.

Snatch (Ex): Against Large or smaller creatures, bite for 4d8+18/round or claw for 4d6+9/round.

Tail Sweep (Ex): Half-circle 40 ft. in diameter, Large or smaller opponents take 2d8+27 points of bludgeoning damage, Reflex DC 41 half.

Spell-Like Abilities: 3/day—*bless*; 1/day—*foresight, geas/quest, sunburst*. Caster level 19th; save DC 21 + spell level.

Spells: As 19th-level sorcerer.

Detect Gems **(Sp):** 3/day—as *detect magic* (caster level 19th), except that the power only detects gems.

Luck Bonus **(Sp):** 1/day—good creatures within a 120-ft. radius of the dragon gain a +1 luck bonus on all saving throws, ability checks, and skill checks for 1d3+36 hours. Caster level 2nd.

Sorcerer Spells Known (6/9/9/9/8/8/8/7/7/4; save DC 21 + spell level): 0—*arcane mark, detect magic, flare, guidance, light, mage hand, mending, prestidigitation, read magic*; 1st—*magic missile, protection from evil, shield of faith, true strike, unseen servant*; 2nd—*cat's grace, cure moderate wounds, fog cloud, shatter, zone of truth*; 3rd—*haste, protection from energy, remove curse, remove disease*; 4th—*charm monster, dimensional anchor, freedom of movement, greater invisibility*; 5th—*dispel evil, feeblemind, hold monster, Mordenkainen's faithful hound*; 6th—*blade barrier, disintegrate, mass suggestion*; 7th—*holy word, limited wish, prismatic spray*; 8th—*mind blank, polymorph any object, symbol of death*; 9th—*imprisonment, storm of vengeance*.

SAMPLE GREEN DRAGONS

Detailed below are twelve sample green dragons, one of each age category. The descriptions include basic personality and encounter notes that the DM can flesh out for his campaign, along with a set of statistics that make the dragon ready to play.

Water Breathing (Ex): All green dragons can breathe underwater indefinitely and can freely use their breath weapons, spells, and other abilities while submerged.

Skills: A green dragon can move through water at its swim speed without making Swim checks. It has a +8 racial bonus on any Swim check to perform some special action or avoid a hazard. The dragon can always can choose to take 10 on a Swim check, even if distracted or endangered. The dragon can use the run action while swimming, provided it swims in a straight line.

Blister
Wyrmling Green Dragon

Blister counts herself among the woodland nobility, along with the beasts of prey. She detests laughter and merriment, disliking elves and positively loathing pixies, grigs, and other carefree sylvan folk. She stalks through the trees, high and low, sometimes winging over the forest canopy, sometimes fluttering among the boles of the trees, sometimes slinking on foot. She has recently located the dwelling place of a band of pixies and has attempted several raids, but the pixies have thus far successfully evaded her attacks. Her last sortie left her entangled while the pixies danced about her and laughed before packing up their meager belongs and fleeing into the forest. Blister has sworn revenge.

Green
DRAGON
Flight
Lawful Evil
Air Subtype
Warm Forest
Underground
Old
24 ft.
Fierce toothy jaws and arrogant crests warn other creatures of the green dragon's reputation for belligerent unprovoked attacks.
Command plants
Plant growth
Dominate person
Suggestion
Detail of neck plate scale showing deep tissue attachment and partial dorsal membrane spine.
Sub-adult
12 ft.
Shed specimen found in forest near suspected lair.
Young
6 ft.
Wyrmling
3 feet

Blister: Female wyrmling green dragon; CR 3; Small dragon (air); HD 5d12+5; hp 37; Init +0; Spd 40 ft., swim 40 ft., fly 100 ft. (average); AC 15, touch 11, flat-footed 15; Base Atk +5; Grp +2; Atk +7 melee (1d6+1, bite); Full Atk +7 melee (1d6+1, bite), +2 melee (1d4, 2 claws); Space/Reach 5 ft./5 ft.; SA breath weapon; SQ blindsense 60 ft., darkvision 120 ft., immunity to acid, magic sleep effects, and paralysis, low-light vision, water breathing; AL LE; SV Fort +5, Ref +4, Will +4; Str 13, Dex 10, Con 13, Int 10, Wis 11, Cha 10.

Skills and Feats: Bluff +5, Diplomacy +6, Hide +4, Intimidate +4, Knowledge (nature) +5, Listen +7, Search +5, Sense Motive +5, Spot +7, Swim +17; Alertness, Wingover.

Breath Weapon (Su): 20-ft. cone, 2d6 acid, Reflex DC 13 half.

Chokedamp
Very Young Green Dragon

Chokedamp fancies himself a deadly aerial hunter who rules the skies above the forest canopy. At this stage of his life, however, Chokedamp stands out more as a cunning negotiator. He has forged a partnership with a pack of worgs whose territory overlaps his own, and through the worgs, he has a loose alliance with a tribe of goblins. Chokedamp and the worgs make a formidable team. The worgs' hunting has improved greatly thanks to aerial reconnaissance courtesy of Chokedamp, while the dragon has collected considerable booty from creatures the worgs have defeated or sniffed out for the dragon. Still, Chokedamp and the worgs distrust each other. The dragon finds the worgs' failure to cower in his presence very annoying; he is aware that the whole pack probably could best him in a fair fight and that annoys him too. Chokedamp also fears that the worgs' goblin allies might raid his hoard while he is absent.

Chokedamp: Male very young green dragon; CR 4; Medium dragon; HD 8d12+16; hp 68; Init +0; Spd 40 ft., swim 40 ft., fly 150 ft. (average); AC 17, touch 10, flat-footed 17; Base Atk +8; Grp +10; Atk +10 melee (1d8+2, bite); Full Atk +10 melee (1d8+2, bite), +8 melee (1d6+1, 2 claws), +8 melee (1d4+1, 2 wings); Space/Reach 5 ft./5 ft.; SA breath weapon; SQ blindsense 60 ft., darkvision 120 ft., immunity to acid, magic sleep effects, and paralysis, low-light vision, water breathing; AL CE; SV Fort +8, Ref +6, Will +6; Str 15, Dex 10, Con 15, Int 10, Wis 11, Cha 10.

Skills and Feats: Bluff +5, Diplomacy +14, Intimidate +9, Listen +8, Search +8, Sense Motive +8, Spot +9, Swim +20; Flyby Attack, Multiattack, Wingover.

Breath Weapon (Su): 30-ft. cone, 4d6 acid, Reflex DC 16 half.

Ottwarslyndanox
Young Green Dragon

Ottwarslyndanox has long been at odds with a small community of elves that live within the confines of the forest that she considers her property. In her younger years, Ottwarslyndanox made direct raids on the settlement, but she was soundly repulsed each time. Now, though she is a much greater force to be reckoned with, she approaches her foes with more caution. She has learned not to expose herself to attack unless she is certain that she has the advantage over her foes. Ottwarslyndanox has respect for spellcasters and magic in general, and she looks forward to the day she can cast spells herself. She is always on the lookout for magic items that might give her an advantage, and she does nearly anything (short of parting with treasure) to acquire a new one.

Ottwarslyndanox: Female young green dragon; CR 5; Medium dragon (air); HD 11d12+22; hp 93; Init +0; Spd 40 ft., swim 40 ft., fly 150 ft. (poor); AC 20, touch 10, flat-footed 20; Base Atk +11; Grp +14; Atk +14 melee (1d8+3, bite); Full Atk +14 melee (1d8+3, bite), +9 melee (1d6+1, 2 claws), +9 melee (1d4+1, 2 wings); Space/Reach 5 ft./5 ft.; SA breath weapon; SQ blindsense 60 ft., darkvision 120 ft., immunity to acid, magic sleep effects, and paralysis, low-light vision, water breathing; AL LE; SV Fort +9, Ref +7, Will +8; Str 17, Dex 10, Con 15, Int 12, Wis 13, Cha 12.

Skills and Feats: Appraise +4, Bluff +6, Diplomacy +11, Intimidate +17, Knowledge (nature) +6, Listen +12, Search +15, Sense Motive +15, Spot +15, Swim +21; Flyby Attack, Heighten Breath, Power Attack, Wingover.

Breath Weapon (Su): 30-ft. cone, 6d6 acid, Reflex DC 17 half (or higher if heightened).

Rynskald
Juvenile Green Dragon

Though he loathes all kinds of sprites and mercilessly hunts those who still dare to dwell in his forest, Rynskald has learned to use some of their tricks against them. He is fond of using illusion cantrips to distract and disorient his foes, and laughs harshly every time a sprite—who should know better—falls for one of his tricks. Of course, he usually stops laughing as soon as he gets the creature in his mouth, but he has been known to chuckle even while swallowing.

Rynskald: Male juvenile green dragon; CR 8; Large dragon (air); HD 14d12+42, hp 133; Init +0; Spd 40 ft., swim 40 ft., fly 150 ft. (poor); AC 22, touch 9, flat-footed 22; Base Atk +14; Grp +22; Atk +17 melee (2d6+4, bite); Full Atk +17 melee (2d6+4, bite), +12 melee (1d8+2, 2 claws), +12 melee (1d6+2, 2 wings), +12 melee (1d8+6, tail slap); Space/Reach 10 ft./5 ft. (10 ft. with bite); SA breath weapon, frightful presence, spells; SQ blindsense 60 ft., darkvision 120 ft., immunity to acid, magic sleep effects, and paralysis, low-light vision, water breathing; AL LE; SV Fort +12, Ref +9, Will +11; Str 19, Dex 10, Con 17, Int 14, Wis 15, Cha 14.

Skills and Feats: Bluff +7, Climb +12, Concentration +17, Diplomacy +12, Hide +12, Intimidate +16, Knowledge (arcana) +7, Knowledge (nature) +7, Listen +17, Search +14, Sense Motive +15, Spellcraft +9, Spot +19; Awaken Frightful Presence, Combat Expertise, Flyby Attack, Power Attack, Wingover.

Breath Weapon (Su): 40-ft. cone, 8d6 acid, Reflex DC 20 half.

Frightful Presence (Ex): 35-ft. radius, HD 13 or fewer, Will DC 19 negates.

Spells: As 1st-level sorcerer.

Sorcerer Spells Known (5/4; save DC 12 + spell level): 0—*detect magic, ghost sound, prestidigitation, resistance;* 1st—*color spray, true strike.*

Klorphaxius
Young Adult Green Dragon

Certain groups of elves have been known to build entire cities in trees, supporting their graceful buildings on platforms among the branches so they seem almost a living part of the tree. Klorphaxius discovered such a city and took a fancy to it, and it is now hers. Her lair is in the largest tree, where she has taken over the palace of the elven princeling who once ruled the city. The palace required some retrofitting to accommodate her Large form, but the sundered interior walls and scattered rubble suit her temperament perfectly, serving as a daily reminder of just how terrible she is.

Klorphaxius: Female young adult green dragon; CR 11; Large dragon (air); HD 17d12+68, hp 178; Init +0; Spd 40 ft., swim 40 ft., fly 150 ft. (poor); AC 25, touch 9, flat-footed 25; Base Atk +17; Grp +27; Atk +22 melee (2d6+6, bite); Full Atk +22 melee (2d6+6, bite), +18 melee (1d8+3, 2 claws), +17 melee (1d6+3, 2 wings), +17 melee (1d8+9, tail slap); Space/Reach 10 ft./5 ft. (10 ft. with bite); SA breath weapon, frightful presence, spells; SQ blindsense 60 ft., damage reduction 5/magic, darkvision 120 ft., immunity to acid, magic sleep effects, and paralysis, low-light vision, spell resistance 19, water breathing; AL LE; SV Fort +14, Ref +10, Will +12; Str 23, Dex 10, Con 19, Int 14, Wis 15, Cha 14.

Skills and Feats: Bluff +12, Concentration +14, Diplomacy +6, Hide +16, Intimidate +19, Knowledge (arcana) +7, Knowledge (geography) +7, Listen +19, Move Silently +15, Search +17, Sense Motive +17, Spellcraft +10, Spot +17, Swim +21; Adroit Flyby Attack, Cleave, Flyby Attack, Power Attack, Weapon Focus (claw), Wingover.

Breath Weapon (Su): 40-ft. cone, 10d6 acid, Reflex DC 22 half.

Frightful Presence (Ex): 150-ft. radius, HD 16 or fewer, Will DC 20 negates.

Spells: As 3rd-level sorcerer.

Sorcerer Spells Known (6/6; save DC 12 + spell level): 0—*arcane mark, detect magic, ghost sound, mage hand, resistance;* 1st—*magic missile, shield, shocking grasp.*

Kallionastiryne
Adult Green Dragon

Kallionastiryne regards every inch of the forest where he dwells as his domain, and he likewise regards anyone who sets foot inside without leave as a trespasser and vandal. His uncompromising defense of his forest has won him the grudging admiration of a few druids; however, Kallionastiryne often grants orcs, giants, or other evil creatures hunting and logging rights, demanding hefty bribes of gold and gems and plenty of flattery as well. Kallionastiryne is not so much worried about the welfare of his forest as he is about being recognized as its owner. Because he regards these deals as little more than temporary agreements with inferior creatures, they seldom last long.

Kallionastiryne: Male adult green dragon; CR 13; Huge dragon (air); HD 20d12+100, hp 230; Init +0; Spd 40 ft., swim 40 ft., fly 150 ft. (poor); AC 27, touch 8, flat-footed 27; Base Atk +20; Grp +36; Atk +26 melee (2d8+8, bite); Full Atk +26 melee (2d8+8, bite), +21 melee (2d6+4, 2 claws), +21 melee (1d8+4, 2 wings), +21 melee (2d6+12, tail slap); Space/Reach 15 ft./10 ft. (15 ft. with bite); SA breath weapon, crush, frightful presence, snatch, spell-like abilities, spells; SQ blindsense 60 ft., damage reduction 5/magic, darkvision 120 ft., immunity to acid, magic sleep effects, and paralysis, low-light vision, spell resistance 21, water breathing; AL LE; SV Fort +17, Ref +12, Will +15; Str 27, Dex 10, Con 21, Int 16, Wis 17, Cha 16.

Skills and Feats: Bluff +20, Concentration +15, Diplomacy +13, Hide +0, Intimidate +25, Knowledge (arcana) +18, Knowledge (nature) +18, Listen +23, Move Silently +20, Search +23, Sense Motive +11, Spellcraft +15, Spot +23, Swim +24; Clinging Breath, Flyby Attack, Hover, Power Attack, Snatch, Wingover, Wingstorm.

Breath Weapon (Su): 50-ft. cone, 12d6 acid, Reflex DC 25 half.

Crush (Ex): Area 15 ft. by 15 ft.; Small or smaller opponents take 2d8+12 points of bludgeoning damage, and must succeed on a DC 23 Reflex save or be pinned.

Frightful Presence (Ex): 180-ft. radius, HD 19 or fewer, Will DC 21 negates.

Snatch (Ex): Against Small or smaller creatures, bite for 2d8+8/round or claw for 2d6+4/round.

Spell-Like Abilities: 3/day—*suggestion.* Caster level 6th; save DC 16.

Spells: As 5th-level sorcerer.

Sorcerer Spells Known (6/7/5; save DC 13 + spell level): 0—*arcane mark, dancing lights, detect magic, ghost sound, read magic, resistance;* 1st—*expeditious retreat, Nystul's magic aura, shield, true strike;* 2nd—*darkness, detect thoughts.*

Kesikasumislox
Mature Adult Green Dragon

As biting as the odor of chlorine that hangs around her, Kesikasumislox's wit slashes her opponents' morale. She has a gift for sarcasm, punctuating every slash with her claws, wing buffet, or tail slap with a snide observation of her foes' weakness. No amount of injury short of unconsciousness can still her tongue, and even on the rare occasions she is forced to flee a fight, she does so with a scathing parting comment. No living creature escapes her contempt, though she has learned to hold her tongue around the oldest green dragons.

Kesikasumislox: Female mature adult green dragon; CR 16; Huge dragon (air); HD 23d12+115, hp 264; Init +0; Spd 40 ft., swim 40 ft., fly 150 ft. (poor); AC 30, touch 8, flat-footed 30; Base Atk +23; Grp +40; Atk +30 melee (2d8+9, bite); Full Atk +30 melee (2d8+9, bite), +28 melee (2d6+4, 2 claws), +28 melee (1d8+4, 2 wings), +28 melee (2d6+13, tail slap); Space/Reach 15 ft./10 ft. (15 ft. with bite); SA breath weapon, crush, frightful presence, snatch, spell-like abilities, spells; SQ blindsense 60 ft., damage reduction 10/magic, darkvision 120 ft., immunity to acid, magic sleep effects, and paralysis, low-light vision, spell resistance 22, water breathing; AL LE; SV Fort +18, Ref +13, Will +16; Str 29, Dex 10, Con 21, Int 16, Wis 17, Cha 16.

Skills and Feats: Bluff +21, Concentration +18, Diplomacy +17, Hide +0, Intimidate +26, Knowledge (local) +14, Knowledge (nature) +14, Listen +26, Move Silently +23, Search +26, Sense Motive +26, Spellcraft +14, Spot +26, Swim +23; Enlarge Breath, Flyby Attack, Hover, Multiattack, Power Attack, Quicken Breath, Snatch, Wingover.

Breath Weapon (Su): 50-ft. cone (75-ft. cone if enlarged), 14d6 acid, Reflex DC 26 half.

Crush (Ex): Area 15 ft. by 15 ft.; Small or smaller opponents take 2d8+13 points of bludgeoning damage, and must succeed on a DC 26 Reflex save or be pinned.

Frightful Presence (Ex): 210-ft. radius, HD 22 or fewer, Will DC 24 negates.

Snatch (Ex): Against Small or smaller creatures, bite for 2d8+9/round or claw for 2d6+4/round.

Spell-Like Abilities: 3/day—*suggestion*. Caster level 7th; save DC 13 + spell level.

Spells: As 7th-level sorcerer.

Sorcerer Spells Known (6/7/7/5; save DC 13 + spell level): 0—*arcane mark, dancing lights, detect magic, ghost sound, mage hand, read magic, resistance;* 1st—*expeditious retreat, magic missile, protection from good, shield, true strike;* 2nd—*cat's grace, darkness, summon swarm;* 3rd—*haste, vampiric touch.*

Othocintlydavarei
Old Green Dragon

Though he is certainly an unlikely ally for good-aligned player characters, Othocintlydavarei has a problem they might be able to help him with. A group of evil druids has taken up residence in his territory, and they have so far resisted his attempts to encourage them to relocate. Their fanatical devotion to the purity of nature threatens to end the logging operation that helps swell Othocintlydavarei's coffers: he has been content to tax the loggers, while the druids are trying to drive them away. He wants to see the meddlers gone, and certainly, the human loggers would rather pay tribute to a dragon than suffer the raids of evil druids and their animal allies. Some sort of cooperation, as strange as it might be, seems almost inevitable.

Othocintlydavarei: Male old green dragon; CR 18; Huge dragon (air); HD 26d12+156, hp 325; Init +0; Spd 40 ft., swim 40 ft., fly 150 ft. (poor); AC 33, touch 8, flat-footed 33; Base Atk +26; Grp +44; Atk +34 melee (2d8+10, bite); Full Atk +34 melee (2d8+10, bite), +32 melee (2d6+5, 2 claws), +32 melee (1d8+5, 2 wings), +32 melee (2d6+15, tail slap); Space/Reach 15 ft./10 ft. (15 ft. with bite); SA breath weapon, crush, frightful presence, spell-like abilities, spells; SQ blindsense 60 ft., damage reduction 10/magic,darkvision 120 ft., immunity to acid, magic sleep effects, and paralysis, low-light vision, spell resistance 24, water breathing; AL LE; SV Fort +21, Ref +15, Will +19; Str 31, Dex 10, Con 23, Int 18, Wis 19, Cha 18.

Skills and Feats: Bluff +27, Concentration +23, Diplomacy +26, Hide –8, Intimidate +32, Knowledge (arcana) +20, Knowledge (local) +20, Knowledge (nature) +20, Listen +30, Move Silently +26, Search +30, Sense Motive +30, Spellcraft +18, Spot +30, Swim +24; Cleave, Flyby Attack, Great Cleave, Hover, Multiattack, Power Attack, Quicken Breath, Improved Sunder, Wingover.

Breath Weapon (Su): 50-ft. cone, 16d6 acid, Reflex DC 29 half.

Crush (Ex): Area 15 ft. by 15 ft.; Small or smaller opponents take 2d8+13 points of bludgeoning damage, and must succeed on a DC 29 Reflex save or be pinned.

Frightful Presence (Ex): 240-ft. radius, HD 25 or fewer, Will DC 27 negates.

Spell-Like Abilities: 3/day—*suggestion*; 1/day—*plant growth*. Caster level 9th; save DC 14 + spell level.

Spells: As 9th-level sorcerer.

Sorcerer Spells Known (6/7/7/7/5; save DC 14 + spell level): 0—*arcane mark, dancing lights, detect magic, ghost sound, mage hand, prestidigitation, read magic, resistance;* 1st—*magic missile, magic weapon, protection from good, shield, true strike;* 2nd—*cat's grace, darkness, hypnotic pattern, summon swarm;* 3rd—*dispel magic, haste, vampiric touch;* 4th—*bestow curse, greater invisibility.*

Giixhosiptor
Very Old Green Dragon

Giixhosiptor loves to play. He spends much of his time in his lair, concocting different games. He ventures out when bored and seeks weak or gullible creatures with whom to play some of his strange games. One of his favorite activities is to lure less powerful creatures, especially adventurers, to his lair. He then tries to trap them, without killing them. After making them give up a large percentage of their magical equipment, he offers it back if they perform some small service for him. Then, he sends them out to run an arbitrary errand, such as killing a chimera, tanning its hide, and bringing him the skin for a rug. When the adventurers return, he is dissatisfied with the result, stating that he had wanted a larger or smaller rug or one that was a different color. He gives the adventurers back the rug and perhaps a single item from their equipment, and then sends them off again on a different, difficult, but equally meaningless task. After two or three such exchanges, either the creatures refuse to continue or Giixhosiptor has grown bored and he decides to eat the creatures with whom he has been playing.

Giixhosiptor: Female very old green dragon; CR 19; Huge dragon (air); HD 29d12+174, hp 362; Init +0; Spd 40 ft., swim 40 ft., fly 150 ft. (poor); AC 36, touch 8, flat-footed 36; Base Atk +29; Grp +48; Atk +38 melee (2d8+11, bite); Full

Atk +38 melee (2d8+11, bite), +36 melee (2d6+5, 2 claws), +36 melee (1d8+5, 2 wings), +36 melee (2d6+16, tail slap); Space/Reach 15 ft./10 ft. (15 ft. with bite); SA breath weapon, crush, frightful presence, spell-like abilities, spells; SQ blindsense 60 ft., damage reduction 15/magic, darkvision 120 ft., immunity to acid, magic sleep effects, and paralysis, low-light vision, spell resistance 29, water breathing; AL LE; SV Fort +22, Ref +16, Will +20; Str 33, Dex 10, Con 23, Int 18, Wis 19, Cha 18.

Skills and Feats: Bluff +29, Concentration +25, Diplomacy +30, Hide –8, Intimidate +37, Knowledge (arcana) +22, Knowledge (history) +22, Knowledge (religion) +22, Listen +33, Move Silently +29, Search +33, Sense Motive +33, Spellcraft +19, Spot +22; Awaken Spell Resistance, Cleave, Enlarge Breath, Flyby Attack, Great Cleave, Hover, Multiattack, Power Attack, Tempest Breath, Wingover.

Breath Weapon (Su): 50-ft. cone (75-ft. cone if enlarged), 18d6 acid, Reflex DC 30 half.

Crush (Ex): Area 15 ft. by 15 ft.; Small or smaller opponents take 2d8+16 points of bludgeoning damage, and must succeed on a DC 30 Reflex save or be pinned.

Frightful Presence (Ex): 270-ft. radius, HD 28 or fewer, Will DC 28 negates.

Spell-Like Abilities: 3/day—*suggestion*; 1/day—*plant growth*. Caster level 11th; save DC 14 + spell level.

Spells: As 11th-level sorcerer.

Sorcerer Spells Known (6/7/7/7/7/4; save DC 14 + spell level): 0—*arcane mark, dancing lights, detect magic, ghost sound, mage hand, open/close, prestidigitation, read magic, resistance;* 1st—*alarm, expeditious retreat, magic missile, shield, true strike;* 2nd—*cat's grace, darkness, detect thoughts, magic mouth, web;* 3rd—*clairaudience/clairvoyance, dispel magic, haste, tongues;* 4th—*enervation, greater invisibility, rainbow pattern;* 5th—*hold monster, mind fog.*

Vaectorfinyairuxo
Ancient Green Dragon

Though he tries hard to be imperious and aloof as a green dragon is supposed to be, Vaectorfinyairuxo has a hard time overcoming his driving curiosity. Other greens sometimes mock him, calling him a "tarnished bronze," because he so often drops the pretense of superiority in order to ask questions about the creatures that should be his prey. He wants to know what their magic items do, what mission brings them to his woods, why they might be willing to die in combat with such a prodigious foe as himself, what they would like done with their remains, who grieves their inevitable demise, and so on and on—often enough, this goes so long that combat simply never occurs.

Vaectorfinyairuxo: Male ancient green dragon; CR 21; Gargantuan dragon (air); HD 32d12+224, hp 432; Init +0; Spd 40 ft., swim 40 ft., fly 200 ft. (poor); AC 37, touch 6, flat-footed 37; Base Atk +32; Grp +59; Atk +40 melee (4d6+12, bite); Full Atk +40 melee (4d6+12, bite), +35 melee (2d8+6, 2 claws), +35 melee (2d6+6, 2 wings), +35 melee (2d8+18, tail slap); Space/Reach 20 ft./15 ft. (20 ft. with bite); SA breath weapon, crush, frightful presence, snatch, spell-like abilities, spells, tail sweep; SQ blindsense 60 ft., damage reduction 15/magic, darkvision 120 ft., fast healing 3, immunity to acid, magic sleep effects, and paralysis, low-light vision, spell resistance 27, water breathing; AL LE; SV Fort +25, Ref +20, Will +23; Str 35, Dex 10, Con 25, Int 20, Wis 21, Cha 20.

Skills and Feats: Bluff +33, Concentration +27, Diplomacy +34, Hide –12, Intimidate +41, Knowledge (arcana) +20, Knowledge (history) +19, Knowledge (local) +19, Knowledge (nature) +19, Knowledge (the planes) +19, Listen +37, Move Silently +32, Search +37, Sense Motive +37, Spellcraft +22, Spot +37, Swim +28, Survival +14; Cleave, Enlarge Breath, Fast Healing, Flyby Attack, Hover, Improved Maneuverability, Lightning Reflexes, Power Attack, Recover Breath, Snatch, Wingover.

Breath Weapon (Su): 60-ft. cone (90-ft. cone if enlarged), 20d6 acid, Reflex DC 33 half.

Crush (Ex): Area 20 ft. by 20 ft.; Medium or smaller opponents take 4d6+18 points of bludgeoning damage, and must succeed on a DC 33 Reflex save or be pinned.

Frightful Presence (Ex): 300-ft. radius, HD 31 or fewer, Will DC 31 negates.

Snatch (Ex): Against Medium or smaller creatures, bite for 4d6+12/round or claw for 2d8+6/round.

Spell-Like Abilities: 3/day—*dominate person, suggestion*; 1/day—*plant growth*. Caster level 13th; save DC 15 + spell level.

Spells: As 13th-level sorcerer.

Tail Sweep (Ex): Half-circle 30 ft. in diameter, Small or smaller opponents take 2d6+18 points of bludgeoning damage, Reflex DC 33 half.

Sorcerer Spells Known (6/8/7/7/7/7/4; save DC 15 + spell level): 0—*arcane mark, dancing lights, detect magic, ghost sound, mage hand, open/close, prestidigitation, read magic, resistance;* 1st—*alarm, expeditious retreat, magic missile, shield, true strike;* 2nd—*cat's grace, darkness, detect thoughts, magic mouth, web;* 3rd—*clairaudience/clairvoyance, dispel magic, haste, tongues;* 4th—*bestow curse, enervation, greater invisibility, rainbow pattern;* 5th—*cone of cold, feeblemind, hold monster;* 6th—*circle of death, eyebite.*

Kranimatraxius
Wyrm Green Dragon

Kranimatraxius firmly believes that the minds of other creatures are hers to do with as she pleases. Weak and pliable compared to the iron will of a dragon, the minds of others are so easily subject to *insanity, feeblemind, mass suggestion*—she can even kill creatures with their own imagination, using *phantasmal killer.* Her breath weapon may be a direct method of slaughtering her foes, but she derives such enormous satisfaction from using her foes' minds against them that she often uses her poisonous gas only as a last resort.

Kranimatraxius: Female wyrm green dragon; CR 22; Gargantuan dragon (air); HD 35d12+280, hp 507; Init +0; Spd 40 ft., swim 40 ft., fly 200 ft. (clumsy); AC 40, touch 6, flat-footed 40; Base Atk +35; Grp +60; Atk +44 melee (4d6+13, bite); Full Atk +44 melee (4d6+13, bite), +42

Green Dragon

Typical Green Dragon Lair

[Size of lair varies with size of dragon]

old growth forest

old growth forest

main entry hidden behind waterfalls

Oblique View

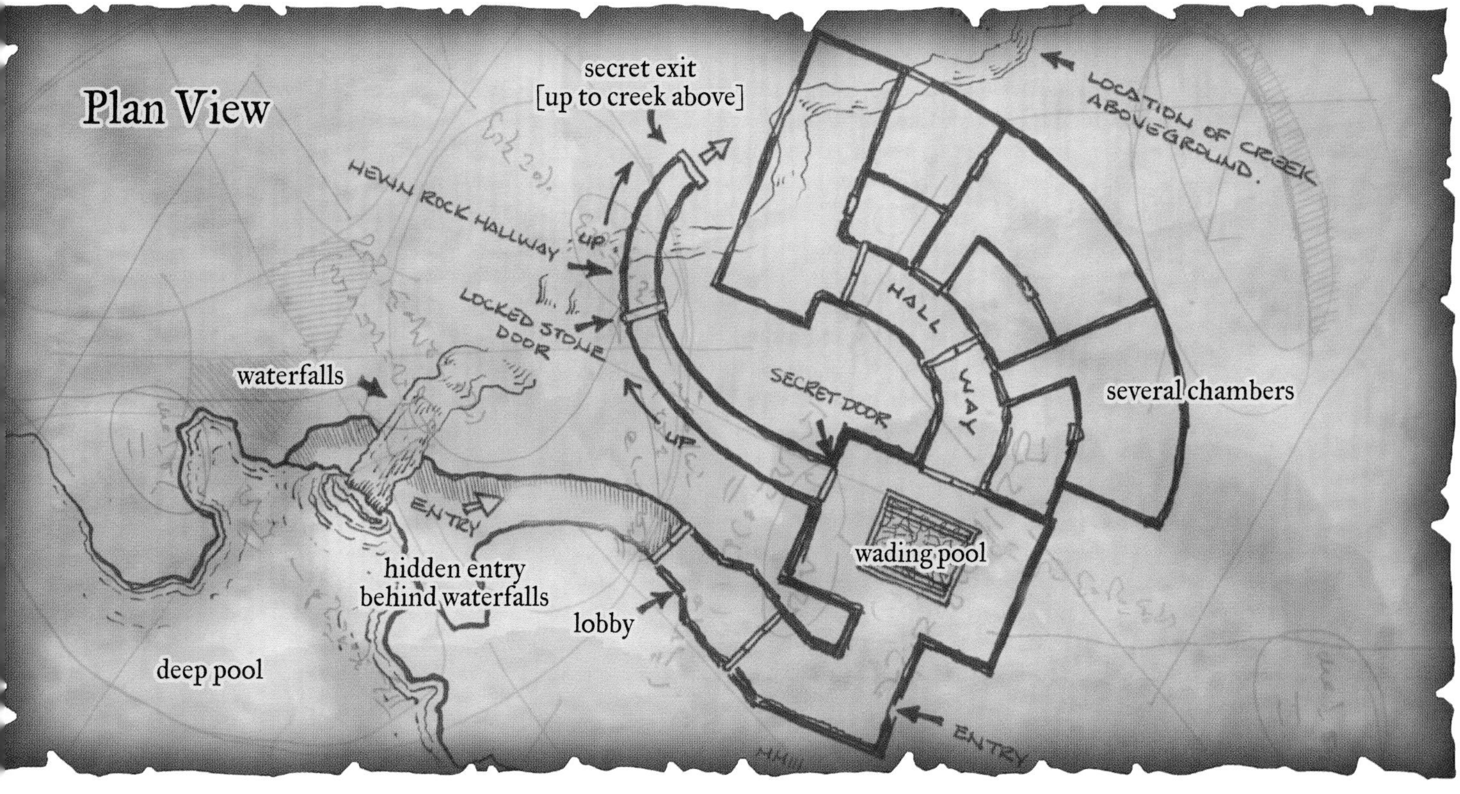

Plan View

secret exit
[up to creek above]

LOCATION OF CREEK ABOVEGROUND.

HEWN ROCK HALLWAY

UP

LOCKED STONE DOOR

HALL WAY

waterfalls

SECRET DOOR

UP

several chambers

ENTRY

wading pool

hidden entry
behind waterfalls

lobby

deep pool

ENTRY

melee (2d8+6, 2 claws), +42 melee (2d6+6, 2 wings), +42 melee (2d8+19, tail slap); Space/Reach 20 ft./15 ft. (20 ft. with bite); SA breath weapon, crush, frightful presence, snatch, spell-like abilities, spells, tail sweep; SQ blindsense 60 ft., damage reduction 20/magic, darkvision 120 ft., immunity to acid, magic sleep effects, and paralysis, low-light vision, spell resistance 28, water breathing; AL LE; SV Fort +27, Ref +19, Will +24; Str 37, Dex 10, Con 27, Int 20, Wis 21, Cha 20.

Skills and Feats: Bluff +40, Concentration +28, Diplomacy +47, Disguise +15, Hide +24, Intimidate +44, Knowledge (arcana) +20, Knowledge (local) +20, Knowledge (nature) +20, Listen +40, Move Silently +35, Search +40, Sense Motive +40, Spellcraft +23, Spot +40, Swim +29; Cleave, Clinging Breath, Flyby Attack, Hover, Multiattack, Power Attack, Quicken Breath, Rapidstrike, Recover Breath, Snatch, Wingover.

Breath Weapon (Su): 60-ft. cone, 22d6 acid, Reflex DC 35 half.

Crush (Ex): Area 20 ft. by 20 ft.; Medium or smaller opponents take 4d6+19 points of bludgeoning damage, and must succeed on a DC 35 Reflex save or be pinned.

Frightful Presence (Ex): 330-ft. radius, HD 34 or fewer, Will DC 32 negates.

Snatch (Ex): Against Medium or smaller creatures, bite for 4d6+13/round or claw for 2d8+6/round.

Spell-Like Abilities: 3/day—*dominate person, suggestion*; 1/day—*plant growth*. Caster level 15th; save DC 15 + spell level.

Spells: As 15th-level sorcerer.

Tail Sweep (Ex): Half-circle 30 ft. in diameter, Small or smaller opponents take 2d6+19 points of bludgeoning damage, Reflex DC 35 half.

Sorcerer Spells Known (6/8/7/7/7/7/6/4; save DC 15 + spell level): 0—*arcane mark, dancing lights, detect magic, ghost sound, light, mage hand, prestidigitation, read magic, resistance*; 1st—*magic missile, magic weapon, protection from good, shield, true strike*; 2nd—*cat's grace, darkness, detect thoughts, summon swarm, web*; 3rd—*flame arrow, haste, keen edge, vampiric touch*; 4th—*bestow curse, crushing despair, greater invisibility, phantasmal killer*; 5th—*feeblemind, hold monster, magic jar, wall of force*; 6th—*circle of death, greater dispel magic, mass suggestion*; 7th—*insanity, power word stun.*

Dimithkarjic
Great Wyrm Green Dragon

Dimithkarjic is convinced that his doom is upon him. He doesn't merely wonder whether death will save visit him soon, he actively expects it. He has known for centuries, he says, that he would not live to see 2,000 years, but he is now only months away, so his imminent demise is inescapable. By no means does this make him a less fearsome foe in combat; he fights as fiercely as he did in his youth. He does not flee a battle, however, since he accepts the fate he believes is predetermined for him.

Dimithkarjic: Male great wyrm green dragon; CR 24; Gargantuan dragon (air); HD 38d12+304, hp 551; Init +0; Spd 40 ft., swim 40 ft., fly 200 ft. (clumsy); AC 43, touch 6, flat-footed 43; Base Atk +38; Grp +66; Atk +48 melee (4d6+14, bite); Full Atk +48 melee (4d6+14, bite), +46 melee (2d8+7, 2 claws), +46 melee (2d6+7, 2 wings), +46 melee (2d8+21, tail slap); Space/Reach 20 ft./15 ft. (20 ft. with bite); SA breath weapon, crush, frightful presence, rend, snatch, spell-like abilities, spells, tail sweep; SQ blindsense 60 ft., damage reduction 20/magic, darkvision 120 ft., immunity to acid, magic sleep effects, and paralysis, low-light vision, spell resistance 30, water breathing; AL LE; SV Fort +29, Ref +21, Will +27; Str 39, Dex 10, Con 27, Int 22, Wis 23, Cha 22.

Skills and Feats: Bluff +44, Concentration +30, Diplomacy +52, Hide –12, Intimidate +48, Knowledge (arcana) +31, Knowledge (geography) +31, Knowledge (local) +31, Knowledge (nature) +31, Listen +44, Move Silently +38, Search +44, Sense Motive +44, Spellcraft +26, Spot +44, Swim +30, Survival +23; Cleave, Clinging Breath, Flyby Attack, Great Cleave, Hover, Lingering Breath, Multiattack, Power Attack, Quicken Breath, Recover Breath, Rend, Snatch, Wingover.

Breath Weapon (Su): 60-ft. cone, 24d6 acid, Reflex DC 37 half.

Crush (Ex): Area 20 ft. by 20 ft.; Medium or smaller opponents take 4d6+21 points of bludgeoning damage, and must succeed on a DC 37 Reflex save or be pinned.

Frightful Presence (Ex): 360-ft. radius, HD 37 or fewer, Will DC 37 negates.

Rend (Ex): Extra damage 4d8+21.

Snatch (Ex): Against Medium or smaller creatures, bite for 4d6+14/round or claw for 2d8+7/round.

Spell-Like Abilities: 3/day—*dominate person, suggestion*; 1/day—*command plants, plant growth*. Caster level 17th; save DC 16 + spell level.

Spells: As 17th-level sorcerer.

Tail Sweep (Ex): Half-circle 30 ft. in diameter, Small or smaller opponents take 2d6+21 points of bludgeoning damage, Reflex DC 37 half.

Sorcerer Spells Known (6/8/8/7/7/7/7/6/4; save DC 16 + spell level): 0—*arcane mark, dancing lights, detect magic, ghost sound, light, mage hand, prestidigitation, read magic, resistance*; 1st—*magic missile, magic weapon, protection from good, shield, true strike*; 2nd—*cat's grace, darkness, detect thoughts, summon swarm, web*; 3rd—*flame arrow, haste, keen edge, vampiric touch*; 4th—*bestow curse, crushing despair, greater invisibility, phantasmal killer*; 5th—*feeblemind, hold monster, magic jar, wall of force*; 6th—*chain lightning, eyebite, greater dispel magic*; 7th—*insanity, power word stun, prismatic spray*; 8th—*mass charm monster, protection from spells.*

SAMPLE RED DRAGONS

Detailed below are twelve sample red dragons, one of each age category. The descriptions include basic personality and encounter notes that the DM can flesh out for his campaign, along with a set of statistics that make the dragon ready to play.

Scorch
Wyrmling Red Dragon

Greedy and destructive, Scorch seldom passes up a chance to bully weaker creatures; he often plays with his prey like some oversized, malicious cat. He takes equal joy in smashing or burning buildings and other things made by mortal hands but too large to carry off. When not spreading destruction, Scorch likes to fly over the countryside at night. He often pauses near towns and villages, sizing them up for future conquests, though he has yet to actually attack a settlement.

Scorch: Male wyrmling red dragon; CR 4; Medium dragon (fire); HD 7d12+14; hp 59; Init +0; Spd 40 ft., fly 150 ft. (poor); AC 16, touch 10, flat-footed 16; Base Atk +7; Grp +10; Atk +10 melee (1d8+3, bite); Full Atk +10 melee (1d8+3, bite), +5 melee (1d6+1, 2 claws), +5 melee (1d4+1, 2 wings); Space/Reach 5 ft./5 ft.; SA breath weapon; SQ blindsense 60 ft., darkvision 120 ft., immunity to fire, magic sleep effects, and paralysis, low-light vision, vulnerability to cold; AL CE; SV Fort +7, Ref +5, Will +5; Str 17, Dex 10, Con 15, Int 10, Wis 11, Cha 10.

Skills and Feats: Appraise +7, Bluff +5, Diplomacy +2, Intimidate +9, Jump +14, Knowledge (geography) +4, Listen +10, Search +10, Spot +10; Cleave, Flyby Attack, Power Attack.

Breath Weapon (Su): 30-ft. cone, 2d10 fire, Reflex DC 15 half.

Raaze
Very Young Red Dragon

Raaze suffers from both vanity and overconfidence. She wastes no time in revealing herself to foes, usually by flying overhead to throw her shadow over a group or by perching in a high place and imperiously demanding that characters behold her magnificent self. She expects lesser creatures such as humanoids to lavish praise upon her and extol her beauty, strength, and grace. If she fails to get the praise she thinks is her due, she attacks. Characters who flatter Raaze must still endure her demands for tribute, and even if they pay up, find themselves invited to flatter her some more. Raaze never tires of hearing about herself, and usually does not let her victims go until they have provided a sum of treasure and assured her that she is simply too magnificent for their small minds to describe.

Raaze: Male very young female red dragon; CR 5; Large dragon (fire); HD 10d12+30; hp 95; Init +0; Spd 40 ft., fly 150 ft. (poor); AC 18, touch 9, flat-footed 18; Base Atk +10; Grp +19; Atk +14 melee (2d6+5, bite); Full Atk +14 melee (2d6+5, bite), +9 melee (1d8+2, 2 claws), +9 melee (1d6+2, 2 wings), +9 melee (1d8+7, tail slap); Space/Reach 10 ft./5 ft. (10 ft. with bite); SA breath weapon; SQ blindsense 60 ft., darkvision 120 ft., immunity to fire, magic sleep effects, and paralysis, low-light vision, vulnerability to cold; AL CE; SV Fort +10, Ref +7, Will +8; Str 21, Dex 10, Con 17, Int 12, Wis 13, Cha 12.

Skills and Feats: Appraise +11, Bluff +12, Diplomacy +3, Hide –4, Intimidate +13, Jump +19, Listen +14, Search +14, Spot +14; Flyby Attack, Hover, Power Attack, Wingover.

Breath Weapon (Su): 40-ft. cone, 4d10 fire, Reflex DC 18 half.

Fylokkipyron
Young Red Dragon

Nothing irks Fylokkipyron like being mocked. Every insult, every syllable of laughter, works its way under his scales like a grain of sand, irritating him until he coats it with a protective layer of seething hatred. The vast majority of his hatred is directed at a very young copper dragon who has dared to make her lair too close to his, a whelp named Rhindani. The upstart provokes him incessantly, and somehow always manages to escape his fury, traipsing away while shouting some singsong insult in his direction. Fylokkipyron spends hours every day plotting his revenge against Rhindani, imagining the various ways he could pull her internal organs out of her body, lingering especially long on that cursed tongue.

Fylokkipyron: Male young red dragon; CR 7; Large dragon (fire); HD 13d12+39, hp 123; Init +0; Spd 40 ft., fly 150 ft. (average); AC 21, touch 9, flat-footed 21; Base Atk +13; Grp +24; Atk +19 melee (2d6+7, bite); Full Atk +19 melee (2d6+7, bite), +14 melee (1d8+3, 2 claws), +14 melee (1d6+3, 2 wings), +14 melee (1d8+10, tail slap); Space/Reach 10 ft./5 ft. (10 ft. with bite); SA breath weapon, spells; SQ blindsense 60 ft., darkvision 120 ft., immunity to fire, magic sleep effects, and paralysis, low-light vision, spell resistance 13, vulnerability to cold; AL CE; SV Fort +11, Ref +8, Will +9; Str 25, Dex 10, Con 17, Int 12, Wis 13, Cha 12.

Skills and Feats: Bluff +7, Concentration +16, Diplomacy +10, Hide –4, Intimidate +16, Jump +24, Knowledge (arcana) +14, Listen +14, Search +14, Spellcraft +7, Spot +14; Awaken Spell Resistance, Flyby Attack, Hover, Improved Maneuverability, Wingover.

Breath Weapon (Su): 40-ft. cone, 6d10 fire, Reflex DC 19 half.

Spells: As 1st-level sorcerer.

Sorcerer Spells Known (5/4; save DC 11 + spell level): 0—*arcane mark, detect magic, ray of frost, resistance;* 1st—*protection from good, shield.*

Kalfyra
Juvenile Red Dragon

Kalfyra is a dragon in search of a lair and a mate. She roams the countryside looking for a likely spot to settle down and eventually raise a clutch of wyrmlings. Relatively personable (for a red dragon), she often stops to talk to travelers or other creatures who might be able to help her. Of course, she often consumes such creatures shortly after the discussion ends, but nobody's perfect. Kalfyra is particularly good at sensing duplicity or weakness in her opponents, and uses that information to her best advantage.

Kalfyra: Female juvenile red dragon; CR 10; Large dragon (fire); HD 16d12+64, hp 168; Init +0; Spd 40 ft., fly 150 ft. (poor); AC 24, touch 9, flat-footed 24; Base Atk +16; Grp +29; Atk +24 melee (2d6+9, bite); Full Atk +24 melee

(2d6+9, bite), +20 melee (1d8+4, 2 claws), +19 melee (1d6+4, 2 wings), +19 melee (1d8+13, tail slap); Space/Reach 10 ft./5 ft. (10 ft. with bite); SA breath weapon, spell-like abilities, spells; SQ blindsense 60 ft., darkvision 120 ft., immunity to fire, magic sleep effects, and paralysis, low-light vision, vulnerability to cold; AL CE; SV Fort +14, Ref +10, Will +12; Str 29, Dex 10, Con 19, Int 14, Wis 15, Cha 14.

Skills and Feats: Bluff +10, Concentration +17, Diplomacy +14, Hide –4, Intimidate +20, Jump +29, Knowledge (arcana) +15, Knowledge (geography) +8, Listen +18, Search +18, Sense Motive +10, Spellcraft +11, Spot +21; Cleave, Combat Expertise, Flyby Attack, Power Attack, Sense Weakness, Weapon Focus (claw), Wingover.

Breath Weapon (Su): 40-ft. cone, 8d10 fire, Reflex DC 22 half.

Spell-Like Abilities: 4/day—*locate object.* Caster level 4th.

Spells: As 3rd-level sorcerer.

Sorcerer Spells Known (6/6; save DC 12 + spell level): 0—*arcane mark, detect magic, ray of frost, resistance;* 1st—*command, protection from good.*

Drachenflagrion
Young Adult Red Dragon

Drachenflagrion collects art objects. He has agents in many communities who seek out such objects, then deliver them to specified locations where he picks them up before bringing them back to his lair. He has his eye on a number of religious relics, but so far has not had the courage to go after them himself.

Drachenflagrion decorates his cave with a variety of interesting objects, from silver flagons to sculptures to tapestries. He protects his lair with liberal use of the *alarm* spell, and uses *obscure object* to conceal new arrivals to his cave for the first week or two (until search attempts are likely to have been called off).

Drachenflagrion: Male young adult red dragon; CR 13; Huge dragon (fire); HD 19d12+95, hp 218; Init +0; Spd 40 ft., fly 150 ft. (poor); AC 26, touch 8, flat-footed 26; Base Atk +19; Grp +37; Atk +27 melee (2d8+10, bite); Full Atk +27 melee (2d8+10, bite), +22 melee (2d6+5, 2 claws), +22 melee (1d8+5, 2 wings), +22 melee (2d6+15, tail slap); Space/Reach 15 ft./10 ft. (15 ft. with bite); SA breath weapon, crush, frightful presence, improved snatch, spell-like abilities, spells; SQ blindsense 60 ft., damage reduction 5/magic, darkvision 120 ft., immunity to fire, magic sleep effects, and paralysis, low-light vision, spell resistance 19, vulnerability to cold; AL CE; SV Fort +16, Ref +11, Will +13; Str 31, Dex 10, Con 21, Int 14, Wis 15, Cha 14.

Skills and Feats: Appraise +21, Bluff +7, Concentration +21, Diplomacy +6, Hide –8, Intimidate +23, Jump +33, Knowledge (arcana) +15, Knowledge (history) +15, Listen +21, Search +21, Sense Motive +7, Spellcraft +12, Spot +12; Cleave, Flyby Attack, Hover, Improved Snatch, Power Attack, Snatch, Wingover.

Breath Weapon (Su): 50-ft. cone, 10d10 fire, Reflex DC 24 half.

Crush (Ex): Area 15 ft. by 15 ft.; Small or smaller opponents take 2d8+15 points of bludgeoning damage, and must succeed on a DC 24 Reflex save or be pinned.

Frightful Presence (Ex): 150-ft. radius, HD 18 or fewer, Will DC 21 negates.

Improved Snatch (Ex): Against Medium or smaller creatures, bite for 2d8+10/round or claw for 2d6+5/round.

Spell-Like Abilities: 5/day—*locate object.* Caster level 5th.

Spells: As 5th-level sorcerer.

Sorcerer Spells Known (6/7/5; save DC 12 + spell level): 0—*arcane mark, detect magic, flare, ray of frost, read magic, resistance;* 1st—*alarm, magic missile, protection from good, ventriloquism;* 2nd—*darkness, obscure object.*

Melniirkumaukrekon
Adult Red Dragon

Ever since a pair of silver dragons slew her parents, Melniirkumaukrekon has held a special place of hatred in her heart for such creatures. She uses every means at her disposal to track down unprotected nests or the offspring of her enemies. She avoids unnecessary risks, knowing that she doesn't yet have the power to face a silver dragon older than her, much less a mated pair. Rather than press a losing fight, Melniirkumaukrekon has no compunction against fleeing the scene, perhaps to return weeks or months later with a better plan of attack.

Melniirkumaukrekon: Female adult red dragon; CR 15; Huge dragon (fire); HD 22d12+110, hp 253; Init +0; Spd 40 ft., fly 150 ft. (poor); AC 29, touch 8, flat-footed 29; Base Atk +22; Grp +41; Atk +31 melee (2d8+11, bite); Full Atk +31 melee (2d8+11, bite), +26 melee (2d6+5, 2 claws), +26 melee (1d8+5, 2 wings), +26 melee (2d6+16, tail slap); Space/Reach 15 ft./10 ft. (15 ft. with bite); SA breath weapon, crush, frightful presence, snatch, spell-like abilities, spells; SQ blindsense 60 ft., damage reduction 5/magic, darkvision 120 ft., immunity to fire, magic sleep effects, and paralysis, low-light vision, spell resistance 21, vulnerability to cold; AL CE; SV Fort +18, Ref +13, Will +17; Str 33, Dex 10, Con 21, Int 16, Wis 19, Cha 16.

Skills and Feats: Appraise +25, Bluff +19, Concentration +24, Diplomacy +20, Gather Information +14, Hide –8, Jump +37, Knowledge (arcana) +18, Knowledge (local) +18, Listen +26, Search +25, Sense Motive +10, Spellcraft +15, Spot +28; Cleave, Flyby Attack, Hover, Power Attack, Recover Breath, Snatch, Tempest Breath, Wingover.

Breath Weapon (Su): 50-ft. cone, 12d10 fire, Reflex DC 25 half.

Crush (Ex): Area 15 ft. by 15 ft.; Small or smaller opponents take 2d8+15 points of bludgeoning damage, and must succeed on a DC 25 Reflex save or be pinned.

Frightful Presence (Ex): 180-ft. radius, HD 21 or fewer, Will DC 24 negates.

Snatch (Ex): Against Small or smaller creatures, bite for 2d8+11/round or claw for 2d6+5/round.

Spell-Like Abilities: 6/day—*locate object.* Caster level 7th.

Spells: As 7th-level sorcerer.

Habitat/Lair
RED DRAGON
Gargantuan
Huge
Large
Medium
Stomach
Back
Leg
Wing
SCALES
Blast Radius
Wing movement in flight

Sorcerer Spells Known (6/7/7/5; save DC 13 + spell level): 0—*arcane mark, dancing lights, detect magic, ghost sound, mage hand, read magic, resistance*; 1st—*alarm, divine favor, magic missile, protection from good, shield*; 2nd—*cat's grace, darkness, shatter*; 3rd—*dispel magic, protection from energy.*

Valinoghtorklax
Mature Adult Red Dragon

Valinoghtorklax is a dragon for hire. Warlords, bandit kings, conquering wizards, and fiendish plunderers of all stripes employ his services to devastate enemy armies and fortifications alike. His mercenary lifestyle sees him crisscross the globe to take part in revolts, uprisings, border wars, demonic invasions, and a variety of other conflicts. He is always paid well for his services, demanding bonuses for slaying enemy leaders. Because of his mobile nature, most of his wealth is portable (or wearable).

His favored tactic is to engage enemies from the air, using Flyby Attack and Improved Snatch to target individual opponents while using his quickened breath weapon to deal rapid-fire devastation.

Valinoghtorklax: Male mature adult red dragon; CR 18; Huge dragon (fire); HD 25d12+150, hp 312; Init +0; Spd 40 ft., fly 150 ft. (poor); AC 32, touch 8, flat-footed 32; Base Atk +25; Grp +44; Atk +34 melee (2d8+11, bite); Full Atk +34 melee (2d8+11, bite), +29 melee (2d6+5, 2 claws), +29 melee (1d8+5, 2 wings), +29 melee (2d6+16, tail slap); Space/Reach 15 ft./10 ft. (15 ft. with bite); SA breath weapon, crush, frightful presence, improved snatch, spell-like abilities, spells; SQ blindsense 60 ft., damage reduction 10/magic, darkvision 120 ft., immunity to fire, magic sleep effects, and paralysis, low-light vision, spell resistance 23, vulnerability to cold; AL CE; SV Fort +20, Ref +14, Will +18; Str 33, Dex 10, Con 23, Int 18, Wis 19, Cha 18.

Skills and Feats: Appraise +29, Bluff +9, Concentration +24, Diplomacy +22, Hide –8, Intimidate +30, Jump +40, Knowledge (arcana) +21, Knowledge (geography) +15, Knowledge (history) +15, Knowledge (nature) +12, Knowledge (the planes) +12, Knowledge (religion) +15, Listen +29, Search +29, Sense Motive +14, Spellcraft +17, Spot +24; Cleave, Flyby Attack, Hover, Improved Snatch, Multisnatch, Power Attack, Quicken Breath, Snatch, Wingover.

Breath Weapon (Su): 50-ft. cone, 14d10 fire, Reflex DC 28 half.

Crush (Ex): Area 15 ft. by 15 ft.; Small or smaller opponents take 2d8+16 points of bludgeoning damage, and must succeed on a DC 28 Reflex save or be pinned.

Frightful Presence (Ex): 210-ft. radius, HD 24 or fewer, Will DC 26 negates.

Improved Snatch (Ex): Against Medium or smaller creatures, bite for 2d8+11/round or claw for 2d6+5/round.

Spell-Like Abilities: 7/day—*locate object.* Caster level 9th.

Spells: As 9th-level sorcerer.

Sorcerer Spells Known (6/7/7/7/5; save DC 14 + spell level): 0—*arcane mark, dancing lights, detect magic, ghost sound, guidance, mage hand, read magic, resistance*; 1st—*alarm, magic missile, protection from good, shield, shocking grasp*; 2nd—*cat's grace, cure moderate wounds, darkness, sound burst*; 3rd—*dispel magic, protection from energy, stinking cloud*; 4th—*fire shield, greater invisibility.*

Sventsorggviresh
Old Red Dragon

Sventsorggviresh passes most of her time in her lair, where she reclines on her vast pile of treasure and feels very satisfied with herself. Always loathe to leave her hoard, she seldom stirs from her lair except when hungry, even then she sometimes cajoles a group of magma, fire, and steam mephits who share her lair into fetching her a snack (or at last locating one for her). She distrusts the mephits, and usually seals her lair with a *wall of force* while she's out hunting. She usually carries her *wand of chaos hammer* in one *glove of storing* and he wand of *fire shield* in the other.

Sventsorggviresh has peppered her lair with *magic mouth* and *alarm* spells to give warning of any intrusions. She has also persuaded an evil cleric she once met to cast some *forbiddance* spells (to prevent extradimensional intrusions) for her. She has since done away with the cleric.

Sventsorggviresh: Female old red dragon; CR 20; Gargantuan dragon (fire); HD 28d12+196, hp 378; Init +0; Spd 40 ft., fly 200 ft. (clumsy); AC 33, touch 6, flat-footed 33; Base Atk +28; Grp +52; Atk +36 melee (4d6+12, bite); Full Atk +36 melee (4d6+12, bite), +32 melee (2d8+6, 2 claws), +31 melee (2d6+6, 2 wings), +31 melee (2d8+18, tail slap); Space/Reach 20 ft./15 ft. (20 ft. with bite); SA breath weapon, crush, frightful presence, snatch, spell-like abilities, spells, tail sweep; SQ blindsense 60 ft., damage reduction 15/magic, darkvision 120 ft., immunity to fire, magic sleep effects, and paralysis, low-light vision, spell resistance 24, vulnerability to cold; AL CE; SV Fort +23, Ref +16, Will +21; Str 35, Dex 10, Con 25, Int 20, Wis 21, Cha 20.

Skills and Feats: Appraise +33, Bluff +25, Concentration +27, Diplomacy +37, Hide –12, Intimidate +35, Jump +44, Knowledge (arcana) +29, Knowledge (geography) +29, Knowledge (religion) +29, Listen +33, Search +33, Sense Motive +19, Spellcraft +20, Spot +26; Cleave, Flyby Attack, Great Cleave, Hover, Improved Critical (claw), Overwhelming Critical (claw), Power Attack, Snatch, Weapon Focus (claw), Wingover.

Breath Weapon (Su): 60-ft. cone, 16d10 fire, Reflex DC 30 half.

Crush (Ex): Area 20 ft. by 20 ft.; Medium or smaller opponents take 4d6+18 points of bludgeoning damage, and must succeed on a DC 30 Reflex save or be pinned.

Frightful Presence (Ex): 240-ft. radius, HD 27 or fewer, Will DC 29 negates.

Snatch (Ex): Against Medium or smaller creatures, bite for 4d6+12/round or claw for 2d8+6/round.

Spell-Like Abilities: 8/day—*locate object*; 3/day—*suggestion.* Caster level 11th; save DC 15 + spell level.

Spells: As 11th-level sorcerer.

Tail Sweep (Ex): Half-circle 30 ft. in diameter, Small or smaller opponents take 2d6+18 points of bludgeoning damage, Reflex DC 30 half.

Red Dragon

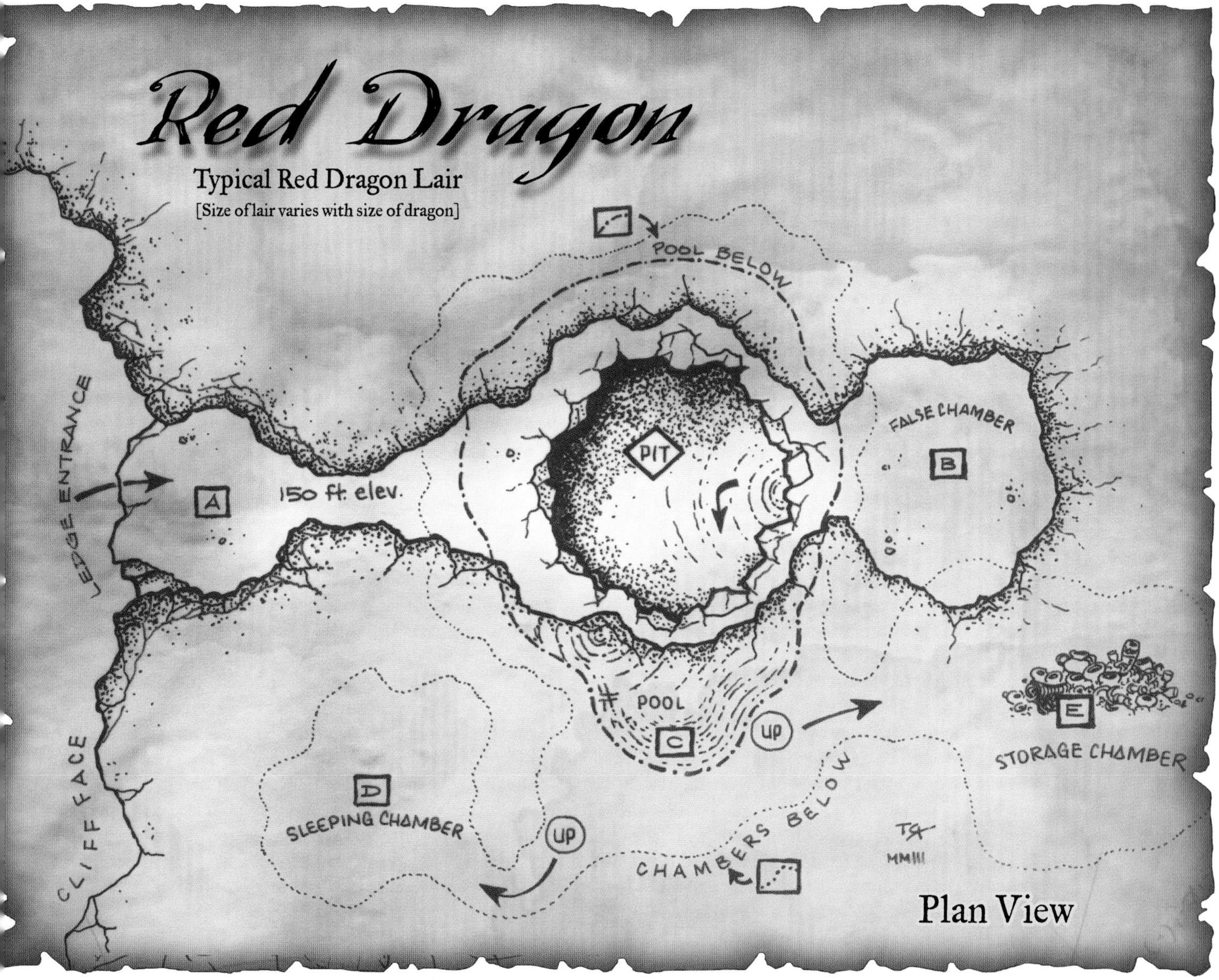

Typical Red Dragon Lair

[Size of lair varies with size of dragon]

POOL BELOW

LEDGE ENTRANCE

A

150 ft. elev.

PIT

FALSE CHAMBER

B

POOL

C

UP

E

STORAGE CHAMBER

D

SLEEPING CHAMBER

UP

CHAMBERS BELOW

CLIFF FACE

TA MMIII

Plan View

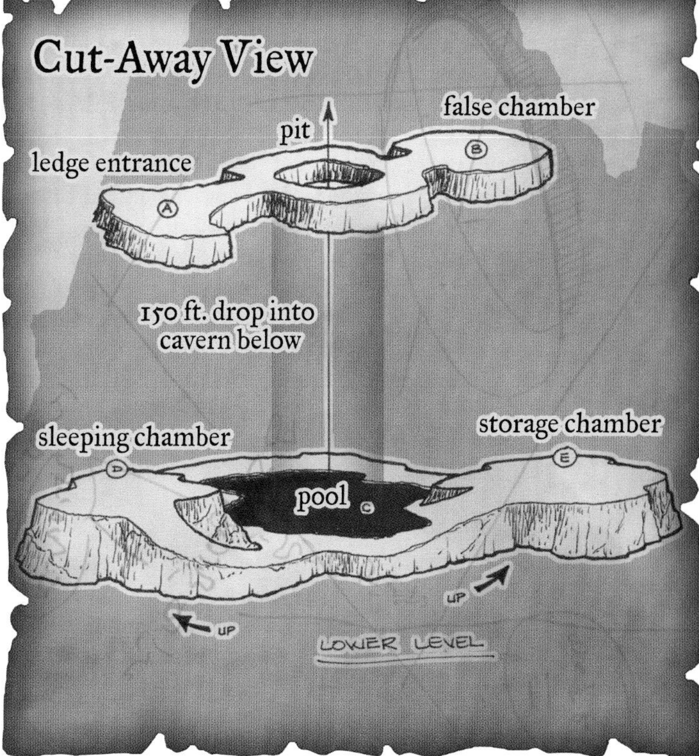

Sorcerer Spells Known (6/8/7/7/7/5; save DC 15 + spell level): 0—*arcane mark, dancing lights, detect magic, ghost sound, guidance, mage hand, prestidigitation, read magic, resistance*; 1st—*alarm, cure light wounds, divine shield, shield, true strike*; 2nd—*cat's grace, cure moderate wounds, invisibility, magic mouth, shatter*; 3rd—*deeper darkness, dispel magic, haste, protection from energy*; 4th—*arcane eye, confusion, phantasmal killer*; 5th—*hold monster, wall of force*

Possessions: *2 gloves of storing, necklace of adaptation, ring of swimming, wand of chaos hammer* (8th-level caster, 28 charges), *wand of fire shield* (22 charges).

Urivayotornotach
Very Old Red Dragon

Urivayotornotach has a pathological hatred of adventurers. He has turned his lair into an enormous deathtrap, fortifying it with pits, tripwires, and the like. His feat and spell selections are aimed at maximizing his adventurer-killing power while simultaneously protecting him from their typical attacks. He has learned from experience the folly of letting pride or dignity interfere with his tactics, and is willing to feign injury or cowardice or otherwise demean himself in ways that other red dragons might not in order to gain a combat advantage. He favors hit-and-run tactics, forcing opponents to bleed off their resources while drawing them ever deeper into his cave network.

Urivayotornotach: Male very old red dragon; CR 21; Gargantuan dragon (fire); HD 31d12+248, hp 449; Init +0; Spd 40 ft., fly 200 ft. (clumsy); AC 36, touch 6, flat-footed 36; Base Atk +31; Grp +56; Atk +40 melee (4d6+13, bite); Full Atk +40 melee (4d6+13, bite), +35 melee (2d8+6, 2 claws), +35 melee (2d6+6, 2 wings), +35 melee (2d8+19, tail slap); Space/Reach 20 ft./15 ft. (20 ft. with bite); SA breath weapon, crush, frightful presence, improved snatch, spell-like abilities, spells, tail sweep; SQ blindsense 60 ft., damage reduction 15/magic, darkvision 120 ft., immunity to fire, magic sleep effects, and paralysis, low-light vision, spell resistance 25, vulnerability to cold; AL CE; SV Fort +25, Ref +17, Will +25; Str 37, Dex 10, Con 27, Int 22, Wis 23, Cha 22.

Skills and Feats: Appraise +31, Bluff +37, Concentration +28, Craft (trapmaking) +18, Hide +2, Intimidate +39, Jump +48, Knowledge (arcana) +31, Knowledge (local) +31, Knowledge (religion) +31, Listen +37, Search +37, Sense Motive +37, Spellcraft +23, Spot +37, Use Magic Device +22; Cleave, Flyby Attack, Great Cleave, Hover, Improved Snatch, Iron Will, Overcome Weakness, Power Attack, Snatch, Suppress Weakness, Wingover.

Breath Weapon (Su): 60-ft. cone, 18d10 fire, Reflex DC 33 half.

Crush (Ex): Area 20 ft. by 20 ft.; Medium or smaller opponents take 4d6+19 points of bludgeoning damage, and must succeed on a DC 33 Reflex save or be pinned.

Frightful Presence (Ex): 270-ft. radius, HD 30 or fewer, Will DC 29 negates.

Improved Snatch (Ex): Against Large or smaller creatures, bite for 4d6+13/round or claw for 2d8+6/round.

Spell-Like Abilities: 9/day—*locate object*; 3/day—*suggestion*. Caster level 13th; save DC 16 + spell level.

Spells: As 13th-level sorcerer.

Tail Sweep (Ex): Half-circle 30 ft. in diameter, Small or smaller opponents take 2d6+19 points of bludgeoning damage, Reflex DC 33 half.

Sorcerer Spells Known (6/8/8/7/7/7/5; save DC 16 + spell level): 0—*arcane mark, dancing lights, detect magic, ghost sound, guidance, mage hand, prestidigitation, read magic, resistance*; 1st—*alarm, chill touch, divine shield, magic missile, shield*; 2nd—*cat's grace, cure moderate wounds, darkness, detect thoughts, pyrotechnics*; 3rd—*deeper darkness, dispel magic, haste, protection from energy*; 4th—*charm monster, crushing despair, greater invisibility, spell immunity*; 5th—*mass inflict light wounds, feeblemind, shadow evocation*; 6th—*acid fog, heal.*

Durtaxsteingakila
Ancient Red Dragon

Durtaxsteingakila may well be the most powerful warlord that no one has ever heard of. She has spent patient decades building alliances with other powerful creatures, from demons to slaadi to dark elves, with the eventual goal of continental-scale conquest. Along the way, she has incited conflict in various locales, each one carefully designed to destabilize a local ruler, weaken defenses, or otherwise make her ultimate goal achievable. In some cases, she has sacrificed her own allies in these battles, but always with a long-term plan in mind.

Despite her many collaborators, no one truly understands the scope of her plan. Many allies don't even know of each other's existence, and in fact, some have even come in conflict with one another. That's just the way she likes it.

Durtaxsteingakila: Female ancient red dragon; CR 23; Gargantuan dragon (fire); HD 34d12+306, hp 527; Init +0; Spd 40 ft., fly 200 ft. (clumsy); AC 39, touch 6, flat-footed 39; Base Atk +34; Grp +60; Atk +44 melee (4d6+14, bite); Full Atk +44 melee (4d6+14, bite), +40 melee (2d8+7/19–20, 2 claws), +39 melee (2d6+7, 2 wings), +39 melee (2d8+21, tail slap); Space/Reach 20 ft./15 ft. (20 ft. with bite); SA breath weapon, crush, frightful presence, improved snatch, spell-like abilities, spells, tail sweep; SQ blindsense 60 ft., damage reduction 15/magic, darkvision 120 ft., immunity to fire, magic sleep effects, and paralysis, low-light vision, spell resistance 28, vulnerability to cold; AL CE; SV Fort +28, Ref +19, Will +26; Str 39, Dex 10, Con 29, Int 24, Wis 25, Cha 24.

Skills and Feats: Appraise +41, Bluff +41, Concentration +29, Diplomacy +47, Hide –12, Intimidate +45, Jump +52, Knowledge (arcana) +27, Knowledge (geography) +27, Knowledge (history) +27, Knowledge (nature) +27, Knowledge (the planes) +27, Knowledge (religion) +27, Listen +41, Search +41, Sense Motive +24, Spellcraft +25, Spot +41, Survival +23; Enlarge Breath, Flyby Attack, Improved Snatch, Improved Critical (claw), Multisnatch, Power Attack, Snatch, Weapon Focus (claw), Wingover.

Breath Weapon (Su): 60-ft. cone (90-ft. cone if enlarged), 20d10 fire, Reflex DC 35 half.

Crush (Ex): Area 20 ft. by 20 ft.; Medium or smaller opponents take 4d6+21 points of bludgeoning damage, and must succeed on a DC 35 Reflex save or be pinned.

Frightful Presence (Ex): 300-ft. radius, HD 33 or fewer, Will DC 31 negates.

Improved Snatch (Ex): Against Large or smaller creatures, bite for 4d6+14/round or claw for 2d8+7/round.

Spell-Like Abilities: 10/day—*locate object;* 3/day—*suggestion;* 1/day—*find the path.* Caster level 15th; save DC 17 + spell level.

Spells: As 15th-level sorcerer.

Tail Sweep (Ex): Half-circle 30 ft. in diameter, Small or smaller opponents take 2d6+21 points of bludgeoning damage, Reflex DC 35 half.

Sorcerer Spells Known (6/8/8/8/7/7/7/5; save DC 17 + spell level): 0—*arcane mark, dancing lights, detect magic, ghost sound, guidance, mage hand, prestidigitation, read magic, resistance;* 1st—*alarm, chill touch, divine shield, magic missile, shield;* 2nd—*cat's grace, cure moderate wounds, darkness, detect thoughts, pyrotechnics;* 3rd—*deeper darkness, dispel magic, haste, protection from energy;* 4th—*charm monster, crushing despair, greater invisibility, spell immunity;* 5th—*mass inflict light wounds, feeblemind, hold monster, shadow evocation;* 6th—*greater dispel magic, heal, mass suggestion;* 7th—*insanity, word of chaos.*

Bheilorveilthion
Wyrm Red Dragon

Bheilorveilthion enjoys personal combat with powerful opponents. As soon as the battle begins, he picks a target within range and charges, using Dire Charge to make a full attack (augmented by Power Attack), combining that with a rend attack if he hits with both claws. This usually reduces the opponent to ribbons, at which point Bheilorveilthion moves on to the next target (assuming any remain in sight after his display of power). It's common for his battles to last only a single round.

Bheilorveilthion: Male wyrm red dragon; CR 24; Gargantuan dragon (fire); HD 37d12+370, hp 610; Init +4; Spd 40 ft., fly 200 ft. (clumsy); AC 42, touch 6, flat-footed 42; Base Atk +37; Grp +64; Atk +48 melee (4d6+15, bite); Full Atk +48 melee (4d6+15, bite), +48 melee (2d8+7, 2 claws), +48 melee (2d6+7, 2 wings), +48 melee (2d8+22, tail slap); Space/Reach 20 ft./15 ft. (20 ft. with bite); SA breath weapon, crush, frightful presence, rend, snatch, spell-like abilities, spells, tail sweep, SQ blindsense 60 ft., damage reduction 20/magic, darkvision 120 ft., immunity to fire, magic sleep effects, and paralysis, low-light vision, spell resistance 30, vulnerability to cold; AL CE; SV Fort +30, Ref +20, Will +27; Str 41, Dex 10, Con 31, Int 24, Wis 25, Cha 24.

Skills and Feats: Appraise +44, Bluff +44, Concentration +30, Diplomacy +50, Hide –12, Intimidate +48, Jump +56, Knowledge (arcana) +35, Knowledge (geography) +33, Knowledge (history) +33, Knowledge (the planes) +35, Knowledge (religion) +35, Listen +47, Search +44, Sense Motive +30, Spellcraft +26, Spot +47; Cleave, Dire Charge, Great Cleave, Flyby Attack, Hover, Improved Initiative, Improved Multiattack, Multiattack, Power Attack, Power Climb, Rend, Snatch, Wingover.

Breath Weapon (Su): 60-ft. cone, 22d10 fire, Reflex DC 38 half.

Crush (Ex): Area 20 ft. by 20 ft.; Medium or smaller opponents take 4d6+22 points of bludgeoning damage, and must succeed on a DC 35 Reflex save or be pinned.

Frightful Presence (Ex): 330-ft. radius, HD 36 or fewer, Will DC 35 negates.

Rend (Ex): Extra damage 4d8+22.

Snatch (Ex): Against Medium or smaller creatures, bite for 4d6+15/round or claw for 2d8+7/round.

Spell-Like Abilities: 11/day—*locate object;* 3/day—*suggestion;* 1/day—*find the path.* Caster level 17th; save DC 17 + spell level.

Spells: As 17th-level sorcerer.

Tail Sweep (Ex): Half-circle 30 ft. in diameter, Small or smaller opponents take 2d6+22 points of bludgeoning damage, Reflex DC 38 half.

Sorcerer Spells Known (6/8/8/8/7/7/7/7/4; save DC 17 + spell level): 0—*arcane mark, dancing lights, detect magic, ghost sound, guidance, mage hand, prestidigitation, read magic, resistance;* 1st—*alarm, chill touch, divine shield, magic missile, shield;* 2nd—*cat's grace, cure moderate wounds, darkness, detect thoughts, pyrotechnics;* 3rd—*deeper darkness, dispel magic, haste, protection from energy;* 4th—*charm monster, crushing despair, greater invisibility, spell immunity;* 5th—*mass inflict light wounds, feeblemind, hold monster, shadow evocation;* 6th—*greater dispel magic, heal, mass suggestion;* 7th—*insanity, reverse gravity, word of chaos;* 8th—*horrid wilting, symbol of death.*

Syzdothyx
Great Wyrm Red Dragon

Syzdothyx desires immortality. Though she dabbled with the idea of becoming a dracolich, she ultimately decided that godhood was her goal. In her most egotistical moments, she styles herself as a rival to the power of Tiamat herself—and her egotistical moments tend to outnumber her realistic moments these days. In the short term, she seeks to gain the attention of the draconic deity Garyx (see Religion in Chapter 2), perhaps becoming an avatar or consort as a stepping-stone to even greater power. The value of her hoard exceeds that held in the vaults of many small kingdoms, but she won't hesitate to use or sacrifice that hoard in pursuit of her dream of divine ascension.

Syzdothyx: Female great wyrm red dragon; CR 26; Colossal dragon (fire); HD 40d12+400, hp 660; Init +4; Spd 40 ft., fly 200 ft. (clumsy); AC 41, touch 2, flat-footed 41; Base Atk +40; Grp +73; Atk +49 melee (4d8+17, bite); Full Atk +49 melee (4d8+17, bite), +47 melee (4d6+8, 2 claws), +47 melee (2d8+8, 2 wings), +47 melee (4d6+25, tail slap); Space/Reach 30 ft./20 ft. (30 ft. with bite); SA breath weapon, crush, frightful presence, improved snatch, spell-like abilities, spells, tail sweep; SQ blindsense 60 ft., damage reduction 20/magic, darkvision 120 ft., immunity to fire, magic sleep effects, and paralysis, low-light vision, spell resistance 32, vulnerability to cold; AL CE; SV Fort

+32, Ref +22, Will +32; Str 45, Dex 10, Con 31, Int 26, Wis 27, Cha 26.

Skills and Feats: Appraise +51, Bluff +51, Concentration +31, Diplomacy +55, Hide –16, Intimidate +53, Jump +61, Knowledge (arcana) +38, Knowledge (geography) +38, Knowledge (history) +38, Knowledge (the planes) +38, Knowledge (religion) +38, Listen +51, Move Silently +9, Search +45, Sense Motive +28, Spellcraft +29, Spot +51, Survival +37; Cleave, Draconic Knowledge, Flyby Attack, Great Cleave, Hover, Improved Initiative, Improved Snatch, Iron Will, Multiattack, Power Attack, Quicken Breath, Snatch, Suppress Weakness, Wingover.

Breath Weapon (Su): 70-ft. cone, 24d10 fire, Reflex DC 40 half.

Crush (Ex): Area 30 ft. by 30 ft.; Large or smaller opponents take 4d8+25 points of bludgeoning damage, and must succeed on a DC 40 Reflex save or be pinned.

Frightful Presence (Ex): 360-ft. radius, HD 39 or fewer, Will DC 38 negates.

Improved Snatch (Ex): Against Huge or smaller creatures, bite for 4d8+17/round or claw for 4d6+8/round.

Spell-Like Abilities: 12/day—*locate object;* 3/day—*suggestion;* 1/day—*discern location, find the path.* Caster level 19th; save DC 18 + spell level.

Spells: As 19th-level sorcerer.

Tail Sweep (Ex): Half-circle 40 ft. in diameter, Small or smaller opponents take 2d8+25 points of bludgeoning damage, Reflex DC 40 half.

Sorcerer Spells Known (6/8/8/8/8/7/7/7/7/4; save DC 18 + spell level): 0—*arcane mark, dancing lights, detect magic, ghost sound, guidance, mage hand, prestidigitation, read magic, resistance;* 1st—*alarm, chill touch, divine shield, magic missile, shield;* 2nd—*cat's grace, cure moderate wounds, darkness, detect thoughts, pyrotechnics;* 3rd—*deeper darkness, dispel magic, haste, protection from energy;* 4th—*charm monster, crushing despair, greater invisibility, spell immunity;* 5th—*mass inflict light wounds, feeblemind, hold monster, shadow evocation;* 6th—*greater dispel magic, heal, mass suggestion;* 7th—*insanity, reverse gravity, word of chaos;* 8th—*horrid wilting, mass charm monster, symbol of death;* 9th—*elemental swarm, energy drain.*

SAMPLE SILVER DRAGONS

Detailed below are twelve sample silver dragons, one of each age category. The descriptions include basic personality and encounter notes that the DM can flesh out for his campaign, along with a set of statistics that make the dragon ready to play.

Alternate Form (Su): A silver dragon can assume any animal or humanoid form of Medium size or smaller as a standard action three times per day. This ability functions as a *polymorph* spell cast on itself at its caster level, except that the dragon does not regain hit points for changing form and can only assume the form of an animal or humanoid. The dragon can remain in its animal or humanoid form until it chooses to assume a new one or return to its natural form.

Cloudwalking (Su): All silver dragons can tread on clouds or fog as though on solid ground. This ability functions continuously but can be negated or resumed at will as a free action.

Nimbus
Wyrmling Silver Dragon

Nimbus has an insatiable appetite for doing good deeds and for learning other people's business. He finds the various tasks and errands that humans tackle every day to be endless fascinating, though he doesn't quite understand why they're so busy all the time.

He often trudges about posing as a human woodcutter, a gnome peddler, or a big, shaggy dog. He gladly renders assistance to anyone who needs it, and he tries anything though he's not always up to the task. He once offered to chop wood for an old widow and nearly chopped off a foot with the axe.

Nimbus: Male wyrmling silver dragon; CR 4; Small dragon (cold); HD 7d12+7; hp 52; Init +0; Spd 40 ft., fly 100 ft. (average); AC 17, touch 11, flat-footed 17; Base Atk +7; Grp +4; Atk +9 melee (1d6+1, bite); Full Atk +9 melee (1d6+1, bite), +4 melee (1d4, 2 claws); Space/Reach 5 ft./5 ft.; SA breath weapon; SQ alternate form, blindsense 60 ft., cloudwalking, darkvision 120 ft., immunity to acid, cold, magic sleep effects, and paralysis, low-light vision, vulnerability to fire; AL LG; SV Fort +6, Ref +5, Will +7; Str 13, Dex 10, Con 13, Int 14, Wis 15, Cha 14.

Skills and Feats: Bluff +5, Diplomacy +9, Disguise +12, Hide +4, Intimidate +5, Jump +8, Knowledge (nature) +12, Listen +12, Search +12, Sense Motive +12, Spot +12; Combat Expertise, Flyby Attack, Power Attack.

Breath Weapon (Su): 20-ft. cone, 2d8 cold, Reflex DC 14 half; or 20-ft. cone, paralysis 1d6+1 rounds, Fortitude DC 14 negates.

Karaglen
Very Young Silver Dragon

Karaglen is a would-be crusader, an occasional joker, and an all-the-time flirt. Often taking the shape of a half-elf youth, she has a penchant for seeking out disputes between nonevil people and using her humor and tact to resolve the situation. While her powers have yet to develop (by dragon standards, anyway), Karaglen often impresses common villagers and low-level adventurers with her comparative skill and maturity. If someone discovers Karaglen's true nature, she often presses the person to keep her draconic origin a secret. She dislikes being the center of attention and prefers to assist others rather than excel herself.

Karaglen: Female very young silver dragon; CR 5; Medium dragon (cold); HD 10d12+20; hp 85; Init +0; Spd 40 ft., fly 150 ft. (poor); AC 19, touch 10, flat-footed 19; Base Atk +10; Grp +12; Atk +13 melee (1d8+2, bite); Full Atk +13 melee (1d8+2, bite), +10 melee (1d6+1, 2 claws), +10 melee (1d4+1, 2 wings); Space/Reach 5 ft./5 ft.; SA breath weapon; SQ alternate form, blindsense 60 ft., cloudwalking, darkvision 120 ft., immunity to acid, cold, magic sleep effects, and paralysis, low-light vision, vulnerability to fire; AL LG; SV Fort +9, Ref +7, Will +9; Str 15, Dex 10, Con 15, Int 14, Wis 15, Cha 14.

Skills and Feats: Bluff +7, Diplomacy +11, Disguise +15, Heal +8, Intimidate +6, Jump +16, Knowledge (arcana) +9, Listen +12, Profession (herbalist) +7, Search +12, Sense Motive +14, Spot +15; Flyby Attack, Multiattack, Power Attack, Weapon Focus (bite).

Breath Weapon (Su): 30-ft. cone, 4d8 cold, Reflex DC 17 half; or 30-ft. cone, paralysis 1d6+2 rounds, Fortitude DC 17 negates.

Namhias
Young Silver Dragon

When older silver dragons try to impress upon youngsters of their race the importance of subtlety, level-headedness, and patience, they seldom fail as spectacularly as they did with Namhias. Some say this young dragon forced his way out of his shell weeks before his hatchmates. Whether that is true or not, Namhias has been in a hurry ever since. Easily angered by injustice or bullying, the young silver dragon rushes into combat at any real provocation. While he does try not to kill those he can subdue, sometimes he forgets the strength of whatever form he is currently in. When not displaying his full might as a young silver dragon, Namhias likes to prowl the mountains in the form of a large, lithe cat or a hulking human.

Namhias: Male young silver dragon; CR 7; Medium dragon (cold); HD 13d12+26, hp 110; Init +0; Spd 40 ft., fly 150 ft. (poor); AC 22, touch 10, flat-footed 22; Base Atk +13; Grp +16; Atk +16 melee (1d8+3, bite); Full Atk +16 melee (1d8+3, bite), +11 melee (1d6+1, 2 claws), +11 melee (1d4+1, 2 wings); Space/Reach 5 ft./5 ft.; SA breath weapon, spells; SQ alternate form, blindsense 60 ft., cloudwalking, darkvision 120 ft., immunity to acid, cold, magic sleep effects, and paralysis, low-light vision, vulnerability to fire; AL LG; SV Fort +10, Ref +8, Will +11; Str 17, Dex 10, Con 15, Int 16, Wis 17, Cha 16.

Skills and Feats: Bluff +16, Concentration +15, Diplomacy +5, Disguise +16 (+18 acting), Heal +10, Intimidate +5, Jump +20, Knowledge (arcana) +16, Listen +16, Profession (herbalist) +19, Search +19, Spellcraft +13, Spot +19; Cleave, Flyby Attack, Hover, Power Attack, Wingover.

Breath Weapon (Su): 30-ft. cone, 6d8 cold, Reflex DC 18 half; or 30-ft. cone, paralysis 1d6+3 rounds, Fortitude DC 18 negates.

Spells: As 1st-level sorcerer.

Sorcerer Spells Known (5/4; save DC 13 + spell level): 0—*detect magic, mage hand, mending, resistance;* 1st—*burning hands, obscuring mist.*

Stratiglynculcies
Juvenile Silver Dragon

Elegant and reflective, Stratiglynculcies has just begun to be amazed at the world around her. An avid traveler, she finds that the humanoid races simply astound her with the amount of knowledge and wisdom they can collect in such short life spans. While she spends much of her time in humanoid form (usually blending in seamlessly with any race or culture), she has been known to assume other shapes in the pursuit of knowledge. Recently, Stratiglynculcies has taken to accompanying good-aligned parties of adventurers in expeditions to unexplored lands or ruined settlements. She often forgets what a "rush" these shorter-lived creatures are in, however, and can be left behind when she spends weeks or even months studying a new find.

Stratiglynculcies: Female juvenile silver dragon; CR 10; Large dragon (cold); HD 16d12+48, hp 152; Init +0; Spd 40 ft., fly 150 ft. (average); AC 24, touch 9, flat-footed 24; Base Atk +16; Grp +24; Atk +19 melee (2d6+4, bite); Full Atk +19 melee (2d6+4, bite), +14 melee (1d8+2, 2 claws), +14 melee (1d6+2, 2 wings), +14 melee (1d8+6, tail slap); Space/Reach 10 ft./5 ft. (10 ft. with bite); SA breath weapon, spell-like abilities, spells; SQ alternate form, blindsense 60 ft., cloudwalking, darkvision 120 ft., immunity to acid, cold, magic sleep effects, and paralysis, low-light vision, vulnerability to fire, spell resistance 16; AL LG; SV Fort +13, Ref +10, Will +14; Str 19, Dex 10, Con 17, Int 18, Wis 19, Cha 18.

Skills and Feats: Bluff +12, Concentration +15, Diplomacy +16, Disguise +20, Heal +21, Hide –4, Intimidate +6, Jump +24, Knowledge (arcana) +12, Knowledge (history) +12, Knowledge (nature) +12, Listen +20, Move Silently +3, Profession (herbalist) +9, Search +20, Sense Motive +20, Spellcraft +13, Spot +18; Awaken Spell Resistance, Combat Expertise, Flyby Attack, Improved Maneuverability, Power Attack, Wingover.

Breath Weapon (Su): 40-ft. cone, 8d8 cold, Reflex DC 21 half; or 40-ft. cone, paralysis 1d6+4 rounds, Fortitude DC 21 negates.

Spell-Like Abilities: 2/day—*feather fall.* Caster level 4th.

Spells: As 3rd-level sorcerer.

Sorcerer Spells Known (6/6; save DC 14 + spell level): 0—*detect magic, detect poison, disrupt undead, mending, prestidigitation;* 1st—*burning hands, cure light wounds, magic missile.*

Lothirlondonis
Young Adult Silver Dragon

In his earliest youth, Lothirlondonis found he could not change shape as freely as his hatchmates. A kindly druid took him in and helped the silver hatchling develop his shapechanging skills. Ever since, Lothirlondonis has had a love for the forest and for forest creatures. He even pays homage to several nondraconic deities of the woodlands (such as Ehlonna) though he does not worship them. Lothirlondonis still spends most of his time in silver dragon shape but sometimes polymorphs into a fey creature and observes travelers who pass through his woods. If they show respect and tend toward conservation, he may aid them or protect them. If they do otherwise, Lothirlondonis does not hesitate to correct them.

Lothirlondonis: Male young adult silver dragon; CR 14; Large dragon (cold); HD 19d12+79, hp 202; Init +0; Spd 40 ft., fly 150 ft. (poor); AC 27, touch 9, flat-footed 27; Base Atk +19; Grp +29; Atk +24 melee (2d6+6, bite); Full Atk +24 melee (2d6+6, bite), +19 melee (1d8+3, 2 claws), +19 melee (1d6+3, 2 wings), +19 melee (1d8+9, tail slap); Space/Reach

Silver
DRAGON
Flight
Lawful Good
Cold Subtype
Warm Mountains
Underground
Old
24ft.
Regal and statuesque, silver dragons cheerfully assist good creatures in need, often appearing as kindly old men or fair damsels.
Feather fall
Polymorph self
Control weather
Control wind
Cloudwalker
Dessicated specimen recovered from slain troll, possibly used as strength totem.
Sub-adult
12 ft.
Detail of front claw.
Young
6 ft.
Wyrmling
3 feet
SARDINHA

10 ft./5 ft. (10 ft. with bite); SA breath weapon, frightful presence, spell-like abilities, spells; SQ alternate form, blindsense 60 ft., cloudwalking, damage reduction 5/magic, darkvision 120 ft., immunity to acid, cold, magic sleep effects, and paralysis, low-light vision, vulnerability to fire, spell resistance 20; AL LG; SV Fort +15, Ref +11, Will +15; Str 23, Dex 10, Con 19, Int 18, Wis 19, Cha 18.

Skills and Feats: Balance +7, Bluff +14, Concentration +18, Diplomacy +18, Disguise +23, Heal +9, Hide –4, Intimidate +6, Jump +31, Knowledge (arcana) +14, Knowledge (nature) +14, Listen +24, Perform (act) +9, Search +24, Sense Motive +24, Spellcraft +16, Spot +24, Tumble +5; Endure Blows, Flyby Attack, Heighten Breath, Hover, Power Attack, Toughness, Wingover.

Breath Weapon (Su): 40-ft. cone, 10d8 cold, Reflex DC 23 half (or higher if heightened); or 40-ft. cone, paralysis 1d6+5 rounds, Fortitude DC 23 negates (or higher if heightened).

Frightful Presence (Ex): 150-ft. radius, HD 18 or fewer, Will DC 23 negates.

Spell-Like Abilities: 2/day—*feather fall*. Caster level 5th.

Spells: As 5th-level sorcerer.

Sorcerer Spells Known (6/7/5; save DC 14 + spell level): 0—*dancing lights, detect magic, detect poison, mage hand, mending, prestidigitation;* 1st—*chill touch, divine shield, protection from evil, unseen servant;* 2nd—*cat's grace, darkness.*

Sallahtuwlishion
Adult Silver Dragon

When Sallahtuwlishion entered adulthood, she resisted putting aside her favorite nondraconic guise, that of a village innkeeper. Now, she still maintains the Silver Goblet Inn but spends only a few days a month there. Most of the villagers know of her draconic nature and cover "Sal's" disappearances, saying to outsiders that she has "gone off to visit relatives" and her adopted daughter runs the place in her absence. Sallahtuwlishion has found herself dragged reluctantly into draconic politics. Because of her willingness to mediate disputes and hold messages (useful talents for an innkeeper), she often finds herself speaking on behalf of older or more powerful dragons and other good or neutral beings.

Sallahtuwlishion: Female adult silver dragon; CR 15; Huge dragon (cold); HD 22d12+110, hp 253; Init +0; Spd 40 ft., fly 150 ft. (average); AC 29, touch 8, flat-footed 29; Base Atk +22; Grp +38; Atk +28 melee (2d8+8, bite); Full Atk +28 melee (2d8+8, bite), +23 melee (2d6+4, 2 claws), +23 melee (1d8+4, 2 wings), +23 melee (2d6+12, tail slap); Space/Reach 15 ft./10 ft. (15 ft. with bite); SA breath weapon, frightful presence, snatch, spell-like abilities, spells; SQ alternate form, blindsense 60 ft., cloudwalking, damage reduction 5/magic, darkvision 120 ft., immunity to acid, cold, magic sleep effects, and paralysis, low-light vision, vulnerability to fire, spell resistance 22; AL LG; SV Fort +18, Ref +13, Will +18; Str 27, Dex 10, Con 21, Int 20, Wis 21, Cha 20.

Skills and Feats: Bluff +15, Concentration +21, Diplomacy +19, Disguise +27, Escape Artist +18, Heal +16, Hide –8, Intimidate +7, Jump +34, Knowledge (arcana) +19, Knowledge (local) +19, Knowledge (nature) +19, Knowledge (religion) +19, Listen +27, Search +27, Sense Motive +27, Spellcraft +18, Spot +16; Flyby Attack, Heighten Breath, Hover, Improved Maneuverability, Power Attack, Recover Breath, Snatch, Wingover.

Breath Weapon (Su): 50-ft. cone, 12d8 cold, Reflex DC 26 half (or higher if heightened); or 50-ft. cone, paralysis 1d6+6 rounds, Fortitude DC 26 negates (or higher if heightened).

Frightful Presence (Ex): 180-ft. radius, HD 21 or fewer, Will DC 26 negates.

Snatch (Ex): Against Small or smaller creatures, bite for 2d8+8/round or claw for 2d6+4/round.

Spell-Like Abilities: 3/day—*fog cloud;* 2/day—*feather fall*. Caster level 7th.

Spells: As 7th-level sorcerer.

Sorcerer Spells Known (6/8/7/5; save DC 15 + spell level): 0—*cure minor wounds, dancing lights, detect magic, mage hand, mending, prestidigitation, read magic;* 1st—*divine shield, magic missile, protection from evil, sanctuary, true strike;* 2nd—*cat's grace, flaming sphere, shatter;* 3rd—*cure serious wounds, flame arrow.*

Livezzenvivexious
Mature Adult Silver Dragon

An unusually "draconic" silver dragon, Livezzenvivexious has little use for other forms. While he takes different shapes for short times, he does nearly all his fighting in dragon form—and Livezzenvivexious does a lot of fighting. Livezzenvivexious loathes evil creatures (particularly demons and devils) and despises evil dragons. Those creatures who worship evil deities also make Livezzenvivexious their enemies. He might use his power to polymorph to get himself into an evil creature's lair or a sadistic cult's stronghold, but when an adult silver dragon appears in their midst, Livezzenvivexious unleashes his righteous fury.

Livezzenvivexious: Male mature adult silver dragon; CR 18; Huge dragon (cold); HD 25d12+125, hp 287; Init +0; Spd 40 ft., fly 150 ft. (poor); AC 32, touch 8, flat-footed 32; Base Atk +25; Grp +42; Atk +32 melee (2d8+9, bite); Full Atk +32 melee (2d8+9, bite), +27 melee (2d6+4, 2 claws), +27 melee (1d8+4, 2 wings), +27 melee (2d6+13, tail slap); Space/Reach 15 ft./10 ft. (15 ft. with bite); SA breath weapon, crush, frightful presence, spell-like abilities, spells; SQ alternate form, blindsense 60 ft., cloudwalking, damage reduction 10/magic, darkvision 120 ft., immunity to acid, cold, magic sleep effects, and paralysis, low-light vision, vulnerability to fire, spell resistance 24; AL LG; SV Fort +19, Ref +14, Will +19; Str 29, Dex 10, Con 21, Int 20, Wis 21, Cha 20.

Skills and Feats: Bluff +15, Concentration +22, Diplomacy +23, Disguise +30, Heal +13, Hide –8, Intimidate +7, Jump +38, Knowledge (arcana) +25, Knowledge (local) +25, Knowledge (religion) +25, Listen +30, Move Silently +8, Search +30, Sense Motive +30, Spellcraft +18, Spot +30, Survival +16; Cleave, Flyby Attack, Great Cleave, Heighten Breath, Heighten Spell, Hover, Power Attack, Recover Breath, Wingover.

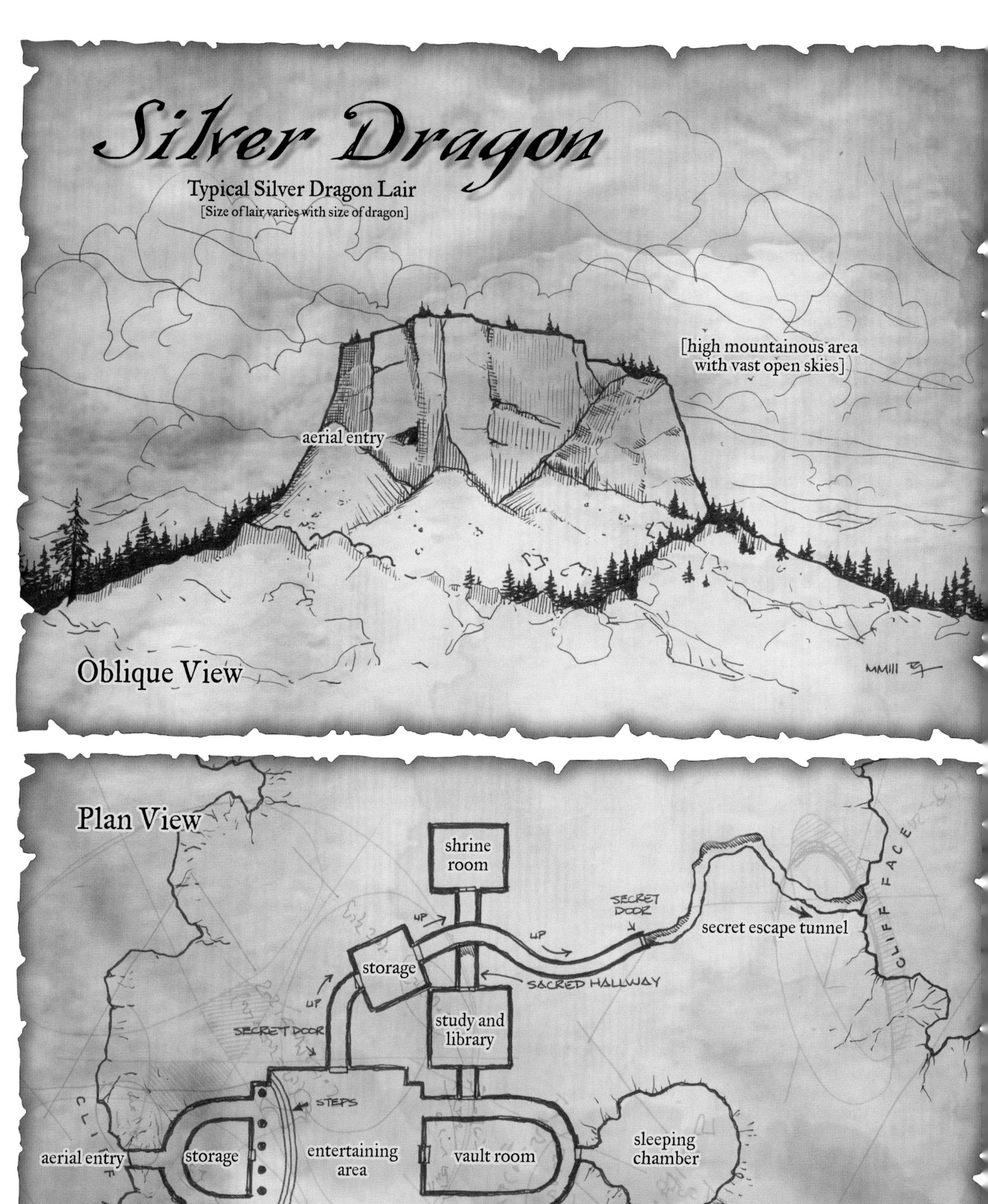

Silver Dragon
Typical Silver Dragon Lair
[Size of lair varies with size of dragon]
[high mountainous area with vast open skies]
aerial entry
Oblique View
MMIII TQ
Plan View
shrine room
SECRET DOOR
UP
UP
secret escape tunnel
CLIFF FACE
storage
UP
SACRED HALLWAY
study and library
SECRET DOOR
STEPS
aerial entry
storage
entertaining area
vault room
sleeping chamber
CLIFF FACE
clinic
clinic
MMIII TQ

Breath Weapon (Su): 50-ft. cone, 14d8 cold, Reflex DC 27 half (or higher if heightened); or 50-ft. cone, paralysis 1d6+7 rounds, Fortitude DC 26 negates (or higher if heightened).

Crush (Ex): Area 15 ft. by 15 ft.; Small or smaller opponents take 2d8+13 points of bludgeoning damage, and must succeed on a DC 27 Reflex save or be pinned.

Frightful Presence (Ex): 210-ft. radius, HD 24 or fewer, Will DC 27 negates.

Spell-Like Abilities: 3/day—*fog cloud;* 2/day—*feather fall.* Caster level 9th.

Spells: As 9th-level sorcerer.

Sorcerer Spells Known (6/8/7/7/5; save DC 15 + spell level): 0—*cure minor wounds, dancing lights, detect magic, ghost sound, mage hand, mending, prestidigitation, read magic;* 1st—*charm person, color spray, divine shield, magic missile, shield;* 2nd—*cat's grace, fog cloud, shatter, web;* 3rd—*hold person, slow, stinking cloud;* 4th—*cure critical wounds, Evard's black tentacles.*

Aesthyrondalaurai
Old Silver Dragon

Known throughout the planes as a master of lore and healing, Aesthyrondalaurai shares her insights with those who can find her. Legend has it that this old silver dragon always takes on a matronly form but seldom stays in one place for long. Still, she does maintain her own lair, high in the mountains, and keeps a strong friendship with eagles, pegasi, and other airborne creatures. When someone seeks knowledge, Aesthyrondalaurai often sends out her friends with clues to her location. If a seeker is persistent enough, he or she can find Aesthyrondalaurai, but it is never easy.

Aesthyrondalaurai: Female old silver dragon; CR 20; Huge dragon (cold); HD 28d12+168, hp 350; Init +4; Spd 40 ft., fly 150 ft. (poor); AC 35, touch 8, flat-footed 35; Base Atk +28; Grp +46; Atk +36 melee (2d8+10, bite); Full Atk +36 melee (2d8+10, bite), +31 melee (2d6+5, 2 claws), +31 melee (1d8+5, 2 wings), +31 melee (2d6+15, tail slap); Space/Reach 15 ft./10 ft. (15 ft. with bite); SA breath weapon, crush, frightful presence, spell-like abilities, spells; SQ alternate form, blindsense 60 ft., cloudwalking, damage reduction 10/magic, darkvision 120 ft., immunity to acid, cold, magic sleep effects, and paralysis, low-light vision, vulnerability to fire, spell resistance 26; AL LG; SV Fort +22, Ref +16, Will +22; Str 31, Dex 10, Con 23, Int 22, Wis 23, Cha 22.

Skills and Feats: Bluff +16, Concentration +23, Diplomacy +35, Disguise +34, Heal +21, Hide –8, Intimidate +8, Jump +42, Knowledge (arcana) +28, Knowledge (geography) +28, Knowledge (local) +28, Knowledge (religion) +28, Listen +34, Profession (herbalist) +11, Search +34, Sense Motive +34, Spellcraft +22, Spot +34, Survival +37; Cleave, Flyby Attack, Great Cleave, Heighten Breath, Heighten Spell, Hover, Improved Initiative, Power Attack, Recover Breath, Wingover.

Breath Weapon (Su): 50-ft. cone, 16d8 cold, Reflex DC 30 half (or higher if heightened); or 50-ft. cone, paralysis 1d6+8 rounds, Fortitude DC 30 negates (or higher if heightened).

Crush (Ex): Area 15 ft. by 15 ft.; Small or smaller opponents take 2d8+15 points of bludgeoning damage, and must succeed on a DC 30 Reflex save or be pinned.

Frightful Presence (Ex): 240-ft. radius, HD 27 or fewer, Will DC 30 negates.

Spell-Like Abilities: 3/day—*control winds, fog cloud;* 2/day—*feather fall.* Caster level 11th.

Spells: As 11th-level sorcerer.

Sorcerer Spells Known (6/8/8/7/7/5; save DC 16 + spell level): 0—*cure minor wounds, dancing lights, detect magic, ghost sound, guidance, mage hand, mending, prestidigitation, read magic;* 1st—*charm person, cure light wounds, divine shield, magic missile, shield;* 2nd—*cat's grace, cure moderate wounds, detect thoughts, fog cloud, locate object;* 3rd—*cure serious wounds, hold person, remove blindness/deafness, remove disease;* 4th—*cure critical wounds, neutralize poison, solid fog;* 5th—*break enchantment, shadow evocation.*

Freilaclanbarin
Very Old Silver Dragon

Nearly eight hundred years old, Freilaclanbarin has yet to reach his full strength and maturity, but he has a ready wit and a clever tongue. Once, it is said, he spent a hundred years in humanoid form advising a dwarven king but then he grew bored with the dwarf's constant desire for wealth. Freilaclanbarin keeps a hoard (as almost all dragons do), but he despises overt greed. Freilaclanbarin often trades with good and neutral creatures, charging a fair price for his knowledge or his treasures, and he builds his hoard through rewards and trade. When Freilaclanbarin does fight, however, he is mighty. He battles from the sky and uses his powerful breath weapon when he can, countering others' magic with his own.

Freilaclanbarin: Male very old silver dragon; CR 21; Huge dragon (cold); HD 31d12+186, hp 387; Init +0; Spd 40 ft., fly 150 ft. (poor); AC 38, touch 8, flat-footed 38; Base Atk +31; Grp +50; Atk +40 melee (2d8+11, bite); Full Atk +40 melee (2d8+11, bite), +35 melee (2d6+5, 2 claws), +35 melee (1d8+5, 2 wings), +35 melee (2d6+16, tail slap); Space/Reach 15 ft./10 ft. (15 ft. with bite); SA breath weapon, crush, frightful presence, rend, snatch, spell-like abilities, spells; SQ alternate form, blindsense 60 ft., cloudwalking, damage reduction 15/magic, darkvision 120 ft., immunity to acid, cold, magic sleep effects, and paralysis, low-light vision, vulnerability to fire, spell resistance 27; AL LG; SV Fort +23, Ref +19, Will +24; Str 33, Dex 10, Con 23, Int 24, Wis 25, Cha 24.

Skills and Feats: Balance +12, Bluff +22, Concentration +26, Diplomacy +38, Disguise +38, Escape Artist +24, Heal +19, Hide –8, Intimidate +9, Jump +46, Knowledge (arcana) +31, Knowledge (local) +31, Knowledge (nature) +31, Knowledge (religion) +30, Listen +38, Search +38, Sense Motive +38, Spellcraft +26, Spot +41, Survival +38; Cleave, Dire Charge, Flyby Attack, Great Cleave, Heighten Breath, Hover, Lightning Reflexes, Power Attack, Rend, Snatch, Wingover.

Breath Weapon (Su): 50-ft. cone, 18d8 cold, Reflex DC 31 half (or higher if heightened); or 50-ft. cone, paralysis 1d6+9 rounds, Fortitude DC 31 negates (or higher if heightened).

Crush (Ex): Area 15 ft. by 15 ft.; Small or smaller opponents take 2d8+16 points of bludgeoning damage, and must succeed on a DC 31 Reflex save or be pinned.

Frightful Presence (Ex): 270-ft. radius, HD 30 or fewer, Will DC 32 negates.

Rend (Ex): Extra damage 4d6+16.

Snatch (Ex): Against Small or smaller creatures, bite for 2d8+11/round or claw for 2d6+5/round.

Spell-Like Abilities: 3/day—*control winds, fog cloud;* 2/day—*feather fall.* Caster level 13th.

Spells: As 13th-level sorcerer.

Sorcerer Spells Known (6/8/8/8/7/7/5; save DC 17 + spell level): 0—*cure minor wounds, dancing lights, detect magic, ghost sound, guidance, mage hand, mending, prestidigitation, read magic;* 1st—*charm person, color spray, divine shield, magic missile, shield;* 2nd—*aid, cat's grace, fog cloud, shatter, web;* 3rd—*hold person, sleet storm, slow, stinking cloud;* 4th—*cure critical wounds, crushing despair, enervation, solid fog;* 5th—*greater command, hold monster, telekinesis;* 6th—*greater dispel magic, heal.*

Asaduanaivakka
Ancient Silver Dragon

Asaduanaivakka Silverstar considers herself a front-line warrior against the forces of evil. She has spent many of her considerable years traveling the world and the planes learning about the constant war between good and evil and she feels it is her time to step up and "do something about it." Occasionally found in the form of a humanoid paladin, Asaduanaivakka inspires and supports those who battle great evil. She has been known to employ lower-level adventurers to battle lesser evils, in the hope that they grow into powerful heroes, but more often, she joins a party of strong crusaders in climactic struggles. She has no compunctions about revealing her draconic nature and often uses her considerable reputation as leverage when seeking to join a party.

Asaduanaivakka: Female ancient silver dragon; CR 23; Gargantuan dragon (cold); HD 34d12+238, hp 459; Init +0; Spd 40 ft., fly 200 ft. (poor); AC 39, touch 6, flat-footed 39; Base Atk +34; Grp +58; Atk +42 melee (4d6+12, bite); Full Atk +42 melee (4d6+12, bite), +37 melee (2d8+6, 2 claws), +37 melee (2d6+6, 2 wings), +37 melee (2d8+18, tail slap); Space/Reach 20 ft./15 ft. (20 ft. with bite); SA breath weapon, crush, frightful presence, rend, snatch, spell-like abilities, spells, tail sweep; SQ alternate form, blindsense 60 ft., cloudwalking, damage reduction 15/magic, darkvision 120 ft., immunity to acid, cold, magic sleep effects, and paralysis, low-light vision, vulnerability to fire, spell resistance 29; AL LG; SV Fort +26, Ref +19, Will +27; Str 35, Dex 10, Con 25, Int 26, Wis 27, Cha 26.

Skills and Feats: Bluff +33, Climb +21, Concentration +27, Diplomacy +46, Disguise +42, Escape Artist +30, Handle Animal +17, Heal +23, Hide –12, Intimidate +40, Jump +50, Knowledge (arcana) +30, Knowledge (local) +30, Knowledge (nature) +30, Knowledge (the planes) +30, Knowledge (religion) +30, Listen +42, Ride +2, Search +42, Sense Motive +42, Spellcraft +26, Spot +27; Cleave, Flyby Attack, Heighten Breath, Hover, Improved Maneuverability, Power Attack, Quicken Breath, Recover Breath, Rend, Shock Wave, Snatch, Wingover.

Breath Weapon (Su): 60-ft. cone, 20d8 cold, Reflex DC 34 half (or higher if heightened); or 60-ft. cone, paralysis 1d6+10 rounds, Fortitude DC 34 negates (or higher if heightened).

Crush (Ex): Area 20 ft. by 20 ft.; Medium or smaller opponents take 4d6+18 points of bludgeoning damage, and must succeed on a DC 34 Reflex save or be pinned.

Frightful Presence (Ex): 300-ft. radius, HD 33 or fewer, Will DC 35 negates.

Rend (Ex): Extra damage 4d8+18.

Snatch (Ex): Against Medium or smaller creatures, bite for 4d6+12/round or claw for 2d8+6/round.

Spell-Like Abilities: 3/day—*control winds, fog cloud;* 2/day—*feather fall;* 1/day—*control weather.* Caster level 15th.

Spells: As 15th-level sorcerer.

Tail Sweep (Ex): Half-circle 30 ft. in diameter, Small or smaller opponents take 2d6+18 points of bludgeoning damage, Reflex DC 34 half.

Sorcerer Spells Known (6/8/8/8/8/7/7/5; save DC 18 + spell level): 0—*cure minor wounds, dancing lights, detect magic, ghost sound, guidance, mage hand, mending, prestidigitation, read magic;* 1st—*charm person, color spray, divine shield, magic missile, shield;* 2nd—*aid, cat's grace, fog cloud, shatter, speak with animals;* 3rd—*haste, hold person, stinking cloud, tongues;* 4th—*cure critical wounds, crushing despair, enervation, solid fog;* 5th—*Bigby's interposing hand, cloudkill, greater command, hold monster;* 6th—*chain lightning, greater dispel magic, heal;* 7th—*Bigby's grasping hand, power word stun.*

Kuulvaysheniruss
Wyrm Silver Dragon

It is hard to think of one of the oldest dragons in the world as a sad, old man, but Kuulvaysheniruss the Venerated has earned that description. For more than a hundred years, Kuulvaysheniruss was the cohort of a mighty paladin in the service of Heironeous, but the paladin was destroyed and attempts to revivify her failed. Now, Kuulvaysheniruss spends most of his time with his memories and doing little. Still, every so often, a particular quest or problem awakens Kuulvaysheniruss's once-lively heart from its slumber and he becomes the powerful dragon songs still sing of. He never takes humanoid form anymore, preferring to battle as he did beside his paladin friend, breathing blasts of paralyzing gas and cones of frigid air.

Kuulvaysheniruss: Male wyrm silver dragon; CR 24; Gargantuan dragon (cold); HD 37d12+333, hp 573; Init +0; Spd 40 ft., fly 200 ft. (poor); AC 42, touch 6, flat-footed 42; Base Atk +37; Grp +63; Atk +47 melee (4d6+14, bite); Full Atk +47 melee (4d6+14, bite), +42 melee (2d8+7, 2 claws), +42 melee (2d6+7, 2 wings), +42 melee (2d8+21, tail slap);

Space/Reach 20 ft./15 ft. (20 ft. with bite); SA breath weapon, crush, frightful presence, improved snatch, rend, spell-like abilities, spells, tail sweep; SQ alternate form, blindsense 60 ft., cloudwalking, damage reduction 20/magic, darkvision 120 ft., immunity to acid, cold, magic sleep effects, and paralysis, low-light vision, vulnerability to fire, spell resistance 30; AL LG; SV Fort +29, Ref +20, Will +29; Str 39, Dex 10, Con 29, Int 28, Wis 29, Cha 28.

Skills and Feats: Balance +7, Bluff +39, Climb +21, Concentration +31, Craft (weaving) +16, Diplomacy +53, Disguise +46, Escape Artist +35, Heal +26, Hide –12, Intimidate +48, Jump +55, Knowledge (arcana) +34, Knowledge (local) +34, Knowledge (nature) +34, Knowledge (the planes) +34, Knowledge (religion) +34, Listen +46, Search +46, Sense Motive +46, Spellcraft +28, Spot +44; Cleave, Flyby Attack, Great Cleave, Heighten Breath, Hover, Improved Maneuverability, Improved Snatch, Power Attack, Quicken Breath, Recover Breath, Rend, Snatch, Wingover.

Breath Weapon (Su): 60-ft. cone, 22d8 cold, Reflex DC 36 half (or higher if heightened); or 60-ft. cone, paralysis 1d6+11 rounds, Fortitude DC 36 negates (or higher if heightened).

Crush (Ex): Area 20 ft. by 20 ft.; Medium or smaller opponents take 4d6+21 points of bludgeoning damage, and must succeed on a DC 36 Reflex save or be pinned.

Frightful Presence (Ex): 330-ft. radius, HD 36 or fewer, Will DC 37 negates.

Improved Snatch (Ex): Against Large or smaller creatures, bite for 4d6+14/round or claw for 2d8+7/round.

Rend (Ex): Extra damage 4d8+21.

Spell-Like Abilities: 3/day—*control winds, fog cloud;* 2/day—*feather fall;* 1/day—*control weather.* Caster level 17th.

Spells: As 17th-level sorcerer.

Tail Sweep (Ex): Half-circle 30 ft. in diameter, Small or smaller opponents take 2d6+21 points of bludgeoning damage, Reflex DC 36 half.

Sorcerer Spells Known (6/9/8/8/8/8/7/7/5; save DC 19 + spell level): 0—*cure minor wounds, dancing lights, detect magic, ghost sound, guidance, mage hand, mending, prestidigitation, read magic;* 1st—*charm person, color spray, divine shield, magic missile, shield;* 2nd—*aid, cat's grace, fog cloud, heat metal, shatter;* 3rd—*haste, hold person, stinking cloud, tongues;* 4th—*cure critical wounds, crushing despair, enervation, solid fog;* 5th—*Bigby's interposing hand, cloudkill, greater command, hold monster;* 6th—*chain lightning, greater dispel magic, heal;* 7th—*Bigby's grasping hand, power word stun, prismatic spray;* 8th—*mass charm monster, whirlwind.*

Nymbryxion
Great Wyrm Silver Dragon

Nymbryxion the Shield of Law seldom visits the Material Plane anymore, preferring instead the uninterrupted sky of the Elemental Plane of Air. If she does travel back to the plane of her birth, she does so in the form of an ageless elven woman with silver eyes. Nymbryxion seldom speaks in either form, preferring to listen and to watch. When she does speak, she cuts right to the heart of any matter and her voice has the power of persuasion behind it. Nymbryxion has been known to visit elder dragons of nearly every type—even chromatic—to advise them on their place in the world. Metallic dragons take her words to heart; chromatic dragons often fly into a rage at her presence but few dare attack her. Nymbryxion is an unbelievably powerful opponent and many creatures of many planes owe her favors. An enemy of Nymbryxion can find few places on any plane to hide.

Nymbryxion: Female great wyrm silver dragon; CR 26; Colossal dragon (cold); HD 40d12+400, hp 660; Init +0; Spd 40 ft., fly 200 ft. (poor); AC 41, touch 2, flat-footed 41; Base Atk +40; Grp +72; Atk +47 melee (4d8+16, bite); Full Atk +47 melee (4d8+16, bite), +42 melee (4d6+8, 2 claws), +42 melee (2d8+8, 2 wings), +42 melee (4d6+24, tail slap); Space/Reach 30 ft./20 ft. (30 ft. with bite); SA breath weapon, crush, frightful presence, rend, snatch, spell-like abilities, spells, tail sweep; SQ alternate form, blindsense 60 ft., cloudwalking, damage reduction 20/magic, darkvision 120 ft., immunity to acid, cold, magic sleep effects, and paralysis, low-light vision, vulnerability to fire, spell resistance 32; AL LG; SV Fort +32, Ref +22, Will +32; Str 43, Dex 10, Con 31, Int 30, Wis 31, Cha 30.

Skills and Feats: Bluff +45, Concentration +35, Diplomacy +57, Disguise +50, Escape Artist +18, Handle Animal +20, Heal +32, Hide –16, Intimidate +54, Jump +60, Knowledge (arcana) +40, Knowledge (local) +40, Knowledge (nature) +50, Knowledge (religion) +40, Listen +53, Profession (herbalist) +30, Ride +2, Search +50, Sense Motive +53, Spellcraft +31, Spot +53, Survival +45; Cleave, Dire Charge, Flyby Attack, Great Cleave, Heighten Breath, Heighten Spell, Hover, Improved Maneuverability, Power Attack, Power Climb, Recover Breath, Rend, Snatch, Wingover.

Breath Weapon (Su): 70-ft. cone, 24d8 cold, Reflex DC 39 half (or higher if heightened); or 70-ft. cone, paralysis 1d6+12 rounds, Fortitude DC 39 negates (or higher if heightened).

Crush (Ex): Area 30 ft. by 30 ft.; Large or smaller opponents take 4d8+24 points of bludgeoning damage, and must succeed on a DC 39 Reflex save or be pinned.

Frightful Presence (Ex): 360-ft. radius, HD 39 or fewer, Will DC 40 negates.

Rend (Ex): Extra damage 8d6+24.

Snatch (Ex): Against Large or smaller creatures, bite for 4d8+16/round or claw for 4d6+8/round.

Spell-Like Abilities: 3/day—*control winds, fog cloud;* 2/day—*feather fall;* 1/day—*control weather, reverse gravity.* Caster level 19th.

Spells: As 19th-level sorcerer.

Tail Sweep (Ex): Half-circle 40 ft. in diameter, Large or smaller opponents take 2d8+24 points of bludgeoning damage, Reflex DC 39 half.

Sorcerer Spells Known (6/9/9/8/8/8/8/7/7/5; save DC 20 + spell level): 0—*cure minor wounds, dancing lights, detect magic, ghost sound, guidance, mage hand, mending, prestidigitation, read magic;* 1st—*charm person, color spray, divine shield, sanctuary, shield;* 2nd—*aid, calm emotions, cat's grace, fog cloud, shatter;* 3rd—*cure serious wounds, haste, speak with animals,* *tongues;* 4th—*cure critical wounds, crushing despair, enervation, solid fog;* 5th—*Bigby's interposing hand, cloudkill, greater command, hold monster;* 6th—*chain lightning, greater dispel magic, heal;* 7th—*Bigby's grasping hand, power word stun, prismatic spray;* 8th—*mass charm monster, sunburst, whirlwind;* 9th—*foresight, summon monster IX.*

SAMPLE WHITE DRAGONS

Detailed below are twelve sample white dragons, one of each age category. The descriptions include basic personality and encounter notes that the DM can flesh out for his campaign, along with a set of statistics that make the dragon ready to play.

Icewalking (Ex): All white dragons can move on icy surfaces as though using *spider climb* (as the spell).

Skills: A white dragon can move through water at its swim speed without making Swim checks. It has a +8 racial bonus on any Swim check to perform some special action or avoid a hazard. The dragon can always can choose to take 10 on a Swim check, even if distracted or endangered. The dragon can use the run action while swimming, provided it swims in a straight line.

Rime
Wyrmling White Dragon

Rime takes savage joy in hunting and is happiest when closing in for a kill. He delights in harrying and killing creatures larger than himself. His favorite prey includes polar bears and the occasional whale, provided he can catch the creature in shallow water where it cannot readily escape. When Rime is hungry, he's not picky about what he hunts.

Rime: Male wyrmling white dragon; CR 2; Tiny dragon (cold); HD 3d12+3; hp 22; Init +4; Spd 60 ft., burrow 30 ft., swim 60 ft., fly 150 ft. (average); AC 14, touch 12, flat-footed 14; Base Atk +3; Grp –5; Atk +5 melee (1d4, bite); Full Atk +5 melee (1d4, bite), +0 melee (1d3, 2 claws); Space/Reach 2-1/2 ft./0 ft. (5 ft. with bite); SA breath weapon; SQ blindsense 60 ft., darkvision 120 ft., icewalking, immunity to cold, magic sleep effects, and paralysis, low-light vision, vulnerability to fire; AL CE; SV Fort +4, Ref +3, Will +3; Str 11, Dex 10, Con 13, Int 6, Wis 11, Cha 6.

Skills and Feats: Hide +22, Listen +3, Search +1, Sense Motive +3, Spot +3, Swim +19; Improved Initiative, Power Attack.

Breath Weapon (Su): 15-ft. cone, 1d6 cold, Reflex DC 12 half.

Hrymgird
Very Young White Dragon

Hrymgird is equally at home in the air or the water. She loves foggy stretches of water, especially if they also have floating ice, protruding rocks, or other hazards. In such places, she alternately swims on the surface or flies just above it on silent wings, looking for prey.

Hrymgird attacks just about anything she meets, except dragons bigger than herself. She has a pugnacious nature and becomes ever more angry as a fight progresses. She screeches insults in Draconic whenever she attacks.

Hrymgird: Female very young white dragon; CR 3; Small dragon (cold); HD 6d12+6; hp 45; Init +0; Spd 60 ft., burrow 30 ft., swim 60 ft., fly 150 ft. (average); AC 16, touch 11, flat-footed 16; Base Atk +6; Grp +3; Atk +8 melee (1d6+1, bite); Full Atk +8 melee (1d6+1, bite), +3 melee (1d4, 2 claws); Space/Reach 5 ft./5 ft.; SA breath weapon; SQ blindsense 60 ft., darkvision 120 ft., icewalking, immunity to cold, magic sleep effects, and paralysis, low-light vision, vulnerability to fire; AL CE; SV Fort +6, Ref +5, Will +5; Str 13, Dex 10, Con 13, Int 6, Wis 11, Cha 6.

Skills and Feats: Hide +8, Listen +6, Move Silently +3, Search +4, Spot +9, Swim +17; Flyby Attack, Hover, Power Attack.

Breath Weapon (Su): 20-ft. cone, 2d6 cold, Reflex DC 14 half.

Kalkol
Young White Dragon

Kalkol often takes to the water, skulking under ice floes and other places where ice meets open water. A tireless hunter, Kalkol also keeps a wary eye out for a band of frost giants that have been entering his territory and stalking him for months, The giants hope to capture Kalkol and force him to serve them as a guard. Kalkol fears and hates the giants. He resents their great strength and their immunity to his breath weapon. Still, he is too stubborn to abandon his territory to the giants, so he remains in the area, avoiding the giants as much as he can.

Kalkol: Male young white dragon; CR 4; Medium dragon (cold); HD 9d12+18; hp 76; Init +4; Spd 60 ft., burrow 30 ft., fly 200 ft. (poor), swim 60 ft.; AC 18, touch 10, flat-footed 18; Base Atk +9; Grp +11; Atk +11 melee (1d8+2, bite); Full Atk +11 melee (1d8+2, bite), +6 melee (1d6+1, 2 claws), +6 melee (1d4+1, 2 wings); Space/Reach 5 ft./5 ft.; SA breath weapon; SQ blindsense 60 ft., darkvision 120 ft., icewalking, immunity to cold, magic sleep effects, and paralysis, low-light vision, vulnerability to fire; AL CE; SV Fort +8, Ref +6, Will +6; Str 15, Dex 10, Con 15, Int 6, Wis 11, Cha 6.

Skills and Feats: Hide +7, Listen +12, Spot +12, Swim +22; Flyby Attack, Hover, Improved Initiative, Wingover.

Breath Weapon (Su): 30-ft. cone, 3d6 cold, Reflex DC 16 half.

Haaldisath
Juvenile White Dragon

Brutal and direct, Haaldisath has survived for this long due primarily to her extreme cowardice. She has just enough wit to avoid capture or death at the hands of more powerful opponents and avoids protracted combat with any foe. If an enemy survives Haaldisath's powerful breath and fends off a pass or two from the air, she flees. She may return, if she has reason to believe her foes have sustained significant damage—or if they approach her lair—but she prefers victims to opponents and a quick meal to a challenging fight.

Haaldisath: Female juvenile white dragon; CR 6; Medium dragon (cold); HD 12d12+24; hp 102; Init +0; Spd 60 ft., burrow 30 ft., swim 60 ft., fly 200 ft. (poor); AC 21, touch 10, flat-footed 21; Base Atk +12; Grp +15; Atk +15 melee (1d8+3, bite); Full Atk +15 melee (1d8+3, bite), +10 melee (1d6+1, 2 claws), +10 melee (1d4+1, 2 wings); Space/Reach 5 ft./5 ft.; SA breath weapon, spell-like abilities; SQ blindsense 60 ft., darkvision 120 ft., icewalking, immunity to cold, magic sleep effects, and paralysis, low-light vision, vulnerability to fire; AL CE; SV Fort +10, Ref +8, Will +8; Str 17, Dex 10, Con 15, Int 8, Wis 11, Cha 8.

Skills and Feats: Concentration +8, Intimidate +14, Listen +15, Search +14, Sense Motive +12, Spot +12, Swim +11; Enlarge Breath, Flyby Attack, Hover, Power Attack, Wingover.

Breath Weapon (Su): 30-ft. cone (45-ft. cone if enlarged), 4d6 cold, Reflex DC 18 half.

Spell-Like Abilities: 1/day—*fog cloud.* Caster level 4th.

Nidhogrym
Young Adult White Dragon

Nidhogrym's overconfidence has led him to a sorry state in life for any dragon. Captured by a small band of frost giants, he's spent several years in captivity, serving a variety of different masters. The giants keep him on a leash of greed: they allow Nidhogrym to keep a portion of all the treasure he helps steal from their enemies, but he must keep it in their lair. He is utterly miserable. Still, he makes up for that indignity with ferocity. Diving out of the air and attacking the frost giants' foes gives him a fierce joy, and Nidhogrym, backed by such powerful "allies," has defeated opponents of greater power than he could normally hope to survive.

Nidhogrym: Male young adult white dragon; CR 8; Large dragon (cold); HD 15d12+45; hp 142; Init +0; Spd 60 ft., burrow 30 ft., swim 60 ft., fly 200 ft. (average); AC 23, touch 9, flat-footed 23; Base Atk +15; Grp +23; Atk +18 melee (2d6+4, bite); Full Atk +18 melee (2d6+4, bite), +13 melee (1d8+2, 2 claws), +13 melee (1d6+2, 2 wings), +13 melee (1d8+6, tail slap); Space/Reach 10 ft./5 ft. (10 ft. with bite); SA breath weapon, frightful presence, spell-like abilities; SQ blindsense 60 ft., damage reduction 5/magic, darkvision 120 ft., icewalking, immunity to cold, magic sleep effects, and paralysis, low-light vision, spell resistance 16, vulnerability to fire; AL CE; SV Fort +12, Ref +9, Will +9; Str 19, Dex 10, Con 17, Int 8, Wis 11, Cha 10.

Skills and Feats: Hide +14, Listen +18, Move Silently +18, Search +17, Spot +18, Swim +12; Flyby Attack, Hover, Improved Maneuverability, Power Attack, Power Dive, Recover Breath.

Breath Weapon (Su): 40-ft. cone, 5d6 cold, Reflex DC 20 half.

Frightful Presence (Ex): 150-ft. radius, HD 14 or fewer, Will DC 16 negates.

Spell-Like Abilities: 1/day—*fog cloud.* Caster level 5th.

Cealdia
Adult White Dragon

Cealdia has survived many years in the frozen northern world by knowing her limitations. She is not the strongest, smartest, or largest predator, and she realizes plenty of creatures exist that are ready and willing to destroy her for a variety of a reasons. She spends most of her time in her lair—a complex series of underground, icy tunnels—and often uses her small magical skills to lure enemies into traps or ambushes. When Cealdia must fight in the open, she prepares ahead of time and prefers fighting from above. She is a cautious opponent and is not above a little judicious bargaining if things do not appear to be going her way.

Cealdia: Female adult white dragon; CR 10; Large dragon (cold); HD 18d12+72, hp 189; Init +4; Spd 60 ft., burrow 30 ft., swim 60 ft., fly 200 ft. (poor); AC 26, touch 9, flat-footed 26; Base Atk +18; Grp +28; Atk +23 melee (2d6+6, bite); Full Atk +23 melee (2d6+6, bite), +18 melee (1d8+3, 2 claws), +18 melee (1d6+3, 2 wings), +18 melee (1d8+9, tail slap); Space/Reach 10 ft./5 ft. (10 ft. with bite); SA breath weapon, frightful presence, spell-like abilities, spells; SQ blindsense 60 ft., damage reduction 5/magic, darkvision 120 ft., icewalking, immunity to cold, magic sleep effects, and paralysis, low-light vision, spell resistance 18, vulnerability to fire; AL CE; SV Fort +15, Ref +13, Will +11; Str 23, Dex 10, Con 19, Int 10, Wis 11, Cha 12.

Skills and Feats: Bluff +22, Concentration +22, Diplomacy +20, Hide –4, Intimidate +3, Listen +18, Search +18, Sense Motive +9, Spellcraft +4, Spot +18, Swim +14; Cleave, Flyby Attack, Hover, Improved Initiative, Lightning Reflexes, Power Attack, Wingover.

Breath Weapon (Su): 40-ft. cone, 6d6 cold, Reflex DC 23 half.

Frightful Presence (Ex): 180-ft. radius, HD 17 or fewer, Will DC 20 negates.

Spell-Like Abilities: 3/day—*gust of wind;* 1/day—*fog cloud.* Caster level 6th; save DC 11+ spell level.

Spells: As 1st-level sorcerer.

Sorcerer Spells Known (5/4; save DC 11 + spell level): 0—*dancing lights, daze, ghost sound, resistance, prestidigitation;* 1st—*reduce elemental vulnerability, true strike.*

Bestlaranathion
Mature Adult White Dragon

Though intelligent, Bestlaranathion proves as capricious as a winter wind and as savage as any wild animal. He has recently learned to speak Common, and has come to think of himself as something of a diplomat. Unfortunately, his efforts at diplomacy usually sink to the level of stark threats, and even when he is able to browbeat an unfortunate creature into some kind of agreement, Bestlaranathion seldom contains his baser instincts for very long and he usually winds up attacking his reluctant allies.

Bestlaranathion frequently roams far afield, and might appear almost anywhere. About half the time, Bestlaranathion simply tries to ambush characters, hoping for a quick kill. The

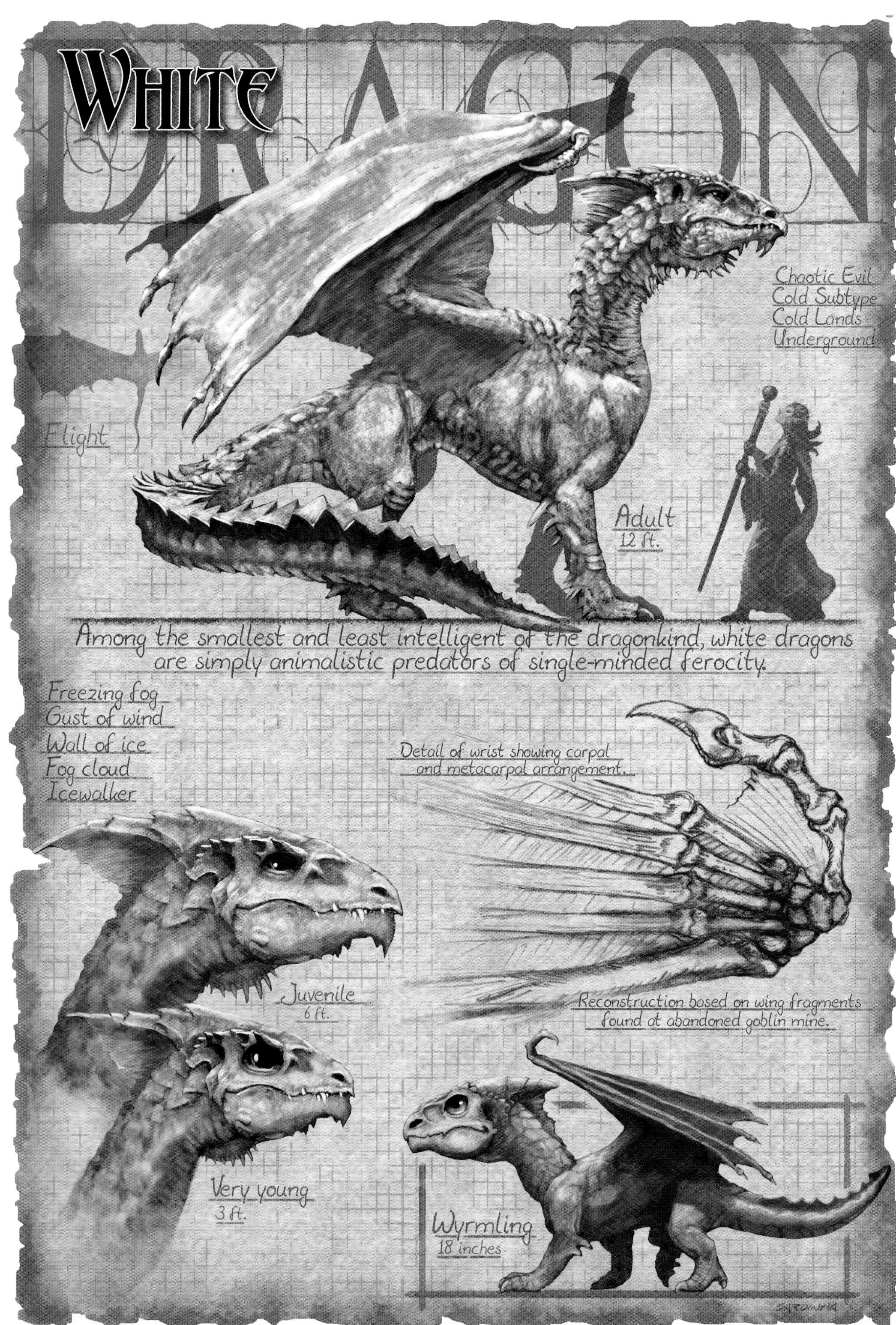
White
DRAGON
Chaotic Evil
Cold Subtype
Cold Lands
Underground
Flight
Adult
12 ft.
Among the smallest and least intelligent of the dragonkind, white dragons are simply animalistic predators of single-minded ferocity.
Freezing fog
Gust of wind
Wall of ice
Fog cloud
Icewalker
Detail of wrist showing carpal and metacarpal arrangement.
Juvenile
6 ft.
Reconstruction based on wing fragments found at abandoned goblin mine.
Very young
3 ft.
Wyrmling
18 inches
SARONHA

rest of the time, the dragon begins an encounter with some show of force that brings his frightful presence into play, but he also makes at least a half-hearted attempt to negotiate with the characters in some fashion. He might demand to know their business, try to extort treasure, or simply converse. Eventually, however, Bestlaranathion's violent nature gets the better of him and he attacks.

Bestlaranathion: Male mature adult white dragon; CR 12; Huge dragon (cold); HD 21d12+105, hp 241; Init +0; Spd 60 ft., burrow 30 ft., swim 60 ft., fly 200 ft. (poor); AC 28, touch 8, flat-footed 28; Base Atk +21; Grp +37; Atk +27 melee (2d8+8, bite); Full Atk +27 melee (2d8+8, bite), +22 melee (2d6+4, 2 claws), +22 melee (1d8+4, 2 wings), +22 melee (2d6+12, tail slap); Space/Reach 15 ft./10 ft. (15 ft. with bite); SA breath weapon, crush, frightful presence, improved snatch, spell-like abilities, spells; SQ blindsense 60 ft., damage reduction 10/magic, darkvision 120 ft., icewalking, immunity to cold, magic sleep effects, and paralysis, low-light vision, spell resistance 20, vulnerability to fire; AL CE; SV Fort +17, Ref +12, Will +13; Str 27, Dex 10, Con 21, Int 12, Wis 13, Cha 12.

Skills and Feats: Concentration +19, Hide +13, Intimidate +15, Knowledge (nature) +15, Listen +22, Move Silently +21, Search +22, Spellcraft +11, Spot +22, Swim +16; Flyby Attack, Hover, Improved Snatch, Power Attack, Shape Breath, Snatch, Spreading Breath, Wingover.

Breath Weapon (Su): 50-ft. cone (100-ft. line if shaped, 25-ft. spread if spreading), 7d6 cold, Reflex DC 25 half.

Crush (Ex): Area 15 ft. by 15 ft.; Small or smaller opponents take 2d8+15 points of bludgeoning damage, and must succeed on a DC 25 Reflex save or be pinned.

Frightful Presence (Ex): 210-ft. radius, HD 20 or fewer, Will DC 21 negates.

Improved Snatch (Ex): Against Medium or smaller creatures, bite for 2d8+8/round or claw for 2d6+4/round.

Spell-Like Abilities: 3/day—*gust of wind;* 1/day *fog cloud.* Caster level 7th; save DC 11 + spell level.

Spells: As 3rd-level sorcerer.

Sorcerer Spells Known (6/6; save DC 11 + spell level): 0—*arcane mark, dancing lights, detect magic, mage hand, resistance;* 1st—*burning hands, reduce elemental vulnerability, shield.*

Yeridajniosjuth
Old White Dragon

Yeridajniosjuth spent many years nursing envy and hatred of those more powerful than she and now this cold and cruel white dragon is in a position for some payback. Rather than settle into a lair and dominate a particular territory, Yeridajniosjuth entertains herself by hunting other dragons and destroying or dominating them. Her favored opponents are young or juvenile metallic dragons (particularly brass or gold), but she is not above attacking red or even other white dragons when she thinks she can win. Yeridajniosjuth's favorite opponent, however, is a more powerful or larger creature—dragon, giant, or anything else—that has been wounded by another. Nothing makes Yeridajniosjuth feel more pleased and superior.

Yeridajniosjuth: Female old white dragon; CR 15; Huge dragon (cold); HD 24d12+120, hp 276; Init +4; Spd 60 ft., burrow 30 ft., swim 60 ft., fly 200 ft. (poor); AC 31, touch 8, flat-footed 31; Base Atk +24; Grp +41; Atk +31 melee (2d8+9, bite); Full Atk +31 melee (2d8+9, bite), +26 melee (2d6+4, 2 claws), +26 melee (1d8+4, 2 wings), +26 melee (2d6+13, tail slap); Space/Reach 15 ft./10 ft. (15 ft. with bite); SA breath weapon, crush, *freezing fog,* frightful presence, rend, snatch, spell-like abilities, spells; SQ blindsense 60 ft., damage reduction 10/magic, darkvision 120 ft., icewalking, immunity to cold, magic sleep effects, and paralysis, low-light vision, spell resistance 21, vulnerability to fire; AL CE; SV Fort +19, Ref +14, Will +15; Str 29, Dex 10, Con 21, Int 12, Wis 13, Cha 12.

Skills and Feats: Bluff +7, Concentration +19, Diplomacy +3, Hide +16, Intimidate +15, Knowledge (nature) +17, Listen +25, Move Silently +24, Search +25, Spellcraft +7, Spot +25, Swim +33; Cleave, Flyby Attack, Hover, Improved Initiative, Power Attack, Quicken Breath, Recover Breath, Rend, Snatch, Wingover.

Breath Weapon (Su): 50-ft. cone, 8d6 cold, Reflex DC 27 half.

Crush (Ex): Area 15 ft. by 15 ft.; Small or smaller opponents take 2d8+13 points of bludgeoning damage, and must succeed on a DC 27 Reflex save or be pinned.

***Freezing Fog* (Sp):** 3/day; as *solid fog* cast by an 8th-level caster except that slippery ice forms in the cloud, creating a grease effect, DC 23 Reflex save to avoid falling.

Frightful Presence (Ex): 240-ft. radius, HD 23 or fewer, Will DC 23 negates.

Rend (Ex): Extra damage 4d6+13.

Snatch (Ex): Against Small or smaller creatures, bite for 2d8+9/round or claw for 2d6+4/round.

Spell-Like Abilities: 3/day—*gust of wind;* 1/day—*fog cloud.* Caster level 8th; save DC 11 + spell level.

Spells: As 5th-level sorcerer.

Sorcerer Spells Known (6/7/4; save DC 11 + spell level): 0—*arcane mark, dancing lights, detect magic, mage hand, read magic, resistance;* 1st—*burning hands , magic missile, reduce elemental vulnerability, shield;* 2nd—*darkness, resist energy.*

Sepsecolskegyth
Very Old White Dragon

Unusually clever for a white dragon, Sepsecolskegyth has a personality like an icy, rusted blade. He is irascible, unpleasant, and thoroughly evil. While his strength assures him of few challengers, Sepsecolskegyth prefers intimidation to overt action. Several tribes of nomadic humanoids pay the old villain tribute in food and treasure, and recently he's even turned the tables on a tribe of frost giants, enslaving a half-dozen or so to do his bidding. When threatened or challenged, Sepsecolskegyth makes good use of his enslaved minions, his breath weapon, and his magic, preferring to avoid direct physical confrontation whenever possible.

Sepsecolskegyth: Male very old white dragon; CR 17; Huge dragon (cold); HD 27d12+162, hp 337; Init +0; Spd 60 ft., burrow 30 ft., swim 60 ft., fly 200 ft. (average); AC 34, touch 8, flat-footed 34; Base Atk +27; Grp +45; Atk +35 melee (2d8+10, bite); Full Atk +35 melee (2d8+10, bite), +30 melee (2d6+5, 2 claws), +30 melee (1d8+5, 2 wings), +30 melee (2d6+15, tail slap); Space/Reach 15 ft./10 ft. (15 ft. with bite); SA breath weapon, crush, *freezing fog*, frightful presence, rend, snatch, spell-like abilities, spells; SQ blindsense 60 ft., damage reduction 15/magic, darkvision 120 ft., icewalking, immunity to cold, magic sleep effects, and paralysis, low-light vision, spell resistance 23, vulnerability to fire; AL CE; SV Fort +21, Ref +19, Will +17; Str 31, Dex 10, Con 23, Int 14, Wis 15, Cha 14.

Skills and Feats: Bluff +8, Concentration +23, Diplomacy +4, Hide +19, Intimidate +20, Knowledge (arcana) +17, Knowledge (nature) +17, Listen +29, Move Silently +27, Search +29, Spellcraft +16, Spot +29, Swim +34, Survival +8; Cleave, Dire Charge, Great Cleave, Hover, Improved Maneuverability, Legendary Reflexes, Power Attack, Recover Breath, Rend, Snatch.

Breath Weapon (Su): 50-ft. cone, 9d6 cold, Reflex DC 29 half.

Crush (Ex): Area 15 ft. by 15 ft.; Small or smaller opponents take 2d8+15 points of bludgeoning damage, and must succeed on a DC 29 Reflex save or be pinned.

***Freezing Fog* (Sp):** 3/day; as *solid fog* cast by a 9th-level caster except that slippery ice forms in the cloud, creating a *grease* effect, Reflex DC 25 to avoid falling.

Frightful Presence (Ex): 270-ft. radius, HD 26 or fewer, Will DC 25 negates.

Rend (Ex): Extra damage 4d6+15.

Snatch (Ex): Against Small or smaller creatures, bite for 2d8+10/round or claw for 2d6+5/round.

Spell-Like Abilities: 3/day—*gust of wind;* 1/day—*fog cloud.* Caster level 9th; save DC 12 + spell level.

Spells: As 7th-level sorcerer.

Sorcerer Spells Known (6/7/7/4; Base Save DC 12+ spell level): 0—*arcane mark, detect magic, light, mage hand, prestidigitation, read magic;* 1st—*charm person, magic missile, protection from evil, shield, true strike;* 2nd—*fog cloud, protection from arrows, resist energy;* 3rd—*dispel magic, lightning bolt.*

Csarivchizzik
Ancient White Dragon

Once an aggressive, active predator, Csarivchizzik has slowed down somewhat with age. It is not a lack of courage or power that changed her ways, but a growing knowledge of the threats in the world around her. Abandoning her lair in the northern mountains, she carried her treasure to a floating glacier far from the nearest coast. Csarivchizzik hunts whales and other sea creatures for food, and harries shipping for sport and treasure. Wisely, she usually attacks from below the surface of the water, erupting upward to spray her icy breath at surprised opponents. Csarivchizzik has a fondness for extraordinarily powerful magic items, however, and she can be lured out of her remote lair by rumors of artifacts in the hands of those unable to defend them from her predations.

Csarivchizzik: Female ancient white dragon; CR 18; Huge dragon (cold); HD 30d12+180, hp 375; Init +0; Spd 60 ft., burrow 30 ft., swim 60 ft., fly 200 ft. (average); AC 37, touch 8, flat-footed 37; Base Atk +30; Grp +49; Atk +39 melee (2d8+11, bite); Full Atk +39 melee (2d8+11, bite), +39 melee (2d6+5, 2 claws), +39 melee (1d8+5, 2 wings), +39 melee (2d6+16, tail slap); Space/Reach 15 ft./10 ft. (15 ft. with bite); SA breath weapon, crush, *freezing fog*, frightful presence, rend, snatch, spell-like abilities, spells; SQ blindsense 60 ft., damage reduction 15/magic, darkvision 120 ft., icewalking, immunity to cold, magic sleep effects, and paralysis, low-light vision, spell resistance 24, vulnerability to fire; AL CE; SV Fort +23, Ref +17, Will +19; Str 33, Dex 10, Con 23, Int 14, Wis 15, Cha 14.

Skills and Feats: Bluff +11, Concentration +26, Diplomacy +13, Hide +10, Intimidate +24, Knowledge (arcana) +18, Knowledge (nature) +18, Listen +32, Move Silently +30, Search +32, Spellcraft +18, Spot +32, Swim +35; Cleave, Dire Charge, Great Cleave, Hover, Improved Maneuverability, Improved Multiattack, Multiattack, Power Attack, Recover Breath, Rend, Snatch.

Breath Weapon (Su): 50-ft. cone, 10d6 cold, Reflex DC 31 half.

Crush (Ex): Area 15 ft. by 15 ft.; Small or smaller opponents take 2d8+16 points of bludgeoning damage, and must succeed on a DC 31 Reflex save or be pinned.

***Freezing Fog* (Sp):** 3/day; as *solid fog* cast by a 10th-level caster except that slippery ice forms in the cloud, creating a grease effect, DC 27 Reflex save to avoid falling.

Frightful Presence (Ex): 300-ft. radius, HD 29 or fewer, Will DC 27 negates

Rend (Ex): Extra damage 4d6+16.

Snatch (Ex): Against Small or smaller creatures, bite for 2d8+11/round or claw for 2d6+5/round.

Spell-Like Abilities: 3/day—*gust of wind, wall of ice;* 1/day—*fog cloud.* Caster level 11th; save DC 12 + spell level.

Spells: As 9th-level sorcerer.

Sorcerer Spells Known (6/7/7/6/4; save DC 12 + spell level): 0—*arcane mark, dancing lights, detect magic, flare, mage hand, read magic, resistance;* 1st—*alarm, burning hands, magic missile, shield, shocking grasp;* 2nd—*cat's grace, darkness, flaming sphere;* 3rd—*haste, protection from energy;* 4th—*fire shield, shout.*

Cheynchaytion
Wyrm White Dragon

One of the most powerful dragons in the world Cheynchaytion revels in his strength. He is wise enough to understand the white dragons' place in the world, but the ancient wyrm has found no threat he cannot overcome. Cheynchaytion enjoys luring challengers into his frozen, undermountain lair where he can use his icewalking abilities and his magic to full effect. Whenever Cheynchaytion travels, rumor of his coming arrives like a chill wind, and he leaves the cold frost of dread behind. Supremely confident, Cheynchaytion loves leaving survivors behind when he attacks—the more to tell of his glory and power.

White Dragon

Typical White Dragon Lair

[Size of lair varies with size of dragon]

Entry View of Ice Lair

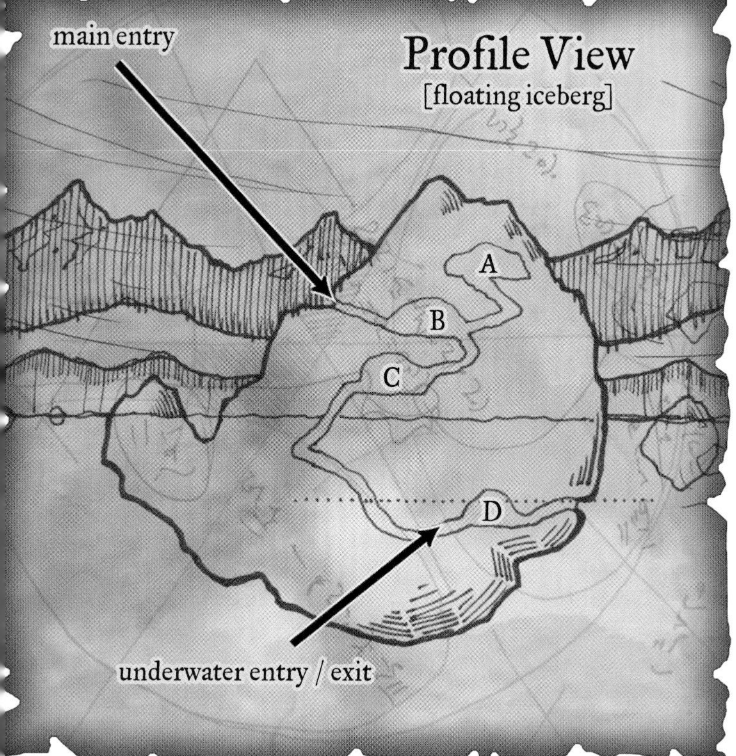

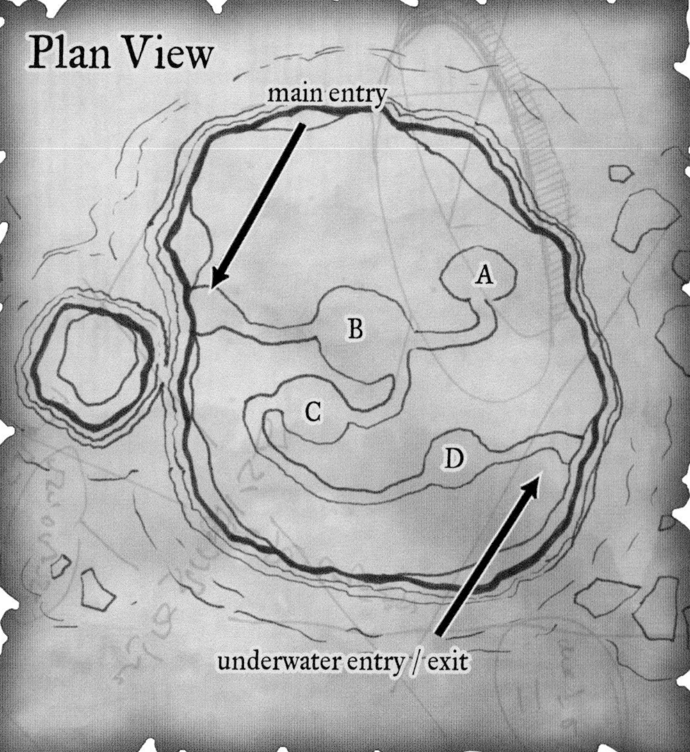

Cheynchaytion: Male wyrm white dragon; CR 19; Gargantuan dragon (cold); HD 33d12+231, hp 445; Init +0; Spd 60 ft., burrow 30 ft., swim 60 ft., fly 250 ft. (poor); AC 38, touch 6, flat-footed 38; Base Atk +33; Grp +57; Atk +41 melee (4d6+12, bite); Full Atk +41 melee (4d6+12, bite), +39 melee (2d8+6, 2 claws), +39 melee (2d6+6, 2 wings), +39 melee (2d8+18, tail slap); Space/Reach 30 ft./20 ft. (30 ft. with bite); SA breath weapon, crush, *freezing fog*, frightful presence, rend, snatch, spell-like abilities, spells, tail sweep; SQ blindsense 60 ft., damage reduction 20/magic, darkvision 120 ft., icewalking, immunity to cold, magic sleep effects, and paralysis, low-light vision, spell resistance 25, vulnerability to fire; AL CE; SV Fort +25, Ref +18, Will +22; Str 35, Dex 10, Con 25, Int 14, Wis 15, Cha 16.

Skills and Feats: Bluff +20, Concentration +27, Diplomacy +17, Hide +9, Intimidate +41, Knowledge (arcana) +18, Knowledge (nature) +18, Listen +35, Move Silently +33, Search +35, Spot +35, Swim +46; Cleave, Dire Charge, Hover, Improved Maneuverability, Iron Will, Multiattack, Power Attack, Recover Breath, Rend, Snatch, Suppress Weakness, Wingover.

Breath Weapon (Su): 60-ft. cone, 11d6 cold, Reflex DC 33 half.

Crush (Ex): Area 20 ft. by 20 ft.; Medium or smaller opponents take 4d6+18 points of bludgeoning damage, and must succeed on a DC 31 Reflex save or be pinned.

***Freezing Fog* (Sp):** 3/day; as *solid fog* cast by an 11th-level caster except that slippery ice forms in the cloud, creating a grease effect, Reflex DC 29 to avoid falling.

Frightful Presence (Ex): 330-ft. radius, HD 32 or fewer, Will DC 29 negates.

Rend (Ex): Extra damage 4d8+18.

Snatch (Ex): Against Medium or smaller creatures, bite for 4d6+12/round or claw for 2d8+6/round.

Spell-Like Abilities: 3/day—*gust of wind, wall of ice*; 1/day—*fog cloud*. Caster level 11th; save DC 13 + spell level.

Spells: As 11th-level sorcerer.

Tail Sweep (Ex): Half-circle 30 ft. in diameter, Small or smaller opponents take 2d6+18 points of bludgeoning damage, Reflex DC 33 half.

Sorcerer Spells Known (6/7/7/7/6/4; save DC 13 + spell level): 0—*arcane mark, dancing lights, detect magic, flare, ghost sound, mage hand, prestidigitation, read magic, resistance*; 1st—*alarm, burning hands, magic missile, shield, true strike*; 2nd—*cat's grace, darkness, detect thoughts, gust of wind, minor image*; 3rd—*dispel magic, haste, protection from energy, vampiric touch*; 4th—*crushing despair, fire shield, greater invisibility*; 5th—*cloudkill, feeblemind*.

Laximyrkcion
Great Wyrm White Dragon

Possessing a general scorn for others' existence rivaled by the most evil demons, Laximyrkcion Iceflame, Scourge of the North has amassed a treasure of such great renown that it attracts hunters from across the planes. Laximyrkcion welcomes these hunters with soul-chilling ferocity and greatly enjoys collecting the frozen heads of any who would challenge her. Fear is Laximyrkcion's greatest joy. Those who struggle to survive under her thrall often inform on or hinder adventurers who would destroy Laximyrkcion and take her treasure, simply because they dread her vengeance. These minions also keep the Scourge of the North informed about happenings beyond her realm, and Laximyrkcion has much knowledge of the world as a result.

Laximyrkcion: Female great wyrm white dragon; CR 21; Gargantuan dragon (cold); HD 36d12+288, hp 522; Init +0; Spd 60 ft., burrow 30 ft., swim 60 ft., fly 250 ft. (poor); AC 41, touch 6, flat-footed 41; Base Atk +36; Grp +61; Atk +45 melee (4d6+13, bite); Full Atk +45 melee (4d6+13, bite), +43 melee (2d8+6, 2 claws), +43 melee (2d6+6, 2 wings), +43 melee (2d8+19, tail slap); Space/Reach 20 ft./15 ft. (20 ft. with bite); SA breath weapon, crush, *freezing fog*, frightful presence, rend, snatch, spell-like abilities, spells, tail sweep; SQ blindsense 60 ft., damage reduction 20/magic, darkvision 120 ft., icewalking, immunity to cold, magic sleep effects, and paralysis, low-light vision, spell resistance 27, vulnerability to fire; AL CE; SV Fort +28, Ref +22, Will +24; Str 37, Dex 10, Con 27, Int 18, Wis 19, Cha 18.

Skills and Feats: Bluff +24, Concentration +30, Diplomacy +28, Hide +24, Intimidate +42, Knowledge (arcana) +25, Knowledge (nature) +25, Listen +40, Move Silently +36, Search +40, Sense Motive +14, Spellcraft +23, Spot +40, Swim +37, Survival +26; Cleave, Flyby Attack, Hover, Improved Maneuverability, Lightning Reflexes, Maximize Breath, Multiattack, Power Attack, Recover Breath, Rend, Snatch, Suppress Weakness, Wingover.

Breath Weapon (Su): 60-ft. cone, 12d6 cold, Reflex DC 36 half.

Crush (Ex): Area 20 ft. by 20 ft.; Medium or smaller opponents take 4d6+19 points of bludgeoning damage, and must succeed on a DC 36 Reflex save or be pinned.

***Freezing Fog* (Sp):** 3/day; as *solid fog* cast by a 13th-level caster except that slippery ice forms in the cloud, creating a grease effect, DC 29 Reflex save to avoid falling.

Frightful Presence (Ex): 360-ft. radius, HD 35 or fewer, Will DC 32 negates.

Rend (Ex): Extra damage 4d8+19.

Snatch (Ex): Against Medium or smaller creatures, bite for 4d6+13/round or claw for 2d8+6/round.

Spell-Like Abilities: 3/day—*gust of wind, wall of ice*; 1/day—*control weather, fog cloud*. Caster level 13th; save DC 14 + spell level.

Spells: As 13th-level sorcerer.

Tail Sweep (Ex): Half-circle 30 ft. in diameter, Small or smaller opponents take 2d6+19 points of bludgeoning damage, Reflex DC 36 half.

Sorcerer Spells Known (6/7/7/7/7/6/4; save DC 14 + spell level): 0—*arcane mark, dancing lights, detect magic, flare, ghost sound, mage hand, prestidigitation, read magic, resistance*; 1st—*alarm, burning hands, magic missile, shield, true strike*; 2nd—*cat's grace, darkness, detect thoughts, gust of wind, minor image*; 3rd—*dispel magic, haste, protection from energy, vampiric touch*; 4th—*bestow curse, fire shield, greater invisibility, solid fog*; 5th—*cloudkill, feeblemind, hold monster*; 6th—*acid fog, greater dispel magic*.

Appendix 1: The Dragon's Hoard

DM: *After slaying the mighty dragon, you loot its cavern. After you've sold everything, the total treasure value comes to 17,562 gp and 5 sp, including identification and appraisal costs.*

Players: *Yawn. What's next?*

If you and your players are becoming bored with hoards, it may be time to spice them up with a little more detail. Few players get excited by finding "six gems worth 100 gp each" or, worse yet, "three art objects worth 500 gp apiece." If you've taken the time to craft a unique dragon, take a few more minutes to craft a unique dragon's hoard.

The three basic components of a treasure hoard are coins, goods (gems and art objects), and items (mundane and magic). Within each of these categories, there are plenty of opportunities to spice up what the PCs find. Next time they come across a hoard, here's what you might hear:

Mialee: *So how do you think the dragon got these silver pieces from the kingdom across the sea?*

Lidda: *Never mind that, I'm too busy prying the emeralds out of this granite statue.*

Jozan: *Hey, Tordek, help me carry this platinum-inlaid teakwood table out of here!*

Tordek: *Sure, just let me finish this cask of dwarven ale I found. . . .*

COINS

The first trick to making a pile of coins seem less generic is to avoid round numbers. After you've determined how many thousands, hundreds, or tens of coins of a type are present, reduce the first digit by one (from 6,000 to 5,000, or from 100 to 90). Then replace each remaining zero with the result of a 1d10 roll.

Example: The DM rolls 2d6 × 1,000 to determine the number of gold pieces in a hoard and gets a result of 7,000. He first reduces this to 6,000, then rolls 1d10 for the hundreds, tens, and ones digits, getting results of 4, 5, and 1. This comes out to 6,451 gp—a nice, nonround number.

In the long run, this method slightly reduces the amount of coinage found by the PCs. If you're worried about this small shrinkage, you can easily add in an item of equivalent value elsewhere in the hoard. For instance, using the example above, you could drop in another item elsewhere in the hoard worth 500 to 600 gp to make up the difference.

Another option is to replace the coinage with another form of currency. Particularly for large transactions, coins aren't a very efficient mode of currency—paper money is easier to transport, and bars or ingots are easier to count.

In most medieval fantasy cultures, paper money is a rarity. However, IOUs, letters of credit, or similar "promises of payment" could easily exist, particularly in a mercantile culture. Such an item is literally worth far more than its weight in gold, but can probably only be exchanged in communities of reasonable size. As a rule of thumb, no IOU worth more than a town's gold piece limit can be exchanged in a community. What's more, unless you're trading it to the person who signed it in the first place, you may only be able get one-half its value in coins or goods (this is up to the DM and the situation). Player characters desperate to get full value might end up traveling from city to city in search of the merchant whose name is on the certificate. Of course, there's no guarantee that the item is genuine (see the Forgery skill, page 74 of the *Player's Handbook*), though you should use this sort of plot device sparingly.

Bars or ingots of metal are particularly common in societies that deal readily in such goods, such as those of dwarves and gnomes. They typically bear an identifying stamp. A typical trade bar of precious metal weighs 1 pound and is worth 50 coins of the same metal.

Trade Bar	Value	GP Value
Copper	50 cp	0.5 gp
Silver	50 sp	5 gp
Gold	50 gp	50 gp
Platinum	50 pp	500 gp

Table A–1: Trade Goods

d%	Goods
01–40	Food, drink, and spices
01–08	Ale, common (3 cp)
09–11	Ale, fine (2 gp)
12–17	Cinnamon (1 gp)
18	Cloves (15 gp)
19–23	Cooking oil, common (1 cp)
24–26	Cooking oil, rare (1 gp)
27–38	Flour (2 cp)
39–43	Ginger (2 gp)
44–48	Pepper (2 gp)
49	Saffron (15 gp)
50–52	Salt (5 gp)
53–62	Tea leaves (2 sp)
63–72	Tobacco (5 sp)
73–84	Wheat (1 cp)
85–92	Wine, common (3 cp)
93–95	Wine, fine (5 gp)
96–100	Other
41–70	Ore or lumber
01–02	Adamantine (100 gp)
03–22	Copper (5 sp)
23–27	Darkwood (10 gp)
28–37	Gold (50 gp)
38–62	Iron (1 sp)
63–72	Lead (5 cp)
73–75	Mithral (100 gp)
76–80	Platinum (500 gp)
81–95	Silver (5 gp)
96–100	Other
71–100	Textiles[1]
01	Cloth of gold (1,000 gp; 10 lb.)
02–04	Cloth of silver (100 gp; 10 lb.)
05–34	Cotton (1 gp; 0.5 lb.)
35–44	Linen (4 gp; 1 lb.)
45–47	Samite (250 gp; 5 lb.)
48–52	Satin (6 gp; 0.5 lb.)
53–62	Silk (10 gp; 0.5 lb.)
63–70	Velvet (15 gp; 2 lb.)
71–95	Wool (2 gp; 2 lb.)
96–100	Other

1 Prices and weights given are per square yard.

As the *Player's Handbook* points out (see Wealth Other than Coins, page 112 of the *Player's Handbook*), most wealth isn't in the form of coins or currency of any kind. It's easy to imagine that a dragon who periodically raids merchant caravans might have a hoard that includes a variety of trade goods. Since trade goods can generally be exchanged for full value, you can replace a quantity of coins in the hoard for an equivalent value of one or more trade goods. Of course, a shortage or surplus of certain trade goods in a particular area can adjust these prices dramatically, at your option. To generate these items randomly, use Table A–1: Trade Goods. Roll percentile dice to determine the category of the item ("Food, drink, and spices" is one category, for example), then roll again for the specific item within that category (such as "Ale, common").The prices given are per pound or pint (except for cloth, which is per square yard).

If you're not interested in variety in your currency, you can even inject a spark of interest into a pile of ordinary coins. Since every coin typically bears the mark of the kingdom, province, or city-state that minted it, simply putting a foreign or otherwise unusual mint-mark on your coins can result in the characters asking interesting questions about how the coins got there. If a dragon's hoard contains platinum coins bearing the imprint of a elf-headed spider, the characters may (correctly or incorrectly) suspect an alliance between the dragon and the drow.

GOODS

Of the three categories of treasure in a hoard, this one holds the best opportunities for making your dragon's hoard an interesting one. After all, there are dozens of varieties of gems and virtually unlimited variations on art objects. In some cases, you may create art objects so interesting that the characters prefer to keep them rather than selling them!

Goods, particularly art objects, provide you with a great opportunity for adventure hooks. Perhaps the characters want to find the creator of a particular sculpture or painting, or the original occupant of an ancient ornate throne.

HOW BIG IS THE PILE?

As the *Player's Handbook* states, a typical coin weighs about one-third of an ounce (50 per pound). But how much space do coins take up, and how big a pile do they make when gathered into a hoard? And do dragons really sleep on beds of coins?

A typical coin measures slightly more than an inch in diameter and is approximately one-tenth of an inch thick. A cubic foot (a volume 1 foot on each side) holds around 12,000 loosely stacked coins.

Of course, coins aren't usually stacked in cubic feet—they're scattered about in piles. A cubic foot of coins fills an area roughly 5 feet on a side to a depth of about 1/2 inch, or 3 feet on a side to a depth of 1 inch or so. That's enough space for a Small dragon to wallow around on, and even a Medium dragon can derive enjoyment from reclining on such a pile.

But larger dragons need an extraordinary number of coins to create a pile large enough to sleep on. A Large dragon needs at least 50,000 coins to create a "bed," while a Huge dragon needs 100,000 or more. Gargantuan or Colossal dragons might require piles of a half million or more coins in order to create a true "bed." And even then, this isn't an enormous pile but little more than a relatively thin layer of coins.

For this reason, most dragons don't actually have beds composed entirely of coins (though some collect copper pieces for exactly this reason). Still, it's nice to dream. . . .

Maybe some of the items are clearly stolen, and the PCs seek a reward by returning them to their rightful owners.

GEMS

Table 3–6: Gems on page 55 of the *Dungeon Master's Guide* has a long list of gemstones and appropriate values. The values given there are for cut and finished stones; uncut or rough gems are worth about one-third their finished value.

A character with the Craft (gemcutting) skill can improve a rough gemstone's value. The raw material cost is represented by the uncut stone. The check DC varies from 10 (for gemstones worth up to 50 gp) to 15 (for gemstones worth 50 to 500 gp) to 20 or higher (for gemstones worth more than 500 gp).

At the DM's option, a check that fails by 5 or more entirely ruins the uncut stone, forcing the character to start over with a new stone.

You can make gems more interesting by making them exotic or restricted. Perhaps the best pearls are retrieved in a certain bay by gnome divers, or maybe the elves control the emerald market. Maybe frost giants in your world use bloodstones for currency, suggesting that if the characters stumble across a cache of bloodstones, it probably came from (or is headed to) frost giants in the area.

ART OBJECTS

Table 3–7: Art Objects on page 55 of the *Dungeon Master's Guide* provides several examples of art objects to place as treasures. But when you're stocking dragon hoards, you can quickly exhaust that list. The tables given here provide the makings for thousands of art objects you can drop into your game with just a few rolls of percentile dice.

To randomly generate an art object, begin with Table A–2: Object Type. Roll d% or select the type of art object you are creating (artwork, clothing, furnishings, jewelry, musical instrument, toy or game, or utensil).

Table A–2: Object Type

d%	Type of Art Object
01–25	Artwork (see Table A–3: Artwork)
26–35	Clothing (see Table A–4: Clothing)
36–40	Furnishing (see Table A–5: Furnishings)
41–80	Jewelry (see Table A–6: Jewelry)
81–85	Musical instrument (see Table A–7: Musical Instruments)
86–90	Toy or game (see Table A–8: Toys and Games)
91–100	Utensil (see Table A–9: Utensils)

Table A–3: Artwork

d%	Type of Artwork
01–15	Bust [1] (H)
16–25	Geometric shape (H)
01–20	Cube
21–40	Cylinder
41–60	Dodecahedron
61–80	Pyramid
81–100	Sphere
26–40	Painting [1]
41–50	Pillar (H)
51–60	Statue, large or life-size [1] (H)
61–75	Statue, small [1] (H)
76–100	Tapestry/wall hanging [1] (S)

1 See Table A–12: Depictions to determine what the object pictures.

Table A–4: Clothing

d%	Article of Clothing [1]
01–15	Boots/shoes/slippers
16–25	Breeches/pantaloons/skirt
26–40	Cape/cloak
41–42	Eyepatch
43–47	Gloves
48–52	Hat
53–55	Helm
56–60	Mask
61–70	Shirt
71–85	Tabard/tunic
86–100	Vestments

1 Roll on Table A–11: Material (Soft) to determine what the clothing is made of.

Table A–5: Furnishings

d%	Type of Furnishing
01–03	Armoire (H)
04–06	Barrel (H)
07–10	Bench (H for bench; S for upholstery)
11–13	Blanket (S)
14–16	Bookcase (H)
17–19	Brazier (H)
20–22	Candelabra (H)
23–25	Candlestick (H)
26–28	Chair (H for chair; S for upholstery)
29–32	Chandelier (H)
33–35	Chest (H)
36–40	Couch/divan/sofa (H for couch; S for upholstery)
41–43	Curtain (S)
44–48	Desk (H)
49–53	Display case (H)
54–56	Footstool (H for footstool; S for upholstery)
57–59	Hourglass (H)
60–62	Lamp (H)
63–66	Mirror, hand (H)
67–69	Mirror, wall (H)
70–71	Pillow (S)
72–77	Rug (S)
78–80	Sack (S)
81–83	Sheets (S)
84–87	Table, dining (H)
88–91	Table, low (H)
92–100	Urn

Table A–6: Jewelry

d%	Type of Jewelry [1]
01–05	Amulet
06–11	Anklet
12–15	Armband/bracer
16–20	Belt
21–28	Bracelet
29–35	Brooch
36–40	Circlet
41–44	Crown
45–51	Earring(s)
52–54	Hair comb
55–57	Hat pin
58–61	Locket
62–67	Necklace
68–71	Pendant
72–73	Periapt
74–75	Phylactery
76–82	Pin
83–91	Ring
92–95	Scepter
96–100	Tiara

1 Roll once on Table A–10: Material (Hard) to determine the item's primary material, then 1d3–1 times on Table A–13: Embellishments.

Table A–7: Musical Instruments

d%	Type of Instrument
01–02	Alphorn
03	Bagpipes
04–05	Banjolele
06–07	Bell, hanging
08	Bones
09–10	Chimes, wind
11–12	Clavichord
13–14	Crumhorn
15–18	Drum
19–22	Drums, bongo
23–26	Drums, kettle
27–28	Dulcimer, hammered
29–32	Fiddle
33–36	Flute
37–39	Gong
40–43	Handbell
44–45	Harmonica
46–48	Harp
49–50	Harp, aeolian
51–52	Harpsichord
53–54	Hautbois
55–57	Horn, natural
58–60	Horn, shell
61–63	Lap-harp
64–65	Lur
66–68	Lute
69–71	Lyre
72–74	Mandolin
75	Organ, pipe
76–78	Pipes, pan
79	Psaltery
80–81	Recorder-flute
82	Shaum
83–84	Stones, wind
85–88	Tabor
89–92	Trumpet, herald's
93	Water-pipe
94–97	Whistle-pipe
98–100	Zither

Table A–8: Toys and Games

d%	Type of Toy or Game
01–10	Chess set (H)
11–20	Dice, pair (H)
21–35	Doll (S)
36–45	Doll, porcelain
46–55	Marbles, bag (H)
56–65	Mobile (H or S)
66–90	Music box (H)
91–100	Puppet (S)

Table A–9: Utensils

d%	Type of Utensil [1]
01–10	Bowl
11–20	Cup
21–30	Ewer
31–40	Goblet
41–50	Mug
51–60	Plate
61–70	Platter
71–80	Saucer
81–90	Tray
91–100	Vase

1 Roll on Table A–10: Material (Hard) to determine what the utensil is made of. In addition, there is a 25% chance that any utensil depicts a person or scene; roll on Table A–12: Depictions.

Table A–10: Material (Hard)

d%	Material	d%	Material
01–05	Bone		
06–08	Coral		
09–12	Crystal		
13–16	Glass		
17–21	Ivory/horn		
		01–12	Boar
		13–24	Cachalot whale
		25–36	Elephant
		37–48	Hippopotamus
		49–60	Hornbill
		61–72	Mammoth
		73–84	Narwhal
		85–88	Unicorn
		89–100	Walrus
22–46	Metal		
		01–02	Adamantine
		03–21	Brass
		22–43	Bronze
		44–61	Copper
		62–65	Gold
		66–78	Iron
		79–81	Lead
		82–84	Mithral
		85–87	Platinum
		88–91	Silver
		92–100	Steel
47–50	Mother of pearl		
51–70	Stone		
		01–13	Granite
		14–26	Limestone
		27–39	Marble
		40–52	Obsidian
		53–61	Onyx
		62–74	Sandstone
		75–87	Slate
		88–100	Soapstone
71–90	Wood, hard		
		01–10	Ash
		11–25	Chestnut
		26–35	Darkwood
		36–45	Hickory
		46–60	Mahogany
		61–70	Maple
		71–90	Oak
		91–100	Teak
91–100	Wood, soft		
		01–15	Alder
		16–25	Balsa
		26–45	Cedar
		46–65	Fir
		66–85	Pine
		86–100	Yew

Table A–11: Material (Soft)

d%	Material	d%	Material
01–40	Cloth		
		01–02	Cloth of gold
		03–22	Cotton
		23–32	Linen
		33–35	Samite
		36–50	Satin
		51–65	Silk
		66–80	Velvet
		81–100	Wool
41–55	Feathers		
		01–12	Eagle [1]
		13–22	Hawk [1]
		23–34	Quail
		35–44	Owl
		45–59	Peacock
		60–71	Pheasant
		72–83	Raven
		84–95	Swan
		96–100	Other
56–60	Feathers, exotic [2]		
		01–03	Achaierai
		04–05	Archon
		06–11	Arrowhawk
		12–14	Couatl
		15–24	Giant eagle
		25–34	Giant owl
		35–44	Griffon
		45–54	Hippogriff
		55–56	Lammasu
		57–58	Lillend
		59–68	Owlbear
		69–74	Pegasus
		75–76	Phoenix
		77–86	Roc
		87–92	Sphinx
		93–95	Vrock
		96–100	Other
61–75	Fur		
		01–03	Ape [1]
		04–07	Badger [1]
		08–22	Bear (black, brown, polar) [1]
		23–27	Beaver
		28–32	Boar [1]
		33–35	Camel
		36–41	Cheetah/leopard
		42–44	Ermine/mink
		45–48	Fox
		49–51	Horse
		50–57	Lion [1]
		58–60	Rabbit
		61–62	Raccoon
		63–67	Rat [1]
		68–70	Seal/sea lion
		71–73	Sheep
		74–79	Tiger [1]
		80–82	Weasel [1]
		83–89	Wolf [1]
		90–93	Wolverine*
		94–95	Worg
		96–100	Other
76–80	Fur, exotic [2]		
		01–04	Barghest
		05–13	Blink dog
		14–26	Displacer beast
		27–34	Girallon
		35–40	Griffon
		41–46	Hellcat
		47–55	Krenshar
		56–61	Manticore
		62–64	Rakshasa
		65–73	Shadow mastiff
		74–86	Winter wolf
		87–95	Yeth hound
		96–100	Other
81–95	Hide/skin		
		01–08	Alligator/crocodile
		09–11	Ape [1]
		12–13	Bat [1]
		14–20	Bison
		21–27	Boar [1]
		28–29	Camel
		30–40	Cow/ox
		41–48	Deer
		49–53	Elephant
		54–58	Horse
		59–63	Lizard
		64–69	Pig
		70–74	Rhinoceros
		75–76	Seal/sea lion
		77–81	Shark [1]
		82–87	Sheep
		88–95	Snake
		96–100	Other
96–100	Hide/skin, exotic [2]		
		01–06	Basilisk
		07–11	Behir
		12–14	Bulette
		15–21	Chimera
		22–41	Dinosaur
		42–56	Dragon
		57–61	Dragonne
		62–68	Hydra
		69–73	Naga
		74–76	Purple worm
		77–79	Ravid
		80–82	Remorhaz
		83–85	Shocker lizard
		86–95	Wyvern
		96–100	Other

1 Roll d%: 01–75 typical animal; 76–90 dire animal; 91–97 celestial or fiendish animal, 98–00 celestial or fiendish dire animal.

2 An article made wholly or partially of an intelligent creature such as a rakshasa or a krenshar indicates much about the item's owner. Usually only evil individuals wear fur of sentient beings. However, small quantities of feathers can be harvested without killing or injuring the creature.

Table A–12: Depictions

d%	Scene
01–04	Battle
05–08	Boats
09–12	Castle
13–16	Children
17–20	Cityscape
21–24	Clouds
25–28	Dancing
29–32	Dragons
33–36	Flames
37–40	Flowers
41–44	Horse riders
45–48	Hunting
49–52	Knights
53–56	Love
57–60	Monsters
61–64	Mountains
65–68	Musicians
69–72	Pastoral
73–76	Religious icons
77–80	Soldiers
81–84	Spellcasters
85–88	Sports
89–92	Trees
93–96	Water
97–100	Weapons

Table A–13: Embellishments

d%	Embellishment
01–15	Carving
16–30	Engraving
31–42	Etching
43–57	Gems
58–72	Inlay
73–87	Mosaics
88–100	Plating

Once you've determined the object type, move to the appropriate table (Table A–3: Artwork, Table A–4: Clothing, Table A–5: Furnishing, Table A–6: Jewelry, Table A–7: Musical Instruments, Table A–8: Toys and Games, or Table A–9: Utensils) to find out exactly what the object is. In some cases, additional rolls on one or more tables may be required, based on the type of object or the sort of material it is made from.

Many of the table entries include a parenthetical label, either H or S, indicating whether the object in question is made of a hard material or a soft material. To determine the exact material, roll on Table A–10: Material (Hard) or Table A–11: Material (Soft) as appropriate.

For additional flourishes, you can roll on Table A–12: Depictions or Table A–13: Embellishments.

ITEMS

Adding mundane items or magic items to a hoard is a good way to spice it up. Dragons with Intelligence scores of 6 or higher are likely to use any items (mundane or magic) that are in their hoards. For instance, a red dragon with a chest full of flasks of alchemist's fire might put the chest in a place where its fiery breath could set the flammable substance on fire.

MUNDANE ITEMS

Table 3–8: Mundane Items on page 56 of the *Dungeon Master's Guide* has an extensive list of mundane (nonmagical) items that can be found as part of a treasure hoard. In addition to these, you can include luxury items such as perfume or incense. Roll d% or select from Table A–14: Mundane Luxury Items. Since the average value of the items on this table is only a fraction of the average value of the items in Table 3–8 in the *Dungeon Master's Guide*, roll 2d8 times on Table A–14 for each mundane item indicated by Table 3–5: Treasure in the *Dungeon Master's Guide*.

Table A–14: Mundane Luxury Items

d%	Luxury Item (Value)	Quantity
01–10	Book, common (5 gp)	2d6
11–17	Book, rare (50 gp)	1d4
18–27	Dye, common (5 sp per pint)	2d8 pints
28–34	Dye, rare (2 gp per pint)	1d4 pints
35–44	Incense, common (5 gp per lb.)	2d8 lb.
45–51	Incense, exotic (15 gp per oz.)	2d4 oz.
52–61	Ink (8 gp per oz.)	2d8 oz.
62–71	Lamp oil (1 sp per pint)	2d8 pints
72–76	Paper (40 gp per ream*)	1d4 reams
77–81	Parchment (20 gp per ream*)	2d4 reams
82–91	Perfume, common (1 gp per oz.)	2d8 oz.
92–96	Perfume, rare (5 gp per oz.)	1d4 oz.
97–100	Soap (5 sp per lb.)	2d10 lb.

* A ream is 100 sheets.

MAGIC ITEMS

It can be tempting to fill a dragon's hoard with an assortment of magic items usable by the dragon itself, such as rings, bracers, potions, and rods. Unless the dragon has ready access to a nearby city in which to purchase such items, however, it probably shouldn't be equipped as well as a typical NPC fighter or wizard. And while any intelligent dragon (one with an Intelligence score of 6 or higher) would be foolish to refrain from using a magic item to its advantage, unlike a typical NPC (whose power often depends on the gear he carries), the challenge a dragon poses derives primarily from its innate abilities, not the treasure it has gathered.

Except in special circumstances, a dragon probably shouldn't use more than one or two magic items out of its hoard. Even if you randomly place useful items, most dragons don't have the ability to identify magic items and thus can't easily determine what might or might not be useful. In addition, dragons have difficulty using many magic items, especially weapons and armor. (See the Rules: Dragons and Magic Items sidebar in Chapter 1.) If you decide to equip your dragon with a variety of magic items, you might consider awarding an ad hoc XP bonus to the characters (anywhere from +10% to +50%, depending on the situation) for defeating it, since the presence of useful magic items probably increases the difficulty of the encounter.

Here's a brief rundown of the utility of the various categories of magic items.

Armor and Shields: Most dragons have no use for such items unless they can assume a form that can wear them.

Weapons: Again, unless the dragon can polymorph or otherwise change its form, most weapons are better off stuck in a pile of coins to look nice.

Potions: Dragons appreciate the value of potions. Dragons with a Spellcraft skill modifier of +15 or better can take 10 to identify a potion, and won't let such items go to waste.

Rings: Dragons can wear magic rings without difficulty. Even if a dragon doesn't know exactly what a ring does, it's likely to wear it for the decorative value alone.

Rods: If a dragon can determine a rod's function, it's probably also intelligent enough to figure out a way to use it in an encounter.

Scrolls: As with potions, a dragon with a reasonably high Spellcraft skill modifier can probably decipher any scrolls in its hoard. If it's capable of using the scroll, it's more likely to use it than to let it decay into dust. A dragon's size may make scroll use tricky, and the DM is free to say that reading a scroll might be at least a full-round action for Huge and larger dragons, or even to say that such creatures can't unfurl a scroll at all. Remember that until a dragon can cast spells, no spells are considered to be on its class list.

Staffs: Like rods, staffs often find use by smart dragons who figure out their effects and can activate them. Remember that until a dragon can cast spells, no spells are considered to be on its class list.

Wands: As staffs, though Huge and larger dragons may have difficulty manipulating such small items (at the DM's discretion).

Wondrous Items: Magic items in this category must be handled on a case-by-case basis. Some, such as amulets, are easy for dragons to wear and gain the benefits from. Others either don't fit, aren't useful, or simply look better sitting on top of a pile of coins. Still, a party is likely to remember the green dragon with a half-dozen *ioun stones* whirling around its head!

SAMPLE HOARDS

Provided below are twenty-seven sample dragon hoards: one each for Challenge Rating 1 through Challenge Rating 27. Each represents approximately triple the expected treasure value of an encounter of that level, as normal for a dragon encounter.

If you use one of these hoards for a creature that doesn't normally have triple standard treasure, reduce the hoard's value accordingly, as given on the table below. For example, the CR 8 hoard is appropriate for a CR 12 dragon with standard treasure, and the CR 24 hoard is used for a CR 28 dragon with double standard treasure.

Hoard CR	Standard	Double Standard
1	—	—
2		1
3	1	2
4	1	3
5	2	4
6	2	5
7	3	6
8	4	7
9	5	8
10	6	9
11	7	10
12	8	11
13	9	12
14	10	13
15	11	14
16	12	15
17	13	16
18	14	17
19	15	18
20	16	18
21	16	19
22	17	19
23	17	20
24	17	20
25	18	21
26	18	22
27	18	23
28	19	24

A total value is given for each treasure hoard in its header line. This figure assumes full normal value for all objects (in many cases, items from the hoard can be sold for only half value by the PCs). Items marked with an asterisk (*) are likely to be used by dragons with an Intelligence score of 6 or higher (smart enough to know what they are and how to utilize them). The gold piece values of individual goods in each hoard are given in parentheses (gold piece values for items are given in the *Dungeon Master's Guide*).

You can easily swap out items in any hoard as appropriate for your game. Unless you specifically desire to give out more or less than the expected value of treasure for the encounter, any added items should replace items of a similar value.

For lairs with multiple dragons, use the treasure that corresponds to the total Encounter Level of the lair.

CR 1 (889 gp, 9 sp, 7 cp)

Coins: 3,697 cp, 113 gp.

Goods: Black pearl (700).

Items: Tanglefoot bag*.

CR 2 (1,799 gp, 5 sp, 5 cp)

Coins: 4,235 cp, 1,972 sp, 505 gp.

Goods: 2 moss agates (11 and 14), amber (90).

Items: Masterwork heavy flail, *potion of detect thoughts**, divine scroll of *doom, hold person,* and *silence.*

CR 3 (2,700 gp, 1 sp)

Coins: 2,511 sp, 179 gp.

Goods: None.

Items: Climber's kit, *potion of eagle's splendor**, *wand of shatter** (21 charges).

CR 4 (3,600 gp, 7 sp)

Coins: 2,307 sp, 370 gp, 59 pp.

Goods: Red garnet (80).

Items: *+1 dwarven waraxe.*

CR 5 (4,800 gp, 7 sp)

Coins: 3,757 sp, 741 gp.

Goods: Blue quartz (9), 2 bloodstones (50 each), fire opal (1,100).

Items: Medium masterwork chain shirt; Medium masterwork short sword, *+1 buckler, potion of nondetection.*

CR 6 (5,999 gp, 9 sp)

Coins: 6,129 sp, 657 gp.

Goods: Amethyst (90), deep blue spinel (600), satin robe with embroidered "M" (50).

Items: Alchemist's fire* (2 flasks), antitoxin (3 doses), *figurine of wondrous power** (silver raven).

CR 7 (7,800 gp, 3 sp)

Coins: 12,163 sp, 1,387 gp.

Goods: 2 eye agates (11 each), coral (50), aquamarine (700), black opal (1,300).

Items: Arcane scroll of *jump, mount,* and *water breathing, wand of ghoul touch** (30 charges).

CR 8 (10,200 gp)

Coins: 1,730 gp, 133 pp.

Goods: Glass music box (90), satin tapestry depicting knights riding to battle (2,000).

Items: *Potion of hide from animals, potion of true strike*, potion of cat's grace*, potion of cure light wounds*, wand of summon monster I** (25 charges).

CR 9 (13,500 gp)

Coins: 4,839 gp.

Goods: 2 obsidian (7 each), 3 white pearls (100 each), 6 amber (150 each).

Items: Arcane scroll of *silent image* and *invisibility*, divine scroll of *detect snares and pits* and *dispel magic*, *hat of disguise*, adamantine heavy shield, *+1 rapier*, *wand of detect secret doors* (35 charges).

CR 10 (17,400 gp)

Coins: 13,680 sp, 2,938 gp.

Goods: Small glass statuette of a wolf (100), marble bust of an infamous wizard (160), small crystal pyramid (700), painting of a pastoral scene (900), silver tiara set with tiny emeralds (1,600).

Items: *Potion of remove fear*, *potion of disguise self*, arcane scroll of *protection from arrows*, *+1 animated large steel shield**.

CR 11 (22,500 gp)

Coins: 6,775 gp, 785 pp.

Goods: 5 obsidians (9 each), 4 carnelians (60 each), 3 red spinels (70 each), 3 red garnets (90 each), 6 deep blue spinels (200 each), 3 star rubies (900 each).

Items: Divine scroll of *faerie fire* and *barkskin*, *potion of jump*, *potion of cure light wounds**, *potion of enlarge person*, divine scroll of *cure light wounds*, *detect evil*, and *augury*, *wand of invisibility** (29 charges).

CR 12 (29,400 gp)

Coins: 3,488 gp, 294 pp.

Goods: Banded agate (10), tourmaline (60), silver pearl (130), violet garnet (400), silver anklet (30), life-size oak statue of a hunting dog (230), crystal bowl and pitcher (300 each), set of mithral wind chimes (400), silver brooch inscribed "To My Beloved Amarathea" (800), holy vestments of samite bearing symbol of Pelor (1,000), gold pendant with ruby (1,700).

Items: Divine scroll of *bull's strength*, arcane scroll of *unseen servant* and *spectral hand*, arcane scroll of *burning hands*, *disguise self*, and *minor image*, *potion of levitate*, *potion of resist energy**, arcane scroll of *suggestion* and *tongues*, *+1 short sword*, *wand of magic missile** (5th-level caster; 34 charges), *+1 frost kama*.

CR 13 (39,000 gp)

Coins: 4,848 gp.

Goods: Tiger eye turquoise (12), 3 citrines (60 each), 2 brown-green garnets (80 each), 2 violet garnets (300 each), 3 golden yellow topaz (400 each).

Items: *Ring of protection +4**.

CR 14 (51,000 gp)

Coins: 19,410 gp.

Goods: 2 jasper (40 each), 4 amber (70 each), golden yellow topaz (300), gold-plated herald's trumpet (90), silver anklet studded with hematite (340), cloak of giant eagle feathers (1,100), mithral bracelet studded with sapphires (7,000), mithral belt studded with sapphires (8,000).

Items: *Potion of displacement**, *wand of mirror image** (15 charges), *wand of cure critical wounds* (25 charges), *quiver of Ehlonna*.

CR 15 (66,000 gp)

Coins: 12,021 gp, 1,683 pp.

Goods: 4 blue quartz (8 each), alexandrite (400), 3 aquamarines (500 each), 2 black pearls (700 each), boarskin cloak (80), silver oakleaf brooch (110), silver ring bearing oak leaf insignia (130), pair of matched crystal goblets (400), bone chair with bearskin upholstery (500), white velvet tunic set with tiny rubies (600), set of ivory and obsidian chess pieces (1,200), platinum wall mirror (1,400), gold bracelet set with emeralds (3,000), life-size crystal statue of pseudodragon (6,000).

Items: *+2 heavy wooden shield*, *staff of swarming insects* (32 charges).

CR 16 (84,000 gp)

Coins: 5,411 gp, 1,839 pp.

Goods: 5 moss agates (8 each), 5 azurites (10 each), 6 hematites (12 each), 5 zircons (40 each), 4 peridots (50 each), 5 jade (80 each), 5 black opals (900 each), silver hand mirror (50), oaken hairbrush inlaid with mother-of-pearl (60), girallon-fur rug (500), pair of platinum bracers (600 each), silver candelabra (700), woolen tapestry depicting the night sky, with diamonds set as stars (1,200), antique harpsichord with keys carved from mammoth ivory (1,600), gold necklace set with lapis lazuli (2,100), platinum wedding band (2,500), platinum wedding ring set with diamond (3,000), platinum scepter set with emeralds (5,000), platinum crown set with emeralds (7,000).

Items: *Potion of lesser restoration*, arcane scroll of *charm person*, *arcane lock*, and *knock*, *golembane scarab* (any golem), *cloak of Charisma +2*, *wand of bull's strength** (48 charges), *+2 keen spear*.

CR 17 (108,000 gp)

Coins: 15,667 gp, 1,421 pp.

Goods: 8 blue quartz (8 each), 4 rhodocrosite (11 each), 8 sardonyx (30 each), 11 moonstones (60 each), 7 golden pearls (110 each), 5 emeralds (1,400 each), mirror of finely wrought and highly polished silver (1,000), silver brazier engraved with crashing waves (1,300), masterwork mandolin inlaid with mother of pearl (1,500), marble-topped oaken coffee table with inset mosaic of elven village (2,000), gown crafted from thousands of butterfly wings alchemically treated to retain their structure and color (4,000), hand-painted table service of triton-crafted coral china covered with scenes of underwater life (5,000), gold necklace strung with rubies (7,000), gold crown studded with rubies and diamonds (11,000).

Items: Divine scroll of *cure serious wounds*, *prayer*, and *remove disease*, *wand of lightning bolt** (38 charges), *amulet of natural armor** *+4*.

CR 18 (141,000 gp)

Coins: 16,905 gp.

Goods: 16 freshwater pearls (10 each), 4 onyx (50 each), 6 aquamarines (500 each), 3 violet garnets (600 each), silver salad fork (20), polished obsidian mug (100), crystal inkwell (110), bronze lamp (110), silver snuffbox (150), silk pillow stitched with gold thread (180), hand carved hickory bookcase with glass doors (200), woolen tapestry bearing holy symbol of Kord (300), 3 gold chains (400 each), pair of gold bracers engraved with leaping flames (500 each), crystal vase (600), mithral hat pin set with tiny ruby (600), silk tunic with embroidered "W" (600), pair of nagahide boots (800), teakwood serving tray (800), painting of dwarf Queen Hammerskjold (900), 2 silver serving platters (900 each), silver anklet with tiny elephant-shaped jade charms (1,200), ceremonial darkwood staff topped with gold orb (1,300), platinum circlet (1,300), gold candelabra shaped like dragon's claw (1,400), silver belt set with ruby (1,400), small onyx statuette of a centaur (1,700), small onyx statuette of a pegasus (1,700), pair of diamond earrings (2,000 each), cape of vrock feathers (3,000), platinum pendant set with three matching emeralds (5,000), gold tiara set with large jacinth (7,000).

Items: Divine scroll of *greater magic fang* and *rusting grasp*, arcane scroll of *magic circle against law* and *detect scrying*, arcane scroll of *bull's strength* and *wall of stone*, *staff of earth and stone* (23 charges), *ring of freedom of movement**.

CR 19 (183,000 gp)

Coins: 32,819 gp, 1,728 pp.

Goods: Velvet bag (30) holding 3 lapis lazuli (7 each), 7 bloodstones (50 each), 6 pink pearls (110 each), 3 black pearls (800 each), 2 sapphires (1,200 each), 2 mithral six-sided dice (40 each), hat with pheasant feather (60), basilisk-hide belt (70), brass ring set with citrine (70), set of 9 clear potion vials in a darkwood traveling case, each with a unique gemmed stopper (90 per vial, 90 for case), bronze ewer engraved with geometric patterns (100), silver cloak pin (140), basilisk-hide boots (150), marble statuette of a gargoyle (150), lionskin cloak (200), gold-plated spoon, fork, and knife with tiny black pearls in handles (300 each), pair of steel gauntlets each set with an amethyst (400 each), life-size marble statue of wyrmling blue dragon (500), antique carpet bearing symbol of Heironeous (600), gold ring inscribed with elven rune for peace (600), mammoth horn capped in gold, bearing scrimshaw depiction of fur-clad orcs hunting mammoths (800), onyx and mother-of-pearl chessboard (800), crystal lamp (900), gold rod of office topped with amber with scarab beetle trapped within (1,000), sword hilt set with amethysts (1,000), intricately carved circle of gold leaves (1,100), pair of gold earrings each set with single black pearl (1,100 each), ocarina carved from petrified mammoth bone, its surface painted with metallic leaf depicting orcs in ritual dance (1,300), cedar music box with tiny crystal dancer inside (1,500), ebony desk with legs carved to resemble a dragon's, plus matching desk chair (1,500 for desk, 900 for chair), silver bracelet set with tiny violet garnets (1,600), embroidered velvet tunic set with bloodstones (1,900), antique darkwood pipe organ with walrus-ivory inlay (2,000), lorgnette on silver chain with cut crystal lenses and silver frames studded with tiny topaz, rubies, and emeralds (3,000), 2 suits of ceremonial gold-embossed full plate armor (4,000 each), two-foot-tall sandstone pillar carved with writhing ruby-eyed serpents (5,000), crystal hourglass filled with diamond dust, each base shaped like a sleeping dragon (one side is gold, the other silver) (6,000), platinum chalice engraved with storm-tossed seascape and set with sapphires (10,000).

Items: *Broom of flying*, *minor ring of energy resistance (acid)**, *ioun stone* (pink and green sphere)*, arcane scroll of *passwall*, *disintegrate*, and *control undead*; *+5 large shield*.

CR 20 (240,000 gp)

Coins: 59,063 gp.

Goods: Eye agate (5), 3 rock crystals (30 each), 7 ambers (60 each), 2 chrysoberyls (110 each), 2 red garnets (130 each), a set of 6 matched chased silver teacups (60 each) with a matching teapot with blue enamel trim engraved with swirling ribbons and geometric shapes (160), steel helm set with two matched moonstones (110), 2 glass cubes each carved with the image of a child's face (130 each), ebony jewelry box monogrammed with "L" (150), gold chain with amber pendant (150), gold bracelet set with amber (200), amethyst bookend (300), oaken quarterstaff banded with silver (400), pair of mithral-toed wyvernskin boots (400), 2 silver armbands (600 each), matched gold earring and nose ring, connected by gold chain (700 for set), 3 silver candelabra (700 each), matched bronze statuettes of a griffon, a pegasus, and a basilisk (800 each), 2 ceremonial gold-plated breastplates, each set with tiny emeralds (900 each), delicate multicolored blown glass lily trimmed with gold (1,000), bloodstone-studded rod (1,500), green velvet cape fringed with giant eagle feathers (1,600), adamantine gauntlet set with matched pair of eye-shaped rubies (1,700), gold-plated hand mirror engraved with cloud castle (1,700), giant-sized beer stein carved from single chunk of marble, with bas-relief carvings illustrating mighty deities feasting and reveling (1,800), three-foot-tall water pipe of beaten gold, its surface chased with entwined dragons, with two smoking hoses of wyrmling red dragon hide (1,900), gold statuette of muscular man with both hands on the hilt of a longsword, its tip planted in the ground at his feet (2,000), platinum thurible bearing symbol of Vecna (2,000), extensive collection of books detailing natural lore (grants +4 circumstance bonus on Knowledge [nature] checks) (3,000), platinum anklet with opalescent blue and purple crystal beads (3,000), pair of diamond-studded belt buckles, one with symbol of Pelor, other with symbol of Heironeous (4,000 each), full-size ornate carriage with silk-lined seats, intricate carvings, and gold inlay (6,000).

Items: *Figurine of wondrous power (obsidian steed)*, *wand of knock* (21 charges), *periapt of health*, *+3 darkwood heavy wooden shield*, *tome of clear thought +2*, arcane scroll of *cloudkill*, *persistent image*, *greater teleport*, *teleport object*, *horrid wilting*, and *prismatic sphere*, *+3 battleaxe*.

CR 21 (261,000 gp)

Coins: 20,211 gp; 4,192 pp.

Goods: 13 hematites (8 each), 10 moonstones (60 each), 5 white pearls (100 each), 13 golden yellow topaz (400 each), 6 violet garnets (500 each), 11 black pearls (700 each), 8 emeralds (900 each), 8 fire opals (1,100 each), 7 star rubies (1,500 each), 3 jacinths (6,000 each).

Items: *Wand of keen edge* (42 charges), *+3 composite shortbow* (+2 Str bonus), divine scroll of *divine power* and *break enchantment*, *rod of metal and mineral detection*, arcane scroll of *fly*, *lesser geas*, and *wall of fire*, arcane scroll of *greater magic weapon*, *lightning bolt*, *haste*, and *confusion*, *ring of water walking*, arcane scroll of *cone of cold*, *crystal ball** (with *see invisibility*), *rod of absorption** (16 levels remaining, 17 levels stored).

CR 22 (288,000 gp)

Coins: 30,818 gp, 1,732 pp.

Goods: 2 malachites (11 each), 3 deep blue spinels (400 each), 5 alexandrites (600 each), 4 rich purple corundum (1,200 each), 3 fine tapestries with silver filigree woven into stitching (100 each), 4 silk pennants embroidered with heraldic symbols (110 each), a pair of dragonfly-shaped earrings made of green glass, blue enamel, and gold wire (200 each), cockatrice-quill pen with petrified pixie head inkwell (400), 4 jade six-sided dice (400 each), teak serving tray with ancient elvish verse inlaid in gold (400), crystal snow globe with wyrmling white dragon claw stand (500), double-stemmed pipe crafted from femur of hell hound (500), gossamer veil set with tiny citrines (500), aquamarine sculpture of cresting wave topped by silver triton (600), ceremonial forge hammer with fire opal set into head (600), painting of halfling cleric of Yondalla wearing vestments of shimmering green (600), finely worked brass trumpet with detailed acid-etching (700), ornate plaque reading "Welcome to Silverpoint" (800), curtain of cut-crystal beads in rainbow colors strung on fine gold chain (900), collection of leatherbound tomes of arcane knowledge (grants +2 circumstance bonus on Knowledge [arcana] checks) (1,000), life-size gold-plated statue of a dwarven defender wielding a greataxe (1,100), mithral-inlaid dwarf keg tap set with emerald (1,300), one-foot-tall marble statuette of elf wizard with crystalline lightning extending from her outstretched hands (1,300), platinum scepter topped by sculpted ivory illithid head (1,300), velvet-lined cherrywood box with gold inlay (1,400), pixie statuette carved from single emerald (1,500), tiny ruby lens set into small gold loop (1,500), wire-posable statue of an elf wearing a jewel-inlaid cloak (1,700), crystal phylactery designed to hold perfume (empty) (2,000), trumpet of unicorn horn with gold mouthpiece (2,100), carving of rainbow jasper that looks like a dragon when held one way and looks like a cat sleeping when held another way (2,600), crystal vase etched with scene of dragons soaring through clouds (3,000), ceremonial dagger carved from single piece of purple amethyst (3,500), gold ring with diamond and inscription reading "Always" (3,500), gold wire spider web with miniature adamantine spider (3,500), marble bust of helmed human with draconic features and sapphire eyes (3,500), diamond-studded belt buckle with symbol of St. Cuthbert (4,000), platinum statuette of robed woman holding open book on hip (4,000), triptych enameled in bright colors on three panels of electrum, showing scenes of devils and angels in desperate conflict (5,000), dragonhide half mask studded with white and black pearls (9,000).

Items: *Rod of wonder*, *sword of subtlety*, *potion of fly**, *ring of water walking*, *wand of cure moderate wounds* (33 charges), *+2 chain shirt of acid resistance*, *ring of protection +5**, *cube of frost resistance*, *wand of greater invisibility** (26 charges).

CR 23 (318,000 gp)

Coins: 55,691 gp; 18,804 pp.

Goods: 6 obsidian (9 each), 5 zircons (70 each), 4 black pearls (200 each), 8 aquamarines (700 each), 9 white opals (1,000 each), blue diamond (3,000), 5 platinum rings (50 each), 4 keys carved from crystal (80 each), intricately carved darkwood cigar box (100), matched pair of gold goblets bearing inscription "Drink in good health" in Elven (100 each), 3 silver armbands bearing onyx lantern insignia (200 each), horse bridle set with moonstones (300), set of silk bedsheets (300), rough-hewn granite statue of dragon with carnelian eyes (400), elegant leaded-glass perfume bottle with pegasus-shaped stopper (600), hickory-framed mirror set with four matching silver pearls (700), jeweled gold statuette of a toad (800), 6 matching intricately carved coral chairs (900 each), collection of leatherbound tomes of religious knowledge (grants +2 circumstance bonus on Knowledge [religion] checks) (1,000), silver-rimmed bone goblet bearing symbol of Vecna (1,000), pair of sapphire earrings sized for Large creature (1,200 each), antique violin with jade inlay (1,300), life-size stone statue of a halfling cleric of Yondalla with hand extended in friendship (1,300), oak armoire with mother-of-pearl inlaid symbols of Boccob (1,300) holding five sets of silken holy vestments bearing symbol of Boccob (110 each), gold brooch set with tiny jacinth (1,400), silver belt studded with red garnets (1,400), fine painting of a golden sunrise in gold-gilt frame (1,500), polished onyx orb cunningly set with garnets, simulating an orrery (1,600), 4 gold signet rings each bearing diamond "N" (2,000 each), intricate amethyst and gold chandelier (2,100), marble altar with symbol of Boccob inlaid in platinum and rubies (2,400).

Items: *Potion of cure serious wounds**, *+1 breastplate of light fortification and acid resistance*, *potion of barkskin** (12th-level caster), *+3 defending bastard sword*, *+3/+3 dwarven urgrosh*, *ring gates*, *pearl of power* (two spells).

CR 24 (348,000 gp)

Coins: 18,030 gp; 3,855 pp.

Goods: 6 deep green spinels (110 each), 7 golden pearls (160 each), 7 alexandrites (600 each), 7 blue sapphires (1,200 each), 3 onyx chesspieces (knight, rook, queen; 10 each), golden metal top that whistles when spun (40), mithral anklet with tiny gold bells (60), 3 iron cubes with different dwarf face on each side (80 each), reversible dire wolf fur traveler's cloak with cloth-of-gold stitching (90), 3 silver anklets with tiny hematites (110 each), black silk skullcap embroidered in silver (200), crimson silk tunic embroidered with leaping flames (200), tapestry depicting great black dragon slaying numerous knights (300), gold cameo of elf woman with elven rune "R" on the back (400), life-size statue of human paladin in full plate armor (400), 3 flawless fist-sized crystal geometric shapes (sphere, cube, and pyramid; 500 each), 3 jewel-encrusted tomes with blank papyrus pages and silver trimmed spines (600 each), gold ceremonial sickle and bowl with engravings of holly leaves (700 each), incomplete set of the Biography of the Grand Tyrant Alonzo (missing book 7 of the 10) (700 gp, or 1,000 gp if complete), silver necklace set with violet garnet (700), crystal hookah sized for a Huge dragon (800), stained-glass chess set (900), pair of platinum candlesticks with elven runes spelling out "May the Light of Corellon Larethian Bless You" (1,100 each), small lead-lined darkwood bookcase with airtight lead-lined doors (1,200), 2 diamond stickpins (1,300 each), gray six-fingered silk glove embroidered with gold and set with tiny pearls (1,300), masterful painting of desolate coastline (1,500), mithral scroll tube engraved with dragons in flight (1,600), dire bearskin rug (1,900), gold-framed crystalline spectacles (2,000), oaken wardrobe carved with ebony skulls on spikes (2,000), ornamental warmask with ruby eyes (2,400), emerald statuettes of male and female lion (4,000 each), ornate 12-candle crystal and gold chandelier (5,000), coral throne upholstered with sharkskin and set with tiny pink and white pearls (6,000), adamantine longsword scabbard set with tiny rubies (7,000), heavy white gold ring set with tiny sapphires (9,000).

Items: *Manual of quickness in action +1, frost brand, amulet of health* +6, staff of the woodlands* (26 charges), divine scroll of *raise dead* and *antimagic field, scarab of protection*.*

CR 25 (384,000 gp)

Coins: 1,752 gp; 10,687 pp.

Goods: 8 moss agates (11 each), 10 bloodstones (70 each), 9 pieces of jade (90 each), 8 amethysts (100 each), 6 golden yellow topaz (300 each), 20 violet garnets (600 each), 6 black star sapphires (1,200 each), 8 star rubies (1,300 each), 7 blue-white diamonds (5,000 each).

Items: *Wand of hold person** (43 charges), *+3 longsword, wand of Melf's acid arrow** (35 charges), *ioun stone** (deep red sphere), arcane scroll of *wall of ice, hold monster, wall of force,* and *Bigby's forceful hand*, arcane scroll of *bear's endurance, cat's grace,* and *slow, +4 greataxe, mirror of opposition, +5 full plate armor of cold resistance.*

CR 26 (423,000 gp)

Coins: 32,050 gp; 1,580 pp.

Goods: 4 freshwater pearls (10 each), 6 red spinels (80 each), 8 pink pearls (120 each), 5 black opals (900 each), 2 gold serving spoons (30 each), set of six bone china salad plates (50 each), set of six bone china soup bowls (90 each), set of six bone china dinner plates (100 each), gold soup tureen (500), darkwood-handled silver hand mirror (600), ivory-inlaid lyre (600), set of six crystal goblets (800 each), crystal pitcher (900), crystal serving bowl (900), 2 gold serving platters (1,000 each), crystal vase (1,100), griffon-feather cloak (1,200), velvet mask studded with rubies (1,300), pair of gold earrings each set with single diamond (1,400 each), gold anklet set with amethysts (1,500), painting of the Battle of Emridy Meadows (1,900), 6 mithral scabbards set with violet garnets (2,000 each), 2 mithral helms set with purple corundum, each bearing the forge-mark of famed dwarven smith Durgeddin the Black (2,100 each), gold flask engraved with "E" (2,200), adamantine idol of Moradin (3,000), 2 blank adamantine-bound spellbooks, inscribed with rearing dragons (4,000 each), pair of silk gloves, each embroidered with a "G" and studded with tiny sapphires (4,000 each), silver flame-shaped brooch set with fire opals (5,000), phoenix-feather fan studded with rubies (6,000), platinum necklace studded with sapphires (7,000), platinum tiara set with diamond (7,000), masterful gold ring set with diamond, 2 matching sapphires (12,000).

Items: *Rod of enemy detection*, gem of brightness*, +4/+2 dire flail,* arcane scroll of *blink, displacement, halt undead,* and *dimensional anchor, wand of knock* (28 charges), *ring of invisibility*, staff of life* (8 charges), *+4 scimitar,* divine scroll of *stone tell, word of chaos, holy aura,* and *sunburst, +2 full plate armor of moderate fortification, mantle of faith.*

CR 27 (465,000 gp)

Coins: 15,985 gp; 1,300 pp.

Goods: 5 red garnets (90 each), 1 aquamarine (500), 5 violet garnets (700 each), 2 black pearls (800 each), 3 blue sapphires (1,100 each), 6 fiery yellow corundums (1,100 each), 4 star rubies (1,200 each), 5 fire opals (1,600 each), 3 blue-white diamonds (3,000 each), 2 blue diamonds (4,000 each), 2 canary diamonds (5,000 each), bright green emerald (6,000), 4 jacinths (7,000 each), set of four intricately inlaid pens (200 each), tapestry depicting trees blowing in the wind (500), obsidian mug (600), horn of cachelot whale ivory with a seascape carved on its side (700), heavy bronze mirror with detailed filigree (750), onyx bowl carved with soldiers marching to battle (750), silver brush inlaid with turquoise (800), tapestry with thread of gold depicting epic battle (900), statue of ship under sail, layered in mother of pearl (1,700), pair of platinum earrings with emeralds (1,750 each), collar set with jade (1,800), obsidian bust of a stately elf (2,000), slippers of basilisk hide lined with white wolf fur, set with sapphires and moonstones (2,400), silver manacles set with jade (3,200), crown set with alexandrites (7,500), pillar of chestnut carved with flames and set with fire opals (10,000), glass scepter with brown diamond and other gems (12,000), marble statue of peacock set with scores of colorful gems (18,000).

Items: Divine scroll of *restoration, control winds, fire seeds,* and *word of recall, wand of ice storm* (37 Charges), *+1 anarchic vorpal scimitar, crystal ball* (with *true seeing*), *+4 breastplate of spell resistance* (15).

Appendix 2: Index of Dragons

The lists in this appendix include all dragons published in official DUNGEONS & DRAGONS products up to the publication of this book. Indexed sources include the following titles:

Monster Manual (MM)

Monster Manual II (MMII)
Fiend Folio (FF)
Monsters of Faerûn (MoF)
Magic of Faerûn (MaF)
Oriental Adventures (OA)
Epic Level Handbook (Epic)
DRAGON® *Magazine* (*Dragon* issue number)
Draconomicon (Dra)

True Dragons

Dragon	Category	Source
Amethyst	Gem	MMII
Battle	Planar	Dra
Black	Chromatic	MM
Blue	Chromatic	MM
Brass	Metallic	MM
Bronze	Metallic	MM
Brown	—	MoF
Chiang lung	Lung	OA
Chaos	Planar	Dra
Copper	Metallic	MM
Crystal	Gem	MMII
Deep	—	MoF
Emerald	Gem	MMII
Ethereal	Planar	Dra
Fang	—	Dra
Force	Epic	Epic
Gold	Metallic	MM
Green	Chromatic	MM
Howling	Planar	Dra
Li lung	Lung	OA
Lung wang	Lung	OA
Oceanus	Planar	Dra
Pan lung	Lung	OA
Prismatic	Epic	Epic
Pyroclastic	Planar	Dra
Radiant	Planar	Dra
Red	Chromatic	MM
Rust	Planar	Dra
Sapphire	Gem	MMII
Shen lung	Lung	OA
Shadow	—	Dra
Silver	Metallic	MM
Song	—	MoF
Styx	Planar	Dra
Tarterian	Planar	Dra
T'ien lung	Lung	OA
Topaz	Gem	MMII
Tun mi lung	Lung	OA
White	Chromatic	MM
Yu lung	Lung	OA

Lesser Dragons

Dragon	Source
Air drake	Dra
Barautha	*Dragon* 284
Cave wurm	*Dragon* 296
Desert landwyrm	Dra
Dragon turtle	MM
Dragonnel	Dra
Earth drake	Dra
Ermalkankari	*Dragon* 284
Faerie dragon	Dra
Felldrake, crested	MMII
Felldrake, horned	MMII
Felldrake, spitting	MMII
Fire drake	Dra
Forest landwyrm	Dra
Forest wurm	*Dragon* 296
Grassland wurm	*Dragon* 296
Hellfire wyrm	MMII
Hill landwyrm	Dra
Hill wurm	*Dragon* 296
Ibrandlin	MoF
Ice drake	Dra
Jungle landwyrm	Dra
Lava wurm	*Dragon* 296
Linnorm, corpse tearer	MMII

LESSER DRAGONS BY CR

Following is a list, in ascending order, of the Challenge Ratings for all lesser dragons. The table on page 288 provides CRs for all true dragons.

CR 1: felldrake, crested; pseudodragon
CR 2: felldrake, spitting
CR 3: felldrake, horned
CR 5: dragonnel; ibrandlin; trilligarg; wurm, Small (any variety)
CR 6: air drake; faerie dragon; plains landwyrm; wyvern
CR 7: ice drake; mardallond; scalamagdrion
CR 8: water drake; Underdark landwyrm
CR 9: barautha; dragon turtle; smoke drake; vallochar; wurm, Medium (any variety)
CR 10: fire drake; ermalkankari; forest landwyrm
CR 11: earth drake
CR 12: ooze drake; hill landwyrm
CR 13: magma drake
CR 14: tundra landwyrm; sunwyrm
CR 15: sea drake; wurm, Large (any variety)
CR 16: jungle landwyrm
CR 17: storm drake
CR 18: desert landwyrm
CR 20: swamp landwyrm; linnorm, gray
CR 22: mountain landwyrm
CR 23: wurm, Huge (any variety)
CR 25: linnorm, dread
CR 26: hellfire wyrm
CR 28: linnorm, corpse tearer

CR Special

Template (CR Adj.)
Dracolich (base +3)
Draconic (base +1)
Ghostly dragon (base +2)
Half-dragon (base +2)
Skeletal dragon (base × 1/2)
Vampiric dragon (base +2)
Zombie dragon ([base × 1/2] +1)

True Dragon CRs by Age and Kind

Kind	Wyrmling	Very Young	Young	Juvenile	Young Adult	Adult	Mature Adult	Old	Very Old	Ancient	Wyrm	Great Wyrm
Amethyst	4	5	7	9	12	15	17	19	20	22	24	26
Battle	3	4	6	8	10	12	14	17	18	19	20	22
Black	3	4	5	7	9	11	14	16	18	19	20	22
Blue	3	4	6	8	11	14	16	18	19	21	23	24
Brass	3	4	6	8	10	12	15	17	19	20	21	23
Bronze	3	5	7	9	12	15	17	19	20	22	23	24
Brown	2	3	5	7	10	13	15	17	18	20	22	24
Chaos	3	4	6	8	11	13	15	16	17	19	20	22
Chiang lung	—	—	—	9	12	14	17	19	20	22	23	25
Copper	3	5	7	9	11	14	16	18	20	22	23	24
Crystal	3	4	5	8	11	13	16	18	19	21	22	24
Deep	2	4	6	8	11	14	16	18	19	21	22	24
Emerald	3	5	7	9	12	15	17	19	20	22	23	25
Ethereal	3	4	6	7	9	10	13	15	16	17	18	19
Fang	2	3	4	6	8	10	12	15	17	18	19	21
Gold	5	7	9	11	14	16	19	21	22	24	25	27
Green	3	4	5	8	11	13	16	18	19	21	22	24
Howling	5	8	10	12	14	16	18	20	22	23	25	26
Li lung	—	—	—	8	10	13	15	18	19	21	22	24
Lung wang	—	—	—	10	13	15	18	20	21	23	24	26
Oceanus	4	5	6	9	12	13	16	18	19	20	21	22
Pan lung	—	—	—	7	9	11	14	16	18	19	20	22
Pyroclastic	4	5	7	10	12	14	16	18	19	21	22	24
Radiant	5	6	8	10	13	14	17	19	20	21	22	23
Red	4	5	7	10	13	15	18	20	21	23	24	26
Rust	3	4	6	8	10	13	15	17	18	20	22	24
Sapphire	3	5	7	9	11	14	16	19	20	22	23	25
Shadow	2	3	5	7	10	12	15	17	18	20	21	23
Shen lung	—	—	—	8	11	14	16	18	19	21	22	24
Silver	4	5	7	10	13	15	18	20	21	23	24	26
Song	2	4	6	8	10	13	15	18	19	21	22	24
Styx	3	4	5	8	10	12	15	17	18	20	21	23
Tarterian	5	7	9	11	13	15	17	19	20	22	23	25
T'ien lung	—	—	—	10	13	15	18	20	21	23	24	26
Topaz	4	5	7	10	13	15	18	20	21	23	24	26
Tun mi lung	—	—	—	9	12	14	17	19	20	22	23	25
White	2	3	4	6	8	10	12	15	17	18	19	21
Yu lung	2	4	6	—	—	—	—	—	—	—	—	—

Linnorm, dread	MMII
Linnorm, gray	MMII
Magma drake	Dra
Mardallond	*Dragon* 284
Mountain landwyrm	Dra
Mountain wurm	*Dragon* 296
Ooze drake	Dra
Plains landwyrm	Dra
Pseudodragon	MM
River wurm	*Dragon* 296
Sand wurm	*Dragon* 296
Scalamagdrion	MaF
Sea drake	FF
Sea wurm	*Dragon* 296
Smoke drake	Dra
Storm drake	Dra
Storm wurm	*Dragon* 296
Sunwyrm	FF
Swamp landwyrm	Dra
Swamp wurm	*Dragon* 296
Trilligarg	*Dragon* 284
Tundra landwyrm	Dra
Tundra wurm	*Dragon* 296
Underdark landwyrm	Dra
Vallochar	*Dragon* 284
Water drake	Dra
Wyvern	MM

Dragon-Only Templates

Template	**Source**
Dracolich	Dra
Ghostly dragon	Dra
Skeletal dragon	Dra
Vampiric dragon	Dra
Zombie dragon	Dra

Dragon-Related Templates

Template	**Source**
Draconic	Dra
Half-dragon	MM